Bluebeard's Secret

THE COMPLETE SERIES

SARAH K. L. WILSON

Cover Illustration: Erion Make
Chapter Glyphs: Emily Crandall

www.sarahklwilson.com
First Edition: August 2024
ISBN: 978-1-990516-52-8

For the one I love best. May this be worthy.
Soli Deo Gloria

FLY
WITH THE
Arrow
SARAH K.L. WILSON

Fly with the Arrow
Dance with the Sword
Give your Heart to the Barrow
Die with your Lord

"There was once a man who had fine houses both in town and the country, a deal of silver and gold plate, embroidered furniture and coaches gilded all over with gold. But this man was so unlucky as to have a blue beard, which made him so frightfully ugly that all the women and girls ran away from him."

- Charles Perrault, Bluebeard,
1697 as translated by Andrew Lang in The Blue Fairy Book 1889.

Chapter One

SOME LAWS ARE TALKED about by all – featured in story and song – and as a result, it's easy to know that if you turn traitor to the king, you'll soon see your head mounted on the battlements of Pensmoore, or if you steal another woman's horse, a hempen noose will be the last to embrace you.

It's not those laws that are the problem. It's the other kind of laws. The laws no one talks about at all.

Like the Law of First Greeting.

And it is those laws that bite you in the end, just like that law bit me.

"Izolda must come to court with me this season," my father had declared one day before riding out on the hunt. When he said that, I had never heard of the Law of First Greeting.

"You must be careful to be very polite to the fine ladies of court, Izolda," my mother warned as she packed my fur robes and velvet gowns into a small chest. "Remember what I taught you. They will all be above your station. Try to be meek. Try not to judge others so harshly. And whatever you do, don't decide to go out shooting or riding with your brothers." She was wiping tears from her eyes, as she always did when one of us left. She would miss us sorely – though even she could have had no idea how long I would be gone for. "Be a good girl. Help the women with their weaving and stitching and they will be pleased with you. You are young and very beautiful." She paused to stroke my face lovingly as she said that. "But trust me Izolda, that beauty will fade in time and you will be sorry if you haven't made use of it while you had the chance. Have some fun. Flirt. Enjoy yourself." She paused as if worried she'd said too much. "But do no more than that because your father will be working very hard to secure a wise match for you. It's high time we found someone suitable. You can't live here forever and you're already nineteen."

"Don't worry so much, Mother," I said, kissing her cheek. I was not worried. I was excited. I never got to go anywhere interesting and I doubted my father would procure me a husband in just one visit.

Since we were a very small martial family on the outer edges of the King's territory, my father would have to be very clever indeed to find a match. I'd be lucky if he found a sober man of forty who still had all his teeth, but I didn't bother to mention that to my mother. After all, I was supposed to be dazzled and delighted by pretty faces at this age and they were supposed to be my folly and ruin. No point in proving that was true.

"Don't forget to check on Brueller in the stables," I reminded her as I put some pine scented soap and a comb in the chest. My mother would forget those. Practical things were not her specialty. "If I am gone, he will have to help Sasa foal all by himself."

"You think too much of horses when you should be thinking of being wed," my mother said with a sigh.

All of that advice, and no mention whatsoever of any Law I must be careful of. No mention that the Wittenbrand might come to the castle, too, tearing through it like a winter storm with all the same icy rage. If she'd said any of that, I might not have even believed her.

Which made sense in a perverse sort of way. If I had been a beautiful but brainless girl of fine fortune and the perfect heroine for a story then I would have been warned of the Law and I would have known not to break it, but I would have been courageous and headstrong and done it anyway. But since I was sensible and calm in a crisis and of mediocre appearance – despite my mother's assurances of my beauty – no one had bothered to warn *me* of a pit that only a heroine could possibly fall into. Girls like me didn't have to watch out for Laws and traps.

The next day, my little bay mare stamped with excitement in the swirling wind and I tried not to tug on her reins even though my own heart was just as exuberant. I was bouncing on my toes as my mother kissed my cheeks. Flurries of snow swirled around her as I said my goodbyes. Her lips were faintly blue in the cold and her eyes were filled with sadness to see us go.

"I shall miss you, my Izolda," she said, pushing strands of my long dark hair back behind my ear.

"We should not be gone for more than a turning of Moons, mother," I said because she always kissed us goodbye like she thought we would all die of the plague while we were gone. My cheeks were hot from her attention already.

If I'd known this would be the last time that I saw her, I would have taken more time to treasure it.

"It's always been you and me standing here holding hands as they go and now it will be only me. I will feel an ache in my heart until you return," she said, and my cheeks flared even hotter. I wouldn't be feeling any aches. In fact, I was so excited to see court for the first time that I could hardly keep my breath careful and measured.

"Be safe and healthy, Mother," I said. "Know that you hold our hearts."

"Be careful not to go off on your own," she said, cupping my cheek in her warm hand. "We don't want the Wittenbrand to snatch you away."

"You know those are only fairy stories." I shook my head, laughing the laugh of the young and hale. I'd been hearing tales of the Wittenbrand all my life, but I'd never seen one and I didn't believe the religious fervor of my people. I cared about facts and logic, not superstition and legend.

"Fairy stories are sometimes true," she said, kissing me again.

My bay stomped and huffed as my mother moved on to my father to exchange goodbyes. He'd end up as red-faced as me if she had her way.

While they were distracted, my brother Svetgin edged his gelding in close to mine as he double-checked the straps holding his bow and quiver in place. He was watching the hills around us as he worked. Winter storms could blow down in a moment's notice and no one took fair weather for granted. Or fair fortune.

"You women fuss too much," he said, rubbing his unshaven face as if he thought there might be a beard there by now. "Men know that traveling is normal and natural."

"How nice for you," I said dryly. "Hopefully all your heavy man-knowledge doesn't make your horse too slow."

"In Pensmoore, we will drink honey ale and dance with big-eyed women," he said smugly, ignoring my jab. "And you may even be favored with a dance, sister, if you can rein in that tongue."

"Big *eyes*?" Rolgrin, my other brother asked, waggling his eyebrows suggestively. Like me, he was dark of hair and eye, unlike Svetgin who had our mother's pale hair and complexion. "Is that what you've been noticing, brother?"

I ignored their banter. Perhaps, were I a boy and able to pick my bride someday, I might be weighing the merits of *eyes,* too. But I was not a boy. I would have to allow my father to negotiate a suitable situation for me and the likelihood of me having any say in it was slim. The likelihood of the man being only double my age was also narrow.

I did not resent my father for this. He was a practical man – I had inherited that from him – and he would choose well. Even if the thought of marrying a stranger he chose for me still put me into a cold sweat.

He had already told my mother that he would prefer a man with enough wealth that we could live without fear of hunger, but too little for him to be tempted to keep mistresses. A man with a good reputation in the court, but not enough reputation to keep him often from his hold. A man old enough to see sense, but not so old as to be unfit company for his daughter. That he considered my feelings in regard to faithfulness and company was a relief. Not all daughters could depend on such good grace from a father.

And since I was an expert at self-control, it would be easy to pretend that what I really wanted wasn't deep, dark eyes and broad shoulders. That daydreams of dashing knights on horseback with flashing swords were only for other girls and not for me. I felt my cheeks growing hot again. Of course, I could manage that.

I sat my mare with a straight back and skillful hands and smiled serenely at my brothers – both younger than I, and yet both more familiar with court. Boys always got the best opportunities. Svetgin had already been to court once before and Rolgrin twice.

At nineteen years of age, I was old to have never been, but my mother was very fond of me and had not wanted to see me married too soon. She had the romantic notion that I may even fall in love or have a whirlwind romance. It was a kind thought – but ridiculous. What had she expected would happen? Had she thought some stranger would appear in the night? Someone dashingly handsome who demanded my hand in marriage for the smallest of dowries? That kind of thing didn't happen outside of stories.

And it certainly didn't happen to minor nobles who had to embroider flowers over the holes in their dresses so that no one at court would know how tight the purse strings had to be in Northpeak.

"Ready to ride, daughter?" my father asked as he mounted his dancing gelding. Storm was too energetic to be a good mount, but he suited my hearty father well. It always surprised me that Father – being such a practical man in all other respects – chose my high-spirited, dreamy mother and then this unsuitable horse. It was a weakness of his. And one that made me all the fonder of him.

If I was allowed to do any choosing for myself, I might choose the same.

The ride from the Hold of the Savataz of Northpeak to Pensmoore City takes eight days, and though we stayed in inns and keeps of other Landholders along the way, we were worn and dirty by the time we arrived. I'd made careful mental notes of each inn we had stayed at. The people as we moved closer to Pensmoore City wore finer clothes – even the commoners. They ate finer foods. Drank finer mead. Their swords and shields showed more polish and their furs less wear from moths and age.

It was foolish to feel smaller just because my father's hold in Northpeak was poorer than these holds of the plains' folk. The sensible thing would be to be glad we were a part of a prosperous nation where many holds were strong and wealthy. After all, if it came to war with the Salamoore or the Aayadmoore along the borders, or the strange islanders of the east, it would be favorable to have such strong allies. And yet, I felt smaller. I felt shabbier. I began to understand what my mother meant when she said my father would have to be very clever to find me a good match. Any dreams I had of a whirlwind romance – however carefully tamped down – were quickly smothered and buried where I could no longer blush in shame that I'd ever had them at all.

In Northpeak, the people held us in respect. Here, we barely garnered a look and those who did look at us often wrinkled their noses. We were plain and bluff people with simple clothing and weapons. We were nothing now that we had left our land.

I could almost feel the smart of being without it – as if everything I had ever been was wrapped up in those trees and snows, and now I was a living ghost haunting these other lands without body or succor.

By the time we reached Pensmoore City, I was eager for any distraction from this constant reminder of my place in the Kingdom of Pensmoore. I tried not to let a stab of jealousy pierce me when we reached the city gates and were spattered with mud by a passing coach. A girl my age looked out between the curtains, her fine golden hair pulled back into an elaborate dressing and a large emerald hanging from a chain over her forehead. Her eyes didn't even focus on us as she drifted by – as if we were nothing more than trees or goats along the horizon.

"We should hurry before night falls," my father said practically. "The steward will be expecting us, and it will make more work for everyone if we are late."

I felt something cold on the back of my neck as he spoke. I glanced over my shoulder through the city gates. The snow swirled thick and heavy, dampening sound and sight like a warm down blanket in the winter. And yet, something felt wrong. Was that a figure I saw in the whirling snow?

There were a handful of shapes that almost looked like men riding horses, though there was something wrong with the horses' heads. I squinted at them, trying to see clearly enough to make out the shapes. Perhaps they were just fellow travelers journeying to court. But if that was true, then why did they leave little shivers along my spine? Something was not right. I had the oddest feeling that winter had opened its jaws and was trying to swallow me up.

I pulled my fur cloak in tighter as if it could shield me from the malice I felt in the swirling wind and the darkening storm.

"Don't dawdle, Izolda," Rolgrin said, tugging on my rein. When I looked back behind my shoulder, there was nothing in the swirling snow except my imagination and a single black raven.

Chapter Two

PENSMOORE CITY ROLLED over the plains like a bank of snow pushed by a shovel. It clumped and heaped, with one building seeming to be built almost on top of the next so that it was as much layers as it was rows. I tried not to gape, but just looking at the high towers made my belly flop. Had the carpenters been wise in their choices of timbers and how to place them, or would they fall down on my head as I was riding beside them? It seemed that cities required a lot of trust in strangers and I was not good at trusting.

And to think, in the darkness, I was seeing only a sliver of the city! These signs – so close I'd barely finished reading one before the next appeared – and the ornaments and cobbles and banners were just a small piece of the whole. It was almost too much to take in. Most of the city and the royal stables passed me by in a blur of grandeur.

We saw nothing of the palace except the back corridors leading from the stable to our rooms and a small part of me was disappointed not to have had the chance to properly gawk.

By the time I was tucked away in a very small but warm room, I was too tired to think of much beyond stripping off my travel-soiled dress, brushing it quickly and readying myself for bed. My head was spinning from seeing the city and I was still just a little queasy at the thought of so many layers of palace above and below me.

At least I had the privacy of my own room. My father and brothers were sharing a room next door, their beds so close that they almost touched.

"Quarters are tight, I'm afraid, Lord Savataz of Northpeak," the Head Steward had told us. "Of course, his Highness welcomes all his loyal landholders and bids you rest and warmth, but the whole of the court is gathering for the princess's presentation ball and that leaves little space unclaimed. We've had to put you in the old servants' wing – to our shame, but no other place was available."

"Do not worry yourself, Head Steward," my father had said. "We are practical people. We are pleased to have a bed and the warmth of a fire. There will be no complaints from us."

The Steward had looked relieved, like a man who'd already dealt with many of those complaints today and was just grateful not to have to repeat the experience. Svetgin opened his mouth as if he was going to complain anyway, but my father stepped on his foot, grinding his heel into the arch, and Svetgin's mouth snapped shut as he gritted his teeth against the pain.

"Do not fear," the Steward said hastily. "They have been thoroughly aired and checked by our head housekeeper."

My father nodded gravely.

I found my room to be well enough, but that night before I went to bed, I opened the small window and looked out into the dark sky beyond.

"If I was a man, I would be a soldier or horse farrier and I would work hard for my kin," I said, trying not to sound too wistful as I looked up at the same moon my mother would be looking at. "But as I am a woman, my lot is to marry well for the good of my family and nation. I only wish that the benefit others receive from the marriage would be in equal measure with my sacrifice in giving it. But since the sacrifice is so great, I expect this cannot be."

A raven gave a cry so close to my window that I gasped, and turned until I saw him there, sitting just a little below the window on the peak of an overhang. I frowned, narrowing my eyes. What was he doing there? If I had been very ambitious, or very foolish, I could have reached out and snatched his black wings. It was almost as if he'd been planning to eavesdrop on me.

Instead, he tilted his head, looking right at me as if he was sharing my secret, and then he flew away in a flurry of black feathers.

I didn't know then that the Wittenbrand are said to watch through the eyes of ravens and hear with their ears. Had I known, perhaps I would have been more guarded with my words. Perhaps, I would have thrown a rock.

I was prompt to rise the next day and carefully brush my second-finest wool gown before dressing, braiding my long dark hair, and joining my brothers and father in the hall. The dress was dark charcoal and perfectly serviceable, and I'd embroidered a pine branch over a tear in the skirt.

"We must attend to men's business, Izolda," my father said gravely. "Can you find the place of women on your own?"

"Yes, Father," I said dutifully, and I was rewarded by his smile.

My feet were eager to explore and the castle was bustling with preparations for the princess's Presentation Ball. It was an affair meant to be so lavish that it would be talked of for the next generation. My mouth was already watering at the thought. Delicacies – and sweets especially – were rare in Northpeak, and if the princess gave me the chance to eat something sugary tonight, I'd be more than happy to play the plain wren next to her bluejay.

I dodged out of the way of rushing servants as I made my way through the castle, peering curiously into the empty rooms. The servants were harried and exhausted even though it was early morning, their arms full of tablecloths or chairs, ducks and geese, cheeses and candles and everything else.

I was far too fascinated and delighted by their preparations to ask after breakfast. Instead, I slipped through the halls letting my curiosity guide me, peeking in at the servants hanging garland in the wide man hall, watching in fascination as a group of musicians practiced in the ballroom, even slipping through the stables and peeking at the grooms tending the snorting horses.

If I was never going to have a ball thrown in my honor then I was certainly going to enjoy Princess Chasida's ball in every way I could, from studying the clever way the servant hid tied-up bundles of fragrant pine bows to sneaking a glimpse at the palace library that was being dusted and cleaned with the fervor of a religious practice.

This might be my only time to see court and I meant to see all of it.

I paused in the stables long enough to slip a carrot to my bay mare and check her hooves. She was in good health and as frisky as I was, and I longed to take her out into the yard for exercise, but I had promised my father I would find the ladies, so I made my way up through the castle, dutifully looking for where the women would be doing the weaving and sewing that would make them all pretty for the coming ball.

I found the women in the ladies' work room. They held little bits of handiwork, and most of them were gathered around piecing a large quilt, but no one was sewing.

"I'll be wearing my hair in the Rouanmoore style," one of them announced to impressed gasps. "My father bought me the pearl combs needed."

They hardly even noticed me slipping into their midst.

"But won't it cover the laced back of your dress?" another girl asked the first one. That set off a flurry of chatter.

I watched one of them practicing her posture, carefully checking to be sure that her figure was displayed perfectly. Another girl had her chin resting on her woven fingers and she was stealing little looks at herself in the large mirror that filled one of the walls. She made little adjustments every time so that she slowly appeared more coy and mysterious as the minutes passed.

I narrowed my eyes and looked around me, shocked to see she wasn't the only one. Well now. Who did the sewing around here if everyone was more worried about how they looked than getting anything done?

Shaking my head, I set into the quilt the group was meant to be sewing. I'd have to do the work of five women to make up for those girls and their careful posing. I glanced around and met the eyes of an older woman who smirked at me. I didn't know if she was laughing with me at these preening girls or laughing at me for working so hard.

After a moment she pointed at the flower sewn over a rip in the cuff of my dress and my face went hot. My embroidery had not fooled her experienced eye.

The girl closes to me dropped her needle and eyed me up and down before turning away again.

Was it possible that they weren't here to quilt at all?

Or was this just how they let someone new know her place was at the bottom of the heap?

"Tell us about the last time a princess was presented!" one of the girls said to an old woman in the corner. She was looking dreamily at the piece she was embroidering – a fanciful scene of castles and flowers. But those flowers were blue. I felt a chill wash over me. I wasn't usually superstitious, but one thing everyone knew was that blue flowers – blue anything – called down trouble. The Wittenbrand considered blue their color and legends said that anyone found wearing it would be claimed by them in soul and body. Nobody with sense wore blue or bought blue or even so much as looked at anything blue in a peddler's cart.

But those kinds of thoughts were just superstition. I knew that. It was just a reflex to be worried about it. There were no Wittenbrand and there would be no stolen souls. I knew better than to believe things that had perfectly reasonable alternate explanations I shook my head at myself and stitched the quilt.

The old woman began to speak. Her voice was surprisingly melodic for a woman of her age.

"The last princess to be presented was Princess Margaretta. And she was your great aunt, Princess Chasida," she said to the girl beside her who sat with a placid smile on her pretty face. Her hair was spun gold and her figure perfect in a blue silken dress. A red gem dangled over her forehead hanging from a golden chain and her eyes were faraway and dreamy like a princess from a storybook. I felt smaller than ever at the sight of her. The old woman was still speaking. "And I was her lady in waiting, as you all know. But that was long before your time.

"The snows were heavy that winter, and the wind bit us, and howled in the trees and it was through the trees that the Wittenbrand came."

I startled at her words. I'd just been thinking of the Wittenbrand and now she told a story about them – it was too strange of a coincidence.

"They took what they willed from us – cattle, horses, gold, and finery. People too. And the tricks they played! Cruel tricks. Things that trapped the mind even when the body was healthy and whole, and tricks that made the body waste away even when the mind was sharp and eloquent. A deal with the Wittenbrand was a deal with death.

"All of the Kingdom of Pen were worried, the wheat was gone, and still there was no spring, and now what was left was being stolen from us. But despite all of that, the King decided to make merry and celebrate the coming of age of his daughter – sixteen-year-old Margaretta. She was in the flower of her youth, young and beautiful with hair like spun sunlight and eyes like slices of a summer lake. He presented her to them all in a gown of gold – a gown much like yours, Chasida, except in color."

Princess Chasida's round cheeks blushed prettily and she glanced across the assembly and sighed. Around me, the other girls sighed with her and again my eyebrows wrinkled. Did none of these girls have any common sense? That thing that let you see through the surface to what was beneath. They all saw a pretty girl sighing beautifully, didn't they? And it warmed their hearts. All I saw was a very spoiled and pretty girl who would be traded by her father for power and influence and a bunch of fools who wished the same for themselves.

My cheeks burned hot at the thought, because I would be traded, too and for considerably less and knowing about it wasn't doing me any favors.

"But that night," the old woman said, "disaster struck, for the Wittenbrand came."

Tales of the Wittenbrand were always full of disaster. No one ever mentioned all the work it probably took to clean up after them. Oh, it might make a fine story to come striding in and tear out the city gate with your bare hands with nothing more said about it but a wink and a smile, but no one mentioned the stone masons and woodcarvers, locksmiths and pursers who had to get involved after that. No one spoke of Jamus, the gate guard who was let go because he couldn't guard a thousand-stone gate without it getting stolen out from under him. No one told those stories.

I chuckled in the privacy of my own mind. If I were a storyteller, those were the stories I would tell, and in those stories I would marry the princess off to someone or something truly hilarious. I would have her marry a toad so that her father could stave off a plague of the creatures, or a fire-breathing steed so her father could equip his military with powerful mounts, or better yet, I would have her marry the Lord of the Wittenbrand and then we would see how much good her sighs and pretty poses were.

In retrospect, it was probably those generous thoughts that led to the curse that fell on me that night.

"What were they like?" the girl beside me asked, clutching her hands to her chest in anticipation.

"The Wittenbrand were far too beautiful – beautiful in the way that the coldest days of winter are – perfect, brittle, and deadly. They swept into our court in silence and in silence we received them. But Princess Margaretta's bells on the end of her golden slippers made a jingling sound, and at the sound of her bell, they froze us to ice and stole away the Princess Margaretta in her golden dress and never have we seen her since."

"But why did they take Margaretta?" the girl beside me asked.

It was a silly question. She'd been there in a golden dress, hadn't she? In the middle of a famine. If the stories of the Wittenbrand were true – that they loved sparkling things and beauty, that they were made of arrogance and haughty desires – then who else would they take? But I did not believe in Wittenbrand or in golden princesses stolen away or in any of that nonsense. Much more likely that this Princess Margaretta had simply run away with a lover or been disgraced and hustled out of sight by her worried family.

Likely, Princess Chasida would wear her fine dress tonight and find herself well-matched to a promising warrior or a prince of a nearby nation, and her life would be well and prosperous. And we would not be frozen unless the servants had forgotten to light the fires in all their excitement.

"Princess Margaretta was bold and bright, unafraid of anything," the old woman said fondly. "It was her bright, bold spirit that drew them in and mesmerized them. They could not help themselves. They were enchanted and so they made enchantment and took her for their own. And when she was gone only one of her golden bells remained in the center of the dance floor."

"Will Princess Chasida be taken, too?" the girl asked.

I almost rolled my eyes. Really? The only threat to Princess Chasida was likely jealous ladies like the one beside me. At least I could be grateful that my meager hopes came with common sense. I had no need to be envious of the princess, since I never had a chance at what she would have. You couldn't be disappointed if you didn't hope for anything.

"She will not be taken," the old woman said, "for one of you will wear the bell that was once Princess Margaretta's and that will prevent bad luck from befalling her."

There was a gasp of horror from around me and really, I would have liked to pretend I thought it was real, but it was obviously staged. They'd all been expecting this.

"But who will wear the bell?" the girl next to me asked, batting her eyelashes and looking right at me.

And that was when my heart sank, because it was immediately obvious to me that the chair I was sitting in hadn't been empty for no reason.

"Luck shall decide," the old woman said. "Look under your chairs, ladies. The woman with the golden bell under her chair shall wear it tonight for the sake of the princess."

Yes. I was clearly the goat who had been staked out for the false mountain lion.

Wryly, I reached under my chair and drew out the golden bell I knew would be there. The room broke into happy smiles.

"Such an honor!" the girl beside me said in a whisper.

"And don't forget to return it when the ball is over," the old woman said placidly. "It's worth quite a lot."

Chapter Three

WE BROKE to eat in late afternoon. The servants had pulled together a hurried lunch for everyone in the dining hall and most were standing to eat or hurrying in and out. The King and Queen had taken lunch in their rooms so no one need stand on ceremony. I looked for my father and brothers through the masses of moving people and as I did, I heard a girl beside me talking with another lady of fine breeding. The girl was the one who had been practicing her poses before the mirror in the ladies' work room. Her voice had the same bell-like quality I expected. Which reminded me, I'd left the bell in the workroom. I was afraid of losing something so valuable. I'd have to remember to go back and get it before the ball.

"I have heard rumors that a special suitor for the princess will be arriving tonight, Lady Allise. Who do you think that could be?" the girl asked, her words clearly concealing the fact that she was quite sure *she* knew who it would be.

"A foreign prince perhaps?" Lady Allise suggested from behind a carefully placed hand. Her bright eyes sparkled and the emerald hanging over her forehead swayed as she whispered. "They say the king has fine hopes for her. Perhaps the foreign prince will bring some of his lords with him and you and I could have our pick for the dancing. Wouldn't a fine exotic lord be exciting? Perhaps they kiss in a different way in foreign lands."

"I've heard that it's not so much a matter of *how* they kiss but that they do it with a passion that would put a Pensman to shame!"

They were giggling together when I caught sight of my family and hurried to join them at the dinner table. My father was glowing with pleasure.

"Two reasons to celebrate, sweet Izolda," he said, ruffling my hair affectionately. "We went to the practice yards with the aim of finding a place for Svetgin in the military and to our delight the commander was there and has offered him a place as squire for one of the King's own knights."

Svetgin grinned at me broadly, barely able to sit still he was so excited. "I will train with Rodham the Brave, Izolda. Is that not wonderful news?"

"It is." I smiled broadly to share his pleasure with him, but I noted the faint tinge of sadness in my father's eyes at the news. He must make this move now before Svetgin grew older if he wanted to secure a strong place for him, but we would all miss my brother. His enthusiasm and boldness were a welcome reprieve from the sternness of our hold.

Rolgrin smiled, too, though I was certain there was envy mixed in his warm congratulations. He must stay and learn the running of the keep and hold for he was to inherit, but there would be no riding out in glorious armor or swinging a sword with fellow combatants. My father already had him working his tallies and studying the rotation of crops for summer.

"But you said there were two reasons, Father," I reminded him, hoping to cheer Rolgrin up. Perhaps the other news was for him. A blacksmith who could make finer swords.

This time the sadness in my father's eyes deepened further. "It so happened that while we were in the practice ring, the Landholder of the Fallowplains arrived with a delivery of horseflesh and we spoke together. He is in need of a bride before the spring and his offer was a reasonable one. You'll find Fallowplains a well-suited place for you, daughter. The hold is close enough that you may visit your family every year and you have always done well with horses – the breeding of which is their main occupation."

I schooled my expression to calm, hiding the sudden flare of panic in me. I felt so suddenly cold that it made my head light. Spring? That was only two months from now. And a return to Pensmoore before spring would be impractical. Which meant he would have me married here and now without even a goodbye to my mother first.

I swallowed down a sudden stab of sorrow. After all, this was very sensible. Even knowing nothing of the man in question, I knew that his status as landholder and the fine nature of his holding was the upper limit of what my father could hope to secure for me. He had done very cleverly indeed.

One sad little passion-tinged hope sunk deep within the waves of my heart. There would be no torrid romances or soaring love affairs for me.

I forced a small smile. "Thank you, Father. It is a fine match."

My father's face softened slightly, and he spoke quietly so he would not be overheard. "I think you will find the man acceptable, also, daughter. He is young at only one and thirty, and his first wife died leaving him no heir. He seems as though he is lonely, but he spoke long and well of horses and the keeping of them, and I think you will find that in his single-minded passion for his work, he is unlikely to have acquired many vices. You can see him there now at the line beside the food tables. He is the man with the long black coat and the short beard."

I followed his nod and saw a large, wide man with a round weathered face and a short blond beard. He was not good looking, but he did not look wicked, and his gaze was turned inward, not lingering on the ladies of the court. I could not ask for better.

"You've done very well for me, Father," I assured him, taking in a long breath. I must ready myself. There was work ahead and a marriage and family to face. Fortunately, the things my mother sent me could serve as a trousseau. and while my future husband looked a little worn, his clothing was of good quality. We would not live in poverty. I could work with that.

Right? I didn't need someone good looking or passionate or brave like a warrior from a story. That was all just window dressing for men who usually thought women were temporary entertainments or bargaining chips. But a tiny rebel part of me had been holding out hope for just that kind of man and it was wailing deep within me, refusing to die quietly. Just die, you fool hope! And would you be quiet while you do it for pity's sake?

"I have promised to introduce you tonight at the princess's presentation ball," my father said earnestly. "Adorn yourself well and prettily, daughter."

I nodded my head, but though I was a sensible girl who knew a good thing when she saw it, I still couldn't help the little pang of sadness in my heart that sprang from a wish to be whisked away by a handsome lover and who would speak golden words into my ear and sigh my name with longing.

I think that perhaps, it was that very wish that doomed me. Along with all the other things, obviously.

Chapter Four

BY EVENING, even *I* was excited for the princess's presentation ball. I had cleaned my traveling clothing and had them packed away again, ready for the inevitable wedding and travel to my new home. I put on my finest wool gown – a deep green, beautifully woven creation of my mother's that hugged my figure nicely all the way to the floor. Over that, my embroidered, sleeveless overdress was laced into place and I carefully braided my own hair in the most elaborate style I knew. It wasn't much. I still looked like the daughter of one of the poorer landholders, but it was my best, and hopefully both my father and my newly betrothed husband would be pleased with my appearance.

I tried very hard not to think of that round face smiling at me. A girl should probably want her future husband to smile for her, but the thought made me just a little ill. It occurred to me that tonight he would be sizing me up like he sized up his brood mares. Would he wonder if I would carry well? If my feed needed to be adjusted?

I took a deep breath. It wasn't sensible to be ungrateful for this opportunity. I would watch for his smile with the same curiosity that I'd employed when I watched the servants set up the ball – and hopefully the same sense of distance.

It didn't do to get too invested in your own life. That only led to disappointment.

I realized as I was leaving my room, that I didn't even know his name. I was going to marry a man whose name I did not know. My heart leapt into my throat again, but I carefully breathed it back down. Vapors and excitements were for girls with money and position, not for those who had to think judiciously of their futures. And not for those who were going to be measured in hands.

My father opened his door, and my brothers exited their room with him. They wore clean, brushed clothing and my father had taken the time to comb his beard. A little shiver of sadness rolled through me. This may be the last time we were all together. After this, I would be married and living in a hold far away and my brother Svetgin would be serving in the King's army.

I hugged him on an impulse.

"What has flown into your head, Izolda?" he said, batting me off. "I'm dancing with beautiful ladies of the court tonight, not sisters!"

Rolgrin was slightly more tolerant. Perhaps he understood what was happening. He let me hug him briefly before hurrying down the hall after Svetgin.

My father was misty-eyed as he embraced me, and he even placed a small kiss on my brow. "Were this your ball and were you princess here you could look no finer, daughter."

I was surprised by his compliment but secretly pleased. It took the edge off the worry I felt as we sallied through the long winding corridors and staircases toward the Great Hall, where the ball would take place. Our rooms in the old servants' quarters were the farthest possible from the hall and I was almost ready to sit down for a while by the time we finally made it into the massive room.

"Lord Savataz of Northpeak and his daughter Izolda," the herald said as we entered.

No one turned to look except for the Lord of Fallowplains who bowed to his companion and strode toward us. I kept my face calm and quiet as his eyes studied me and I saw them linger on my hips.

Yes, get a good eyeful. They're very narrow indeed if you're comparing them to a horse.

It was hard not to feel resentment as he clearly was checking for the pink of health in my cheeks and any sign I could breed well, but I was being unfair to him. He must be clever in his choices just as my father must. Perhaps he had married for love the first time and had come to regret it when his wife died without providing an heir. It was a sad thought and I tried to tell myself it was true if only because it made me feel compassion toward him rather than anxiety.

"Lord Savataz," he said, bowing slightly to my father.

"Lord Danske, may I present my daughter Izolda."

Lord Danske bowed nicely to me and I forced my lips into a smile.

"Greetings to you, my Lord. It is a fair night." My voice sounded too fragile. It should be strong and powerful. It should tell the world I held the reins of my future strongly in my hands. Instead, it told them I was terrified.

"May I be bold, beautiful Izolda," the Lord of Fallowplains said awkwardly, clearing his throat partway through his speech. "May I, ahem, be bold and request a dance from you this evening? The akul, if you would favor me, as it is the only one I know."

No one may now say that I do not have the restraint of a saint. No one. Because the akul involves a great deal of prancing and those who dance it look like they think they are horses. And still, I did not snort a laugh or so much as twitch a lip.

"It will be as you please, my Lord."

"You may call me Leonid," he said, and for a moment he looked like only a nervous man and not a Lord arranging a marriage for himself. I softened.

"If you prefer not to dance, Leonid," I said gently, "I do not require it of you."

He sagged with relief.

"We should suit admirably, if you don't think me too bold in saying so, Izolda." He looked around nervously. "If you don't mind, I'll beg my leave for the moment. I was called away to the stable – my horse had a hot leg and none of the fool stable boys noticed – and so I missed eating at midday. It has left me ravenous."

He was gone as soon as I was done making my bow. I was trying very hard not to imagine life with the ravenous Lord Fallowplains – or Leonid, as I supposed I would have to get used to calling him.

"Daughter?" my father asked, watching me carefully. "You are pleased with the match?"

"Of course," I said with a smile. I was about to take his hand when the herald spoke again and this time, the whole room went still.

"The King, the Queen, and Princess Chasida!"

We fell into bows and curtsies but not before I caught a glimpse of Princess Chasida. She was indeed the sparkling gem of the nation. And she had not brought bad luck on herself by wearing gold like her great aunt Margaretta. Instead, she was dressed in a gown like a sparkling cloud that flowed around her such that it made her look half magic. It was made entirely of blue cloth. Blue.

I was not superstitious, I reminded myself as I sank into my curtsy. But I was also very glad not to be wearing blue. It was so much worse than gold.

I had barely managed to rise when a finger and thumb grabbed my ear, pulling me to my feet, and I looked right into the eyes of the old woman from the work room.

"The bell, girl," she hissed. "Where is the bell?"

Chapter Five

I RUSHED FROM THE BALLROOM, not even stopping to give my father an explanation for my strange behavior. I'd forgotten the bell! And while I didn't believe in any of these superstitions, there was just something about tonight with the Princess so bright and beautiful, and the whispers and the wind howling around the castle and that blue, blue dress that was making shivers run up and down my spine like a squirrel on a tree branch.

I lifted up the skirts of my woolen dress and sprinted down the empty corridors and up the lonely staircases. Every noble and servant in the castle was in the ballroom or the kitchens or the coach house right now. There wasn't a soul to slow me.

My breath heaved in my lungs when I finally reached the work room. I snatched the bell from under my chair where I'd left it and paused for one gasping breath to look out the wide window.

I could hardly make out the rooflines of the surrounding buildings. The wind roared cold and harsh, sending gusts of glittering snow puffing with its every movement. It was cold enough that the snow sparkled like shredded diamonds and frost filled the air. I couldn't even see the moon above.

I thought I heard hooves on cobbles and a shout from below, but I didn't recognize the harsh consonants of the words. Perhaps the princess was going to receive a foreign prince after all.

I drew in a second rasping breath and then spun on my heel and paused.

Somehow, impossibly, I could hear the swell of the orchestra, through the open workroom window, and for a bare moment I thought I had turned to confront a dark-haired girl with high color in her cheeks and a sharp, intelligent look in her grey eyes. But it was only my own reflection in the large mirror.

I shook my head and sprinted back down the halls and through the stairways and corridors, my feet echoing loudly through the empty castle wings.

I slowed as I drew nearer the Great Hall. I needed to catch my breath. I must be a sight after that run. The bell jangled merrily as I carefully patted down my braided hair and tucked a loose strand behind one ear, the sound of the bell the only thing I heard.

Jingle. Jingle. Jingle.

My heart was slowing down. My breathing returning to normal.

I plastered a cheerful smile on my face.

And then hesitated.

Why could I hear the bell so clearly when I was just outside the hall? Shouldn't I hear the orchestra? The party?

I stepped past two men standing on either side of the doorframe, their eyes fixed on something within.

And then I froze.

Everyone in the room was standing perfectly still and silent, though they swayed slightly, their chests rising and falling just enough to tell me this was not a trick of my imagination or a spell.

I had a perfect view of the ballroom from the door, almost as if someone had parted the crowd just for me.

I saw my father first, a look of panic on his face as his eyes met mine. I had to tear my gaze away so I could see the rest. I could not find my brothers in the crowds, but I was surprised to notice that my betrothed was watching me with an identical look on his face to that my father wore, as if he, too, was worried for me. It was surprisingly endearing, and it warmed me in a pleasant way. Perhaps being married to Leonid would not be so bad after all.

But I snatched my gaze from his, too, looking to see what was going on.

My bell still jingled slightly as I took a step forward and finally saw King Feolin Pensmoore and Queen Illandre Pensmoore standing just in front of their thrones on the other end of the room. It was as if they had risen in surprise only to find themselves stuck on their feet. They were mirror images of shock – each with a hand reaching toward their blue-shrouded daughter who stood before them facing the ballroom. Her face was so pale that I was afraid she might be dead, and her lips were as blue as her dress.

Her mouth quivered slightly as if she longed to speak but was fighting against an equal longing to keep silent. A single tear streaked down her cheek.

But it was not the princess who had my full attention.

It was the five men standing in the middle of the room. Foreigners, for certain. The crowd had parted so that there was a ring of empty space all around them, and at their very center there stood a man, no taller than all the rest, and yet somehow he seemed to take up more space.

If I were being quite honest – which I probably wouldn't be no matter what the circumstances entailed – he was almost exactly like the fantasy man I'd envisioned falling passionately in love with. The one I was currently trying to mentally murder in my psyche. That one.

He had the same strong shoulders and neatly narrowed hips. He had the same corded arms and sharp jawline. The same black hair and dashing good looks. The same sharp expression that seemed to stab to the heart of your secrets. The exact same smirking irreverence that so often painted my imaginary lover's face.

He was tailor made for my dream-world, except for one small detail that I would certainly never have added.

He had a blue beard.

Not blue like a jay, but blue like a hound or a horse. It was trimmed so close to his face that it was more stubble than beard, and yet I felt frozen by it.

Only the Whittenbrand wore blue.

And it was with that thought that I realized they were all wearing blue in varying shades. Some of their clothing was dusky dove grey-blue and some a powerful peacock. Some a thick blue-black that was so dark it was nearly midnight, and some a light, airy blue that sang of faraway oceans.

The man with the blue beard wore a coat of that deep midnight with a high collar and a small white neckerchief at the throat. He wore a waistcoat under it that clung to his frame in a way that made me swallow. It was a brilliant cerulean. His breeches were just as revealing as the vest and were a smoky Prussian. I did not let my gaze linger on those.

If there had been any doubt about who these men were, all doubt was removed.

Legends had come alive. The Wittenbrand were here.

The bearded one – who I was beginning to think of as "Bluebeard" – made a sudden move toward the princess and wrapped his hand around her throat.

He was inhumanly quick and inhumanly graceful. It was as if a pillar of smoke had come alive and leapt at her. Or perhaps, as if a falcon had morphed into a man. Or whatever a Wittenbrand was.

"So beautiful," he said silkily. "Will you not greet me, Princess? Have you not prayed for a powerful husband, and one rich as sin besides? I have gold of such quantity that your father could fit his soldiers in golden breastplates and greaves. Your mother could sew it into the gown of every maid in the castle. You could gild your very walls with the stuff. Will you not speak and greet me as one of your own?"

His eyes seemed to dance and laugh at her.

The princess's throat bobbed as she swallowed. Her eyes met mine across the room, filled with terror and, when she noticed the tiny golden bell in my hand, filled with hate.

And she was right. I hadn't been here with the bell and now the Wittenbrand were here to snatch her away. But why was no one speaking? Were they under some kind of a spell?

I took a step forward, not sure what I could do and yet feeling responsible to do *something*. After all, it was my error that had allowed all of this. My oversight. My tardiness.

I couldn't let her suffer for me.

I took a second step, and the bell sang out. Bluebeard spun, releasing the princess, and stalked toward me.

In Northpeak, we lost a man almost every year to cougar attacks. I couldn't help but think – as he took that predatory step toward me – that perhaps the men who died were so fascinated by the cougar that they couldn't run or even scream. I knew I was.

He tilted his head, his eyes lighting with delight.

"What a singular golden bell you bear, maiden. But your manners are very poor. Will you not greet a visitor to your King's court?"

My eyes met his. His were blue – of course – and so light they were almost white. My stomach flipped as I realized they were the eyes of a cat, not a human, with black slashes for pupils. They pierced into my own and I could hardly look away.

"Will you not speak and bid us welcome?" He bit his full lower lip after he said that, his cat's eyes dancing as if he were laughing at a joke I hadn't heard.

It seemed suddenly as if he were balancing along a high branch. A bare movement on either side and he would fall to his death, and only my greeting might prevent that. People in such a dire state had a tendency to do wild things. He took a step backward and grabbed the princess by the hair, jerking her head back and exposing her throat.

"Or perhaps we'll wait and see what you say when we're done with this pretty trinket."

My heart leapt into my chest, racing so hard that my breath was coming in ragged gasps. All my fault. If he killed her, it would be on my head, and all because I disregarded a silly princess and her silly friends.

The only sensible thing to do was to try to calm him down.

"I greet you, foreign Lord, and wish you well on this winter night." My voice as clear as a crystal bell. Where had that voice been when I met my betrothed?

As if my words had broken a spell, Bluebeard dropped Princess Chasida. She fell to the ground in a heap, sobbing loudly. Around me, there was a sigh that sounded almost like regret or guilt. My eyes narrowed. Something was going on that I knew nothing about.

Bluebeard smiled – a wolfish, wicked smile.

I felt something tighten in my chest that I couldn't identify. My hand reached up to clutch it, but I'd barely managed a gasp of my own before I caught the eye of my father. His mouth was hanging open in an agonized expression. He took one stumbling step forward and suddenly Rolgrin was there beside him, supporting his arm and whispering urgently in his ear.

"The Law of Greeting," Bluebeard said, his grin widening so now he reminded me of a fox. His eyes seemed to be fixed on me still, which made no sense. What was the Law of Greeting?

Though they had started breathing and murmuring again, the court was still. But this time it was not the frozen stillness of fear, it was the waiting stillness of anticipation. Fear crept up my spine like a slow spider.

To my shock, the Lord of the Fallowplains moved forward, a determined, purposeful look on his face.

"You may not take her, Wittenbrand," he declared. His awkwardness had been shed, and in this one moment he looked like a hero of legend rather than a backwoods breeder of horses who needed an heir.

I bit my lip and tasted blood.

Bluebeard's grin turned to fury. "By the Law of Greeting you know I may take whatever greets me upon my arrival. It is the long-standing agreement between the Court of Pensmoore and the Wittenbrand."

My heart stuttered painfully.

"But you haven't been here in generations," the King said, finally speaking. He had positioned himself before Princess Chasida, shielding her with his own rather substantial body. As if she were still in some kind of danger. Maybe she was. No one had bothered to teach me about the Law of Greeting. Maybe there were more laws I did not know. I was finding it just a little hard to breathe.

"Be glad I have not," Bluebeard said softly, his low voice rumbling like the thunder of a coming storm. "I could have visited you many times over the years and yet I have reserved this moment for a special need. I have come for a bride."

A *bride*?

"The girl is promised to me," Lord Fallowplains – Leonid – said, striding through the crowd toward Bluebeard. My eyes widened and my hand reached up to clutch my chest over my heart. I had not expected so much loyalty from a man who had only just met me. My father had chosen very well indeed.

So why was I still finding it so hard to take a breath?

Bluebeard smirked. "Well, now the promise is broken by the Law of Greeting. Be on your way, hale mortal."

"I will not," Leonid said, swallowing nervously. "It is my life for hers. You will not take her."

He was within reach of Bluebeard now, arms crossed over his chest, squaring his stance, his round chin thrust forward. I had thought he was a large man when I met him, but he seemed small in front of Bluebeard, even though he had four inches at least on the Wittenbrand.

Bluebeard sighed and made an expression of distaste. "What is this? A duel? Over a woman not yet your wife? How horribly last century. I thought we'd moved past that. Haven't we moved past that, Sparrow?"

One of the figures with him snickered unkindly.

Leonid cleared his throat. "I am offering a duel, yes."

"No," I said quickly. "You don't need to do this for me, Leonid."

He made a gesture to quiet me, and Bluebeard snarled.

"Do not silence my betrothed, mortal." His hand shot out, grabbing Leonid by the neck and shook him so quickly that I hardly realized what was happening. Leonid's large head snapped back and then forward like a doll in the mouth of a very large dog.

Princess Chasida screamed so loudly that I heard nothing else and her guards finally came to their senses, rushing forward to surround the royal family.

Bluebeard flung Leonid's limp body aside and I struggled to see him. Was Leonid dead or merely unconscious? How had Bluebeard done that with just one hand? To a man larger than he was?

My hands flew up over my mouth and the little golden bell dropped to the floor, rolling across the shining marble to Bluebeard's feet.

Bluebeard snatched the bell up, bouncing it on his palm like a toy. It rang every time it struck his palm again. Like a death bell signalling to the town that someone was gone.

Around me, people were shuffling backward, making the gap around me wider and wider. I looked to my own father and he looked back at me, sadness and resignation in his face. Resignation. That was what hit me so hard. What was he going to do? Was he going to try to step up and fight, too?

I shook my head at him, but he took a determined step forward.

I glanced at Leonid. He was very still on the ground. I wasn't certain if he was dead – but he might be. I glanced back at my father pushing through the crowd, his face drained of blood. If I didn't do something fast, that would be him, too.

"I will be your bride," I said. The words had tumbled out of me so quickly that everyone seemed to freeze, listening. "I will be your bride and go from here with you. Only let me say goodbye to my family, and gather my things, and let there be a proper wedding before I leave these lands with you."

Because if I was going to lose everything, I should at least be sure we were properly married and I was not to be a slave or a concubine.

“Done.” Was that sorrow I saw in Bluebeard’s eyes as they met mine? It must have been a shadow because his eyes immediately shifted to trickery as he turned to the King. “Go find whatever holy man you use and bring him here. There will be a wedding before the hour is gone.” He turned to his own men. “Sparrow, Grosbeak, gather her things and take them to our mounts. When the ceremony is completed, we ride.”

"This man was so unlucky as to have a blue beard ... Adding to their disgust and aversion was the fact that he had already been married to several wives, and nobody knew what had become of them."

- Charles Perrault, Bluebeard,

1697 as translated by Andrew Lang in The Blue Fairy Book 1889.

Chapter Six

THE KING CLEARED HIS THROAT. I couldn't even see him anymore behind all his guards. "By the Law of Marriage, you must spend at least one night with your new bride under the roof of her guardian. Since she is of my land, this castle may stand in stead of her home."

Bluebeard waved a mocking hand. "Is it not night? Have we not spent it here beneath your roof? Why ask me to meet conditions that are already met?"

The King's voice sounded strained. "We have laws, and you have laws. The Law of Greeting is where they meet. If you ask us to respect that law, we must respect all the laws."

"This was not required of me the last time I came to claim what is mine."

"A different man was King then. Perhaps he had less fortitude than I do. We will honor the laws. But we will not be dogs before you rolling in the mud. We have laws of our own and we will uphold them. Be ye noble or craven, of sound purpose or twisted, she will be your bride but only if you marry her properly."

My legs felt weak beneath me. The realization that I was actually going to marry this man – that the King was negotiating that the marriage be legal and binding – was suddenly becoming far too real. I met my father's eyes across the room, and I let one moment of my fear show, let him offer his strength in the shared misery in his own eyes, and then I dropped my hands from my mouth and stiffened my spine. I lifted my chin and forced my face into a calm expression. I could be sensible about this.

Bluebeard was here right now in the Court of Pensmoore. He had already killed my betrothed. My family would be next, and then the simpering girls from the workroom, and the King, and Queen, and Princess Chasida, who was having hysterics on the royal dais, and the soldiers and grooms and servants and everyone else. I had no doubt that he and the four others with him could accomplish that. No doubt at all. They wouldn't swagger in here demanding brides – and talking to kings as if they were grooms – if they couldn't enforce their will. Which meant that if I cared for my family and had compassion on these other people, if I cared for the stability of our nation, then there was only one sensible thing to do and that was to marry this foreign blue-bearded murderer and keep them all safe.

It was even a clever match. After all, I was the daughter of a very minor house, and quite dispensable, and he was a threatening foreign lord. A foreign lord of the Wittenbrand. He was one of the strange long-lived beings of legend who scared us in tales told on long winter nights. He was one of the ones rumored to steal children from their cribs and carry off grown women to be their wives. I paused at that thought.

Well now. It was hardly a rumor, was it? It was happening to me. Perhaps I'd been too quick to label things superstitions when they were not.

I'd barely finished the thought when my father and Rolgrin finally made their way to me.

My mouth was very dry.

"You don't have to do this," Rolgrin said as soon as they'd joined me. He shot a furious look at the Wittenbrand, his sword hand grasping at the empty spot on his belt. No one had worn weapons to the ball.

Bluebeard heard him and leaned toward us in a very feline way. One of his eyebrows quirked upward like he was going to share a delicious secret. "If she does not, then the Law of Greeting says that your kingdom is mine from the stones to the rooftops. Every speck of dust of this place will belong to me, and then I could still marry her – and every other woman in this land – for she would be mine, too."

I shuddered.

"But then why have you never done this before?" Rolgrin demanded.

He was young and furious, determined to protect me. I shot my father a worried look and he put a hand on my brother's shoulder.

"Who says I have not?" Bluebeard asked. "I'll take that man's lying tongue."

My eyes were so wide now that they stung.

"Princess Margaretta," I gasped. "You were the one who took her."

"Was that her name?" Bluebeard asked indifferently. "Golden-haired round little thing, like that girl who wears our colors so boldly?"

He spared a glance for Princess Chasida and her bright blue dress. I almost thought I saw a glimmer of disgust on his face. He must not like to see mortals wearing his color without warrant.

"I hardly remember her," he said indifferently, and Chasida shrieked in terror.

My father's face grew whiter and I grabbed his other hand, hoping he would see sense.

"Girls are married all the time for the safety of their nations," I whispered to him. "Usually they are princesses and not lower nobles, but it does happen. Even with people like us."

I was surprised by a clinking sound behind me. To my shock, a pair of the King's guards were there with Svetgin between them, locking him in manacles.

"What –" I gasped, and then the King's guards moved fast, ripping my brother and father from me and chaining them with Svetgin. "What are you doing?"

I felt suddenly bereft.

It was the King himself who spoke. As his voice echoed out to me, I realized that the hall was emptying. The pretty girls in their dresses were gone. The band was nowhere to be seen. The Queen was helping the hysterical princess out of the room and most of the guards were going with them.

Chasida gave me a look of pity before she was escorted out the door. She had stayed silent. She had known the law. I didn't know if she pitied me for being ignorant or being a fool but at least I hadn't had hysterics in front of everyone. And that was something I could comfort myself with in the wee hours of the night.

"We don't want anyone else to die, Izolda of Savataz. I'm sure you can understand that." The King's tone was not unkind. "It's for the safety of your brothers and father. They cannot decide to do something heroic under lock and key. They cannot be killed by the Wittenbrand if we keep them from being fools. I promise you, fair lily, I will release them all the moment you and your bridegroom are out of sight of the city walls. Until then, they will be kept comfortable, but they will remain under guard."

One glance back at the red in my father's cheeks told me the King was wiser than I had guessed. My father *had* been planning to fight for me. Perhaps he had been waiting for the right moment or for Svetgin to join them so they would be three to five. Either way, in that moment I was grateful to the King. My mother would get to keep two of her three children and my father as well. This was better. Rolgrin was but seventeen and Svetgin only fifteen. They did not need to die for an older sister when they hadn't even tasted life properly.

One death in exchange for their lives – and also the lives of thousands of others – was a small price to pay.

"As you say, my King," I said respectfully, and he gave me a rueful smile. His craggy face and reddish nose looked almost comforting. Which was saying something. Truly, this was an odd day.

The King hadn't left the dais. Now he gestured, and my family was carefully brought to one side below the dais.

"If we are to have a wedding, let us do it properly," he said stiffly. "The bride's family are on this side. And the bridegroom's on this side."

Bluebeard chuckled, still bouncing my golden bell on his palm like a cat playing with a toy.

"I do not think you wish to see my family, little King. They would give you nightmares that may kill you in your sleep."

He rubbed his blue beard and considered me in a way that made me think again of a cat. This time, of one eyeing a mouse. I stood even straighter to show him I was no mouse. He smirked.

He could smirk all he wanted. I was not the one with a horrendous blue beard or the need to trick people into marrying me. I'd had someone who actually wanted to marry me.

I shot a guilty glance to where Leonid lay – lifeless – on the ground. I wanted to believe he had merely swooned. I was almost certain I was wrong.

He'd been a good man, though I'd barely known him at all. He hadn't deserved to die honorably defending a woman he'd only just met. He deserved far better. What would his hold do now with no heir and no

Lord? I felt a stab of worry for them, but I must not let that distract me. There was nothing I could do to help, and I knew the King would take care of them. He would install one of his best knights there to manage the hold and people, and in time the wound would heal. Though likely Leonid's horses would miss him for the rest of their lives. I had a feeling that they were very attached to him.

"Gathering wool?" someone whispered in a rough voice at my ear.

I startled and turned with narrowed eyes to see the wicked glint in Bluebeard's.

"I was mourning the death of my betrothed before marrying another. It seemed fitting. Especially since my new husband was his slayer." I made my words icy cold.

"Is that who that was?" He said the words like they were maple candy he was turning over on his tongue. "Your betrothed. What a shame. You could have borne his gigantic babies."

"You know he was," I said acidly. "He told you so."

"I wasn't listening. I rarely bother listening to mortals. They speak and speak, but in the end, they just die before they're even done talking," he said, waving a hand languidly. "Speak to my riddle, fair mortal. What keeps you waiting until it dies?"

"Hope?" I asked.

He chucked in delight. "A better answer than mine. I was going to say 'kings.' Can we get on with this ceremony?"

"Yes," the King said, and I saw the bitterness souring in his eyes – but there was relief there, too, and guilt whenever he glanced at my father. He knew how close he had come to seeing his own daughter wed this way. And he knew that he'd have no trouble from my father over it. My father was a loyal King's man. He'd be loyal to the point of death. Even now. Even when his daughter stood substitute for the princess in a wedding meant to protect the kingdom.

Someone shoved an old man in a robe forward and I startled. I was too deep in my own thoughts. Had my heart ever sped this fast before?

He looked priest-like, but I wouldn't know. We only had monasteries up in Northpeak and the monks only came out in the summer to sell honey mead and, three other times a year, to sing to us of holy things and perform marriage and death rites all in one big batch. They preferred to divide life into slices like a goodwife with a pie.

The old man tottered slightly, blinking as he looked around him.

"It's a wedding, brother," the King murmured.

"Ah yes," the old priest said, "And we'll do the traditional vows, of course."

"No." Bluebeard snapped the word. Behind him, his men shuffled like nervous horses.

Of course, he wouldn't want to do traditional vows. There was no way this ravager of kingdoms and thief of maidens was going to promise fidelity to me.

"You promised the marriage would be legal," the King prompted. "There must be vows."

And for just a moment, I saw a glimmer of pain in my enemy's eyes. Now, what was that? I had a mind to draw it out further and examine it. It could be useful in keeping me alive.

"I have never said vows before," he said in a way that made me think of snakes hissing.

"But you will say them to me," I said firmly. I didn't need the king to stand up for me. I could stand up for myself. "Or we will not be wed."

He looked at me for a very long time and behind him, one of the men spoke in a language I did not know. It sounded like a curse.

Bluebeard bit his lip and then said, "And what will you give me in return, mortal woman?"

"The same vows," I said, my cheeks flushing. "You give me yours and I give you mine. Is that not what marriage is?"

There was a glitter in his strange cat's eye, as if he'd never considered such a thing, and for a moment his hand strayed to the hilt of his sword. My breath caught in my throat. I didn't dare let it out. I had the feeling I was a heartbeat away from him drawing the sword and slicing my throat, but after a moment he tilted his head slightly to the side and then he laughed.

He smirked. "I will offer the vows of my people."

Behind him, one of his men shut his mouth with a loud click and the other gasped.

I darted a glance to him. There were three remaining, as one had gone to gather my things. All three wore stony expressions on their beautiful faces. They were all of swarthy of skin and hair with brilliant blue cat's eyes – but while their coloring matched and their beauty was similar, each had his own appeal. One was a woman. One had a huge scar that twisted up from either side of his mouth. My future husband seemed taller than the rest of them – though he was not – and with his blue beard and a scar that cut down across one brow, he looked the roughest and cruelest of all.

"Then let us say our vows together," the priest burbled happily. "The groom may begin."

Bluebeard was staring at me like I should realize how significant this was. He leaned forward slightly, looking as if he might leap at any moment. Seeing as it was my wedding, I was very cognizant of its importance.

"As long as rivers run and moon shines, as long as the earth has bones and death has claws, as long as the ages pass and fail – that long shall I be husband to you. Flesh of my flesh and bone of my bone you will be. Spirit of my spirit, heart of my own heart, fall what may, we shall be one. Your days shall be mine and your happiness my own. My body I dedicate to none other. The bounty of my wealth is yours. If ever it be otherwise, may I waste away with sickness and may famine eat my strength, and may my enemies overtake me, and siphon from me the blood of my life."

Well, that was somewhat extreme.

Perhaps I should have been horrified. A smart girl would have been. But mostly, I was just fascinated. This vow was deeper than any I'd heard before. It seemed to match the tightness that had surrounded my heart since I spoke my greeting. It was just as immobilizing. Just as binding. Just as deadly terrifying.

"And now the wife," the priest said. "Say your vows, kind lady."

I looked at Bluebeard and paled.

"It was you who wanted a real marriage and I have complied with your wishes, you ambitious climber." He said the words like he was spitting them. "You ask for things above you and I have granted them and now you reject my gift?"

"I reject nothing," I said carefully. I didn't know why he thought this was some kind of maneuver on my part, but I wasn't ready to see blood spilled over it, and there was violence in his eyes. "But I will need your help. The words are unfamiliar to me."

With his prompting, I repeated his vow.

"As long as rivers run and moon shines, as long as the earth has bones and death has claws, as long as the ages pass and fail – that long shall I be wife to you. Flesh of my flesh and bone of my bone you will be. Spirit of my spirit, heart of my own heart, fall what may, we shall be one. Your days shall be mine and your happiness my own. My body I dedicate to none other. The bounty of my wealth is yours. If ever it be otherwise, may I waste away with sickness and may famine eat my strength, and may my enemies overtake me, and siphon from me the blood of my life."

I felt a chill wash over me at my words. When I glanced behind me, my father's face was wet with tears and my brothers' expressions were sickened.

"And so, I declare, man and wife," the priest said, still seeming to be oblivious to our situation. "And you may kiss your bride."

"There will be no kisses," Bluebeard said.

And for that one thing, I was thankful to him.

Chapter Seven

"YOU SHOULD SAY YOUR GOODBYES NOW," Bluebeard said, his shining cat's eyes never leaving my face. He had an odd look on his face like he was trying to read my mind right through my skull. "We leave at first light. I think that counts as spending the night under your roof, little King."

The King's mouth tightened but wisely, he said nothing. What could he say? We all had heard of the power of the Wittenbrand – even if I'd been a skeptic until today.

A thousand years ago, they waged a war against humans and nearly destroyed us completely. We still didn't know why they'd called a truce and relented. We only knew that we were bound by some old treaty to allow them into our mortal courts if they asked it and to provide a tithe to them if requested. And apparently, there was this Law of First Greeting no one had told me about and now a Law of Marriage no one had seen fit to mention. Because obviously, you wouldn't mention it to the one person who likely should have been told. Where would the fun be in that?

Whoever had designed this world of Kings and Wittenbrand had been like the ladies in the workroom – not very interested in the consistency of their work.

I kissed my father's cheeks gently, ignoring – for the sake of his pride –

that they were so wet and his eyes so glassy that he likely saw only a blur instead of a daughter.

"Your honor is not besmirched," I whispered to him. "Tell my mother that you did all you could do and paid a high price for the sake of the kingdom. And do not forget that the King owes you now. It could have been his daughter who was taken. Be sensible. Demand a knighthood for Svetgin and a good bride for Rolgrin. Tell my mother that I love her and will miss her and that she must not blame any of you."

"My Izolda," my father began, but I kissed his cheeks again, embraced him, and his voice broke. He need not say anything, for I knew his heart and that he loved me and that he wished beyond anything that he could save me from this.

"I absolve you of any guilt," I said. "Live in peace."

I kissed each of my brothers and murmured to them, "Live well and be prosperous. Your sister is proud of you."

They seemed stunned as they spoke the words of goodbye back to me, their voices hollow with shame and their faces pale as death.

In time, they would forgive themselves. There had been no way they could protect me from this. I had sealed my own fate. It would have been silly to think otherwise or to expect the impossible from any of them. A part of me found it interesting that they had been willing to risk me to a marriage that only had a dice roll's chance of success as long as it was within a world they were comfortable with, but they were terrified to offer me to this foreigner and found it shameful, though the risk was similar to me. The difference was only in degrees and not in kind. For all I knew, this inhumanely beautiful monster also loved horses and spent his time breeding them. For all I knew, he could also be so obsessed with them that he thought of little else.

It was unlikely, but still possible.

But even though I could see all that, I loved them too much to want to leave them with sadness or shame.

"Cheer up, my father and brothers," I said bravely, "for though I may never see you again, you have given me in marriage to a foreign lord for the sake of our nation and should feel no shame in it. Indeed, I'm sure your King and country thank you."

I looked at the King. He swallowed and his face turned red almost instantly. There. I'd planted a sliver into his mind. He would always remember how he owed my family a debt.

Oddly, he leaned in for a fatherly kiss on the cheek. "Go with our blessing, daughter of Pensmoore."

And then I turned and faced my fate.

My new husband wore a strange expression on his face and a darkness in his eyes that made my heart speed, and my knees turn to jelly. I took one wavering step before I forced the iron of my will into my legs and managed a straight back and steady steps again. It took an effort of will that consumed most of my energy.

We were all silent as the King himself led us down a short corridor to a suite of rooms as fine as his own – perhaps they were his very own.

"Your men will be given appropriate accommodations," he said tightly. "And you are free to leave at dawn, having consummated your marriage and made a legal binding out of what has been offered nation to nation."

And now it was my face that was hot as fire as I realized why he'd insisted on a night beneath his roof and a wedding chamber for us both. And if I'd been irritated at my people for trading me off as tradition demanded, I was even more horrified at a King who offered my innocence up as the price of security for his kingdom.

And yet the practical side of me was impressed. It was a very tiny price for a kingdom to pay for security. And it cost the King almost nothing at all. He was getting a very clever bargain. Even if my cheeks flamed at how it would be paid. I doubted I could be so cold.

I did not meet his eye as my new husband growled in answer and opened the door.

"How hospitable," he spat. "Your laws, mortal man, are as delightful as your city."

The King seemed mollified by that – which was ridiculous. Could he not see that the Wittenbrand mocked both his laws and holdings?

At Bluebeard's curt nod into the room, I entered the suite before him and managed to hold myself together long enough for him to follow and lock the door behind us.

After that, it was all I could do to make it to the nearest flower pot before losing the lunch I'd hurriedly eaten at midday when my life seemed settled, and the supper of dried meat and hardtack I'd eaten on the road the night before, when I'd been excited to see the city for the very first time.

With the contents of my stomach, I brought up every hope I'd ever had of living a happy – or even a quiet and relatively peaceful – life.

"How very mortal of you," Bluebeard said with a grimace when I was done. He shoved a pitcher of wash water toward me and strode away as I dutifully washed out my mouth.

I was grateful he'd given me the whole jug. One more glance into the room and at the massive four-poster bed with its thousands of pillows and silken bedcoverings and I was heaving up the last of the acid in my belly. It turned out I needed most of the pitcher to rinse my mouth before I made it any farther into the room. Just the sight of that bed was enough to make me queasy again. I wasn't ready for this. Not with a man who had just killed another with his bare hands. Would he snap my neck, too?

"I will promise you very little beyond what promises have already been made," Bluebeard said from a chair by the fire, where he was reading a book entitled *Marvels of Modern Accountancy,* "but I can promise you this. I will feed you food that sits better in your stomach and has not soured. The ladies of my court do not spend most of their time bringing up what has been fed to them."

At least he thought I'd eaten something bad. That was a good thing. I swallowed down another wave of nausea. I doubted he'd be pleased if he learned the real reason for my sudden attack of illness. I didn't have much experience with men, but likely the idea that I was sick at the thought of him consummating our wedding would irritate him.

At the very least.

Possibly even enrage him.

The sensible thing would be to hide my feelings on the matter.

It was hard to do when he was already half disrobed, his jacket and shirt unbuttoned and open to his breeches and one of his legs slung up over the arm of the chair.

I looked around the room warily – trying to put my eyes on anything other than him. He was not entirely human with his too-quick movements, his flickering facial expressions, and those strange eyes mesmerized me.

He twitched his nose just a little when he spoke like a cat might. But none of that took away from the very masculine lines of his body or the way his muscles – laced with silvery scars – were taut and well disciplined. No, it would be unwise to let surface things influence my opinions of the violent murderer who had married me. If I did that, then I'd be like those girls preening in the mirror and I'd fall into a worse trap than I'd fallen in already.

It was worrisome enough to be married to an unpredictable man of violence. It would be much worse if I allowed myself to let my emotions swirl when he was around. A clear head was my last weapon.

Better to focus on the room. It was massive – which gave me a lot to look at. Bigger than my parents' apartments and all of their children's put together. It was also grand – filled with objects of curiosity and fine craftsmanship. I could spend all night going from one to the next and not have time to give each its proper due. They were stored on shelves and in cases, on little tables and in opened chests. The chest nearest me held a helm and mail shirt made entirely of gold and adorned with gems made to look like peacock feathers. It was utterly impractical – and beautiful as a summer's day.

There was a wide door to one side, and I could see through it a brass tub and stack of cloths for drying. The enormous bed sat on a raised dais, a window with a small balcony on one side of it, and a huge fireplace with a roaring fire on the other. Beside the fireplace were a pair of high-backed chairs and a stack of books.

Bluebeard was skimming the books and then throwing them into the fire one by one. I tried very hard not to be appalled. It didn't work. Instead, I bit my lip.

He was not just a murderer, but also a book murderer, which felt similar in an odd way.

"Not a single worthy page in the lot of them. As if economics is not a black art of magic controlled by a few demon summoners. And this one! A treatise on morality. From a group of people who sell me delicious young women as brides for nothing more than the promise not to kill them."

He looked up at that and smirked. I tried to keep the fear from my expression as I opened my mouth to ask him how old he was, but he raised a hand to forestall me and leapt up from his chair, flinging the book he'd been holding into the flames. They burst into sparks that shot out into the room like a thousand orange stars.

He was in front of me – inches from me – in a heartbeat. His finger covered my lips and his beautiful eyes looked into mine. All of a sudden that tightness in my chest drew me to him as if I had been fitted to a yoke pulled inexorably to his breast by a dozen oxen. I fought the feeling and kept my feet firmly planted in place.

"As of the moment we were married, the spell of magic and its curse has fallen upon us," his voice oddly breathy. "I must warn you not to break the spell under any circumstances, or the curse will come to pass and with it, the goodwill I have for your people will end. I will turn on this place and ravage the cities and lay waste to the towns. I will burn every home and any place where two sticks have been set on one another. I will sow the fields with salt so that no crops will grow. I will slaughter the inhabitants and lay them out head to foot across the kingdom and write in their blood that these souls were lost because of Izolda of Savataz. Is that clear? Don't speak."

I swallowed, nodding carefully. He was a madman.

"Good. I see you understand perfectly." He smiled one of his foxy smiles.

I understood *perfectly* that he was utterly insane.

"There are terms to our marriage that go beyond the vows," he said.

Even I knew that. Why did he think I was vomiting into the flowerpot?

"I have not the patience to tell you all of them."

What a surprise. No one had bothered to tell me *any* of them, which was how I ended up here.

"Would you like to hear one term, though? The one that matters most tonight?"

I had to look away from his eyes. They were too intense, as if he could peel back my layers and expose my core.

I looked nervously at the bed, but he caught my chin between his finger and thumb and brought my gaze back to his deadly and beautiful face.

"The curse is this – I may not speak a word to you in the day and you may not speak a word to me at night or the spell will be broken and, with it, our marriage. You must heed me on this."

I blinked at that. Stunned by such a very strange request.

"And if the curse is triggered, I will have to enact the horrors I just enumerated. Do you understand?"

I nodded. But seriously, the threats were going to have to slow down or I was going to pass out from how ill I felt.

"I think that will do for tonight," he said, releasing me. His eyes seemed to be weighing me like he was going to purchase me by the pound. "I didn't ask my men to bring your things here and I don't think I will. Take something from the King's wardrobe to sleep in."

He nodded to a tall armoire, and wordlessly, I stumbled to it and opened it. Robes of silk and fur in every color known to man, embroidered with scenes of hunting and fishing filled the wardrobe. All of them could have fit three of me. I stretched an arm out to take one and he reached past me, snatching up a royal blue robe in shining silk that was trimmed with white fur.

"I've changed my mind. You should wear this," he said with a wink.

Icy cold shot through me.

I paused for a moment, not taking the robe. I'd agreed to the silence and agreed to the marriage. But if I didn't put my foot down somewhere, I'd be nothing more than a doormat. I looked him squarely in the eyes and reached past the blue robe to pull out a gaudy bright red one trimmed with orange fox fur, and covered all over with scenes of a particularly bloody hunt.

I turned on my heels and went to the dressing screen without looking back, though I heard his growl behind me. As I stripped out of my dress and wrapped the robe around me, the growl turned to a laugh.

I hung my dress up carefully and stepped out from behind the screen, the hood of the robe pulled up over my head.

He smirked and gestured toward the bed. "I'll take the chair. Go to sleep. It will be a long ride tomorrow."

Wait. What? He wasn't going to ... My cheeks heated again.

He raised a single eyebrow.

"Fifteen wives I have had of mortal blood and fifteen wives have worn what I told them to wear that first night. But I sullied myself with none of them and I will not sully myself with you either, even though you are clearly no mortal woman but rather a demon sent to torture me."

And with that insulting declaration, he stalked over to his chair and sat down much more energetically than necessary, picking up yet another book, cursing, and throwing it into the flames.

I seized the opportunity, ran across the cold flagstones, and flung myself into the massive bed, gathering the blankets around me like the walls of a keep and burrowing into them so that nothing of me showed but my eyes.

I do not know how long I waited like that, afraid and close to being ill again, as he cursed at book after book, but eventually, sleep stole me away more thoroughly than the Wittenbrand could.

Chapter Eight

THE NEXT MORNING, I woke still shrouded in blankets. My legs ached from being curled up under me all night and my eyes were surprisingly puffy. I wiped them awkwardly. I might have been crying in my sleep and I did not like that at all. If he'd seen that, it was a sign of weakness.

The sun was not yet up, and Bluebeard was asleep beside the dying fire, his head hanging over the high back and his mouth wide open as if he were a particularly expensive fly trap.

By the candle clock on the wall, it was five bells of the morning.

I crept from the bed, slipped into the bathroom, and poured water quietly to clean myself. It was cold – of course – and brisk in the winter room, but I scrubbed myself carefully and wiped away all signs of tears, combing out my long hair and braiding it in an elaborate double-woven braid – the fanciest I knew how to make.

I was not vain. I knew well enough that I was not the fairest girl of the court.

My face was long rather than round, my eyes tilted slightly instead of wide and large, and my mouth had an unusual bend to it, so it often looked like I was smirking when I was not. And my figure – such as there was of it – was more bony than properly curvy. I had a serviceable body and a face that expressed my thoughts, and a woman could hardly ask for more when she had her health and family.

My thoughts stuttered at that part because I no longer had a family, though I did have a very strange husband.

I would simply have to make do with him.

And, I would have to look the best I could, and hold my head high, so that I at least kept my dignity, even if all else had been plundered.

I turned, meaning to collect my dress, and gasped when I saw Bluebeard leaning in the door.

"You move very quietly for a noble woman," he said, narrowing his eyes. "I don't know if I trust that."

I bit back the response that rose in my throat. I was hardly the untrustworthy one since I was not the one who was going to be stealing *him* away today.

He raised an eyebrow. "Don't speak."

I was trying not to speak, but it was very hard to keep all my questions inside.

How long had he been standing there? Only long enough to watch me braid my hair or long enough to watch me washing myself, too? I tried to think back to how much skin might have been shown and I couldn't remember. I'd thought I was alone. I dared not make that mistake again.

"Be that as it may," he said with a strange, almost hungry look in his eye. "I will need to stop speaking to you when the sun rises, so I must remind you that if anyone asks, you should tell them that we consummated our marriage, or they will think this wedding was a sham."

I felt my face heat at the thought of confirming that to anyone.

He paused, rubbing his short blue stubble with one hand. "I see you are of two minds about it. Well, there is still time." His expression turned wolfish. "If you prefer not to lie about it, we can consummate it now, and then you can blush prettily about the truth instead of a lie. Does that suit you, wife?"

It did not suit me. At all.

Though I did find myself swallowing a lump in my throat that hadn't been there a moment ago. This was the first time that a very beautiful man with his hair tousled from sleep and had lounged against a doorframe and suggested an intimate act to me. And it was the first time I'd been called 'wife.' It was a powerful word – a word that left little chills running up my legs.

I needed to remind myself that he was not human, that he had stolen –

or perhaps bought – me as one might acquire livestock, that he had ridiculous rules about our lives together, that he had threatened the death of thousands if I disobeyed, and that he had likely killed the honorable man who had tried to defend me. That last part cleared my head admirably.

I shook my head and he smiled as if he'd just solved a problem and expected to be congratulated.

"Well then, that's cleared up. Tell them I was a delight. Tell them I was a better lover than any you could have imagined."

He seemed absolutely sincere about that. I felt my jaw dropping in shock. As if I would ever say any of that!

He turned and padded back into the room, and I realized his feet were also bare and that there was something strange about them. It almost looked as if the floor was mossy where he had stepped. Ridiculous.

He looked over his shoulder and called a parting shot. "Speak to my riddle, wife of mine. Or rather, don't, but do contemplate it. What does the ship feel when the tide turns? What does the bird wish when the wind shifts? What does a man think when his fortunes reverse?"

He didn't stay to wait for the reply, which was good, because I might have been tempted to answer with the only answer I could agree with right now – *fear*.

I shook my head and dressed quickly before any other dangerous offers were made to me.

But I couldn't help but think that I was biting off more than I could possibly chew with this husband I'd acquired. Even if he didn't kill me before the week was over – which he very well might – he may just break me and leave me in pieces.

I needed to wear my good sense like armor and keep a close watch.

True to his word, at the first ray of dawn, Bluebeard rose and bathed himself. He had none of my concern for modesty, and one glance at the bathroom told me to keep my back firmly to the door. I fed the fire in silence, trying very hard not to remember what I'd seen in the split second I'd noticed him in there. He was my husband, and I supposed there was no harm in looking, but he had also been very clear that he was my enemy and his sheer beauty was a weapon he could use against my maiden mind. I would not so easily fall into its trap.

I didn't turn when he was done until he tapped me on the shoulder and smirked, waggling his eyebrows at me.

"I suppose we're leaving now," I said carefully, testing to be sure it was allowed and wouldn't end in sudden bloodshed and rampage.

But he didn't even acknowledge that, merely slipping on his boots and jacket as if I were a fly buzzing around his head. "I have a lot of questions. About things you said last night."

Still nothing.

"Perhaps tonight you can tell me why you've had fifteen wives. It seems an inordinate number for one man to have, don't you think? Are they still living? Am I to meet them?"

What had gotten a hold of me? It was a *very bad* idea to poke at the man who held my fate in his hands. And yet the longer he was silent, the bolder I felt.

"And if they are dead, did they all die of being around you? That doesn't recommend your company."

At that he looked up, fixing me with a devilish glare made all the more devilish by how the sunlight caught his nearly white cat's eyes. I gasped and he leapt up, seized me by the throat, licked his lips, and hovered so close to me that for a moment I wasn't sure if he was about to break my neck or kiss me. He released me suddenly and strode to the door, opening it so hard and fast that it hit the wall, bounced, and nearly smacked him on his smart behind.

Well, then. No more teasing about the wives, perhaps.

Unless he really bothered me.

I followed him out into the hall, where his men were already waiting. Two of them held my chest and the female one had a saddlebag in her hand. She was armored the same as the others, and for a moment I was envious of her thick armor and sharp sword. I could use a sword like that.

"Let's see her things," Bluebeard said briskly.

They opened my chest.

"What are you doing?" I asked. But, of course, he couldn't respond to me. He just started throwing my plain dresses to one side and the pretty to the other. I had very few of either, but it made sense. If we were traveling by horseback, then we would need a light load.

"At least let me take the necessities," I said, pushing past him to take a small woven bag of soaps and combs and other needed things from the chest and put it in the bottom of the bag. I added my handkerchiefs and reached for a plain shift.

He ripped it from my hand, snorting, and took a lace one from the chest instead. Something my mother had added to my chest, for reasons unknown to me.

"That's impractical," I objected. "There's hardly enough there to keep me warm!"

He batted me backward and to my horror, shoved the lightest, fanciest dresses into the saddlebags, and threw the practical gowns aside.

"Wait! You've left all the useful ones."

I scrambled for the warm woolen shifts, but he kicked them aside, tossing my fur-lined cloak to me. I caught it and put it on. At least it was warm as well as pretty. To my surprise, he added a book to my bag. A book of tales. One from our room last night that he had not chosen to burn. He did not choose a single practical item except a small mirror.

"Leave the rest," he ordered his men. "My wife will ride on my mount with me."

"I have a very good bay mare of my own," I objected. "She is well suited to traveling and will be no bother."

It was like he didn't even notice my words. He strode past and his men fell in behind him as if they practiced walking down corridors together. His female warrior was no different. She didn't even look twice at me as she snatched up my saddlebags.

I stood frozen in place until they stopped, waiting for me.

One of the Wittenbrand turned – a little too quickly for a human. "Will you come, or must you be carried, girl?"

"My name is Izolda," I said, clenching my fists at my sides.

He grinned a creepy grin, with those scars that cut up from his mouth, like the grin of a toad. "Must you be carried, Izolda? I have stolen many a mortal from this world. I can sling you over my shoulder and have you dreaming pink dreams and sighing purple sighs before we reach Wittenhame."

In answer, I hurried to catch up to them. There would be nothing more undignified than being carried by them out the doors and through the city like an ill-tempered child. And I didn't want to know anything about pink dreams or purple sighs.

If there were servants in the halls, they ducked out of the way before we reached them. I saw a streak of black dart into one door and a white apron edge into another, and both doors were quickly shut.

"There was only one welcome for us in this Hall," Bluebeard said the third time it happened as one of his men put a hand to a sword hilt. "And it was the only welcome I required."

And the only welcome that could doom me to losing my life, but we wouldn't mention that.

He paused and his men paused with him in the empty, vaulted corridor. I looked up at the groin-vaulted ceiling. I still wasn't used to the grandeur of this place. And perhaps I never would be, since I was unlikely to see it again.

Bluebeard looked to the man right beside him. "We are not all armed as we should be for the journey."

His man looked curiously from one of them to the next, his brow wrinkling and with good reason. They were all very, very armed.

Swords hung strapped across backs or down the sides of their legs. One man had a small axe at the waist and another a quiver of silver arrows and a bow. Bluebeard had his own quiver and bow and a sleek sword at his waist. Their weapons – oddly enough – were made almost exclusively of a metal that shone like bronze. Little knives were strapped at the tops of boots or their hilts peeked teasingly out jacket cuffs. Not a mote of iron was on the lot of them.

And there was only one of us who was not armed.

"He means me," I said after the silence stretched out. "I am not armed."

"We don't arm mortals. We never have," the man closest to him said.

"We will arm this one," Bluebeard said. "As soon as possible."

His men frowned in a way that looked close to rebellion, but they touched the opposite shoulder with a hand, and it looked like a salute.

Interesting. So, he wouldn't talk to me, but he was ... sort of caring for my needs. In the most ridiculous way possible. I could have used my chest of warm dresses – or even just one of those double-thick wool woven gowns. Instead, he'd tossed those, kept the lace, and now he was acquiring a weapon for me. He was a puzzle.

That paused my thinking.

He was a puzzle I was going to have to figure out if I had any hope of making my life last longer than the ride to his lands. That was my goal. I must pick this Wittenbrand apart and know him up and down.

It was the only way to survive this madness.

The king was waiting for us in the Gatehouse with most of his court arranged behind him and a line of palace guards in front of him.

I craned my neck, looking for my brothers and father, but I could not see them. Bluebeard whispered to one of his men and the man grabbed me roughly by the arm and pointed to a balcony above. My father and brothers were there – their chains removed but naked blades pointed at them from four guards.

I waved up at them and schooled my face to calm. They would prosper and be at peace – as long as I was wise and did not tempt them to action.

"The marriage has been completed?" the King asked, looking at me.

My cheeks flamed and my eyes widened. I was not sure what to say.

"It must be completed, by the Law of Marriage," he insisted and behind him one of the girls tittered nervously.

A sinking feeling stabbed through me at that. But when Bluebeard's eyes shot to the offender, his hand gripping the hilt of a sword, I raised a staying hand.

"All the Laws have been fulfilled, my King," I said.

There was a growl behind me from my husband and one of Bluebeard's men leaned in close. "No wife of my master calls a mortal their King."

I swallowed, waiting for a tremor of fear to pass, and I was surprised to see that the king was doing the same thing.

"I do not know his given name," I said cautiously, "nor have I the right to use it. What would be a proper mode of address?"

No one answered my question.

Without looking at me, Bluebeard met the King's eyes and made a declaration.

"The agreement of the ages has been met. Peace will remain with you until we meet again. Do not forget the Laws."

"We thank you," the king said, and maybe his voice was a little breathy when he said it.

"Where is the sword?" Bluebeard asked with a frown.

"Sword?" the King asked, perplexed.

"The marriage sword, as is tradition the morning after a wedding. Where is hers?" Bluebeard looked around at everyone nearby with his brows drawn down and fury on his face.

The King snapped his fingers and one of his guards rushed forward. There was some whispering and then after a few minutes, a fine sword was produced in a silver-worked scabbard. The king tried to hand it to Bluebeard, but he scoffed.

"No, *she* gives it to me so that no knife may cut our bond. Do you not exchange swords in this barbarous mortal world?"

My husband was nearly shaking with some sort of pent-up emotion that I read as rage.

The King offered me the sword with an air of great care, and I offered it to Bluebeard just as gingerly.

He grunted in satisfaction, accepting the sword and scabbard and slipping off one of three belts he was wearing, adding the sword and scabbard to it.

He knelt before me so suddenly that I gasped, and in a moment, he was unbuckling a second sword from his waist – one the length of my forearm and made of that odd coppery metal. It was very finely made indeed. He wrapped his arms around me and as my face went hot – again! – he placed the belt around my hips and tightened it before buckling the sword on.

"It is done," he declared to those around.

That was it and then he was striding through the gates and one of his band – the woman – was guiding me out behind him, and I couldn't tell if she had my arm to guard me or to keep me from lingering. I shot one last look at my brothers and father on the balcony and then I was torn forward again, being hurried through the gatehouse and out to the mist beyond.

Oddly, it seemed as though Bluebeard's men had formed a ring around me rather than him – as if it was my life they were guarding. I shook my head but then stopped. As ridiculous as that might seem, I was certain that it was fact. For some reason, I was valuable to them. And that they thought I was in some kind of danger.

"It shouldn't be misty," I said aloud. "Not after all that snow."

No one listened to me. That was starting to be the new normal. Instead, Bluebeard gave a piercing whistle with his fingers in his mouth while one of his men spoke low and fervently to the gate guards. He came back with a pair of daggers on a man's belt and handed them to Bluebeard, who – without any ceremony at all – turned and slipped his arms around me a second time.

I gasped and one of his eyebrows rose like he found me amusing. The belt slid around me, and he buckled it for me in the front. Even buckled on the tightest hole, it hung loosely over my hips. He made an irritated sound in the back of his throat, produced a knife from his sleeve, and cut a new hole for me before cinching the belt.

"Thank you," I said, because what else did you say? I was very well armed indeed and almost half again as heavy as I'd been an hour ago.

Around me, there were looks of approval – as if I'd been undressed until this moment and someone had taken the time to clothe me decently.

And then I caught sight of our mounts.

They appeared through the mist blazing a bright white and shaking snow from their beards, their red eyes flashing. They were antlered elk. Massive ones – but they didn't seem anything like the elk that we hunted in Northpeak. They were half again as tall, for starters. Their coats were the blue of my new husband's beard and their antlers were inlaid with gold and silver. They were saddled and haltered, and I gasped as Bluebeard put his hands around my hips and threw me up onto the back of the nearest beast.

"The answer to your riddle," I said, looking down at him, "is fear."

He sucked in a breath, bit his lip for a moment as if something was bothering him and then leapt into the saddle behind me. Before I could catch my breath, we were off.

Chapter Nine

"ARE WE GOING TO YOUR HOME?" I asked, though I knew he would not answer me. In the deep fog, I had lost track of his followers and I could see nothing but fog and elk and the hands of my husband on the reins on either side of me. He rode with me pressed against him and if I tried to wiggle to create a space between us, he pressed me firmly back to him again.

"In the mortal world, we have stories of people stolen by the magic of the Wittenbrand. Stories of how they come back and they are never the same."

I glanced over my shoulder and saw there was a small yellow bird on his head. My eyes widened as four more landed on his shoulders and head.

"You seem to be very attractive to birds," I said dryly. It was a worrisome characteristic for a man who reminded me so much of a cat.

He lifted a single brow in response and I could almost imagine him saying, "Just birds?" because that seemed to fit with the kind of person who had suggested I tell everyone at court what a delight a night with him had been for me.

I turned back around, trying to think. I was married to a man who either currently had or once had fifteen wives. I did not know his name or the names of his friends, the name of his court, or why he had such a penchant for human brides. I needed to know these things before I could decide what to do next.

There was no sound of the elk's feet on the ground and it worried me that we seemed to have been riding in a straight line since we mounted. That should have taken us straight into the side of a building or the castle wall. But we'd been riding for hours with no breaks and no lifting of the fog. I had a very eerie feeling that magic was involved, and I didn't like the idea of that at all.

"What is the name of your kingdom?" I asked him. I glanced over his shoulder and he gave me an acidic look. "Oh, I don't expect you to answer now, but it might be gracious of you to inform me of the most basic information when eventually you find your tongue has loosened ... what are you doing?"

I slapped his hands away. He had taken my braid and had begun to unweave it. I snatched it away and quickly rewove the braid.

Were the Wittenbrand obsessed with hair? And birds? I tried to remember what I knew of them.

Most of the tales were meant to terrify. That, at least, seemed accurate enough. There were the tales of travelers who were lost in a winter storm. They may find that they had stumbled into the lands of the Wittenbrand and when they returned to us, they were not the same. They dreamed strange dreams and saw visions with startling accuracy. Some would be gone for twenty years and not age a day. Others would be gone a day and return to us elderly and withered.

There were the tales meant to convince us they were at the heart of every problem – every stolen pie, every woman with child while her husband was on a long journey, every illness sweeping through the town. All those things were laid at the feet of the Wittenbrand.

Though I couldn't imagine Bluebeard stealing pies, I *could* imagine him poisoning them. My face flamed when I moved down my mental list. I shot him a dirty look over my shoulder and his smoldering gaze matched mine. No, I would not think of unexpected pregnancies. My cheeks were already hot enough.

He certainly didn't look like he spread illness. He'd been fastidious about his cleanliness and he smelled so sharply of cedar that I thought he might keep sprigs in his pockets.

Every strange occurrence in our world was blamed on the Wittenbrand and every bit of magic came originally from them.

And yet.

My father had never seen one until now. And neither had his parents or their parents.

I knew nothing about him or his people.

The Wittenbrand had just been a story to me. Something to explain when things went bump in the night. Something to blame misfortune on. Something to curse when the crops failed, and the lambs were stillborn, and a man died without an heir.

I paused there and thought sadly for a moment about the man who had died without an heir just last night. The man who had died trying to protect me.

I sniffed back a tear, and a finger reached out and turned my chin until I was looking into a pair of very light blue eyes. They narrowed with a frown at my tear. I knew what he wanted to ask.

"You can hardly murder someone who sprang to my defense last night and then expect me not to mourn him. And you can hardly expect me to leave my family forever without shedding a tear."

He glowered.

"Perhaps, when we stop tonight, you'll deign to tell me where we are going and what you plan to do with me. I find it very hard to know how to feel about all of this when I do not know how I will be spending my days."

He ignored me, releasing my chin and wrapping one of his arms around me to snug me close against his chest. I was about to object when he kicked the elk and it lurched forward, leaping like a deer over a fence, its antlers bobbing. And yet, the ride was perfectly smooth. I looked down to try to see the ground, but it was swallowed up in mist.

There would be no answers from my new husband. So. I would need to concentrate and investigate if I was going to find out the nature of what the Wittenbrand were or why they had ventured into the human world to get me.

Why did people go a long way to acquire an item? They did that for precious things. But if he'd done this fifteen times already, it hardly seemed that mortal brides were rare. I remembered a knight who had visited us telling of the cargo that came off a ship in Porthaven. He'd claimed to see pearls the size of my fist and eaten a creature with a hard red shell.

Eaten. I shivered. I hoped very much that I was not meant to be a delicacy.

He had my hair out of its braid again and he was running his fingers through it as if he was charmed by the length. This time, I let him be. If he was a cat obsessed with a strand of yarn, then at least he wasn't a cat ripping the heads off sparrows.

The rest of the morning was spent in silence. I had nothing to say to my captor and he could not speak to me. It was hard to make conversation with someone who could not speak back, and I couldn't discuss my hopes and dreams about a future that was more opaque to me than the mist.

I judged it to be close to noon when we landed somewhere. It worried me that it felt like landing. One moment, the elk was carrying me without a jostle or lurch and the next moment, the sound of thudding hooves met the earth, and I was jarred in the saddle. This entire journey seemed incredibly impractical and I wasn't sure how to operate in a world that was so odd.

A large spreading tree was just ahead of us, ringed in grass. Two of my husband's followers were already there and one was kindling a fire. I could only see a few strides in any direction, so wreathed were we in mist.

We slowed to a stop and Bluebeard dismounted, helping me down graciously. As the elk's back was nearly half again as tall as me, it was still a rough landing.

"We need to move faster," the man by the fire said. He was the one with scars around his mouth that made it look like he was grinning twice. "I'm getting an itch between my shoulders. The game will begin soon and on it rides the fate of this mortal world."

"You should be nervous, Vireo. We did not plan to spend a full night in the mortal world," Bluebeard said

"Then why do it at all?" Vireo grumbled. He was filling a kettle with water. "You shouldn't have taken Wittenbrand vows with her or agreed to their Marriage Laws. Not only are you wasting time, but you're also tying yourself like never before."

His mouth shut with a snap as another one of the Wittenbrand arrived, pulling food from his pack as if it had been arranged ahead of time. His hair was longer than the others and pulled back into a knot at the back of his head. He grinned in a wicked way, almost leering when he came to me.

"Do you want to eat?" he asked, leaning against the tree as he offered me a small loaf of bread.

I did want to eat, but I didn't trust this Wittenbrand.

"They call me Grosbeak," he said, letting the name tumble over his lips like he was kissing it.

I looked away sharply. Had he no respect for Bluebeard? Or was my new husband not powerful enough to keep his men in check?

"You could call me that, too," he pressed.

There was a growl from the fire and when I looked back, Grosbeak had his head bent low.

Bluebeard handed me a small mug of hot tea with a dark look on his face as if I had been the one to start that conversation.

"Speak to my riddle, Grosbeak," he growled, his eyes never leaving mine. "What has one hand and one eye?"

Grosbeak laughed, as if the riddle didn't bother him at all. "Me, if I push you too far. Is that what you want to hear, Arrow? I can be a good Wittenbrand. I just don't have to *like* it."

Arrow. So that was what his men called him, but that didn't mean it was his name. I liked Bluebeard better.

I sipped the tea carefully, watching Bluebeard from the corner of my eye. His moods changed faster than the weather – faster than my brothers' moods when they'd first begun to grow beards. And last night he'd killed poor Leonid. He could shake me to death just as easily. I needed to be very, very careful about what I did next.

"We must move more quickly after we eat," Bluebeard said, his voice more growl than the sound of a leader commanding troops. What manner of man was he? "The Sword will make every attempt to catch us while we are vulnerable."

At that comment, Grosbeak side-eyed Bluebeard so briefly that I almost didn't notice it. Did my husband see that? It put me on edge. Like the look you get from a town cur right before it bites.

"Is my husband a prince in your land?" I asked Vireo.

The woman at the fire snickered. She'd been quiet until then.

"In a manner of speaking," Vireo said. "Though he may wish otherwise. He is the Arrow of Wittenhame, Lord Riverbarrow, and a prince of Wittenhame, though not blood to the Bramble King. He flies to the heart at the order of his Sovereign – as we all must for the great game."

He was a prince? And an arrow? And a lord? But he didn't wish he was a prince, so I would avoid that part. It still made me feel a little dizzy. It was strange enough to be married to a foreign lord, but princes were dangerous. People wanted them dead.

"The Arrow?" I asked carefully. "That's an odd designation. Is it like a knight?"

I didn't want to infuriate my new husband. I wouldn't mention the prince part.

"Not quite," Vireo said, considering. "Close, but a little more significant than that. He is lightning rod and blade, both." At my confused look, he rolled his eyes at Bluebeard and then sighed and turned back to me, addressing me as you might address a particularly annoying child. "There are several named roles in the Wittenhame. Your husband is the Arrow. Your task should be to meet them all and figure out what they do without troubling me to explain it."

"Do you think it's unlikely that I will?" I asked. His tone had suggested it was an impossible task.

"The Arrow has had fifteen wives. You are only the most recent. None of them has lived long enough to complete that task."

A chill came over me. I knew I was in danger with this husband and his strange, barbaric followers, but I had expected I would at least survive – however miserably. I had assumed too much.

"Did he kill them? The other wives?" I tried to keep my tone bold instead of terrified.

"All but the one just before you. She died by her own hand."

"Did she have a name?" I asked.

He shrugged as if he didn't care. Around us, the sound of the others eating was all I could hear. They were watching us intently as if our conversation was entertaining.

"How long ago?"

"Six months ago."

I gasped. "So soon?"

"There is a toll you pay for being married to the Arrow. A price for marrying him. It is possible that the price will be too steep for you to complete even that small task. It's possible it will be too steep for you to see tomorrow."

He didn't sound particularly concerned about that.

I shivered in horror. Six months since his last wife died and he was already married to me. And his friends – if that was who these were – thought nothing of the fact that I might not survive through the night.

I glanced over at Bluebeard, but he did not seem to be paying attention. He was jingling the little golden bell for a yellow bird, drawing it ever closer as it fell slowly under his enchantment until it crept right up and sat in his hand. He closed his fingers around it so suddenly that I flinched. And then opened his hand and the bird flew away.

"He certainly seems keen on marriage," I said lightly. "And what is my role as his wife? Am I to be some kind of Arrow?"

That earned me a harsh laugh from the whole party. I noticed that Bluebeard did not laugh. Instead, he looked longingly after the bird as if he wished he could fly away with it.

"You, an Arrow? I think not," the woman Wittenbrand said. "The Arrow is our Backwards Man. While everyone is moving forward, he is walking backward and that is how he can see the future – because he's facing it."

"That doesn't make any sense."

"What does?" she asked with a wink.

"And what of the rest of you? Are you his court?"

They all laughed at that and she answered me. "We're bound to him by blood and oath – like your sworn arms men but deeper than that – and he'll spill our blood if we falter. We do his bidding and kill by his word. Does that make us his court? I suppose it does. His Court of Fools."

I swallowed, wondering at that. He was like a prince. And these were like his knights. But none of them acted like that at all.

"Leave off, Sparrow. We need to get moving," Bluebeard said, throwing the water from the kettle over the fire. It hissed as if it were a living thing being smothered.

He was tending to his mount when the first arrow flew through the air, landing in the moss beside the fire.

"To horse!" he cried, and I was thrown to the back of the elk before I could gasp. It stamped its blue foot and sprang into the mist at almost the same moment that Bluebeard hugged me to his chest. It was almost as if he was huddled around me to protect me from the arrows – but that was madness. What was one more wife when you'd had fifteen?

Chapter Ten

THE ARROWS DID NOT relent even though I couldn't see our pursuers. They flew and flew until I wondered if they were magical in some way. Twice, our elk shrieked, stumbling to the side. Each time, we pierced the mist to where another of the Wittenbrand were riding and nearly collided with them.

I tried not to scream as I clenched my jaw tight and held on to the saddle with all my might.

Bluebeard cursed in his own tongue as an arrow sliced so close that it nicked the elk's neck, leaving a thin streak of red blood.

My heart was in my throat and it made my chest ache every time I heard the sound of the arrows hitting trees or grass nearby.

Slowly, the arrows grew more sparse and then eventually stopped.

"I would like very much to know who is shooting at us," I said as calmly as I could, but there was a tremor in my voice that betrayed me.

There was no response, of course. Perhaps, I would learn to be quiet, too. I shook my head wryly to myself at the thought. My father had hoped to find me someone who would be good company. I could almost guarantee that his choice would have been far, far better, even given the fact that all our conversation would have been of horses. I could have learned to enjoy that. I rather liked horses. Perhaps, in time, Leonid would have come to value my thoughts on the matter. But none of that mattered now.

I had a mute for a husband during the day and a villain by night. Perhaps we'd find our own things to discuss – but any discussion we had would be like mailing letters to play a game of merels.

We slowed after what felt like hours. My muscles were stiff from tensing at every turn and I was grateful when Bluebeard practically shoved me off the elk. The poor thing had two arrows in its flank, and he turned, ripping one out.

"I'm going to walk that way to – to relieve myself," I said, pointing to a nearby patch of bushes, barely discernible in the fog.

He spun, frantic-eyed at the same moment that Grosbeak's elk plunged from the mist to join us.

"A good ride, Arrow. It's been long days since the Hunt chased me in the mists of memory, and here I am running beside the famed Arrow." He paused, glancing from one of us to the other, realizing that neither of us was listening.

"I'll only be a moment. It's just that it's getting urgent." I felt my face heating. Still, Bluebeard stared at me with intense eyes, his hands holding that one bloody arrow.

"I'll take her," Grosbeak said, seeming to understand what I meant. "No Wittenbrand arrow will fell her while in my care."

Bluebeard didn't seem convinced, but I shook my head and stalked to the bushes. Some things just couldn't be ignored forever. Even for very practical girls – maybe especially for very practical girls.

I found a well-sheltered spot between the bushes. When I'd finished, and I was tucking my cloak back around me I felt something in the pocket.

Odd. I hadn't put anything in there. I fished it out and found a small fabric packet tied up in string. With care, I unfurled the packet and found a little round, dull mirror smaller than my palm with eyes stamped all around it and a thin letter. I jammed the mirror back in my pocket and opened the seal on the letter. It was written in a magnificent hand.

To Izolda Savataz of Northpeak,

Though your marriage to this foreign lord comes as a surprise to all of us, it is our royal hope that you will choose to act as our eyes and ears in the Wittenhame. Were this a usual wedding of convenience, we would have had time to provide you with adequate tutelage as to what to observe and how to report it, but as this is all done in a great deal of haste, we can only send you this mirror and hope you can use your good sense to note what might interest us in the courts of our ancient neighbors.

The king wanted me to spy. I felt a chill at the thought. But the letter was not finished.

As you are your father's daughter and therefore must be loyal as he is, we trust you will accept that this is your role without question, just as we will honor your father without questioning why you were the one chosen.

The threat there was fairly explicit – the implication that I had greeted Bluebeard on purpose, knowing what that would mean. I didn't even think he believed that. It was just a courtly bargaining chip. And then the offer: spy, or we'll blame your parents for your failure. I would have accepted that, but the King could have offered his own daughter – or even himself. After all, Bluebeard had not specified a young woman must be the one to offer the greeting. Perhaps the fat king could have been the one riding an elk nestled in the lap of my dear husband. I had to suppress a snicker at that image in my mind.

This mirror is the only way we have of contacting you, but its magic is weak. Be ready with it on midsummer night.

Midsummer? That was six moons from now! Was he mad?

And then it was signed with the King's royal signature.

I was not fool enough to keep the letter. I buried it with the waste. But I kept the mirror. I had a decision to make about whether I would use it. Under normal circumstances, I would be insulted at the suggestion that I would spy on any husband of mine. But this husband had murdered a good man in cold blood last night. It was hard to weigh whether it was he or the King who best deserved my loyalty now. And, of course, there was the threat to my family.

A hand reached through the bushes and drew me out so quickly that I was still gasping when I came face to face with Grosbeak. His eyes glittered as he pulled just a little harder than he needed to and I stumbled.

"We're stopping for a moment while the mounts are tended. And I doubt the Arrow will notice you gone for a few more moments. So. Let's see how well you play games, mortal."

I tried to find my voice, but it came out a little too high. His pupils – narrow slashes rather than the round of human eyes – were expanding and I felt like I was caught in the gaze of a snake.

"What kind of games?"

"My favorite kind of all," he said with a nasty grin. "The kind that leaves scars."

"I'm not interested," I said curtly. I tried to rip myself from his grip, but he held me fast.

I opened my mouth to scream and his hand slammed around it, cutting off all sound. He had my back to a tree before I knew it and I squeezed my eyes shut knowing that whatever happened next, I would be powerless to stop him. I was defenseless in his grasp, tiny as that bird in Bluebeard's hand and just as easily crushed.

I knew my eyes were welling up with tears, but to my shame, I couldn't stop them any more than I could stop my panicked breathing. He was tugging my skirts up and I tried to shift to the side, but he had me pressed too hard against the tree. All my struggles were not enough to move even a bare finger-width.

I opened my eyes, frantic to find a way out – any way at all. And then his blade was out, copper bright in the light and my heart was hammering in my ears. Pain blossomed in my upper thigh as the blade cut into the tender flesh. Stars shot across my vision and I gasped in agony.

He was knocked away. One moment his face was hardly a breath away from mine, the next he was gone. My hand felt for my thigh, clamping tightly over the welling wound. Tears flowed and my breath came out as a shudder. My blood was thick and hot, pouring through my fingers. I fell to the ground as if my very life was seeping out of me.

And there he was – my new husband – kneeling with one knee on Grosbeak's chest as he removed his head from his body with a single slice of the slightly curved, silver-inlaid sword the king had given him. Horror flashed across his face. He sprinted to me, and for the barest moment, I thought he was coming for my head, too. Instead, he dropped his blade on the mossy ground and ripped my hand from my leg, cursing violently.

I heard voices as the others arrived, but my eyes were caught on Bluebeard's. He gritted his teeth like he was dying to say something and then with a hiss of frustration he put a hand on my head, and everything went black.

Chapter Eleven

I BLINKED awake to find myself lying on a soft cloak with another one wrapped around me. With my face pressed to the ground, the scene in front of me looked odd until I realized the Wittenbrand were digging a grave for the headless corpse of Grosbeak who had tried – perhaps – to kill me. That's what it meant to try to cut the femoral artery in the leg, right? I'd heard of men on the plains who were gored by wild boars and bled out in minutes when that artery was sliced by a tusk. That could have been me. So, why wasn't it? I felt for my leg and hissed when I found the flesh completely smooth.

My hiss drew Bluebeard's attention. He threw down his shovel and strode across the cold ground to sink into a crouch beside me. He examined my face with what looked like concern and then offered a hand up. I realized, belatedly, that it was his cloak I was wrapped in on top of my own.

"Let's speak these rites and get out of here," Sparrow said as she threw the body into the pit they'd dug. They seemed horrifyingly unaffected by the death of their comrade and a new chill tore through me. Was life of so little value in the Wittenhame?

Bluebeard took my hand gently and placed it on his arm, guiding me to stand beside the grave. The gentleness tore something loose in my mind and made me want to laugh hysterically. That one, ridiculous contrast made everything else seem that much more insane in comparison.

"You were taller than me by almost a hand," Sparrow said and then drew a finger down forehead, nose, and chin in some kind of sign.

"You were the lord over the Mudhills and you owned a herd of Clay Horses," Vireo said soberly, making the same sign.

What sort of memorial was this? I felt my eyes widening.

"You were husband to Derlia, now deceased, son of Gorath, also deceased," said the only one whose name I still didn't know. His eyes were dark, and he shot a poison glance at Bluebeard. Maybe not everyone was as calm about this brutal murder as the rest. He made his sign grimly.

"You were a traitor and likely a spy, but you played cards as well as any I've known. And you died with me owing you two silver," Bluebeard said grudgingly, making his sign. He threw two silver coins into the grave.

All eyes turned to me. I supposed I was supposed to say something. But there was very little I knew. Seeing as Sparrow had only mentioned his height, I could say anything, really. Height. I again felt the hysterical urge to laugh. He was shorter now, wasn't he? What was wrong with me? I was losing my mind. And they were all still staring at me.

"You were very quick with a knife," I said acidly, and there were nods of agreement around the circle as I made the sign the others had made.

"Cover him up while I settle my wife on our mount," Bluebeard ordered in a low, furious tone. "When I find out who has betrayed me, it will be more than their head that I take from them."

The man whose name I still didn't know looked up at that. "Maybe no one has betrayed you. Maybe he just acted on what we were all thinking. You shouldn't have married her in our way. You never have before. How are you supposed to spend her if she is your Wittenbrand wife?"

"In the same way that I spend them all," Bluebeard said, and his hand on mine was suddenly cold as death. "I was married to them all or none of this would work."

"You weren't married to them our way. You didn't give a vow. You didn't put them in your room for a night. We took them from this world, you kept them sleeping the pink sleep until we crossed, then we brought them to your home, and you put them in their rooms and that was it. They lived out their brief days like birds in a cage. But this one you keep awake. And you ride her in front of you. You act as if she is your wife in fact as well as name!" The look of pure hate on the other man's face made me shy away. "Put her in the hole with him. Go back and get another. One like the others. The Bramble King will approve. We all will."

"I'm collecting heads today, Ibis," Bluebeard said, looking away into the distance as if none of this meant anything to him. He drew my bell from his pocket and bounced it on his palm, rolling it over his knuckles like a man at the fair might do with a coin. "Would you like one of them to be yours?"

The other Wittenbrand looked away and spat and Bluebeard moved with inhuman speed. The bell fell into a sleeve and disappeared, and he scooped me up into his arms and strode through the mist to where the elks huffed in the cold under a sprawling clump of cedars. His elk bore two wounds from arrows in his haunch but seemed unconcerned as it tore up frosty grass.

Bluebeard set me delicately on the elk's back, arranging me in the saddle in a way that seemed fussier than I thought my situation warranted. I was very light-headed. So light-headed that little sparks danced across my vision, but I was not in immediate danger. He turned to retrieve something, and I gasped. There was an arrow stuck in his shoulder.

This would be shocking in any circumstance, but this man had killed and buried another, healed my wound by some sorcery, and carried me through the woods – all with an arrow shaft stuck in his flesh.

"Your shoulder," I gasped out. "Let me help you."

He grunted impatiently, reached up to where it stuck out of his shoulder and broke the shaft close to the skin with no more than a single grunt of pain.

My hands flew up to cover my mouth. If he had been my father or my brothers, he would be sweaty and white-faced, laid out on a table while someone cut the barbed head from his skin.

Bluebeard winked at me, looking for all the world like the beautiful devil the monks spoke of – the one who thought so highly of himself that he fell from heaven into the underworld. And then he was gone, striding through the woods.

He returned with a grisly trophy, the head of Grosbeak, hanging from his hand by its long, blood-drenched hair. I gagged into my hands but fortunately for me, I had nothing in my stomach to vomit up. I had the most terrible precognition that I might need to stay light on the meals for the days and weeks to come.

He leapt into the saddle behind me, still clutching the head, shifted until we were pressed against each other again, and then made a satisfied sound and flicked the reins. Our elk leapt back into the mist as if it carried riders holding heads in their fists every day of its life. Maybe it did.

A wave of nausea rolled over me at the same time that my hysterical laugh bubbled up. I couldn't hold it back this time. And why should I? If I was going mad, then what was the point of hiding it?

"Is it always like this with you?" I asked as my teeth chattered together.

He tilted my face around to see his – oh so gently, as if he were a lover and not a monster. I felt his palm reach up and cup my face and then everything went dark again.

"This little one here is the key to the closet at the end of the great hall on the ground floor. Open them all; go into each and every one of them, except that little closet, which I forbid you and forbid you in such a manner that, if you happen to open it, you may expect my just anger and resentment."

- Charles Perrault, Bluebeard,

1697 as translated by Andrew Lang in The Blue Fairy Book 1889.

Chapter Twelve

WHEN I AWOKE, it was dark. I opened my mouth, but a hand clamped around it.

"Remember, you must not speak to me."

I thought about biting his hand, but then what? Would he chop off my head, too? I certainly was no match for him with the sword he'd given me.

"We are about to land at the Evergreen Inn. I will take a room there for us. I stole a few of your hours to heal you, but that is not real rest, and you will still need sleep to refuel yourself. Do not speak to the denizens of the inn. Do not speak to the Wittenbrand who ride with me. I will tell you what you need to know when we are in private again."

I would have been more resentful of those orders if I hadn't still been in shock over watching a man beheaded after he tried to kill me. My head swam at the memory of his bronze knife cold on my thigh and then the hot pain that followed. Little stars still danced across my vision. I'd lost a lot of blood.

I was very, very careful not to glance to my left. I caught occasional glimpses of Grosbeak's severed head out of the corner of my eye. I didn't want a better look. Every glimpse made me feel ill all over again with a kind of gripping queasiness that made all the illness I'd felt so far pale in comparison.

The elk touched down in a flurry of snow, landing in front of a well-lit inn with a jolly green sign and snow frosting the roof and the edges of the diamond-paned windows. Music poured out from the common room – a tin whistle and a snare, a woman's lilting voice, and the sound of clapping and foot-stomping. I realized, with a start, that it was a human inn.

Had we not been traveling to the Wittenhame?

And yet, here we were in what was obviously a human town. Rooftops with curling smoke spiraling white against the black sky made a sloping curve down the hill from the inn. In the distance, the wide moon shone on the glare ice of a lake. Through the diamond-paned glass of the inn, regular people were dancing and laughing, red-cheeked, smiling, and whole. They wore bright reds and yellows – both men and women – and the women wore bonnets embroidered heavily around the brims in bright colors. Their pale braids hung down from these bonnets, like spun gold against the scarlet and marigold of their clothing.

Rouranmoore. I'd heard of this nation. But it was many days' ride from my home and then one must take a boat across the wide channel. My breath froze in my lungs. That misty world we'd traveled through – had it somehow been outside our world? And now we were dipping back in to rest at a common inn?

I made a strangled sound in my throat.

"Don't fret, pretty wife," Bluebeard whispered in my ear. "No harm will come to you while you are with me and I will be with you until the end of your days. You are far too precious to leave without protection."

I gave him a long, dry look. I wanted to say that the only protection I needed was from him. But that wasn't entirely true, as evidenced by the head he still carried in one hand.

I looked at him and then glanced at the head and then back to him again.

"Oh no, bell of my heart, the head I keep. It is my due." He winked one of his terrible cat's eyes and I shuddered.

He was going to bring the head into the inn.

My cheeks flamed with the horror of it, but he snatched up my spare hand, kissed the back of it, hopped down from the elk, and drew me into the inn as if nothing was wrong at all.

And what could I do? Could I steal the elk and run? I looked over my shoulder at the exact instant that it winked out of sight. One moment it stood, stamping in the snow, the next minute it was gone. No, I could not steal our mount. Could I run out into the snow? In these clothes, I would freeze to death before morning, but even if I did not, he was inhumanly fast, and the snow was deep. I would leave tracks and he would find me so quickly that all I'd get for my trouble was my new husband's distrust. I would simply have to bear all this.

Bluebeard strode straight to the bar where a man a head taller than him and twice as wide was polishing glasses and watching the dancing with an indulgent smile.

"A room I'll have and a dram of your wine," Bluebeard said.

"There are none to be had," the man said without looking at us.

Bluebeard set the severed head on the counter and looked the man full in the face while around us the dancers slowed to a stop and the tin whistle squealed a wrong note.

"Three decades and four years ago there was a man who operated this inn by the name of Rubken. And that man asked me for a barrel of wine that never runs dry. And in exchange, I asked him for a room always kept free for me. Now ... I ask *you* ... is there a room? Or is there an empty barrel?"

The man went pale as a ghost. "There's a room, of course, noble Wittenbrand. And food to go with it. My daughter Sarcha will take you there immediately."

He must not have cared much for the poor girl to offer her up like that. It seemed a lot of men were willing to offer up their girls rather than bear the risk of the Wittenbrand themselves. I raised an eyebrow.

The innkeeper snapped his fingers and a girl with eyes round as those of a fresh-caught fish hurried over, wiping her hands on her tidy white apron. She bobbed a curtsy and practically ran up the stairs with Bluebeard striding behind her. I had to speed up to almost a trot to keep up with them.

Bluebeard had kept the head. The thought of sleeping in the same room as it made something inside me start to whimper.

The room the girl showed us was on the highest floor and took up the entirety of it. It was long and low, with an exposed beam ceiling and the thatch right there sitting on the rafters. It had its own separate bathing chamber with a door that locked. Someone had white-washed the walls nicely and even put a braided rug on the floor beside the bed. A fire burned hot at one end of the room and a wide hearth surrounded it.

Sarcha bobbed another curtsey and then she was gone, running down the stairs as if her life depended on it. My legs itched to follow.

Bluebeard set the head down by the door and stalked to where I stood by the fire.

"I can understand being upset over the misunderstanding with your betrothed." He paused as if thinking. Oh yes, it was night now. He could say his piece. I straightened, lifting my chin to show I was not afraid. It was a lie but I would need to get very good at lying to be around this man. "Well, I really can't, but I can *try* to understand. What I cannot at all fathom is why you would be upset about Grosbeak over there."

He flicked a finger at the head. It rolled slightly to the side, looked up, and scowled at him.

"You'll have to wait on vocal cords, Grosbeak. I've about used up my reservoir of magic."

I gasped, my hands flying over my mouth. The head was still alive? And now it turned its furious gaze on me. I backed up until my shoulders hit the wall. Bluebeard scowled.

"Don't be such a fainting violet. He has no limbs. He cannot harm you or betray you now."

I was in hell. I was being punished for sins uncommitted and crimes unrealized. That must be what this was. My breath sawed through my lungs, leaving them ragged.

Bluebeard pulled the bell out of his pocket as if it was significant, and bounced it on his palm a few times, biting his lip before looking over at me with what could almost be a soft expression.

They'd been right about the bell. It really did attract the Wittenbrand. A laugh swelled in my throat, threatening to escape. It took all my presence of mind to force it back down.

He strode over until the tip of his nose nearly touched mine. He placed his hands either side of my face, palms flat against the wall, eyes looking deeply into mine.

It was impossibly unfair that he smelled of lavender and his breath – which ought to be rank from travel – smelled of mint. It was also impossibly unfair that his blue stubble had not grown at all and was just the right length to make him look more rakish than anything else.

My breath hitched in my throat.

His eyes twinkled as if we were about to share a delicious secret. It was all I could do not to tremble slightly at his decided beauty and the uncommon way his ears came to a very faint, barely-there point. He reached into his shirt with a sudden motion and pulled out a small golden key on a chain around his neck. Drawing it off, he placed the chain over my head instead.

His fingers trailed lightly over my throat and I shivered. My good sense was screaming to me that now I was mixing fear and attraction and if I wasn't careful, I'd be drunk on them, and once drunk on that deadly brew, I may never be able to feel one without the other – which would be very dangerous indeed.

I agreed, but there wasn't much I could do to prevent it. It was carrying me along like a swollen river after the spring melt.

His hands pulled away and settled back to the wall on either side of me. I swallowed and reached for the key so I could focus on something – anything – other than the powerful man caging me between his arms.

The key felt heavy, and when I lifted it, I saw it was the length of my pinkie finger, crafted of woven gold as if someone had magicked a thousand fine wires into a key instead of stamping one in a mold. It was impossibly fine workmanship, incredibly valuable, and it weighed far more than it should have.

"You will wear my key as some women wear rings," he whispered as his cat's eyes locked on mine. There was a sudden desperation in his eyes when he said, "but whatever you do, you must not enter the room the key unlocks. You must not open it. You must not use the key at all. Do you understand me?"

I nodded nervously and he exhaled a long, desperate breath.

"I have tried. Let it be known and remembered that I have tried." He looked like he was in turmoil as he spoke, his eyes thick with something very like pain. Unconsciously, I reached toward him, stopping myself just before my hand touched his arm.

No, no, Izolda. You must not be sucked into his story. That will only complicate things. Remember who this man is – a murderer, a trickster, and a thief. And do not be drawn by pity or anything else.

"Well then, that's the day," he said briskly, startling me, and leapt from where he stood to the bed in a single massive jump, as if he were a large cat jumping on prey. He kicked off his boots and threw himself under the covers with so much violence that I could hardly catch my breath.

My mouth was still hanging open when there was a knock at the door. I had the foresight to draw my sword before opening it, but it was only Vireo.

"Your bag, Lady Arrow," he said with a smirk, handing me my saddlebag.

"Thank you," I said a little breathlessly.

"It's not a gift," he said harshly. "It is payment for the entertainment earlier. I haven't watched the Arrow claim a head in so long that I almost forgot that he collects them. The opportunity you afforded will keep me entertained for many nights to come."

I took the bag wordlessly – because what could you possibly say to that? He *collected* them? Like interesting rocks or trinkets?

I was very careful to bar the door before I slipped my sword back into the scabbard, snuck into the bathing room and barred that door. That done, I sat on the floor, and sobbed until I could sob no more.

"Then she took the little key and opened it, trembling."
- Charles Perrault, Bluebeard,
1697 as translated by Andrew Lang in The Blue Fairy Book 1889.

Chapter Thirteen

THERE IS ONLY SO MUCH CRYING a girl can do, and eventually, I sobbed myself to sleep. I woke with a muzzy head and looked out the window of the bathing chamber to see it was still dark. I changed into the nightdress in the bag – the ridiculous filmy lace one that Bluebeard had chosen – and worked to wash my dress of dirt and blood. It was the only practical one I had, and it would have to do for tomorrow. If Bluebeard left the inn in the same hurry that he'd entered it, I'd have to be ready to leave in the space of a heartbeat.

When the dress was clean, I did the only sensible thing a woman in my situation could do. I drew the key out and wondered to myself how one could use a key to open a door that was not there. I examined it from every angle, searching for clues and finding nothing. There seemed to be a very small bow and arrow placed somehow under the golden wires but that gave me no clues. There was no writing on it, no symbols, nothing to give away what manner of door it might open.

I put it between my thumb and forefinger, miming turning a key as I considered it.

To my shock, the air in front of me shimmered and then a rectangle of space opened up in front of me. I dropped the key in shock, and it fell to the end of the chain, thumping hollowly against my chest.

In my mind, words seemed to whisper as if the room before me was welcoming me.

I am sudden death to calm.

My roar breaks the hush.

My song, the mind's somnolence.

I was no longer looking at the bathing chamber. Rather, I was looking into a large room with no windows. It was lined with fifteen glowing pillars set in alcoves, and before each pillar was an open book chained to a pedestal reader. The center of the room was carpeted with the layered skins of many animals I recognized and many I did not. I would not like to meet the one with the orange and black stripes on a dark night, that was for sure. Neither would I like to meet the scaled one with the very long jaw.

Each book glowed a faintly different color than the next so that some were pinkish and some golden, some spring green, and some the purest white. One was even faintly purple. And each book matched the glow of the pillar behind it.

At the very end of the room was a very large hourglass with the top bulb completely empty and the bottom bulb full of what looked like uncut garnets. As I watched, the hourglass slowly spun until the top bulb was now the full one. The first garnet hit the floor with a clatter, and then someone began to pound on the bathing room door. In a panic, I leapt into the mysterious room.

The pillars, it turned out, were not pillars at all. They were women, frozen in place, eyes shut as if they were sleeping, but utterly still. They stood on pedestals that brought their feet to the height of my waist.

I stared in horror at the one nearest to me, whose face was bathed in a very soft pink light. She was wearing a golden dress and had a face so much like Princess Chasida's that they could be sisters. And one of her shoes was missing a golden bell.

I raced to her alcove and reached for her, but my hand met something that felt smooth and slick as glass surrounding her. There were no seams, no top or bottom, as if the once-living Princess Margaretta had somehow been blown into invisible glass. She still looked nineteen years old. The same as me.

My belly rolled uncomfortably at the thought.

I hurried from her to the next girl – a girl with a very impressive figure and flowing dark curls. Her red dress dipped low in the front in a way that made my cheeks hot.

I rushed on to the next in line – a girl with sharp, authoritative features and a very bulky dress with an elaborate belt as thick as my forearm ringing her waist. Her hair was white – but her features as young as my own. The book on her stand was signed on the exposed page and a tiny brass plaque on the alcove she stood in bore the same inscription. Ki'e'iren. Was that her name?

The next woman was curved perfection with full lips and cheeks and such an abundance of curls as I'd never seen before. She wore a two-piece costume too indecent to wear in society and her skin was flawless wherever it was exposed.

I fled down the line of beautiful women – one after another, stuck in perpetual beauty forever – as the pounding on the bathing door finally turned to the sound of wood cracking and splintering.

They were his wives, I realized. The wives of Bluebeard, encased in … magic?

Dead. All dead. And there was one empty pillar with an empty pedestal and no glow in either located right next to the door.

Was it getting hot in here? I felt almost faint with the heat.

By the time I reached the hourglass, my breath was caught in my throat and little white stars were dancing across my vision. I collapsed in front of it as Bluebeard strode through the room, his face a thundercloud.

"Where trouble is, look for the woman," he growled, his lip twisting up in a way that made his beautiful face look like a devil's. "Speak to my riddle? What creature must plumb every depth, turn every stone, tempt death and defy him to his face and all that only to reap what she never sowed and gain what she never earned? Whose curiosity devours like an army of locusts and mind seeks out danger as a man seeks out a lover? I will answer for you – it is a wife."

He reached the place where I was crouched on all fours, reached down, and pulled me up by the roots of my hair so that I was looking into his eyes.

"I had hoped to spare you this, Izolda." Fury and pain filled his face. "Do you long to dance with death? Does your heart yearn for the barrow before its time? Fifteen times before, I have watched this story unfold. Fifteen times before, I have given a key, and fifteen times before, it has been turned in the lock. I had hoped that perhaps you were too clever to fall into this trap, but oh how you have disappointed me, wife."

He turned my head with my hair and pressed my face to the glass, his chest heaving with his infuriated breath.

"The proverb says, "*Teach us to number our days.*" See these garnets? They are the days of your life, Izolda. And because you opened this door, they are mine now irrevocably. Mine to spend as I want. Mine to rule over. Mine to direct. And when they are gone, you will be on that last pedestal and your days will be no more."

I knew my eyes were wide and pleading. I wanted to speak more than anything. No, I wanted to stop crying even more. It was humiliating to let him see me cry.

"Your tears cannot save you," he whispered, his gaze catching mine, and for a moment his fury faded away, replaced by a dull misery that ached out of him and seeped into me. "Even *my* tears will not save you now. You are well and truly trapped by magic too great for you. All that now remains for us is to see how we will spend the time you have."

He swept me up into his arms as if I were his lover rather than his enemy and carried me from the haunting room. As he went by the last pedestal, I saw that it now bore my name. *Izolda Savataz.*

When we left the hidden chamber, the door vanished as if the room had never existed at all.

Bluebeard carried me through the ruin of the door, through the horrible room of the inn where Grosbeak's eyes followed us, to the large bed where he laid me on the mattress and stepped back for a moment, catching his lower lip between his teeth before he tugged up the eiderdown and tucked it under my chin.

"Sleep, treacherous one. You cannot break our hearts more tonight."

For the second time, I cried myself to sleep.

Chapter Fourteen

I WOKE to a hand clamped over my mouth. I barely bit back a scream when I saw Bluebeard's pale cat's eyes staring into mine.

Something slammed against the door and wood crunched behind us.

"No time to dress, wife," he said, shoving my fur-lined cloak into my hands and the pair of belts with my sword and knives. "Hurry. They've found us."

His blue coat and shirt were completely unbuttoned and untucked, revealing skin so crisscrossed with scars that I gasped at the sight of them. They were worse the more skin I saw. What had happened to him? Another key – silver – dangled on a chain around his neck. I shuddered, wondering if it led to the same kind of place as the golden key hanging inside my lace nightdress did.

I finished clasping the cloak and buckling on the belts over my filmy nightgown at the same moment that Bluebeard slung my saddlebag over my shoulder. He had his own hanging over his.

"Hold this for a moment," he said, trying to pass me Grosbeak's severed head.

I shook my head violently. I was *not* going to carry the head!

The door shattered and fell into the room with a boom. I jumped, squeaking in an embarrassing way in my surprise.

Little bits of wood and straw rained into the room like a sandstorm. I backed up until my head hit the thatch roof above and Bluebeard threw the head back at me as if he expected me to catch it. I dodged out of the way, letting it hit the ground with a dull thump. I had my limits. I was not going to cart around a dead head for him – especially not one that was scowling up at me from the floor. Just the thought of it made me ill.

But there was no time for being ill.

Two men leapt into the room, and Bluebeard's curved swords appeared in his hands as if by magic. He was so fast! One of them was his own bronze sword and the other was the one the King had offered for me to give him, inlaid in silver and sharp as winter. He spun the swords on either side of his body, as if he were a performer for the King's court and not a man in the room of an inn.

The men brandished their own swords, not bothering to be dramatic. They were human just like me. Dressed like minor nobility – just like me. They were both breathing heavily, as if they wanted to be there as little as I did. The younger of the two – barely older than my own brothers – caught sight of me and cursed vehemently.

"He has already taken another."

"This has never been what you thought it was," Bluebeard said silkily. "You still have time to leave. I don't want to kill anyone."

The other man – this one older and bearded – spat. "We don't believe your lies, kidnapper."

"I keep trying to tell you all that I'm not a kidnapper," Bluebeard said through gritted teeth, but there was no time to say more. Both men attacked as one and his swords whirled in his defense. He fought like he was dancing, a quick step back and then another to the side. The blade in his left hand came up and twisted just so, flinging the man on the left backward. Then a step forward, a pivot, and he knelt with precision, sword up just in time to block the double-handed swing from the other opponent. He stepped forward twice, still on his knees – knee to foot, knee to foot, sword up like the thrust of a horn. He tossed the inlaid silver sword up in the air in a way that made it spin and then caught it by the grip so that it curved back along his forearm. He lunged to his feet, his first sword blocking a fresh blow, followed quickly by a back-handed slash from the sword now facing the wrong way. Blood sprayed across the room, coating our bed.

My hands found my face, my breath coming out in a rush. I didn't even think of the sword or knives on my belts. I wasn't thinking at all.

Hands seized my shoulders, covering my mouth. I barely bit back a scream and then I was yanked up through a hole torn in the thatch and pulled onto the roof by Vireo. He threw me in one motion onto the blue elk stamping and huffing on the thatch. In front of him, Sparrow sat her elk, and there was one other elk with a long, dark bundle slung over its back.

Vireo ducked through the thatch again, came back with the severed head of Grosbeak, and strapped it behind my saddle. I didn't move to stop him. I could hardly keep myself from shaking head to foot already. I didn't know if it was the searing cold or the shock of another attack – of more bloodshed. Vireo took my saddlebag from me with care, as if he thought I might bite at any moment, and attached it to the side of the saddle where it belonged.

"There was one more of you," I said through chattering teeth.

He nodded his head to the bundle tied to the saddle of the riderless elk. "The Brotherhood of Stolen Sisters killed Ibis on our way here. They took us a bit by surprise tonight."

"I thought you were immortal. I thought you didn't die."

"We die neither by age nor by disease, but violence and poisons may end our lives like a string of pearls severed. Who would have thought they could guess we'd be here on this of all nights?" Vireo said with a savage grin. "Never a dull moment when you ride with the Arrow. Always an adventure."

"You consider death an adventure?" I asked. My tongue was thick between my frozen lips. The lace nightie was not warm enough for a winter's night.

Vireo cocked his head to the side, brow furrowing. "What else would you call it, then? Is it not the great adventure? The sea each must one day sail?"

He'd just finished with me when Bluebeard vaulted up onto the roof, flicking the blood from the tips of his swords and then wiping them on the thatch.

"Thatch shouldn't hold something as heavy as an elk," I said, my teeth still chattering. Hysterics didn't make sense. I needed to stop them at once.

"It's magic, wife of the Arrow," Vireo said, winking this time. "Get used to it."

Bluebeard sheathed his swords and threw something at Vireo, who caught it and examined it. He was close enough that I could see it, too. It was an iron medallion with the words "Forever the Faithful" etched on the back and a pair of crossed swords on the front.

"Brotherhood," Vireo said with a nod, as if he'd been expecting it. He glanced at Bluebeard as my husband mounted behind me, his hot breath gusting across my neck. "Dead?"

Bluebeard didn't answer directly. He made a whooping sound, both Sparrow and Vireo replied with the same as Vireo hurried to mount his elk, and then we were leaping into the sky. I bit back a scream, but we did not plummet to the ground outside the inn. Instead, we disappeared once more into the thick mist, the elk seeming to run through it as if they were running on a well-packed road.

The frosty air bit through my lace nightgown until my skin smarted all over like little needles were being jabbed into every inch of my skin. The night sky above us was crystal clear, the stars spilling across it like a spray of water on a hot summer day – glittering, bright and sharp in beauty. Our elk's breath gusted into the air, almost tinkling from the cold. My breath gusted with his, like a silver chain hanging from my mouth and nose. My eyelashes froze together a little and I had to wiggle my nostrils to keep them from freezing.

Bluebeard reached around my throat, and I froze, terrified that he might strangle me right here, drain me of days, and put me in that room with all his other wives.

He tossed my long braid over my shoulder and I felt the lightest brush of something warm on the back of my neck before my cloak fell, pooling between us. I grabbed for it frantically, but already he was slipping a dress over my head – I reached my arms through the woolen sleeves, greedily grasping for warmth, and as I tugged it around my hips and under my bottom, he already had the cloak back up and was clasping it around my shoulders. It was a narrow warmth, but more than nothing.

"You are likely wondering what those men wanted," he whispered in my ear. "I shall salve your curiosity. They want you."

A chill shivered through me. But how could that be? Who in the world would want me?

"When you opened that door – against my warning, I might add – you unlocked my access to your days and now I may spend them as I please. Each one opens for me new powers and skills I cannot access otherwise. I had but a bare brush of them before, but now they are my possessions, every one. Your kind have stories about the Wittenbrand and the great feats we may accomplish – but magic, my glorious wife, has a price, and the price is paid by the wielder. He pays with his life. He pays in the length and breadth of the days allotted to him. But a married man is one with his wife. And as one, I can pay with your days. With the allotment of your life's breath and the span of your soul's time on this garlanded globe."

And that explained why he had sixteen wives. Sixteen seemed awfully excessive, even for him.

I glanced back at his sharp, pale eyes. They had a fey look to them but even with his blue beard, he didn't look much older than thirty years. And if he was only thirty years old – or perhaps even thirty-one – and assuming he'd begun wedding wives as early as fifteen or sixteen and that there were no overlaps between his marriages, then he had spent the life of a woman for every year he was an adult. My heart seized inside me. Did I only have a year left to live? Did I have less? Perhaps he drained a wife entirely and then bided his time for a year before he was finally driven to take another. He did not seem like a man much given to self-control.

My brow wrinkled. But hadn't he spoken to the man last night of having been there a generation ago? And had he not stolen Margaretta, who would be aged by now had she lived? Perhaps he was far older than he appeared and more frugal than I guessed.

"The Brotherhood of Stolen Sisters wishes to spare you this."

My heart leapt, startled from fear by this sudden burst of hope. If they came for me again, perhaps I ought to lend them aid. Perhaps if I did, I could go home and leave this strange husband and his terrifying plans for my future. Surely, my king could not fault me for wanting to live the year out. He would not punish my family if Bluebeard was dead and unable to come for me.

And all Bluebeard's threats about razing my lands and slaying my people would die with him.

Something soft was flung around my neck. Bluebeard buttoned it in place, the very tips of his fingers brushing my throat in a way that made me shiver – and not from the cold. It was a fur collar, I realized, thick enough to be a scarf. It must have come from his own bags.

He whispered again in my ear, his words tickling my heart in a way I didn't find at all comfortable.

"You tantalizing creature. You mad folly. You unravel my careful plans and bring care into my unraveling. And yet, I must use you as I have used the rest of my wives – even having given my vow and all that such portends."

I pulled forward, away from his words, but he only leaned with me so there was no gap at all between the warmth of his body and my back. No gap at all between his gusting breath and my frozen ear. No gap at all between the squeeze of his thighs and my seat on the elk. Something tightened in my belly.

"I have decided to offer you something I offered none of my other brides – just as I offered you a marriage vow when I did not offer them the same."

I screamed "*no*" in my head, but he could not hear my fierce denial. And he could not see the tears that might have been fear or might have been rage that froze on my cheeks as quickly as they fell.

"I offer you an alliance. Work with me, wife. Do not be merely something I use up and put away in that closet you found. Be some*one* who weaves this dangerous gilded web with me. A true partner in the spending of your days and the rending of your years." He paused and I felt a light tug on my braid. I frowned, turning, and realized he was fiddling with the end of it again. "You're a wise woman, wife. I can see that about you. Likely, you're thinking about whether it is shrewd to betray me to my enemies. I assure you that it is not. Your best hope of deliverance is in the arms of the very man you loathe. Think on it. I do not need the answer immediately, but I will need it before we next enter the lands of mortals."

Though he was my enemy, his dearest desires in conflict with my own, his offer gave me pause. Had I not wished that someone would see me as an equal, that I could be more than a bride married to a disinterested husband? That in marriage, I could do more than simply sacrifice myself for nothing? And here he was making me an offer of just that. How perverse that it would be him to offer me such a gem when it was also him who wanted to ruin everything else that I loved.

Something made a growling sound in the heavy mist surrounding us and I looked toward it, startled out of my own brooding. A dark shape was moving precisely beside us, neither ahead nor behind – so close that I felt I could reach out and touch it. It rumbled again with the promise of dismembering us in due time.

"Mist Lions," Bluebeard whispered. "They rise again, and all such monsters will rise the longer we linger. We must join the Wittenbrand at the Turning of Ages, the Game of Crowns, and we must join them soon or time itself will begin to unravel."

Well, that sounded like a bad thing. He was just full of pleasant news today.

"I must play the game. For if I do not, this world will be ravaged by those who do. And who knows what evil they may unleash or what chaos may come to rule the mortal realm? And I must take a day from you, wife," he said, flicking my ear sharply.

My hand sprang to my ear, clasping it against the sting. I almost cried out an objection, barely catching myself in time. Instead, I turned, letting all my fury fill my face so he could see how I felt about being randomly mistreated.

His eyes were dancing when I turned, his smile mischievous, like a boy caught stealing sticky buns. My lips were parted in a snarl, but to my shock, the moment I was fully turned around, he leaned in and caught my lips with his own for a sudden, shocking kiss.

I had never been kissed on the lips before. My mother kissed me often on the cheek or forehead, her kisses maternal and safe. My brothers or father had, upon occasion, given me the rare minimal kiss on the cheek, as if to get it over with as quickly as possible so that no one might think they actually felt affection of any kind toward me.

But this was my first ever kiss on my lips and it was far, far sweeter than it had any right to be. Especially since it was coming from a man who had not only murdered fifteen wives but was dead set on murdering me.

Delicious warmth mocked the frigid night and tantalizing softness dazed me. It was as if he was shaping my lips into a clay pot with all the firm delicacy of a potter caressing the clay. I melted against him despite all my good judgment, my common sense lost in the momentousness of the act.

He drew back, and for the barest second his nose nuzzled against mine, and his forehead gently touched against mine, as if in apology for what he'd stolen this time.

And then he was leaning back from me again. I faced forward as fast as I could.

That was a very, very bad idea. Kissing did not stop with kissing. My mother had been clear about that. Kissing, she claimed, nearly always started an avalanche like the wrong note sung in the mountains and it ended – if it ever ended at all – with fat babies and lines of inheritance.

My face was hot at that thought.

"I always try to give as much as I take," Bluebeard said lightly and I wondered if those other girls had blushed as hot as I was blushing at his kiss. I wondered what they'd given him after that. And if he really had given back just as much in return.

But I could hardly be jealous of a string of dead women, right? After all, I had known that Leonid had been happily married before me and the fact had not left me envious but had made me feel secure in the fact that he was capable of some measure of care for a wife. So why should I feel cheated that Bluebeard had been married before? That he had likely kissed all those women – and more – before, while I had only ever had this one stolen kiss? Perhaps it was merely the imbalance. Perhaps if I kissed the rest of the Wittenbrand he'd brought with him, it might even the balance. But the thought did not help at all and I felt certain that the action wouldn't either.

I bit my lip in irritation. I was being impractical. But so was he. Sixteen wives was far too excessive! And taking kisses from any of them just seemed like an excess too far.

I would be judicious about this. I would not be jealous and I would not remember the feeling of his lips on mine. I would, instead, set my excellent mind to the puzzle of how I should betray him to the Brotherhood of Stolen Sisters, thus making both my King and my family safe while securing some length of future for myself. I let out a long breath and let out all my jealousy and foolishness with it.

I was nearly at ease again when I heard Grosbeak's gravelly voice, and all semblance of composure fled as I covered my mouth to hold back a shriek.

Chapter Fifteen

"IF YOU THINK GIVING me a voice will make me your ally, Arrow, you can think again."

I gasped and craned my neck backward. The voice really was coming from Grosbeak's head. Little gold sparks were popping one by one out of the top of his head like corn popping in a kettle over a fire. They fell to either side of the elk's blue flank, falling into the mist and disappearing.

"I think it will, enemy of mine," Bluebeard said contentedly. "You will soon find that being a head with no body is a boring existence – unless someone finds a way to make it interesting for you."

"I'll chew up your boots and spit them out in a thousand pieces," the head said in an ominous voice. "I'll bite your toes off and laugh as you stumble in your own blood. I'll scream your location to the heavens until vengeance rains on you like the fires of heaven!"

To punctuate his claim, he began to shriek – terrible, soul-shivering screams that struck to my very core. I tried to plug my ears, turning my head away to look ahead again, but it made no difference. Bluebeard ended his screams with a dull *thunk* – but not soon enough. The shadowy lion closed in, leaping for us.

It did not look like the fawn-colored lions I was used to in the rocky mountain clefts. This creature was a silvery-white with jagged black stripes across its fur and a double pair of white feathered wings. It leapt for us, its wings giving it extra lift.

This time, Grosbeak's scream was pure terror.

Bluebeard hunched forward, whipping the reins and the elk leapt ahead. He leaned around me, low so he was hanging almost off the saddle to the right. His sword slid from the scabbard with ease – the sword I'd given him for our wedding – and then he was whirling it in his right hand like a pinwheel.

A lion from that side leapt, wings extended, and he sliced it onto ribbons without slowing at all. Its keening scream faded behind us.

A second lion leapt, teeth and claws gleaming for the brief instant it became solid instead of ephemeral. Bluebeard's sword severed its head cleanly from its lion body, and a tiny, giddy part of me wondered if we would keep that, too. Perhaps we'd tie them all behind the saddle to add growls and purrs to Grosbeak's screams.

And then pain filled my world and I screamed, too.

I tried to look behind me, but I was caught in place, agony ripping down my back.

Bluebeard cursed loudly and then shifted behind me. His blade whipped around my body like my hair on a windy day. Something screamed – a high-pitched animal squeal – and then all was silent except my agonized breath huffing into the night.

I clutched the saddle, eyes gritted shut. I needed to breathe. I needed just a breath. Each attempt was agony.

Slivers of ice and fire shot up and down my back turning my bowels to jelly and my head to a fizzling mass of chaos.

"Blood of gods and mortals," Bluebeard breathed, and I thought that maybe he was pulling the edges of my cloak aside, but I couldn't tell. All my senses were directed at the searing, endless pain in my back.

"You're clever with the blade, I'll give you that," Grosbeak said grumpily. "But you always let things come to a head. Why didn't you kill the lions *before* they attacked? You could, with all that power just waiting to be used."

"Everything deserves to act before it is judged," Bluebeard said distractedly. There was a note of concern in his voice. "Can you hold on, you stern creature?"

"Of course, I can't. I have no arms." Grosbeak's voice was still bitter.

"I'm speaking to my wife, adversary," Bluebeard said but I barely had the wherewithal to nod my head. It was taking all my strength just to hold myself up in the saddle.

"We'll have to go straight to the Wittenhame, I suppose," Bluebeard said reluctantly.

"And then everyone will know you've made me your creature for no reason but your own pleasure!" Grosbeak crowed. "And they'll know you had to cave and take a short cut!"

"And they'll not lift a finger for you, fool," Bluebeard growled before whistling sharply twice. On either side of us, his men closed in, riding their own elk. Sparrow's elk had claw marks on its hind flanks. Vireo was still flicking blood from his blade.

"Mist Lions," he declared. "If they are waking then there are worse things yet."

But he seemed resigned to it and so did Sparrow, their eyes hard and focused into the mist.

"No," Bluebeard said, sounding a little guilty. "We'll use the key."

Vireo's mouth dropped open and he shut it hard, his eyes widening so suddenly that I thought he might have bit his tongue.

"You've shown us the fruits of rebellion," Sparrow said with a nod to Grosbeak's head, "but even with that trophy I am gravely tempted not to follow."

Bluebeard shrugged. "Suit yourself. My wife needs aid. The lion tore her back."

Sparrow leaned in a little, and I felt cold on my back as if Bluebeard were exposing the flesh to the cold. Sparrow looked green when she pulled back.

"Scars and sires," she cursed. "And with the horns of the Hunt still in my ears."

"We must ride the dangerous paths to reap the gift of speed," Bluebeard said grimly. "Do not die before your time, my practical wife. It would be far too dramatic an end for you."

I gritted my teeth. I'd never want him to know that I absolutely agreed with him.

"What's he planning to do?" the gravelly voice of Grosbeak asked from behind me. "Please, fellow Wittenbrand, assure me that our great Arrow does not plan to dole out madness."

The others were silent. Which should make me worried, but all I could think of was the pain.

"Just watch the rear," Bluebeard muttered. "Call out if you see more lions."

"And if I see horrors beyond the pits of hell? What shall I call out then?" Grosbeak spat back at him.

"Don't worry," my husband told him, "I don't plan to ride past any mirrors, so you won't need to report your ugly visage to me."

Sparrow snickered but then she turned sober. "Maybe you should brace the girl."

The elk shuddered as his feet hit the ground and Bluebeard leapt from his back to a fallen tree just peeking out of the mist where we had temporarily landed. I clutched the pommel of the saddle, feeling sweat break out all over me despite the way my breath still left a spectral plume in the moonlight.

He reached around his neck to pull out the little silver key and looked right at me.

"Every Lord of the Wittenhame has a key like this one. We usually prefer the long ride through the lands of dreams that connect the mortal world with the Wittenhame. It is faster than any human road and contains only limited nightmares."

That must be this fog we kept riding through. Even injured, I could work that much out.

"Just turn the key already," Grosbeak moaned. "No one wants the lecture."

"I do," I said between gritted teeth. "And I have all my limbs, so I win."

A startled laugh escaped my husband's lips and he smirked as he finished his explanation. "I told you there's a price to all magic. This magic can take us directly and immediately to the courts of the Wittenhame. But we each pay a price for its use."

"And the price is insanity, yada yada," Grosbeak said from behind me. "I swear, you cut my patience off with my head."

"The price is a *piece* of your sanity," Bluebeard said gravely. "Fortunately, you seem to be the most sane person I've ever met. You have plenty of sanity to spare."

"Have the rest of you used the key a lot?" I asked Vireo.

He snickered. "Are you asking if your dear husband is insane? Because the answer should be obvious – a thousand times, yes. Now, quit stalling like a girl about to make her first kill and let the Arrow use the key to the kingdom, yeah?"

I swallowed and tried to nod. Instead, it was just a flinch. Little white stars danced over my vision. Again. I was nearly killed a lot when I was with Bluebeard. And he hadn't even tried to kill me himself yet.

Bluebeard gave me one last, grave look and laid his hand briefly on the back of my neck. "Courage now, you solemn creature."

Then he lifted the key – and just like when I had opened the door to his wives' chambers, he turned the key in the air and a door opened before us.

It was like someone had cut a neat door with a curved top out of the air itself, only on one side it was entirely different from the other. On our side, it was the foggy land – the dream world? – and on the other, I saw the glimmer of lights and heard the sound of tinkling laughter. But the door rippled like a troubled lake, as if there was a thick window set into it.

Bluebeard seemed to grit his teeth and then he dropped the key back into his shirt and took a step forward, pulling the elk to follow him through the door. I opened my mouth to protest but then shut it with a click as he disappeared into the rippling view of – whatever it was he'd stepped into. It wasn't sensible to fear something just because it was foreign and hard to see, and yet I felt shivers of dread as the elk stepped forward.

"Whatever pain you're feeling, Lady Arrow, will be nothing compared to the madness of stepping through that door," Grosbeak said, cackling to himself as if he wasn't stepping through with me.

I clutched the saddle horn as my face hit the bubbling surface and I gasped.

Someone was screaming so loudly that I couldn't process any other sense. Screaming, and screaming and screaming.

I looked to the side and saw Bluebeard smiling at me. He was speaking, but I couldn't hear him through all the screaming. And then his head fell off, rolling to the ground.

What happened next wasn't precisely a series of events or visions. When they passed, I couldn't have described any of them later, but I had the sensation that I had experienced a hundred tiny horrors. My hands shook as if they could remember something my mind did not, and my heart was heavy and laced with a sadness deeper than I'd felt before.

I jumped at the sound of the elk's feet on the gravel below and my wide eyes came up to see Bluebeard – with his head on again – trying to speak to me.

After a moment, I realized that the person screaming so hoarsely was me.

I stopped abruptly, but I couldn't entirely calm myself. Instead, I was making tiny little keening sounds one after another. Bluebeard seized my face between his hands.

"Izolda," he said sharply. And then, again. "Izolda!"

I managed to stop the hysterical sobs so that they were only very heavy breathing.

"There, see? I told you it wasn't so bad. You're still mostly sane."

He laughed in a way that made me wonder if he was.

Then, he let go of my face and I realized I had tears running down my cheeks. They stung in the cold. On either side of me, Sparrow and Vireo were hunched in the shadows, eyes staring into nowhere, their expressions dull and aching.

"It's almost dawn," Bluebeard said, not even waiting for them to snap out of their mirrored shock. "We need to move."

Chapter Sixteen

OUR ELK WERE STANDING on a wide, flat blue stone, snow drifting over it like a bridal veil. The moment that Bluebeard's elk stepped beyond it, the stone disappeared and a crash like cymbals made me startle despite the pain of my back.

Angelic and harsh all at once, a choir began to sing, their voices first soft and then growing louder and louder, containing within them the anticipation of spring which slowly rose into the blast of dawn light scouring the earth and from there into a roar as though a tempest were rolling across the horizon. While I saw no owners of these voices at all, their song overwhelmed me. I caught very few of the actual words, except for the occasional "glory," "power," or "prince." But I didn't need to hear the words. The very tone spoke of magnificence, of fealty, of worship.

The chorus combined with my pain to leave me in a trance-like state of feverish dizziness.

As the elk stepped farther, nearly dancing in his precise steps, red and white petals fell out of the star-bright sky, filling the crisp air as if to celebrate the entry of a conquering prince into a great city. They fell around, in front and before us, creating a carpet of petals for the elk to walk on.

I blinked hard, sure I was hallucinating through the searing agony I fought in my daze. But when one of the petals landed in my lap, I picked it up and stared at it through glassy eyes. It was velvet soft and fragrant between my fingers.

We emerged into a thickly wooded area wreathed in white snow. The world became bright in a strange, too-white way that was nothing like sunrise or noon.

Before us, something like a white marble altar stood and at its center, a single all-white flame burned. Within the flame, a brilliant white arrow was stuck into a jagged stone.

To my shock, my husband leapt from the back of his elk and ascended the steps of the altar in a way that seemed both reluctant and reverent all at once. He bowed low, making obeisance with a gesture and the flame seemed to flicker in greeting. All at once, the singing stopped.

"And so Wittenhame greets her princes," Vireo said wryly.

My shock must have shown on my face. "What is that?"

He snickered. "The Wittenbrand. The white flame? Did you not know of it before? Teeth of the gods, but mortals are a stupid breed."

There was an irritated tick like someone had *tsked* out of the side of their mouth and then Bluebeard was there beside me.

"Watch your tongue, Vireo, or I'll feed it to Grosbeak."

"I shall eat it with relish!" Grossbeak said from behind us and I shuddered and then froze. Even that tiny movement brought tears of suffering to my eyes.

Bluebeard mounted behind me and Vireo's voice was a little more respectful when he said, "Welcome home, Prince of the Wittenbrand."

Bluebeard grunted. We were moving again before he began to whisper to me.

"Let me tell you a story, wife of mine."

And I found that the words of his story seemed to ease the pain of my wounds, so I listened intently.

"The Wittenbrand are called so for the great White Flame of the Wittenhame. No one can tell how the Flame came to be or why it shows favor to some and not others, but all here respect the flame or see ill luck follow. And it is whispered from nurses to their charges and from the lips of mothers to daughters, and the words of fathers to sons, that one day, blood will be spilled on the Wittenbrand. The brand will turn gold and on that day a great hero will arise and he will pluck that arrow from the stone and he will be marked with white and chosen by the Wittenbrand to lead the people to an age of glory."

I wanted to know if that meant people went around slicing their fingers and touching the flame to see what happened. It sounded like the kind of fool thing people would do.

Bluebeard sounded chagrined when he said, "Of course, I've been with the lads to test if anyone's blood could change the flame or pluck out the arrow. They make a bit of a game of it from time to time – particularly now at Eventide."

Of course.

"And it is said that when the Wittenmarked one comes, he will bring us milk and honey to eat, and all will dance for ten years in joy at his coming."

"Tell her another one," Grosbeak said from the back of the elk. "One that's not old and dry from the telling. Played-out stories are no way to win a lass."

"Perhaps if you'd stuck to stories, you'd still have your head," I growled.

Bluebeard laughed, a lovely, tinkling laugh, and then he whispered to me, "And the Wittenmarked will marry the finest woman of the Wittenhame, for she will have been revealed to be true of heart and pure of spirit. And all the land will see peace once more."

As he finished his tale, we left the thick woods, the elk still walking on fallen petals and through heaps of soft snow. We took a turn in the path and I gasped at what was laid out before us.

The forest had not melted away from around us, rather, it had gotten larger so that we were as mushrooms on the forest floor. Around me, between the massive boles of the trees, were the oddest houses. They were small and crooked as if made and then left to dilapidate. They grew moss and fungus all over them, and each was moving. One was strapped with a great band to the back of a toad. Another seemed to walk on four legs of a pair of storks. Yet another, rumbled happily on the back of a painted turtle larger than a palace.

Bluebeard whistled and a house fluttered over to us, half flying and half hopping across the ground. It had grey, tufted bird's feet and a pair of wings on either side that looked like ruffed grouse wings. It was a tall, twisting affair, thatched on the roof and covered all over with thick chartreuse moss and clinging lichen.

"Here we are," he said, and leapt from the elk, snatching Grosbeak's head from the back of the saddle and tying it to his belt by the hair. Then, he gently lifted me from the saddle.

I moaned at the movement. My back was pure agony. My vision swam with the pain as he eased me from the saddle. For a bare moment, I could hear nothing, and I missed the orders Bluebeard was giving his men. I had the sensation of movement as my eyes squeezed tightly shut and my jaw clenched even tighter, and then he was carrying me up steps. I opened my eyes in time to see him opening a round blue door painted with constellations and then he carried me inside.

"None can cross the threshold of a Wittenbrand house without invitation or magic," he whispered in my ear and despite the agony I was feeling, there was also a little thrill at his words. "In my home, you are always welcome, wife."

He was surprisingly tender in how he welcomed me – or perhaps my senses were merely dulled by pain.

He set me on my feet, and I stumbled to one side, catching myself on a tree – an actual real tree – from which coats and hats were hanging. The inside of the house was much larger than the outside. At any other time, that would have bothered my sense of order. Right now, it was just one more thing I observed and then ignored. Pain has a powerful way of concentrating the mind so that all else seems but a needless detail.

This room was so full of things – shelves stacked so full of books that they were jammed in every which way and crammed into every gap. A series of stuffed birds lined up on the top shelf and arranged in order from largest to smallest. A stuffed wolf beside the bookshelf that I was certain was looking straight at me. Beside him, a window as tall as me was thrown open, but the view from outside it was not at all the view from where we had just left. It showed mountains drifted with snow and bright stars above, swirling with color. The curtains to either side were deepest blue, dappled with silver. And after a moment I realized the silver in them was actually little lights winking and twinkling at me. I'd only examined half of one wall when Bluebeard set Grosbeak's head down on the bookshelf and began to throw off his bloody clothing.

"And now you choose," he said, tossing his sword into an urn as tall as my waist and carved with mostly-naked men grappling with dragons. I would have found them shocking any other time. Right now, they were merely another useless detail. "I can stitch your back with silver thread, and it will heal quickly and soundly, but it will pain you. Or, we can spend a day of yours and I can heal you instantly."

The jacket was next. He tossed it to the floor as if it were nothing. And then his white shirt – stained with blood. Should I be worried that he was undressing before me? I couldn't remember. There was only the pain and the time before the pain.

He whipped off his white shirt, gathered it with the jacket, and walked past me to where an open hearth contained a merrily dancing orange fire.

He threw the clothing in the fire, tugged off his boots, and threw them in, too. They went up in bright red bursts and coiling black smoke and then a puff of smoke filled the room. The fire made a sound like a belch and said, "Thank you."

I must be losing a lot of blood. I was imagining things. Like how utterly beautiful my new husband was without his shirt. He wasn't a large man, but he was all corded muscles and white silvery scars from the waistline of his leather pants to his closely trimmed black hair.

"I bet you'll choose a day,'" he said, stripping off his stockings and sending them into the greedy flames. I could have sworn a flame that looked very much like a tongue licked them up. "But before you do, think hard, my wife."

I was starting to like it when he called me that. No, that couldn't be right.

He turned his silvery eyes to me, and they glinted brightly, reflecting the dancing flames. "A day is a precious thing. Who can say how many you have been allotted? It is easy to spend them like water for trinkets, only to realize too late that you've used up all your precious days on nothing at all."

He plucked a twisted red bottle from the tangle of a human skull and a shed snakeskin wrapped in a string of pearls above the fireplace. Unstoppering it, he poured a single drop onto his fingers and then promptly began to smack his day-old blue beard with his hand. The scent of cloves and cedar filled the room in the most appetizing way. Having done that, he ran his hand through his very short hair like a bird preening its feathers, and then replaced the bottle.

I was still staring at him with wide eyes when a raven flapped down and landed on his shoulder. I gasped and looked up. And up. And up. I could not see the ceiling of this house. What I could see was a chandelier made of deer antlers and strung with black pearls and dripping yellow candles. And ... was that an orange cat sitting in the chandelier, hissing at me?

Bluebeard smacked the raven away, irritably.

"Not now," he chided. "Report later."

"I'd take the day," said Grosbeak from his spot on the shelf. He sounded oddly content, as if he was resting now that he had been set on a shelf. "Pain is never worth the price. What is one day for the loss of it?"

"You tell us," Bluebeard said easily. "You are out of days, so you would know best."

"I'm not out of days, I am simply short one body," Grosbeak sniffed. "Don't you want to ask me 'Who sent you?' or 'Why did you try to kill my new wife?'"

"I never ask questions I already know the answer to," Bluebeard said, smacking the lintel over the fire with the palm of his hand. A hidden compartment sprang out. I didn't think my eyes could grow bigger, but apparently, they could. He drew out a spool of thread, that was indeed silver, and a needle that looked to be made of the same material. "Make your choice, wife."

I bit my lip. Even if this thread really did heal me quickly, I would still be in pain the whole time. And what would that be? Weeks? Days? Or I could give a single day and it would all be over.

My head throbbed with the agony of my shredded back and sweat slicked my forehead. But Bluebeard was right. I did not know how many days I had left. What if I offered just one and then I missed something important?

I pointed to the thread and the half-smile he offered me was triumphant.

"Up on the desk," he said, gesturing to a desk the size of two beds stuck together. It was heaped with parchment and quills, ink bottles and books. Books open. Books shut. Books on top of parchment, and under parchment, and in stacks, and in what might have been stacks before they fell into whatever they were now.

I stared at the mayhem. There was no way *to* get up on that mess even if I wanted to. The raven fluttered down and landed on the edge, tilting its head at me.

Bluebeard looked from my wide eyes to the desk and back, and then he stepped forward, and very gently removed his cloak from my shoulders and threw it into the fire.

"Thank you," said the fire.

"This will hurt," Bluebeard said, and he almost sounded sorry for that. But then he lifted me up so suddenly that I couldn't even catch a breath, flipped me in his arms so I was face-down, and leapt.

The leap was impossible. A man his size could not leap into the air from a standing start with a full-grown woman in his arms and land on a desk higher than my waist.

But here we were.

He laid me down on the heaps of papers, and then with a rip that made my cheeks suddenly hot as a sizzling day in summer, he smoothly separated the back of my lacy nightdress all the way down to my waist – and I could only hope no farther.

From the shelves, Grosbeak whistled, and my face grew even hotter.

"Only three claws tore your back," Bluebeard said, ignoring Grosbeak and sitting beside me on the desk cross-legged as his gentle hands worked their way down the slashes on my back. "One is barely two inches long, but the others are longer and deeper."

He breathed across my torn skin and his breath felt cold like the first snows of winter. I shivered.

"Easy now, wife. Easy." He ran a hand over my head and hair as if calming a snorting stallion and then he reached for the needle and thread. "They're horrible wounds, but we'll soon have you stitched. I have marks like this myself."

I remembered those scars, decorating his whole body like netting.

I felt the bite of his needle when it entered my skin, and I clenched my jaw against it, feeling a fresh wave of nausea kick through me and sweat slicking my fists and face in a wave. Had he stitched many people before? I wished I could ask him and hoped he would say yes – because it would mean he knew what he was doing – but also no – because then this would be a rare thing around him instead of a regular occurrence.

The room swam. I tried to look at the papers right under me to keep my mind from dwelling on what he was doing to my back. They were poetry, I thought. One was some ode to snow on tree branches and another one described the wonder of frost on window panes. I had expected something more along the lines of bribe letters or threats. The poetry surprised me.

I lifted my head just a little and saw a door behind the desk that seemed to lead into a dark corridor.

"I wonder how many rooms are in this house," I said a little faintly.

"Best not to ask," said Grosbeak from the shelf. "In a Wittenbrand house, that might change with his mood. It could be large as a palace today and then just this room tomorrow."

I was starting to think I was in a world where I didn't know the rules. And that worried me.

"This is not a very sensible place." I felt like I was pushing through a heavy quilt just to speak the words. "Where does the food come from?"

"Dreams and dreamers," Grosbeak replied glibly.

"Not farms and farmers?"

"Now, what would we want with farms?" Grosbeak asked. "The people on farms are dull. They do not dream of flying like a bird or being gutted by a unicorn. Their thoughts are entirely of crop rotation and putting up carrots for winter."

"Maybe that's because they like staying alive," I said wryly.

"You can't live at all with such a lack of imagination," Grosbeak said. "That's just surviving."

"I don't think you're in a position to scorn those who want to survive," I said coldly.

"Well, I might be dead," Grosbeak said, "but I still am more alive than they'll ever be."

And as horrifying as he sounded, I thought he might be right.

"Let me tell you a tale," Bluebeard whispered in my ear as he set a stitch. I was grateful for the whisper for it distracted me from the pull and tug of his needle. "It's a tale of star-crossed loves. Two warring clans lived side by side."

As he spoke, I could almost see a vision of the tale he was telling me in my mind. Focusing on it eased the pain once again and I found myself sinking into the story.

"They hated each other with the hate you must feel for those who keep accusing you of things you never did and then killing your relatives for it."

That was understandable. I hated the Wittenbrand and they'd only killed one man, who I had met that same day. He wasn't even family.

"Then one day, a Cavr'l was working on a stone wall between their lands when a Hy'lil set on him, and their fight was harsh and swift until the hood of the Hy'lil fell free and her bright red hair shook out long and brilliant. And the Cavr'l's eyes widened and he let go of her cloak and she scampered away."

I felt his needle drawing through my skin and I tried not to whimper at the added pain.

"But the next time their two clans tangled, when she rose from ambush with them to smash the heads of the Cavr'l, the head she was meant to smash had raven black hair and the eyes of the stranger who had let her go, so she did not slay him but pretended to miss her mark."

His gentle hands were drawing my skin together as he worked but despite his gentleness, I could not help the tears that swelled in my eyes and brimmed over onto his poetry.

"The winter grew cold and harsh, and she went out hunting and found nothing. Her belly was empty, and her hands froze to the bone, and she dared not go home to look at her family and their empty eyes and empty bellies unless her hands were full. So, she collapsed against the wall and lay down in the snow to die there, and who should happen to be on the other side but the Cavr'l with the dark eyes? He had with him a brace of hares. One, he gave to her, and their eyes met, and an understanding was made."

I leaned into his words and the rich cedar and clove scent that surrounded him and I tried to think of nothing else.

"And from that time on, when the two were out hunting, they would meet at the wall and share what they had, and also share warmth that turned to kisses, and kisses that turned to true love."

True love was something I would never have. So why did the mere thought of it melt my heart the way the Cavr'l's had melted his enemy's?

"But in the spring, when the snow melted and the clans turned to warring again, their families discovered them one night, wrapped in his cloak, and perched on the wall and though the lovers tried to explain, they were ripped from each other's arms and cursed."

I felt him tie a knot, tugging at my skin in a way that made me bite my own lip.

"And from that day on, the Hy'lil was woman all day long and a red fox at night, and the Cavr'l was man all night long and a dark raven in the day, and never may they speak to one another or find solace in feverish kisses. Except for that one moment at the edge of dusk and dawn when they are both human for the blink of an eye, and sometimes when they meet there, the clouds turn pink for blushing at the passion of their kisses."

He tugged another knot and I bit back a cry.

"Stay still now," he said, stroking my head again, and then a smell of camphor filled the room – pungent and intense.

I winced as he spread cold ointment over my wounds and then again as he pressed something soft against them.

"You'll need to sit up so I can wind the bandages around you." He was so close as he whispered to me that his lips almost grazed my ear.

I sat up with great care, my stitches smarting and the pain a dull constant like the ache in my heart from where my family and home used to be. Like the betrayal in my memory when I saw all those dead women encased in magic. Just like that.

I managed to get myself upright, clutching the front of my nightdress to me. It was tattered and ruined. His hands reached around me and under the dress, grazing the bare skin at the bottom of my rib cage as he ran the bandage around me and wrapped it around my back and then again, and again. It was such an intimate gesture for two strangers. Two strangers who were married to each other. I found it hard to reconcile this Bluebeard with the gentle touch, who never once tried to put his hands in intimate places while he worked, with the one who had so easily lopped Grosbeak's head off and stolen my first kiss from me.

"I think something backless," he said when he was finished with the bandage.

I found him at the side of the desk, rummaging in the bottom drawer. He pulled out a dress made of some soft, rippling material that caught the light and somehow softened it to cling to every curve beneath. It was a soft grey-blue, and trimmed in fox fur at the cuffs and the edge of the high collar. Thick black embroidered scrollwork covered the bodice and fell to spider legs across the full skirt. The back of the bodice was open in a wide keyhole that would have shown most of my back had it not been wound with bandages.

From beside it, Bluebeard pulled out a pair of soft leather boots with very sturdy soles and strong laces. They were so different from the dress that my eyes widened. These were practical boots for living and working in, and while they were finer than those I usually wore, they were just as sensible. I could run or gather firewood in these without worrying about turning an ankle.

"There are underthings in the drawer," Bluebeard said, looking over his shoulder casually at me. "One of my other wives had a whole batch ordered right before her last day."

Those words tore away all the softness and intimacy, shredding it like wet paper. I should never forget I was his sixteenth wife. I should never forget that none of this was real.

He reached over to me and popped something into my open mouth. In surprise, I bit down and tasted mint.

"I'll leave you to dress," he said, snatching a knit hat from the coat tree and jamming it over Grosbeak's head right down to his nose. "No peeking."

He paused in the doorway and then turned back to me. "When dawn comes, I will need your answer, wife. Will you work with me or no? Think hard on what you will say."

Then he strode through the door and I watched him prowl down the long, dark hall like a cat going out for the night. I half expected to hear him yowl when he reached the other end, but when all that met my ear was silence, I chewed my soft, gooey mint candy with my eyes as wide as saucers.

Chapter Seventeen

AFTER A MOMENT, I came to my senses. Who knew when he would return? I should dress before then. I scrambled painfully down from the table and put on the odd clothing that had been left for me. It was a long, agonizing affair. Every movement tugged and pulled at my stitched skin and my tears flowed freely as I carefully shrugged on the ridiculous dress.

Twice, I had to hold onto the desk to catch my breath and clear my head. Would I work with Bluebeard? Did I dare say no? Did I even want to? Here, so far from the mortal world, spying for my king seemed ridiculous. What would I say? That the houses had wings and the fires spoke and if he found a man to pull an arrow from a stone it would fulfill their prophecy?

I laughed hoarsely at myself for even thinking of it.

The dress was far too fancy for everyday wear and I missed my practical woolen shifts and embroidered overdresses. This one would be cold – especially in the back, despite the fur trimming the keyhole. If I hadn't been in a torn nightdress, I would never have worn it at all. But while I did indeed find a blue silk slip – fortunately, it had a very low back and was trimmed in lace so that if a little peeked into the keyhole of my dress it would not look out of place – there were no other dresses.

I frowned as I put on the slip purchased by another woman. It worried me that it fit me perfectly. But it was impractical to be fussy when it was my only option and utterly superstitious to think that its dead owner would resent me for wearing it. Or for marrying her husband, for that matter. When I was done, I marched over to Grosbeak, and delicately pulled the hat from his eyes.

"Bluebeard may know why you were trying to kill me, but I do not," I said to him. I needed an ally here. One I could be sure wouldn't run out on me. "And if you don't tell me right this instant, I will throw you into the hungry fire."

There. That should get me some answers for once. I needed to be smart about this. I wasn't used to fires that belched or bodiless heads, but I could still find ways to be sensible in a nonsensical world.

"Bluebeard? Is that what you call the Arrow?" His snicker was nasty. "Oh, he'll like that. I guarantee he will."

"Fire or confession," I insisted.

"You won't do it, a big-eyed wisp of a thing like you with tumbling dark waves of hair – oh, you're a pretty one, and you can hold your tongue, but you're mortal, and all mortals are but a blossom that lasts a day and then is gone. You've no value at all. You're just a stone in a game of merels. Something to sacrifice. Something to use. The Arrow will use you for your days. I planned to use you to delay him."

"Delay him?" I asked in a deadly voice.

"I'll say no more."

I lifted his head by the hair and held it as far from my body as I could. It was heavier than I'd expected and lifting it pulled at the stitches in my back so that tears brimmed in my eyes again.

I took three wavering steps toward the fire before he hissed.

"I'll talk." The words came out in a rush. "I'll tell you why."

I finished walking to the fire and set his head on the hearth. His eyes were wild. "Not here. It's too hot here. Don't you know that corpses burn?"

"You're not a corpse yet," I said in a cool tone. "But you could be."

"Yes, yes, I understand." He looked resentful. "It's about the Great Game of Crowns, the Turning of Ages. They play it every five hundred years and it's due to be played again. Tomorrow. If the Arrow does not arrive in time, he does not get a seat at the table. If he does not come with magic, he will surely lose the game. So, I tried to kill you because it would force his hand. He would either have to play without magic – for he draws that from you – or he would have to go and find a seventeenth bride and marrying takes time. The mortals like it done right. Either way, he's out and he can't win and ruin things for the rest of us."

He was right, I realized, suppressing the cold fear that washed over me. I was only a tool. A thing. Or at least, that's what I was to them. But imagine if you were trying to use a tool and it came to life? What if the axe started to chop at you or the blade twisted in your hand? I might be a tool to them, but I was a living tool. I would find my way to chop.

Besides, Bluebeard had asked me if I was on his side, and would he do that if he only saw me as a thing? Unless maybe it was a way to keep his things orderly and malleable. I frowned as I thought.

"And was this plan your own?" I asked, keeping all that out of my cold voice.

"Of course not. I worked for the Sword. Your husband will know that by now. It's no secret that they are rivals."

So, Bluebeard had powerful enemies. Which meant I did now, too.

"And now you work for me," I said.

"I *certainly* do not."

I lifted his head by the hair again and moved it closer to the flames. The fire murmured something that sounded a bit like begging.

"Not the fire, not the fire!" Grosbeak pled.

I pulled him back.

"I know perfectly well that terror only gains you obedience while the fearful thing is there," I said calmly, marching him back to the bookcase and setting him down there. He was still steaming.

I walked over to a small alcove where someone had thoughtfully placed a bowl and pitcher. They were both encrusted with round, red gems. Uncut rubies, I thought. I ignored the king's ransom I was using as a tool and washed my hands thoroughly. Dead things were disgusting.

"What is it that you may still want, dead as you are?"

His face took on a thoughtful expression. "Revenge on your husband."

"Besides that." Hurting my husband would not help me at all.

"There is nothing besides that," he declared boldly.

"Very well, then I will find some other ally."

I moved back to the desk, examining the papers there. Anything to keep me distracted from the grip of the pain in my back.

"Perhaps ..." Grosbeak let the word hang in the air, but I didn't take the bait.

I kept shuffling papers and reading them as I went. My husband was very fond of stories. Not a single paper here was nonfiction. They were all tales or poems, songs, or stories. How interesting. What sort of a man did that make him inside his mind? He was both murderer and poet, brigand and storyteller.

"It's possible that I also want revenge on the Sword for putting me in this position," Grosbeak admitted eventually.

I turned to him and smiled.

"Your smile is crooked," he said. "And your face too narrow. And your nose is too thin."

"And you're a bit on the short side these days," I shot back.

He snorted.

"I will give you revenge on the Sword if you work for me. Be my ally. Be my helper."

"Why do you want that?" he asked suspiciously.

"I am new to this world and I can't ask my husband questions in the night or receive his answers in the day. You can help with that."

He pursed his lips, seeming to consider my words.

"You will never get revenge for me on the Sword," he said eventually. "It is impossible."

"Nothing is impossible if you approach it with systematic logic and careful observation," I said as I flipped through my husband's papers.

"You must get it for me before the Game of Crowns is finished," he said. "Or our bargain is void and I will spill your secrets to all who listen."

"Done," I agreed.

"What is done?"

I turned to look at Bluebeard. He was leaning against the doorway, one shoulder propping him up as he examined his nails. He wore a midnight blue jacket thick with bronze frogging across the breast and narrow, tailored blue trousers with bronze scrollwork running up the outsides of the legs. The jacket was hanging open and under it, he wore a white shirt trimmed in red fox fur that he'd left open and a tailored vest embroidered with arrows of many styles. Again, he'd only buttoned it partway, as if to show he didn't care. Most of his chest was left exposed so that his many crisscrossing scars were bare to the world on the surface of his pale skin.

I looked him up and down and raised an eyebrow at his smirk.

"Yes," he said, "I'm a fine specimen of a Wittenbrand. Now, what deal has she struck with you, Grosbeak?"

Oddly, he had the tiniest cut on his cheekbone under his left eye and a thread of blood ran down his cheek. His leaning had turned into something that looked more menacing.

"Only that I am to be her creature," Grossbeak said bitterly.

"In exchange for?" Bluebeard asked, stalking forward and rubbing his beard with one hand. It was so short now that it was nothing more than stubble, and yet he had not shaved it completely. I wondered why. Maybe there was something wrong with his skin underneath.

"She said something about revenge," Grosbeak muttered. "And she needs some way to carry me. She doesn't seem keen on holding me by the hair."

Bluebeard barked a laugh as if this was a great joke and disappeared down the hall. When he returned, he had a lantern pole and a length of sky-blue ribbon. The lantern pole was the length of my leg with a decorative counterweight in the shape of a raven taking flight behind the handle, and a large lantern hanging from a chain on the other end. Bluebeard flung it onto the desk and began working to remove the lantern.

"I like this idea, wife. Perhaps Grosbeak can be of practical use to you. He knows this world enough to avoid the worst pitfalls. And if you fail her, you speaking pumpkin, you gourd of words, I'll feed you to the fire myself."

"Thank you," said the fire.

Bluebeard left the lantern on the desk and stalked over to Grosbeak, studying him as if deciding how to affix him to the end of the chain. It had a hook to hold the lantern. He gave a one-shoulder shrug and then began to dig the hook into Grosbeak's scalp.

Grosbeak grunted in pain.

I looked hurriedly away and tried to catch my breath. I was a practical girl. I was used to dealing with things as they were and not trying to imagine what they could be. Imagining, dreaming – that only made it harder to focus on what was in front of you. But all of this was pushing me to the very edge.

"Oh," Bluebeard said offhandedly. "There's a book in the top drawer of the desk. Would you fetch that?"

I was glad for a practical task. I opened the top drawer and found a book bound in blue leather. Everything was blue for these people. I was starting to long for red or yellow or any other color at all. By the time I'd turned back to my husband, he had Grosbeak fitted on the end of the pole and a ribbon tied to the tip where the chain hung down.

"There. That's delightful." He looked very satisfied with himself before he turned to me with a fierce glint in his eye. "The book is for you. You should keep it in the room the key opens."

At those words, a stab of fear shot through me. He could make me do a lot of things. He could dress me and bring me to homes carried on grouse wings. He could force my silence all night and be silent all the day long, but he could not make me go back to that place. I would not look his other wives in the eyes again or feel the horror of watching an hourglass measure my days.

I crossed my arms over my chest and gave him my most mulish look. There were limits. And this was where I'd set mine. Even if I felt a little sick to my stomach.

He was like the shadows when he slid across the floor to me, taking my shoulders in his hands and leaning in to whisper in my ear. I shuddered at the intimacy. This man was violence and desperation, intensity and focus. I did not like being the center of that focus.

"The book must go on the pedestal. Fail me in this and I will be sorely grieved."

He expected to slowly kill me and for me to spend that time ... writing about it? Was that what this was?

He was insane. *That* was becoming obvious.

And his strange beauty as he hovered beside me glaring – all that coiled muscle waiting to spring, all those lean, hard lines – well, that did nothing to dull the danger and fury in his every look.

"Put the book in your private chambers, fire of my eyes. The chambers my key opens. And do it quickly for we are already late and there will be a penalty."

He drew back enough for me to see the threat in his eyes.

I swallowed, took out the key, and opened the door while he still held my shoulders in his grasp. The moment it was open, he released me, and I stumbled inside, trying not to cry with my frustration. These moods of his, harsh and fierce one moment and gentle the next, were impossible.

I set the book on the empty stand, the one nearest the door. My eyes clouded with unshed tears. I was furious. At him. At this situation. At everything. And fury made you do stupid things. I couldn't afford stupid things right now.

I took long breaths and dulled my fury, dashing the tears from my eyes. And that's when I saw a tiny roll of paper tucked into the ledge of the stand for my book. There, in the tiniest letters possible, someone had written, "open me."

I unrolled the tiny paper. Someone had written a note in tidy, round script:

All is not as it seems.

You'll be fine if you listen to him and stay out of the way.

It's not that bad.

M

I glanced at the stand next to mine where the brass plaque bore the name "Margaretta." She was dressed in soft gold with round, pink cheeks, long blonde hair to her waist, and a figure that would have looked good in any dress – but especially this one which made her round curves elegant and princess-like. She was almost shockingly like her niece, Princess Chasida. The family resemblance ran strong in their female line.

And she'd been kind enough to leave me a note. I felt a warmth at that. I wondered if it could possibly be true. Could this really not be so bad after all? Or was Margaretta just such a sweet girl that even being married to a monster hadn't shaken her?

I tucked her note into my book, my heart suddenly uncertain. It was easy enough to listen and stay out of the way. Perhaps I should follow her advice – at least until I knew more.

I looked around me furtively and snuck over to the first girl – the one on the other side of the horseshoe-shaped configuration. Her clothing was of a fashion I didn't recognize and the cloth was rough, the weaving not so fine as mine. I thought that perhaps this was Bluebeard's first wife.

Like the others, she was almost shockingly pretty, with delicate skin, a sea of freckles, and very long, straight hair the exact color of a fox. Foxes were embroidered all over her rough dress and a fox fur stole hung from her shoulders.

I opened her book and flipped quickly through the pages. There was nothing in it except for a small paragraph on the first page. Not even her name.

The paragraph was a riddle. It read:

I am sudden death to calm.
My roar breaks the hush.
My song the mind's somnolence.

What a strange thing to choose to write in your book. Nothing personal. No message to her family, just this strange little rhyme. Something about it tickled my memory. Hadn't I heard it before?

Shaking my head, I left the room and the strange women who had preceded me behind.

Chapter Eighteen

I STEPPED out of the room and the door shut behind me. Before it had closed, Bluebeard crossed to me, lightning-fast and I didn't even have time to flinch before he flicked his wrist, and something cut my cheek just below my eye.

I gasped, barely biting back a cry, and my hand rose to touch the wound. He caught my hand in his, his chest heaving with emotion and his gaze latching on to mine so that I couldn't look away from those icy grey eyes if I wanted to.

"It's my mark," he said, turning his head ever so slightly and tilting his chin upward so I could see how the blood had dried into a very long tear-streak on his cheek. "Would you refuse it thus? You are my wife. You will wear it with pride."

I swallowed and nodded. After all, it didn't hurt too badly. A wife bore troubles for her husband and bore his name. Bearing his mark was no great thing.

He nodded sharply as if he approved of me and then spun toward the door of his home. He moved as he always did – with a kind of barely suppressed energy, as if he would have liked to run the width of Pensmoore and was only just holding himself back.

The sun was still not quite up when Bluebeard flung open the door to his home.

"In less than an hour," he proclaimed to me, "the sun will rise and with it will dawn my silence. So, think on this, wife. I want you near me until we return to this home of mine. The world of the Wittenhame is a dangerous place and I dare not let you be stolen from my grasp."

I gave him a wry look. After all, he only wanted me near to protect his investment. I was his well of power. It was like leaving the house with a bag of gold. You'd be a fool not to keep it near.

"Ah, here is my band," he said, snatching my free hand to escort me down the steps of the house.

The house stayed relatively still as we made our descent. I tried to keep Grosbeak steady on the end of the lantern pole so that he didn't swing into the railing.

"I think I might be ill," Grosbeak groaned.

"You'll get used to it," I said firmly. "Keep your eyes on the horizon. It helps with motion sickness."

"Where did you learn that?" he moaned.

"My father took me on a ship in the sea once. It was a mortifying experience."

We reached the bottom of the steps, but Bluebeard did not let go of my hand as he inspected the double row of ten men on either side of the path. They stood in crisp blue uniforms that looked rather like Bluebeard's but with arrows sewn up the arms in gold stitching and one across the breast with a whorl of scrollwork around it.

Vireo stood at their head, looking as if he'd hurried into his uniform, and Sparrow was on the other side of the rows, her head held high.

"Ibis?" Bluebeard inquired.

"Given to his family for rites."

Bluebeard nodded sharply.

"All accounted for?" he asked, raising an eyebrow. There was a dangerous tone to his voice.

"For now," Vireo replied, looking back and forth between me and Grosbeak. "What are you doing with the traitor?"

"My wife has made him her pet."

Vireo's eyebrows shot up and Grosbeak protested, "Here now!" but Bluebeard continued.

"We'll make our formal entrance. We need to hurry."

Vireo leaned in, concern etching his features. Across from him, Sparrow leaned in, too, an identical concern on her face.

"You bring her with you?" Vireo whispered. "Her who is mortal and key to our success?"

"I do," Bluebeard said, his lip curling.

"You've not done so before, Arrow," Sparrow said respectfully, but there was anxiety behind her eyes. "Far be it from us to question you on this, but would it not be better to bind her to her rooms as you did with the others? You could post us as guards. I would volunteer."

"Speak to my riddle, Sparrow," Bluebeard said with a dangerous smirk. "Who has a bed but does not sleep? Who has a heart that does not beat?"

"The dead," she said, her eyebrows raising into a wry expression.

"And anyone who questions me on this," he said, pulling back and raising his voice. "We move with speed. Fall in."

And hurry we did.

I had expected Bluebeard to let go of my hand, but he kept a tight grip on it, and though I knew he would one day kill me and that he only kept me close because I was worth so much to him, I couldn't help but take a little comfort from the warmth of his grip as he led me through this strange world of his.

It was a puzzle that he had decided to keep me close. Sparrow's suggestion was very practical. If I was the magical equivalent to a well-stocked larder, didn't it make sense to keep me far from danger and guarded? And yet he'd reacted to that as if she had struck his face.

I shook my head and tried to take in the details around me. My brain kept trying to pretend that I was doing it so I could report on this world to my king. The rest of me knew that was a pleasant lie. My king could not cross into this world. He could not walk through the land of dreams or cross through the barrier of madness. I was too far gone to ever see another mortal again. I needed to adjust my thinking. I was weak and vulnerable as a hare in the snare. My only protection, a madman and murderer. But he did seem to want to protect me, and that was not without value.

And if I were to win his favor and extend my life, I would also have to pay attention.

The Grouse House, as I couldn't help but think of it, had taken us to the base of a strange cluster of blue and pink-tinged white fungus that rose so high in front of us that they dwarfed the palace of Pensmoore.

Icicles thicker than my waist hung in solid waterfalls from one level to the next and pooled onto the ground, shining dangerously in the moonlight. The edges of these falls were clouded and frosty but the center portions were pure and transparent, and I found my eyes following the intricate pattern they formed as they rippled down the cluster of fungi.

To my horror, I realized that I really could see into the ice, and in its depths hands reached toward me and faces thrust forward with eyes and mouths gaping as if people had been frozen within the depths of the ice as they tried to claw their way free. And what people they were – for some had wings and some had claws, and some had the feet of hinds and goats.

I froze for a moment as the horror of their presence sank in. They were real people – I knew this somehow – not illusions. And they were trapped forever in the ice.

Bluebeard pulled me along after him, closer and closer to their last resting place. I did not want to go toward that ice.

But there was no way to avoid it. For it was to the fungi that we were hurrying as we made our way around the icy falls. Sounds of loud partying and celebration trickled down from the various levels and a wild dance spilled out around the base of the fungi as people whirled in the moonlight to the sound of fiddles and drums and tin whistles.

My feet were starting to grow lighter and my steps quicker as we drew near, as if my feet, too, wanted to join the dance despite my brain screaming at them that it was a terrible idea.

The moment the dancers caught sight of us, they froze, and then a cry went up.

"The Arrow! The arrow flies!" The tune changed, and a singer began to chant in a silken song, her words otherworldly and beautiful as they spread over the people. Each ear it touched seemed to warm to the tune and the people joined in with the song.

Fly with the Arrow,
Dance with the Sword,
Give Your Heart to the Barrow,
Die with your Lord

Bluebeard nodded to them as they sang and then some left the singers and the dancers and crowded around us so that his band escorting us had to make a path for Bluebeard and me to walk in. I could hardly hear the singing for all the cries of, "Arrow! Arrow!"

And if ever you be broken,
And gasp on the ground,
Hold up your fine token,
And join with the sound

Bluebeard turned to me with shining eyes, biting his lip as if he was planning something, and then he spun me around quickly as if we were dancing, too, and dipped me low. At the bottom of the dip, he seemed to pounce, like a cat on a songbird and he stole a kiss from my lips right there in front of the crowd.

My heart leapt in my throat. I couldn't breathe. I wasn't sure I wanted to. The pain in the tears on my back was agonizing but it mixed with the sweetness of his kiss in a way that made my head spin. He tasted like the sweet mint he'd eaten and his eyes were dancing when he pulled away and drew me back to my feet. I was still gasping when he made a throwing motion over the crowd on either side and people leapt to catch tiny blue sparks as they flew out.

To my shock, each person who caught one seemed to change.

Sing for your Sovereign,
Bow to your Dream,
Make Haste for the Fallen,
Rise in Esteem

One man with the feet of a faun leaned heavily on a cane, but when he caught the spark in his hand, he dropped the cane and leapt six feet into the air. Another woman, hacking and coughing to nearly double, caught a spark, and her brown-bark face cleared and her moss green eyes relaxed.

And if ever you be broken
And gasp on the ground,
The word may be spoken,
And salvation found!

We were almost to a door carved into ice and steps working their way through that doorway when Bluebeard held up his hands.

"No more today, my friends. I am spent."

And then he led me through the door and the sound of song and merriment began to fade as we climbed the steps. I paused on a stair and looked a question at him, and he scratched under his collar irritably.

"Five days," he said after a heartbeat. "Their healing cost five of your days."

I felt my face freeze as stone-cold as the ones pressing toward the surface of the ice behind him. They looked like they were trying to come through the wall to seize him and drag him into the ice with them. I felt the exact same way. But it was hard to begrudge others their health – even knowing that they were spending *my* days to get it.

I simply shook my head. It was only five days. But he'd spent them like candy, while he had wanted to save one to avoid healing me. Were these people so much more precious than I was?

A servant in a strange livery of leaves and brown swaths of fabric, with a crown of dried oak leaves around his tousled blond head, and strings of acorns across his chest, rushed up to us and made a hasty bow. His cat's eyes were wide, and his pupils narrow.

"My Lord and Prince, mighty Arrow," he said, his big eyes growing even larger as he spoke. His ears formed tight points at the end. His lips were very full for a man. "Please make haste."

He led us up the steps in the ice. After a moment, we reached a landing and an open door leading to a shelf of the fungus where the dancing continued, but here it was slow and sweet and couples swayed in each others' arms as tiny little multi-colored lights flitted around them.

Bluebeard guided me past the door. "We must make haste. We have but minutes until the dawn."

"Please," the servant begged from two steps above us. He swayed a little as if he wanted to sprint up the steps and was only holding himself back for our sakes. Tension filled his voice. "Please, the rest are seated."

They certainly started their days early if they were already partying before the sun came up, or maybe we were so very late that they'd been partying since yesterday and this was simply overflowing into today.

Along the stairway, portraits were hung. I paused slightly at the first one. A fair lady with hair like the servant's, and a crown of golden oak leaves. Her skin glowed like it held a candle inside, and her eyes – while blue – seemed almost to glow gold as well. She had a superior smile on her face that made me think of Princess Chasida. I did not like that smug look in her eyes. Those were eyes that would gut another woman and sell her meat at the market.

"That's Lady Tanglecott," Grosbeak informed me.

"She looks like she eats other women for a tea snack," I said precisely, and he snickered, to the horror of the servant two steps above us. The servant gasped and looked toward Bluebeard.

I chanced a glance at my husband, but his expression was carefully neutral.

The next landing showed me a feast so mouth-wateringly opulent that I couldn't prevent my belly from rumbling over the whole roasted pig and the scent of toasted nuts and berry pie.

"As I said, wife," Bluebeard growled as if I had spoken rather than my belly. "We have but minutes to spare."

I nodded and hurried on with him.

"There will be food up above," the servant said, a little breathless. He kept running a few steps up and then running back down to be sure we were following him, and then running up again. My father had a dog like that once.

We passed a series of other portraits like the first, all cruel-looking Wittenhame. Each one more other-worldly and inhuman-looking than the next.

I stumbled when we came to Bluebeard's portrait.

"Lord Riverbarrow," Grosbeak explained derisively. "Him who is called The Arrow. A prince among the Wittenhame."

I paused this time even though my husband's hand pulled at me. Because he looked so eerie in this portrait – so pale and so blue and so very inhuman that I felt choked at the reminder that I had married someone who was not of my world at all. On his cheek was a single red tear. Just like the one I bore.

"Hurry, wife," Bluebeard murmured, and to my eye, his pale skin looked blue among the ice and glowing fungi.

Something glinted in Grosbeak's eye and then he spoke.

"You call her 'wife,'" Grosbeak laughed, "but do you know what she calls you?" It felt to me like an act he was putting on. His voice sounded just a shade too high and his emotion just a tinge too desperate.

"What?" Bluebeard growled as he led me past two more landings.

The servant hopped from foot to foot as if he badly needed a quiet moment in the back house.

I was growing weary of all the stairs and every stitch in my back felt like it was pulling, but I didn't dare pause. Even if the servant hadn't looked about to cry, leaning against the wall was out of the question. It would mean leaning against the poor victims trapped within it.

Instead, I dug deep inside, battling both the pain of my stitches and the nausea and light-headedness that made it hard to concentrate.

Grosbeak remained silent, his expression turning smug. He was getting the reaction he wanted – though I didn't know why he wanted it.

We rounded another corner and Bluebeard spun me so my back was to the wall, but though his actions were full of frustration, he was careful not to press my wounded back against the ice . He let go of my hand and braced himself against the wall with a hand on either side of my head. He peeked a little look out at the worried servant on one side and his anxious men on the other, as if this was some grand joke that he was wasting time when he should be hurrying.

"You have a name for me, you stone-faced certainty?" His eyes were lit with some emotion I couldn't understand, and his lips parted slightly in anticipation. "It's not 'honey' or 'darling,' is it?"

I lifted a single eyebrow. I thought he said he was in a hurry. And even he should realize I was not a girl who would call him that.

"Please, for the love of the wind's name and the forest's caresses, please!" the servant begged, swaying side to side with urgency.

Bluebeard frowned as if he'd heard my thoughts and then tilted his head to one side, his cat's eyes still teasing. "It's not 'illegitimate son of a donkey' either, is it? What might that name be, wife of mine?"

I lifted the other eyebrow. Did he really want me to break my pact and speak aloud to him?

He waited a heartbeat before smiling savagely and winking at me.

"My prince?" Vireo said nervously. Now he sounded as nervous as the servant. "The edge of darkness lifts."

"I shall hear the name at dawn, fire of my eyes," Bluebeard murmured for only my ears to hear.

I tilted my head as if asking, "But will you?"

Bluebeard growled in his throat, snatched my hand back, and led me up another spiral of the stairs to where they finally came out to a wide balcony. We stepped up into the bright moonlight there, where the thick lip of fungus made a fine, long hall looking out over the Wittenhame all around.

Though a fall from the edge of the fungus lip would be fatal, no railing was erected, nor a low wall. No provisions were made at all to guard guests.

A long table was laid out, made of woven bones and a tangle of interwoven weapons – bows, axes, swords, and anything else I could think of. Around it, were chairs that left my pulse racing. Who in all the world would choose chairs like these? I feared the stains on the dark wood were not made of age but of blood. Leather straps were dangling from them as if someone had once been strapped to them – or may still become imprisoned there.

The servant who had led us bowed until he was bent almost in half, and on either side of the door, a pair of other servants bowed in the same way.

They murmured something, but I was not listening to them. I was not even looking at the people surrounding the table as Bluebeard hustled me toward the one empty chair – the one at the end of the table.

I was looking at the figure seated at the head of the table.

He looked like a very large man – a head taller than Bluebeard and twice as thick. He was seated on a throne made of bones I didn't recognize – large bones that were almost bird-like, or maybe lizard-like – and both he and the throne were half-encased by the ice of the wall. Frost covered what was still unencumbered by ice, coating his eyelids and his beard, decorating his grand crown with a lace of frostwork. His eyes were half-closed and his voice was speaking very quietly – and yet it seemed to fill the room.

"... wait no longer," it said slowly as Bluebeard drew me to the table. Someone had scattered fat white and blue hyacinths all over the table and everyone's drinks were interspersed with the sonsy blooms. "Only those who are seated ..."

Bluebeard sat so quickly that it almost didn't look graceful – the first ungraceful movement I'd ever seen from him – and he pulled me down to sit on his knee like a child.

"...now, will be qualified to enter."

And when Bluebeard breathed out, I realized he'd been holding his breath.

Around the table, everyone else seemed to let out a breath, too, though their sighs sounded more like disappointment or resignation.

All the other eyes were on us. And they were the eyes from the portraits leading up the stairs.

"Did you feel the lack of my presence? Was it a howling wind echoing through your hearts?" Bluebeard asked lightly, throwing his leg up over the arm of his chair casually. He looked for all the world like a cat coming in late after a night of prowling.

Someone farther down the table growled.

A thrill of fear shot through me and with it the very strong desire to be ill for there was murder in every set of those eyes.

Chapter Nineteen

"LET THE GAME DAWN," the sovereign's voice announced, and then his eyes closed as if he were going back to sleep.

"That's our sovereign," Grosbeak hissed to me. "He rules all of the Wittenhame. Any seated here could be his successor – if they earn the role."

I swallowed and very carefully did not touch the blood dripping down my cheek that everyone around the table was staring at.

Out on the horizon between the great trees, the first golden ray of dawn split the sky.

"You've married again," one of the men halfway down the table said, putting his feet up among the hyacinths as he spoke and crossing the ankles of his knee-high patent leather boots with delicate care.

I noted that he was absolutely not looking at Grosbeak's head and Grosbeak was looking very attentively at him, his mouth a straight line of fury. This, then, must be his master.

He wore a jacket like Bluebeard's, but it was crimson and trimmed in white. I counted three swords on his person. Two were crossed over his breast as if to show just how very addicted to swords he really was. He put his hands behind his head and leaned back in his chair as if he were going to fall asleep right here. Maybe they all were. After all, the man encased in ice seemed to be somnolent. Every now and then, his great face twitched under the frost as if he were dreaming.

Servants began to move quietly between those sitting, bringing steins, mugs, and glasses that steamed or seeped or bubbled depending on what manner of brew was within. One seemed to be hissing and another gave off a whine like a kettle at a boil. Those sitting around the table barely noticed the drinks or the servants, simply accepting them or waving them off as they chose. Bluebeard took a steaming, thick drink of a very pale green that smelled powerfully of mint. He must really like that flavor.

"And who exactly did you marry?" one of the women asked. She had dark hair and was missing two fingers and an ear. She'd placed a pair of small bearded axes before her, wedged into the table as if she thought she'd need them at a moment's notice.

Across from her, another woman laughed – one with pale blonde hair, but I barely looked at her hair. My breath froze in my throat when my gaze turned to a pet she was feeding from her hand. There was one on either side of her and they were silvery-bright, striped with black slashes, and bearing four small, feathered wings on their backs.

I froze, my eyes widening at the sight of them. Would I find my own flesh under their claws?

"I'm still finding out," Bluebeard said coldly, shifting me so that I had to meet his eye.

His gaze locked onto mine as a ray of gold washed over his face.

He wanted me to tell him what I called him to myself. His name. I could see the frustration building behind his visage just as it built in me when I couldn't speak to him in the night.

I bit my lip and thought about it. If I told it to him right now, it would tell him I was on his side, but it would also tell him that I could be cowed into doing whatever he said.

"I respond better to honey than to stings," I whispered. But I did not say his name, and though his lip twitched irritably right where that little scar nicked it, there was nothing he could say because dawn was bathing the sky.

"Do keep this one around longer than the last one," the man in the red coat said. He was missing the smallest finger on his left hand. "I like the taste of her spirit. Like black pepper and limes."

"You can still taste the spirits, Sword?" Bluebeard said with innocent eyes. "And here I thought you lost that ability in the last game."

There was laughter around the table and the Sword's expression went stiff. He was not amused.

Bluebeard caught my eye and there was something steely in his. He held my gaze and reached for the cords tying my cloak. I shied away but his free hand grabbed my knee and pinched it – hard – as if trying to tell me wordlessly to allow this.

I swallowed. It felt like a power game. And I was the one being made to look foolish. But showing my wounds to the table – which was what would happen if he removed my cloak and my backless dress showed everyone my stitched flesh – didn't make any sense to me. Why bother? What did it prove?

I was angled on his lap so that my back was to the table. I took a deep breath and judged the calculated look in Bluebeard's eye. He was planning something. If I wanted to know what it was – or know about any of this so I could report it to the King – then I needed to play along. I gave an infinitesimal nod and let him loosen the string.

The cloak fell to the floor and behind me I heard a gasp.

"Someone has not been playing very nicely with his toys," the Sword drawled. "What a naughty boy. You should be conserving her. You'll need every bit of her you can barter."

Barter? Fear shot through me, and Bluebeard – his eyes still locked on mine – gave such a tiny shake of his head that I wasn't sure I'd seen it at all.

Someone cleared his throat – a man seated opposite to the Sword. He wore an opulent plum doublet with a jagged collar and golden powder surrounded his eyes. Unlike his fellows, he wasn't missing any fingers or ears.

His eyes held a calculating glance as he said, "As youngest and newest to the table, it is on my oath to offer the bones for the telling of the fates."

"Offer the bones then, boy," Bluebeard said in a bored tone. "Don't bore us all with talking about it."

Again, there were snickers, but the Sword spoke sourly. "We wouldn't have waited here until the exact last second if you hadn't delayed, Arrow. Your snide remarks notwithstanding. To be frank, I grow weary from a long night of indulgence. And you are its maker, not its victim."

The young man swallowed, looking back and forth between them as if waiting for someone to give him permission to move. Eventually, the woman from the first portrait I had seen on the stairs – Lady Tanglecott – raised an imperial hand. She was the one with the mist lion pets. Just glancing at them made my mouth taste sour. I did not like turning my back in their direction.

"Throw the bones, Coppertomb." She sipped on her pink drink and tiny pink sparks flew off of it when she blew on it, leaving black singes on the table and any clothing they hit.

The young man looked grateful. He lifted a horn up above his head and then stood, swirling it carefully in his hand before dashing the contents onto the table.

They looked something like dice but double the length and half the width. They were dark in color and etched with white, and they all landed face down except one.

Everyone around the table stared for a long minute at that one piece before Coppertomb gathered them up again with care.

The eyes of the Sword lit with what I thought might be pleasure or anticipation, but everyone else was properly stone-faced.

"What did that mean?" I whispered to Grosbeak.

"Shhh," he whispered back. "I'm concentrating."

"Leash your pet, Lord Riverbarrow," Lady Tanglecott said, and around me there were snickers. I realized, to my horror, that she was referring to me. My face felt hot.

"If I ever took a pet, Lady Tanglecott," Bluebeard said with care. "I would be sure to choose one that would claw your eyes out. And I don't mean those tame kitties you keep beside you. I think I would require something nearly as fearsome as I am."

"Enough." The word was cold, and it came from the other woman at the table – the one missing the eye and two of her fingers. She twirled one of the ones left in her dark hair. "We know the game. All that remains for today is to choose the playing piece. I grow weary and my pillow calls to me, so let's have this done and be off to our beds so that when darkness descends again, we are ready for the hazards."

"Why the hurry?" a man from the other end of the table whispered. He hadn't spoken until now, and he still didn't look up from a book he was reading. His head was crowned with antlers and his feet were up on the table just like the Sword's.

"I prefer my moves made in the game, not in boasting before it begins," the dark-haired lady said.

"I agree with Lady Wittentree," Lady Tanglecott said.

I committed the name to memory. If I was going to give a report on midsummer night, I would need all the information I could gather – surely, this was what he must have meant by spying. For we had no information about their rulers or courts or ways and that was something that I alone could discover for my people. And if I chose instead to throw in my lot with my husband, these details would make me a more canny ally.

"Bring the pieces," Coppertomb said nervously, and a pair of servants hurried through the ice door bearing a large copper cauldron between them on a pair of poles.

The servants wore padded gloves and long leather aprons, and they were both red-faced and sweating. After a heartbeat, I realized they were mortal just like me.

They struggled forward with the heavy cauldron and placed it alongside the table, next to Bluebeard. I could feel the heat of the cauldron from where I sat as the servants retreated, bowing and sweating, as they backed away from the swirling pot. It looked as though it were full of molten lead, and the top was streaked and crackled with impurities.

To my utter shock, Bluebeard thrust his left hand into his mug of minty drink and then into the molten lead beside us.

I screamed, clutching my throat. He was going to lose his hand. Cold sweat broke out across my brow and I leapt up from his lap, backing up to make space for him to crumple.

He did not crumple.

Along the table, vicious laughter rang out. Bluebeard brought his hand out and opened his fist to reveal a little figure in his palm. It looked exactly like the king of Pensmoore but it was the size of my index finger. Whoever had carved it had made his costume and features so perfect and so carefully detailed that he looked alive. That streak of grey in his hair was exactly as in life.

To my horror, the tiny figure blinked at me and then opened his mouth and screamed in silent, writhing agony.

"Pensmoore," Bluebeard announced casually, showing the others.

I clapped my hand over my mouth and he pocketed the piece, motioning to me with his hand to sit on his knee again.

His hand was untouched. Not even pink from the heat.

I felt like I might faint. Or perhaps be ill. Or perhaps throw myself off the edge of the fungi to end this madness. This could not be happening. Maybe I was still trapped in that wave of madness between the worlds. Maybe I'd never managed to get free of it.

Bluebeard's strong hand whipped out, snatched my wrist, and used it to guide me back to his knee.

The Sword was already getting up, swaggering over to the pot. He plunged his hand in the beer stein and then into the cauldron and came out with a glittering princess wrapped in silver swaths of fabric.

"Aayadmoore," he said easily and sat again.

Behind him, a man in mason clothing began to tap chisel and hammer against the wall. Above him, I realized, were lists of countries and players. Tanglecott was listed beside Fraedrann. But the nation of Fraedrann had died in a terrible plague that swept the nation hundreds of years ago. My brow furrowed. What was this list?

The man's chisel began to tap and I could have sworn he was writing "Pensmoore" on the wall. My blood felt like ice.

"Ilkanmoore," Lady Tanglewood announced as she made her way back to her seat. The dark figure in her fist struggled, tiny arms and legs flailing.

"Rouranmoore," Lady Wittentree announced, leading a man made – it would seem – entirely of white roots that formed hair and beard and clothing. Two blue eyes peered from under the mass of roots while Lady Wittentree dipped his hand for him. When it emerged she announced, "And for Lord Marshyellow we have Moravidmoore."

Antlerdale never looked up, merely showing his piece to the others. Only the Sword's mutter of "Ptolemoore" tipped me off to who he had chosen.

"They play against each other," Grosbeak whispered to me. "The fates of mortals are their pieces and the whims of chance their dice. Although, that should be obvious to anyone possessing half a brain."

A thickly built man with jutting lower incisors and very thick black hair pulled his hood back and emerged from behind Antlerdale. I didn't even notice him until he moved. He swayed as if he were under the influence of a substance.

"Gods have mercy," he muttered as he reached in and then cursed when he pulled out a woman with thick layers of skirts and a tall, conical hat on her head. "Qaramoore."

And that left only Coppertomb who hurried over, carefully soaking his hand in water until the sleeve was wet and the Sword was waggling his eyebrows at him, before reaching in and out as fast as a blink.

"Leaving me with Salamoore," he said, seeming relieved. But hadn't that been inevitable if it was the only piece left? The expressions on the other faces around the table suggested that maybe it was not.

The sovereign at the head of the table opened his eyes again, and the room fell silent. His voice – again – was authoritative, though barely louder than a whisper.

"Play resumes at Peak of Night."

Chapter Twenty

IT WAS like a wildcat had been let loose in the room. The moment the Sovereign closed his eyes again, the Lords and Ladies of the Wittenbrand scattered.

Some leapt from the side of the fungi ledge. I gasped at that, but no one seemed concerned. Perhaps they could fly, or maybe they were athletic enough to twist and land on another ledge. Some rushed out the door. Some moved to watch the stonemason etching their names in the rocky wall, chatting loudly about the results of the nations drawn.

Bluebeard helped me up, leaving the cloak on the floor. Did he want my back on display? I opened my mouth, and he pressed a finger to his lips as if the two of us were sharing a delicious secret. I pressed my lips together tightly to show him how irritated I was. I was not cattle. I was not a prize dog. I was his wife, and if that meant to him that he could use me as he liked, to me it meant that I was his equal and deserved to be treated as such.

But I could wait until we were in private to tell him that. I could wait until it was just the two of us. And then I would show him how to treat his wife.

He'd wanted an answer on whether I would work with him. I wanted an answer on whether *he* would work with *me.*

I let my eyes glitter with suppressed anger but before I could do more than look at him, an icy hand touched my back and I flinched in pain.

Something fumbled at my wrist. I spun in time to meet the gaze of the Sword. Something about the way he was looking at me made my mind go numb for just a moment.

Bluebeard's hand shot forward and caught the Sword's wrist, hauling his hand from my back. "Look all you want, but please don't touch," he said smoothly.

"Why ever not, Arrow?" the Sword asked, leaning smoothly against the woven table, his hip jutting out saucily as if he was completely at his ease. He picked a bloom up from the table, twirling it between finger and thumb before burying his nose in it. "It's not like you really touch them. You're more frigid than winter's bite."

"And more ruthless," Bluebeard countered. "I'll take more than your fingers if you touch her again. You'll be thinking fondly of the black of frozen flesh the frost steals when you compare it to what I demand in payment."

The Sword bit his lip at me and then the corner of his mouth turned up. "I think she's received the message."

He sauntered away, leaving Bluebeard standing there with his chest and fist thrust forward as if he were on the verge of giving chase. His lip curled up a little and he reached to take my hand.

Which was when I realized someone had tucked something into it. A scrap of paper, if I wasn't mistaken. I slid it between my fingers and offered my other hand to take his. Bluebeard whistled as he guided me down the steps and out of each doorway. His band joined him again, one by one, as if drawn by his low whistle.

They weren't the only ones. Little birds fluttered down, landing on his head and shoulders and singing sweetly in harmony with him.

"A fine showing," Grosbeak murmured. "The nations are all key ones and very close to one another. Close enough for the opening moves to be very interesting. They may already have agents in each others' courts. It will be a fine Turning of Ages this time around. Very fine."

"Are they truly playing on behalf of the nation whose leader they chose?" I asked Grosbeak, and was surprised when Bluebeard's hand tightened on mine. It wasn't painful, but more ... tense ... as if he feared the answer to this question.

"Haven't you heard tell that the Wittenbrand play games with the fates of men?" Grosbeak asked me.

"I've heard the rumors."

"Now you get to see it. A real game with real people and nations as the markers. If your nation is lost, you lose."

"What do you mean by lost?" I asked weakly, conscious that Bluebeard was squeezing my hand even more tightly – and that in his other fist he held the king of my nation in miniature.

"Ever heard of the Eldenheim? The Corrindale? The Xan Tharan?"

"I have not," I said, licking my dry lips.

"Well, there you go then. Lost means lost."

Lost. My family. My home. My nation.

He held their fate in his palm.

Quite literally.

Which meant he must not fail. If he failed, he would lose everything I loved. Every*one* I cared for. And that meant that if I turned on him and gave him up to the King of Pensmoore – if that wasn't him shrunk to the size of a finger and stuffed into my husband's palm – then far, far worse would happen than simply me losing my life and all my days. And what if our king didn't know about this? Maybe he should be told that much at least. It was hardly betraying anyone to tell him about his own fate – and possibly the best bit of information I could glean for him.

I felt dizzy.

At the last door, Vireo rejoined us.

"So," he asked my husband, "What is it to be then? I had a herd of pigs riding on famine."

"Famine?" I gasped. My eyes were so wide they were beginning to sting.

"War," Bluebeard said quietly. "It's to be war."

The band around us seemed grimmer somehow, their faces hardening, grips tightening on sword hilts. Did that mean they would fight?

"We're ready, Arrow," Sparrow said grimly.

"The flat tokens that Coppertomb threw determined the game," Grosbeak told me. "Famine, Pestilence, War, or Cataclysm. The games of the lives of men. Cataclysm is my favorite. Very dramatic. Most of it is determined by chance. War is the most strategic. It favors the thinkers and plotters. Like the Arrow here, or the Sword."

I risked a glance at my husband's face and shrank at what I saw there, for that was not concern or horror. In the lines of his face were anticipation and giddy eagerness. He couldn't wait to start. And if he lost, then everything would be lost to me.

Despite the frigid air, I felt hot all over.

"And could he have chosen not to play?"

Every eye was glaring at me now.

Grosbeak laughed. "Well, if he didn't play, he would no longer be a prince of the Wittenhame. He would forfeit his lands and people. Any claim he has laid on the mortal world and any magic he may derive from his claims there would be lost. He would lose his position and someone else would claim it. Vireo perhaps, or another Wittenbrand. Whoever made the claim would have to pass through a series of trials to take the role, but there would be many who would try to do that. If you don't play, then you are no prince of our land."

"Are we returning to your home, my lord Arrow?" Vireo asked crisply, refusing to look at Grosbeak or acknowledge the assumption that he was next in line for Bluebeard's position.

"Immediately. My wife needs feeding and sleep."

"And tomorrow?"

"You know none of us may act until the bets are placed," Bluebeard said briskly. Our escort shoved through the last of the stumbling dancers in the snow below the bottom steps. Around us, the day was bright and merry but the Wittenhame were stumbling to their homes nearby, putting their hands up to shield their eyes from the morning sun as if it was offensive to them and not the golden delight of the heavens.

"Others may choose to act sooner," Vireo replied, stone-faced.

Grosbeak chuckled. "You know the Sword will cheat. He'll already be sending messages. Nothing you can prove – just little things to pave the way."

"I am not the Sword," Bluebeard said menacingly. "I am so much worse than he could dare to be."

The Grouse House took that opportunity to make an appearance, fluttering down from one of the trees and landing in front of us so inelegantly that I was afraid it would crash.

Without a word, Bluebeard swept me off my feet and into his arms and marched up the stairs.

"Get sleep and food into you," he called over his shoulder. "And be back here before first dark. We have planning to do and strategies to make."

He yanked the door open and stepped inside with me still in his arms, pausing only when he saw there was barely room to stand inside.

"My people," he said, his voice ragged. "You have come to me."

My jaw dropped at the various people assembled in the room. Some sat or stood on or flapped over the desk. Some on the bookcases. Others on the hearth. The rest of the floor was packed with people of every size – one nearly the size of an oak tree, others so small they rivaled my fingernails. They had wings, or webbed feet, or horns that curled, or spiraled, or were straight. They had large, sharp teeth and broad, flat teeth. Some had papery skin like birch bark and others were ridged like a maple tree. Some hovered on dragonfly wings and some bore bird wings tucked modestly behind their backs. Some presented wide antlers and some hair like dandelion frills.

Bluebeard glanced at me, an odd expression on his face that looked almost like pride – but that could not be right. After a moment, he seemed to realize that he couldn't speak to me, so he spoke to them.

"This is my newest wife, Izolda of Pensmoore. I present her to you."

"Lady," the nearest one squeaked – a woman, perhaps? – who was shaped like a porcupine and completely covered in quills. "We thank you for your sacrifice."

And then they all swiveled away from me and toward Bluebeard and she spoke again. "We came together, but I was elected to speak. We suffer, Lord of Riverbarrow. All down the River the old ways die and the folk die with it. Our trees are cut, our swamps drained dry, our flowers plucked. We wane and die, we waste and grow hollow. We cry to you for salvation."

"Patience, my folk," Bluebeard said, but his face was pale and for the first time since I met him, he seemed afraid. "I work to buy it all back and make you free."

"We know you care, Lord of Riverbarrow," the porcupine lady said. "But we dwindle. Some of us are the last of our kind in your lands. And we fear that if you do not act quickly, there will be no folk for you to save."

He ran a hand over his face, and I could have sworn his lovely eyes were wet with tears. The blood streak on his cheek smeared and he bowed his head.

"I hear your words, my folk. And I listen. Please have faith in me for a little while longer."

They nodded gravely and then passed him one by one, leaving out the door. Each of them touching him as they left – as if just touching him would work some kind of magic.

Furtively, I stole a look at the tiny paper rolled up between my fingers.

I nearly dropped it in my shock. I could have sworn that the Sword had given it to me, and yet it was in my brother's hand. It read:

Izolda,

We will come for you. Have no fear.

Svetgin

My brother's words, in his hand. I looked up quickly. None had seen me reading the paper except Grosbeak, who raised a single eyebrow and smiled nastily. But even though I knew that my husband must win in this game with the lives of men, I couldn't help the glimmer of hope that seeing my brother's words drove into my heart. He knew where I was. He was coming for me.

Could that even be possible? He had sent a note – a feat I'd thought impossible. Perhaps the only limit here was my own imagination.

The last of the folk trooped out the door and Bluebeard shut it behind them, leaning his head against the doorframe. His shoulders slumped as if he was carrying a terrible load.

I ought to fight with him. I ought to tell him he was terrible and cruel and disrespectful and all the other things I'd observed since he put me on the back of his elk and ridden through the madness into this wild world. But how did you kick a man who was already so far down?

"I'll give you a hint," I said calmly, setting Grosbeak on the bookshelf.

Bluebeard spun and looked at me, his eyes blazing a question and irritated at my interruption all at once.

"The name I call you comes from a color," I said calmly.

His forehead wrinkled in puzzlement, but he no longer looked defeated.

I strode over to the edge of the fire and picked up one of the books on the hearth. Its name was on the spine. *Marvels of Modern Accountancy.*

Wait. Hadn't he thrown this book in the fire when he was reading it the night we were wed?

I shook my head. It was just a strange coincidence. I'd had a lot to think on that night. I couldn't trust my memory about the details.

Bluebeard moved to sit at his desk, poring over pages of what looked like poetry as if there were answers there. He opened his hand and put the little king down on the table so that he was standing, facing him. His feet were attached to a lead disc, so he could not move but he bellowed silently, shaking a fist. It made something cold seize in my chest.

No, I would not be the puppet of the little king. I needed to seal things with my husband. I had married him. He held my nation in his palm. It was with him that I must forge some kind of alliance.

"I would like to speak to you, husband," I said calmly.

He did not look up.

I swallowed.

This was going to be hard to manage when he couldn't speak to me but harder still if he wouldn't even look at me.

He gestured to a table in one corner of the jumbled room that was laden with food. I was not hungry. Okay, I was hungry, but I was not going to eat until I made my point.

"It's important that we talk." I made sure my voice was very clear.

He still didn't look up. He took out a pen, dipped it in an inkpot and began to write. I peeked over his shoulder. He was writing poetry. The fate of my world and the lives of those wild folk hung in the balance and he was writing poetry.

I shook my head and took a deep breath. Calm, Izolda. Losing your temper now will help nothing.

I waited and waited for what felt like an hour and still, he did not look up or even so much as glance toward me.

I needed to get his attention. I put my hands on my hips and then immediately let them drop again. The pain in my back was too intense. I was swaying on my feet from exhaustion and anxiety and hunger. I needed to eat and I needed my bed.

But if I left things like this, night would fall again and my voice would be lost to me before I could do anything to change what was.

The room was full of items – books and trinkets. Curiosities and precious things. The raven flapped over one bookshelf, tempting me, but it was important to choose things that were valuable enough that he'd notice but not so valuable that it would hurt him.

The raven walked across the desk and tilted his head at Bluebeard. My husband paused his writing and tilted his head in a mirror image of the bird, his cat's eyes flashing in the fire. So, he would not pause to hear me but he would pause to stare at a bird?

I shook my head. Well, that settled it.

With care, I strode to the hearth and picked up *Marvels of Modern Accountancy*. I cleared my throat and then threw it in the fire.

"Thank you," the fire rumbled, puffing up to twice his height for a moment before calming back down.

Bluebeard's head whipped up and he looked at the fire and then at me. I picked up the next book and this time I read the title aloud.

"*Crop Rotations: How to Account for Them Without Making Your Head Spin*. Clever."

I threw it into the fire. Sparks puffed into the air and the fire belched loudly.

"Thank you."

Bluebeard dropped his pen and rushed across the room as I picked up a third tome.

"*A Head Above the Rest: Ancestry of the Landholders of Pensmoore*. Well, don't they think a lot of themselves."

Bluebeard's hand caught my wrist before I could throw it into the fire. His eyes blazed into mine.

"Don't like the disrespect of having your books burned?" I asked Bluebeard acidly. "Well, I don't like disrespect either. I'm your wife. I am not a broodmare to be auctioned off to the highest bidder. I am not cattle to be traded in and stalled. I am not a pretty necklace to be bought and placed within a jewelry box. I am a living woman with a mind and abilities and there are things I can offer you."

"She speaks as though she possesses something I do not already own, my fire," Bluebeard said, shooting a glance at the fire.

"Yes, my master," the fire said.

"You drew my king from the molten lead," I said, catching his gaze again and looking into it with enough intensity to hold it. "You carry the fate of my nation in your hands."

He tilted his chin up arrogantly.

"And you carry the fates of those wild folk who came here to plead with you," I added, and he softened just a bit, his face relaxing slightly.

I felt my own brow furrowing. *That* was the path to his heart? This strange, violent man cared about that odd collection of creatures more than anything else? It was ... surprisingly endearing.

"You think I am only of value to you for the days of mine that you can spend to get what you want."

He raised an eyebrow in response.

"You are wrong. You asked me if I would work with you. My answer is yes. But will *you* work with *me*? You will find it much easier to get what you want with me as your ally rather than your enemy."

He raised the other eyebrow as if he didn't believe I could be his enemy.

"I could speak during the night and take your magic away," I threatened. His grip on my wrist tightened, his eyes blazing with deadly warning. "Yes, you'd kill my family and nation, but you might already do that with foolishness in this game of war you are playing."

"She speaks as if I believe that she would doom us both, my fire." His voice was low and insinuating.

"Yes, my master," the fire said. "But have a care. There is a fire in this one. Like recognizes like."

"Have I mentioned you are a rare fire beyond mortal worth?" Bluebeard said.

"You have not, my master."

I flicked my wrist and the book sailed into the fire's maw. He consumed it with a burst of orange flame and Bluebeard clenched his jaw so tightly that I heard his teeth click.

"Thank you," said the fire.

"That's what happens when you compliment things," Bluebeard said sourly. "It goes straight to their heads."

"Yes, my master."

I cleared my throat again.

"I can make your life miserable in a thousand small ways, husband. I can distract you from your purpose. I could even take my own life – and then what would you do? Would you have time to find a new bride?"

"Tell me she wouldn't do that," Bluebeard called to Grosbeak. "Tell me she has more sense than that."

Grosbeak opened his eyes and blinked slowly. "I doubt it. She took me on as a pet. That's hardly sensible."

"Ah, but had she not, you would have joined the heads of the other traitors in my crypt. An interesting prospect to be sure, but not quite as interesting as the fate she has granted you."

His crypt? He really did collect the heads of his enemies? I suppressed a shiver. There wasn't time for that when I was trying to make a point.

"I'm not asking for anything that doesn't benefit you to give," I insisted.

Bluebeard used his grip on my arm to lead me from the fire to the table full of food. He scooped up an apple.

"Care to eat, Grosbeak?"

"I do not, Lord Riverbarrow. I would like to sleep." Grosbeak promptly followed his words with closed eyes and a snore that could not possibly be real.

Bluebeard huffed and bit the apple, dropping my wrist.

I leaned in close. "Have any of your other wives helped you? Have they found ways to goad your enemies or sing the harmony to your melody?"

He shot a glance my way out of the corner of his eye. His eyes were rimmed in dark lashes, shockingly pretty for a man's.

"I am starting to think that they did nothing but sit in this house as you wiled away their days," I challenged.

He looked at me, chewing the apple and raising a single eyebrow.

"They did?" It was meant to be an exclamation, but it came out like a gasp. "But what did they do with themselves?"

He gave a one-shouldered shrug as if it was hardly his concern and tapped the key around my neck as if I could get all the answers I wanted if I just went and read their hideous books. Which I supposed I would have to do ... but I wasn't done with him yet.

I shook my head as he reached for a chicken leg but watching him eat was making my stomach rumble. I caught up a thin piece of bread that smelled of cardamom, lavished it with butter, and bit it. It was gone in moments and I followed it with dried plums and honeyed carrots, parsnips in mint sauce, a blue-veined cheese, something hot and bitter that poured from a kettle, and sweet spiced nuts that melted in my mouth. And when I'd eaten my fill, I met his eyes again and he was grinning at me as if my appetite amused him.

My cheeks grew hot, but I was not done. I leaned across the table, swallowing the terror inside me. I could do this and see some measure of freedom before my untimely death, or I could live shut up in this house for the rest of my days ... with the warm fire and all the food and the books that seemed to never end. I pushed that thought aside before it became too tempting. I wasn't naturally bold or aggressive, but I needed him to hear me and to listen and if drama and bold words were the way he communicated, then they were probably the way he could hear me. I must use them or suffer for not using them.

"Only a fool leaves his sharpest sword behind when he goes into battle," I said, catching his eye. "Only a fool leaves one of his oxen behind when he goes to plow. Only a fool gets married in his second-best shirt. If you don't make use of me properly, then you've wasted what you have, and if you fail at whatever it is you are trying to achieve here, then you'll have no one to blame but yourself. Why bother asking me to work with you if you only plan to use me as your tool and not your equal?"

He chewed his food, watching me carefully, and then he took my hand. To my utter shock, he kissed the back of it and then winked at me. He stood and led me over to a settee beside the fire, sat, and motioned for me to come closer.

I watched him warily. It bothered me to no end that one of us must always be silent. It made me say more than I would usually say. And also less.

It was like a burr under my dress, like a splinter in the arch of my foot, like a buzzing mosquito in the small hours of the night.

He took my other hand and drew me so that I sat on his lap, straddling him, and then he smiled.

"I don't know what game this is," I said, still wary and worried. This intimacy was not what I was asking for. "But I would like an answer. Will you treat me like an ally? Will you show me the respect I deserve and see that I can work with you?"

He nodded very solemnly, his blue eyes locked on mine, and when I nodded, too, he smiled wickedly, and began to play with my hair.

I moved to get off his lap and he shook his head. He was tying little knots into my hair, oddly enough.

I might as well let him. I'd gotten what I asked for, after all. If all he wanted in return was to make a rat's nest of my hair, I'd still made the better bargain.

The fire felt good against my sore back and it was nice to sit without the wounds touching anything. The soft movement of his tying knots in the lengths of my hair began to lull me to sleep. I leaned forward enough that I could rest my forehead against the padded back of the settee. He made a sound in his throat that sounded almost contented.

And without meaning to, I drifted off to sleep.

Chapter Twenty-One

I WOKE in the middle of the day. There was a knot in my stomach that made me feel like I was going to throw up. I pushed myself up from where I was slumped on the settee and pain flared through me like shards of glass under my skin. Sweat broke across my forehead.

I gasped, wavering on the edge of the settee. I'd fallen asleep half on top of Bluebeard and half on top of the settee. He was still sitting, head thrown back, breathing through his open mouth. It was shocking to see him so vulnerable, but I knew he was – that he'd left himself utterly at my mercy.

I could kill him right now if I wanted to and be free of him and his world of horrors.

I swallowed.

I could slit his throat before he woke. I could strike him on the head with the fire poker.

And then what? I would be a murderer just like him. My nation would be trampled in the game the Wittenbrand were playing. And it would be my fault.

I staggered to my feet. No. I'd told him I would back him. I'd made vows to him of marriage. I'd made my choice. Now came the part where I saw it through.

I was careful not to wake him as I stumbled out of the main room toward the dark corridor. I didn't know what was in the rest of the house, but I was hoping to draw a cool bath and ease the pain of these stitches.

I snuck past Grosbeak who was snoring on the shelf and carefully eased my way into the darkness. The corridor had no windows and I stubbed my toe on what turned out to be a staircase. I crept up it, step by step. The faintest sound of birdsong seemed to echo with each step, but there were no birds on the spiral stairs and eventually, they arrived at a wide, airy room.

It was as odd a room as I'd expected from this house.

A four-poster bed was strung with vines that formed a canopy and hung all around it in verdant tangles. From the vines bloomed such a display of coal-black flowers that the bed seemed to be made of them. They fluttered in a non-existent breeze, their petals dropping all around and fluttering through the air. To my surprise, they smelled faintly of vanilla.

Boots and gorgeous clothing were strewn everywhere, and among them were various swords, staves, bows, stacks of books, and more arrows than I could count. It was as if someone had been living a life in this room one layer on top of the other, on top of the other, without ever cleaning the layer below, or even checking to see if anything was growing inside of it.

My fingers twitched with the desire to tidy.

But this wasn't a room like one you'd find in a house. One wall was completely missing, showing a shoreline where waves rolled in one after another to smash against the rocks. The other walls were hung with thick tapestries and bookshelves jammed full of books and odd items, just like down below. Also like the room below, the ceiling was hung with a wide chandelier dripping with fat wax candles, and the ceiling above was so high that all I saw was darkness and mist.

To one side, the stone floor smoothed into slick rock and a pool was formed with water tumbling into it from a stream that started halfway up the stone wall. It steamed as though it was hot, and set beside it was a full-length mirror and a small table with a teapot and delicate cup.

To my surprise, the teapot was warm.

"Well, this is a curious place," I said.

"What do you find so curious?" asked the gargoyle at the top of the mirror.

I jumped. Little chills raced up my spine. But after a long breath, I answered him.

"There is hot tea but no servants."

"The house provides what is needed." I could have sworn that the gargoyle sniffed disdainfully.

"And if I drink the tea before he wakes?" I asked.

The gargoyle made a horrible face like children do when they are trying to terrify you. When I said nothing, he eventually replied.

"More will appear when he wants it, child of foolishness."

Well then. It only made sense to enjoy it if there would be more for him later.

I began to strip off my dress and then paused.

"I shall close my eyes," said the mirror, closing them but then opening just one a small sliver.

I shook my head. But I was being absurd. It was only a mirror.

I pulled off my dress, unwound the bandages carefully, and slipped into the stone pool. Every part of me hurt, from head to toe. The water made my wounds sting worse than ever, but at the same time it seemed to soothe them, so I stayed in the water, carefully nibbling on the toast and drinking the hot tea. If I couldn't sleep then I could at least take care of my body in other ways.

I needed to think.

Last night had gone well, all things considered. Bluebeard had agreed to respect me. I had settled in my mind that I would work with him. Note or no note. But if I was going to keep his respect, I would have to prove myself to him. What could I do that he couldn't? How could I make myself useful?

I pondered the question as I bathed and then I stepped out of the pool and found a somewhat clean pair of blue breeches and a loose white shirt with arrows stitched all over it. Dressed in these, I felt considerably better.

I felt my back with careful fingers. My stitches were no longer hot and puffy. They still stung, but they also itched. Bluebeard had been right. His silver stitching had quickened their healing.

Sitting down on the edge of the bed, I basked in the light coming from the beach on one side of the wall. I wasn't fool enough to walk through to it. For all I knew, it would leave me in another world. And I was on the second story of the house, so the sand that was drifting into the edge of the room and mixing with Bluebeard's discarded things made no sense at all.

I couldn't stay here, of course. This was his bed, in his room. I would just sit for a moment to catch my breath. The warm sun began to relax me. Okay, I would just lie down for a moment and catch my breath.

I woke to the hooting of an owl and something that sounded like splashing. It was evening again.

"Ah, you're awake, fire of my eyes," Bluebeard said, his voice low and sultry. I blinked my eyes open and immediately shut them. Then, like the gargoyle, I cracked just one open a little bit.

The mirror snorted.

"Only you would enter *this* room, you devilish sensibility." He was sitting in a tufted chair beside the fire, one leg thrown over the arm of the chair with nothing on him but a pair of rumpled breeches. He had the teacup in one hand, his smallest finger on that hand pointed out delicately as he sipped. "You step where no one else dare pass."

I blinked, confused.

"The nightingale stairs decide where to bring the person who steps on them. Faithfully, they have carried fifteen brides to their own rooms and beds, but you, they have brought to *mine*."

I sat up. After all, he was the one who chose to sit half-naked while I was sleeping here. He could hardly feel modest now, could he? He was sipping his tea and reading a book called, *Avoiding Military Defeat and Assassination: Don't Lose Your Head.*

"I rather like you in my clothing," he said, watching me with a possessive gleam in his cat's eyes.

I felt my cheeks heat as I stole a little peek at him. He was made entirely of muscle and scars except for a dusting of dark hair over his chest and forearms that made my mouth unaccountably dry. It must have been whatever was in the tea I drank. I licked my upper lip and tried not to think of tea or of hair that clung to hard muscular planes. No, I definitely wasn't thinking of that.

Keep a clear head, Izolda. You may have agreed to work with him, but you know this marriage cannot exist in truth. You are simply working together. Besides, you have never let a pretty man turn your head before and you don't need to start making a fool of yourself now.

His hair was damp and little beads of water flecked his cheeks. I realized, with a feeling I wanted to hope was horror, but was something else entirely, that there were wet footsteps leading from the bath to his chair. I could have woken any time while he bathed.

Could you blush all over your body? I thought I might be.

"Your bag of things is over there, wife," he said, pointing to my saddlebag on the other side of the fire, "if you prefer something of your own. I don't know why you would. Your taste in clothing is sinfully plain."

My eyes widened. My things!

I hurried to them and to my delight, I found one of my woven dresses and tabards crumpled in the saddlebag, along with underthings and woolen socks. I was almost crying with the relief of something from home when I felt his eyes on me and turned to see him look suddenly away, his cheeks stained with sunset.

"Is it really too much to ask that you give your whole life to me?" he said, clearing his throat as if he were having trouble concentrating. "Is it really too much to ask that you risk the same way I do?"

"Mirror," I said, crossing to where the gargoyle looked down at me. Below him, I could see Bluebeard scowling in the reflection. "Tell my husband that sacrificing your wife's wellbeing isn't nearly the same risk as sacrificing your own."

"I'll tell him no such thing," the gargoyle said haughtily.

"What if there was a reward that came with the risk?" Bluebeard asked, tilting his chin.

"Mirror, tell my husband that if there is a reward, it would have to be vast to equal the risk to my life and future."

"I will not be your messenger," the gargoyle growled. "You are abusing me most sorely."

"Oh, the risk is great, I'll agree," Bluebeard said, his voice turned to coaxing. "So, let me offer you the greatest reward I can imagine to match it."

I quirked an eyebrow at him.

He grinned as if we were sharing a joke. "Me."

"Mirror, tell my husband that I already own him body and soul. That is what marriage means."

"That's torn it!" the gargoyle shouted and then he closed his eyes furiously and pursed his lips in concentration. The mirror went black and he was gone.

I heard a wet sound behind me and turned to find Bluebeard right there, leaning in close. I kept my eyes firmly on his and definitely nowhere else. But my cheeks felt hot enough to melt that lead from yesterday.

"There's owning and then there's possessing, you sober monstrosity," he whispered, leaning in so his lips brushed the shell of my ear. "You own me, as I own you, but I offer you more than that. Take this risk with me – offer your life up – and I will give myself to you beyond vows and bonds. I will give you heart and mind and my very soul."

I pulled back so I could look into his eyes, frowning. An offer like that was too extravagant. No wonder he lived in a little cottage instead of a palace. He had no sense of how to make a good bargain.

Maybe that was what he needed me for.

The predatory look in his eyes stole my breath away as he lifted my hand toward his lips. I expected him to kiss the back of it as a lord might. Instead, he caught my index finger in his teeth – not enough to hurt but enough to *suggest* he could hurt me. At the last second, his teeth released the tip of my finger, and his soft lips wrapped around it instead as his bite turned into a kiss. He let it slide between them and away and as my finger left his lips, he gave me a devilish smile.

"Now, I've put you on equal footing, my wife. You have offered your life in a gamble for the future. I offer you my soul. Do we have a bargain? If we do, then we have equal risk and equal reward."

It was what I wanted, wasn't it? Then why did my throat feel so dry?

I could not explain it, but I felt like I was at a disadvantage here.

He lifted his hand and offered it to me, as if to seal the bargain. Shaking, I took it. I hardly knew why. Why gamble for something I wasn't sure I wanted? Why gamble for something that technically I should already own? And yet my heart raced at the thought, and I could barely suppress the shiver that ran through my core.

"We have an accord," he said with a fierce grin. "And we are late. The bids are supposed to begin at Peak of Night. I have held things up, but I cannot dally forever, or they will begin without me. So, dress and adorn yourself for a spectacle, for I have a task for you that will let you help me just as you offered to do."

"Oh," he said stalking across the room, reaching for something that hung over a dressing screen. "And wear this, my bride. We need all the spectacle we can muster."

He handed me a filmy dress made of the finest silk and lace I'd ever seen and then pointed to a dressing screen in the corner. I looked longingly at my own dress in my other hand, but he snatched it away and threw it over the mirror.

"Quickly, unless you wish to lose one of our landholds before the game has even begun."

That was all he needed to say. I hustled around to the back of the screen and began to dress in what he'd given me. It had a corset, but no back – to my relief. The boning of the corset merely kept the bodice in place, leaving my wounds free to air and heal.

Designed to look like a breastplate, the corset was trimmed in silver with sections that looked like overlapping plate armor. It fell to a frothy skirt and the lace at the top of the corset draped around the neckline in a way that hinted more than revealed. Dark and mysterious, the entire expanse of the full skirt was sewn in what looked like a battle scene, complete with charging horses, flying arrows, and dying corpses. I wasn't sure if I should be impressed or horrified. I felt a little of both.

The people in the scene, I realized, were both human and Wittenbrand. And the Wittenbrand seemed to be leading them or cheering them on from behind the frontlines. I hoped it was not a picture of what was to come.

I strapped my sword belt back on over the dress. I was going to have to find someone to teach me how to use the sword.

I paused as I tucked the golden key into my neckline. Seeing it made me think of the riddle that the first of Bluebeard's wives had left behind. I was almost certain it was the words I'd heard when I first entered the room myself.

I am sudden death to calm.

My roar breaks the hush.

My song the mind's somnolence.

Was the answer a scream? That seemed appropriate for this strange land. But if that was the answer, then why had the first queen written it down? Was it some esoteric way to tell us she was screaming inside? She could have just come out and said that.

I shook my head and stepped out from behind the screen.

Chapter Twenty-Two

IF I'D KNOWN THEN about the kinds of rituals the Wittenhame loves, I would have been a lot more nervous to see another of them. I might have even demanded a lesson in using the weapon at my side. But I was still flushed with pride at my triumph in securing my husband as an ally and I had not yet realized that even together we were not enough to rival this world.

Bluebeard had dressed in a midnight blue doublet slashed with crimson. He'd re-cut his cheek and with a quick flick of his little knife he recut mine so that the blood could drip and form that long red teardrop that apparently told everyone who we were. I gritted my teeth at the sting. For the sake of my nation, I could bear a tiny wound.

He looked grimly pleased and devastatingly handsome as his black hair shone with water and his short blue beard clung to the sharp angles of his face. There were tiny threads of silver at his temples and I wondered yet again exactly how old this husband of mine was.

His cat's eyes gleamed and narrowed. They made my stomach do little flip flops as if this were my lover escorting me to a feast rather than my co-conspirator leading me to battle.

I gave him a tiny nod.

"You look well, wife," he said, his eyes gleaming with something I couldn't quite place. "Did I mention that your sword has a name? I called it Angstbite when it was mine."

He led me down the stairs to the room below.

I lifted Grosbeak's pole and he yawned dramatically. "Ready to go?"

"For all the good you did me last time," I said sourly. "You were supposed to be a help to me, but you said nothing about what was going on and I had to figure it out on my own."

"Yeah, yeah, don't get too big for your britches."

"I'll remind you," I said primly, "that you do not wear britches and therefore require my good graces – which you will only have if you remain useful."

I was still frowning when Bluebeard draped a white fur stole over my shoulders. The ends of it had pockets for my hands and there was a deep hood attached.

"Keep your back visible," he said, looking at me like he was weighing me with his eyes. He raised the hood so it framed my face. "Yes, I think that's best. Let them all see your wounds."

Just the mention of them reminded me of their steady ache. I tried to push the thought aside. As long as I concentrated on other things, the pain of the cuts was easier to bear.

"We must make a grand entrance. When we arrive, I will make a bold move. If you want to be a help to me as you've said, then it would be good if you played along." He lifted an eyebrow. "Do you agree?"

I nodded. This was one way I could prove my worth to him. This, and maybe solving the riddle.

He offered me his hand and I followed him out the door and into the night.

"Why does everything happen at night?" I asked Grosbeak.

"In the Wittenhame, we live in the shadows and dusk and we sleep in the heat of the day."

I shook my head as I looked up at the crystal-clear stars. They splashed across the sky like a handful of snow flung into the air. Low on the horizon, the full moon clung to the edge of the earth as if afraid to show its face. Perhaps even the moon was wary of this mad place.

The Grouse House had moved while we were inside it, and now we were situated in a forest made entirely of tall, purplish mushrooms. They glowed just enough to make out their outlines in the darkness.

Bluebeard offered me a hand and leaned in close. "You're as wild-looking as this land and as lovely as the night and yet you feel as real as a stone in a world of shimmering shadow. You are cold iron to my Wittenbrand magic, hard bronze to my wafting vapor, heavy lead to my tumbling feathers. Anchor me, you obelisk. Keep me tethered to what is real."

It was an odd request, but it made sense that he would make it. Who wouldn't want to be firmly planted in reality? I nodded solemnly and then, with eyes that held a warmth I didn't recognize, he swept me into his arms.

"Ride with me to Hazard Hall. We have amusement to set to flight and revelry to take captive."

He leapt and we landed on something living. As he settled me on its back in front of him, I realized – to my surprise – that we were riding a black salamander with little flecks of blue in its shiny skin. It skittered along the ground so quickly that it almost felt like flying as we slid through the mushrooms all around. The salamander moved in a serpentine pattern so it looked as if we were hurrying straight for the stalk of a mushroom, only to suddenly avoid striking it as we veered in the other direction, and then the process repeated itself. I had to close my eyes to keep from being ill.

But closing my eyes was no help at all. It only made me more conscious of Bluebeard at my back, his warm body and all its hard and soft parts pressed against me. If we could be allies, couldn't we also be friends? If friends, why not a married couple in truth?

My cheeks flared hot at the thought.

There were the other wives to think of.

And the fact that when he had run me out of days, that I would be replaced by yet another girl who would look at my blank book with scorn and wonder if she should try to find happiness in the arms of this beautiful, wicked man while she could. The thought made me feel both cold and hot at the same time. And it also made me feel like a fool.

No man, no matter how pretty or fascinating, was worthy of having me for just a time. I wasn't a trinket to be enjoyed for an evening and discarded. I was more like a marriage sword, to be worn with honor for all your life.

I frowned at the thought. I wore Bluebeard's sword at my side, and he wore the one I'd given him. There had been a variety of weapons in his room, but no other fancy swords. No other marriage swords. And there had been none in the room with the wives. Had none of them exchanged swords with him?

"Keep your eyes open," he whispered in my ear. "When your days are limited, you shouldn't waste even an hour of one of them. What if that hour is your very last?"

I wanted to ask him how a salamander was awake in such cold weather – didn't they sleep the cold months away? – but once again my question would go unanswered. If I could change one thing about my predicament, it would be that. To be able to speak and be spoken to was a gift I'd never fully realized before. I missed it sorely.

By the time we reached Hazard Hall, I was sick to my stomach and my head was spinning – but I'd enjoyed every minute of the ride. I'd let myself really look as the mushroom-covered landscape melted into a land with a mantle of snow and then went from flat to rocky and from rocky to the edge of an endless lake – calm and still as a summer pond and rimmed in giant cattails coated in frost. The edge of the lake was stiff with a ledge of ice, but a few steps out from the shore the water was still warm, and it lapped against the ice like a lover stealing kisses again and again.

We rounded a tuft of reeds and the sand of the beach opened to a cove where someone had painstakingly set blue stones into patterns that formed a mosaic in the sand. At the apex of the mosaic was a high stone that made a kind of platform or maybe an altar. It was set against the surrounding cliffs.

Beside it, a blue banner hung, with the names of those competing in the games and the nations they would represent emblazoned upon it. I saw Bluebeard's name immediately. Riverbarrow – Pensmoore.

On the other side of the rock, another banner hung that said "Hazards" at the top, but the rest of the banner was empty.

Behind the rock, set into the cliffside, the Sovereign slumbered. But this time he was not encased in ice, but rather mostly buried in sand, as if someone had begun to uncover him before growing bored and wandering away.

The other competitors were already arranged below the altar at a table heaped with so many kinds of food I couldn't have guessed at what some of them were.

The Sword was hacking flesh from a fish large enough to swallow me. His blade had carved through its silver, crackling skin to the soft orange flesh below. Beside him, Coppertomb bit into a golden apple and Marshyellow poured two separate jugs into one stein – one with a stream of silvery liquid and one with bronze.

And around them, tiered as they climbed the cliffsides, were the Wittenbrand gathered to watch. Their tables were also laden with food and each table was lit by a forest of white candles – some taller than I was. Some as thick as trees. Clusters of them wove between the tables and tiers of them in the spaces between groups of people. Thousands ringed the altar and the table where the players sat. Dancing and glinting, the lake reflected their light back to them in long smudges of brightness across its calm surface.

But in the shadows, I saw people whispering, and others kissing, and still others fighting with blades or fists. There was laughter everywhere and the occasional scream and something about the whole event that felt like the edge of a nightmare when a pleasant dream turns to something malevolent.

I shuddered and Bluebeard gripped my hand in his as he helped me down from the salamander.

"Do you think what you see is madness?" Bluebeard asked as I caught sight of a man grinning with teeth stained red. I could only hope that wasn't blood. "Then think about those folk you saw in my home. They wanted my help. Do you remember that? The people you're looking at right now are why they need help. These people took their whole lives from them."

"Lives worth no more than a beetle's," Grosbeak said from his place at the end of the pole. "Don't listen to your grandstanding husband, Izolda. The people you are watching now are those the gods truly love. The Tuathan. The true princes and princesses of all living things. And today they place their bets on the great game that will determine the fates of all the rest. If that isn't power, then what is? And having that power makes them almost immortal. It certainly sets them above all mortal ken."

"I think I preferred your pet when he didn't talk so much," Bluebeard said. "But do not fear. I have a use for him that will make listening to his ravings well worth the pain."

"You make it seem, Grosbeak," I said, "as if these people are not people at all but merely living versions of stories."

To my surprise, Bluebeard spoke, his eyes far away so that it looked like he was speaking to himself and not to me.

"We *are* stories. There's nothing more to us. This world we live in is no more real than any other. Life, death, these are ephemeral things no more solid than the steam that wafts from your cup of tea. We can none of us prove the world we see is the same as the world another sees. Our minds take in the sights but then they interpret those things into a story told just for us. We hear, we see, we touch, and our mind translates it to a tale. By rights, our hands should pass through each other, no more solid than the space between the stars. But one day, when we fly from this earth like the arrow loosed from the bow, we will enter whatever life comes after, and all we will have to bring with us will be the story – for that is what we are. We are the story of our choices, our grim failures, our crippled successes. We are the story of our molten passions, our loves and hates, our tears in the silence. We are the story of how others touched or shunned us, of loves returned, revenges enacted. When all flesh and glory melts away and there is nothing left of us, we will be only the story going on to what comes next."

I shivered at his words. No wonder he was willing to spend other people's days so blithely if he thought we were nothing more than stories. Did he think he was writing *my* story? If he did, he should think again. I would not let it be written by anyone else but me.

Bluebeard took something from a saddlebag hanging across the salamander's back. I hadn't even seen it was there until he slung a quiver over one shoulder and quickly strung a bow. The salamander dipped its head to my husband and slid away.

Bluebeard winked at me when he was finished.

"They call me Arrow and with good reason, wife. I fly just as fast and true."

I watched him as he arranged them the way he liked. He looked like an arrow himself – he was so slender and pointed and quick in his movements. His eyes flashed in the candle-light with intelligence and charm. If he hadn't been a murderer, I'd be proud to be a wife to a man like this. If he hadn't been so terribly unpredictable, I might have even liked it.

True to form, he reached for me, surprising me as he drew the wild curls of my hair forward with a gentle touch, making sure my back was exposed. Then he took my hand, lifting an eyebrow as if asking for permission, and when I nodded, he tucked it into his arm and began to stroll toward the party.

"So, what's your plan?" Grosbeak murmured. He was swaying in time with my steps, his expression flickering from worry to intensity and back to worry again. What would it be like to have your fate so much in the hands of another?

"You shall see and understand soon enough," Bluebeard murmured.

But I had other ideas. "Tell me what gossip you know about the players of this game, Grosbeak," I said. "Surely, you must know something."

"Ah! Finally, you are tapping into my potential. I can help you here. The Sword is – of course – a formidable player. Sharp and brutal, he will strike first and hardest. He is not known for finesse or spycraft."

Bluebeard snorted.

"Didn't he turn you on the Arrow?" I asked, watching Bluebeard stiffen a little out of the corner of my eye. "That seems like spycraft."

"Some people make it easy to betray them. The selfish. The arrogant."

"Keep talking," Bluebeard said in a low, calm voice that hinted at violence. "And we shall see whose arrogance makes them easy to betray."

He stalked beside me in a flowing stride that made me think of a black cat crossing a courtyard. His eyes were everywhere as if he were memorizing the position of each person and object in the riotous revel.

"Coppertomb is known for his callowness. This is his first time playing. They say he murdered his father to take his place. He used bitterbark poison – a woman's weapon."

I laughed and Bluebeard shot me a surprised glance. "Is the insult in the death or the manner? You make it sound like it was worse that his death was womanish than that he was killed."

Grosbeak frowned. "Dying should be dignified. Look at how well I did it. The grandest of kings could not have surpassed me."

"At least we know your skills," I said glibly. "So, we should watch our cups around Coppertomb."

"Watch your cup around everyone," Bluebeard murmured. "You have no friends here but me. And possibly Vireo."

He nodded to the side and I saw Vireo with Bluebeard's band, playing a game of cards around a low table. There were already empty steins around them, and a half-eaten three-tiered cake to one side. Frosting dripped down like a waterfall across the cut side and my mouth watered. There was even a round orange fruit on top of it.

"In fact, it would be better if you didn't eat or drink anything until we return home. And now – no more gossip. We are nearly there."

We kept our eyes on the head table as we made our way forward, our path determined by the forest of white candles. They made the journey surprisingly warm in the frosty night and kept me from shivering despite my backless dress.

I heard murmurs as we passed tables and dancing couples. People were watching us.

At first, I thought it was because I was carrying a severed head, but after a while, I realized they were whispering about my back.

"Claws," someone said, curiosity thick in his voice. "Do you think he marked her on their first night?"

"Why not?" his companion asked but her voice sounded intrigued. "He looks the type to mark what's his."

My face was hot when I realized what they were saying. They thought my husband had done this to my back – and rather than being repelled by that, they were intrigued.

When we reached the table, it was Lady Tanglecott who greeted us, her neutral expression unshakable.

"Will you bring your wife for every round, Riverbarrow? It seems somewhat gauche."

"Where I go, she will go, and what I despise, she shall despise also," he said lightly, but I noticed that everyone at the table was watching us. "Besides. I need her to set my target. Put your new pet over on that table, wife."

The large table was facing the crowd with all the players seated along one side of it. A place had been left for my husband at the end nearest us. Just one chair, I noted.

Off to the side past the far end of the table was a smaller table bearing a washbasin and towel and it was to that table that my husband gestured as he strode off in the opposite direction, fiddling with the string of his bow as he walked.

"Take one of those golden apples and put it on Grosbeak's head, sun of my world," Bluebeard continued lightly. I noticed he liked to give me extravagant pet names when he was being particularly overbearing.

I picked up two of the apples from the table and my eyes met the Sword's as I plucked them from the heap. I could eat the second one. There is no way they'd poison an apple on their own table.

"Just because you married him, doesn't mean you need to stay with him," the Sword drawled. "My claws may be bigger, but I don't feel the need to mark what is mine on the outside."

It was the words 'on the outside' that left me shivering. What sort of marks would he leave on the inside if I took him up on this offer? My eyes narrowed and I said nothing, simply gliding over to the table that my husband had indicated.

"Set the apple on his head when you have him in place, jewel of Wittenhame," Bluebeard said as he took an arrow from his quiver, looking down the shaft as if to judge how it might fly. "Grosbeak was a friend of yours, if I am not mistaken, Sword."

The Sword's mouth tightened. "No friend of mine."

"How odd," Bluebeard said, but his voice sounded more like a threat than a simple observation. "We Wittenhame cannot lie. And yet, I could have sworn he was a friend. Perhaps he was merely your plaything. As he is now the plaything of my wife."

"Don't let him do this to me," Grosbeak hissed. "He'll shoot me!"

"You're already dead," I said practically as I removed the wash basin from the table and set his head down on it.

"It will still hurt. And I will be humiliated." His hiss grew sharper. "You heard the Sword disavow me. They will all laugh at my torment."

I didn't feel the least bit bad for him. And yet I paused. My husband had asked me to play along to prove my loyalty. He was trying to make a spectacle here for all to see. Perhaps there was a way to show him how useful I could be. A way he hadn't even thought of himself.

"You sent me a message," Bluebeard continued as he chose a second shaft. "And in that message, you suggested I cannot win this game because I do not sacrifice enough. I am no risk taker, you said. You know every move I make before I make it, you said. Did you see this coming? Step back, wife."

I stepped back at the same time that the arrow flew, striking the apple on Grosbeak's head. He screamed, his face distorted with terror as juice sprayed across his face and the apple fell to the ground, pierced straight through with the arrow.

The crowd roared.

Bluebeard had their full attention. He made a little bow.

"Set up a second apple, wife. Once may be a coincidence. Twice will show my skill."

"I stand by your cowardice. What skill does it take to shoot at someone already dead?" the Sword said from his seat. He'd thrown his feet up onto the table, leaning back in his chair. "You won't take the risks I do. Which is why you won't win. And when I do, I will raze the ground of Pensmoore – I'm sick of how you treat it like your own fiefdom, snatching brides from there and letting your wild folk roam their bogs and woods."

He did? My brow furrowed.

He considered my land his?

"I can guess your every move," the Sword said.

"Did you guess this one?" I asked in a clear voice as I set the second apple not on Grosbeak's head but on my own.

There was a delighted gasp along the table, and when my eyes met my husband's, he had a look on his face as if he'd just found a particularly fine vintage of wine in his cellar he had not realized was there. He barely seemed to be able to tear his eye from me as he drew another arrow from the quiver.

He broke eye contact long enough to look down the shaft and then his gaze swung to mine again. He was drinking me in like I was life in a cup. He was watching me like I might evaporate with the dawn. Maybe he believed I would. After all, I was made of story to him. And I'd just given him an excellent story.

The party, I realized, had gone utterly still. I risked a glance to the side and saw they had all stopped their games of chance, their dances, their music, their trysts, and were arrayed to watch the spectacle before them.

My body was shaking all over, my head suddenly light.

He'd proven he could do it. Logic told me he could do it again. Logic was not working on my body, though. It was telling me that I needed to relieve myself. Promptly.

"Eyes on me," Bluebeard said as if he were seducing the entire crowd, but his words were for me, and as my gaze met his he gave me more instructions. "Hold your breath and watch me."

My fate was in his hands. But it had been there since I had greeted him. It only made sense to trust him with it again. The worst he could do was kill me. And he'd already promised to do that eventually.

I drew in a long, steadying breath. Despite my flawless logic, my knees were shaking, and my abdomen felt like water being sloshed around.

He drew his arrow. The point seemed aimed right at my head.

I couldn't help it. The tiniest moan of fear escaped my lips.

He raised an eyebrow.

I held my breath. I tried to keep my eyes on him, but I couldn't help the delicate scream that tore from my lips when the arrow loosed.

I heard it zip through the air. Heard the sound of it pierce the apple over my head. Felt apple juice spray across my scalp and the pulp of it fall into my hair.

I hadn't even shut my mouth when a second zip disturbed the air above me. An arrow took the apple a second time, splitting it right down the center. The halves fell to either side of me, bouncing off the fur of my stole.

Grosbeak cursed as loudly and vehemently as I wanted to, while around us the crowd cheered. Their voices washed across us over and again like waves smashing the shore. He had given them a spectacle. And they loved spectacles.

"I'm willing to place my hazard now," Bluebeard announced to the crowd. "And any sane man will be betting on me. My wife certainly did!"

That got him a laugh and another cheer. At the table, the Sword scowled grimly. He'd taken his feet off the table, but just like Bluebeard, his eyes never left me, as if he could steal me away by the power of his will and ruin all Bluebeard's plans in a single stroke.

There was a sudden chime, and everyone froze. The Sovereign spoke from his place half-covered in sand.

"Peak of Night is upon us. Make your hazards."

Chapter 23

THE WITTENHAME, it would seem, took gambling very seriously indeed. The moment their Sovereign had finished announcing that they could make their hazards, a pair of creatures with large wings and hunched backs hurried to either side of the altar. They threw something at the ground that went up in a burst of bluish-white flame and continued to burn as they each pulled a silver cord and released a banner.

To the left of the altar, the official hazards of the players would be recorded. To the right, the official hazards of the spectators. I expected that list would be considerably longer.

The players rose, almost as one, to walk toward their banner. Bluebeard removed the string from his bow and approached me before he joined them.

To my utter shock, he kissed the top of my head almost reverently and murmured, "What courage. What blazing, maddening courage. You were right, wife of mine, you do make a better ally than an enemy. Wait here as I place my hazard."

And then he was gone. I gathered up Grosbeak and took him to the long table.

"I'm outraged that you did that to me," he sputtered. "Outraged."

There was still a little apple in his hair. I flicked it out and tried to ignore how tired I was and how much my back ached. There was no time for self-pity. If my husband's competitors had left anything incriminating at their table, now would be my chance to find it – and they had left so many things that I needed to move quickly to see if there was anything of value.

"I could have died, you know. He's not the best shot in all of history, just the best shot there is right now! And how did you know he wouldn't miss and kill us?"

"I guessed," I said.

I hadn't known. It was a calculated risk. I was the kind of person who took calculated risks because it was sometimes the only way to get ahead. You just had to be sensible about it.

"Guessed? You guessed? You gambled with our lives!"

"My life," I corrected. "You already lost yours by taking a stupid risk. I rather think that betting against Bluebeard – as you did – usually doesn't work out for people quite as well as betting on him winning does."

He was sputtering incoherently when I set him on the table and pretended to be grazing off the lavish food while I made my way slowly along it. I popped a grape in my mouth and looked over what Lady Tanglecott had left behind. A tiny fabric bag sewn with mouse skulls. A fan with a design of rats on it, their tales intertwined in a terrifying knot. A stole made of very delicate fur in a light brown color.

"Lady Tanglecott seems fond of rats," I murmured, but there was nothing here to lend me any guesses about her strategy. Her purse contained only a handkerchief and some mortal coins.

I moved on, plucking a tiny pickled egg from the dish and popping it into my mouth as I looked at what Lord Antlerdale had left behind. It was a book.

Mist and Memories: The Memoirs of Lord Antlerdale, the cover read.

Wait. It was a book about him? I flipped open the cover.

"Don't think I don't see what you're doing," Grosbeak whispered. "And if you don't hurry, you're going to be caught. You won't find anything in there. The Arrow would have a copy of that book just like everyone else. Antlerdale gives them out like candy at a Nightwatch feast, and only the kindest of the Wittenhame agree to take a copy anymore. That's people who publish their own writing for you, forever hawking that tripe to everyone else."

I made a sound in the back of my throat, but I left the book and hurried onward, plucking a strawberry from the plate to hide my actions as I examined a hat left by Bluffroll. It was a simple, broadbrimmed black hat. Nothing of interest there except for the dried snakeskin tied around the crown of the hat.

I sighed and moved on to where Lord Marshyellow had left a walking staff as tall as he was. It was topped by the dried head of a cottonmouth snake, its mouth open and a small hat fitted to its head that matched the one Lord Bluffroll had been wearing exactly.

I shook my head. The Wittenbrand were an eclectic kind with the same taste in items you'd expect from a mad wizard, but there was nothing here that might help my husband.

Coppertomb had left nothing behind. Not even a hat or wrap. Wittentree had left a pipe carved to look like a small angry man.

The Sword had left his own copy of *Mist and Memories: The Memoirs of Lord Antlerdale.* And that was all. In frustration, I sat down and began to chew on a roll.

"I told you," Grosbeak said, rolling his eyes. "Everyone has a copy. And you'd better get out of here before Lady Tanglecott places her bet and comes back here."

"Why do the players place bets anyway?" I asked. "I thought that was for spectators."

But I was hardly paying attention to the answer as a thought occurred to me. Grosbeak said only the kindest people still took copies of Lord Antlerdale's book. But the Sword was not a kind person. What was he doing with a copy?

I opened the book casually. It looked the same as every other. The title was on the first page. Lord Antlerdale had signed it.

"They have to have skin in the game. Literally. Those are the rules. They must bet with pain, or loss, or not at all. That's why some are missing eyes or ears or fingers from past games. Did you not notice?"

"Bluebeard is not missing anything," I said, opening the book and flipping through the pages. It was the right book. It hadn't been replaced with secret messages or hollowed out to hold something precious.

"He's missing wives," Grosbeak said a little nastily. "I'm sure you've noticed."

In the margins of the book, someone had written with pencil in a tiny, precise hand.

Raw timbers, ten carts full

Bridge builders tackle

Cart and horse

Wages

Cost: five hundred silver pieces, to be delivered when job is complete on the Alder River

Now, this was interesting.

"See," Grosbeak was saying, "Lady Tanglecott has bid her left hand. She must be very certain. I would have expected a finger or two, but the whole hand?"

I wasn't paying attention to their horrible game or the sudden burst of cheering around us. I was paying attention to those margins. The Sword had paid for a bridge to be built. And the nation he had received bordered Bluebeard's – mine – with only a river in between.

Six tons of quarry stone

Barges

Cable

Sail hands

Cost: three hundred gold sovereigns drawn from the coffers, half in advance

"You'd better hurry! She's on her way back. And look now! Antlerdale has bet his northern estate and one of his antlers."

There was a smattering of applause but nothing major.

"Why bid at all?" I asked. "Or why not bid something insignificant, to mitigate risk?"

But I was still distracted. These were the Sword's logistics notes. This one, I was sure, meant he was blockading a port somewhere. Logistics would tell us exactly what he was doing. I needed to read and remember as many as I could.

Cloth, uniforms, stitchery: five hundred gold sovereigns

How many uniforms could you get for that?

Stables and hands. Seven hundred and fifty silver pieces

I should have attended my father's lessons to my brothers about managing estates. I felt hot all over as I tried to remember how many horses you could house for a silver piece. How many uniforms could be made of a gold piece? This was all important.

My lips moved as I tried to memorize each entry.

"The highest bidders get the opening moves. And advantages. The key is to either convince your opponent to bid too high and thus, bleed him hard when you win, or to drive him to bid too low in his fear of how high you will go. There's no point making a huge bet if you are sure your opponent will outbid you. Usually, for instance, the Arrow is quite conservative. He bids the life of his wife."

"What?" I looked up then, my fingers still jammed in the book.

"Well, you had to know you were going to die soon," Grosbeak said unapologetically. "Maybe he'll keep *your* head on a ribbon, too." A hand clamped down on the back of my neck and I leapt in my seat.

"And what, pray tell, are you doing, mortal?" a silken voice asked me.

Chapter 24

THE THING about allies is that they never end up being the people you expect. The same is true for enemies. Which makes them hard to distinguish.

I looked up into the cold eyes of Lord Coppertomb. His hand was soft and delicate, like he didn't perform even the lightest of tasks with it.

"Only competitors are allowed to be at this table," he said but there was a glint in his eye.

"I was only hungry," I said, popping an olive in my mouth. I chewed it deliberately, looking at him the whole time. Beside me, Grosbeak began to hum.

"What is your name, child of dust?" he asked, his plain face inscrutable. Almost everyone in the Wittenhame was either incredibly ugly or gloriously beautiful, but he was the one person here who was neither. He could have passed for human if he clipped the ends of his ears – and not even a very noticeable human if he wasn't dressed in cranberry uncut velvet and draped in strings of beads made to look just like human molars. My mind stuttered over that. I knew full well that they weren't made at all. They were taken. From people's mouths. I could only hope they were already dead.

"Izolda of Northpeak," I said calmly, keeping my face clear of any emotion. I had to remember that he was one of the players of this deadly game of lives, too. "What did you hazard for the game?"

"A finger," he said with a small smile. "And a month in a woven cage. I need no grand gestures for my debut game."

I suppressed a shudder. I knew how nature worked. If I seemed scared, the predators would gather.

"And you, Izolda, have already paid a price, haven't you? They say that those who fly with the arrow burn hot and bright and fast. And then they are gone. Like a shooting star in the sky."

"They say many things," I said coldly.

"Did he tell you that he has had sixteen brides before you?"

"Fifteen."

"She's not a fool, Coppertomb," Grosbeak said from beside me, breaking his hum for long enough to sneer.

A flash of irritation crept over Coppertomb's face, but Grosbeak only began his tune again.

Coppertomb turned his back to Grosbeak. "Then you know he will spend your days as water for his purposes."

I took another olive and ate it very slowly, trying to appear as though my heart wasn't racing so fast I could hardly breathe. But it was a lie. All calm in the face of this madness was a lie.

"He holds my nation in the palm of his hand," I said slowly.

Coppertomb looked surprised, but there was something off about it, as if he was very poor at performing and trying to make up for it.

"Oh. He's playing for your nation? It must seem noble to you – a woman who has never seen the game played before." I felt my face growing hot. I was not a fool and did not appreciate being spoken to like one. Coppertomb leaned in very close so that he could lower his voice almost to a whisper. "But what you don't know is this: he doesn't need to win to save your nation. In fact, he'll spend them like water just like he'll spend you. The faster he's out of the game, the sooner your people can go back to their normal lives. No plotting. No warring. No assassinations of minor nobles."

"What do you mean?" I asked, holding the next olive between my finger and thumb. My heart was beating so hard it felt like it would burst.

"We play this game to win, but we don't play it for the sake of the mortals. If one of us loses and the nation they were playing is still intact, then the country is left alone. We have no need to send our armies there. It's essentially out of play. If, for instance, your husband was delayed and missed his turn, that would be the end for him. And there would be no war in Pensmoore at all. No young soldiers dying on the field, wailing for their mothers. No children starving or women weeping. Just peace while the rest of the world battles it out."

I couldn't help myself. I saw the faces of my parents and brothers as he spoke. My heart galloped like a runaway horse.

"And wouldn't that be nice for you," I said acidly. "You could win."

"So, could you," he said slyly, as if letting me in on a joke. "I could send you home to be with them in such a way that he could never come after you again. It would be better for him. He could go attend to his folk. I've heard they have been much neglected as he's been amusing himself with wives. You could return to yours and comfort their hearts. Your nation would remain at peace. And all he would sacrifice is a little pride and one wife."

"Except that he's about to hazard me in this game and if he loses, my life is forfeit," I said.

"Let's watch and see," Coppertomb said, taking my shoulders gently in his hands and turning me so I could see the list of bets.

It read:

Tanglecott – left hand

Coppertomb – left pinkie, a month in a woven cage

Antlerdale – one antler and his northern estates

Bluffroll – a brace of stallions, his three consorts, a toe from the left foot

Marshyellow – a public flogging, a month of poisonings but not unto death

Towerrock – the child of his sister, his left eye

Riverbarrow –

I felt like I was holding my breath. I was going to burst. I was going to break apart.

And then the announcement.

"Lord Riverbarrow has bid –" There was a long pause as if the announcer had not expected what he saw here. "His immortality."

A gasp filled the air, and the shock was so intense that Grosbeak stopped his humming. Even I did not know what to say.

"See now?" Coppertomb whispered. "I can read a man's heart through his face, and I knew this year it would be different – that he would need your magic so much that he didn't dare bet you."

Was that the true reason? Because it felt as if he had taken a death sentence for me, and I did not know how to feel about that. My eyes sought his across the crowd. To my shock, his gaze met mine and something shot through me that felt exactly like lightning and fear all rolled into one.

"If I take your offer, he will lose his immortality," I said, and I was surprised to find my voice trembling.

Coppertomb's laugh sounded almost derisive. "What do you care if he loses something you never had? He will become like you. Is that such a terrible fate?"

It was not. I'd known many people who had lived and died natural lives. There was no shame in it.

"Think on it," Coppertomb said. "It is a solution to all of our problems, and if I use his magic to achieve it, it can be done with haste and perfect attention so that no one gets anything less than what they deserve."

"His magic?" I echoed. I felt stunned.

Coppertomb's hand drifted to my stricken back. I flinched from his touch. He must not have realized he was hurting me.

"Your days are represented somehow in his lair," Coppertomb whispered as Bluebeard began to stride toward us through the crowd. His brow was furrowed. "Bring me but one of them tomorrow at the Opening Spectacle and I will accomplish everything I have promised you."

I swallowed as he drifted away, and in my mind, I saw myself taking one of those garnets and giving it to Coppertomb.

"I don't trust him, and neither should you," Grosbeak opined.

But would it really be so terrible for all of us if I took this third way? The only one who would lose would be Bluebeard, and like Coppertomb said, he would only lose something I'd never had. It hardly even seemed like a loss when you put it like that.

"I can see you lying to yourself even though your back is turned," Grosbeak said. "It's fun, isn't it? Swallowing your own deceit? I always thought so, and then I ended up dead."

"I am not you," I said calmly.

"No, you're even more naïve."

Chapter 25

HUSBANDS, it turned out, could be jealous even if their wife is nothing more than an ally in purpose.

We spent as little time at the event as we could. Bluebeard looked troubled, his eyes constantly flicking over to Coppertomb.

"Tell me what he said to her, Grosbeak," he whispered when the hazards were all made. "Tell me why she looks so pale."

"Or what?" Grosbeak asked. "Will you kill me?"

"There are worse things than being dead," my husband said through gritted teeth.

We were standing off to one side while he drank a small, foaming drink. He didn't offer one to me, and I didn't take one. My stomach had been rolling with nerves since Coppertomb spoke to me. To have a choice – a real, actual choice that could change everything – was both intoxicating and terrifying. Because whatever I chose tonight, it would seal the other path forever. Either way, I would be risking my family. Either way, I would be risking myself. And on top of that, I had given my word to Bluebeard that I would work with him. How could I betray him when he had not been faithless to me?

"Name one," Grosbeak countered.

"I shall name three. I could put you in a den of fire ants and let them leave you in stinging agony. With no hands to claw them away and no way to run, you would endure them long past your breaking point. I could make a death mask of your face with molten lead. Very slowly. One layer at a time. I could set you in a cupboard under my stairs, wrap your head in a towel so you could neither see nor hear and forget I put you there so that you may spend all of eternity with only your own thoughts for company."

Grosbeak did not answer, but he looked very green. I understood that feeling. I was swaying on my feet.

Eventually, Bluebeard sighed. "Enough. I will take you both home. Neither of you is much of a benefit to merrymaking."

He led us through the party, past screams, and chases, and bouts of swordplay. Past people laughing and drinking and feasting upon strange fruits. Past others passionately kissing in each other's embrace. Someone threw a crown of white flowers on his head and he left it there, slightly askew, as if he had already had too much of the wine.

And for the first time, I wasn't terrified. I felt as though I had a door I could open and step out at any time and that feeling gave me a coating of armor.

We had almost left the party behind us when we reached one last couple lurking in the shadows behind a rock. One of them looked up and as the candlelight caught her face, I realized it was Lady Wittentree.

"Leaving so soon, Riverbarrow?" she asked. Her teeth looked red and for a moment I worried she had not been kissing the man beside her, but harming him. But then he stepped out into the light and he was such a great ogre of a fellow, marked all over with green patterns, that I did not fear for him.

"The revelry grows tedious," Bluebeard said lightly.

"If you think to take an ally, consider me," she said, to my surprise. "Send that pretty one to deliver it. What is his name? Vireo?"

"I'll think on it," Bluebeard said, and then we were hurrying into the night and he was pulling me along as fast as our feet could carry us.

In the darkness, the laughter and screams seemed to echo everywhere.

"Sometimes I feel it, too," he whispered to me as we hurried into the velvet night. "The feeling that it's swallowing me up and I'll never be free of it."

I shivered. And then something landed in front of us. I sagged in relief when I realized it was the Grouse House.

Bluebeard swept me off my feet and mounted the steps two at a time, slamming the door behind us. I expected him to put me down then, but he murmured, "Leave Grosbeak to his napping here."

I set the head on the nearby bookshelf and Bluebeard carried me up the spiraling staircase, speaking barely above a whisper as the darkness caressed us.

"Your bravery touched me. My heart is not entirely ice. That someone – anyone – would choose to stand with me without bargain or coercion ... You should know what it means to me. Though I do not have means to express it, I will have you know it all the same."

Guilt made my mouth dry. I didn't deserve his praise when I was seriously tempted by the thought of betraying him.

We reached the top of the stairs again and found ourselves in his cluttered bedroom with the tall black-bloomed bed and the strange mirror, only now the open wall was showing a frozen lake with dancing bright lights across the crystal sky slung over it. The room was not cold despite the howling wind outside the open wall, because the other wall contained the hearth and the familiar fire. But this fire was twice as large as the last time we'd been in the room, and seemed to be dancing in tune to the howl of the wind.

"My fire," Bluebeard said tiredly.

"My master," the fire replied.

"Your greeting warms my heart as your flames warm my skin." Bluebeard turned to the bed and sighed. "There's still only one bed," he said tiredly. "I would have thought the house would realize there were two of us now. Ask the mirror and it will give you clothing for bed."

I went to the mirror and cleared my throat but before I could speak, it spat out a filmy white shift.

"Perhaps something with more fabric," I suggested shyly, my eyes glancing at that one bed. Bluebeard was beside it shrugging off his sword and more daggers than I realized he was carrying.

The mirror made a motion that looked like a shrug and spat out a long, trailing black nightgown made of a fabric so sheer it was nearly invisible. I sighed. It was so much worse than the shift.

Shaking my head, I went behind the screen, took off my dress and sword, and pulled the shift over my head. It was backless, too. Everything I wore these days was.

When I emerged, Bluebeard was sitting on the edge of the bed with a small clay pot in his hand. He motioned for me to join him.

I swallowed as I crossed his cluttered floor. Did he mean for us both to sleep in that bed? Had our strange way of sleeping the night before emboldened him? Would he want ... I stumbled over the thought. To make matters worse, he was sitting there in only a thin pair of woolen trousers that hugged his legs like a second skin.

He saw me noticing and shrugged. "The mirror has odd tastes sometimes."

My face felt so hot that I wondered if I would need the fire.

"Lie down here," he said, patting the bed beside him.

I froze.

He looked at me, puzzled, and then his brow cleared in understanding and he sighed. "I want to tend your wounds. They do not look well to me."

I relaxed and nodded, making my way to the bed and lying down where he asked me to.

"With your back to me so I can rub in the ointment," he murmured, gently twisting me to where he liked. Then, he draped quilts over my legs and up to where I could hug them to my chest. "I can never understand why the house thinks a view is important when I sleep, but it never fails to provide one."

From where I lay on the bed, all I could see were the black blossoms hanging from the bed and the strange bright lights dancing over the pale snows beyond. I watched them weave and shudder, mesmerized by them.

After a moment, cold ointment touched my back and I flinched.

"Easy. Easy there," he whispered to me as if calming a horse. "I must snip these stitches yet."

And yet, I did feel easier at his touch. It was light and while it certainly hurt my wounds, it was more sore than painful. They would heal. After a moment, his hands warmed and I leaned into the touch as he tended me, cutting the stitches and tugging them free and then soothing the skin with his salve. After long minutes, his hands left my wounds and began to gently knead the skin around them and up into the muscles of my shoulders and neck. I didn't know if this was part of his healing, but if it was, then it certainly was working. My whole body seemed to lose its tension, melting into his ministrations until I was certain I would let him do this forever if he wanted.

"I want to thank you, wife of mine, for coming to my aid. Speak to my riddle – what do you do with a sudden ally? An asset you didn't know you possessed?"

And I was imagining things, too. For a moment, I could have sworn I felt his hot breath on my neck and the faintest press of lips to my hair. But that was just dreams beginning before sleep had come. After a moment, I was pulled under into an exhausted rest where I dreamed of stolen kisses with a husband who had never had any other wives and had chosen me for love alone. And though he acted nothing at all like the man I married, he looked just like him and it made my heart hurt in a curious way I had not thought possible.

I woke in the pale light of pre-dawn to find him sleeping beside me, sprawled on his belly, the quilts wrapped around his waist. The fire drowsed in the hearth, snoring slightly with a burst of sparks whenever it did, and the rippling lights beyond had danced themselves away and left heavy snow drifting through the sky like fat feathers.

I blinked myself awake and found the chamber pot and a wash area in one of the doors leading out of the room. I cleaned myself up and leaned over the basin, thinking.

I didn't really want to think, if I was being honest. I didn't want to make a choice about what Coppertomb had offered. Partly because I was worried that Grosbeak was right, and I shouldn't trust Coppertomb. And partly because I was worried that even if he was right, I might still be tempted to snatch at the chance for everyone to be mostly happy.

It was the sensible solution. Falling in love with my captor was not.

I looked in the long mirror over the basin and took a deep breath. I was a mess. There were still knots in my long hair that Bluebeard had tied. My small shift was rumpled from sleep and the blood on my cheek had smeared in the night. I washed my face and took a long breath.

I didn't like to admit it to myself, but I was beginning to be almost attached to Bluebeard. It was likely only because he was fascinating. Everything he did was dramatic and vibrant – even among a people so dramatic that you could find death or glory around every turn. They made my head spin and my mouth feel dry – and he was worse than the rest. Taking that from him seemed like a crime.

But when I drew the golden key from its place between my breasts, I imagined all the other girls who had done the same thing. Murdering them had *also* been a crime. He would soon murder me, too. Would it just involve the stealing of all my days so that I collapsed on the floor lifeless because I had lost all my time, or would it have to turn ... grisly? There had been no marks on the girls in the room. But what if he'd magically erased those? What if I was destined to die at his hand? Would it be ghastly and terrible? I swallowed down a knot of fear.

And if I chose to stick with his plan, then when he was done with me, he would take another bride and do the same to her.

Maybe I didn't have to choose yet, but maybe I could be prepared. What would it hurt to have one of the garnets ... just in case?

But even making that decision felt like making *the* decision. I took a long breath and turned to go back to bed and then stopped. Why not just go into the room and take a look at it again? Maybe I would see something that would make sense of all this. It couldn't hurt. And avoiding the place didn't make all those other girls just go away.

I drew the key out, turned it in the air, and stepped lightly into the room that opened before me.

I was struck again by the incongruence of it – and the horror. It was a room outside of time and space and my husband used it to store the bodies of the women whose lives he'd stolen. How many of them had slept in his bed like I had last night? How many of them had he gently tended like he'd tended my wounds? My stomach twisted at the thought. It was bad enough when men were faithless, but worse when they killed the very women they were meant to be faithful to. Just looking at them nearly decided me.

I strode across the magical room to the eerie hourglass and worked my way around it. How would I steal a garnet from it? They were mine – my days and nights stored away within. And yet, they felt utterly inaccessible. I reached forward and set my hand against the glass bulb at the top. To my shock, my hand pressed right through the glass to the gems on the other side. My head spun and I felt ill – it was like seeing my own flesh cut up in front of me. Frantically, I snatched one of the garnets and drew it out, keeping it pressed tightly in my palm as I slumped to the ground and pressed my forehead to my knees. My breath wouldn't slow. I was getting lightheaded.

With a thrust of my will, I forced myself to concentrate. I mustn't let it get the better of me. It was my day to spend as I liked. If I gave it to Coppertomb ... well, it was mine to give. And if I kept it for myself, wel,l it was still mine.

And yet, somehow, I didn't think that Bluebeard would feel the same way.

I stumbled back to my feet, my head still reeling. Apparently, stealing your own days was no easy task. I felt like I was intoxicated as I stumbled along the line of women. I kept glancing up at their clear, flawless faces, wondering if their spirits were watching and judging me. What would they have done in my place? None of them had betrayed Bluebeard, or they wouldn't be here. Was that because they didn't have the choice, or had they chosen to be faithful where I was thinking about faithlessness? Had they – possibly – loved him?

The thought put a stab of anger through my heart, and I froze at the feeling. Ridiculous, Izolda. To be jealous of women who had no more say in this than you did. To think you owned any part of him and could feel threatened by another's claim. Foolish. To want to own any part of him. Foolish and more foolish. I was falling down a fool's hole that I'd dug for myself, and the thought of that made me shake my head at myself.

Just to prove that I wasn't jealous, I opened the nearest book at random. It belonged to a woman who stood right beside Princess Margaretta. She had a very impressive figure clad in a silky dress that clung to every curve. I felt my cheeks growing hot just looking at her there, encased in his magic. It was like she might come to life and outshine me right here and now.

I opened her book at random and read a page from it.

I have always been considered a beauty. Desired by all.

Well, that part wasn't very surprising.

Princes from faraway lands had already come just to dance with me. Just to exchange heated looks and hidden kisses. So, when a lord of the Wittenbrand came to steal me away to be his wife, I was not surprised. An exquisite bride requires a rare groom.

I looked up at her again. She certainly thought a lot of herself.

Imagine my shock at discovering I was his fourteenth bride. To say it was an affront to my dignity would not be enough. I was horrified.

I felt a pang of sympathy. I had been horrified, too.

But I was not a fool. I never have been. I read the journals kept by those before me and I saw no hint of real attachment between them and their master.

Now that, actually, was quite interesting. And there had only been one more bride after her. Had he really not loved any of them? Not even a little?

So, I did what any thinking woman would do. I set out to seduce him.

Not what *any* thinking woman would do. I could think just fine, and I was seducing no one.

I started with fine foods and cut flowers. With well-thought compliments and careful turns of suggestive phrases. He proved impervious to suggestion and insensible to romance.

What? I was blushing just reading this.

Perhaps a more direct course of action was required. But my touches were rebuffed, and my kisses turned aside. In frustration, I revisited the journals of the others, looking to see if I had missed something. But if any of these others was somehow his one true love, it is not recorded on the pages of their journals. Nor is any hint of that in his home.

I snuck into his bedroom – you can coax the stairs to bring you there if you offer them pretty trinkets – dressed for love, but he took some time returning, so I searched it top to bottom and found no relic of the other wives there. No abandoned earring or lock of hair. No love missive or article of clothing. It was all his own property, all masculine.

She was certainly a bold one!

I grew bored and went back to the great room and when he found me there, he told me he was tired. When I offered to help him into bed, he told me he was perfectly capable of helping himself. When I offered to undress him, he looked as though he thought I was crazy. When I abased myself completely and told him I would do anything, anything at all for his pleasure, he told me he had left a cord of firewood outside the door and if I were to stack it in the shelf beside the fire, he'd certainly be grateful for my efforts. Then he took me by the elbows and gently shoved me away from him.

My eyes were huge. He'd done that? I doubted many men would. Particularly not when they were already married to the woman.

I was perplexed. Who would not be?

That night, emboldened by what might be the final option, I stripped down to my skin and waited in a bath of hot water and rose petals in his room. I had the mirror produce a bright, shining copper bath. You can get it to manifest any number of things.

She was relentless. I knew I should stop reading, but now I couldn't put it down. I wanted to know what was next. Where would these attempts end?

When he entered the room, his nose was in a book and he did not see me until I rose from the steaming water like a goddess from the depths.

I risked another glance at her and her very impressive figure. Yes, goddess seemed like an accurate descriptor.

He strode forward and lifted my wet body to his, and I thought I had finally won. I was just starting to smile in triumph when he threw me out his bedroom door. I skinned my knee on the floor and was just getting to my feet when he came out a second time ... and threw the bathwater after me. I was left there sputtering, drenched, and rejected.

I covered my mouth to keep the laugh from escaping. I could see him doing that. I could see him striding back into his room and asking his fire to dry him.

I am not one to retreat from what I desire easily, but this man is too much for me. I have resorted to entertaining myself as I may, by flirting with his followers when they come here. If he feels any jealousy, he does not show it.

And now I felt bad for him. My face was burning with emotions I couldn't even put names to.

And I write this for those who come after me, so that they don't make the same mistake I did. It was humiliating for me to experience such depths of rejection, and I can assure you it will leave a bitter taste in your mouth to have the same happen to you. And it will, for none can outstrip me in beauty and desirability.

She was certainly right about that! If this happened to me, I would never live it down.

Was her whole journal like this? Curious, I flipped to the first page and found inscribed on it the same riddle that the first bride had in her book.

A sudden idea seized me, and I left her journal on the pedestal and hurried down the line, looking at the first page of each of the books.

And there it was.

The same riddle.

I am sudden death to calm.

My roar breaks the hush.

My song the mind's somnolence.

They each began the same way but in a different hand. Each of these women had heard those same words. And they'd faithfully written them down. And now that I was looking for them, I spotted them carved in a ring where the wall met the domed ceiling. The riddle was carved between roses and stars and strange symbols so that you had to either have them on your mind in order to see them. But it was plain as day.

Could one of the others have solved the riddle? But if they did, then wouldn't they have recorded the answer somewhere?

I shook my head in frustration. These were nothing but foolish guesses, and I had bigger problems to solve than riddles in books. I needed to decide whether to give Coppertomb my day.

But even though my mind should have been on that, it kept drifting back to the riddle as I left the room, crept back to the black-flowered bed, and crawled under the bright quilt.

The fire flared for a moment in a fiery yawn. I cuddled down into the warmth of the bed and let the rising sun's rays lull me to sleep as my mind turned the riddle around and around, looking for any kind of crack in its edges.

Chapter 26

THE NEXT TIME I WOKE, it was to a surprisingly soft touch, and Bluebeard's cat's eyes regarding me carefully. He winked one of them and put a stack of clothing beside me.

"I have things I must say to you," I said blearily, and he sat down on the edge of the bed. I struggled to sit, wincing at the pain in my back.

I was surprised again when he helped me up, his hands strong and gentle and his dark lashes framing his cheeks as he looked down. His face was so close to mine that I could have kissed him if I pleased. Which was utter nonsense. Would I even be thinking that if I hadn't read about the fourteenth wife's attempt to seduce him? Would I ever consider it if he weren't so terminally beautiful that it hurt to look at him in the bright afternoon sun?

He bit his lip as he watched me, as if he was as nervous in this moment as I was.

"I don't know why you look nervous," I said irritably. "I am the one who has never been married before. You've had at least fifteen other women in your bed."

He raised an eyebrow condescendingly as if to dispute the matter. Maybe the journals hadn't been lying after all. I felt my cheeks growing warm – again.

"But that is not what I want to talk about." I paused and he sat back a little as I took the clothing from him so that I had something to do with my hands. Maybe I should take a page from his book. "Speak to my riddle, husband."

His answering grin was boyish. I would never get over how young he looked despite the blue beard.

"Who builds a bridge and does not use it to cross a river? Who gathers supplies to blockade a port with no intention of blockading it? Who orders uniforms for men who will never fight?"

He looked intrigued when I began and hungry when I ended my words, leaning forward as if his nearness could encourage me to speak more.

It did.

"While you were bidding, I took the liberty of investigating what your opponents left at the table," I said calmly. "People often forget that what they choose to keep or do not keep as possessions says a great deal about them. The Sword kept a book he shouldn't care about. And inside, he had notations. I can write them down for you. I remember them clearly."

He huffed a laugh through lips made soft with something that looked like a combination of pain and relief. His eyes met mine and a tiny thrill shot through me at the look in those liquid grey cat's eyes. In a human, that might almost be longing that he was letting me see behind the shutters of his eyes. Longing mixed with elation.

He held my gaze for a moment and then dove off the bed, moving too quick for a human and scrambling through the layers of his things. He came up like an otter with a fish in its mouth, holding an inkpot, a pen, and a half-filled page of crossed-out words and trailing verse. He flipped the parchment over, put it on a book and pushed everything toward me.

I took his quill, met his eyes with a proud look of my own, and began to faithfully copy everything I'd witnessed in my careful, clear hand.

"I am a good wife to have," I said coyly, and the smile he gave me in return looked sly. More than ever before, I wished he could speak at the same time as I could. This game where we each played mute was like chewing rocks for breakfast. I misliked it.

It ate at me constantly – termites to the wood of my mind.

"And by the way, I have a name to offer the sword I gave you. You called mine Angstbite. Yours can be Edgeworthy."

He barked a laugh.

When I was done, he kissed my forehead, gestured to the bath as if inviting me to take one, and left with the words I'd written.

I'd kept my left hand closed that whole time. The moment he was out of the room, I opened my palm and looked down at the rough-cut garnet concealed within it. It felt like a crime to be holding it. After that moment of his joy bursting from him so infectiously, it also felt like a betrayal.

But I kept it with me as I stripped out of the clinging shift and dropped into the hot pool. I kept it on the little tray beside the bath as I drank the steaming tea from the little teacup and tried to hold it like he did with my pinkie finger out. I kept glancing at it furtively as I washed my hair and then came out and dried my body with the cloth folded beside the stones of the pool. I donned the clothing Bluebeard had left for me – a tight pair of plum-colored velvet breeches, a tall pair of sturdy black boots, a creamy brocade doublet slashed in plum and sewn with gold, and a frothy white tunic sewn all over with downy grey feathers.

I was not in the habit of wearing breeches like a man. It made me feel bold. Just like my words that morning had.

I arranged my curls so that they framed my face in wild spirals – the best I could manage to make it do – and put the garnet carefully into a tiny hidden pocket of the doublet.

My marriage sword was nearby, and I strapped it on with hardly a thought. Perhaps I could convince Bluebeard to teach me to use it so it would not only be a decoration.

I made my way down the winding stairs, listening to the birdsong, and paused halfway down. I was growing used to this house and this world. If I was honest with myself, I would have to admit that I was even growing used to my feral husband. The thought should make me very careful. Instead, it brought a feeling of warmth rushing all through me.

And perhaps it was that moment, thinking those thoughts in complete betrayal of my original self, that doomed me the second time.

In the main room of the house, Bluebeard's band was clustered around his desk, poring over a map. Vireo studied Pensmoore, his index finger jammed right over Northpeak in a way that made my heart skip a beat. What was he planning with my home?

He spoke excitedly to the man next to him. "Five hundred. That must be the number of his new recruits and if he already has more uniforms being sewn for them then they'll be trained by the time we make our first move. We should expect that his will be the bridges. He'll need one to reach Southfallow. That has to be his first move."

"But why block the port off?" the other man said, shaking his head.

They were matching in their blue doublets and cat's eyes, and they both were eating from a spread of food all around the map as they spoke.

Sparrow looked up and caught my eye with a smirk as she took a delicate bite from a very tiny boiled egg.

"To keep his navy safe until he's ready to use them," Bluebeard said, considering the map. "He's planning to set against us the swollen weight of his empire like a river running after the melt of spring. Like so many, he exposes his vulnerability in his boldness. It will leave his rear unguarded. If we could just see our way clear to finding an ally to attack him there while he goes after us, then he'll be caught in a vice."

"Unless he's already persuaded the others to work with him," Vireo argued. "They'd love to see you unseated, Arrow. We all know the Bramble King favors you."

"The Bramble King favors no one," Grosbeak muttered bitterly from his place on a high shelf. Someone had elevated him so he could see the map over their heads.

"Is that the name of the Sovereign?" I asked from my place on the stairs.

Bluebeard froze, his eyes locked on me. Was he so surprised to see me? I lived here, too.

Vireo coughed, looking from Bluebeard to me and back. "As you say, lady, so it is."

"And you are tracking the Sword's plans on the map," I added.

"As you say," Vireo said, looking again to Bluebeard.

Bluebeard was still frozen in place, his eyes drinking me in as if he was watching for something. It made my cheeks hot. What would he be looking for in me? Betrayal? I had not yet planned to do that. And on top of it, I had proven to be a worthy spy.

"When do we make our first move?" I asked shyly.

"After the opening event – a grand showing of all the players and their retinues to kick off the games officially," Vireo said, his brow beginning to furrow now when he glanced at his master.

One of the others snickered and Bluebeard blinked suddenly and looked back at the map.

"A ball then?" I asked, face hot, trying to seem sophisticated and calm rather than off-balance. Why did my husband look at me so strangely? Was he that grateful for my spy work? It had only been common sense and a showing of good faith.

This made them all laugh. "A mortal might throw a ball, lady. But not the Wittenbrand. We prefer to show ourselves off in other ways."

"Like what?" I asked, crossing to the table and boldly helping myself to one of the spiced sweet buns. It was still steaming as I tore off a piece to bite.

His grin seemed eerie with the scars arching up from it. "Tonight, we will ride in the Spectacle. The competitors will choose two companions to ride with them on Wittensteeds which live a single night and then wither and die. We will ride them fast and hard and at each interval, a target will be high and far from the path. We must make a shot with an arrow. At the end of the night, the competitor whose arrows have pierced closest to the mark of each target will receive a boon. And all of Wittenhame will have seen us ride and shoot. It's an honor to be asked and I will ride with pride. As will Sparrow, I suppose, since Grosbeak has proven traitor."

"No," Bluebeard said firmly, and his eyes lock on mine again. There was something in them that I could not decipher. Something deep and swirling. "No insult to you, Sparrow, but you will be preparing for our first move against the Sword. We will not wait for him to strike us. We must strike first." His gaze returned to the map. "Here and here. Come, let Izolda advise us on her father's defenses and that of his neighbors. We will be relying on his ability to withstand attack from the sea."

I moved to his side and he leaned over the map to show me. As I leaned with him, his breath washed over my skin, making me shiver.

"If Sparrow does not ride with you, Arrow, then who will?" Vireo asked with a dangerous note to his voice.

"My wife will ride with me," he said, his eyes still on the map.

"Ridiculous!" Vireo snorted. "You jest."

"I do not jest today, but if you prefer that I did, then speak to my riddle. Who has two smiles and still makes me frown?" Bluebeard looked up and met Vireo's eyes, and I felt myself drawing back as their gazes locked. Vireo looked furious.

"Why begin down the path of a fool today, Arrow?" Vireo snarled. "You've never been one before. No fair ankles or delicate wrists have turned your head from battle. These mortals are to us as blades in the battle – we need them, but without us wielding them they are nothing."

Bluebeard made no reply, but I could see he was considering Vireo's words. I pulled back, taking a step from the table. I'd been a fool to think this could be a true partnership. Watching Bluebeard with his own made it so obvious that leading these people was what he was born for, and they were all faster and stronger and smarter than I was. Vireo made perfect sense. There was no reason to bring me when he had these others who were better.

My back hit the bookshelf and I hugged myself as I watched them all leaning in toward the growing conflict instead of away from it as men usually did. All but Sparrow, who rose unnoticed and made her way to stand beside me.

"You've never done this before," Vireo said, emboldened by Bluebeard's silence. "Why bring one of them into things now? Why dress her for a hunt instead of in silks to look pretty on your arm? Why involve her in your schemes?"

"Who do you think got us this information, Vireo," Bluebeard said mildly.

"You've stirred up a nest of wasps, mortal," Sparrow whispered beside me, looking casual, as if she'd chosen to stand beside me entirely at random.

"Then make her your spy. Dress her even prettier and foist her on your enemy. Don't bring her into our councils like this." Vireo gestured at the map and the silent men ringing it. They were watching him with intensity in their eyes, hanging on every word. "Don't offer her your secrets. You never have before. You know that they make you vulnerable. You can't afford to care if they live."

"I did not mean to cause such distress," I whispered back to Sparrow.

"Did you know," she said, "that he doesn't need to kiss you to take your days and use them as his own?"

I felt my face grow hot. Why else would he kiss me if not for that?

Vireo seemed like he couldn't stop now if he wanted to. "You can't afford to care if your wives are harmed. You can't afford not to use them up. And yet you have given this one true marriage vows. Don't deny it! I was there! You've given her a place at the table with you – not just at the events, but here where you discuss strategy. They whisper about it at every door of the Wittenhame! They roar with laughter when your back is turned. Your enemies have noticed, too. You have drawn their eyes to her. I saw how Coppertomb spoke to her last night. I saw how the Sword keeps one eye on her at all times. And worse yet – the fire suggested you tucked her into your bed last night!"

"Is that all?" Bluebeard asked in a low, dangerous voice. I felt my mouth go dry.

"We don't care who you bed," Vireo said in a low voice. "It's none of our business – so long as it isn't your wives."

I didn't mean to gasp, but I did. When Bluebeard turned to look at me when I did, there was something unreadable in his eyes – something that looked a little like fear.

He spun back to Vireo and in a voice so low I thought it might turn into a whisper, he began to speak, leaning over the table until his nose almost touched that of the other Wittenbrand. I could almost feel the violence crackling in the air, like lightning waiting to form.

"What has a head and no body?" my husband growled.

"Grosbeak," the Sparrow said with a laugh. She didn't seem at all worried by what was happening, and a quick look around the group told me that none of the rest of them looked particularly shaken either. They looked eager – like they were anticipating a particular treat.

"And what might soon have a body and no head?" my husband pushed.

"Vireo, if he doesn't remember why they call you 'Arrow,'" Sparrow drawled.

Vireo stormed out of the house, slamming the door loudly. The fire whooshed in response.

"Insulting!" it roared, flaring up.

Sparrow shook her head. "He's riled. That's all. Grosbeak was a friend."

"I could still be one," Grosbeak said from his perch.

Sparrow snorted, not even looking at the head. "No one else feels like that, Arrow. An exhibition is just a game. Take who you like." His eyes narrowed as he grinned. "Only let us win this game with you and we will be pleased."

There were murmurs of agreement from the others around the table, and my speeding heart began to slow. It would be fine. They would not all betray him just for me.

Bluebeard shot me a slightly guilty, slightly embarrassed look and then gestured toward the chair Vireo had been sitting in. I settled myself into it and Sparrow settled in with me.

"Now tell us, lady," Sparrow said with certainty in her voice. "Were there any other notations in the book?"

The rest of the afternoon was spent in strategy. The rest of the group seemed pleased enough as Bluebeard hammered out the details of how they would begin and what they would do to achieve it, what moves their competitors were sure to try, how they would counter. I offered what information I could about the land I'd come from and otherwise kept mostly quiet.

Bluebeard glanced at me often, an unreadable look in his eye. More than ever, I wished we could just speak honestly together. There was so much I would ask him. Every now and then, I felt the garnet in my hidden pocket, or remembered Vireo storming away, and I wondered if he had been right. Maybe I wasn't good for his master. Maybe I would ruin him.

And I also wondered if what Sparrow said was true. I'd thought he was kissing me because that was how he stole my days. Was it possible that he did it only because he liked it? Was it really true that he had married me in a different way, as his men had been complaining about since it happened? And if those things were true, was it possible that I could be his ruin like his enemies hoped and his followers feared?

Chapter 27

I'M NOT GIVEN much to anxiety or supposing, but even if I had been, it would not have saved me from that night. There are some boxes that once opened, do not shut again. Some jewels that, once stolen, cannot be returned.

This time, as Bluebeard took my hand to lead me to the Spectacle, I wanted him to be able to speak to me so badly that I could almost taste it on the tip of my tongue. He looked me deep in the eyes and smiled a wicked smile full of promises he planned to break.

I left Grosbeak behind. He could not ride with us.

"She'll need both hands for her mount," Bluebeard told him. "She can't bring you."

But I was worried about leaving him on a shelf in the Grouse House.

"She could leave you in her secret room," Bluebeard suggested, and so that's what I did. I brought him into the little room and left his head on the pedestal meant for me.

"You can't just leave me here in a sepulchre," he raged. "It's filled with the bodies of the dead."

"Then you'll fit right in," I'd said shortly.

And so I stepped out into the evening beside my vicious husband and joined hundreds of people running like rain from the hills into a stream toward where the Spectacle would begin.

Rough wooden booths had been set up around the starting line and already – though the sun was only just sinking in the sky – they were lit from within. They roared to life as people served out strange drinks of every type – some that steamed and some that growled and some that turned the drinker's nose purple. There were booths with tight-wound breads and booths with evergreen wreaths to wear around the neck. One sold candies that were swirled white and red – so bright and glossy I could hardly believe they were real. Another booth had calling birds with tails almost as long as a man was tall. Those who bought them set them on a shoulder and the birds' tails trailed behind their owners like the train of a fancy bridal gown.

My eyes were wide as Bluebeard led me toward the event, but I stopped him just before the sun dipped below the horizon.

"Whatever happens next, you should know that you have my full confidence," I said.

If only I could be sure that was true of me, too. I was not at all confident in myself or in my own mind.

He gave me a puzzled look but waited a heartbeat as darkness took the place of golden sun, and when there was no more trace of gold in the sky, he looked at me with dangerous eyes and said, "Speak to my riddle, portentous one. Why do you wish me luck as if you think I will need it?"

But by the way his eyes glinted, I could tell he was joking. He had no notion of the garnet in my pocket. He had no idea that I was balanced on a knife's edge between loyalty and betrayal.

With a laugh, he threw a cloak around my shoulders – deep blue and rippling like the night, trimmed in white fur around the hood and the edge, and then he drew me along with him toward the event.

The Bramble King – the Sovereign – was buried this time in snow and lit with bonfires at his feet. He watched sleepily over a scarlet line along the ground. Along the line, the other competitors already stood, their two chosen companions accompanying them. Vireo was already waiting for us.

He scowled when he saw our linked hands, but Bluebeard nodded to him and Vireo seemed to relax, as if he hadn't been sure whether he would still be welcome and was mollified to find that he was. It didn't seem very practical to keep a man so close who disagreed with you so vehemently, but Bluebeard greeted him, letting go of my hand to clasp his.

I was waiting to see the steeds we would ride. I had experience riding horses, and I even thought I could ride the elk that Bluebeard favored. But to my surprise, Bluebeard lifted up a handful of snow and blew on it, and from his breath, three pawing stallions sprang to life. They were made entirely of snow sparkle and frost, as if he had thrown the light snow into the air and it had simply decided to choose this form on the way down. They tossed their glittering rainbow manes and shook themselves, straining forward as if it were only his will holding them back.

"They respond to commands," Bluebeard told me. "'Halt' to stop. 'Forward' to go, and nudges of the knees to turn them."

All down the line, the other competitors were blowing on their handfuls of snow, but I privately thought that none of them had steeds quite so snorting and restless as Bluebeard's and certainly none of them were as shaggy and powerful looking. Perhaps there had been a storm in his breath but only calm summer breezes in theirs.

"I will guard your back to the end, brother," Vireo murmured as he mounted his steed. "Do not see my disagreement as disloyalty."

"I never did," Bluebeard said with a small smile.

He offered me a hand and I took it, meeting his gaze as he helped me into the saddle. He looked excited, barely containing his energy as he prowled from my mount to his, his eyes on everyone around him, looking for weaknesses. If I had to guess, I would say this spectacle would be fun for him.

The horses were far higher than I was used to, and though they were held back right now, I could feel in their magic bodies a desire to run that outstripped anything else I'd felt in a mount before. It was disconcerting to be able to see through them, catching only the movement and edges of their being in the glitter of shining snow, but I was determined to prove I was not afraid. If I chose loyalty to Bluebeard, he would need to know he could rely on me, and he could not rely on a coward.

The look he gave me from the back of his pawing stallion was one of both challenge and something that almost looked like respect. For one awful moment, I wondered if I could leave him even if I wanted to. I may never find a man who looked at me like that again. In Pensmoore, my best hope had been a man who would give me the dignity of marriage and children and – if I was very lucky – be faithful to me. Here, now, I could stay with this man who gave me devilish looks and bright magic horses and enchanted clothing and wondrous spectacles. And what if that meant my life was short and over before the winter? Was it really so bad to live thirty years in six months? Was it really a bad bargain?

Everything in me was screaming inside me that it was a very bad bargain, but when I looked into his glittering cats' eyes, I didn't believe any of it.

He whispered to his horse and it moved in close to me so that he could lean from the saddle and speak in a low whisper.

"Izolda, your beauty draws from me a confession I would not normally make, but I bare my throat to you. I am not certain that I can save your land as you hope. There, I have confessed it."

I felt my eyes going wide. He'd never seemed to lack confidence before.

"No," he said, shaking his head. "It is not that I think I shall lose, but rather that sometimes to win you must sacrifice everything. It is possible that I will need to destroy what you love, to let it burn and wail and die, if I am to win. I think it best that you know that before we start."

My mouth fell open, betrayal stark and bitter in my mouth.

A horn blared, haunting and dramatic, and Bluebeard's horse reared.

He shot me a last look, torn and haunted, and then he cried, "Forward!"

His sparkling mount it dashed across the line.

"Forward!" I called in a hollow voice, realizing the race had begun.

But the cold air streaming across my face could not compete with the ice solidifying my heart.

It was all I could do to cling to my horse's gossamer mane as he rushed forward, hot on the heels of Bluebeard's stallion. Beside me, Vireo cursed loudly, clinging to his own steed like a lamprey on the side of a fish. Even with my hesitation, we'd been first off the line.

We galloped up a narrow forest path between rounded boulders and groping pines, turning tightly to cling to the hill from the one direction, only to double back and cling in the other direction. The horses were wild, almost screaming as they ate the ground under their feet at a jolting, furious pace, nearly missing the turns as their hooves scrabbled over slick stone and tufts of grass.

I kept my gaze forward and clung tightly to the horse, letting him have his head. There was no way I could hope to steer him. I could only hope that he kept following Bluebeard's horse and was not lost in the tight turns and narrow trails.

My heart was in my throat, my cloak swirling behind me, my knuckles white where they gripped the icicle mane.

My husband was ahead of me. He rode with all the grace of a big cat – as if he had plucked this horse from the night sky and set it ablaze with his passion to bear him where he chose – which he had, I supposed. How many days had that cost me? Did I even care?

I should have been terrified. My heart should have been in my throat – and it was a bit – but there was also something else stealing over me. Something I hadn't expected. Elation.

I had never thought I would love the danger of a night ride like this one – and yet I did. Oh, how I did. All my inhibitions fled from me and it was just me and the horse and the ride, flying down the trail like an arrow loosed from a bow. There was no difficult decision. There was no betrayal. Just a magic horse and me and the ground below and the air above, forever.

I let out a delighted whoop and heard Vireo curse again from behind me.

I tried to catch a glance of him over my shoulder, but I saw nothing more than a blur of rider on horse and a vague impression of someone else very hot on his heels.

I had to turn again to catch my breath.

We neared the top of the high hill, where snow glazed the tops of rocks and trees like an iced bun. The moon was creeping high in the sky, and though it was small during this cycle, it seemed brighter than ever, flooding the landscape with its stark white gaze.

Bluebeard spoke to his horse and it reared, too excited to want to halt – even after racing up a hill so steep that I felt winded just thinking about it.

He drew the bow and arrows from the hanging quiver at the side of his magical saddle and fitted an arrow to the string.

I looked into the distance as Vireo pulled up beside me and there it was, the target. A ring of licking white fire surrounding what must be a solid target for the arrow to hit. It was far enough away that I wouldn't be able to see the arrow strike, but Vireo pulled out a long telescope and opened it, lifting it to his eye.

Bluebeard loosed the arrow and Vireo cried out in delight.

"Middle ring!"

But it wasn't Vireo that Bluebeard looked at with a wicked gleam in his eye, it was me. He grinned, and I found myself grinning back even as my heart was ice inside me. Our eyes met and for just a heartbeat I wondered what it would be like to be married to him in the normal way – the way where joys like this could be shared. My heart ached worse than the tears in my back at the thought of it.

"Now, how is that for shooting, mortal wife? Have you ever seen the like?"

I wanted to tease him, wanted to remind him that I had let him shoot an apple from my head, but I dared not.

Vireo glanced at me. "I swear, Arrow, your wives leave tingles down my spine with their eerie silences and long looks. How you put up with it is beyond my ken."

Bluebeard frowned at Vireo, but he said nothing in my defense, simply calling to his horse, "Forward."

My face was burning with shame as the sounds of the next competitor warned me he was hot behind us. Vireo's horse leapt forward, and my horse was a heartbeat after as irritation simmered within me.

I could hardly be blamed for my silence when I'd been warned not to speak – ordered, even. Did he think that I didn't want to break the silence? Did he think I liked being mute when I had so many things to say?

But now some of the fun had been leeched out of the ride and while my horse still danced and leapt beneath me, its semi-translucent muscles bunching and lengthening with every stride, I did not revel in it as I had. I'd been given a bitter drink and told to swallow. Did he really mean that about sacrificing my family? Perhaps it had only been more drama. But could I be truly equal to the man while under this curse? While subject to his whim? I'd been fooling myself.

We rode down a steep hill and crossed an ankle-deep stream with ice crusting the edges, turning round a great tree's trunk and up through flowers encased in diamond frost that towered over my mortal head. And still, I was stewing.

I wanted to speak – of course I did! I wanted to congratulate him, to provoke him, to tease him. Did they think me less because I showed restraint for his sake?

I ground my teeth. If I could, I wouldn't just speak, I would demand, I would riposte, I would roar.

Roar.

We leapt over a low fence and I barely concentrated in time to stay astride the horse as he made the jump. The moment his diamond feet hit the hard ground again, my mind was back to spinning.

Roar.

That was in the riddle.

I am sudden death to calm.

My roar breaks the hush.

My song the mind's somnolence.

Could it be possible that the answer to the riddle was speech?

It was written in every journal – as if daring us to break his rule. If this was truly the answer to the riddle, then it was a gauntlet the magic had thrown down to each wife. One that had never been picked up. But why would it do that? Who had written those words in the room and why did it whisper those words to each of us? Had it been a ruse all along?

When he'd bid me silent, he'd said outright that we would lose the magic if I spoke out of turn. No wonder no one else had tried. And yet ... this poem was written everywhere in the very heart of the magic he had possessed. What if he hadn't created the room, only brought his brides to it one by one? What if he was as much in the dark as we were about the provenance of the magic or the rules surrounding it? What if he'd been lied to?

I shook my head. I felt confused ... but also curious.

Behind me, something snorted and I glanced over my shoulder to see the Sword right at my heels, his beast flaring with little bursts of fire.

"Forward," I whispered to my horse, leaning over its neck. "Forward."

The horse sped onward, but up ahead I'd lost sight of Bluebeard and Vireo. I'd been too occupied with the words of the riddle.

I heard a crack behind me, and my horse leapt forward, screaming.

I glanced back to see the Sword gaining ground. He was almost beside me now, a whip in his hand. He struck my horse with it and a tiny tear formed in the starlight-and-snow of my horse's hindquarters.

"Off on your own, mortal wife? What a delicious surprise!"

"Drawing their swords, they ran directly to Bluebeard. He knew them to be his wife's brothers ... but the two brothers pursued and overtook him."
- Charles Perrault, Bluebeard,
1697 as translated by Andrew Lang in The Blue Fairy Book 1889.

Chapter 28

I WASN'T sure what I was expecting him to do. Maybe whip me? Maybe speed by?

I didn't expect the shove when it came, hard and fast.

I fell from the back of the horse, smashing into a tuft of frozen flowers and hitting my shoulder hard against the ground.

I tumbled, momentum still at work, and then finally stilled, disoriented, head whirling and back screaming.

I forced myself to my feet, breathing hard. The pain of the impact only hit me as I tried to straighten. My entire left side – shoulder, ribs, arm – was in agony. Snow clung to me, melting and seeping through my clothes. And yet, as I saw the Sword plunging around the corner ahead, the pain seemed less important than what he was doing. He was tucking his whip into his belt and drawing his bow.

I knew, without knowing how, that he planned to use it on something other than the target.

Something nudged me from behind, and to my surprise, my horse was there, his velvet frost-nose pressing against my uninjured shoulder.

"Kneel, friend, and I will mount," I whispered.

He knelt and I scrambled onto his back as the Sword's two companions thundered by on horses that were mixtures of frost and flame. They were neck and neck as they took the corner ahead.

"Forward," I whispered, and my horse stood, reared, and pawed the air in a single motion.

I held on with gritted teeth as he plunged up the moonlit track, banking around the corner. As soon as we rounded the bend, everything before me stood out in the stark relief of the moonlight.

I gasped, my heart racing as I saw it all, my breath puffing out of me in ghastly clouds.

Vireo was down on the side of the trail, chasing after his horse. It looked like he'd been thrown on the corner. The Sword's two companions thundered off the trail toward him, their steeds kicking up clouds of snow as they galloped, whips at the ready and glinting in the moonlight. They were not playing fair.

That left Bluebeard alone and far ahead, his horse standing still as his back arched and he took aim with bow and arrow toward the second target.

Behind him, the Sword had stopped, too, his bow at the ready, arrow nocked. But he was not aiming at the target. He was aiming at my husband.

I couldn't get there in time to stop him. Or to do anything to warn my husband.

I could call his name and warn him. But only if I believed the riddle. Only if I thought I'd really solved it.

But something was sticking in my mind. Bluebeard had warned me personally not to speak or all would be lost.

And there was that last line speaking of "the mind's somnolence."

My heart was racing, my head seemed to spin, but there was no time to make a clever decision or be sensible about this. If I did not speak, it might be too late.

What good would any amount of magic do him if he were dead?

I opened my mouth, summoning all my courage.

And in that flash of a moment, my heart spoke to me.

The mind! The mind! It's in the mind.

I shut my mouth with a snap and thought with all my might.

Behind you! Bluebeard! Behind you!

Bluebeard's arrow flew from his bow and in the bright moonlight I saw it go wide from the target as he spun on his horse's back and ducked so quickly that it seemed to all be one motion. The Sword loosed at the same moment and his arrow flew over my husband.

He was fitting a second arrow to the string when a hand grabbed me from behind, spinning me.

"I've found you just in time, wife of the Arrow." Coppertomb's voice sounded triumphant.

"The Sword attacked him," I said stupidly, not sure how he came around the corner without me noticing. I felt like I was in shock, like Bluebeard really had heard my voice in his mind. How else would he have known to duck? The importance of it – the possibility of it – changed everything.

Coppertomb's horse was huffing in the cold, its frosty body filled with dark swirls like eels living within it.

He leaned in close so that I could feel his warmth in the cold of the night, and his hands grabbed my jacket.

"Your day. Give me your day and let your brothers come and save you, or it will be too late. In a moment, the Sword will slay him, and your life will be forfeit with his. Only give me your day, and there is still hope for you."

"My brothers?"

I needed time to think. I needed time to consider what this new development might mean.

"You've done something. I can see it in your eyes, mortal. You are as open books to the Wittenbrand. You've broken your marriage somehow, haven't you?"

"What?" I peered toward Bluebeard but all I saw was his horse wheeling in the snow as the Sword took another run at him, sword held high. There was no sign that I'd done anything other than warn him.

"If your marriage was not broken, don't you think the Arrow would draw on your days to save himself now?" Coppertomb said impatiently. He grabbed my chin between a thumb and forefinger and turned my head back to the battle. "Look!"

In the distance, Bluebeard was battling the Sword – blade to blade. There were no bursts of light or strange occurrences, just the ring of blade on blade.

Could it be true? Had speaking within my mind been just as devastating as speaking with my mouth would have been?

"You've been a fool," Coppertomb said, confirming my thoughts. "Don't make it worse by continuing on that path."

"No," I began, but I was too distracted to notice when he grabbed me and started to pat at my pockets.

"Here!" he said, triumphant as he drew the garnet from my doublet. "Was that so hard? Mortals try to complicate everything."

He threw the garnet to the ground and when it hit, the earth shook and then tore open.

My horse screamed, rearing up.

It leapt over the tear in a cloud of starlight, wrenching me from Coppertomb's grasp.

His curses rang out behind me, but my horse's hooves pounded over the frozen ground as it tried to outrun the tear in the ground. Out of the fissure spilled dark figures that looked like armed men. They were dazed and stumbling, some of them calling out or raving like madmen.

"To me! To me!" Coppertomb cried, waving his arms to them.

I didn't know if he was rallying the men or trying to call me back, but my horse had a mind of its own and it was thundering straight toward Bluebeard.

Bluebeard raced toward the Sword. As I watched – shocked – he stood up on the back of his horse, crouching as the stallion galloped. The Sword had his weapon ready, aiming to sweep at Bluebeard's legs. But as he struck, my husband leapt to the Sword's horse, knocking his opponent off with him.

They rolled across the ground, sliding over the light skim of snow.

I put my hand over my mouth as my horse plunged toward them.

Bluebeard was going to break his neck. And then I was going to trample him.

He popped up from the ground and found his balance, wavering slightly. My breath hitched in my throat. A little sound like relief escaped my lips.

At his feet, the Sword reached for him – but too late. My horse galloped close at the same moment that Bluebeard lunged, leaping in a way that seemed almost effortless onto the back of my horse and then leaning almost over me as he clung to my horse's bright mane.

"Bluebeard?" he asked, horror in his voice. "This is what you name me?"

I squirmed on the horse's back so I could see him there, leaning over me like a black cat riding a charger.

You heard me. I … I solved the riddle.

His laugh was long and low. "Wondrous as it is, I do hear you, wife of mine, fire of my eyes, despair of my soul."

Coppertomb says I have broken our marriage.

"I think not. I feel your days. I can still reach for them. What riddle do you speak of?"

There was a riddle the room told me when I entered. It is written on the walls and in every book.

"A riddle," he said, his voice growing bright as if something had just finally made sense to him. "And it told you to speak to my mind?"

I thought so.

I looked up at his face – at the utter elation I saw there. He did not look angry at all.

He looked down at me for a half of a heartbeat and then back up again, but that tiny fraction of a second had shown me blazing pride and something that looked almost like fierce affection mixed in.

"Speak to my riddle, wife of mine. What manner of woman solves a puzzle that fifteen before her could not solve?"

The type who listens, I said dryly, but I didn't feel proud or smug. I felt nervous. I had not betrayed him by speaking aloud – but I had betrayed him far worse when I snuck into the room and stole one of my days. Even if I hadn't given it to Coppertomb with my own hand, he had it now, and he had used it to practice magic.

We plunged into a copse of trees and Bluebeard pushed the stallion onward as branches beat us from every direction.

"Something hunts us, solemn wife. Something not of this world."

Behind us, I heard a yell.

"They went in here!"

Our horse crashed into a small, roughly circular glen, bathed in moonlight. Light, swirling snow in flakes as tiny as dust motes whirled around us.

Bluebeard urged him to the center of the glen, and he drew his blade, one hand on the mane, one on the hilt of the sword.

"Do not fear, Izolda. You are under my protection wherever trees breathe and forests take root, wherever rain falls and water floods over the earth, wherever the angry wind blows or the rocks groan with age, there you are mine and always will be," he said in a low, dangerous way.

I met his eyes, but I did not see fear there. Instead, my pulse quickened for another reason entirely. He was looking at me with such open vulnerability in his eyes that it made me gasp.

"I have waited decade upon decade for a wife who is my equal – for a true partner in this adventure of mine." His lips quirked teasingly. "I had not expected her to mock me for my blue beard."

I wanted to answer him. I wanted to return his assurances with my own. But my words cleaved to the roof of my mouth. We had already been betrayed – and I was the traitor. I did not deserve his loyalty or his faith in me.

"They're here!" someone called, and just like that we were ringed by dark figures, coming out of the trees, their shadowy weapons raised and faces enshrouded in the dark hoods of their cloaks.

They charged before I had the chance to scream, weapons raised.

Our horse reared, pawing the ground, and I clung to his mane, Bluebeard at my back. My body pressed flat against his warmth and my breath hitched in my throat. I felt his breath coming hot and fast, his heart pounding through our clothing as it matched the speed of mine.

The horse crashed back to the earth and the fight began as Bluebeard clashed sword to sword, making our horse dance around to avoid contact as he fought.

I clenched my jaw, trying not to bite my tongue. Trying not to scream. I didn't dare distract him.

He was nimble and quick, his short sword lightning-fast as it swept a blade aside, twisting and flicking and sending it from the hand of an attacker. He was moving to the next one as I was still watching the first fall back – unarmed now.

Bluebeard urged the horse ahead at the exact right moment to get under a man's guard and then he plunged his blade through a chink between the man's breastplate and shoulder armor. We spun in a circle and his horse kicked back. There was a scream as the man charging us from behind fell to the ground, clutching his broken arm, his battle-axe skittering away across the frozen grass.

I didn't dare close my eyes. I didn't dare let myself scream. I was worried I might forget to breathe

Bluebeard moved like lightning, like time didn't touch him, like he was made of magic and wishes and songs of bards. He danced and wove and wheeled, one with the horse, one with the swirling snow, one with the night. And in his eyes, there was fierce violence and something that looked all too much like obsession. He lived for this, I realized. He loved it far too much.

Perhaps his men had not been joking when they said he collected heads.

And then someone cried "Hold!"

I gasped as Coppertomb rode out from the forest on his shadow-caging horse. The ring of soldiers encircling us drew back. All I could hear was panting breath and creaking leather and the squeak of boots on snow.

"There you are, Arrow. And with your lady wife, I see." Coppertomb looked far too smug. A shot of terror rippled down my spine. Bluebeard flicked the blood off the end of his sword, wheeling the horse to keep everyone in sight. "You should have stayed by my side, Izolda. It's harder to bring you to your brother with an angry husband crouched around you."

"Brother?" I gasped.

A dark figure stepped out from the ring, his shoulders back and head held high. He threw back his hood.

Svetgin.

It was both him and not him. My hand flew to my throat.

He looked to be thirty years old. Worn and filled out, his muscles bulky, his eyes narrowed in thought and a wicked scar decorating one cheek that looked old – a decade old. And yet it had not been there last week.

"Izolda," he said in wonder, looking at me as if he had seen a ghost. "You have not changed."

"What is this?" Bluebeard asked, his words thick with fury.

"Your lady wife gave me a single day – a day to save her family and her nation and free herself from your grasp."

"That's not –" I started.

"Shh," Bluebeard said gently, laying a finger over my lips. I bit his finger. He didn't even flinch. He merely turned to my brother. "You are here for your sister?"

Bluebeard tilted his head as he watched Svetgin and Svetgin stood a little straighter.

"We come for all the brides you've stolen."

There was a murmur from the rest of those in the ring, and with that murmur, I realized who they were. The Brotherhood of Stolen Sisters. And they had found a way into the Wittenhame because of me. Because of my betrayal. Because of the garnet I had stolen.

"My other wives have passed through this life," Bluebeard said calmly. "Izolda is the only one who still lives."

"Then we come for their revenge," Svetgin said harshly, his once boyish features twisted in a way so unfamiliar to me that they did not seem to be his at all.

Bluebeard turned my face gently toward him, his finger still on my lip. "Tell me only this, wife. Did he take your garnet, whether by your hand or by force?"

His grey cat's eyes held a depth of sadness that twisted in my belly. His finger left my lips.

He did, I said in my mind, feeling my eyes welling up.

Bluebeard's lips crashed into mine so unexpectedly that I didn't know what was happening at first and then he was kissing me with devouring passion so that I could hardly think, hardly breathe. Desire welled up in me, rising to match his. He moaned slightly into my mouth as if he was breaking apart even as he kissed me. I kissed him back, torn by the agony of my own betrayal. I was breaking, too, shattering apart even as I clung to him. A deep ache started in my heart and flooded through my body.

He broke away, leaving me gasping, his expression vulnerable and aching. His fingers caressed my cheek – longingly, almost lovingly. "You are beautiful, my betrayer, light of my eyes, breath of my lungs. For you, I would bend an oath and break the skies. Let that kiss be the memory you take of me as you leave me to my fate."

And then hand ripped me from the saddle and the sparkling snow horse under Bluebeard collapsed and dissipated in a puff of sparkling motes.

I couldn't see him – couldn't see anything as I was wrenched away, my hood pulled over my eyes, and dragged across the snow in strong, muscled arms.

I thought I might have screamed, but that, too, was muffled by my cloak.

Blade met blade in a sharp clang. A loud curse was abruptly cut off and then cries filled the air growing more and more frantic. I kicked and elbowed and lashed out wildly against whoever was holding me.

And then my brother's voice was in my ear, lower and rougher than I remembered. "Easy, now. Easy. We'll have you home soon. Trust us."

Someone smashed a cloth over my face, and everything went black.

Dance
WITH THE
Sword
SARAH
K.L.
WILSON

Fly with the Arrow
Dance with the Sword
Give your Heart to the Barrow
Die with your Lord

Chapter One

THE LAW of Greeting bound me to him. The Law of Unraveling stole me away.

No one had told me about that law, either, but something in my bones already knew about the dark law that streaks all our memories with tiger-striped charcoal. It's the law that tells us nothing lasts forever. The law that reminds us that you can't account for everything that might happen before it does. The law that determines that if something bad *could* happen … then it will happen.

And it was *tha*t law which stole me away. That, and my own foolishness. For in this, as in so many things, I was author of my own undoing, crafter of my own sorrow, grand architect of my own destruction. I had betrayed my husband and with him, I had betrayed myself.

And though I tried to pull my way free of my brother's grip, though I tried to wrench the hood from my face, all I received in return was his firm rebukes and gentle shushing.

"Hush, Izolda. You have suffered a great harm and you are mad with it. You are drunk on magic. You will come back to sanity soon enough."

Sanity? I was sane as any other. Saner than him, perhaps, as I had not spent my life hunting a lost sister.

Sane or not, my heart felt like a patchwork quilt torn asunder by giant hands. One half flapped in tatters reminding me of my family and hearth, urging me to think of a brother's love so deep, so protective, that it crossed the walls of the world to come and snatch me from the hand of death.

But the other half fluttered and snapped and forced to my mind the look on my husband's face and the agony in his eyes as he bent to kiss me before I was torn away from him. It forced me to remember his hearth with its living tenant fire and his people with their fates caught in his hands.

And these two halves turned from torn halves to gnashing wolves that chased each other round and round in a vicious circle until I could not tell which was eating the other and which I wanted to survive. But with every bite that one tore from the other, it tore a chunk of flesh from my heart.

Eventually, the hood fell from my head and though Svetgin still held my arms tight at my sides, I could see again.

My breath gusted into the air in little puffs of lamb's wool, hanging so innocently for a bare moment before being snatched away by the wind as we rode.

We rode through the darkness on a well-traveled road, the moon – shockingly large and yellow for all that it was the lesser light of the heavens – coated the snow and trees with vermeil. It gilt each of our compatriots so that their horses looked as if by a snap of the fingers they could be frozen and placed on the mantle of a great room for the entertainment of guests centuries to come.

Each face I saw was human and grim as though they had ridden through death's halls and plundered the depths of hell itself – as I supposed they had.

And I was the trophy they returned with – a plain human girl made less plain by this strange mortal light.

I saw no sign of my husband and heard no echo of him in my mind.

But my brother spoke of him as we rode, his voice stuttering slightly as the horse's trot jarred us. "You'll forget whatever that reprobate did to you, Izolda. In time, you'll heal from it. I'll secure you a good husband. A sound one. One who does not steal you away. And our name will be cleansed of the reek of ill luck."

"I'm already married," I said through frozen lips. My words sounded too soft, too intangible.

"It wasn't real," Svetgin said. "It wasn't to a real person. It was like being married to death. You'll see. You'll understand. You just need time."

But time was what he was taking from Bluebeard because if my husband did not have my days, then he would not be able to play the Great Game of crowns and fates, and if he didn't play, all would be lost for Svetgin and for Pensmoore and for the mortal world.

An owl hooted in the shadows above and I shivered at his aching call. But still, the horses kicked up sprays of gilt snow like showers of cider and the shadows danced to the heavy drums of the hooves beating the ground. The snow was sharp-edged and sugar-slick as it is in late spring when winter tries with all her heart to cling to the world she's lost.

I tried to squirm in my seat to look behind us. Had they taken anyone else? Did they have Bluebeard back there somewhere?

My heart, my heart, what had I done? I'd betrayed him, I'd offered up life for death and full arms for a breast bereft of life.

But Svetgin held me fast, whispering, "Almost there. Almost there," as the hours bled one into another.

My heart beat as hard as the hooves of the horses and my breath raced so fast that I tasted blood in my breath, but it wasn't until we rounded the corner of a cliff that it was truly snatched from my lungs.

Before us, seated next to a river rushing with spring swell, stood a tower capped in a peak like a spiraled onion. I had heard of the peaked towers of Aayadmoore, but never see one before.

"Our allies," Svetgin told me, sounding relieved. "The Towers of Aayadmoore."

Within the tower was a light, and the light glowed through the stripes that spiraled vertically through the onion tower top. They must have been made of panes of glass cut to fit the curve of that tower peak. But who had such mastery at their disposal and why would they use it for that? The spiraled windows threw light across the ground around us, and shadows, too, and because of how the onion was curved, the light looked like claws trying to shred us to pieces.

"Why are we not in Pensmoore?" I asked, trying to keep my voice steady. If I objected too strongly – if I seemed anything other than grateful to have been wrenched from the arms of my husband – he would think I had gone mad. Something inside me prickled, warning me that no good could come of that. They locked mad women away in towers, didn't they?

I watched the tower and tried to clamp down on the voice whispering in my head that it was already too late, that my ruddy-cheeked brother had brought me here to live and die out my days in that tower top above.

I could taste the lack of magic in this world as one tastes burnt garlic on the back of the tongue. The colors of the indigo forest were less vibrant, the scents of pine and spring-melting snow less pungent, the timbre of voices less shivery. It was as if I had sucked the juice from a piece of summer melon but left the flesh unbitten. It was a pale miserable thing where once it had been bright and full and I itched with the loss of it – a ghost limb no longer mine.

Hooves pounded on the road, turning from the dull thudding of iron shoe on ground to the harsh clop of iron shoe on cobble. We were among the houses like a dog among grouse – sudden and predatory. I half expected them to scatter – but no. Only the houses of the Wittenhame flew. These buildings were nothing more than false teeth in a craven man's jaw – lifeless, ill-fitting, a shade of what could be.

Men in uniform let us pass through iron-wrought gates, saluting as if to superiors, and then we were in among closer, darker buildings seeming to crawl with military uniformed men like a hive of bees arranging itself for conquest.

And of course, this was so. I tried to remember who had pulled Aayadmoore's name for the Great Game. Was it not the Sword? Was this not his pawn in that game of kings and fates?

The sound of forges working into the night rang out, but there was too much bustle and hurry, too many moving bodies and animals for me to count or keep a tally of what we would face if ever we were again free.

We reached the dread doors of the palace far sooner than was reasonable. Far sooner than I would have liked. And Svetgin – finally – released my wrists as he drew me from the back of his mount. She huffed, shaking her matted grey mane, and rolling her horsey eye at me as if in reprimand for the scent of magic that clung to me still.

I shied back from her and found myself suddenly surrounded by the men who had kidnapped me and brought me to this foreign place. They formed up around me like an honor guard, leaving Svetgin in the middle with me as we were greeted by a man with a snowy white beard and the air of a chamberlain.

He bowed deeply. "We honor you, Brotherhood of Stolen Sisters. We honor your bravery. We honor your success."

There was a murmur from those around me that sounded like agreement.

"Please," the man said, "follow me. Refreshments have been prepared for you. The Lord Saberac has sent word that he is on his way and will offer you audience as soon as he arrives."

We were led into the tower and to my surprise, it was richly decorated – so richly that it seemed like too much. No one needed so many silken hangings, so many gilt doorways, so many small curiosities on tables and shelves, in corners, and lining the walls. They combined with the cloying smell of rose water to make my stomach clench within me.

But it was not long until we found the small dining room set aside for our use – and, I noted – guarded by soldiers whose uniforms did not match my brother's, nor any of the other men in our escort. Svetgin followed my eyes and whispered, "The hospitality of Aayadmoore is generous, is it not, sister?"

I offered a close-lipped smile. If ever there was a time to keep my lips closed, it was now.

"Is our mother well?" I asked him cautiously, but his face fell.

"Dead these ten years past," he said quietly, grief painting his face. Something lurched in my chest – something wild and painful that hurt and caught and tore at me.

I had been very fond of my mother. She was everything I was not in all the best ways.

"Father?" I gasped.

"Last winter the cough took him."

He wouldn't look at me now, wouldn't meet my eyes. I felt my lip trembling.

"Rolgrin?" I asked, barely able to choke out his name.

Svetgin coughed, trying to disguise his emotion. "The same cough a week later."

"Then you are Lord Savataz," I said and it felt like I had swallowed a lump of porridge too quickly and it was lodged in my throat.

"You are the last of my family," he said helplessly, and he seemed glad for the chance to turn away from me to other things.

The men sat without delay, feasting on the roasted meats and vegetables and toasting one another with wine for their great success – all but a spare few whose wounds were being treated in the room beside ours. And though my worried brother offered me a plate and then tried to ply me with morsels of his own, I did not eat or drink as if it were this world rather than the world of the Wittenbrand that might trap me within if I tasted their food or drank their wine. Already I felt trapped by it, caught in a nightmare I would not wish on my worst enemy. My family gone except Svetgin, and he so changed I did not recognize his heart.

The thought of eating made me ill, but the speculative looks of the men around the table when they eyed me made me more ill.

"You'll find a groom for her then, Savataz? A lordling of your nation?" one of them asked in an accent I did not know. He was not much older than I was. Far too young to be the brother of any bride my husband had taken.

I looked around the table. With the exception of one older man who stared at his lamb with hollow eyes and my brother, none of these men could be truly a brother or father of those he had taken. Was it a mantle passed from father to son, then? Carried through the years like a prized axe or a medallion of note?

"Indeed," Svetgin said firmly but when the man opened his mouth again my brother gave him the slightest shake of the head as if to silence him, and his mouth closed with a click. They deferred to him. Good. That meant we wouldn't see trouble from them.

But I froze when four men came in an hour into the feast, their hands shaking and eyes haunted.

"Is it done then?" the one who had inquired about my future asked, but he was waved off irritably by the newcomers who did not eat but buried themselves deep into their cups.

What were they waiting for? Could it have something to do with Bluebeard?

I watched them all with great care until the little chamberlain returned, his eyes bright as lingonberries and his smile more oily than the lamb dish.

"The Lord Saberac has sent a gift for the rescued lady," he said, bowing to my brother. "He will gather you forthwith to the top of the tower but bid me present this, first."

There was a gasp from around the table as the chamberlain held out a gold dress trimmed in olive green. It looked like the overly decorated room we were situated in. It looked like something a princess might wear to a fancy ball – but not a Pensmoore ball with that low V cut so deep into both the front and the back that it would brush my waist at either side and a pair of ribbons that ran to a heavy gem collar from the sleeves and across the shoulders to keep it up.

"A grand gesture," my brother said, looking at the garment warily.

"And yet I find I am clothed well enough and far too simple a woman to wear such finery," I said, sparing him the need to turn down the dress. My heart seized in my chest at the sight of that dress. Whoever wore it would be collared like an animal and no amount of gems could make up for that.

"You'll wear it all the same, fair lady," the chamberlain said smoothly, "and it will suit you well, for today is your wedding day."

A gasp went up around me and two of the men whooped, clinking their glasses.

"I'm already married," I said calmly. Surely, they'd realize this was a mistake.

"Her wedding day?" Svetgin asked, looking between the shock on my face and the excitement of his fellows.

"The Lord Saberac has declared he will marry your sister himself, Svetgin Lord Savataz, honoring you and erasing forever the shame of your house."

My heart sank at the look of relief on my brother's face. There would be no help from him. He was as relieved as if he had been told a death sentence had been lifted from his neck.

"And my living husband?" I pressed, needing to know the answer, and dreading it all the same.

"The Lord Saberac wanted you to be well assured that he would take care of that complication."

Chapter Two

WHEN I HAD BEEN CAGED within the dress and in the confines of its heavy collar, the chamberlain led us up spiraling stairs to the top of the tower. Two of the older men led the procession, bearded chins tilted upward in pride. They took time to brush their coats and give their sword hilts a quick polish while I was dressing. Such care inspired me to wonder who this Lord Saberac was that he had inspired such devotion in his men.

Curiosity pressed upon me, a leaden weight on a stack of papers, until I finally bent to its demand.

"Who is Lord Saberac?" I ask my brother as we mounted the stairs.

Even here, the iconry was heavy and rich. Such alcoves were set into the wall beside the staircase as could rival any collector's. Each alcove housed a sword of a different design, their designations and the battle they were known for displayed on plaques beneath.

In the center of the staircase where one could peek over the banister to the floor far below, there was a hanging display of more swords held at fanciful angles so that it could almost be imagined that they battled one another without any need for a man to direct their blows. I held my breath for the barest moment, daring one to move, to scrape metal upon metal, but no. They were locked in eternal struggle in this high column of blade brothers, entangled forever in enmity but they were mortal wrought and mortal displayed and would not spring to life and skewer us as they might in the Wittenhame.

I swallowed down worry. My practical eyes told me that so many swords spared for decoration means there were many more already in the hands of deadly men. It was that I ought to focus on and not the whims of the master of this tower who used perfectly good tools as fanciful decoration.

I forced myself to think past my fear. What did it say about this man that he hoarded gold to line his walls and swords his towers? Surely such a one would feel entitled. Those with much often felt they were due much more.

He had certainly helped himself to a bride thinking that was his due.

I gritted my teeth against a knot of fear in my throat. I had already been forced once into a marriage not of my choosing and though I had betrayed Blubebeard, he had not betrayed me. He had not laid a finger on me in any way that would cause me pain or grief. Something about this sword-lover made me think I would not be so lucky twice.

"The honored Lord Saberac saved this city two decades ago from a terrible flood," Svetgin said in an undertone, finally answering my question. "He arrived hours before it came with a dire warning to flee, but the people had not enough boats or carts to take their things with them, and so in his generosity, he provided ships and carts to load their precious things and keep them safe throughout the flooding. This city is wealthy because of his help."

"He had ships and carts waiting?" I asked, trying to keep the thorn from my words. Surely, I was not the first to notice how convenient that was for him. A flood was easy enough to cause if you had large horses and men to craft a dam and then burst it.

"He had been on a mission to bring sacred icons to the Seer of Tides and was returning, his fleet and carts emptied of their wealth."

I gave my brother a long look and trembled at what I saw because his face glowed with admiration and devotion. He did not see the obvious – that anyone can cloak their intentions with claims of reverence or that it was easy to be the savior of a city if you were the one who set it up for disaster.

I bit my lip and phrased my next question with care. "Surely they paid him for such a service? When they owed everything to him?"

"He would not hear of taking the riches they wished to lavish upon him," Svetgin said and for the first time since I had seen him as a man, he had some of his boyish energy back, some of the spark back in his step and gleam in his eye as if this story brought back memories of his youth. "We heard the tales even from where I was stationed with the army in Pensmoore. How he took only a tenth for all his trouble and expense. How the people were so grateful at such humility that they turned over to his use this tower and the keep below. There was little else on our tongues that spring."

"Indeed," I said noncommittally but to me this sounds like a Wittenbrand trick, and a simple one at that, for with a single swindle this man has bought for himself a reputation, a palace, and enough wealth to fund an army.

And now he had selected me as a bride. Why?

"It is a great honor to be his bride," Svetgin assured me. "An honor so deep we will never be able to repay him."

"Perhaps we could offer a tenth," I suggested and tried very hard to keep the bite from my tone.

Ahead of us, the chamberlain opened tall, gilded doors and proclaimed, "The Brotherhood of Stolen Sisters, the Pensmoore Lord Savataz, and his sister who is to be bride to the Lord Sabarac, Izolda of Savataz."

The Brotherhood swept into the room, carrying Svetgin and me in with them. The room was large and wide and the dawn outside the narrow windows broke in a red line across the horizon as if someone was gutting the dying sky like a brook trout.

I was wrong about the windows. No glass filled their empty settings. The wind, taking advantage of this, swept in – an uninvited and cold-fingered guest. The Brotherhood positioned themselves carefully as they spread out, keeping real metal behind their backs and not empty sky or tumultuous breezes. In this horrendous dress, the cold air kissed my skin with toothy bites, leaving me prickled and wary.

And as the Brotherhood opened up and out like an untimely flower caught blooming, I stole my first look at the man standing at the heart of all of this theatre.

I reeled back a step, gasping, prevented only from collapsing completely by my brother's firm hand on my arm.

"Well now, little darlin', I knew my collar would fit that pretty throat, but I wondered if you'd set it there yourself or have to be fitted for it," the

Sword drawled. He stood where the bloodred dawn could highlight the edges of his golden hair and cheeks, making it appear as if he had dusted himself with dried blood.

He wore scarlet brocade as another might wear ermine, the jacket lined with sealskin and unbuttoned to the waist like he thought he was Bluebeard – or perhaps was imitating him. His thread-of-gold lace-cuffed shirt was equally unbuttoned, showing a pale swath of hairless chest and chiseled midsection. I thought perhaps it was meant to look attractive. Instead, I found my tongue-twisting back in my mouth as if I'd eaten something rotten.

In one hand, he held the pole on which Grosbeak swung. He gestured to it with a smirk. "I brought to you your trinket – a pretty for my pretty."

"Run, Izolda," Grosbeak warned me – the words running out in a single breath before the Sword flicked his wrist and Grosbeak's severed head swung on its chain and struck the wall so hard there was a meaty *thunk.*

I swallowed down bile.

Svetgin cleared his throat awkwardly.

"Ah, my brotherhood, my knights, my crusaders in this cold dark world," the Sword said, sounding both sincere and mocking at the same time. He pulled a mother-of-pearl comb from his pocket – a cleverly designed little item, and combed back an errant lock before continuing. "You've succeeded where all else have failed and you have brought back behind this mortal veil one of your stolen sisters."

There was a ragged cheer as the Sword played to his audience, posing so that he was leaning on the post that held Grosbeak's severed head like a conquering king looking over his kingdom.

"And from it," he drawled, "you have snatched this artifact of devilry – this evidence of the evil of the man you begged me to help you conquer."

Another cheer.

"And I … I will honor that boldness. I will honor that bravery. I will honor the men with the intestinal fortitude of *bulls* who tore into their enemies and snatched back from them this prized lady. And I will honor you by marrying your stolen sister, sealing her honor, and removing from her the stain of her unholy marriage. And she and I will dance at our wedding before all my friends. What say you?"

His blue eyes twinkled, and I realized that by some magic he has made them look mortal.

The Brotherhood around me cheered, and my brother cheered loudest of all – almost as if they were under a geas, but I knew no magic was at work upon my companions except the magic of hope and ambition that sometimes make fools of otherwise moral men. I was deep in thought because I realized that what I said next would determine not just my own fate, but possibly the fate of Pensmoore, because the Sword wasn't playing for Pensmoore. I knew that. He was playing for Aayadmoore, and with it, the fate of our entire world.

I was so caught up in weighing my words that it was a moment before I noticed the chairs placed behind the Sword. They looked like upholstered thrones. One faced toward us, but the other was facing away, and chains were strung across the lowest point of its high back and those chains were very minutely moving. They appeared to be iron.

"But before I fulfill that promise," the Sword said, eyes glinting. "There is the matter of a fiend who needs to be dealt with."

He set Grosbeak's head down and with one wrenching movement, turned the backward chair around so that we could all see the occupant of it. And if I was not afraid before – and oh, but I was – now, fear took up a home in me, hollowing me to the core.

In the chair, chained with heavy iron, sat my husband, his beard blue and his bright eyes flashing. The red sunrise edged his chair in ghost flames so that it looked as if he were lit on the pyre, set ablaze with holy judgment.

His gaze was only for me. It found me from across the room and clung to me.

"And now I win the game, Arrow," the Sword whispered.

"Speak to my riddle, Sword," Bluebeard said with a twist to his mouth – his lip was split and bloody and a tiny trail of red rolled down and dripped from his chin. "What has blunted points and a blunted mind? What gold without to hide rot behind?"

"I'm done with your riddling," the Sword said, and I thought that maybe he'd forgotten his audience now that he was looking only at his enemy.

Quick as the tongue of a snake, he flicked a knife out and sliced through my husband's jacket and shirt, ripping them away from his body so that his silvery-scarred skin glowed lightly in the red dawn.

He spun, remembering us again.

"Long have your courts and kingdoms respected the strength of leaders who can vanquish their enemies completely. Today, you will help me vanquish yours."

"No," I said, clear as a bell. I hadn't come up with a speech. I didn't know what to say. And I had no weapon or clever idea, and yet the idea of standing here silent while Bluebeard was at this Wittenbrand's mercy wrenched something in me. I could not do it.

The Sword prowled over to me, a cat waiting for his moment to pounce, and just as I knew he would, he waited until he was only inches away before his hand shot out and gripped my throat. He did not squeeze. He merely held it.

"Your sister is bold, Savataz. Is she not my willing bride?" Dangerous, was the gleam in his eye.

"Of course she is," my brother said, looking shakenly between him and me, and I wondered if he remembered the day that was years ago for him but only a short week for me, when I had been stolen from him the first time. It had been a lot like this. Only that time an innocent man had died for me, and this time it would be my Wittenbrand groom. "There is no need to threaten her."

But I would not be spoken for any longer.

"There *is* a need for threats," I said smoothly. "The Sword has the right of it. For if he marries me against my will, I will do everything I can to turn all things against him. I will poison every dish and turn every blade. I will not rest until he is forever resting."

It was not a practical thing to say. The sensible thing to do would be to wait while he did as he willed to Bluebeard and then quietly allow him to marry me and keep myself still and composed until he inevitably grew bored and moved on to other things while I escaped his notice. And yet, I found that with my husband behind him, beaten and chained, practicality was slipping through my fingers.

The Sword patted my cheek and Svetgin tensed beside me. "Ah Izolda, your mind is twisted by all you have suffered. Is that not so, Lord Savataz?"

"It is," my brother said vehemently. "Blood and bone, but it is."

"And here, I wish only to spend her days as her ruthless rogue of a husband did – only for better, purer things."

My stomach flip-flopped.

"Hold her fast against her madness, Savataz. Hold her fast or I will not be responsible for what comes to pass."

My brother grabbed my arms firmly, standing behind me. "Is this necessary, Lord Sabarac? Can she not retire to some calm place while this necessity takes place?"

The Sword smiled lightly. "I think not. She must witness this death if she is to be my bride. I am told she says she is already married. Well. So she is. It is said in the long story of the founding of humanity that a man was born of dust and breath and from him was plucked a single rib – formed to be a woman. 'Why a rib?' it is asked. So that she may be close to his heart, closely tucked under his arm."

My brother sounded fervent when he said, "And so Izolda will be to you, only do not make her watch you slay her captor. She is already shaken, and women are gentle creatures."

Obviously, my brother had not married.

The Sword leaned in close and whispered to Svetgin, "Hold her, or she will pay with him, as will you." I felt the shock in Svetgin – in how he held me in wooden hands as the Sword whispered then in *my* ear. "And if you so much as flinch I will have you wear a rope of your brother's intestines as a garter at our wedding."

He drew back enough to meet my eye and then kissed me chastely on the cheek.

His kiss burned. Like a living thing I could not dislodge. Like a leech latched upon my face.

I quivered with fury.

Behind the Sword, someone cut our dialogue by yawning very loudly.

"If you're about done, Sword, I grow weary of theatrics," Bluebeard announced. "Dramatic talkers so rarely do dramatic deeds."

Chapter Three

THE SWORD WHIRLED and his blade leapt from his scabbard as if it were alive. He tossed it in the air, let it spin three times, and then snatched it from the air, holding the hilt in a backhand. I barely had time to catch my breath before he had it spinning again, but this time, I ignored his trick. I didn't need to watch men show off. I'd seen enough of that to last my entire life – short as it may be.

"Stand him up," the Sword barked, gesturing to the Brotherhood men closest to Bluebeard. "Mind his chains. The ones on his wrists must remain."

The Brotherhood scrambled to obey and there was an edge of anticipation to their actions that I did not like – the brightness of raven eyes and crow beaks just before they fall upon the fallen.

Why was Bluebeard doing nothing? I knew he was powerful. I'd watched him take the head from a man like another might pluck an apple. I'd watched his magic heal grievous injuries. I knew he didn't need to let himself be manhandled, and yet, he did. And all the while, his light cat's eyes were locked on mine, never wavering. As if he were speaking some wordless ballad to me in his every stillness.

"Hold your sister, Savataz," the Sword said, his voice again both sincere and mocking. Perhaps he was insane. It would explain so much. "Remind her not to flinch."

But I was not a swoony girl. I would not faint or flinch. Not even for this.

It took all my willpower not to grimace when the Brotherhood men stepped back, leaving Bluebeard standing on his own, hands trussed before him. Where the iron chains had touched his skin, the skin was red and puffy as if he'd been burned. His lip and one of his eyes were swollen and darkened.

Even so, he watched me, his eyes never wavering, that single line of blood down his cheek looking forever as if he had shed a single crimson tear.

The Sword leaned in toward Bluebeard and whispered something to him, and I knew what it would be – it would be an identical threat to the one he'd made to me. I knew it like I knew my own name. He was that predictable.

And then he danced back a step, the lightness in his feet holding a strange joy incongruous with the moment, before his blade flicked, *swish, swish, swish,* and my husband's clothing fell to the ground, leaving him in nothing but his iron chains.

I felt my cheeks flame, but I held his gaze as he held mine.

"You're not my type, Sword," he drawled. "And that was my favorite pair of buckskins. You owe me five gold pieces for those, though I'll forgive you the shirt. It was last season's fashion."

"When I'm done here, I'll owe you so much more than five gold pieces," the Sword hissed and to my horror, I felt anticipation growing in the air around me. I risked a glance to the side and saw the Brotherhood men were tense – but not with the tension of those about to fight but with the tension of those about to savor. They wanted my husband's pain. They wanted it very badly.

"How comes it, Lord Riverbarrow, that you are the same as any mortal man when stripped of your finery? Shall we toss a coin for his fate, men?" the Sword asked, rolling his sword handle around his forearm in a neat trick that made it appear almost as flexible as leather instead of pure steel. "You can call the toss, Arrow."

"Heads," my husband said, smirking at Grosbeak whose eyes flicked back and forth between him and the Sword as if he was watching a game of shuttles. "I collect them, you know."

"Not anymore you don't," the Sword said with a laugh but as he produced a gold coin, Bluebeard's eyes locked on mine again.

I swallowed at the intensity there and then gasped when his mind met mine with speech.

Speak to my riddle, wife of mine.

I thought we'd lost that when we left the Wittenhame.

My mouth was suddenly very dry.

What must he think of me, he who had been stripped bare by his enemies and paraded before them in chains because of me. Because I took a single day of my life and allowed it to be stolen by his enemies. Tenson danced down every nerve.

Who cuts out my heart and wears it as her crown? Who holds its shattered fragments in her palms?

Anguish wrung my heart like a rag.

I gasped. His eyes – blood of gods and men – those eyes. They gutted me. And yet, I could not lie to him. I could not betray him in that, too.

I do, I said.

And before I could say anything else, the Sword's blade spun through the air again, and this time when he caught it backhanded, he spun with it and plunged it directly into Bluebeard's side with a slow flourish.

A scream tore from my throat, but Svetgin held me fast, not letting me so much as move an inch.

My husband's gaze was still locked on mine. It glazed over for a moment as pain washed over him. He coughed, blood spattering from his lips in tiny droplets.

Through gritted teeth he spoke, enunciating each word with care.

"It's a good sword, Towerrock, but I do so hate it when they stick."

A foul expletive tore from the Sword and then he twisted the blade and a moan twisted from Bluebeard's mouth with his movement. The Sword leaned over my husband trying to free his blade, and I bit hard on my lip until blood wetted it as I tried with all my power not to move, not to flinch.

Husband of mine, I reached for him with my mind, but found only pain. *Master of my fate.*

But why was I holding myself back from flinching when the Sword had already done his worst? For what could be worse than this?

"No," I gasped, wrenching against Svetgin's powerful grip. "Leave him. Take my life instead."

The Sword turned to look at me and nausea rippled through me at the look of sheer delight on his face, but more than that, at what was in his hand. He sheathed his sword, cupping his prize in his palm.

"How do you sever the wife from the husband? A puzzle for the ages. And one I have solved, friends," he said.

Behind him, Bluebeard fell to his knees, chained hands moving so that his bare arms could cup the ragged hole in his body. His eyes caught mine once more. In them, violence and certainty, fury and agony all mixed up in a poison so potent I could feel it from here.

I'm sorry. I'm so sorry. Tears streaked down my face, but my mental voice could not call back my betrayal. It could not bring back his life.

His eyes glassed over, and his head slumped forward.

A sob choked in my chest.

"Hand me the gold item you see beside you, Knight Wheavon," the Sword ordered and one of the Brotherhood passed him an item that looked very much like a crown. But it was fitted with a locking bracket and into that bracket, the Sword slotted his trophy. It fit perfectly into the swirling metalwork meant to hold it – a ghastly, white rib, streaked in the blood of my husband and wrenched from his breast by this mad Wittenbrand. "Death may not be enough to sever the tie between man and wife. This I know. But what if I take back what is hers by right? And what if I take it for myself? The ancient rib from which woman was formed. Poetic, don't you think?"

Triumphantly, the Sword crowned himself with the bloody crown.

"I need no marriage vows to own you, Izolda Savataz. You are already mine."

But I didn't care what he did – he and his bloody trophies. I didn't care what claims he made on me. There was only one man I cared about. And as I watched him, my eyes burning with unshed tears, he looked up one more time and I could tell the effort cost him, naked, ruined, and murdered as he was. His mental voice was still clear even though it was faint as a whisper.

One bone of mine he has taken, and yet in the marrow of each of the rest is the song of your name.

And before I could say anything in return, he lurched to his feet, slipping in the pool of his own blood, and without a word, he leapt like a dog into a lake – full-bodied and joyful – out one of the gaping spiral holes in the side of the tower.

I wanted to scream. I did. But it was like the scream was stuck inside me, like it was screaming me and not the other way around.

The Sword cursed loudly. And I could not understand why, because my Bluebeard was gone – fallen to his death. No, *leaping* to his death.

A monstrous choice.

The room swam with my tears. I dashed them angrily aside and now – now! – Svetgin released me so that I could wipe them, and I bolted to the gaping hole in the tower, not caring that my skirts trailed through my husband's blood, searching for his pale body on the rocks below.

What I saw instead, was the wings of a great raven – greater than I'd ever seen before – glowing with the gold of the bright dawn. My breath hitched in my throat at the sight of him. On his back, he carried the Arrow, Lord Riverbarrow, Prince of the Wittenbrand, and the one man who I had just realized owned my heart.

Chapter Four

I WATCHED the Sword fighting to compose himself and for just a single moment his eyes flickered like he couldn't control whatever illusion made them appear human and then he turned to the Brotherhood. His calm smile didn't even appear forced. He was very, very good at hiding his emotions. I made note of that. I might need to remember he could do that.

My mouth was dry as dust. I ran a thick, dull tongue over my dusty lips.

"Well, we had a little of our own back before the end, did we not brothers?" There were murmurs around us and the Sword half-bowed his head. "You all know why I came to you – how I had a sister stolen from me. How I was determined to stand with you – to finally lay hand on the inhuman creature who was stealing our sisters. Our revenge has been met and now I will honor Svetgin's sister with the marriage promised her. One that is blessed, chosen by her family, and a haven to her and her children."

I did not believe a word he said. I watched him from the side of my eye – the gore-flecked bone in his crown drying as he spoke. A scrap of flesh hung off it, fluttering when he turned his head too fast. He'd need that mother-of-pearl comb again to tidy his hair when this was done.

One thing, I knew. I had not lied. If he forced me to marry him, I *would* find some way to kill him. I had not thought myself a murderer before I was stolen away to the Wittenhame, but the death of such a one would not burden me with guilt. And I had seen better men slain before me.

My hands flexed and unflexed as I thought about the open swirl of window I stood beside. I could feel the breeze stirring over the waking city below, sucking at me as if calling me into its embrace. The hot white of full-blown dawn washed warm over me as if the sun wished to offer succor, as if the sky itself wished to bless me, or maybe to welcome me.

If I tried to push him over the edge, would I go over, too?

Could I do that?

My thoughts raced, mounting to a conclusion. My parents were dead. My only living brother caught in the fist of a mad Wittenbrand. My husband named me betrayer.

I swallowed and now the dryness of my mouth was tickling my throat.

I was not done living. Not yet ready to end my life intentionally. No, I would be sensible about this. I would bide my time and find a more subtle means of murder – a means that would achieve my ends without taking my own life with it.

They'd been speaking behind me as I weighed the worth of my life, but now someone cleared his throat gently and I turned to see my brother. There was a look of compassion in his eye as he offered me a hand and also – was that an edge of terror. Did he begin to realize what he had dragged us both into?

"Come, Izolda, the priest is here."

"You know your Lord Saberac is no good man, do you not, Svetgin," I asked gravely.

He did not look me in the eye. "You have been promised to him. I cannot change it now."

I tipped his chin toward me with a single finger, and he met my eyes reluctantly.

"The moment you leave this room," I breathed, "Run as far and as fast as you can go, brother, and do not look back to this place. Not to save me. Not to come to the aid of a friend. Not to carve out your revenge. Or you will be caught into this spider's web with the rest of us and you have seen now for yourself that the only way free is with the price of much blood."

He swallowed, but I did not want to hear his response. I wanted to leave my words to sit heavy on him – a mantle he could not dislodge.

I turned. And when I did, I was surprised to see that already Bluebeard's blood had been scrubbed from the floor and his chair removed.

A priest in full raiment stood with holy chalice in hand and beside him, the Sword had posed himself, one hand behind his back like a lord at a ball.

I could see no reason why the Sword would want to marry me. Was it only to spite Bluebeard? Or did he really think that he could spend my days, too?

My brow was furrowed as I lifted my blood-soaked hem and stepped to where the priest and the Sword waited.

"I do not wish to remarry," I told the priest.

"It matters not, lady," he said seeming unconcerned. "We care not for your whimsical Pensmoore ways here in Aayadmoore. Your guardian has sworn you as bride. Your bridegroom accepts you as such. You have no will nor wiles here." Well, then. It seemed there were madder lands than even the Wittenhame. The priest turned to the Sword. "Have you paid the price to the guardian?"

"I have," he gave a confident smile as if he was a true bridegroom sure of his suit and not a monster wearing the rib of my husband for a crown. "By the rescue of Izolda Savataz – led by me – I have obtained the right of marriage."

"And do you confirm he has paid in full?" the priest asked my brother.

"I do," my brother's voice was shaky.

I had no allies in this room.

Except one.

I stole a look at Grosbeak. His head had been all but forgotten by everyone assembled. A strange and horrible curiosity to the mortals and a traitor to the Sword. He frowned at me and then winked. I thought that must mean he was still with me – still my creature, or guide, or whatever he was to me.

It gave me the courage to keep my head high.

"And do you assembled here declare that you are witnesses to this agreement and covenant between these two houses?" the priest asked.

There was a murmur of approval amongst the Brotherhood. I turned to look in every eye. They had lived their lives and possibly given their fortunes in pursuit of sisters lost long ago to them. And yet now they blithely gave a woman away unwillingly to a husband not of her choosing. My tongue curled on the bitterness of irony – thick as the scent of blood still lingering in the air.

"Then by the authority of crown and kingdom, you are husband and wife," the priest said.

A shiver of fear rushed through me as the Sword's calm façade cracked and a look of predatory anticipation filled him. He hunched forward slightly, as if he wanted to reach for me and was only just stopping himself, and then the predatory look shifted to one of concentration and then confusion.

"They're not there," he whispered. "Not there. But they must be." He shook himself and looked at the priest. "Fully married? Man and wife?"

"Yes, indeed," the priest said, beginning to move toward the door. "And may you have many years of prosperity together and heirs of your body to maintain your line."

My second husband's hand shot out and caught the priest by the collar. "You're certain, priest?"

The priest raised an eyebrow, and the Sword removed his and with a slight nod of his head that was almost an apology.

"You're as married as any other man in Aayadmoore. As much as priest and ceremony can make you, at any rate."

There was an edge to the Sword that almost looked like panic and for a moment I was confused and then my lips parted as I understood. My days. He thought to secure them by marrying me. He must not be able to access them as Bluebeard had.

He crossed to me in a single step and grabbed me by my hair yanking me close to him. "Where are they? Why can I not feel them?"

I gasped in pain, but I said nothing. I would not help him. Not even to understand what was so very plain to me – that he could not steal my days from Bluebeard and that if it were in my power, I certainly would not give them up.

His brow furrowed and then cleared, and his bright eyes shot up to me in sudden revelation. Ice ran cold through me. That look in his eyes was too close to the one I'd seen there right before he took my true husband's rib.

"Out," he said, his voice like a sword cutting through the air. "All of you, out."

"Out, my lord?" Svetgin asked nervously. "Will we not toast the happy couple?"

"But we are not a couple yet, are we, Savataz?" the Sword growled. "We are only half married. Married by ceremony but not by deed."

My brother's face paled as understanding dawned and I felt myself go suddenly lightheaded, too. I'd been spared the cruelty of an unwanted wedding night once before. It seemed I would not be spared again.

Chapter Five

"YOU DISHONOR my sister with such boldness, sir," Svetgin said and something like hope sprang into my breast.

"I said, *out*," the Sword roared, backhanding Svetgin when he took a step forward. The movement pulled my hair and I blinked back tears, grabbing the Sword's fist in both of mine as I tried to keep my head close enough that he wouldn't yank out all my hair by the roots. "A deal was made, Savataz, and a bride given. Would you claim now that you have been cheated?"

"I thought you were a good man," Svetgin said thickly, cupping his cheek with one hand. "A man of honor."

He reached for his sword, but one of his fellows slammed the hilt back into the scabbard, giving my brother a silent shake of the head in warning.

"Come, Svetgin," another said. "Leave him to his wedding night."

"That is my sister. And he speaks of her like she is property," Svetgin said, chin trembling.

"You sold her to me as property," the Sword said, dragging me with him as he stalked forward. "You offered her up to me as mine – her inheritance and her body to be used by me as I will. What did you think you were doing when you made our bargain?"

My brother's face went deathly pale – as if he had just realized what he'd done. As if he'd just realized that this day is a mirror to the last day that he was held back by others and I was sold away. Only this time, a whole nation wasn't saved with my innocence. This time it was only a ragged patch on his reputation. It must be a terrible thing to realize you are a fool and have been a fool all your life.

I tried not to judge too harshly knowing how painful that must be, but it was hard not to condemn with the Sword making threats against my person.

I swallowed down a burst of fear. I must not let myself imagine what would come next or it would paralyze me. My husband lost a rib for my betrayal. I would lose my dignity and my agency and the last shreds of my innocence.

No, I must not think of it.

I wanted to be ill.

I wanted to be dead.

I closed my eyes for too long and it was only the yank of the Sword tugging me again by the hair that snapped them back open. Blood and spittle flew across my face. He had hit my brother again. Stark red blood on a shining floor. Harsh bruises blooming on a swollen lip.

"Take your treacherous brother away," he said to the Brotherhood. "And leave me to my wedding night."

What is it in a man that leads him to do what he says he will never do? What is it that makes him go against what he has proclaimed to be his virtue? Is it shame? I thought it might be, for there was shame in every face as they dragged my brother away, ignoring his cries and pleas.

I shook so hard my teeth rattled as the men left – every one of them refusing to look at me, refusing to let their eyes stray on what they were about to allow.

It was shame that filled me from brim to bottom the same as it did to them. Deep, terrible shame. For I could not blame anyone for what had happened but myself. If I had not taken that gem from the hourglass, I would not be in the mortal world now. If I had told Bluebeard what his enemies were planning, I would be with him still, he would be uninjured, and he would have the head of any man who so much as touched me.

The door shut with a snick and the Sword did not wait before flinging me against the remaining chair. The world reeled as I hit it, striking so hard that the chair toppled, taking me with it. I blinked back pain and tears as pain blossomed in my back and head and one of my shoulders from where I had struck the ground.

I was sprawled across the chair, the room spinning around me in a whirl of gilded metal and bright sunlight.

I needed to find my feet.

I needed to get a weapon.

I scrambled to my feet, tripping on my dress. I was like a newborn kitten. None of my limbs was obeying me.

"I'll have those days, mortal," the Sword said, looming over me. "I'll have them if I must take your tainted mortal flesh to mine every night from now until the end of the Game."

He worked at the remaining buttons on his jacket and then flung it to the side, turning to his shirt and with each item he removed I felt fear coil deeper in me, swelling up within me until thought was squeezed out entirely and only terror remained to gibber at the back of my mind.

I felt something like a prick of surprise – or possibly rage – in the back of my mind but there was no room for any thoughts of that. I had seen a chance.

I sprang, leaping as far and fast as I could go, and snatching up Grossbeak's pole in both my hands. I held him out in front of me like a talisman.

"I don't like this! I don't like it at all!" Grossbeak shrieked.

The Sword dropped his shirt to the ground and looked up, surprise and then delight flooding his features. He drew his sword silently from the scabbard, stalking forward.

"A little dance before we couple, mortal girl? A little game to get the blood flowing? I'll play your games, but know, I will not hold back. I will take you to wife bloody and broken if I must, or if you surrender, I will relent and leave your skin in one pretty piece."

"We both know I'm not very pretty," I said, trying to space my feet out well to give me room to maneuver.

"And yet, your value lies elsewhere. How many mortals have I tried to take days from? And none has given up a single one. And yet my rival has married sixteen women and taken their days, taunting me with his added power." Here it was. The reason his teeth were clenched. The reason he stalked me and made me prey. "I will have what is his. If he can take them from you, then so can I. And I will wring them from you by whatever means I must."

"I don't stand up well to sword slashes," Grosbeak interrupted as I held him higher, his voice trembling. "I really think I should warn you about that. I won't last very long as a weapon."

I ignored his panic, waiting. I knew the Sword was not a patient man. He would not hesitate in striking first.

I had judged the Sword accurately. He whipped out a single thrust and I batted it away with the pole from which Grosbeak hung. The chain rang against the blade and Grosbeak screamed. "Gourds of the Netherworld!"

I spun backward, keeping the lantern pole high.

"You'll not have me," I told the Sword firmly when Grosbeak's echoes had faded. "Not as wife or as anything else."

"I have had many things that uttered the same," the Sword said languidly.

I was not skilled with the sword. I was not large enough to make this a fair fight even if I was. And on top of that, it was clear he was very skilled – and toying with me. He stretched out the showy musculature of his arms and shoulders as he moved, glancing at himself from time to time in the small stand mirror to one side of the room as if he enjoyed the sight of himself playing with me as much as he enjoyed the game.

I fought determinedly, using every scrap of energy I had to parry his thrusts and turn his blade. I was light on my feet and had good balance, but that wouldn't have been enough even if my newly healed back had not made me stiffer in movement than I would have preferred.

"I have enjoyed this game, mortal girl," the Sword said, "but now I run low on patience. Let's have this marriage completed that I may spend your days as I must."

And this time when he thrust his blade it narrowly missed my head. It was all I could do to dodge away but his quick second strike knocked Grosbeak's pole from my hands, ringing the metal so hard my fingers buzzed with the strike.

His sword hilt crashed against my cheek before I could gasp, sending me spinning. I hit the ground hard, not even sure which parts of me had struck, only that I must find my feet again or all was lost. I scrambled upward, my heart racing, too filled with the urgency of the moment to feel the pain of my injuries.

The world reeled and spun as if I were in a small boat instead of on land.

I'd just made it to my feet when his hand shot out and seized my throat. He took two steps forward, driving me backward. I tried to squirm from his grip, but my feet slipped, tangled in my too-full skirts. No wonder he put his women in these dresses. They were as immobilizing as chains. The thought felt foreign in my pounding head.

He pinned me against one of the winding wall sections, his grip around my throat like iron. I grabbed his wrist in both hands, fighting against it. I couldn't catch a full breath. My throat ached from his grip.

And now panic flared in my belly. I had thought to fight – and if it had looked as if I might fail, then to fling myself from the tower. I had not thought he could so easily overpower me, and a sense of furious futility wrenched through me.

His eyes were bright and mad. He would have no pity on me until he'd claimed what he came for.

"Enough with this dance, let's see it done with," he snarled.

A knock came – sharp and urgent – again and again.

"What?" the Sword roared.

"Lord Saberac! Lord Saberac, it's urgent!"

His face flushed crimson. "Not urgent enough to disturb me. Leave!"

Again, the wild knocking, and the Sword spun, though his hand kept my neck pinned to the wall.

"If you interrupt me at my sport a second time, I will take your head!" he roared.

"Lord Saberac, they are at the tower gates and will soon overwhelm us!"

"Viscera of the seas!" he cursed and his hand dropped its grip leaving me to slump to the ground.

I heaved, all my suppressed terror suddenly spilling out.

He flung himself away from me and toward a window so that he had a hand on either side of one of the openings while his whole body leaned out and over to survey the land below. A stream of curses turned the air a vibrant blue.

Curious – too curious, since it was curiosity that led me here – I crawled to the edge and looked down below.

The ground crawled with figures in the stark black uniforms of Pensmoore. Their banner flew over them, snapping in the morning wind. As I watched, the air over one part of the city shimmered, and then a tear – as if in a piece of cloth – opened and men poured from it like water from a hole in a bucket. As fast as they arrived, they made war upon the city, tearing guards from their posts, skewering horses on their spears, and kindling angry flames. Watching them aged me a year in the blink of an eye.

"Psst, lady," Grosbeak whispered.

His pole was right beside me. With trembling hands, I reached for it, barely catching it in my grip.

A blow sent me sprawling backward, head ringing.

"Do you see what you've done?" the Sword asked, his words deadly quiet compared to how he'd roared at the messenger – but I was much more terrified of this quiet Sword. "You've distracted me as my enemies close in."

I tried to reply but nothing came from my crushed throat except a croak. I clutched at it, panic flaring. I had no voice to even scream.

He took a stalking step toward me and froze, a look of utter terror painting his face as he looked up at the window. A shadow blocked the bright morning sun, and a voice rang out.

"Sword!"

I pushed up to my elbows just in time to see a cloud of colorful songbirds – birds of every size and color and kind – fly in through the open window in a rainbow burst. They bore a great burden on their many tiny bodies – my cat-like husband. A cacophony of fluttering filled the air, a thousand lacy wings caressing the strands of the winds as he arrived in their flurry, prince of wings, sovereign of wind.

A single blue feather drifted to land right in front of me as my mouth fell open in awe.

In one hand, he gripped his sword. With the other hand, he tossed a severed head at the Sword.

"Yours. I believe."

My eyes were full with the sight of him, my heart racing.

He was arrayed in fine clothing and finer weaponry. Which alone was stunning when he'd left here only perhaps an hour ago and then he was both naked and mortally wounded. But though he was dressed, there was a bloody red stain across his side, soaking shirt and jacket and trousers in bright crimson.

My eyes flicked from that to the head as the Sword caught it. It was – or at least had been – Knight Wheavon, the member of the Brotherhood who had handed the Sword his crown. Bluebeard's eyes never took it in at all. They were all for me.

"This," Bluebeard said, striding toward me, "is mine."

He offered me a hand with a questioning quirk to his eyes, but I did not hesitate at all. I grasped it firmly and let him pull me to my feet. I snatched up Grosbeak from the ground while I could. He was my only weapon.

"I thought you collected these," the Sword said, staring at the head. His voice tried for nonchalant, but only managed hollow.

"Heads or wives?" Bluebeard asked flippantly. "I collect both. But while I'm happy to give you that head as a gift – a tip of the hat from one competitor to the other – if you harm my wife again, I shall not suffer you to live, rules of the great Game aside."

The Sword looked up, and for a moment his eyes sparkled like he meant to attack Bluebeard, and yet, there was fear in his movements. Perhaps Bluebeard unchained was an entirely different thing.

"My city is being ransacked. My bride stolen. If you think this is over, Lord Riverbarrow, you have not thought at all," he said, instead. "I will make war on you. And it will not matter that killing you would lose me the game because I will revel in your suffering for the rest of your shortened life. I will take from you every slice of life you wish to taste and sour it with the life's blood of everyone you love."

"Then I suppose it's a good thing that I love so few," Bluebeard said, spinning me suddenly and lifting me in his arms like a bridegroom carrying a bride. "Next time you try to steal a man's wife, you should confirm that she wants to be stolen. A woman taken against her will is never truly yours."

The Sword sneered. "You would know, Arrow."

"You're a tasteless unworthy thing, Sword. I spit you from my mouth."

He lifted me into the air so suddenly that I barely had a chance to gasp, and then we were carried out the window on the backs of hundreds of colorful songbirds, their songs and cries below us punctuating every movement, leaving the Sword behind with a dead man's head in his hands, a look of shock on his perfect features, and my husband's rib in his crown.

Chapter Six

BIRD SONG CAN BE ephemeral and uplifting or insistent and obnoxious. Here in the sigh of the wind and the gasp of the air, it carried the melody of relief. Having never been a bird, I had never flown, and yet it was not the curiously unsteady sensation of flying that gripped me now but the warring fears within me. Somehow, though they opposed one another, that only increased the power of each one over me.

I was terrified of the conflict unrolling underneath me, the tiny bloody figures rolling across the ground or lying slain in final repose were like the denizens of a particularly gruesome tapestry. But I was just as afraid of flying up so high above them even though that meant avoiding the conflict. Could these little birds truly hold us? What if they perished in the attempt and we – also – fell to our deaths. My face hurt from where I'd been hit – aching so much I feared one eye might swell. If a single blow could do that to me, what might bearing so much weight do to these small birds?

And this was not my only fear. I was utterly terrified of what the Sword had planned to do to me – both in ravaging my physical body and my spirit. But I was nearly as afraid of what judgment Bluebeard may have in store for me now that I had betrayed him and put him in a position to be mortally wounded. It was only his retrieval of me that had saved me from the Sword, but what fury must he feel for me now?

I must be practical about this. It was good to fly rather than to fall. It was good to be rescued rather than ravaged. Whatever came next, I would deal with that. I would not borrow trouble that was not mine to take.

"I didn't marry him willingly," I said to Bluebeard, hoping he would accept that small offering. Just because you are starting to realize that the current of your heart turns to someone, doesn't make it easy to bare that heart to them.

He did not reply. It was, after all, day. And he did not speak to me in the day. But he'd spoken to me mind to mind, and he could do that, so if he wasn't speaking, then he probably did not wish to.

And yet, I had things to say. Keeping secrets didn't work if you wanted to be someone's ally. Or friend. Or wife.

I swallowed.

My father always said that if you wanted to ride a spirited horse, you must seize the reins firmly and keep a solid seat.

I felt a pang of sadness at the thought. He would never say that again. Never offer his other practical, bluff advice. And I needed it now more than ever. How did you make amends with a wild man who both thought he possessed you and saw you as his betrayer?

Carefully.

You did it carefully or you didn't manage it at all.

I swallowed and took the reins in hand firmly.

"I originally thought to spy on you," I said, keeping my tone calm and frank. Emotion would not help matters. He would just think I was trying to manipulate him. Even with my calm tone, his hands tightened around me. "My king asked it of me."

I met his eyes, and he raised an eyebrow. I had forgotten that he didn't want me to call the King of Pensmoore "my king." I cleared my throat to cover my error and continued.

"It seemed reasonable at first. And then I met your people and I decided I did not want to spy on you. I wanted to work with you."

Bluebeard had a remarkably expressive face. It seemed paler than usual, nearly green, but the way his lips twisted conveyed all his distrust so clearly that he might as well have said "liar" right then and there.

"When Coppertomb suggested that I steal one of my own days, I was tempted to try. After all, having some small part of my fate in my own hands had an appeal. Would you like someone else to own every one of your days and to spend them as they pleased?"

His face seemed to soften slightly at that, but he still shook his head disdainfully as if I should have known better. And, of course, I should have. Still, he remained silent.

We were flying away from the city now, flying low over the river that divided Pensmoore from Aayadmoore. I could feel the spray of water on my face we were so close. If the birds dropped us, we would rush down the rapids and be dashed on the rocks. I could almost feel it happening, see it step by step in my mind's eye.

I wrenched my gaze away and back to him.

"I didn't plan to give him the garnet. Not in the end. In the end I decided I wanted to work with you – to be your ally. Maybe even your friend."

He remained silent.

I sighed. "I suppose that is over now."

And he did not disabuse me of the thought, he merely tore his gaze from mine and looked toward where we were flying.

The birds dipped lower and lower and when we reached the bank of the river on the other side, they suddenly let loose, scattering in a hundred different directions.

It was hardly a fall. Almost more of a stumble.

But Bluebeard's arms lost their grip on me, and I sprawled in the tufted grass along the gravel shores before I realized he was beside me, eyes closed and face paler than death.

The wings of hundreds of birds flapped around me, brushing my face and arms and hair as they dispersed and leaving behind a flurry of falling feathers in white and black, brown and gold, blue and scarlet. They fled like my hope – spooked and scattered.

When I could see again, there was Bluebeard, passed out on a thick tuft of grass, his face pale as death. His birds had fled with his consciousness.

I sat up, rustling the tall grass.

"You promised me revenge on the Sword, and yet at your first encounter you let him trounce you completely," Grosbeak complained from where he lay. He kept spitting between words as the sandflies we kicked up tried to swarm in his mouth. "Useless! You had to be saved by the Arrow! No Wittenbrand woman needs a man to save her."

"I doubt there are any who need a useless woman to carry them around or shake the flies from their mouths, either," I said wryly, shooing the flies away and setting his head upright so he could watch me. "Any tips on gut wounds?"

I pushed Bluebeard onto his back, ignoring how beautiful he was in near-death, like the memorial painting of a battlefield after a great victory.

I unbuttoned his fox-fur-lined shirt and pulled it from his trousers so I could get a better look at his wound. Flowers sprung up around him. The tiny plants pushing through the earth and tumbling up toward the sky before blossoming into white with purple hearts and purple with yellow hearts. There were a hundred of them where he'd passed out, and more surrounding him before I was able to so much as expose his skin. What did it mean to be married to a husband who did this to the land and sky? Whose very presence made it come alive?

I shook my head. Wounds didn't tend themselves and I needed to get to work. Someone had put a rough bandage around his side and even set it with silver stitches, but two of the stitches had pulled loose and his entire belly and leg on that side were drenched in blood.

"Looks like he stitched himself. That's his silver thread. For all the good it did him," Grosbeak sneered.

I felt a chill go through me. Had he been unable to heal himself because he didn't have access to my days? But no, the wound was crusted a little as if it was trying to heal.

"It looks days old," I muttered. "But it was no more than an hour ago that he was ripped apart."

"It was days for *you*," Grosbeak snorted. "Or did you not notice that time is a game for the Wittenbrand?"

"What do you mean?" I asked, trying to clean Bluebeard's wound with a piece of my dress. There were so many layers of skirts that surely one of them could be spared.

"Did you not notice that mere days in the Wittenhame were years here in the mortal world?"

"That did seem to be clear when I met my younger brother as a grown man and learned my parents were dead," I said acidly.

"Don't give me that tone, mortal. It works just as easily in the other direction. Your Wittenbrand husband must have used his key when he fled on the raven. And gone home. And there he would have dressed his wound and clothed himself before returning to bring the armies of Pensmoore directly to the Sword's door. That must have cost you."

"Cost *me?*"

"Well, it's your days he spent, isn't it? Feel any older? Maybe seeing your first grey hair?" he snickered.

"What?" I glanced at the braid tumbled over my shoulder and gasped. There *was* a white thread in it. Just one.

"I'd guess he took a whole year to make that little trick happen. Maybe even more." Grosbeak laughed. He always sounded particularly nasty when he laughed – especially when his laughter was aimed at me.

I opened my mouth to object and then snapped it tight. It was hardly sensible to complain now – when complaint would do me no good. Hardly practical to complain when he'd brought that army for the purpose of freeing me. Though the cost seemed too high for the gain. My possession of myself and my innocence – while of incredible importance to me – did not seem like something others should die for.

"Why didn't he spend them to heal this wound, then?" I asked sharply. The bleeding would not stem with my bandage no matter how tightly I wrapped it and I had no other supplies. Worry made my voice tight and annoyed.

"Well, that's the Arrow for you. Disgustingly noble at the worst possible moment. He won't take from you for himself, but he'll take and take if he thinks it will be good for you. Typical."

"He thought a war would be good for me?" I asked icily.

"They were *already* at war. It was only a matter of who took the opening strike."

"And my husband thought it should be him."

Grosbeak rolled his eyes. "Is that the Sword lying bleeding on the ground? You don't call stealing the Arrow's rib a strike? Did he steal your brain when I wasn't looking?"

I ignored him, but I couldn't keep my telltale cheeks from heating.

"If you're just about done fussing with a wound that won't heal, you should come and look at my head," Grossbeak said. "I think he fractured my skull back there."

"And what can I do about that?"

Grosbeak grunted. "Fine. Then look to yourself. You have a shiner, and a split cheek, and your shoulder is nothing but one huge bruise. And I'm being a gentleman and not mentioning that neck. Actually, if you were wondering if mottled purple was your color, now we know. It isn't."

I gave him a death glare and sat back staring at Bluebeard. He was still bleeding. I had not helped matters much. And we were sitting on a riverbank across from a war with no supplies, no shelter, and no way to make a fire. By nightfall, we would freeze to death. I was already cold in the chill spring air with only this flimsy dress for cover. I was not the kind of girl who sat down and cried when things got tough but I was sorely tempted to change that.

"What I would really like to know," I said irritably, choosing frustration over despair, "is where Coppertomb was in all of this. *He* stole the gem. *He* brought the Brotherhood. So why were they answering to the Sword?"

"Not his style," Grosbeak said. "He likes to work from the shadows. The manipulative voice behind the activity. The puppeteer. The slithering snake."

"Delightful."

"Likely, he struck a deal with the Sword to snatch you for him. Coppertomb's a new player, but he's coy as a girl trying to marry into wealth. He'll be lurking in the shadows nearby. Mark me on this. If you want to help the Arrow, you should keep an eye out for him."

A horse whinnied somewhere nearby.

I froze, wishing I could make myself small.

"Are you hiding? Are you hiding from a horse?"

I put my fingers to my lips to silence Grosbeak. There was someone there. And what did he expect me to do? Use my terrible sword skills to take them down? No. The practical thing to do was to be quiet and hide here.

"You're going to let us all freeze to death along a riverbank because you're afraid of a herbivore?"

He was right. A horse might not have a rider. It might be tied along the riverbank and loaded down with supplies. And some of those supplies might be medical supplies.

With a sigh, I scooped up Bluebeard's sword and lifted my skirts with my other hand.

"If you leave me here, I swear I'll scream."

"If I am to take you, you bodiless rogue, then you must promise silence," I whispered.

"You're starting to sound like your husband."

"Promise." I shook his chain.

"Nngh. Promise."

We stalked silently into the trees together.

Chapter Seven

THERE WAS something about being back in Pensmoore that made my skin tingle. I was only a few strides from the river – a few strides into the land of my birth and it had etched itself into my mortal fibers in such a way that I could feel the pull of it tangling into every beat of my heart. The trees leaned forward to touch me with their waving branches. The grasses caressed me. The earth rose up to meet me. Gladness, deep and full filled me just from the resonance of the land to my presence. What would it have been like if I had lived a whole life here? Raised horses? Kept a keep? Bore and raised children for ... what was his name? Leonid? Already I was forgetting him – a cruelty he did not deserve when he'd given himself to save me.

It was with these gloomy thoughts that I emerged from the trees that lined the riverbank and out into a rolling field. The field was broad and deep – so much so that I could see all the way to where the river curved back on itself and to the fine bridge positioned there.

I had not been wrong about the horses. There was one tied to a tree not far from here. He rolled his black eye at us – as horses do when they have no other way to express anxiety – and stamped a foot.

He'd earned his right to be worried. Beyond the horse, filling the road beyond the field and packing the bridge to its limit before spreading out on either side, was something out of the Wittenhame.

Only in dreams do you see such mad things as this. I blinked twice to be sure I was not dreaming, but the ache of my throat and jaw told me certainly that what I saw was true. An army with inhuman, cold eyes marched up the road carrying fierce weapons. I bit my lip at the sight of them. Their bodies were flat – as if they were made of carding or parchment. When their eyes moved or features flickered, it looked as if they were suddenly painted on in a different configuration – so they did not so much move as shift from pose to pose.

I froze, my ruined throat throbbing as I swallowed nervously.

"There's a move you'll never forget," Grosbeak said, taking in their patterned red and white uniforms just as I was. They were all the exact same inscrutable pattern in a mirror image from bottom to top. "A playing card army. I haven't seen one of those in ... well, never, but it was said that one was used in the Great Game of Crowns and Thrones five ages ago. It's red, so it probably belongs to the Sword. But why did he need your days if he could conjure up *this*?"

Why, indeed?

"I thought the Wittenbrand's color was blue?" I said.

"Oh, aye, but it is, but the Sword seems to think he needs his own personal color and for him, that is red as the crimson tide he drains from his enemies."

"How charming," I said dryly. "And it still doesn't explain why he wanted my days."

"He means to wound me, bodiless curiosity," Bluebeard murmured from behind me and I had to clutch my mouth with a hand to keep from yelping.

Though he spoke to Grosbeak, his lips were mere inches from my ear. He'd snuck up on us as soundlessly as if he didn't even ripple the air. I spun, looking him up and down. How was he on his feet after losing so much blood? He was still pale. He was still drenched in blood from his wound.

He swayed slightly but kept to his feet.

"The horses are mine, Grosbeak. Left here before this little adventure. We'll race the playing cards to the heart of Pensmoore."

Ridiculous. I scowled at him and took the key from my bodice. "If you can walk, then you can walk yourself into your room of wives with me and rest there. You're in no shape to ride anything right now."

He smirked at me and took the key, but he didn't open the door, instead, he tucked it back into my dress, his fingers brushing the neckline in a way that made my cheeks hot as a blacksmith's furnace and limped to the wild-eyed horse. I watched the army warily, but they did not turn aside to us.

"Stop dawdling," Grosbeak complained. "They won't stop for us. They obey orders and there's no one here to order them to go after us. We're safe enough."

They still made me nervous. Like a snake you could see slithering in the grass not far away – no matter that it was not poisonous, there was always the fear that it might be.

Bluebeard caught my hand and drew me to the horse. The stallion stamped a wary hoof, but Bluebeard stilled him with a hand, reaching into a leather-tooled saddlebag and drawing from it clothing, which he handed to me.

"This is your horse. You put him here," I acknowledged. "That's very practical of you."

He didn't reply, but he reached into the other saddlebag and drew out a clean shirt, changing swiftly despite the severity of his injuries. I glimpsed other bruises and cuts on his exposed skin while he dressed and when he was done, he looked at me with a raised eyebrow.

"I know you can speak to me," I said, steeling myself for the worst.

His eyes tightened into narrow slits, all the more worrying in their cat-like regard. And then he did speak.

Faithless and Feckless you may be, but I am not. Though you sell me to my enemies, still I honor you as wife. But speak to my riddle, you sensible monstrosity. Why will the ruffed grouse refuse to be tamed? Why will a plant not grow in salted soil? Why does the heart refuse to trust?

Just looking at his expression left my mouth dry but if ever I wanted a chance to still be allies, now was that time. I took a long breath and said what I must.

"I have seen how you are a violent man, killing whomever you please, and dealing with each according to your own judgment."

His head cocked to the side. *And you thought that wrong? When have I ever been anything but good to you? Did I not just snatch your skin from the flayer?*

"You have been other than good to many people," I said, twisting the clothing in my hands. "But I own that I am in your debt and the debt is so great that I cannot repay it."

You cannot judge how I treat others because you are not them. Tell me, have I ever betrayed you? *Ever been violent or unjust or cruel to* you?

He took a step forward as if he couldn't help himself. My lip trembled.

"I cannot tell you yes."

He was inches away now, leaning in, his own lips trembling over ragged breaths. I could almost taste his breath in mine, that ever-lingering hint of mint bidding me to lean forward into it.

Then tell me no, for my ears long to hear my justification.

"You have never been cruel to me," I whispered and I gasped as his hand grabbed my waist and drew me against him so suddenly that I couldn't catch my breath before he leaned in and stole away a kiss. It was gentle but swift, sweet but bitter.

But you have broken off a shard of me with your betrayal and left in me a never-healing wound. And yet, I have purchased you with my rib, sealed our vow with my sacrifice, and made you utterly my own. And how shall you honor this, fire of my eyes? How shall you meet my fervent devotion?

"It won't heal?" I gasped. He hadn't let go of me, though his kiss had ended. I wanted more, as if one kiss was just not enough – which was insane since he was almost as dangerous to me as the Sword – whether married to me and my rescuer or not, for when this speech of his was done, he would sweep me back into his mad ambitions and this gamble of his to save my land and people.

The Sword marked me with water-tempered Wittenbrand steel. And such a mark by one Wittenbrand to another had no cure I know.

"Then you'll die?" I was aghast resting my hand gently on the uninjured part of his waist. He half-closed his eyes, leaning into my hand as if he liked the feeling and then he sprang away, snatched his blade back from my hand, and slid it into his scabbard – so sudden that he left me reeling at the shock of his changing moods.

I have grown attached to my immortality. It would be a shame to lose it now. Dress, you sober monstrosity. I brought you clothing from home.

I changed hurriedly, confusion topmost in my roiling emotions. I was relieved to be rid of the Sword's horrible dress with its collar and imprisoning skirts and I was surprised by what Bluebeard had brought me. It was blue – as everything he owned seemed to be – but it was more akin to his clothing than what he'd given me before. There was a frothy, rabbit-trimmed shirt, a pair of dark, fitted trousers, high, ruddy boots, and a periwinkle jacket embroidered all over with little figures. When I looked closely at the fabric, I blanched. The jacket seemed to depict the Sword, sewn carefully with his scarlet coat and golden curls, but each depiction of him was the size of my first finger and in each one he was being killed in a new and more gruesome manner so that long consideration of my jacket would turn the stomach of even the staunchest warrior.

I put it on hastily, trying not to look too discomfited. At least it fit well. The fur-lined collar went up to my chin and the sleeves widened over my hands with a fur cuff that gave enough warmth to battle the spring chill. Across the waist and breast, someone had set a number of purely decorative straps and buckles in the same ruddy leather as my boots. It made me look formidable. It was a statement that I found I enjoyed almost too much.

"Thank you for the clothing," I said quietly.

Courtesy of the mirror. Bluebeard shrugged from where he stood as I dressed, his back to me, his eyes studying the playing card army. There seemed no end to them. *He seems to love the Sword as much as I do. Though I reserve my greatest fury for young Coppertomb who thought to entomb me in my own affections. I will enjoy disabusing him of the notion of his cleverness.*

I cleared my throat and he turned as I lifted Grosbeak again.

"No clothing for me?" Grosbeak asked and we both ignored him. "Not even a hat? You stopped to get her a full wardrobe."

I faced Bluebeard squarely and drew myself up to my full height.

His eyes sparkled at that with something that almost looked like hope.

"You ask for loyalty. You ask that I match your sacrifice with my own." I nodded. "You're right to ask me for that. I promised you I would be your ally. I broke my promise. But what can I give you when you already possess everything that is mine from the clothing on my back to my very hours and days? What can I give you when I have married you, and taken your home as mine, and left the remains of my family behind? What else is there to give?"

Your heart remains your own.

"And is that what you would have of me? The one last thing that I maintain of my own?" I was proud of myself. My voice did not shake at all.

Yes, he prowled toward me like a big cat stalking prey in the high grass. *I would have the whole of it dedicated only and always to me.*

"It is not so easy a thing to do. I cannot cut it from my body and place it in a crown for you," I said dryly. "And I cannot prove that I was tricked – that I did not intend to betray you, that I will not do it again."

Prove it to me by not *being tricked again. Prove it to me with no more betrayals. Prove it to me with the gift of your heart.*

Once more, he was inches away, and I thought he might kiss me again but instead, he blinked as if coming awake from a dream, reached into his pocket, plucked out a bone whistle the length of his thumb, and played a single note.

If you cannot gift it in whole, then gift it in slivers and I will reassemble it within my own breast and guard it there in the sanctuary of my immortal soul.

I opened my mouth, meaning to answer – though what did a person say to *that*? – when a drum rolled fast and certain and out of the shadows Bluebeard's band appeared. With their arrival, the moment was lost, though not the offer or the promise.

Chapter Eight

IT WAS Vireo who crashed through the trees first, riding one of the ghostly elk of the Wittenbrand.

"You whistled?" he asked, flicking blood from the end of his naked blade. His brow was sweat-slicked, and his elk stained in streaks of red, his feet blackened with ash and soot.

"The sacking of Aafgaard?" Bluebeard asked crisply, mounting in a single movement despite his pale face and bleeding side.

Aafgaard must have been the city we just left.

"We hit them hard and fast," Vireo said. "A raid, not an occupation. And his enchanted cards were already on the move when we hit, just as you planned." He pointed at the army of playing cards still marching by. "It will take them some time to deal with the damage and bury their dead. Enough time, perhaps to deal with his enchanted soldiers before they arrive at Pensmoore City."

My eyes widened. That army of magical ... things ... was headed to Pensmoore City. And they were so set on it that they had not turned back to defend Aafgaard. I swallowed. That was my people we were speaking of. Perhaps not my actual family anymore – and my heart hurt for Svetgin at the thought of that. Had he survived the battle I'd just escaped? – but Pensmoore was still my home and the idea of them being overrun by this playing card army upset me in a way I couldn't fully explain.

Bluebeard offered me a hand up to ride pillion, but I shook his hand away and mounted myself. He shouldn't be pulling me into position. He shouldn't be riding at all in his current state. He was going to make his injury worse.

I was settling myself when Sparrow's elk emerged from the forest, running to join us. She had a haunted look in her eyes as she crossed the field.

"You should stash her back at your house or in one of those rooms you carry around with you," Vireo said, gesturing to me, as they waited for Sparrow. His mouth twisted, his eyes on me. "You need her days, perhaps, but she's no friend to us now."

"Is she not?" Bluebeard asked, suddenly frosty.

Sparrow pulled her elk in, her breath gusting and her cheeks flushed as if she'd just ridden hard and fast.

"Will you declare that she is still your bride when she has sold you to your enemies and slain you alive?" Vireo asked, his voice full of disbelief. He did not even look at Sparrow as her head swiveled back and forth as she watched the other two speak. "You've paid in blood and pain for her treachery."

I felt my face grow hot. He was not wrong. The practical thing would be to keep me out of their way where I could do no more harm.

"Does the earth have no bones then, Vireo?" Bluebeard asked. His voice was the voice of the winter when it rolled down from the high passes. "Have the tides ceased to ebb and flow with the breath of our sovereign? Have the ages ceased to pass and fail, and the waters below the earth risen up and swallowed her whole? Is this what you have come to me to declare?"

Vireo shifted uncomfortably in his saddle. "You know I have not."

And now my husband's voice snapped like a whip. "Then understand this – that we remain one, and if she has sacrificed a piece of my flesh, then that was hers to give – for my body is dedicated to her and to no other."

Vireo's mouth dropped open, forming the beginnings of unspoken words before discarding them, trying again, and then finally settling into furious horror.

"If you're done questioning our lord, then I have news," Sparrow said, letting her elk step closer to Bluebeard's horse.

It was a measure of Vireo's shock that he let her push past him. Our horse stepped sideways uncomfortably. I patted his flank to calm him. He and I were the two mortal creatures here. We needed to stick together. Grosbeak swiveled on the end of his pole, eyes bright with cunning as he absorbed every word.

"Speak your message, Sparrow."

"I went to the drop point, but the messages there are not good. Rouranmoore pleads with us to ally. Ships from Quranmoore and Salamoore are spotted just off from the Rouranmoore coast. Either we make her our ally, or she will be lost by the next moon."

Bluebeard cursed violently.

"I was just leaving with that message when the Bramble King raised the silver flag," she continued, her face growing more sober still.

Bluebeard and Vireo froze, all other thoughts forgotten.

"I missed it?" Bluebeard asked, face white.

Sparrow shook her head, "I hope you'll forgive my ambitions, but I ..." she seemed to have to take a breath to say this next part. "I stood in your place to receive the message."

Bluebeard and Vireo were so still that my nerves shuddered.

"Oh ho!" Grosbeak roared, unconcerned by our consternation. "You've a rival, Vireo! She declares a loyalty you don't feel, doesn't she?"

"Shut that garish slash you call a mouth, Grosbeak." Vireo muttered but his face was flushed, and his hand kept gripping the handle of his sword.

"What does it mean that she took the message?" I asked calmly.

"Don't tell her," Vireo snapped, his outstretched finger pointed at Grosbeak. "She betrayed us once and she'll do it again."

Bluebeard snapped his fingers and the flesh on Vireo's pointing hand crumpled suddenly as if it had aged, and aged, and then died and was nothing more than desiccating flesh on useless bones.

Vireo gasped, pulling the hand back and clutching it to his chest.

"You're a fool, Arrow," he spat, so furious he was vibrating. "She's not one of us. Not born to us. And she's done nothing worthy of us. She has no place among us. Quote your marriage vows to me all you want but I cannot fathom why you would give her your loyalty over me – me, who has been with you these past hundreds of years – or Sparrow who has done the same."

"I married her in the Wittenbrand way," Bluebeard said so quietly that I barely heard the words, and Vireo had to lean forward to hear them. "You saw it, for you were in attendance. It is a thing I have never done before and will never do again." At that, Grosbeak gasped as if utterly shocked by his words. Bluebeard's voice grew louder and became authoritative. "In so doing, I have shifted my poles and turned the tides of my heart, I have made her north star and center, a treasured treasurer, a well of souls. And those who would call me friend must honor that or they dishonor me. What say you, Vireo? Are you still among my band?"

"I am," he spat it so quickly that I barely caught the words, but I did catch my husband's snap of his fingers.

Vireo's hand was instantly living flesh again. He sagged as it was restored.

"Gather up the creature they call a king and bring him to meet me at the war camp," Bluebeard instructed. "We shall join you there as quickly as it is possible and make what plans we must."

Vireo nodded, but his face was still twisted as if in pain as he rode away on the white elk.

We watched him go, the air around us as thick as a down-filled bolster.

"In receiving the message on his behalf," Grosbeak said distinctly, breaking the tension, "Sparrow has sealed her fate with her lord's. If he fails, she will fail with him and receive the same forfeit – her immortality."

Shock is a thing that tastes of vinegar. My eyes widened as it washed over me, and I met Sparrow's eyes. She nodded curtly but she was not hostile to me as Vireo had been – merely indifferent.

"And if she succeeds?" I breathed.

"She will have a taste of the same reward," Grosbeak said, smiling in his speculation.

"Lord Riverbarrow," Sparrow said formally, ignoring us. "The Bramble King invites you and all the others to solve his riddle. He had put a personal stake into the turning of Ages this time. For while you play your everlasting game, he offers another within it."

"And what is his riddle?" Bluebeard asked.

"I am the culmination of desire, the fruit of death. I am the summit of loss, the passing of weight. What am I?"

"And was there any more to it?" Bluebeard pushed.

Sparrow nodded. “As he was closing his eyes he whispered, ‘His glory fades.’ Does that mean something to you?”

Bluebeard tapped his chin. “Perhaps it does. Lead the way, Sparrow. We ride for the war camp.”

Chapter Nine

OUR ROUTE AVOIDED the card army, but at the first village we found, Bluebeard stopped and signaled to Sparrow who dropped down and ran into the nearest house. I felt a pang of homesickness at the sight of the hamlet. It reminded me too much of home. The small houses were thatched with the same steep roofs, the same type of ridgepole was stuck through the thatch with its figurehead carved on the end to protect the entrance to the house. A similar thatched roof was set on poles over the community well in the center of the village. I remembered drinking from a well just like that when my father brought me on his inspections of the outer villages. I could almost taste the goat's cheese and radishes I'd been fed.

"I thought we were in a hurry," Grosbeak complained.

"If I had to guess, I'd think she was warning people who still have living bodies to take theirs somewhere safe," I said, pushing back a wave of homesickness.

"What does it matter if they survive? They're only mortals."

I let the words hang in the air a long time before I replied. "Perhaps I'll find a new pet. One with more compassion. A polecat, perhaps, or a scorpion."

Grosbeak grunted. "Don't expect apologies from me. I neither give them nor receive them."

But I was annoyed enough to stuff his pole through the saddlebag strap instead of holding it myself. It would be a rougher ride, but I wouldn't need to apologize since he didn't accept apologies.

A man ran out from behind the house before Sparrow had returned. He flung himself to the dust in front of Bluebeard's horse and something in me tightened. He was too close to the stallion's hooves and Bluebeard had chosen a horse just like himself – arrogant and fierce. What if he kicked the man's head in? His hands were worn from farm work, but someone had carefully patched his shirt. He was loved. He would be missed.

"Mercy on us, lord of the Wittenbrand," he said.

"I am not here to judge but to warn," Bluebeard said. "An army spreads across the land, marching not far from here to the west. You should flee further east. Your village lies too close to their path."

The man bobbed his head, eyes still downcast. "Are you Lord Riverbarrow? The patron of Pensmoore?"

Bluebeard grunted. "Where have you heard that name?"

"From my grandad when I was just a tad on his knee," the man said hurriedly. "He told a story from his own grandfather of a one who had stood for our lands long ago, keeping us safe from the wrath of the earth. Was that you, Lord of the Wittenbrand?"

My brow furrowed. In my time, I had met people who feared the Wittenbrand and spoke of them in hushed tones. I'd seen them send peddlers off with loud curses because they sold blue garments. I'd heard the whispered hushes when a storyteller tried to spin a story of their lands for a night in a warm bed. But I had never met anyone who was so close as this to worship.

"What is it you ask of me, mortal," Bluebeard asked.

"Patron, help me. My son is gravely ill."

Behind him, there was a sudden commotion as Sparrow left the cottage. Spilling out behind her were children and women dashing in every direction. Heeding her warning, they were gathering what they could to take with them as they fled.

"Why think you to ask me for healing?" Bluebeard asked.

"You're the patron for our lands – you stand for them. You plead for us before your own sovereign. Won't you plead now? Are you not one with our lands?"

Bluebeard smirked. "Through my wife, I am indeed. Ask her if she is willing. I shall abide by her choice."

The eyes of the man looked up to me, pleading and vulnerable.

"My boy," he pled, his voice rough with unshed tears. "Please."

Bluebeard's eyes rested on me, too, and when I met them, I nodded firmly. I did not care what price he took and of course, there would be one.

"Bring your son here," Bluebeard demanded.

The man rose, gesturing urgently behind his back. A curtain in the window twitched. We'd been watched all along.

And then a pair of men came clambering out of the cottage, a blanket held between them. A small boy lay pale and sweating on the blanket.

Bluebeard set his mouth grimly as if he could feel the boy's twisting pains. He wiped a hand over his face and then leaned toward me and took a kiss delicately from my lips.

Gasps of relief and shock filled the air. When my head was no longer spinning, I looked down to see the little boy standing up and leaping into his relieved father's arms.

"Sparrow," Bluebeard barked. "Manage the warnings, or I'll be stripped of her days before their needs."

Sparrow bowed her head slightly as Bluebeard kicked the stallion. The great beast leapt forward, and in a moment, I'd lost sight entirely of the happy child and his terrified village. I'd lost sight of Sparrow or the people she was warning. I didn't need to see them. Their faces were engraved on the lids of my eyes, and I saw them every time I blinked. My husband had the power to heal anyone – everyone. He could heal all the world.

"I suppose one might say I'm greedy to hold such power to my breast, wouldn't you say, Grosbeak," Bluebeard said as if reading my mind. He must hate having to speak to me through our go-between, though why he didn't just simply speak to my mind was a mystery.

"I ... take ... every ... opportunity ... to insult you ... Arrow," Grosbeak managed, his head pounding wildly at the end of his chain without my grip to soften the blows. Served him and his smug immortality right.

"Indeed, you do," Bluebeard said. "But still I have decided to impart wisdom to you. For I have but one wife now, and I must bargain every blessing I can from her days before they are gone and used, and I am left bereft."

His explanation was clearly for me but why didn't he say it within my mind?

"You've granted her ... a ... great honor ... never before seen ... that a mortal ... would live with the Wittenbran ... d ... as wife," Grosbeak agreed before shaking his lips like a horse, letting spit fly in every direction.

I grimaced.

"And yet, though she is now my heart, I will spend her like water through a net," Bluebeard said ruefully. "I will spend her land and perhaps even that boy she just gave a day for. I will spend, and spend, and spend even if it takes the last drop of my own blood to accomplish what I must."

I shivered. For I knew it was true, but what could be of such value that he would give everything for it? Forget the sovereign's puzzle – *this* was the puzzle I would need to figure out. Especially since my violent husband promised me his enduring commitment one minute and that he would use me up for this mysterious purpose in the next.

But as we galloped away from the little village, a realization dawned over me. The last time I had ridden across the landscape of Pensmoore, it had been on the way to Pensmoore City where my father was bent on finding me a match and the most I could hope for then was a man who would be kind to me and if I was truly lucky, might even be faithful. I had hoped for respect. I had not thought it reasonable to expect love.

And here I was married to an unpredictable Wittenbrand who had not just given me marriage vows but had declared I was to be considered his equal and his most precious associate – though I had neither earned my place through birth nor deeds. It was a respect that was more than I could have hoped for. It was a position higher than I'd ever hoped to reach.

And what was I to do with all this loyalty? What was I to do with all this honor?

The weight of it troubled me.

Perhaps, I should try to be more than an ally. Perhaps I should consider that he truly wanted me to be his wife.

Was it possible that with respect we could have ... companionship? Deep friendship? Sometimes the way he spoke made me almost think of love. And I knew my heart was slipping over the edge of it, but it would be willfully ignorant to let it. He was an impulsive, energetic person – ingenious, vibrant, and horrifically violent. Did he know what love was? Would he love as violently as he lived?

The thought of it stuck in my throat like the bone of a fish and I could not dislodge it no matter how hard I beat at it or tried to press from every side. Before I could dislodge it, I would need to know what it was he felt so desperate for that he was willing to give my life.

Bluebeard was wandering just as deep down his own mental paths – or I assumed as much for he did not speak.

Morning came and went and still we rode. He moved me to a spot in front of him so he could play with my hair again, tying little knots as we rode in silence, but though the forest acted strangely around him – the birds whirling up in the trees as if greeting a friend, the branches waving to him and flowers springing up anywhere he set a foot – still this land was to the Wittenbrand like a garment beat against the rocks too many times. The color had seeped away and with it, my sense of place and home. What was this place to me now? What loyalty did I owe it? What part of my heart did *it* have?

But thinking of that brought to mind the face of that small boy and I could not say I did not care because spikes of compassion shot through me at the thought of him fleeing with his father – healed but not safe. Someone must stand for these people. And Bluebeard had offered me the choice of how to spend my day – to offer or withhold it from the boy. What did that mean? Did it mean he was offering me the chance to be an equal with him in standing for my nation? Was I the right choice for that?

Lost in thought, I pondered all this. And Bluebeard played with my hair. We rode easily together, moving in concert, easy near one another despite our painful injuries and stiff limbs.

Sparrow would warn the villages behind us, so Bluebeard pushed his horse hard, gaining ground until we passed the marching playing cards. He winced from time to time, grasping his wounded side, but when I reached to check his injury, he shook his head, moving my hands aside.

"It's awfully quiet," Grosbeak announced when the hours grew long, and then he launched into a rowdy tavern song.

Bluebeard shut him up with a cuff to the cheek.

"That hurts, you know. I still feel pain!"

"So do I," Bluebeard said. "Your voice saws through my nerves worse than the Sword's blade ever could."

After that, Grosbeak remained silent.

We found a stream wending through the meadows at midday, a small bridge crossing it on the road. A bird trilled in the trees as our horse's hooves struck the bridge and Bluebeard cocked his head to the side. And then another trilled. He frowned, turning our horse off the road and into the trees.

"What is it?" I whispered.

He pressed a finger to my lips, listening.

We'd come out to a little clearing, and in the center of the glen on a cut stump, someone had placed an egg the size of my hand woven from grass.

Bluebeard tilted his head slightly to the side, eyes glittering. This was not right. You did not just see woven eggs sitting in clearings in the mortal world.

I looked from side to side, suspicious.

And there it was. A boat flipped over but half-submerged along the river. It should be pulled properly up on the shore. And over there, someone had hastily hidden chopped firewood behind pine boughs.

But Bluebeard was already urging the horse forward.

Ambush! I cried in my mind, trying not to alert the predators waiting for us. *Ambush!*

Nonsense.

He wasn't listening.

I turned in the saddle and shoved him backward with all my might. His eyes widened as he lost his seat, and then turned his fall into a flip and landed in the soft grass at the same moment that a crossbow bolt *thunked* into my shoulder.

Pain flared through me, roaring and overwhelming. I tried to blink it back. Tried to clear my head but I was already being dragged off the horse and into the bushes. I fought against my captor, blindly, desperately.

Easy. Easy now.

It was Bluebeard. I drew a shuddering breath, but his hands had left me, and all I saw were his boots as he stood beside me, and then even they were gone as he leapt from sight.

I shoved down a wave of nausea fighting the pain and the sense that I needed to get up and *move.*

I pushed up to hands and knees, buckling and seeing red at the pain in my shoulder that came with that movement.

I was just in time to see Bluebeard leap like a cat onto the back of a man holding a crossbow and bolt. My husband swayed as he plunged his sword into the man's neck and then spun to land in front of a second man, sword neatly slashing his throat.

Bluebeard spun again, already on to the next attacker and the next, a whirlwind that sent out streaks of blood instead of raindrops.

And all I'd done was ... well, I'd done nothing, as usual. Why did he want me along when he was better off fighting alone? I did nothing but slow him down.

"Psst ... Izolda," Grosbeak said. He was lying on the grass beside me. He must have been dropped in the attack.

I looked up muzzily just as a crossbow bolt thunked beside me. I needed cover. I needed it now. I couldn't find any. The trees were all too far away.

There was a scream, and when I looked over, Bluebeard was severing a man's head from his body. He scooped it up, two heads in one hand now as he stalked forward. But his enemies were everywhere, coming out from under the overturned boat, leaping from their hiding places in the rushes, and dropping down from trees like deadly bats.

"Psst ... grab me first!"

First? Before what? But I couldn't think – the thoughts wouldn't come – so instead I obeyed, snatching Grosbeak's pole up.

"The door! Go through the door!" he said.

Door?

"The key is around your neck."

"Oh. Yes." I fumbled for it, but my right arm was barely working now.

Bluebeard backed up to us, holding off three men with his fine swordsmanship and the help of the heads he held in one hand. Raising them kept blows back easier than a shield would.

"Come on!" Fear filled Grosbeak's every word, slicing into my foggy brain.

I found the key as another bolt hit the ground just a finger-width from Bluebeard's foot. My heart was in my throat, pain spiking through the rest of me in raw-mawed bursts.

"Open the door!" Grosbeak screamed.

I opened the door, remembering to grab the horse, and stumbled into the room.

"Bluebeard!" I called as I fell to my knees on the floor. Panicked breathing made my words rough-edged. "Bluebeard!"

The door was closing behind me – I didn't remember doing that last time. I'd saved Grosbeak and the horse and left the most important person behind. Horror roared through me like a forest fire.

And then he was there, crashing through the last sliver of open door before it closed, the heads he'd taken held in one hand and his bloody sword in the other.

I'd never seen anything so beautiful.

I was smiling as the world went dark.

Chapter Ten

I WOKE to gentle hands tending me. Someone had balled up the rug made from the striped creature and pillowed my head on it. One would think that would be luxurious, but it smelled of dust and dead animal. That same person had set out the three severed heads in a row beside me and put Grosbeak's on the end of the row.

"You should know that I would display very poorly," he said sourly, his eyes not on me. "Especially now that I have been hit, and knocked against walls, and used as a sword."

"You do not need to be pretty. You need only remind my enemies of my power."

Grosbeak snickered. "Is that what your mother told you?" His eyes settled on me. "Oh, she's awake."

The hands moved and then suddenly Bluebeard's cat's eyes came into view. They searched my face intently as he spoke in his mental voice.

"We've ruined another jacket. It seems I will need to employ a tailor exclusively for you – maybe even a dozen of them. You'll leave me destitute in the cost of clothing."

"It can be mended," I said faintly through gritted teeth. A moan escaped them despite my best efforts. My shoulder was radiating pain.

"Easy now. Easy." Bluebeard said, running a hand over my hair. *"Don't move until we've drawn this bolt out of your shoulder."*

"You're talking to me again," I gasped. "You wouldn't speak before."

"In the mortal world, our speaking between minds requires the use of magic, and I will spend a single one of your moments on such expressions. No thought I have is worth their expenditure."

It seemed sweet. But also very much something a man would think. As if leaving me to stew on what he might be thinking or wanting wasn't spending my time and efforts already.

"But you'll speak to me here." Little black spots danced over my vision. Don't pass out again, Izolda.

"In this little pocket of the Wittenbrand, magic lives free. I can spend enough of it to speak in your mind without spending your moments."

Well, that was fair enough. "Can you help my shoulder?"

My words came out more pleading than I'd hoped.

"Of course, he can," Grosbeak snickered. "He could heal you from any ill if he used up your days. But he won't do that. He needs them all for some grand plan of his. By the way, have you seen this place? It's creepy. And I'm saying that as someone who has a gaping wound at the end of his neck and possibly a fly infestation starting up."

"They're his wives," I said weakly. I must have lost some blood to feel so weak. I tilted my head just enough to look up at the nearest wife. Princess Margaretta with her tiny, pinched waist and her big golden curls.

Grosbeak snickered again. "And now, with you here, the collection is complete. I knew some of these mortals. Or at least, I saw him carry them into the Wittenbrand crowned with his flowers and carried in his arms."

Was that a stab of jealousy I felt at the thought? Or was it just the agony of a bolt in my shoulder. I swallowed against a dry throat.

"I'm going to draw out this crossbow bolt," Bluebeard said in my mind. *"We're lucky. It is not deep, though it struck bone and that may be a problem. But crossbow bolts are thrown like a dart with a heavy head, not launched like an arrow. People are often misled into thinking that they're more powerful than a good bow, but it's simply not true. The rogue was too far out of range and his dart hit your shoulder and penetrated through clothing and flesh but it has severed no major blood vessels and not caused the damage it would have if it had been a broadhead with a proper bleeder point."*

"I remember how bright his eyes were with each of them – as if he had found a lost pearl," Grosbeak said, unaware of the conversation in our heads. "And now he stands them up in rows like little silver spoons in a case." I shivered but Grosbeak didn't stop as if he needed to say his piece and could not stop himself. "Did you know that we grew up together? The Arrow and Vireo and me? We tried to pull the arrow from the stone. We stole magic from open flowers and wrung little charms out of pixie wings. And now look at us."

"You betrayed me, Grosbeak," Bluebeard said grimly. "You deserve what's been done to you ten times over. A price paid in blood."

"She betrayed you, too. I don't see you claiming *her* head, though you've claimed her whole self, I suppose. What's her penalty? What's her price?"

"I paid her price myself in my own blood," Bluebeard growled, gesturing at his wounded side. "And I will go on paying it forever."

I gasped, tears springing to my eyes, and he froze.

"You've made me neglect my wife," he growled at Grosbeak. "Remain in silence or I will kick you across the room."

But my wound was not why the tears sprung to my eyes. It was his words that cut so deep. I had not known there would be a price for trying to cut myself free of him. But of course, there was. Of course. And of course, he had paid it. And wasn't he trying to pay some kind of similar price on behalf of his beleaguered people and mine?

Tears marred my vision, but I could just make out him producing a knife and stroking my hair again.

"I must cut this quarrel out. Be brave, wife."

I clenched my eyes shut as the knife sank in, and gritted my teeth together as the pain started, breathing hard and fast as he cut the quarrel free. The pain was a glass shard in my shoulder, cutting me even after the true damage was passed. It took long breaths before I could so much as open my eyes again.

"As I suspected. It may have bruised your bone, and ravaged your flesh, but this will heal. Stay still now. I've thread and needle in my bag."

"Did you see the woven egg?" I asked him, trying to distract my mind as he drew thread and needle from his bag and cleaned them both.

"It smelled of mint."

Interesting. I hadn't noticed that, but I *had* noticed his particular fondness for mint.

"Do you think it was the Sword?"

"Too soon. We'd only just fled him."

"Coppertomb, then?"

"It was likely the mortals. Not all of them appreciate their 'patron.'"

"I don't think so," I whispered as the needle but my skin. "I think that someone plans to murder you, husband."

He froze. Had I said something wrong?

He leaned in close so that his lips were bare inches from mine, and I could feel his breath against my lips.

"Say that again." His mental voice was a caress. I shivered at the sound of it.

"Someone plans to murder you. Husband."

He shivered, eyes closed and a smile on his face. *"That, I could listen to all day long."*

"You love to hear of plots on your life?"

"I love to hear you address me as husband."

"In this place where fifteen others have done the same?" I couldn't keep the wryness from my tone.

His face fell and he returned to stitching my flesh. He'd cut my coat and shirt away from the wound and they gaped open lending to the strange intimacy of him mending my body for me. If it was a loving thing to mend a coat for your beloved, was it not more loving still to mend her flesh?

"I hate this place," he confessed. *"Each face you see is a failure of mine. Each book, the story of my dereliction. Think you that the wound in my side will never heal? This is a thousand times worse for it is the wound in my soul that cannot heal – the plan hatched a thousand years ago that has failed and failed and failed."*

"And what is the plan, exactly?" I asked, anticipation filling me. This was it, at last. I could feel the edges of it as if by understanding this one thing, I could understand everything about him.

He looked down at me and his lips parted on his inhumanly beautiful face and for a moment I thought he might answer. His cat's eyes were wide and vulnerable, and they made his tousled hair and thickened blue beard look almost boyish.

But he shook his head. *"No. Not now. I will not confess this yet. For though I have borne the sorrow and agony of your betrayal in my own flesh, I dare not open this to you, also, lest you plant your traitor blade in its back and destroy us all."*

I gasped and he shook his head and returned to his methodical stitching, his touches against my skin gentle – oh so gentle – but his words had wounded me far more deeply than any quarrel could.

He was just to judge me. Right to protect himself from me. So, then, why did it hurt so much? Why did it wound so deeply?

I bit back tears. Ridiculous, Izolda. You have let him mislead you with pretty words. You are no more the trusted wife than Grosbeak is.

"That was a trap back there," I said, changing the subject to something where I could be helpful. "And it was not a trap laid by mortals. Nor, as you have stated, was it likely laid by the Sword or Coppertomb. Which means that one of your other rivals is trying to assassinate you and that they know the exact way to draw you in."

His mouth twisted wryly.

"*What makes you so certain?*"

"No mortal would be lured into an obvious trap by nothing more than a grass egg."

He laughed – to my surprise. "*They did not contend with my mortal wife's eyes. But you are not wrong I think.*" He lifted the quarrel with care and to my shock, the arrowhead evaporated in a puff of purple smoke. "*This is laced with Sapporous a Wittenbrand poison that saps away control over magic. You, being mortal, are unaffected.*"

"But it would have rendered you helpless," I agreed.

He shrugged – the motion of his tightening muscles reminding me that he had more danger in him than just magic – and flung the shaft to the side, drawing out a soft cloth from his saddlebag and winding it around my shoulder.

"*If they wish me dead, they will have to send better assassins.*"

"If you wish to live, you might think about knowing where their assassins will be," I countered. He needed spies. More of them and better than what he had.

He took up another of the rugs – a sheepskin dyed purple – and draped it over me for warmth.

"*Sleep now,*" he suggested. "*And in a few hours' time, we will mount the horse and gallop through the door and hopefully they will have dispersed or will be so startled that we will be free and clear.*"

"Will time pass differently here, as it does in the Wittenhame?" I asked and he shrugged.

"*Sometimes it does. And sometimes it does not.*"

I nodded but the gesture felt hollow. He did not trust me enough to confide in me – not even enough to tell me whether we could trust time in this place. Buying my debt to him with his own blood, elevating me to a respected position – these were gifts. But without his confidences, without his trust, what did they matter?

I shifted and squirmed, and while the pain in my shoulder ate at me like a furtive mouse with a block of cheese, the doubts in my mind ate at me more. For with every day that I stood by my husband's side, I lost the ties to my own people, to my own past. Svetgin was back there somewhere. Hopefully, he had survived the attack on the city. Hopefully, the Sword was not angry with him for my escape. I could have allied myself more fully with him. I could have chosen the Sword over Bluebeard and sealed my chance to live again alongside my brother.

But I had chosen my husband, and though he had chosen me in some ways, there were still rooms in his heart locked so far away that this little key could not open them. I could not still my anxious mind to rest with that forever chewing away at my edges.

After long minutes, a hand reached out and touched my arm and I shifted enough to see that Bluebeard had settled down in his own bundled rugs close enough to touch me.

He left his hand on my arm, and though it did not heal the gnawing or fill the hollowness in my breast, it was just enough comfort to help me surrender into sleep.

Chapter Eleven

IN THE TALES told by mothers to their children through the ages of my land, there is always a common thread – in every happy ending there are the seeds of the next tragedy and in every deep calamity there is still the possibility to wrench happiness from the clawed fingers of fate.

I woke to my fate staring intently at me with his cat's eyes glowing like twin stars.

"Your injuries must be checked, and needs attended to as quickly as possible, and then we will leave this haunted cavern – this place that makes my belly roll and my heart lurch – and face our enemies full in the teeth."

"When you say 'haunted cavern' are you talking about this wedding gift you gave me?" I offered dryly. "If I knew you thought so poorly of it, perhaps I would not have accepted it. A husband's gifts are meant to show his regard for his wife."

My own belly was lurching, the muscles around the quarrel puncture stiff and agonized. I tried to sit and blinked back tears.

"And so my gift does, for does not laying bare my failures make me vulnerable to your knife? In drawing back my shirt and leaving you a clear path to my heart, do I not offer you what I would give no other?"

"You gave it to fifteen others," I said gesturing to those very women, still and ominous on their pillars. My face felt hot as my body fought to heal me.

He made a brushing motion with his hand as if I was missing the point and then reached out to help me sit up.

"Today's ride will be hard on you. But you are made of strong fiber and a copper will. I think you will survive it," he said as he carefully removed my jacket. His hands quick as they worked to undress me and my cheeks burned so hotly I feared they would be damaged as he stripped the layers separating us. This time their flush was not from my injury.

With a touch so delicate that I barely felt it, he loosened the ties of my shirt and slid the rabbit-lined collar down over my shoulder so he could tend my wound there. I held the rest of my shirt up with blushing modesty, watching as he unwound my bandage and then frowned.

"This wound is not mortal wrought, as you well know, or It would have healed more by now." He blew on it, startling me and sending a rush of heat through my core. *"One of my fellows has tried to assassinate me. But which one? That is the question. And it needs an answer."*

He bathed the wound, wrapped it again, and then gently turned me around so he could loosen my ties even further and let my shirt slip down my back to my waist while I clutched it to my breast with a trembling hand.

"Your back is healing, though. I will snip these silver stitches for you later, wife, but they need salve now. You should know the scars have a longevity beyond the healing."

"Scars do not bother me," I said, my voice trembling.

He leaned around me in the sudden way he had and caught my chin, looking into my eyes as if he'd find the answer to a riddle there.

"If they do not bother you, then why do your cheeks flame scarlet? Why do you tremble with every breath as if you are afraid I will set you to fire or rip you apart entirely?"

My gasp was involuntary but the way his lips parted in response to it was enough to unfurl the last shreds of certainty I still had.

"You said you do not sully yourself with mortal brides and yet here you are, undressing me piece by piece."

He frowned. *"Your innocence is safe with me, wife. Have I not told you so?"*

"Did you say the same to all of them?" I asked, gathering courage under the clouded eyes of all the other brides he'd had. "Did you look each of them in their lovely faces – so much prettier than mine – and tell them you would not share their favors?"

"Each of them heard the same from my lips." His eyes were still drinking in mine – still trying to draw something out that I didn't know was there. It was not helping with the blushing or with the flipping and spinning of my belly.

"But why?" I gasped.

"I made a vow of chastity."

"What?" I asked and now he ducked his head, as if somehow embarrassed, and he retreated around my back as if he were safer there. "For how long?"

"As long as it takes."

I felt the sting of salve as he applied it to my healing back.

My mouth felt dry. "But whatever for?"

"I have been awaiting my true bride and the wait is worthy of the maiden."

What should I say to that? What should I say, looking out over all the others, standing imperiously on their pillars, faces blank in death, eyes glazed with the passing of all their dreams, perfect bodies preserved forever?

He was not entirely the monster I thought he was. Not entirely, but still, it was there. He had not taken *everything* from them, but he had burned their days like logs in a fire. And yet, that gesture, that nod to their humanity and value – that he had not also used them for his own amusement – it made my heart ache with some emotion I could not name.

"Then I hope that you find her someday," I said in a small voice as his fingers traced the healing wounds of my back, applying this healing salve of his.

His touch was so delicately soft that it was like a lover's caress. Was it the first time he'd traced patterns on a woman's back? Was he as new to the way it pulled at his breath in the same way that I was new to it?

He cleared his throat and pulled my shirt back up for me and I felt the strangest feeling of regret as he helped me back into my jacket and all the tight tension that had filled my every muscle lessened. With the lessening, the pain in my shoulder flared hotter.

"It will be a hard ride for you, but ride we must," he said in my mind, changing the subject as if we hadn't just shared an intimacy. *"But we must ride out now, before we lose the element of surprise. We'll prepare, mount the horse, and then you'll turn the key, and we'll gallop from this place at full*

speed. My hope is that they won't be able to respond fast enough to stop us. And then we'll ride hard and fast to the war camp."

I nodded, taking a sip of water from a waterskin he offered me.

"We only slept an hour or two at most. They shouldn't have had time to gather reinforcements."

He was back to being a lord of the Wittenbrand – intense, strategizing, unafraid.

And I was back to being Izolda, not sure if I was sowing seeds of peace or reaping a whirlwind. With Bluebeard, I was probably doing both.

"I need to look at your wound before we ride," I said, reaching for him, but he batted my hands away.

"There's nothing that can be done for that, fire of my eyes," he told me mentally. *"A Wittenbrand wound it is, and a Wittenbrand wound it will remain."*

I raised an eyebrow but left him alone. If he wanted to keep bleeding through his shirt like an endless blood spring, well, he was a grown Wittenbrand and he could do as he wished.

In a matter of minutes, we were mounted again. Bluebeard set me to ride behind him.

"I plan to fight my way free, and I don't want you to take any more quarrels for me," he explained as he offered me Grosbeak's pole.

My bodiless friend woke with a scream and then blinked several times. "Oh, we're still here. How disappointing."

"Where did you think we'd be?" I asked, braiding my mussed hair as Bluebeard tied the heads he'd collected to the saddlebags behind me. He was tying them by their hair, which felt far too similar to what I was doing. I hoped I didn't end up a bodiless head.

"Heaven. Hell. I know not, but not in your lover's death closet."

I glanced around at the spacious room, its denizens keeping their silent, judging watch. The hourglass at the back of the room made a tinkling sound as one of my garnets broke free and fell to the bottom bulb of the glass. The room was many things, but not a closet. I shivered, glad to be leaving it again.

"Keep your tongue in your mouth or lose it, too," Bluebeard growled at Grosbeak as he mounted. "You're traitor to your people and a blemish on your family name."

"You would know," Grosbeak said sourly. "It was you who killed my father after he cheated the Duskatain. And yet, can a Wittenbrand cheat? Is that not *who we are?* Is it not how we soar in this world? To ask us to do otherwise is to ask a leopard not to wear spots. *You* are cheating. I know you are. That's what this grand plan of yours is really – some way to cheat at the great game of crowns. Or maybe to cheat death once more. But you condemned him for the same. You were barely higher than his waist when you took his head and claimed the Duskatain as your redeemed vassals. You took half my birthright that day. You took my family name. So don't talk to me about blemishes."

Bluebeard cuffed him coldly and I froze as he growled into Grosbeak's face. "Don't talk to me at all."

And then he drew his blade and said, "My wife has named this blade true. Edgeworthy she was called, Edgeworthy she shall be. Brace yourself, traitorous Grosbeak. We've heads to free from bodies today."

"*The key, if you please, wife.*"

With a shaking hand, I drew the key out of my bodice.

Ready or not, here we come.

I turned the key in the air and Bluebeard kicked the stallion with a cry of, "Ha!"

Chapter Twelve

WHEN I WAS A SMALL GIRL, my mother would tell us the story of the Wild Hunt.

"Deep in the darkest place in the forest," she would say, "rides the Wild Hunt. Led by the Redblood Stag and mounted on antlered wolves, the Wittenbrand ride to kill, and rend, and tear. Each visage is hard as stone, carved by the wind and their cruel acts. They sniff the wind and then they streak out in each direction. They are falling stars, wandering planets, heavenly demons bringing the gift of death. And if they smell mortal flesh they pounce, ripping, and tearing, and shredding to pieces." And then she'd pounce herself, tickling us like mad before falling restless into the blankets beside us and saying, "But I will keep you safe, little bugs."

There was no mother to keep me safe this time, no one but Bluebeard.

I turned the key and we leapt from the hidden room back into the forest clearing. Someone screamed and then men were scattering in every direction as I fought to remember to turn the key again and close our little room. It shut just in time, almost slicing one of our ambushers clean in half. He drew back, sword rattling as he drew it from the scabbard. I spun then, ignoring his cry to keep my eyes on what we were doing.

Warriors rushed in from every side, knocking over supplies and spooking horses in their hurry to get to us. Bluebeard leaned to the side, scooped up the woven grass egg that had lured him there in the first place, and tossed it back to me, and then his eyes turned on our attackers and I braced myself. I was just in time to grab his waist with one hand as the stallion reared, coming down hard on a screaming warrior.

They were not all mortal, I noted. Just as many had antlers or wings as regular mortal features. Just as many were dressed in the decadent, maddening styles of the Wittenbrand as those who wore doublet and hose or the colors of livery.

I gasped as Bluebeard cleaved the first head from shoulders – an antlered head, I noted. After that, it was a haze of spattering blood and screams, of bodies launching toward us with clawing hands, or sharp claws, or edged weapons.

My husband fought and fought with the grim determination of the reapers at harvest, hurrying to bring in crops before rain or frost rotted them on the fields. He spun the horse with a deft hand tangled in the reins while his sword arm flicked and danced, weaving like a master at his loom – only instead of weaving cloth, he wove death, and he wove salvation.

I was too occupied to watch every detail. I rode pillion, gripping with my knees as I thrust and jabbed Grosbeak's pole at anyone who slipped past Bluebeard's dancing attacks. There were few, but for me, even a few were enough to keep me on edge, heart racing and muscles stiff as I desperately swung and blocked. My shoulder burst with pain for every movement, and doubly so for every impact. I was certain I'd torn the stitches Bluebeard had so carefully set in my flesh.

The world around me was nothing but noise and people, motion and clawing forest branches in one wooden hue or another blending to a tapestry of fear and pain.

"I bite! Do you hear me, I bite hard!" Grossbeak snarled right before he sank his teeth into a mortal's ear. The man screamed, and there was a ripping sound. I did not look. I did not want to see. By the time I was swinging Grosbeak again, he was spitting out the ear.

"That's right! Run! Run back to your mothers!" he screamed as our horse plunged through a gap in our attackers, plummeting through the woods. "Oof! That was a branch! Do you know how much that – oof!"

I hurried to pull his head in closer to the horse's flanks as we sped into the hot late afternoon sun and back to the road, branches whipping us as if they were our enemies, too. The horse thundered down the road for far longer than I thought a horse could take before Bluebeard finally drew him into a walk.

He flicked the blood from his sword and paused to wipe it.

"This does not look right to me, Grosbeak," Bluebeard said, glancing over both Grosbeak and then me as if checking for injuries before returning his gaze to the ground. I suspected he spoke to my friend so he could speak aloud to me without breaking the rules.

"I see the footprints of the card army, and I expected that, but what do you see here?"

"Men and beasts fleeing the army," Grosbeak said. "Nothing to be concerned about."

"No small footprints. No cattle other than horses. Where are the villagers that Sparrow warned?"

"Perhaps they went a different way."

"Why then, do I see so many men and horse tracks?"

Grosbeak's expression was like a facial shrug. "It's a road. There are tracks. I'd be surprised if there weren't."

Bluebeard grunted but he stayed quiet as we rode, and he shushed Grosbeak when he tried to sing a ribald song.

"Something is amiss, betrayer of mine," he growled.

Our pace sped quicker with every turn until, as the sun began to burn a sulky copper, we turned on the road to where the landscape on either side opened up into a wide grassy field.

I gasped.

It was almost too much to take in.

We had emerged behind the playing card army – hundreds, maybe even thousands of small figures were spread before us in formations, but the edges of the formations bled out across the land as they thundered toward a retreating army of men on the far side of the field opposite to us.

Bluebeard cursed.

"Tell your mistress to hold onto you tightly, Grosbeak," he ordered. "It seems I must spend a week of her life today."

And then he raised a palm and a rip tore through the air ahead of us.

I balked at what I saw there, my palms instinctively clammy, my breath coming far, far too fast until my head went light and woozy. If I'd known where we were going today, I would have stayed hidden away in that little room of dead wives. If I had known we were on the path to this, I would have cowered behind their corpses and watched my days run slowly out one by one rather than be here and now.

I forced down that feeling and clenched my jaw tightly. I could see I must be practical about this. There was nothing that could ever stop Bluebeard from racing into danger and if I was his wife then I must accept that I would be forever rushing in with him. I held onto the lantern pole with a shaking hand, straightened my back, and forced myself to breathe as our stallion leapt like a trout through the slice and into the fray.

We'd emerged where the playing card army rolled over its opposing mortal army like surf on sand. The stallion barely kept his feet as a wave of them crashed into him, it was only Bluebeard's clever riding that kept us upright as he shifted and guided with rein and thigh.

I swung my lantern pole at the nearest attacker, knocking him back – to my surprise. He was lighter than me, vulnerable even to my weak attacks. But though they were vulnerable, they were deadly fast. Three more filled the gap where one had been, and now I had three to battle instead of one.

"To me!" Bluebeard roared. "Men of Pensmoore! To me! Stand with your patron!"

And as he called to them, he steered the stallion to face the army and raised his hand, a wave of air bursting from it and knocking the cards back and into each other.

They're shuffled now, my brain offered. A stunned thought, but all I could manage beyond simply reacting and reacting again as the cards gathered themselves up again and clambered forward, their focus on just one point now – us.

Their painted faces shifted so rapidly from expression to expression that I wondered how they kept them from falling off entirely and they moved with the nausea-inducing flexibility of paper and a strange, almost side-to-side movement like a snake. Up close, the paintwork on each card was utterly incredible in both detail and design, each one a work of art and each one very subtly different.

Bluebeard flicked his hand again, such a small movement for the result. Flames erupted among them, catching their paper aflame so quick and hot it stole my breath away and leaving them in smoldering heaps around us. They weren't human – not even animals, just things made for trouble and evil – and yet I still flinched from how easily Bluebeard shredded and ignited them. He drew his sword, slashing and hacking as he roared his song, "To me, to me, to me!"

I grabbed the whistle that hung around his neck and blew.

He said nothing about my breach of his person. Maybe he had nothing to say or maybe he was simply too busy battling for our lives.

The cards fell before him, cut or hacked to bits, or trampled by their fellows.

For a long moment, I thought it would not be enough. For a long moment, I thought we would be trampled anyway, dragged under by the pull of so many thousands of bodies.

It was just us in that moment, just Bluebeard swinging his sword with business-like determination and a grim set to his mouth like he was doing something unpleasant. And just me behind him, swinging Grosbeak out to catch any cards he missed as my bodiless friend screamed at the top of his lungs.

"No! No! Not the cards! No!"

And then they were there, masses of mortals rushing up beside us, dressed in the colors of Pensmoore, weapons flashing in the fading sunset.

"For the Arrow!" Someone cried and we surged forward as one, knocking cards aside, trampling them underfoot. They were just cards, right? Just cards. So why were they a threat at all?

A mortal beside me cried out in agony and I looked to see his arm severed at the elbow, a card with a red edge plunging past. The card slid easily through a second man's wrist before two other mortals skewered it on swords and slashed it to pieces.

I was going to be ill. I needed to be away from here. Anywhere else. Anywhere else at all.

"Fight harder!" Grosbeak scolded, bringing me back to reality.

I fought down my nausea, and with all my strength, I swung the pole.

If I'd been on my own, I'd be dead a thousand times over, but my husband turned every blow aimed at me. He was like five men fighting at once, a flurry of blades and movement.

Vireo rode up beside us.

"I beg your forbearance, Arrow," he said breathlessly, flicking a pair of cards aside. "I was a fool to leave you."

"So you were," Bluebeard agreed. "And a fool to lead the mortals to battle here."

"We did not pick this place. We met them on the road, but they drove us back to the fields."

Bluebeard stiffened and by now I knew him well enough to understand. He was furious.

"How many have you lost?"

"We had no time to count. We were routed. The men are scattered."

"Forward!" Bluebeard roared, ignoring Vireo and leading the men himself.

He was right to do so. They rallied to him, hope blazing in their eyes. Man after man joined him, helping him as he pressed their enemies back, flung them to the ground, and trampled them under his stallion's black feet. He fought them, wave upon wave, a sea of enemies, but even the sea itself could not stand against my husband. He was rage and darkness, martial power and fury, death loosed upon the earth. And though his own side bled furiously, still he fought onward.

"If you'll not stand me as your brother, then bind me as your vassal," Vireo said when he surfaced again from the fray. "Give me one more chance, brother."

"Peace," Bluebeard roared, shifting his reins to his sword hand and reaching across. Vireo clasped his hand. "Round up those who are scattered and bring them to the flanks of the Sword's folly. We'll dash them against the rocks and rid ourselves of this monstrosity."

"As you say, my Prince," Vireo said, sketching a bow, but though he had clasped my husband's hand, there was still a cloud of worry on him as he rode away. I would be worried, too. Bluebeard had claimed Grosbeak's head for less loss of life.

"To me, men of Pensmoore!" Bluebeard called, "to me!"

We turned back to where the mass of cards was pushing and pressing. I was soaked through with sweat already. Every muscle ached and my shoulder was fiery pain, agony in my living flesh. Blood poured down my sleeve to match the blood staining Bluebeard's side and thigh as I sucked in deep breaths through my nose, just trying to stay upright.

But though we had the men with us, though they sped to join their patron and fight alongside him, even so, we were outnumbered. The first stab of fear hit me when I saw a mortal beside us stumble and fall – not from the cards, but from sheer exhaustion. The fear turned to terror when ten more stumbled with him.

"Up," Bluebeard cried, "Up."

But they were beyond encouragement. They were almost beyond life. I could see what was coming, see the falling comrades, see the cards wash over us, knowing it was too late – just too late to stop it. Disappointment was bitter on my lips as I slipped a hand around Bluebeard's waist. One last touch to savor before we both fell and were sliced to ribbons by the raging cards.

A horn sounded on the far slope ahead of us and to the left. A second horn matched us, ahead of us and to the right.

But horns could not save us now.

And then there was movement over the left hill. I squinted at the sight and gasped. Mortals. An army of men thundering toward the fray and at their head was Sparrow, her sword arcing before her in a bright crescent.

"Sparrow," Bluebeard breathed, relief strong in his voice, too.

On the other hill, Vireo thundered down, the men he'd found thundering with him.

"We're saved," Grosbeak said – sounding almost as if he feared for his life, too. Though how he could fear when it was already taken, I didn't know. "We're saved."

But he was right. We cut them down like a field of grass before the mowers.

Until there was only one. Standing alone before the Arrow. His drawn mouth worked across his card surface and then – in a way that sent chills down my spine – the Sword's voice spoke through him.

"What have I done behind your back while you were killing this army, Arrow? Where is the knife planted and how are you bleeding?"

Then the card crumpled to the ground, still and lifeless and across the landscape, every ruined card disappeared. What manner of magic could have sustained them and then ruined them?

Around me, a cheer went up from ragged throats and heavy hands – so tired they could barely lift up in salute. No one else was looking at such good news with sideways eyes. There was only relief and gratitude.

"The Arrow! The Arrow!" they roared – one name on a thousand tongues.

"Let's go find that missing human king," my husband growled. And I did not think he meant to congratulate him.

Chapter Thirteen

IF I'D IMAGINED a war camp, I would have imagined a grim set of low tents with little to eat perched atop a hill where a watch could be set on every side. I would have imagined a few stoic men clutching weapons and dreaming of home.

What we found when we rode into this war camp bore little resemblance to what I had imagined. There were tents and fires to be sure, but the tents were made of fine canvas and painted with the crest of Pensmoore – a black horse galloping over a field of green – and trimmed with careful stitching.

Where I had expected grim conditions, instead there were roaring fires and servants bearing trays of food and wooden chairs on which to sit and tables on which to dine.

Certainly, there were pickets – fine lines of well-bred horses I couldn't help but approve of as we walked by – but they were tended by grooms. And certainly, there were apothecary tents where moans and screams were common, but they were pushed off to the side and away from the boisterous clamor of the celebration going on in the camp when we arrived. Indeed, one would hardly know a devastating defeat had only narrowly been escaped just a short ride away from here.

We were on foot, Bluebeard insisting that our horse was too weary to carry us after the mad dash and then the battle – and he seemed correct, though our horse held his head high and did not stumble despite his sweaty flanks and neck and the heavy gusts of breath stirring the black hairs in his nostrils.

Night fell moments before we reached the camp – sudden as an ambush – and Bluebeard leaned in close so that I could feel the brush of his rough cheek against mine as he whispered. It sent a little shiver of pleasure through me that almost disguised the teeth-clenching ache in my abused shoulder.

He whispered so low that I could barely make out the words. Certainly, they could not be stolen by ears not meant to hear them.

"I must dance a pretty jig here, fire of my eyes, for it is a fine line between respect and resentment, adulation and abhorrence and I must keep to the former and fend off the latter. I fear I shall be distant to you as I tend to this, but fear not, you remain my wife and ally. And so, I beg you not to speak mind to mind unless we must. I fear you tap some unknown source with this strange speech we share, and I do not wish to waste it, or it will not be ready at hand when it is most necessary. Simply stay near me and when all this is passed, I will take you from this place of war and to a better nest in which to rest."

I opened my mouth, and he laid a finger over my lips. I nodded my agreement instead, remembering belatedly that now that the sun had set, I must not speak to him. The inability to argue voice to voice – or even just discuss chafed like a wet strap against the skin.

I had no desire to speak to anyone else. Seeing so many dressed in the colors and sigils of my people made my heart sick for Svetgin.

More than that, the sight of my people – sharpening the shorter, stouter blades of home, their beards trimmed in the way of Pensmoore, their accents ranging from the roll and sway of the east to the quick clip of the west, the scents of their foods as much like home as my mother's keep – drew from me a homesickness that turned my heart in my chest. I felt deeply the years that had passed, and they left a blackened scar across me that was so tangible I felt sure that were I to expose my skin I would see it somewhere upon the pale expanse.

I watched the men with a heavy heart – my people, and yet not mine. I watched the shadows just as carefully, certain that at any moment I would awaken in Bluebeard's house and this place would all be a fitful dream.

I was still thinking that when a groom came and took Bluebeard's horse. I disentangled Grosbeak from where his pole had been propped in the saddle. He was fast asleep – snoring in a way that seemed inconceivable in a dead man, but who was I to say how the dead ought to sleep? Certainly, they slept the deepest of any of us.

Bluebeard snatched his trophy heads from the saddle before the groom led the stallion away, and in the commotion, the people nearest us noticed who he was and the battered army marching at his heel.

A cheer went up through the people left behind.

"Arrow! The Arrow! Patron Saint of Pensmoore!"

When had they added that part? They said it with such conviction, as if each of them had known it since birth, and yet I had been raised among these people and though I'd known to avoid the color blue and that the Wittenbrand stole people away and soured milk and were the source of every stillborn calf and foal, I had never heard one of them called "saint" or "patron." I had never heard anyone shout in joy at their arrival. Indeed, had they not all cowered back from him when Bluebeard came to take me for his bride?

It was that moment of adulation, that cheer that was still echoing, repeated again and again as we entered their midst, that glassy-eyed worship – it was that which severed a string I did not know was tied to me. Was it loyalty? Was it belonging? I couldn't put a name to it yet, but even so, I was certain that something had broken that was once strong. Something was flapping loose in the wind that had once been tightly bound. I prodded at the feeling in my heart as a tongue might prod a missing tooth, feeling the pain of the loss but also the sense that something new was emerging where it once had been.

There was a movement in the crowd like a rolling wave, and then, emerging with lantern-bearers on either side and a gaggle of older men in kaftans and trousers – and even one in a long robe – following behind, emerged the King of Pensmoore.

He had aged poorly.

His eyes were rheumy and his dark hair a hoary, yellowed white. His face twisted with what I read to be suppressed fury.

"Who leads my armies into battle? Who makes demands of me and mine?"

Everyone froze, the inner layers first and then, slowly, whispers rippled outward as the celebration stilled and all paused to see what would be said next.

Bluebeard pulled something small from his pocket and bounced it on his palm. The action unsettled the King so much that he wobbled, catching the arm of the man next to him for support.

I strained my eyes to see what had caused his discomfiture and Bluebeard paused, opening his palm before him so that we could see what was in his hand.

It was the tiny king figure he had pulled from the molten lead at the start of the game. He bounced it one more time on his palm and the king's face blanched under the redness of cheeks and nose.

"What devilry is this?" he gasped as the tiny figure stilled and then arched in agony, twisting and squirming in Bluebeard's palm, his tiny face twisting into the most precise lines of agony. No sound came from his open mouth, though the flesh of his face seemed to strain back from what must have been a tortured cry.

The king's eyes were transfixed on Bluebeard's palm, and he was not alone. Everyone who could see – or strain to see – that little figure was staring at it breathlessly. I felt a knot forming in my own throat. They were going to murder us.

Grosbeak snorted in his sleep.

"I hold within my palm the future of this nation," Bluebeard said in a low voice – a voice that was barely loud enough to be heard.

I could hear the people around him swallowing as he spoke, all their gazes looking toward his. His cat's eyes glimmered with bright moon-like reflections in the lanterns.

"I hold the fate of its king in my grasp," he continued. "And here we arrive, blooded and parched from a battle. We slew, on behalf of Pensmoore, the playing card army sent by the patron of Aayadmoore. But we were victorious only after it slew five villages, leaving not a soul alive or even enough of one person to bury and be sure it was them." I gasped at this and heard my gasp reflected in the gasps of the crowd. How had I not heard that? "Would you have preferred that army marched across the breadth of Pensmoore, slaying all that came in their path? Slicing them to shreds like cabbage for sauerkraut? Is this your wish? Do you envy the cabbage his due? Does the carrot catch hold of your envy?"

Someone snickered in the crowd, but others shifted uncomfortably, eyes wide. They were watching, eyes sweeping back and forth from the king to my husband, and I caught the moment when they seemed to be teetering in the middle, as if their loyalty perched on a fence post.

"I do not spend freely," Bluebeard said, and his words were met by whispers as they were passed back through the crowd. "Not lives. Not men," he gestured here to the men in the column behind him. "Not kingdoms," here a vague wave to the king. "Not even wives."

And though he did not point at me, all eyes turned to me.

"She's one of yours, if you'll remember," Bluebeard said. "Your blood, your kin."

He beckoned to me, and I came forward. He caught my hand in his and looked into my eyes considering, as if deciding whether to do a thing. We were allies. He should know that by now. I nodded to him. Whatever it was, I was ready.

And like that, quick as a serpent, he moved. The tiny king figurine was flipped into the air so that it tumbled end over end like a juggler's ball, while he drew his knife and slashed my palm, tucking the knife away before he caught the tiny king again. He tucked the king in his pocket, too, scooped up a handful of dirt from the ground below, and rubbed it into the wound on my palm and for a moment I felt utterly woozy. The ground around me tilted and then came up to meet me and it was only a pair of strong hands catching me that kept me from falling flat on my face.

Bluebeard spoke – and yet it sounded as if his voice was layered with another voice, as if two voices spoke at once in unison. And with it, I heard the sound of a great thrumming, like a long, deep, throaty heartbeat.

"Blood to earth, branch to bone, she holds your heart, she holds your home. Within her lies your fecund earth, within your hills, her blood brings birth. Now two are knit and one there be, the roots below the flowering tree."

And then the words passed, and my vision cleared and when I blinked back to awareness, I realized I was held up by Bluebeard's grip alone, clasping my upper arms. Around our feet, vines wrapped up to waist level and silky flowers the size of my hand hung in white decorative bells.

I could almost hear them tinkling as the heartbeat faded with the earth. I sucked in a long breath and once more, Bluebeard's beard tickled my cheek as he whispered so low, I could barely hear him.

"Take a moment to recover yourself. I have spent nigh on a year of your life in sealing the land with you. Surely, you must feel the loss."

I did feel the loss. But why would he spend so much on *that*? What was the point of it?

My lips thinned out into an angry line. When it was my turn to speak again, there was going to be a pointed discussion about the spending of days and exactly how much could be spent without at least consulting me. After all, they were *my* days he was spending. *My* years. And maybe he'd given a rib for me, but he'd have to ask if he wanted to carve decades off of me like the breast meat of a roasted goose.

But his action had certainly done one thing. There was only a pause for a single moment and then the roar of approval from all around him was so loud, so overpowering, that it immediately made my head ache and ears ring. The king flinched back from it, quickly smoothing his face to hide expression.

"Come, patron," he said with false gladness when the thunderous approval died enough to hear his words. "You'll dine with me tonight – you and your lovely lady wife."

And for the first time since my arrival, his eyes shot toward me and the look in them was not happiness, nor approval, nor welcome at all but a baleful fire that might have scorched me to the ground if it were not for my powerful husband and his mercurial favor.

"As you say," Bluebeard said lightly, turning slightly so he could share his wink and smile with all the onlookers. "Provided there is no shredded cabbage on the menu."

Chapter Fourteen

ENTERING the king's tent as hot food was served brought back memories of eating at his table in Pensmoore City. The scents were identical and little flashes of my father's proud visage, and the excited energy of my brothers' movements kept stealing over me. I had to brace myself against them in an effort to keep from being overwhelmed. My best help was Grosbeak.

"Pitiful," he muttered as we entered and were seated. "Mediocre. The ways of mortals turn my stomach."

"You have no stomach," I said idly as my eyes tried to take everything in at once. There were almost no women and what few there were bobbed and curtsied, serving the tables, eyes downcast. Those in the tent must not have heard the commotion without, for they were deep into their cups, drinking as if it were a race to the bottom of a keg.

I shifted painfully. The ride and the battle had not done me well with my injury and I was lightheaded and exhausted as well as in constant, throbbing pain just as insistent as the words of my bodiless friend.

"Then it turns my sense of taste," Grosbeak grumbled. "I still have that, do I not? The ability to judge ridiculous and pathetic from noble and worthy."

"I should hope so, or you are of no use to me," I said, but my brow was furrowed because the scene in the tent didn't look quite right to me, and I couldn't figure out why. Perhaps it was only pain clouding my mind.

Silence seemed to blanket me, and I paused, realizing belatedly, that the king and his council were regarding me with wide eyes, frozen in the act of entering the tent.

"You speak to a severed head," the king said, as if each word was being spat from his mouth. "You. A Savataz of Northpeak. You have no proper decorum. You are no lady of this court."

The censure in his voice was grim and with it, something inside me rebelled. What did I care if he judged me? I judged *him* for selling me to a man he both feared and hated to save his own daughter's skin. I'd been grateful to him up until now – thankful for his insistence that I be properly married when Bluebeard had come for me, but I saw now that it wasn't from a generosity of heart.

"How *is* Princess Chasida these days?" I asked, my face and voice a blank canvas. "Did she marry? Is she well? Has she children?"

The king's face flushed red. It seemed he was still capable of hearing my meaning. But the flush drained from his skin after a moment and he shook himself as if waking for a dream, paused, and there was a calculated gleam in his eyes as he said, "Indeed. And we should speak of it, as you were such dear friends. Please, go on without me, beloved advisors. Eat and be merry together and show our patron guest the pleasures of my table."

His advisors entered as they were bid, my husband coming up on their heels like a wolf behind geese.

Bluebeard's eyes narrowed and he looked at me. I lifted an eyebrow. The king was not very subtle. If he wished to pretend I was friends with his daughter as an opportunity to tell me something, surely we must both want to know what that something was.

"Stay where I can see you both," Bluebeard ordered, shooting a daggered glance at the king.

The way the king of Pensmoore's face turned to a light maroon told me he was biting down fierce retorts and maybe even fierce actions. He should bite harder. I'd seen Bluebeard take a head for less than the insults the king had offered so far.

Speaking of which, my husband set the heads he was carrying on the table before him as he turned to speak to one of the kaftaned advisors. They were looking worse for wear. If he insisted on dragging his trophies around, he should take better care of them.

I was curious about what he would say to an advisor. Was it simple pleasantries, "Oh, yes, I have more at home, but these will be an excellent addition to my collection" or was it more serious talk such as, "Since I'm your patron saint, I think a monument is in order"? I couldn't listen from here, even if the king wasn't drowning out my eavesdropping with his hissing words but I was curious about how Bluebeard spoke to mortals when he wasn't taking them as wife or removing their heads.

"You were sent as a spy to his house," the king hissed.

"I was sent as a tribute," I corrected him, coldly.

"But the note I sent and the mirror – "

"Were worse than useless." I turned away from my husband to face the man who ought to have been my sovereign and my protector. "And what shall I tell you, my king? That the Wittenbrand have carved up the world and they will fight now using the nations as the playing pieces on their board?"

"I'd prefer you didn't lie or make up wild stories," he hissed. "I'd prefer you acted as a loyal daughter of Pensmoore. Did I not tolerate your father and brothers in court all these years because of you? Do you not owe me now more than this?"

We were pressed against the tent wall, lost in the crowd of people, even though he was king, and I found my eyes straying from his face as if he were no more important than a nattering neighbor rehashing the same gossip he'd already told me thrice. There was something odd about the room. It was bothering me. And yet I couldn't identify what it was.

"Tolerate?" I asked, keeping my voice as cold as I could. "This is your message for me? That the sacrifice of my life for our nation bought my family a mere grudging tolerance? I thought you were going to tell me about Princess Chasida."

He waved a hand. "She's well of course. She has four children who are healthy. She married a prince of Ptolemoore and our trade has been beneficial. She's fat with fortune and health."

I let that hang in the air as I studied the crowd. It was the serving girls, I realized. They were too beautiful. Far more beautiful than me, though that wasn't the point. The point was that they were extremely comely and yet they were out here tending the army instead of safe at home. They were covered from head to foot, so it was doubtful they were camp followers. Why, then, were the most beautiful women I'd ever seen – with the exception of the Wittenbrand and Bluebeard's other wives – serving the king's table here? There was not a dull face in the mix. Not a single one. Surely that was odd.

"You can hardly blame me for selling you for peace," the king said, grimly. "What is it if one woman dies for the sake of an entire nation? What is her life worth when stacked against those others? What loyalty do I owe her or her family for merely doing their duty?"

It's strange how quickly a strong root can wither and die. I had thought I was rooted to these people. I had thought that root could hold and feed me all my days. An anchor to my past and to my self. I thought to shelter in its shade and sleep in its embrace, safe from the horrors of the world beyond. But now, it had crumbled to chalk in my hands. And though Bluebeard had tied me to the land and the land to me, I felt no kinship to this man, or his ways, or his court. I felt only a deep antipathy. Any loyalty within me for Pensmoore was long lost.

I was about to say something cutting to him, when Bluebeard lifted a drink from a tray carried by the most stunning serving woman I'd ever seen.

I left the king and ran towards him, screaming in my mind.

Don't drink it! Don't drink!

To my relief, he set the drink down. Now that I looked, I realized that the men around the table were not so deep in their cups as I had thought, but rather that someone – or several someones – had been serving them something ... off. One of the nobles clambered onto the table, eyes glassy, a song on his lips. He laughed wildly as I reached Bluebeard's side.

"What is it?" my husband asked at the same moment that the man fell from the table and lay there, motionless in the ground.

"What manner of mortal madness is this?" Grosbeak echoed.

"Poison, Grosbeak," I said. "The kind only the Wittenbrand have. The kind that makes you mad with emotion."

A second man was already clambering on the table to the shouted horror of the guards. But I didn't look at him as Bluebeard turned to me and then back to the chaos around me and then back to me again.

"Brilliantly noticed, fire of my eyes."

Vireo joined us, emerging from what had been a peaceful crowd only moments ago but was now bubbling with fear and aggression.

"Watch yourself!" a man nearby warned a chair was thrown across the room, breaking with a crash.

"Take my wife away from this madness," Bluebeard said, shoving me into Vireo's arms. "Take her somewhere safe until I call you. She is right – as she so often is. My enemies are plotting my death. This time, with poison. We must put an end to this underhanded deceit before they take something more valuable than my playing field or the ribs in my side."

I wanted to tell him to be safe. I wanted to tell him that I hadn't given the king any new information – that I was still his ally and wife. I had to settle for silence as he tucked a stray lock of hair behind my ear and whispered.

"Obey me in this one thing, wife. Go with Vireo and do not fail to follow where he leads you. Swiftly now, all is unraveling."

And then Vireo seized me by the arm, drew his sword, and led me into the night.

Chapter Fifteen

"WHERE ARE YOU TAKING ME?" I asked Vireo. He had led me through the chaos of the camp, his sword drawn as if he expected an attack at any moment. I saw no reason for such concern.

The poison had been grim, but it had been in the king's tent and surely such a poison would be costly and limited to where it could do the greatest damage. Out here in the camp, no one would spend their resources on a few common mortals. Most were already in their tents, sleeping or moaning in pain from the injuries dealt them. Those who remained had strung chunks of witch's hair moss over the entrances to their tents – a sure sign that patron saint or not, Bluebeard and his small band made them nervous.

We could easily join them, huddled by a campfire, and no one would notice. I could even moan in pain quite genuinely. I was already blinking back tears as he tugged on my hand. Each tug pulled at the wound in my injured shoulder.

Those mortals we encountered looked up from sharpening swords or eating a savory stew. The scent of it wafted to me, making my stomach rumble and clench. It had been more than a day since I'd eaten.

As we passed a ring of men eating around a fire, Vireo snatched up a chunk of bread from a communal bowl and a skin of water and shoved them roughly at me. The fiddle one of the men had been playing squealed to a stop.

"Eat," Vireo ordered me, glaring at the men as if to demand that they insult him so he could return the favor. "Continue with your music, mortals, this is none of your affair. Something quick and joyful, I think. I loathe your dirges."

The violin stuttered back to a start – a stumbling, leaping melody that was half jig and half terror.

I stuffed the bread into my mouth, eating as quickly as I could as struggling to swallow down the water while holding Grosbeak's lantern pole. I would not put him down. If I did, he'd be lost to me and I would be alone with Vireo and I did not trust the Wittenbrand, even if my husband called him brother and forgave him for his temper.

I was just glad not to hold his hand anymore.

"Yes, that's how to feed her," Grosbeak sneered. "Bread and water like any other prisoner. The Arrow won't like it if you care for his wife so poorly."

"Bread and water can't easily be poisoned," Vireo said, and then turned to me, his voice snapping like a flag in high winds. "I'm taking you somewhere safe as I promised. I have no silver key to take us straight to the Wittenhame, so we will ride as we have ridden before."

"Is it safe to go back?" I pressed. "Time passes differently there."

He snickered in an evil way. "What does it matter to you, mortal wife of the Arrow? You are but a treasury of days for him to spend as he wishes. My only fear is that he will reach for one and find it is missing."

"Then perhaps we should not spend my days in futile travel," I said dryly. I had only just returned to the mortal world, and I did not want to go back to the Wittenhame. Especially not without my husband to guard me against its many horrors.

"Time marches on with or without you. You can no more stop spending days than the sun can stop rising. Perhaps the sun stands even a better chance than you do, being a great light of heaven when you are only a wisp of mortal life."

We were well into the tree line now, and the dark branches crowded out the last scraps of light so that I stumbled often, barely catching myself.

I was not certain I should follow Vireo into the darkness, but when I weighed my options, there were none better. If I turned back, I risked falling into whatever revenge Bluebeard might be setting out on the Wittenbrand who had attacked him, or on the court of Pensmoore, or whoever else he blamed. He would think me safely away and could easily harm me by accident. If I managed to find his side without harm, he may very well turn me around and send me back again with Vireo by stronger means and feeling all the while that I had betrayed him once more.

There was no place for me among my mortal kin. The king had made that certain in his speech to me. And there would certainly be no place for me in Aayadmoore with my brother – unless I wished to be at the mercy of the Sword again.

There was no way forward but through, so through I must go.

Vireo grunted each time I fell, but he did not turn to help, and he did not slow his pace.

"If you kill me in this forest," I said calmly, "I do not think it will go well for you with your master."

He spun and grabbed me by the throat. It was already bruised and aching from the last man to do it. My heart sped like a rabbit caught in a trap, as if the heart itself knew time was short and was rushing to beat as much as possible before the end. But underneath that fear was a cold fury at the feeling of his fingers around my neck.

"Do not presume to tell me what is best for me and do not call the Arrow my master."

Grosbeak snickered cruelly. "You could be a head on a pole, too, Vireo. He likes collecting heads from anyone who bothers her, and he didn't stop her from claiming me. He'll smell the truth. You know he will."

Vireo cursed and released me. "Just stay close," he growled. "Are you not glad to be free of him?"

I was not glad, I realized. I was likely safer away from him, no longer a bargaining chip or tool, but leaving his side felt like being wrenched from my home.

We reached a clearing a few moments later where three saddled and antlered elk stamped in the moonlight. Tiny bells tinkled from the chains hung between their antlers. A pang of remembering shot through me – the memory of the last time I was stolen away on a frosty elk. But that time I had been mounted with my husband.

"I will not share a mount with you. You ride alone," Vireo announced, to my relief. The longer I knew him the more wary he made me. I did not trust his jealous looks or calculating eyes. Did Bluebeard not see in him what I did? Was he blind somehow to a man who clearly was oriented due self?

"Are we riding those misty paths all the way to the Wittenhame?" I asked as I mounted the elk. The elk stood very still, allowing the trespass, though he snorted crystal breaths into the air through his twitching nostrils. I found his huffing quite charming.

"I know a shorter path," Vireo growled. "You'll need to stay close on my flank, so we reach it in good time."

"You have no key," Grosbeak reminded him. "So, what shortcut do you speak of? You don't mean a colossus? That's madness, brother."

Vireo spun despite being mounted and slapped Grosbeak so hard that his head swung on the pole, and I had to hold on with all my strength not to lose my grip. My mount shifted uncomfortably under me and then lowered his head and bellowed.

"We ride," Vireo said and put action to words.

My elk followed but now my mind was full of questions.

"What's the colossus?" I asked Grosbeak.

"A huge statue. Have you heard of them? Figures of Wittenbrand who have fought as patrons of the nations in the past and won. They usually leave a colossus behind to mark the spot and then the colossus serves as a key to and from the Wittenhame."

"Then why didn't Blue – " I caught myself, "the Arrow use one last time? He was in a hurry then."

"They come out in odd places – sacred places where the Wittenbrand are vulnerable. Had he done that when he was rescuing you, then you may have died before he took a single day from your life."

"I thought Vireo was supposed to be bringing me somewhere safe. That's what the Arrow told him to do."

"I thought so, too," Grosbeak said ominously.

It didn't take long until I realized we were headed south toward Aayadmoore. We charged down short roads and then cut across country to hit them again.

"Vireo," I called after several hours of him riding ahead of me, circling back to urge me on when I fell behind. I considered if I should try to lose him, but even the smallest hesitation was immediately noticed and I did not have reins on this elk, it merely followed Vireo's mount wherever it went. There would be no riding off on my own. "Are we going to Aayadmoore?"

"We're going to the Wittenhame. I did promise the Arrow to keep you in a safe place, didn't I?"

His smirk worried me, and I remembered how he chafed when Bluebeard had brought me to the various events in the Wittenhame, how he'd stormed off when Bluebeard hadn't listed to his advice, how he'd somehow been losing that battle only for my husband to win it when he wasn't looking.

"Should I trust you, Vireo?" I asked him calmly.

In fairytales, the girls never ask that question. Maybe it's because they know they will be lied to, so why ask at all. Or maybe it's because they fear the answer will be exactly as they expect. Or maybe because they have other things on their mind like spinning straw into gold before everyone they love perishes. But I have always found you can learn as much from lies as from the truth, so I asked.

He shot a sharp glance at me, and I could tell he wasn't sure what to say next. And then a look of cunning crossed his face.

"Bargain with me, wife of the Arrow."

"What bargain would you strike, you who calls himself my husband's brother."

He made a clicking sound of disapproval from the side of his mouth. "I call myself nothing that I do not have the right to claim. But now heed me, mortal woman, for I shall offer this only once. I do not know what madness has seized our prince that he has chosen you. You are not lovely like his other wives, and yet he has married you properly. I would think he would want to choose a woman who would distract his enemies more fully."

"I suppose beauty does serve a purpose," I said calmly. I did not need it rubbed in my face that I was not beautiful, though people seemed to think that bringing it up put me in my place. I knew my place. I did not require reminders and it was not where people thought it was. "The beautiful are meant to be looked at while the rest of us get on with the business of making a life."

There was an arrogant tilt to his head when he answered me. "We Wittenbrand do not prefer to work. We'd rather bargain or fight, steal or kill."

"So it would seem. And do you think this makes you our superiors?"

"I think our long lives and magic do that. The only good a mortal serves is as a pawn. And you've been a poor pawn to my prince, the Arrow.

Already, you have lost him a move in the game and a rib. I would see better things for him."

It might have been a valid point if he hadn't stolen my girlhood, my future, my prospects, and my days. It seemed an even trade to me.

"And so you are pleased to see us separated," I pressed, still suspicious.

"I am pleased to see you out of his way. Don't you think that is for the best? Don't you think he is better off without you?"

"I think that if I am out of the way, I cannot help him. Was it not I who saw the drinks were poisoned by those very beautiful women? My skills have helped him more than once. Perhaps *you* are the one who sent the poisoners, since you seem so taken with beauty. Are they not who you would have chosen to deliver your draught?"

He pulled his elk in so quickly that the poor creature rose on hind legs, pawing the air before settling again. Reaching out, Vireo seized the front of my jacket and pulled me in close.

"Don't think to blacken me in your husband's gaze. It will not happen. I am no rival of mortals."

I refused to succumb to fear, not even when his belt knife flicked up and scratched at my throat.

"None can be your rival unless you let them, Wittenbrand. Do you call me rival? Is it not you, then, who has made me so? I have only the power to terrorize that you have gifted to me."

He huffed a frustrated breath and released me, and I tried to be subtle in how I checked my throat. Only a small nick. It was bleeding, but not badly. It stung, but only enough to remind me that I must be very careful with this Wittenbrand. He was not my friend. Whether he was a friend to my husband remained to be seen.

"You can be killed and snatched from him, and then what will he do for days? How will he win his battle?"

"He's encountered that problem fifteen times and had no problem finding a solution," I said dryly. "Here in the mortal world, it should be easy enough to find a girl to greet their patron saint."

He grunted, but I was worried now. There was no reason for him not to kill me.

"Do you wish to bargain to see your brother again?" he pressed.

A stab of worry filled me. Was that where he was taking me?

"If you bring me to him, you will betray the Arrow," I couched.

"How disappointed the mortal man must be to have spent his entire life seeking you only to be abandoned by you in the final hour. I am given to understand that gratitude is considered seemly in mortals."

The final hour? Worry gnawed at me at his words. Did he know something I did not? Had my brother died there with the Sword?

We burst through the tree line to where the river flowed before us, only here there was a guarded bridge not far upstream. The soldiers patrolling there wore the ruddy uniforms of Aayadmoore. How did he intend to cross it? He could not fly on the backs of songbirds as the Arrow had.

"What would you have of me, Vireo?" I asked, hoping we could finish this talk before he took me somewhere truly dangerous. "What would you bargain for?"

He stopped his elk, suddenly, and my elk stopped with it. The moonlight limned them both in bright edges and their breath was matching ghost-like gusts hanging in the air with every breath. And for the first time since the day I'd met him, Vireo reminded me of Bluebeard. It was the vulnerability, I realized, the way he seemed to be baring himself to me.

"You asked for a real marriage, and he gave it to you, and now it is killing him. He ought to have burned through you and made his move and remarried all over again, do you understand? Can you follow this reasoning with me?"

An image of Bluebeard stripped naked, his rib torn from his side came to mind and I swallowed, my throat too dry for it to be any relief.

"Yes," I whispered.

He leaned in closer. "I would not see you humiliate us before mortals, but you make a laughingstock of my prince. His other wives never did that. It is this that drives me forward and bids me appeal to your reason."

"I don't care what the others did," I said, putting as much defiance into my voice as I could. But I did care about not humiliating him. I was surprised by how much the thought of that stung. Was he flinching inside with every choice I made? I hadn't noticed that, but then again, he was opaque to me as clouded glass.

"Hear that?" Grosbeak taunted from the end of his chain. "She doesn't care what you think!"

"Ignore the ghast," Vireo said, his voice low and trembling. "He's dead. Nothing he says can be something new, he can only regurgitate old things."

"You're a regurgitated old thing!" Grosbeak spat.

Vireo ignored him, and now all of him seemed to tremble and not just his words as he pushed his argument. "The Arrow says you are practical – that you have the magic of seeing things and knowing their use." That was magic? "Would you not employ that for him? Would you not wish to serve a purpose his other wives did not? To be more than decorative? To be helpful? A benefit?"

And now he was striking close to my heart because I *did* want to be useful. But I did not trust Vireo and I did not want to work with him. He would betray me – of that I was certain. He would knife me in the back, given half a chance, or push me from a cliff. Or ... well, the Wittenbrand had many ways to kill. I did not need to imagine them all.

"Is that what all this is about? You want me to be useful? You want me to help you help him?" I pressed, because I needed time to think about what to say. Bluebeard had urged me to follow him. He'd urged me to obey this one thing.

I gritted my teeth against how that stuck in my throat. I didn't want to trust Vireo. I didn't want to follow him anywhere. But I also did not want to betray my husband's trust a second time.

"I wanted to give you these hours we've been journeying to think. To realize what has been happening. It makes me sick that he doesn't trust me anymore," Vireo said in a low voice. "Sick to my very heart. Do you know what I have done over the years to purchase his confidence?" He shook his head wildly. His breath was coming too fast as if everything depended on this. "Surely, you must want redemption, too. Are we not the same, you and I? Are we not both proven unreliable? Proven treacherous? Don't you want to wash that stain from your hands? And you can. You could spy for him in a way that no one else could. You could gather information. You could use the false expectations of others to hide in plain sight."

"The king of Pensmoore asked for the same thing, but I was of little use to him," I said, still cagey. I could follow him without truly trusting him. I was a practical girl. I could do this practical thing.

"Were you really trying?"

I shook my head.

"The next time someone tries to assassinate him, you'll know in advance. You'll know before anyone else. Wouldn't you rather be useful than a decoration? Wouldn't you rather prove your worth?"

I remained silent. He seemed to talk enough for two of us.

"Then bargain with me. We both have so much that needs forgiveness," he pled. "Give me your word that you will come with me willingly to the place I am taking you and that you will trust me and stay with me until you are shown this useful path, and in return, I will make you useful. I will give you a better understanding and a powerful role in this Game of Crowns and Thrones. What say you, Izolda Savataz, wife of the Arrow?"

"I wouldn't do that," Grosbeak warned, his voice rising in pitch as if he was catching Vireo's desperation like a disease. "You can't trust a traitor."

"I'll follow you without a bargain," I said coolly, unwilling to be swept away in their drama.

Vireo leaned in close. "Bargain with me, or do not follow at all."

I bit my lip. I'd been given one order and one only. To follow. Did I dare make this bargain in order to obey? But I did want to prove to Bluebeard that he could trust me, and I wanted to trust him. And the only way I could do that was by following his one request.

"You'll live to regret it!" Grosbeak warned. "Or worse yet, you won't live at all."

"Yes," I agreed, ignoring my friend. "I accept your bargain."

And I couldn't have said why, but Vireo's answering smile worried away at the edge of my mind like a puppy on a fresh bone.

Chapter Sixteen

"THEN WE ARE IN AGREEMENT," Vireo said, pulling a key on a light chain out from within his shirt. It gleamed silver in the moonlight. "And we have no more need of hours of pretense at riding across this dull mortal land."

"Where did you get that?" Grosbeak gasped, horror in his voice as his eyes watched the key.

Vireo turned it quickly in the air and a door leapt open.

"Don't go through the door, Izolda," Grosbeak said with trembling lips. "Ask him where he – "

His words cut off as Vireo cuffed him so hard that he spun in a spiral on his chain.

"Come, wife of the Arrow," Vireo said, his voice suddenly cold after the warmth of his arguments. "You promised to follow until the plan was revealed."

I could not have done otherwise. The pressure of our bargain clamped down on me and bid me move as he had ordered. I did not so much as lift a finger to protest, though my skin crawled as he led my mount behind his and stepped through the door.

The key had looked just like Bluebeard's key into the Wittenhame. Had he stolen it? Had Bluebeard given it to him in order to more easily spirit me away?

All question of the provenance of the key vanished as the elk took a second step and the madness hit me.

The world stretched and pulled like rope under tension, and I was unmade and remade in a blink of an eye, my mind seeing a thousand tiny visions like slivers of mirror that reflected a world I did not know and then were jammed directly into my brain. Agony filled me and I tilted my head back as I screamed.

It was over as fast as it began, but though we stepped onto the other side and through the madness, I couldn't help the endless whimper shuddering through my lips or the way my hands both clung white-knuckled to Grosbeak's lantern pole, or the way I was shaking like the earth when it quakes and nearly breaks apart.

I hardly noticed the arrow jammed into the stone, for there was no music this time and no golden light. No singing or petals falling from the sky.

There was nothing that greeted us as it had greeted Bluebeard – as if the Wittenhame rejected our entry. I clenched my teeth and forced myself to stop making such terrified sounds as Vireo pulled my elk along behind him – not toward where Bluebeard's house had been last time, but in the other direction.

Around us, the carpet of leaves and moss on the floor of the Wittenhame seemed to rustle and crawl. I watched it, half curious and half trying to claw my way back from madness. It wasn't until long minutes had passed, that I realized there was something under there following us as we moved. I thought I caught a glimpse of a slug, but after a moment, I realized they were white roots.

I opened my mouth to ask about it but was cut off when Vireo cursed under his breath and kicked his elk into a run. We ran – the roots running alongside with us – until the forest opened itself wide and I realized that ahead of us the land dropped off abruptly and I could see far into the distance where the land rose to meet the horizon in that familiar blur of land kissing air. There, in the vague shapes so far past sight that they had forgotten they could be seen at all, a thousand small rainbows glinted and danced, and my eyes played tricks on me that told of faerie dust and faerie gold.

"I hate this part," Grosbeak gasped as we thundered forward.

We weren't stopping. We were going to plunge right over the cliff.

I gripped Grosbeak's pole and tried to gauge how to leap from the back of a moving elk, but I saw no way to jump without my momentum carrying me over the cliff. I'd have to jump without the assurance it would work. I tensed my muscles, prepared to leap – and then the elk was in the air, I'd missed my chance, and we were flying through the air, off the cliff, over the valley of waterfalls and rainbows.

A bright light flashed across my vision, and we landed hard on rock.

The elk scrambled, his hooves trying to find purchase, and then he crumbled under me like a sandcastle washed away by the sea. I gasped as my feet hit the ground, my mind bending to try to see what was happening. One moment an elk had been under me and the next thing I knew it was gone.

The injury in my shoulder flared hot and painful and the smaller cuts in my back echoed the pain, leaving my mouth opening and closing like a fish drawn up from the depths. Catch your breath, Izolda. Just one good breath.

Just in front of me, Vireo had his face in his hands, little sobs sawing out of him.

"What did you see in the valley?" Grosbeak asked me in a rusty voice – the kind of voice that sounded like he'd buried his entire family.

"I saw," I said, pausing to lick dry lips. "Waterfalls and rainbows."

His laugh was snapping sticks and broken bones. It went on and on. When he recovered himself he snorted. "Hear that, Vireo? She saw rainbows and waterfalls."

"What did you see?" I asked, catching that breath finally and letting it fill me and ease some of the pain.

"Everyone I knew burning and blackened by the flames of hell," he flung the words out like a curse. "And though I doubt our Vireo will tell us what he saw, you can see it was not rainbows by the way he holds his shoulders so tight."

I blew out the long breath. More Wittenbrand magic. I didn't want to guess at what it meant.

And now we were here. On an island made of fierce slabs of upturned granite and dead, white trees like pillars smashed into place by the hand of an angry god. Pale lichen etched itself across the rock faces and tiny evergreens tried hard to replace their dead and worn brethren above. And all around, as far as I could see, there was only grey water and grey sky. The water was in a temper, dashing itself against the granite shore as if it, too, wished to leap over a valley of rainbows.

"What is this place?"

"You don't want to know. Or maybe you do. What do I know? You're the one who made the soul-forsaken bargain with him." Grosbeak sounded sour.

"I saw the key," Vireo rasped, looking up at us with his startling blue eyes, madness as thick in them as cold lard the morning after a feast. He scrambled over and grabbed me by the hair. "And as I thought, it's you. It's *you* all the way through. Come."

As if I had a choice. He dragged me by my long braid over the rocks which were more vertical than horizontal. He was half-frantic in his stumbling climb, his free hand grasping at rocks and bushes as he tore a path through the landscape. We were following the lapping waves, skirting the edge of the rocks where someone had scraped strange runes into the black lichen that grew along their side next to the water. I could not read them, and I almost thought that I should not try.

"This," Grosbeak said grandly as he swung on the end of his chain, narrowly missing small, gnarled cedars and jutting deadwood, "is the Isle of Burning Guilt. Any who make a vow here are bound by the denizens of this place to fulfill it or die trying."

How charming.

"Are we still in the Wittenhame?" I asked, "And could you stop dragging me by my braid, Vireo? I don't see how I could escape this place even if my mount hadn't melted like spring snow."

"Yes," Grosbeak said at the same time that Vireo said, "No."

And so, I was half-dragged along the rocks as I fought to keep my feet so that my hands and knees were scraped, my shoulder wound was open again and bleeding hot against my skin, and my temper just as damaged.

We only slowed when we stumbled upon a Wittenbrand sitting on a rock by the edge of the water, his eyes hollow, white hair flowing down his back to tangle in the pale, dead reeds that rustled along the bank. On either side of him, two sharp-eyed Wittenband stood, arms crossed, eyes looking in every direction. They were his guards, I realized, as I recognized him from the Great Game of Crowns.

"Bargain with me, rock," Lord Marshyellow croaked. "Bargain with me for your fate and you shall be as men who live a few days and then weep for eternity."

He looked up, suddenly, and his eyes lit as he saw me.

"I did it," he said, a vague smile lighting his empty face. "I made a mortal."

"That's the wife of the Arrow, Lord Marshyellow," one of his guards murmured. "And look, here is Vireo of the Arrow's band, here to turn his coat as promised."

Turn his coat? A stab of fear shot through me – I'd been right about Vireo – but it was Marshyellow who looked panicked.

"Then the poison didn't work. But I thought that certainly he would be tempted by more pretty wives. And what is this you wear, wife of Arrow?"

I looked down at my clothing, ripped and torn from being half-dragged over the rocks. It seemed fine to my eyes otherwise. I was dressed. Certainly, the clothing was blue, but Bluebeard had given them to me himself. They should not cause offense.

"Is that the Sword depicted thus upon your jacket?" He shuddered. "It is, it is, I remember now."

"It's just decoration," I said carefully. I was uncomfortable around those who were already mad. They made me doubt my own sanity.

"No, the memories! Stop the memories! I cannot take them." He closed his eyes, clutching his head as if he was in pain and Vireo made a frustrated sound in the back of his throat.

"Take off that fool jacket, Izolda," he snapped.

I looked back and forth between them. Vireo was here with another competitor for the game. And already there was talk of him turning coat. I gritted my teeth, irritated that I was right about Vireo. He'd pushed me into a bad bargain and even if I'd gone into it with open eyes, knowing what he was, I still didn't like playing the pawn. They meant to use me as they wished and I would not bear well under their usury.

It was time to draw a line. I'd promised Bluebeard I would follow, but I was not a child. I was not a slave. I would not be treated as such.

"I plan to wear it, Vireo, and wear it with pride. Would you have me do otherwise?"

Vireo cursed.

But before he could bring me to heel there was a call from within the forest.

"If you plan to bargain with us, then join us. And if you do not, then flee this Isle while you still can before your souls are bound forever."

Chapter Seventeen

"IT'S TOO LATE NOW. Your fate is on your own head," Vireo hissed as he led me to follow the voice.

"Good thing we have an extra head between us, then," Grosbeak muttered.

Behind us, the two guards were helping the distraught Lord Marshyellow up so he could follow us.

We clambered through a tumble of rocks and found ourselves on a huge, roughly level, expanse of dark granite. It was ringed by broken white trees, long dead, forming what looked like a ring of broken teeth or a crown made of broken bones.

Perhaps in another time, I would have considered what it meant to meet inside a broken crown. Today, I was too intent on who waited for us there. Through the broken spikes, we saw two figures. One, I expected after seeing Lord Marshyellow, but one I did not.

If I had told the king of Pensmoore about this meeting, he would not have believed me. He would have thought it was fanciful musings of a foolish girl. If I had told him that he and the other kings and queens of man were nothing more than pawns – that the real fate of the world and everyone in it lay in the palms of a scarce few Wittenbrand and that every tiny move they made left the fates of our nations tumbling into chaos, ruin, and death – he would have thought me insane.

The knowledge should have meant power for me. Power to stop it or twist it or ... something. But knowledge is not always power. Sometimes, it is only the marker over the grave of the future you thought you had.

A throat cleared, and I returned my thoughts to what was before me – the meeting of four allies. That they were here for something of import was clear from the fire burning in the center of the ring – a strange orange fire edged in thick smoke that poured like milk, heavy into the air and across the rock, and then vanishing. The Wittenbrand stood equidistant to each other as they waited and Vireo took his place easily in the ring with them, Marshyellow being herded into his place, as well.

Lady Tanglecott was one of the two waiting for us, her white-winged mist lions flanking her on either side and her golden oak crown reminding us that she was battling for the place of sovereign just like the rest. It was her who surprised me. I had expected her to be the type to fight alone.

Coppertomb, on the other hand, did not surprise me. My betrayer sat tidily on a small folding stool made of carved bones and a swath of black silk. The bones appeared to be femurs. I did not want to think too long about where they came from. Perhaps, he had tricked their owners into giving them up as he had tricked me. Betraying their very limbs as I had betrayed my own heart.

"You are late, Vireo," Coppertomb said calmly. "You promised you could get the job done and done quickly."

"There were complications," Vireo argued.

"After I handed her to you? Threw her into the mortal world for the taking?"

"The Sword was there," Vireo complained. "You said nothing about him."

"You couldn't handle dancing around him? You couldn't think to use his endless rage to fuel your desires? And yet you tell us you are fit to sit at our table, to take your prince's place as Lord Riverbarrow."

I gasped, freezing in place. But why was I surprised? Why was I shocked when I new what was at his core. Simply saying it out loud did not make it worse.

"Told you," Grosbeak grumbled.

"Silence, ghast. You were not invited here. The Arrow should have put your head with his others," Coppetomb said with a twist of disdain to his mouth.

Tension filled me. Bluebeard told me to follow – but how far would he expect me to go? Had he meant me to serve as a spy for him or had he truly trusted Vireo? Did I trust *him* enough to carry this ruse out all the way? I clenched my jaw so hard I feared it might break. I'd have to see this through. It was only sensible to gather what knowledge I could about our enemies. It wasn't sensible to trust that they wouldn't kill me afterward, though. Was a meant to follow that far? To let my own throat be cut in sacrifice? I hoped not.

"I'm not the Arrow's pet. I'm *her* pet," Grosbeak grumbled.

"I said, *silence*." The words were whisper-quiet. "Now that we're all here we must be quick. If any of the others catch word that we've formed an alliance – that we have means to remove them from this Game – then they'll form their own alliances, and the Game will quickly devolve into a blood sport."

"Isn't that what War is?" Vireo asked sourly. "A blood sport?"

"It can be," Coppertomb agreed. "When it is fought poorly."

I looked away from his blazing eyes, my heart sinking because he'd beat me once before and used me to set a trap for Bluebeard and if I was here before him again, then he must want to use me again. Had Bluebeard realized what position his edict would put me in?

Vireo kept a tight grip on my braid, but as I looked down, I saw something small in the grass by my feet – a tiny grass-woven egg the size of a quail's egg. It was so close to my foot that I was surprised I hadn't accidentally stepped on it.

I tried to stoop to retrieve it, but Vireo hauled up on my braid.

"Still, Izolda," he hissed.

"Can I not fix my boot?" I asked quietly. "Better now than when you want to move."

He grunted, releasing me just enough to let me bend. I fussed with the boot and scooped up the egg when I was done, hiding it in the palm of my hand. Maybe Vireo hadn't fully lied to me. After all, I was getting information for Bluebeard, wasn't I? If not in the way I'd expected.

"I prefer to fight my wars on my own terms," Coppertomb said with a smug smile. "I prefer to poison the enemy before I sneak into his tent."

Was it he who sent the poisoners to Bluebeard, then, and not Marshyellow? Or perhaps they had worked together – as much as Marshyellow worked at all.

"Then it's time that you explained why you've sent this dog to fetch the Arrow's latest wife," Lady Tanglecott said, looking bored. "I'm not as amused by posturing as you are. Do you want him to chase after her?"

"I had hoped to seize his power from him," Coppertomb said, hands steepled under his chin as he watched me. "Killing her will only give him the opportunity to marry again."

"The Sword tried to marry her, and that did not break the bond," Vireo reported.

"But if we keep her from him, perhaps that will be enough," Coppertomb mused. "He must have some proximity, must he not, Vireo?"

"I believe so," Vireo said solemnly. "And he seems to be more powerful when she is by his side. Keeping them apart can only help. The Sword is determined to sever their tie."

"Then send her to him," Lady Tanglecott said smoothly. "Let the Arrow and the Sword squabble over her like dogs over a bone, and while they fight, we will pick over their holdings and over their carcasses."

Coppertomb smiled and then Marshyellow began to laugh and laugh as if the greatest joke had been told. His attendants rushed to him, but he waved them off.

"Back Yarrow, back Frost. I need not your aid," he gasped. "Still laughing."

Coppertomb sighed. "That's well enough with me, Lady Tanglecott, but we must bind her lips then, too. We'll seal our pact as it always is done and seal her with it. And if she fails, Vireo, then she fails on your behalf. You'll not sit with us at the table. You'll not sit at all."

Vireo frowned, his unhappiness apparent, but he still rolled up his sleeve with the others and Coppertomb carved a rune into each of their arms with the tip of his dagger – a rune that looked a lot like the writing in the lichen on the rocks. The fire flickered and the milky smoke poured out of it, sweeping around our feet, pooling there and then flowing upward to wreath the broken crown.

"The girl?" Vireo asked when Coppertomb did not carve mine.

"The blood oath doesn't work unless she means it and she won't. The wraith will be enough," Coppertomb said as if speaking to a child. "Come now, let us make the vow."

And then together they spoke – Marshyellow a beat behind the rest.

And as they spoke, I thought I saw figures and faces in the strange milky smoke.

"We swear by blood and smoke, on pain of guilt and fire, that we four are bound now to work as one, to overthrow our enemies until none are left, and to keep this pact sacrosanct to us. Or may the mist consume our souls. And we swear by the denizens here to be bound to their rule in secrecy, silence, and purpose."

And as if their words had triggered something, five figures detached from the smoke – ghostly wraiths with human faces and open mouths, their eyes white and opaque. They drifted, one to each of us, and the girl who stood beside me was thin as a wrung cloth, as flickeringly translucent as the smoke, and horrifyingly cold.

"And may the Bramble King have mercy on us all," Lady Tanglecott said, and then she blew into the fire and strode away through the shattered tree crown. Flames danced in her path and the wraith attached to her broke away from the smoke and hovered over her left shoulder, hanging down across her back like a nosy relative watching her every movement.

"Bramble King. Mercy." Marshyellow had barely spoken the words when his attendants took his arms and guided him through the trees in a different direction, the flames licking across their path, too. His wraith spun around the three of them like a skein of wool.

"Bramble King have mercy," Coppertomb intoned, making a two-fingered pious gesture, and then blowing into the fire. His eyes were cruel and cold when he turned to Vireo. "Get her to the Sword by tomorrow at noon or I'll take back that key and turn you over to your master."

"I don't respond well to threats," Vireo said, but his voice was weaker than it should have been.

"Then you shouldn't have made an oath on the Isle of Burning Guilt," Coppertomb said with a shrug, and he turned on his heel and strode in a third direction, flames spreading out from his path like licking tongues. His wraith danced a jig behind him and turned to make a rude gesture at us before he disappeared into the smoke and flame.

"Our turn now," Vireo said grimly. And he seemed shaken when he blew on the fire and then spun, hauling me through the tumbled rocks to the water's edge. "Hurry. Bramble King have mercy. We must put distance between ourselves and the flames. The entire island will burn to seal our vows."

"What have you bound me to, you viper?" I asked him.

"I've bound you to silence, nothing more."

"And you're selling me to my enemy as bait for a trap. A trap for the Arrow!" I said as we scrambled across the rocks, the fires licking at our heels. I shouldn't have bargained with him. I should have tried to follow some other way. Coldness filled me, deep and oppressive. I'd bungled things again. Even in trying to follow whatever plan my husband had for me, I'd opened myself up to this. "You said I would be useful. We bargained for it!"

"Think back to what I said," he answered as he grabbed my braid again and pulled me with him into the grey waves.

Behind us, the entire island was a conflagration as the dead wood embraced the cleansing flames. I had a sensation of cold on my left shoulder and when I shifted to look, the ghastly face of the smoke girl was looking right back at me. I screamed, and her mouth opened wide in imitation. The scream echoed out over the waters.

"Wraiths," Grosbeak grumbled from his place on the end of the chain. "I hate wraiths."

My breath was coming too fast. I tried to twist away from the spirit, but she bent around me, following the way my head turned so she was still in my peripheral.

I was going to scream again. I could feel it bubbling in my throat. I fought the sensation. It was not practical to scream. Screaming only opened my mouth and left me vulnerable. I needed a plan. I needed a way to reasonably deal with this Wittenbrand madness.

Vireo tugged my braid again, dragging me deeper into the water so we were knee deep and then hip deep and then chin deep.

"I said you would be useful," he gritted out as we fled the flames. "I never said *who* you would be useful to."

Chapter Eighteen

FORTUNATELY, we didn't have to go deeper into the water than that, for the lake was no more than chin deep. Vireo dragged me through it by my braid and I had to keep all my concentration on not stumbling, and holding Grosbeak's head up over the water, and so I passed through that dark lake with only a few glances over my shoulder at the burning island or the wraith who hovered over my shoulder.

We reached the other side and began to rise up from the water, Grosbeak spitting weeds out from between his teeth – I'd dunked him more than I thought. We slid over algae-coated stones, slowly climbing from waist level to knee level, and I tried to speak.

"Back there," I gasped. "You swore me to secrecy about – "

But before I could finish the sentence, the wraith wrapped an icy hand around my mouth and twisted so that her huge, dead eyes looked into mine as she shook her head.

I shivered and then retched, fighting to push her off of me so that I could vomit. In my frantic fight, I lost Grosbeak for a moment and had to recover him, dripping, from the lake.

Vireo watched it all with a stony face, not even letting go of my braid as if I were a horse that might spook and run.

"You were bound to silence at the island," he said when I was left, panting, gasping, and clinging to my lantern pole, one hand thrust out to try to hold the ghast at bay. "Were I you, I would not try to speak of it again."

I stood completely still, frozen into place, the only sound the trickle of the water running off me and whisper of the wraith right behind me.

I watched him for a long moment and then I shivered.

"Why are you trying to replace –"

The hand covered my mouth again and I gagged on my own words. I wanted to bite it. I wanted to scream. But I had a terrible feeling that if I opened my mouth the creature would reach right down my throat.

"Vireo's a cold devil who was meant to be the Arrow's closest companion," Grosbeak informed me. "You stood over my grave, Vireo. Do you not see the irony? I turned on a man I once called friend, and tried to kill his bride. You've turned on him the same way and yet you stood over me and spoke words of remembrance as if my death was justified. Should I speak some over you now?"

Vireo's reply of, "Silence, revenant," seemed half-hearted.

But Grosbeak's words were putting steel back into my spine. I'd survived the wound he'd inflicted and now he was my creature. Surely, I could do the same with Vireo. I held my back straight as we emerged from the water.

"He was good with a blade and better with a lie," Grosbeak intoned as if he really was at Vireo's funeral. "He had no patience for the dead though they'll be required to have patience for him now."

"I bid you silent, and silent you will be on this matter, or I'll carve out your dead tongue," Vireo threatened, but he seemed shaken, and as I looked at the crumbling cliff along the shore of the lake, I could see why.

We were not alone. We were being watched by the cliff – for deep in its sandy wall, half-hidden by slides of sand and tumbles of wildflowers, was the dreaming Bramble King. His eyes eased open, watching us, and Vireo froze and then bowed jerkily, terror making his movements choppy and abrupt.

"His glory he fades," the Bramble King said barely audibly. "His glory. Fades."

And then he closed his eyes again, shook himself, dislodging a fall of sand, and opened them again intoning, "I am the culmination of desire, the fruit of death. I am the summit of loss, the passing of weight. What am I?"

"I don't know," Vireo said through thick lips. He stumbled backward, losing his grip on my braid. "Come, Izolda," he hissed. "Come away."

"What is your riddle for?" I asked the King, tilting my head to the side.

He winked at me, and his eyes glazed over with white, and he ceased moving.

I thought I might know the answer to the riddle. I thought I might have an idea of what he was offering, though I did not think he was offering it to me.

"His glory fades," I muttered to myself just as Vireo managed to snag my braid again and drag me away.

I was still pondering his riddle when we clambered up the beach and made our way deeper into the Wittenhame, leaving lake and beach behind and entering the tall wood until we were lost among the roots of the trees that stood higher than the sky.

Last time I was here, there seemed to be magic everywhere. Now, there were armies everywhere. And though flower petals fell down from the sky in a constant fragrant rain – as if this was the wedding of Spring and Summer – still this world felt empty and dark compared to the last time I was here. Some sweet magic had been torn away just as my husband's rib had been torn from his side.

"This is what your husband ought to be doing." Vireo's eyes were poisonous as he looked back at me. "Look at Lady Tanglecott's mounted Lions."

He gestured to where a column of Wittenbrand mounted on actual mist lions rode out from a tear in the sky. They rode four abreast, their white mounts clawing at the air and snapping at anyone who got in their way. White fur lined in the burnt gold of an orange blossom heart was striped jagged charcoal lines but neither light nor shadow disguised the power of bunching muscles and the way their lips curled up in black arches and revealed the scimitar curves of ivory teeth. My back twinged at the thought of one of them getting near me again. I couldn't believe that the men dressed in flowing purple and seated on saddles of gold were not immediately consumed by their own mounts but they hardly seemed to notice the beasts under them. They rode with eyes ahead and voluminous banners flying behind them.

And then we were descending into the chaos.

A group of Wittenbrand wearing Coppertomb's drab colors drilled in firm precision around a long cylindrical device. One end of the device smoked and sputtered, but it was not that end they were avoiding, but the other. They worked in perfect synchronicity as if they performed a dance.

I barely had time to gape before Vireo spun us in another direction and we were nearly crushed against a party of Wittenbrand marching to a steady whipcrack. They cracked their whips in unison, taking a step behind the whips, spinning, and then cracking again until they leapfrogged each other, jammed naked knives between their teeth, and then spun again. They smelled of sweat and onions.

I was struck dumb turning from one group to the next.

"But are they not at war in the mortal world?" I whispered to Grosbeak as we wove through the crowd. I barely had time to digest one sight before another filled my vision.

"Of course they are. This display is for intimidation. A reminder of what you go up against. A reminder of how strong and brave we are – we will not merely spend our mortal pawns in battle, we will fight ourselves. Or, most of us will." He sounded proud. "You wanted to play the game, Izolda. You wanted to break free of the Arrow. Now you see what that means. The rules are death by drowning, by fire, by enchantment, or by sword. What choose you, now?"

"I choose not to die," I said between clenched teeth.

"That was my choice," he replied, nodding sagely – though how he did that when he hung from a chain, I did not know. "It worked out well for me, as you can imagine."

I bit back a curse.

Okay, Izolda. Think. You wanted to be a spy. You wanted to find practical ways to defeat your husband's enemies. So. Do it. Watch and learn. Find ways. What would a mortal learn from this that a Wittenbrand wouldn't see?

I kept my eyes open as we whirled between displays, watching fire-breathers spout like baby dragons and a series of knife throwers strike targets the size of wine corks hanging from their friend's ears. And I knew the answer to my question.

We were in trouble – we mortals. So much trouble.

I swallowed down heavy despair, thicker than cold grease in my throat.

What hope had we against the powers arrayed against us? Who could deliver us from this coming death?

Someone stepped in front of Vireo – a familiar figure with antlers and shaggy green moss all over his body. That was one of Bluebeard's people, wasn't it?

"Stand aside, Cornelis," Vireo growled. "I've no time for you."

"The rumors say you plan to take the place of the Arrow as our prince, and yet you have no time for us?"

"Neither now nor if I ever take that place."

I was so distracted that I didn't notice there was someone standing behind me.

"Feeling misty-eyed?" a voice whispered in my ear. "No, don't turn. He's busy now. Just take this message."

I felt something slip into my palm – the same palm that held the egg – while Vireo shoved Cornelis aside.

"Know your place, Cornelis. You're folk. Underfolk. That's all you'll ever be."

"That's not how the Arrow sees us, Vireo," Cornelis called after us as Vireo pressed back into the crowd. "He sees us as people. He cares about our peace."

Vireo stopped and whirled back to shout at Cornelis, which gave me a chance to see the whole band of them there – the strange folk I'd seen in Bluebeard's house. Some were walking, shambling trees. One was a fox in a vest and hat. A few had antlers or hooves or tails. They seemed smaller out here among the Wittenbrand. Dimmer. As if they'd lost their life just a little.

I stole a look at the paper in my hand.

"We're with you," it read. "For the Arrow."

And I could see it was true, shining out from their eyes as they watched Vireo with restrained fury and me with pity.

"And is he here?" Vireo roared. "Is he raising an army? Is he vanquishing his foes? Or is he saving mortals? Did he spend all his resources on peace for his *folk*?" He spat the last word. "You. This mortal girl. The mortal world. You're all his undoing. He's a soft fool and you've killed him with your own hands."

And then he was storming away and dragging me with him and this time I went willingly because I couldn't look into their crumpling faces without crumpling inside myself. We all meant well – these folk and me –

and we all weighed on him against our wills. Even my obedience felt like a betrayal to my husband.

"And how do you like the Wittenhame on your second trip here, Izolda?" Grosbeak asked as if a cheery conversation was the right choice when Vireo was glowering and tugging me by my braid so that I feared it might come out at the roots.

"I wish I had a fairy godmother to whisk me away like in a tale for children," I said, my eyes stinging. But even if she did, there was no fleeing this. "This place seems dimmer and darker than the last time I was here."

And it was true, for while it was still violent and bloody – I was relatively certain that one of the vendors was selling jackets made of human leather and there was a card game going on that we'd walked by where the competitors were betting fingers and toes – it had lost the sense of purpose and wonder that had been mixed throughout that violence before.

"Hear that, Vireo? She says it's darker. Less magical," Grosbeak said.

Vireo grunted.

"Would you say it's *lesser*, Izolda?" Grosbeak pressed. "Pathetic, even? In comparison, of course, to what you saw before?"

"Perhaps," I said, drawing the word out in my uncertainty. "Certainly, less lively, less vigorous."

Grosbeak laughed nastily.

"I can still sew your mouth shut, revenant," Vireo muttered, but he seemed preoccupied as we finally emerged from the press of bodies and pushed toward a building that looked like a tangled crown sticking out from the forest floor. It was the size of a palace and gilded from top to bottom as if the owner had said, "Try for blindingly ugly, but I'll settle for merely gaudy if I must."

"The Wittenhame, my dear Izolda," Grosbeak said, as if he were delivering the most delicious gossip, "is much like the valley we leapt into to find the Isle of Burning Guilt. You, as a mortal, cannot shape it, though some features like the valley reflect the inside of your mind. But the rest of the Wittenhame is affected by those mortal souls residing there. As the prisoner of Vireo, you are seeing *his* Wittenhame, just as when you came here as wife of the Arrow, you were seeing *his* version of this place."

Oh.

Oh.

Well. That explained Vireo's attitude.

"Shhh," I warned Grosbeak. He wasn't making us any friends.

"I'll be rid of you both soon enough," Vireo growled. "And good riddance, for I have plenty more that needs my attention."

Grosbeak nodded gravely. "Like proper grooming. Or dying messily on the Arrow's blade."

"Laugh all you want, you two damned souls. It matters not to me," Vireo said as he tugged me roughly forward and knocked on the gilded door. It was made entirely out of hundreds of interwoven blades. "You're the Sword's problem now."

Chapter Nineteen

THE SWORD, it turned out, did not answer his own door, nor was his home as welcoming as Bluebeards for while Bluebeard's ceiling seemed to reach up endlessly into the starry sky, the Sword's castle seemed to reach *out* endlessly into one gallery after another.

He was a collector. And were I not in fear for my life, and if I did not have such utter disdain for a man who would snatch away my innocence just to test a theory about a rival, I would have been deeply impressed.

We were led by a silent butler through the Sword's halls, passing through a gallery so long it could hold the entire palace in Aayadmoore within its walls. It was decked out, floor to coffered ceiling, with portraiture. Tiny miniatures no larger than my palm were side by side with portraits so large they dwarfed me, their elegant gilt frames thicker than my waist. And while one might think that no one could take time in thinking of the place for each one of so many thousands, there had clearly been careful intent regarding the positioning so that a fierce expression was followed by one that countered it with disdainful arrogance and then that again was belied by a face of such virtuous innocence that I found myself pausing to wonder if it could be real or if the designer had intentionally revealed the hypocrisy by placing it beside that particular counterpoint.

I leaned in closely to examine one, and to my horror I realized that the curling hair around the face was real hair set into the paint and the frothy lace around the neck was made of human teeth.

And that was only one gallery.

"Ohhh. Fancy," Grosbeak commented appreciatively. "I've never seen such a collection of death portraits before. A sheer delight."

Somehow, his comments seemed to cheapen each room as if his very admiration lessened them. I was grateful for any distraction that might turn my mind from wandering how a "death portrait" was made and with *what.*

No better was a room of gnarled, shrunken bodies that Grosbeak claimed were called "mummies" arranged in various poses with blades stuck through them as if they had died and then been frozen in the pose of their deaths.

Our legs tired and our eyes wore dim from seeing horrors by the time we reached the heart of the palace. Were a connoisseur granted both access and a pair of scribes to assist, still he could not have cataloged the room of tiny miniatures crafted to look perfectly lifelike in expression and fashion – and posed in such a way that made me shudder and close my eyes, begging whatever merciful god there may be to take the memory of what I'd seen away. He would have been just as put upon to try to catalogue the hall that was a series of waterfalls falling from one tier to the next with walkways weaving between them and trees dripping with flowers leaning over the paths as if trying to catch a lover's whisper. Interspersed among the flora had been gold-cast statues of Wittenbrand and when my eyes had widened at the sight, Grosbeak had snickered with delight.

"The Gilded Falls. There's a legend about how he trapped those and brought them to his house. I thought it was merely a story."

"I would think he'd want to display those golden statues somewhere more visible," I said.

Grosbeak snickered. "They stay where they are. That's the beauty and horror of it. The waters turn any living thing that touches them into gold. If you creep closely you can see schools of fish at the bottom of the pond – but I wouldn't recommend getting close enough that the spray could touch you."

Perhaps, were I another woman, I might find such grandeur impressive. Perhaps, I might be flattered to find myself mistress of it – married to the owner of all I surveyed.

But just as in fairy tales told to children, I had an inkling that as easily as this wealth had been accumulated, it could be snatched away, and with it, no happiness had been bought, no joy fostered, no longevity purchased for the heart. Just as the false marriage the Sword had forced on me was hollow, so these horrifying luxuries were hollow with it.

And though the butler was well dressed in clothes far finer than those worn by the King of Pensmoore, and though he looked mortal to my naked eye, but for the greenish tinge to his skin, still anxiety knifed its way through every nerve of my body as we drew closer and closer to the Wittenbrand who had made himself my mortal enemy as surely as he had made my husband such.

We found him in the middle of an enormous ballroom, directing his staff of hundreds as they prepared what appeared to be a feast.

"Ah, you've brought my wife, Vireo," he said casually as if I hadn't been ripped from his grasp and then stolen away from Bluebeard's. "I believe the price of retrieval was my support on your bid for a seat on our council, hmm?"

"As you say, Prince of Wittenhame," Vireo said woodenly, and I was surprised by how still his face and body were – almost as if he were petrified in fear.

"I'll throw in an invitation to dance here tonight," the Sword said, sweeping a gracious bow – but a very shallow one that was almost mocking in how he sketched it. "After all, you were prompt, and she seems to be as unharmed as any of us. All of Wittenhame will dance at my Petal Ball tonight for the dawn of the Second Move."

His grin was toothy and dangerous, and I realized that within the spills of flowers and ornamental flowers his staff was arranging, there were a variety of traps – some large clamshells with spiky teeth like the cruel ones meant to catch the leg of a bear and some tiny little things barely larger than my fingernail. I was no fool. Those tiny ones were likely just as deadly as the large ones.

Take note, Izolda. Do not stop to smell the roses.

My heart was racing so quickly that I couldn't quite control it. Little spots of blackness danced over my eyesight, and I knew I must calm myself or risk fainting. But I needed a plan. I needed it now. It needed to be practical, and it needed to keep the Sword from molesting my person.

I could think of nothing. Reaching for thought was like trying to hold air in the hand.

"You're outdoing yourself, Sword," Grosbeak said, breaking the tension.

"I've raided a thousand gardens over a thousand centuries for these," the Sword said with a satisfied smile as he waved an elegant hand at the sprays of flowers draped or wreathed or carefully woven over every surface of the room, even including the many arched doors. "But none compare to the flower who will walk in on my arm into the Petal Ball tonight."

"Like you, I often find an enchanted partner to be the best," Grosbeak said but I knew there would be a barb by the tone of his voice. "A woman spun from a rose blossom has skin softer than a petal and she doesn't stab you in the back. Wise choice."

"My choice is wise indeed," the Sword said coldly. "For I shall display to the Wittenhame how I have stolen the Arrow's wife and made her my own. You may go now, Vireo. And mind the traps. It would be a shame to attend my ball with only one leg. It would set us one partner shy for the dancing."

He waved a lace-cuffed hand idly and then turned on me.

I could stay silent. I could refuse to speak or to cry or to run or to show my fear, but I couldn't keep my breath even and calm. Not even though I fought it with all my strength.

"You've played the coy and blushing maiden, mortal girl, but now that time is passed," and with shocking speed, his hand darted out and pinched my ear and with even more surprising strength, he wrenched me off my feet and began to drag me over the marble floor by the shell of my ear.

Pain filled me, pounding through my head. I caught his wrist with one hand, holding tight to keep my ear from being torn off, and with the other I clutched Grosbeak's pole as he was dragged along with me. Tears stung my eyes, but I would not scream. I would not.

I needed an opportunity. Some chance to get away.

And then I saw it.

We were passing an open door of what must be a library. All I could see was a wall of books. But libraries were always huge and this one would have plenty of places to hide.

With a quick twist, I hurled Grossbeak's head into the open door and then flipped hard, rolling to the side like a pickerel on the line and flipping from the Sword's grasp – the fish spitting the hook.

I tumbled, rolling across the slick floor and through the door. I could feel each bump and bruise, but I refused to acknowledge them as I scrambled to my feet and slammed the door shut before the look of shock had left the Sword's face.

With quick hands, I locked the door. There was a bar, which I set quickly into place before the first knock hammered against the thick door.

"If you think a door will keep me out, little mortal, you should think again," the Sword drawled.

It would be okay. I had time. I just had to hide in the library.

I scooped up Grosbeak's pole.

"Nnngh. Why did you throw me like that? I'm a head, not a stuffed ball for children to throw!" he moaned.

I ignored him. This was our chance to escape. Spying was not a good fit for us after all, and we'd seen plenty enough to tell Bluebeard.

I ran down the shelf of books – it was barely two strides long – and turned into a tiny padded alcove for reading.

"There's only one shelf in this library," I gasped, shocked.

Even my father's library was bigger, and we had not money for many books with our horses to care for and a keep to manage.

No. This couldn't be right. The ache in my healing shoulder intensified and when I pressed a hand to it, it came away wet. Flinging oneself across a hall to bounce and roll was not a winning strategy for healing wounds.

The Sword pounded on the door again, making the lonely books quiver on their shelves.

"I'm sorry, did you take your second husband for a reader?" Grosbeak asked sourly. "He struck you as the type to contemplate life and consider the nuances, did he?"

I gritted my teeth. My plan was failing fast.

"Let me in, Izolda Savataz!" the Sword roared. "For I will make you my wife this time and no cloud of birds will swoop in to stop me."

The monster was outside my door, clawing his way in. How would I keep him out? How?

"He's going to get in. He's going to get in," Grosbeak chanted and I didn't know which of us he was cheering for at that point.

The frame of the door splintered with a chilling crack.

"If you can't keep him out, let him in, let him *in*," Grosbeak screamed and then burst into hysterical laughter. You'd think the one who had only his head left would learn to keep it in a crisis.

I rolled my eyes at him, but as the bar across the door broke in half, I seized on his suggestion and drew the little key from my bodice.

He was right. This wasn't the only place to which I could flee, and if I couldn't keep the Sword out, then I really should let him in – all the way in.

I drew out the key, twisted it to unlock the room, and fled inside.

It was only when I glanced over my shoulder to see if he was following that I remembered the ghast riding just over my shoulder. She winked at me and that alone was enough to make my breath gasp harsh and raw in my lungs.

Chapter Twenty

"HERE HE COMES, HERE HE COMES!" Grosbeak shrieked as I ran down the line of wives, looking up to their impassive faces as if they could see, as if they could guard, as if just by having them there as witnesses I could derive some kind of strength from them. They had each been where I was before. In a manner of speaking. Certainly, the Sword had not stolen them from Bluebeard, but that had not saved their leaking days.

My days trickled down from the top bulb of the hourglass, the garnets ringing like tinkling bells as they fell and hit their fellows. My husband must be spending my days even as I ran toward them. I could only hope that he was spending them on something useful and not on trying to rescue me.

And just like that, steel snapped my spine straight and I felt like I could breathe again.

I was a practical girl.

I could deal with this sensibly. So, what did a sensible girl do when confronted with an enemy bent on her destruction? She found a way to dissuade him.

I took up a stance in front of the hourglass and crossed my arms, trying to look like I knew what I was doing. Like I belonged here. Like he didn't. And it was easier to do because it was true.

"What manner of mausoleum is this?" the Sword asked as he slunk into the room, hand on the hilt of his sword, his eyes wary. He stepped like a cat in a new place, his graceful movements so close to my husband's, that my traitor heart beat double for a moment. I forced it back to calm.

"Behold," I said, grandly – because he was grand and I was beginning to realize he could respect nothing else, "The brides of Bluebeard. And what, lordly Sword, do they have in common?"

"They have all passed this life," he said, awe in his voice and something that looked like enjoyment. It took me a heartbeat to identify it. It was admiration – one collector admiring the collection of the other. "I see the charm."

"And what else do you see? Surely, you, a great collector, can see the similarities," I said.

"They're each more lovely than the last," he said, his voice distant and wondering as he reached out and touched the edge of Princess Margaretta's dress.

I flinched. It felt almost as intrusive as if he'd touched the hem of my own garment. My fellow brides were not here for his amusement. My thoughts stuttered for a moment as I realized that perhaps that was why Bluebeard kept them in this room that held the hourglass. Only another bride could know what they had suffered. Only another bride could pay them the honor they were due.

The Sword lingered over Corinnian, a particularly lovely bride whose full figure gave her an air of majesty I would never possess. He paused, arrested, and then his eyes whipped to mine.

"Except you. You are an aberration in a perfect set."

His brow furrowed in confusion.

"Do you note their books?" I asked, drawing him in with my mild tone, setting my own trap among the flowers. If only it would work. If only he did not see it before it was sprung.

He laid a hand on the closest one and I flinched as he flipped through the pages.

"They speak of their lives with Bluebeard," I told him, my voice smooth as a storyteller's. "Of their secrets. Of the one thing you don't know about them."

I was betting that he wouldn't read them. A man with such a pitiful library wouldn't read, would he?

"How he takes their days as his own," the Sword breathed in reverent wonder, hunger in his tone.

It took every bit of my self-control to keep surprise from my expression. He must be desperate indeed to reveal himself to me so.

"They are virgins one and all," I say, my voice low and calm, hoping he might forget it was me talking at all. "Untouched by Bluebeard, despite his marriage to them. Untouched by any man."

He looked up sharply at me and I was surprised as his expression turned from suspicion to hope. He flipped through the book in his hands – and I knew which one it was. It would tell of the wife who tried to tempt Bluebeard into her bed, failing again and again.

He read it as a starving man eats a dinner laid before him – devouring it without pause. And then he looked up at me and the relief on his face was stark.

Had he feared what he would do to me as much as I had feared it? The thought made him seem more human to me. More vulnerable. More like someone I could understand.

"And so, I have a choice," he said and all the compassion I'd just discovered in my heart withered away at his words. "A choice on which weighs so much."

He tapped his lip with one finger, regarding me and then regarding the other brides again before returning his eyes to me.

"If I defile you, I will rob him of his secret power, rendering you useless. But if I do such, I will also keep that power from my own grasp."

He tapped his chin.

"Perhaps it was that you were married twice." He was nodding now to himself. "You will have your marriage to him annulled. We will see a priest. And then you will marry me again. It is only the vows that keep your enchantment from my grasp. I had not thought that they must be removed before others were added." There was certainty in his eyes now. "Yes, this is so. And you will return to him the key to this room, for it is not yours and it never will be." He smiled. "Yes, that will work. That will suffice."

He put down the book and started to stride away, spinning in place to say one more thing to me.

"You'll attend the Petal Ball with me tonight and I expect that you will show your loyalty to me with your eager feet in the dances and your eager smile at my side. Have not a fear for what you will wear, as I shall provide that. Think instead of resting. The rings around your eyes are dark with sorrow and you are not one of those women in whom grief works beauteous wonders. Don't leave the library. I will retrieve you at dusk."

And then he was gone – out of the room of wives, and out the door of the library, and I heard the sharp snick of bolts being thrown and the heavy *thunk* of the bar on the other side of the door being set in place.

I leaned heavily against the hourglass as if embracing my own days might make them last just a little longer – or run out right now – and I hardly knew which I wanted more. I simply let the cool glass against my cheek give what comfort it could.

"Well, that went smoothly. Who knew you were such a savvy negotiator," Grosbeak said. "But you'll need a plan before the Petal Ball. When Bluebeard sees you on the Sword's arm, he may well behead you both. Trust me, it's not as glamorous as I make it look."

My eyes went wide.

"He'll be there?" I asked, my voice choked with worry.

My battered friend grinned.

"Of course. Like the Sword said, half the Witenhame will be there."

"And I won't be able to tell him about the isl – "

The specter wrapped her hand around my mouth, frowning as she shook her inky head.

"Exactly," Grosbeak said, almost smugly. "I've gotten to like you, Izolda, and yet I've always been a passionate admirer of melodrama. I believe you're about to deliver for me tonight. I can hardly wait."

Chapter Twenty-One

I SEIZED upon this opportunity to finally examine the egg. There was really nothing else to do.

It was woven of grass and light as a feather and though I held it up to the light and peered at it from every which way, I could not determine what might be within the weaving for there was neither shadow nor profile to hint at it and it was not heavy, nor did it make a sound when shaken.

"Where do you pick that up?" Grosbeak asked curiously. "'Tis an odd little thing."

Eventually, I resorted to breaking it open – a difficult thing to do with an egg so tightly woven. I had to grasp each side and pull – and when I did that, it flattened the woven egg so much that I was certain there could be nothing inside and I was ruining this uncanny bit of craftmanship for no reason at all.

Eventually, though, the strands of grass shredded and the egg tore in twain, and from its hollow grassy depths arose the smell of fresh-turned fields and a voice that sounded so much like the Bramble King's that I looked around the room, thinking he might be right beside me.

It sang,

"*Fly with the Arrow,*
Dance with the Sword,
Give your heart to the barrow,

Die with your Lord.

"And if ever you be broken
And gasp on the ground,
Hold up your fine token
And join with the sound,

"Sing for your sovereign,
Bow to your Dream,
Make haste for the fallen,
Rise in esteem,

"And if ever you be broken,
And gasp on the ground,
The word may be spoken
And salvation found."

It was the song I'd heard from the crowd when the Arrow arrived for the opening of the Game of Crowns. And now that I heard it again, different words and phrases stood out to me than they had last time.

Perhaps, it was because when the words faded a very tiny item was found in the scraps of grass after all – a tiny golden bell, as small as the nail on my forefinger and forged with such precision that all I could think of were tiny jewelers hammering it out. It hung from a little clip meant to be fastened into hair and after a moment of thought, I clipped the tiny bell into my dark locks.

It did not ring when I moved. It made no sound at all. And there was something about that so immensely chilling that I shivered with the thought of it.

"It's only an egg from a Springtide Hunt," Grosbeak said disappointedly. "I'd hoped there would be something special inside it."

"Isn't the little bell something special?" I asked, surprised by his reaction.

"Not really. It doesn't even ring. And the song is just that old folk ditty.

Who would ever give their heart to the barrow? No one falls in love with the dead."

"Aww, Grosbeak, don't give up so easily," I said lightly, troubled even more now by his words and trying to hide it. "I'm sure there's a bodiless lady out there somewhere."

"Yes, in your husband's vaults," he said sourly. But I pretended to be absorbed in repairing my braid in the reflection of the hourglass because I didn't want him to see what was churning in my brain.

I saw this place differently than the Wittenbrand did. What was normal to them was a wonder to me and that gave me an advantage because since all of this was new to me, I did not overlook any details.

Which was how I was sure that the Bramble King's little riddle was simply understood.

I am the culmination of desire, the fruit of death. I am the summit of loss, the passing of weight. What am I?

It seemed obvious to me what he was saying. He meant this game that they were all playing to be a hunt for his successor. After all, did they not all want to reign? And could that not only be accomplished by his death? And inheritance was, indeed, a passing of weight at the very summit of loss.

But it was more nuanced than that because I was certain that he had left these eggs to be found along with his riddle and while his riddle told us *why* this hunt mattered, *why* this game mattered, it did not mention how it was to be achieved. And while that might be as simple as winning all the wars and wiping my mortal brethren from the maps of this age, it might be something that was more obvious to me than to them. It might be contained in that song. That simple, folksy song they thought nothing of. After all, why else would the Bramble King have sung it? And what could this bell be but the token in his song?

I would keep it close just in case. I would hold it fast. And if no one – not even Grosbeak – realized why, then all the better. It was more beneficial for me to be thought a child wearing a trinket than to show that I understood.

The nice thing about being beneath notice was that nothing else was beneath *my* notice.

But though I turned the second riddle over and over in my mind, I had no answers when the Sword came to retrieve me. For while the first riddle that opened the second was simple enough, the second riddle was far more complex to decipher.

The Sword was decked out even more splendidly than he had been before. His jacket was made of the actual open blossoms of red roses, the scent of them filling the air and clinging to his finely wrought face and curling gold hair. He'd even twined contrasting white roses around the scabbards crossed over his back and hanging from his left hip.

"My blossom," he said, offering me an arm with a smile as if he was my husband in truth and not my tormentor. "Let us see you dressed."

I did not take his arm. "I'm fine in the clothing I wear," I said, not even looking at my torn and bloody clothes.

"I think not. I am not bringing Death's scrub maid to the Petal Ball, but rather my delicious trophy of a wife. Come." He raised a challenging eyebrow, his arm still held out.

If this was a battle of the wills, perhaps it was better to surrender now and fight back when he least expected it. Holding in all the things I wished I could say to snub him, I instead took his arm, careful not to crush the roses as I let him lead me down the hall.

I closed the door of Bluebeard's chamber of wives behind me and carried Grosbeak's pole in my other hand. The Sword scowled at my friend's head swinging back and forth.

"If you are to be my wife, you must give up such pedestrian accessories," he said in his arrogant drawl.

"If you think you are my husband, it would do you well to give up thinking you can determine my actions," I said and I hated that I sounded a little breathless. He was a powerful Wittenbrand. He could slash me apart with that sword. He could take my life in an instant. I couldn't stop him.

But I could stop him from taking my dignity. I could, at least, do that.

He brought me to a small parlor decorated in scrollwork panels of white and gold. The room was empty of furnishings except for one full-length mirror. And for a moment, I startled, because the mirror looked very much like Bluebeard's mirror except for the moon-shaped face gilt on the apex of the mirror rather than a gargoyle. It yawned dramatically and then opened its eyes.

"Dress my wife in a gown that bares her soul to all," the Sword drawled.

"I'd really rather not," I said sternly.

"Well, aren't you a fearsome bore," he huffed. He turned back to the mirror. "We'll compromise. Dress her as the fearsome bore she is but make it elegant. And captivating. I'll have no wife of mine look the drab."

I stared at him. Compromise? From the Sword. If he could compromise in this, could he be reasoned with on the field of battle?

"What are you staring at, mortal?" he chastised me. "Walk through the mirror!"

I startled at his fierce hiss and then pulled myself straight and strode through the mirror. I closed my eyes at the last second, not daring to look when I crashed into the glass, but there was no crash and I found myself on the other side feeling – heavier.

I looked down and gasped. The mirror had given him exactly what he'd asked for – at least in its own way. The dress was of a fine dove-grey silk that buttoned with tiny black buttons right up to my chin. Tight sleeves reached down to loops that fitted over my middle fingers. There was hardly a breath of flesh exposed anywhere. Modest. Boring. Totally inappropriate for something called the "Petal Ball." Or it would be if that were all.

It was not all.

The skirts of the dress were very full, and they pulled up at the front to be so short they were barely decent, exposing the edges of frothy cream petticoats – and three snapping grey and white wolves. They seemed – somehow – constrained by my skirts so that they could not leave the bell of the full skirt. They could not move more than a few inches to lunge and snap at anything nearby.

I should have feared they would turn on me and devour me, but my first thought was for Grosbeak, and I barely pulled his pole up high enough in time as the middle wolf snapped at his head.

"Go back through the mirror!" he gasped. "Nothing with wolves, mirror! Scars and sires! It's for the forest-forsaken Petal Ball, not a raid on the north peaks!"

But the Sword had already looped his arm around mine again.

"Perfection," he said with a suave smile. "We're the beauty and the beast of legend. I, of course, am the beauty."

"Of course," I said dryly, but his grin seemed to take it for a demure.

"'For none could learn to love a beast,'" he quoted smugly.

But I wasn't listening. My attention was entirely taken with the door at the end of the hallway.

"Your party must begin soon," I said awkwardly. "But where are the guests?"

For the hallway was utterly empty without even a servant in sight, though blossoms hung in garlands along the hall.

I would not want to be those servants tomorrow. My arms felt tired just thinking of all the work of hauling the flowers away and sweeping up the petals, filling sacks with them, and bringing the sacks to carts to haul away. Even an army of servants working until their arms and backs ached could hardly clear away so many flowers before they began to rot, and the stench of rotted blossoms would fill this palace from bottom to brim. It seemed, somehow, a fitting tribute to the lord of these halls.

"They are arriving through other doors. My palace has many," he drawled, playing with the hilt of the sword at his side. "Be not anxious, I have timed our arrival to perfection."

And when he hauled the woven-sword door open – a door taller than three of me standing on each other's shoulders – he was proven correct. His ballroom was almost filled to the brim.

Where once there had been a sweeping expanse of marble floor, now there were costumed people in gowns and suits so grand I could hardly take them in. A woman near me wore a dress made of a hundred doors and whenever one opened, a tiny mouse would pop out and scurry to another door, opening it in turn, and disappearing inside. Little hints of her flesh or underthings peeked out at every open door and I was already blushing for her when I tore my eyes away to the next costume. This was a Wittenbrand man with a very tall hat of ringed-tails sewn into a tall, flat-topped contrivance. Thunder made his whole hat quake and then every so often a tiny burst of blue-white lightning would crackle out from the hat and into the crowd causing shrieks and laughter in equal measure.

I ripped my eyes from him, too. There was no time to take in every outlandish costume, my wolves seemed almost tame in comparison, except that they kept the crowd back from me. I ought to wear such a dress at every social outing for just that effect.

I forced myself to take inventory of the room. The doors that had been shut before were open now, and each of them was as high and wide as the one we'd arrived through. The vistas they displayed in their open portals stole my breath more than the fashion, for each seemed to enter a different world – one a pale beach with white sand and azure sky as far as the eye could see. Another a thick jungle of heavy fronds and howling creatures, still another showed a rocky coast at midnight with the high moon full-blown and shining and another still rippled with the yellow glare of the desert.

But here, in the great room decked out for the party, where drinks both iced and steaming were flowing freely and flirtation mixed with challenge and laughter with the occasional pained scream, here, the room was so overflowing with blossoms that petals in pinks and purples and whites rained down on us, a fragrant blizzard with drifts to match below.

"My kingdom," the Sword said proudly, sweeping his arm to display the room to me, and just when I was beginning to realize that one wall – made entirely of petals – showed the figure of the Bramble King half-submerged in petals as he drifted and dreamed, the Sword added, "And those who will soon be my subjects."

And a chill rolled through me because that meant he knew what the riddle meant, too, that he knew this game was a game for winning the Bramble King's throne and he was playing to win just as my true husband must be.

That alone should have been enough to freeze me in place and burn me to a black cinder – but it was nothing compared to the jolt of terror-laced delight I felt when my eyes tripped over a gaze across the room – a gaze of light blue cat's eyes above one single streak of scarlet blood staring right at me as if it could pin me in place.

I froze and beneath those javelin eyes and one corner of a mouth turned upward as its owner rang a tiny golden bell – the bell he'd scooped up when I dropped it at the moment of our first meeting. Like magic, the crowd grew silent – all except the Sword who was growling in the back of his throat.

The Sword's face had gone scarlet, but my husband, my daring, wild husband looked down on him with a smirk as he announced to the room, "The flower, lovely in her grace and delicate in her scent is but a promise. I care not for the promise, but for the fruit of it."

And with a strange sign made by twisting the fingers of one hand and drawing them down before his face and then a flick of his wrist, he turned every flower in the room into bursting ripe fruit.

My breath caught with all the others, but not in wonder over fat blushing fruit, but in guilt, as I listened to the words he spoke, for *I* had promised him the world and fruited nothing but bitter betrayals.

Chapter Twenty-Two

THE SWORD MUTTERED A CURSE. "One day I will make him eat refuse for every time he has upstaged me."

But then he forced a bright smile on his face as he seized my hand and led me to the very center of the room. He plucked a small comb from his breast pocket – the delicate thing I'd seen before made of mother of pearl and inlaid with emeralds. The teeth of the tiny comb were no straighter than a crone's. He ran it through his curls for a moment before tucking it away and as if the action had gained him courage, he spoke with a voice both loud and carrying.

"Friends, enemies, Wittenbrand," the crowd turned from Bluebeard to him, their eyes bright with what I thought must be a glimmer of Grosbeak's taste for melodrama. "Welcome to my halls and I hope you don't feel the need to change my décor so dramatically, as some have." Around us, the crowd laughed nervously. "The Second Move is upon us and with it, a time of celebration. And so, I beg you to be my guests this night and abandon all that is beyond these walls as we dance the night away."

He extended his free hand in open welcome and then snapped his fingers. The music started, though I could not tell where the pipers and players were hidden.

"Lady," the Sword said, bowing to me. One of the wolves tried to snap his arm off, but the Sword kept far enough back that it could not reach him

– a feat since the three wolves were positioned across the front of my dress, joining in the music with the steady thrum of their growling. "We will dance, of course."

I opened my mouth to refuse him, but he leaned in close, avoiding the wolves, and whispered. "I still think divorce is for the best, but the other ways of dealing with you have not been removed from the table. Humor me."

I glanced at him, as he leaned toward one of my ears, glanced to the other side to the dark wraith settled there with a finger over her lips, and then back again. In the stories, a person had a devil on one shoulder and an angel on the other. No one had ever told me a story about a person with two devils competing, but it seemed I would be the central character in this one.

"Do you know the *akul*?" I suggested, but he only laughed and slipped himself behind me, clasping his spread hand over my belly in a way I found far too familiar and then taking my free hand in his.

I gasped, my cheeks heating immediately. But then I realized that the dancers around us were positioning themselves likewise.

Beside us, Lady Wittentree paused with her partner, her skirts whipping and snapping around her like a ship's sails in a storm. Every so often a black, white-tipped breaker would roll out from them and crash like surf upon the ground around her, leaving a brackish trail everywhere she went. She seemed to wink at me, though it was hard to be sure when she had only the one yellow eye.

"I asked for the *aconda*," the Sword said smugly, "both because I prefer not to be unmanned by your wolves while I dance, and because I have a feeling that a certain fruit-loving prince may not like this dance."

"Of course, you chose that dance," Grosbeak said from his place on the end of the chain, "since it involves hiding behind your woman."

"Silence, pet." The Sword adjusted his crown slightly, as if to emphasize the rib contained within it.

"Will the next dance involve you dramatically leaving those you vowed to protect out on their own to be cut off from their people?"

"I'm afraid I don't know that one, cursed specter," the Sword said coolly.

I ignored them both and looked up again, letting my eyes steal a quick look at Bluebeard. I gasped all over again as his eyes pierced into mine. I'd been using the common expression "steal a look" all my life, but this glance, this gaze, really felt like theft. I felt I robbed him of something private to him, for the look in his eyes as I snatched my glimpse of him was the look of a man bereft.

Without breaking eye contact, he held his hand to the side, and Lady Tanglecott took it, swaying to position herself – and her accompanying snow lions – in front of him for the dance.

A stab of jealousy burned through me. Lady Tanglecott wore a dress made entirely of white feathers and every so often a band of double rainbows appeared around her waist or arm or thigh as if she were an angel from the heavens. If our apparel reflected our souls, what did that say about her? Or me, for that matter.

The music began, and the Sword stepped me through the dance. It was easy enough to follow with him leading despite the twisting feeling in my guts. His body pressed up against my back, his hand tightened across my belly. I felt more of him than I would have liked against my back and his nearness gave me a queasiness that highlighted how this dance was yet another betrayal of mine against my furious husband. Yet another dagger in his etched back. It should be for some purpose at least.

"Have you planned your second move?" I asked the Sword, as if making conversation.

"I planned all of this decades ago, before your father's father was making sons." He jogged me to the side with the other dancers.

To my shock, I realized this was no court dance. Beside us, Lady Wittentree spun suddenly, pulled a comb from her hair, loosening the sharp blunt locks, and then stabbed it into the side of her partner. He gasped, doubling over the wound as she tossed him to the side and then with an eager smile, found a new partner to spin her through the dance.

She was not the only one. I caught a glimpse of a pair locked in what first appeared to be a passionate embrace, but I realized after a moment that the lady's eyes were rolled back, a tiny dribble of green fluid falling from her parted lips. Poisoned.

Just as many dancers escaped the fate, though the dipping and spinning and weaving and ducking were not all part of the dance, but part of a more deadly dance between partners. A dance of life and death, celebration and destruction rolling in a tide of horror.

"And is it going according to your plans?" I asked, a little breathlessly as laughter and a teasing tone rolled over us from nearby. How did they laugh and flirt in the middle of ... this?

"There was only one thing I did not have – but that fault is mended now," the Sword said slyly as he guided me out from him and spun me in a whirl, my canine protectors snapping at his knees and groin as he danced both with me and away from my wolves. I was piteously glad of them. The only defenses I had were these skirts and my bodiless token. "I required only a powerful bait. A way to lure the incorruptible. Who would have thought she'd be a grim-faced mortal?"

"I surprise even myself sometimes," I said dryly, but my eyes were wide as I watched the dance unfolding around us.

"First time dancing with a Wittenbrand?" the Sword drawled. "It's a spectacle no mortal court could contain."

"If by spectacle you mean an embarrassment," Grosbeak complained. "No one is putting in much effort. I'm seeing injuries and illnesses but where are the guts strung like garters? Where are the rains of blood? You'll have to replace your whole staff after this debacle, Sword. I almost think people are enjoying themselves."

To my horror, I thought he might be right. When I looked around us, the people dancing and fighting – blocking blades, turning blows, and still keeping a tight rhythm, a steady stream of careful steps and spins – seemed to be enjoying themselves. There were as many passionate kisses as there were attempted murders. As many winks and laughs as poisoned dusts flung in the face of the other. Was this just how they danced in this mad, mad place?

But it was impractical to kill off half your court every time you had a celebration ... wasn't it?

I found the question disturbing. The Wittenbrand seemed to set as much value in life as in anything – they only saw its worth for how they could make use of it. It bore no intrinsic value on its own.

"It's the Second Move, dead man. We need every player alive for the fun to come," the Sword drawled to my best friend. "Don't rush me. There will be rivers of blood in good time."

"Psst. Izolda," Grosbeak whispered as the Sword whirled me again. It was hard not to hit people with Grosbeak's pole as we danced, his head swinging wildly toward the other dancers. Hard to avoid their blows and stabs and strikes as they danced and fought with wild looks in their eyes and lips parted with delight. "Your bridegroom comes. Him with the wounded side and fiery eyes."

And then, as the spin landed me neatly with my back against the Sword again, I was suddenly face-to-face with Bluebeard – almost chest to chest with him. My breath came so fast that the little black buttons on my dress strained in the effort of holding my lungs encased.

"Do you mind? We're dancing," the Sword said drawing out the syllables slowly, but the laughter in his voice told me this was the exact outcome he had hoped for in using me as bait. "And the mortal dances so well."

Bluebeard reached out and for a moment I thought he might be about to draw me to him. I started to melt, to sag toward him, but I was wrong. He snatched one of the roses from the Sword's jacket and as he brought it to his lips it became a strawberry.

"I thought I turned all the flowers to fruit," he said. "Perhaps yours have not the ability to be more than decorative, Sword."

He bit into the strawberry with his fine white teeth and my breath caught at his nearness. Oddly, one of the wolves whined, sitting back on its haunches and despite his very close proximity, none were trying to bite him. Perhaps they, too, recognized his reign over me.

"Too sour," Bluebeard declared. "Unripe. Callow."

"That you came all this way to insult me is flattery enough," the Sword drawled. "Had you no one else to feed you, Arrow?"

"Not for the hungers that drive me, Sword," Bluebeard said, but his eyes were not on the Sword, they were on me and if my heart was racing before, it was thundering down the track now. He reached up and touched my cheek with the gentlest touch of a single fingertip. "Enough of this dalliance wife. Come back to me. I've missed your somber face."

The Sword laughed nastily. "She's within my embrace right now, Arrow. And possession in the Wittenhame is the law. She belongs to me."

"Mm." It was not assent, and he still wasn't looking at his rival. His very gaze made me feel hot all the way through. "We are not our own – any of us. Come, dance with me, wife."

He took Grosbeak's pole from my hand and offered his other hand to me.

"I don't much fancy being passed about like a party favor," Grosbeak complained as the dancers ebbed and flowed around us, no more interested in this conflict than the dozens of others breaking out across the ballroom.

"I'm trying to *see*! Do you know how hard it is to keep score with this chain swinging me about like a drunken sailor?"

"Is that wound of yours still bleeding, Arrow?" the Sword asked with delight in his voice, and I realized that in offering me his hand, my husband had exposed his bleeding wound. It still seeped a fresh, angry crimson.

A tiny shudder of protective fear ran through me. Always, I made him vulnerable.

Bluebeard leaned in close so that his forehead almost touched mine – almost, and yet not quite – and I wanted it to touch mine. I wanted to feel forgiveness in the touch.

"I'll ask again, and then I will leave if you give no answer," he whispered. His hot breath gusting over me like the winds of spring, carrying away the last resistance of the ice. "Dance with me?"

I grabbed his hand before he could take the offer away.

"Always," I mouthed.

And then suddenly, I was knocked to the side, only keeping my balance by the hand Bluebeard held. Pain blossomed in my face, my head, my neck. I wrenched my hand from the Sword's and put it to my split cheek, cradling the ruined flesh.

In his hand, the Sword held a dagger, the pommel dripping with blood.

I gasped, stumbling, my wolves snarling and snapping, and almost dragging me back toward my attacker.

"There, now do I have your attention, Arrow?" the Sword asked, his voice smooth and venomous. "Take her if you want. Dance as you will, but I know I'll leave my marks on her, too, just as you have. I'll snatch her back when I'm ready and I'll dance this dance of blood and passion with you until one of lies entwined with death at the feet of the other. And it will not be me, for I have not given my heart to the possession of a rotting mortal, already dead in the view of centuries. Dance with me, Arrow, for you are weak and soft and your white belly is showing with the hole where your rib once graced it."

"I already have a partner," Bluebeard said smoothly, drawing me close to him – chest to chest instead of with me in front of him, and he moved so that his wounded side was exposed to the Sword, guarding me with his broken body. My wolves calmed at this. "And she's prettier than you, Sword, so you're out of luck."

"You won't heal from the wound I gave you," the Sword snarled. "And you won't leave this room with your mortal talisman. I've enchanted every door against her escape, so roar all you want, but you have no bite here in my palace."

And then he strode away flicking blood from the pommel of his dagger, and I was left in Bluebeard's arms. He spun me out, slowly, watching me through eyes I could not read, and then spun me back to him, but while those around us fought a dance of passion and power, his handling of me was almost tender in its gentleness, achingly sweet in how he moved me so that it was his own back that was exposed to the other dancers and not mine.

He danced silently, his eyes on mine, his lips parted slightly, as if he had so much to say that he didn't dare say anything at all. And never, not for even a moment, did he stop looking at me, as if he were reading me like the most enthralling of books.

We were clear across the room, dancing slowly toward the huge fire that burned in an alcove along the wall, when the voice of the Bramble King cut through the festivities. It was barely more than a whisper and yet it sliced through the noise like cutting puppet strings.

"I declare the opening of the Second Move," he said, and then his eyes closed, and he retreated, vanishing into the flowers.

Where the Bramble King had been only a moment before, a tear formed in the wall and Coppertomb strode out of it. He was tidy and dapper and well dressed – not at all decadent in his choices. And his crisp appearance sent a chill down my spine. And though I wanted to be still and watch what he did next, I found I could not stop dancing – almost as if my feet were enchanted to dance until my slippers wore out like a girl in a tale.

"Tanglecott," Coppertomb announced, and for a moment I thought he wanted to say something, but he only pointed at her and then stepped aside and through his tear in the wall a bright streak leapt forward that looked almost like a dog, except that it had six heads, growling and snapping.

It lunged forward, scooping up the nearest screaming dancer and shredding her between the snapping jaws of two heads. And oh how I wanted to stop dancing, but my feet would not still. My heart would not calm.

"To the hunt!" Tanglecott cried in return from her side of the ballroom and then her snow lions leapt toward the six-headed dog and the party – such as it was – devolved into screaming, flight, and the drawing of weapons.

A sound filled the room. Screaming cicadas. And then, with the horrific sound of a hundred thousand sets of wings, they were everywhere, filling the ballroom in a mad cloud of vengeance.

"These parties always seem to end like this," Grosbeak said, but it wasn't a complaint, it was pure delight in his tone. And that tone turned my stomach.

"It's time we left, wife of mine," Bluebeard said mildly. "Unless you wanted to dance more?"

I met his eyes with mine and my eyes must have been doubled in size.

He nodded gravely as if I had replied, and then snapped his fingers and the room grew and grew until it seemed the dancers around us were giants and their screams made the whole world shudder. We barely dodged away from trampling giant feet as he danced me toward the flames – double my height now.

Just when I feared we would be burned up he called out, "My fire!"

"My master," said the fire.

And the world went red, red, red, and hot as shame.

Chapter Twenty-Three

A HAND LED me gently through the licking flames and then, with a sound like fabric tearing, we stepped out of the fire and into my husband's house.

Home, home, home my mind sang as the raven croaked and swooped down toward us, landing on Grosbeak's head.

"Love of forests and dales, would you get that thing off of me?" he protested.

Home, home, home, my heart sang as Bluebeard turned and said, "Thank you, my fire."

"A pleasure, my master," the fire growled, sparks spurting upward as he spoke.

Home, home, home, my heart sang as Bluebeard spun me to face him and raked my body with his gaze. I opened my mouth and he closed it with a single finger laid across my lips.

"It's evening, fire of my eyes. Your silence is required." One of my wolves snapped at him and he reached down and shut its mouth, pinching its snout together with his hand just like he'd closed my lips. "Hush now, pack of the night, wolves of my wife, guardians of my princess."

They obeyed immediately.

"That was the best Petal Ball I've been to in years," Grosbeak said with a happy sigh. "It's a shame we had to leave just when the fun was beginning."

"Say the word and you may return, O my enemy," Bluebeard told him distractedly, but his eyes never left mine. He gently touched my split cheek and I winced. "Days or silver thread, wife?"

I pointed to the thread in its hidden place, and he made a smug sound that might have been a rueful laugh. Now that he was here with me again, I couldn't help the almost intoxicated feeling I had at his presence. He sang to me like a song only I could hear. And it was brighter and stronger now that I'd seen his world without him – vicious, washed out, and blood-soaked – and seen the love for him in the eyes of his folk.

"Sit, while I do the honors," he said, and so he cleaned and stitched my wound, and as he did, he spoke to me. "I hope that you learned something of value, wife, so that your ill-advised dalliance with the Sword – or should I call it what it truly was? – your attempt at *spying* did not go to waste."

My eyes widened and he gave me a saucy half-smile as he threaded the needle with silver. I had only been there because I was following *his* order to follow Vireo. Did he really believe I'd betrayed him? And yet it had felt like a betrayal even though it was not.

"Speak to my riddle, wife," he said, looking up through the fan of his eyelashes. My breath caught in my throat. "What arrow sits better in the quiver than flies in the air? What spirit is better bound than set free? What sword is better kept in the sheath?"

"*None,*" I admitted in my mental voice.

"And you are better left to fly free and seek your mark," he murmured. Touching the sleeve of my dress which was wet with blood. "We will tend this a bit later, I think."

"She's a great spy," Grosbeak said his words snapping like my wolves. "Wasn't at all in danger – again – when the Sword tried to steal her virtue. Again. You don't seem too worried about that, Arrow."

"Why should I worry with you to defend her, Grosbeak?" Bluebeard asked, cleaning my wound with gentle hands. I tried not to flinch. "Why would I worry when I know my very sensible wife is craftier than the trickiest of the Wittenbrand?"

"You *should* have worried," Grosbeak argued. "Vireo betrayed you! He dragged her into a conspiracy. We thought you would blame her for that!"

"And he will be punished for what he did," Bluebeard said coolly as he set the first stitch. Tears stung my eyes. "But think you that I did not know what was in his heart? If I did not, would I have charged him with her care? Would I have asked her to follow him where I could not? He was most certainly planning to betray us. I hope only that my wife saw what was needed."

Grosbeak and I both gasped at once and my husband quirked an eyebrow.

"You thought so little of me, wife? You thought I'd send you away to be protected by a traitor? To be watched over by a twisting reed? That I had misjudged both him and you by so far a distance?"

I shook my head, stunned. He was making no sense. He knew all this? Then why did he not prevent it from happening?

"I did think so. And like Grosbeak said, I thought you would blame me later even though I was only obeying your request. I thought you would feel betrayed."

"Not so," he breathed as he set the second stitch, sending a little shiver over my bruised skin, and then he spoke this part into my mind so that it would stay between us. *"I have given you my trust, wife. And though I cannot yet entrust to you all my purposes, I do trust your heart and value your loyalty."* He switched back to speaking aloud. "My enemies plot and plan and think I do not know, but now my austere aspect, my sober visage, you can tell me all they have sworn you not to tell. Now, you can tell me what ways they threaten you and what means they use to try to tempt you into their arms. I would know the fullness of what we face."

I saw – I began, and then the specter was there, leaning around my shoulder and wrapping her clammy hand around my mouth, and to my shock I could not speak with my mind, either.

"Back creature," Bluebeard said, flicking the wraith away. She sulked over my shoulder but pulled her hands back in close.

"They've sealed you with a wraith." Bluebeard's eyes were bright with excitement. "Now, why would they do that unless you had something interesting to tell me? But you cannot tell me, or she'll choke the life out of you. Not even with your mind." He bit his lip in an inviting way. "That does complicate things. It wasn't the Sword, I gather. Secrecy is not his style. Nor Vireo for that fool would not think to seal you so."

"Not the Sword," Grosbeak confirmed. "And I grow weary of waiting for my revenge on him. Why will neither you nor your mortal wife slay him and get it over with?"

"You know as well as I do that if I slay him by my own hand, I will forfeit the game," Bluebeard said, sparing a quelling look for Grosbeak. "Is that what you'd have me do? Give up my immortality for your petty revenge?"

"Revenge is better than a thousand days of life."

"If you say so. I suppose you would know best, dead as you are."

"Then treat with Izolda, and convince her to kill the lout," Grosbeak muttered. "She is remarkably peaceable, even when pushed."

In answer, Bluebeard set the last stitch on my face, picked up Grosbeak's pole, and set him on the bookshelf across the room from me. "I am done speaking with you, corpse. I have a wife to attend."

He threw a cloth over Grosbeak's grumbling head and returned with a little pot of salve, leaning in close so that I could feel his breath as he spoke.

"I've had enough of your pet for the time being, wife, and there are things we need to say to one another." He ran a hand over his short beard nervously before meeting my eyes with his unsettling cat's eyes. "I seem to be forever short on time. But I must spin more time for this. Somehow."

He took my hands in his calloused ones, as gently as you might take a child's, but I saw him wince as he turned, the wound in his side soaking the side of his clothing. I flinched as I looked at it and he met my eyes.

"Never mind the blood. It is no matter. Listen, wife, my enemies gather around me. I know not who to trust. Tanglecott has offered me an alliance, but should I agree?" He shook his head as if he was confused and I opened my mouth only to have the wraith clap both her dark hands over it. Bluebeard flicked them away irritably. "She seems now to be at odds with Coppertomb, but this could be a ruse. I cannot know yet."

He drew me down to sit on the hearth with him as the fire crackled merrily behind us and a tiny clock on his wall burst open while a bluebird sang out from it to tell us the hour of the night.

"But there are things I *can* tell you and I must tell you some of them now. Give me your ear, wife. I have planned this turning of the ages for a very long time," he said and as he spoke, I could almost feel him weighing every word, deciding what he could trust me with and what he needed to keep to himself. "It's my one chance to get this right. The only chance there will ever be. I think I have my pieces in place, my moves chosen with care, my strategy firm, but now you are here, and you change everything, bringing order into my chaos like a pole jammed through the spokes of a wheel."

He shook his head again, but whether it was to clear it or out of denial, I didn't know.

"*Then you trust me still?*" I probed, disconcerted by this turn of events. I'd expected anger. I'd expected hurt. I had not expected admiration and plotting.

"Why would I not when you have not betrayed my trust?" he asked, seeming as confused as I was. "I know well enough your limitations, my mortal ally, but you wanted to work with me and I have decided to have faith that you can – nothing can grow if fenced too tightly."

"*Oh,*" I said with my mental voice. It seemed far too small a thing to say for the enormity of what he'd revealed – that he had accepted me as his partner in this so fully that he was willing to let me try to work at his side. I swallowed down a sudden dryness in my throat. This trust – unexpectedly vulnerable – touched something in me I hadn't felt in a long time. Family. It felt like family.

His next words came out in a rush.

"You must understand. I have people depending on me. I did not grow up like other Wittenbrand. I was abandoned, alone. Taken in by kindness from time to time but just as often kicked in the teeth. When my time came to become a man, I carved out for myself lands in the Wittenbrand by deception and sword and arrow. And to those lands, I invited all who, like me, were without a place – the wild things, the forgotten things, the things of strange innocence. But to command a thing brings the necessity to care for it, and to care for it brings the necessity of command, and if I lose this strange gamble every Wittenbrand I have ever sheltered, each one I have succored – down to the smallest and last – will be without shade again – hunted, slaughtered, tortured for fun. Do you understand why I must fight so hard? Why I must not fail them?"

I nodded.

"Too much rides on this, Izolda. Too many souls look to me. I cannot fail them. Have you seen this land through the eyes of the Sword who wishes to snatch you from me? Have you seen how he would remake the Wittenhame in his image?"

"*I have,*" I said, and my words just didn't seem like enough. I wasn't gifted in speeches as he was.

He sighed, as if frustrated that his words, too, were simply not enough. He ran a hand through his hair.

"I was a boy of fifteen, shaggy-headed and dreamy-eyed, when I found this house and the fire took up residence here. And what did you say to me, fire?"

"Feed me, my master," said the fire in his deep, rumbling voice.

Bluebeard placed a piece of wood carefully on the fire and kept speaking. "And so, I did. And so, this house was made, bit by bit, hope by hope, in simple requests granted and simple hopes made new. And when I took my first head at sixteen, I kept that head to advise me, and so my Vault of Wisdom was crafted. And when I was a daring youth of seventeen, coming now into my ambition, seeing for the first time what I might achieve if only I dared, I stole for myself the first of my blushing brides. And now here we sit, you, this fearsome wife of mine, you, this traitorous heart that will not simply rest, you who constantly runs headstrong into every danger – here you sit with me. And here I pour out my heart to you in hopes that for once, instead of returning it to me in shards, you will return my hopes with a little of your own heart."

My breath caught in my throat.

"You love your people," he said thickly, and his eyes shone a little too brightly, though he wasn't looking at me – almost as if he couldn't. "Love them enough to give yourself as my bride. Love them enough to keep giving even now when they have traded you away and treated you as chaff on the wind. And surely you, my severe partner, my stalwart bride, surely you will understand what it is to let your life's blood seep out with every beat of your heart for your people and your land."

I blinked back a tear that was trying to form because I did understand. Even now, with my parents gone, and Svetgin so confused, and my king showing his hatred of me – even now, I wanted my people safe and well. And I would, indeed, give what I must to achieve it. I felt in him a spark of recognition – two fires knowing they burned on the same fuel.

His voice trembled as he added, "Surely you must see how I will give of my own flesh to have you, to keep you, to buy you back from treachery. Surely you understand that you are without price or equal to me."

I could not speak and even if I could, I was not so eloquent and I did not know what he was to me – only that when he was not there the world felt dull. And so, instead, I leaned forward and kissed him gently.

His answer to my kiss was so violently delighted that my breath stuck in my throat. He caught me up, crushing me to him, his kiss devouring my lips as if he could not possibly get enough and when I had been so very kissed that I was not sure I could breathe at all – that I thought perhaps my stitches may have torn, that the wolves of my dress chased each other's tails snarling and snapping, he finally let go and drew back.

"If anyone can light the Wittenhame ablaze, fire of my eyes, it will be you," he said and he sounded almost despairing. "What have you done to me? You have broken what was whole and torn down what was walled up."

I bit my lip, not sure what to make of that. I'd thought to seal our alliance. To show my willingness to remain his wife. Instead, I had somehow invited a fire into our friendship just as he had once invited a fire to live in his home and this fire – like that one – had one thing to say: "Feed me."

"Come now," he said, his voice husky and breathing ragged. "Let us free you from this wraith that blocks your sweet lips and think together on how we shall fit your straight lines and sharp edges in my serpentine tide. We will adjourn to my vault and consult those who came before."

And he seized my hand and pulled me along after him like a boy bent on showing me his collection of frogs. And I hardly knew what I would say when it finally was my turn to speak again because he had surprised me and surprised me until I hardly seemed to know what manner of man I had married at all.

Chapter Twenty-Four

"BRING YOUR PET," Bluebeard suggested as I walked past Grosbeak and I snatched him up as we went by. "It would be good to remind him how fortunate he is to have been adopted by you."

Bluebeard leaned down and picked up a leather sack that had been placed by the front door, balancing it easily on one palm despite the heavy look of the thing.

"Oh, I know this already, Bluebeard," Grosbeak said happily. "The drama she brings is exquisite. I have never tasted the like."

"You will not call me that," my husband said with a scowl.

"Why not? It's her name for you," Grosbeak said lightly.

One of my dress wolves whined like a dog being disciplined and Bluebeard reached down to caress its head, settling it. Leaning down brought him closer to my face and he leaned in so that all I could see were his pale eyes and teasing smile.

"Is that your name for me, you somber visage?"

Yes, I said with my mind.

"Then I shall wear it with pride and grow this beard you are so fond of to my knees."

I'd rather you didn't.

"No, it is settled. I never go back on my word," he said, pulling me to the staircase. To my surprise, they were sloped into a descent instead of ascending into the stars. Which was crazy since this house had no cellar. Even so, we began our descent down the dank-smelling, moss-fringed stairs. "I shall grow it long and with pride."

But you didn't give your word! I protested in my mind. *Please, reconsider.*

Although why I was asking him not to hide his pretty face, I couldn't have said. Wouldn't it be good to have it hidden, to be able to disguise himself from his enemies? To be able to disguise his beauty from me where it wouldn't make my stomach flip and my breath catch at the worst possible moments?

"I like the look of your pouting lips, wife. I will, I think, defy your wishes more often simply to provoke so stirring a sight."

I shook my head at him as he laughed and then put his shoulder into a heavy wooden door at the bottom of the stairs.

He heaved and the door opened into a high-ceilinged room. Dusty light filtered down in beams and to my surprise, green moss coated the walls, and long vines curled around anything they could, swathing it in emerald and giving this place a curiously fecund look. Tiny blue flowers sprouted on the vines. A comfortable-looking tufted chair and ottoman had been placed facing one wall. They were well worn, as if someone had sat here, again and again, looking up at the wall. To one side, the fire burned bright and hot, though not hot enough to dry up the wet air or bright enough to light the shadowed corners. It was a homey place that felt like curling up with a good book and a hot drink on a winter evening.

The wall the chair faced, however, was completely occupied with shelves carved straight from the earth and rock. They were rough-hewn and as my eyes slowly adjusted to the low light, the occupants of the rough-cut shelves were finally revealed.

They were heads. And more heads. And more still. Rows and rows and rows of them reaching up to where I could no longer see them, they were so high.

I struggled not to gag at the sight, though I should be used to decapitated heads by now.

It was like a witch's cottage in some grim tale, or a cavern where a gorgon might rule, or the cave of treasures in which a single coin must be searched for to pay death his due.

I shivered at the sight of them, for it seemed my husband had not been exaggerating when he said he collected heads. And he had not been merely acting on a whim when he animated Grosbeak's head, for he drew from his leather sack a new trophy and placed it, almost reverentially on the shelf at shoulder height. And as he set it in place it shivered and woke.

I gasped as I saw who it was.

Vireo.

He'd been alive only hours ago and now here he was, being placed on a shelf with hundreds of others. A chill shivered through me.

"Did you ask Vireo to care for your bride after all?" A head off to one side asked. It was a greenish color with dark matted hair and lower incisors that stuck up past the upper lip. I gasped at the sight of him.

"You can't do everything," Bluebeard said lightly. "Sometimes you have to send someone to do it for you."

The speaking head snickered. "And has that ever worked out for you?"

Bluebeard laughed ruefully. "Never even once."

"And yet you still offer villains chances and blackguards second tries."

I moved to place Grosbeak on the ottoman but stopped when he gasped. "Please. Don't set me down. I fear you will not pick me up again. Please. I see my father there on the shelves."

"You fear joining us, son?" the green-faced head asked, snickering. "You fear the fate you earned for yourself? How did *you* betray the Arrow?"

Grosbeak seemed choked when he answered. "I tried to kill his bride."

This time, the laughter filled the room. Every single head laughed, except for the scowling Vireo.

"Are you all traitors, then?" Grosbeak asked, terror lacing his voice with sharp edges.

"Every one of us," the green-faced head said. His accent was thick and coppery. It made me think of rolling hills and tan-colored skies. "As you well know."

But though his voice was warm, my skin chilled to goosebumps. Because I was a traitor, too. I deserved this wall, too.

And when my husband turned from his task and faced me, my eyes strayed to the wound in his side – the ever-present evidence that instead of taking my head, he'd let them take his rib. That instead of giving me what I deserved, he took my treachery in his own flesh.

I swallowed, fighting not to feel faint.

"What do you think of my councilors, wife of mine?" he asked.

I held his gaze, but I said nothing for I was bound to silence, and I did not speak with my mind for I was afraid that any word I said might condemn me. At another time, I could have claimed I had acted for my parents, for my land. At another time, I could have claimed I had never meant to act, that my wavering indecision could not be held against me even if it had offered opportunity to my enemies. But I could not argue that looking back at it. From this new vantage it seemed, at best, poorly thought out and unfounded and at worst, true betrayal.

I licked my lips, nervously.

"They're a sight to see, Arrow," Grosbeak said with a nervous laugh. "A sight that chills the bones. But why seek their counsel when clearly you were the wiser man?"

"Clearly?" Bluebeard asked, but his eyes were still on me.

"Well, ha ha." Grosbeak really must be worried he'd be put on the shelf. I'd rarely heard him so obviously pander to anyone. "They're the ones on the wall and you're the one talking to them. If they were wiser than you, they wouldn't be dead."

"Mmm," Bluebeard said, and it was neither agreement nor approval, but his gaze was unwavering as if bidding me here and now before these fearsome visages to make my case for what I did or join them. I had no case to make. The only sensible thing left was to offer what I could.

Surely, there is some way I can atone for what I did, I said in my mind, bound up in sudden fear.

His eyes softened, and to my surprise, he kept our conversation private.

I have already made atonement for it, bride of mine. Speak no more of treachery. Wear not a dress of shame.

He stepped forward and to my utter shock, he took my hand and raised it to his lips, tickling it with his light beard as he kissed my palm.

"Sit with me, now, as I take the wisdom of my councilors," he said softly, guiding me to the chair, and offering me a hand to settle into it. He pulled the ottoman to the side and perched on the edge of it, side by side with me. His breeches, soaked with his own blood, began to stain the light tufting of the ottoman.

"Speak you, my enemies," he said, addressing them. "Speak your wisdom to me, for the Second Move is upon me and I fight to see my way forward."

"What is your dilemma?" a female voice asked. I peered up into the darkness to see a woman with golden hair and a silver crown speaking to him. Her eyes were closed as if she slept.

"The Sword seeks to divide me from my wife and my power, to take it for himself and to snatch up her lands as he does so, for she has been married also to the land and what mars her, mars her country, what breaks her will shatter it, and what heals her, mends its ills."

"An interesting problem," another head replied, snickering. "You could not have prevented this by hiding her away as you have done before?"

"He married her the Wittenbrand way," Vireo's head said, filled with scorn.

His words were greeted by laughter – but not, I realized, directed at Bluebeard. All the eyes of the heads on the wall were slanted toward Vireo in the middle. There was one that struck me as odd. It was the beautiful head of a woman with flowing green hair tangling around her head and flowing down to the shelf below. Over one ear, her hair was held back with a single mother-of-pearl comb decorated with emeralds. She looked as though she had been drowned.

"You who were friend to the Arrow, first in trust, first in esteem – you betrayed him over this?" one of the heads said.

"He betrayed me for my place. To win royal blood for his own veins," Bluebeard explained. "But his treachery is no matter now. Speak, Vireo, and tell me what it is you vowed on the Island of Burning Guilt."

But even now, when Vireo opened his mouth, a dark spirit burst forth, spinning around his severed head just once and then pasting both hands over his mouth.

"He's warded," the green-faced head said, certainty in his tone.

"As is my wife," Bluebeard said, frowning. "And together they know who the conspirators are, but I cannot make either speak or the specters will destroy them before any answer can slip out. Which means I must find other ways to detect my enemies and run them afoul. Who now will prophesy and what will you say to me?"

They look at one another and then one of the heads speaks, "If you wish to remove the specter, you must break the tie that binds the conspirators."

"I've already killed Vireo," Bluebeard said coolly. "Would death not break the conspiracy?"

"It would seem not," the same head said. It was long and thin with a yellow cast to its brown skin. "It would seem the conspiracy stands without your former captain."

"Hmm," Bluebeard seems unhappy. "Does anyone else have a word to speak?"

A female head cleared her throat and when I found her head on the shelf, she was a square-jawed woman with a tangle of red curls around her head. Her eyes were glazed and white as if she had been blind in life as well as in death.

"Keep your token close," she intoned. "Keep it at hand."

"Is that a prophecy?" Bluebeard asked when there seemed to be nothing else coming.

"Yes," they agreed in unison.

He looked at me, licking his lips. Did he think I had to do with that token? I shot a glance to Grosbeak. I thought that if I had something that could be called a token, it would be him. He was, after all, my symbol for defeating enemies and finding friends. My symbol of everything both gruesome and magical in this strange Wittenhame.

"I must ride out to battle the Sword and his mortal armies once more. Have you advice for that?" Bluebeard asked and there was a formality to his words that made me wonder how they made prophecies and gave advice. Did he come down here often and keep them informed or did they have their own ways of seeing what was happening in the worlds beyond this dank cellar?

"Make an ally of Wittentree," one of them said. A man missing an eye with a grievous scar where it once had been.

"Can I trust her?" Bluebeard pressed.

"Who can say?" the man asked with a laugh. "It matters not. She is to be your ally in this or the threads will not wind the pattern and our weaving will collapse unformed."

Bluebeard grunted.

"And the battle?" he pressed.

"The woman, the wife," the redheaded seer said, her cloudy eyes seeming to light from within. "She must lead your troops in the Battle of the Bairn."

"How will I know this battle?" Bluebeard pressed.

"It will come in red. Scarlet in sign, crimson in cast. It will be apart from where you are."

"Have you no more than this?" Bluebeard pressed, and his eyes looked pained as he spoke.

"No more," they intoned together. "Even our wisdom has bounds."

"Mmm." Again, he sounded neither approving nor content.

He rose, offering me a hand up from the chair.

"Then I'll bid your leave until next time, Vault of Wisdom," he said, bowing elaborately. After a brief pause, I bowed, too. It was always best to remember your manners, after all.

"I'll have my revenge on you, Arrow," Vireo wheezed, finally finding his voice again from his place on the shelf.

"Will you?" To my surprise, Bluebeard did not seem to share the chill I felt at those words. He tilted his head slightly. "Do not take my mercy for weakness, Vireo."

"Mercy?" his former friend growled. "You call this mercy?"

"Your death was fairly earned. You'd scorn it now?" My husband's voice was cold. "That I kept your head and invited you to my council, offering entertainment and the chance to be of use instead of the burning fires of hell – that is the mercy. I have given it. And I can take it away."

And with that, he spun and swept out of the vault, and I found myself hard-pressed to keep up with him, even though I ran, my wolves howling under my skirt all the way to the top of the steps and into the front room beyond.

Chapter Twenty-Five

I STUMBLED, breathless, as we reached the top of the stairs, my cheek aching, my shoulder aflame, and my legs tired. How long had it been since I last slept? I felt as if I could hardly stay upright anymore.

Bluebeard steadied me, taking Grosbeak's pole from my weary hand and jamming it into an urn close to the door that housed a collection of long items. I glimpsed a walking staff with a toad on the top of it, a pair of unstrung bows, and a shepherd's crook. The toad winked at me with a leering smile on its amphibian face.

"Sit. Stay," Bluebeard ordered Grosbeak. Grosbeak scowled back but said nothing as Bluebeard drew me to a place near the fire and began to strip off his party clothes, throwing them into the flames.

"Thank you," said the fire, puffing a little black cloud for each item. "Thank you, master."

He was down to his breeches when he stopped stripping and seemed to realize what he was doing.

"You're shivering," he said, scratching his beard irritably. His movements were impatient, like he was holding himself back from acting. "We need you fed, the stitches removed from your back, need you bathed, and given time to sleep." He blew out a long breath. "There's no time. There's never enough time."

I laid a hand on his arm. He was wasting more than enough time with this litany when we could just be getting on with it.

"*There's time enough for what matters,*" I told him mentally.

"Every day of yours is precious," he protested, shaking his head as looked up into the vaulted ceiling and snapped his fingers.

A raven flew down and landed on the desk. Bluebeard looked at the raven, tilting his head one way and then the other, and then stepping back as the raven leapt into the air. Bluebeard hurried to brush his parchments aside to form an empty space on the desk. But despite his haste, I caught a glimpse of one that read,

"Solemn visage, somber stone,
Your steady gaze anvil to my sword
Wrench from me now my steady home
And to your breast press this ..."

I wished I could have read the rest. It had been on the top of the papers as if it had been recently written. Had he been writing poetry while I was with the Sword? The thought was ... odd. Not planning? Not fighting? Writing poetry? When would he have found the time to do that?

And was it ridiculously conceited that I thought it might be about me?

"And because your time is precious," he said, snapping me out of my thoughts, "wasting even a moment of it seems to be a luxury I cannot afford and dearly wish to avoid. So. We must cram every bit of what is needed into these few hours we steal."

There was a muffled cry and the sound of furious flapping of feathers, and then a pair of ravens descended carrying a heavy cloth between them. They set it on the desk, screamed, and flew back up into the star-filled sky in a flurry of black feathers. Even the arrival of dinner was a dramatic production here.

I opened my mouth and shut it again with a click as Bluebeard untied the knot at the top of the cloth and opened it, revealing fresh-baked bread, rounds of cheese, and a variety of fruits and roasted vegetables.

"There's never meat if you ask them for dinner," he said, looking slightly chagrined. "I hope you don't mind. They find the idea of delivering cooked meat offensive and if you insist on meat, they bring you what they would eat, and trust me, it will make you wish you had not asked." He grimaced. "Don't even think about asking for eggs."

He must have taken my shock for disapproval. His cheeks burned hot under their layer of beard.

"Here," he said, gesturing to a cleared off spot on the desk. "Sit. Eat. I will remove the silver stitches from your back as you eat, and I will talk to you about what we will do next." He sighed. "Three things at once. Surely that must satisfy even the most stringent of task-masters."

I had no idea why he was so worried about my days. Had he not spent them as often as he liked? And now he was obsessed with using each minute well? But I was very hungry, and the bread smelled of home and of snatching little loaves from the hot pan while Cook scolded me, so I took my place on the desk and tucked in. He rummaged in a desk drawer and came out with a little pair of sewing scissors and a large knife.

I froze.

"The scissors are for the stitches," he explained as if this made perfect sense.

I swallowed the mouthful of bread and gave him a level look.

Don't tell me that the knife is for the cheese, I told him with my mind. *Because if you do, I won't believe you.*

He'd already clambered up onto the desk and settled himself behind me, crouched on a stack of books and papers as if he were an oversized raven about to scold me for requesting a dinner of eggs.

The knife flashed in the firelight and then suddenly, he seized the back of my collar, and I heard a ripping sound. My back felt cold.

"The knife was for the dress," he said as if it were perfectly obvious.

I liked that dress.

"You may have all the dresses you like, fire of my eyes, but not if they are given to you by the Sword," he said and there was a glimmer of violence in his eye when I turned to meet it.

I held that gaze and silently fed a piece of cheese to one of the wolves curled up around my knees. He returned my silent stare for a half a beat, and I wondered what he would do. Would he be angry?

His sudden laugh made me want to laugh, too. He shook his head and then carefully moved my braid over my shoulder so he could look at my back. It felt better. It didn't pain me anymore. Not like my face.

"These need to come out. They've done their work already," he whispered, and his breath made the hairs on the back of my neck prick up.

Perhaps, were I a different kind of girl, I might have had thoughts of lust at a beautiful, well-set-up man crouched behind me, shirtless and running gentle fingers over my back – especially knowing he was my husband and nothing was forbidden to us.

I did not feel that way.

Rather, I felt like pulling away.

It was not that I didn't trust him with my safety – I did. Not that I didn't believe he was trying to help me by taking out the stitches – he was. Not that I thought he would take advantage of me – I did not. He'd proven again and again that he was nobler in nature than that.

No, my sense of wariness came from fear that anything between us could not last. He claimed he had some masterful plan in this strange dance of crowns and thrones but we'd both come close to kissing death. And even if we both survived, what then? Could a Wittenbrand live peaceably with a wife as a mortal man did? Could he come home to eat and settle in to speak of the day with her? Would he not grow bored of my mortality day after day? That would only lead to heartbreak for me and humiliation. Perhaps it was better to avoid it completely.

What should I make of this man who had given me his hand in marriage, and his rib, and his loyalty, and his vows for seemingly no good reason?

I peeked up through the curving branches of the multi-tiered chandelier, looking past the glowing eyes of the cats strutting through the waterfalls of candlewax and up even further to where the raven had returned and I thought back to another raven long ago who had sat by my window as I spoke aloud my lack of hopes and prospects.

One raven was much the same as another. It would be foolish to think it was the same one. More foolish yet to think that such a one could report to my husband.

And yet.

And yet, I had stood there, looking out over the sleepy city, and told the world that I would prefer to be married off for some kind of good and not just convenience. And if someone had heard, then they had answered, because what greater good could there be than saving your nation?

"*Were you there with the raven when I confessed that I wanted more from this life?*" I asked him tentatively with my mind.

He bent around me to meet my eyes and he winked, disappearing again to work on my back.

"Why did you think I was pleased when you greeted me, Izolda Savataz?" he asked lightly. "We shared a kinship, we two. Both of us want our lives to mean something. Both of us want more than comfort or ease. Both of us married for something greater."

"*And is that why you married me in the Wittenbrand way?*"

I felt an unexpected touch on the back of my neck, soft and warm. A kiss. A shiver of surprise drifted down my spine.

"Among other reasons, my solemn monstrosity. That, and your judging eyes,and your sober refusal to bend, make you the straight line to my wanderings, the plumb to my troubled depths, the anchor to my bucking ship."

His hands left their work and drifted, taking liberties as they combed through my hair and ran down my shoulders and arms, lightly, softly, in a way that made me think of where else I could allow them to go. I swallowed and held myself tighter.

I picked at the last crumb of bread and winced as Bluebeard pulled a particularly tough stitch out.

"Easy now, easy," he whispered. "Almost done. Have patience now."

All the kinds of things you breathed to children, to hurt animals, to troubled souls. And yet there was a solidness to his voice that went deeper than iron, deep into the veins of the molten earth.

"Let me tell you a story," he said as he worked, and it made me think of the way he'd told me a story when he'd put these hundred stitches in place. "Of a time when the world was new, and she grew life by the word of the creator and sprung from his chest as he lay on his back in repose among the stars. And as he breathes, her oceans move, her tides come and go, her stars spin and set her courses. And when he smiles, she feels warmth and sunshine, and when he cries, she feels it in the rain."

I flinched steadily as he worked, but he knew what he was about because the story soothed the bite and pull as he worked.

"And one day man began to dig, dig, dig, deep into the mountains, down, down, through the caves, seeking the heart of the earth. And when they reached it, they went further still, for it was not gold or iron, silver or diamonds that they dug for, but for power. And when at last they found the hidden pools of midnight power in the belly of the earth, they dug them out and pulled them loose, and thus they dug out the rib of the creator and wrought in him a grave wound, a mortal wound, a wound edged in evil and self-focus so that it may never heal, and always until this day the creator bears the festering mark of man's pride. From it have spread all the evils of this world and the land has been washed over a thousand times a thousand with the tears of those who have felt it and the tears of him whose body was broken by them."

"*And what happened to the men who dug?*" I asked with my mind because I did not want to say, "Just like me." Or to ask if there was any saving of those who had done the digging. I knew without asking that there would not be.

He moved from the last stitch on my back to work on my shoulder, restitching the stitches I'd pulled there and binding the wound. It felt hot and angry where he touched it.

"They were consumed by their own hearts."

"*And is there any hope for the creator, or will he die and the world with him?*" I did not know why I was taking this so seriously. It was only a story. It was only a myth. So why did I feel a chill greater than his breath on my back as he worked, more than the shiver of stitches coming loose from my flesh? Why did it feel so real?

"There is always hope," Bluebeard whispered, and I felt almost as if I could feel his lips pressing against the skin of my back and his shadowed chin scratching against the delicate skin of my neck where it met my shoulder. "There is always redemption."

"*Even for me?*" I whispered in my mind.

"Especially for you. But I would think you would stop musing on worthiness and on whether you must pay for your betrayal. Is guilt sensible? Is self-recrimination a practical skill?"

I felt my cheeks growing hot. He was right. I was being ridiculous.

"If I have forgiven you, who can say otherwise? If I have set you free of these impractical burdens, are you not free indeed?"

And this time I was certain it was his lips I felt pressed up against the wing of my shoulder.

And for just a moment we both kept perfectly still and let ourselves rest in that moment.

"*Why do you kiss me so often?*" I asked with my mind.

"Because every kiss may be the last," he whispered before he shook himself and said, "They're out now and we have much to discuss. Come now, you must bathe, and we must speak before you can sleep, for I fear that you will be snatched from me again before I have had the time to confer with you. Always, time is our worst enemy, stealing away what is most precious to me."

"*Don't you have less of my time to spend, the more of it you stay with me?*" I asked, wondering if he'd make sense of those jumbled thoughts. What I meant was that he could spend all my days and marry again quickly and have more days at his disposal. But I paused for a moment, because hadn't he suggested that I would be his last bride?

"Were I to spend them with no constraints, I would spend them all exactly like this," he said, and he leapt from the desk in a sudden burst of energy, swept me off in a flurry of papers, and then carried me up the singing nightingale stairs with my wolves howling all the way.

Chapter Twenty-Six

"YOU PLAY THE HIS NIBS' seven in this hand if you want to save your queen," Bluebeard said as he laid down a King's Nibs. I was struggling to keep up with the cards and the conversation at the same time. I'd played a little before – mostly with Svetgin and Rolgrin when we were younger. It wasn't fashionable in the Pensmoore court to play at cards. But playing cards seemed to help Bluebeard think, so he had us spread across the wide bed, playing a hand as he talked to me.

It was not what I'd expected he would want to use his bed for. The sense of that hung heavily between us – as if, while we played cards so innocently, both of us were thinking about what games could be played that required no cards at all.

The stairs, of course, had taken us back to his room. No number of protestations would take us anywhere else – though I did not think Bluebeard had his heart in his threats.

I had bathed hastily in private, minding my many wounds, and then – while Bluebeard fed my poor wolf dress to the fire, howling and all – I had drawn a new outfit from the mirror. The mirror spat out a nightdress of silk lined in fur. But it was not to be outdone by the Sword's mirror and it had produced a nightdress with a mink collar. The mink's eyes moved like it was alive. I hesitated to put it on, but it was that or sleep in my underthings – and besides, the mink was in a staring match with the dead girl hovering over my shoulder. I didn't mind if they both wanted to keep an eye on each other.

"I'd apologize that there is only one bed for two people," Bluebeard had said dryly when I finally made my way to it, "but seeing as you have brought two more with you, I can hardly see you objecting."

"When can I get rid of this horrible dead specter?" I'd asked with my mind. *"It's not like – "*

She had put her hand over my mouth even though I was speaking with my mind. I tried to bite it, but she tasted of rot and grime, leaving me choking and trying to spit with her hand still over my mouth.

To my shock, she was ripped away and I could breathe and clear my mouth of the taste of her. Over my shoulder, I had seen my husband shaking her by the scruff of her neck.

"Play nicely, specter. I could make you wish you were not attached to my wife. I could make you wish it with every last wisp of that scrap of a soul."

The specter had drawn back, lifting her hands and then very obviously clasping them together as if to promise good behavior and the shaking had stopped.

I played a different card than the one he was coaching me to play. I didn't like having my moves dictated to me.

He shook his head as he played his next card and snatched my queen away. "You don't want to lose the queen," he said meeting my eyes. "Ever. That's the first rule."

I felt a strange shiver at his words. He meant them to mean more than advice at cards. He meant he was planning to keep me safe. Or maybe just keep me. Or maybe both. Which was very practical of him. This steady cycle of finding and marrying wives must have taken a lot of time and effort. If he could learn to be more careful in using up my days, he could save himself a lot of wasted energy.

"In the mortal worlds," Bluebeard continued, laying his discarded cards face up and arranging them off to the side to illustrate his words, and then taking up strands of my hair to play with as he spoke, "we are lining up for battle. The Sword has marched the Aayadmoore straight across Salamoore, which he could only do if Coppertomb had allowed it. He appears to be making for Rouranmoore. But why? Why drop his never-ending siege of Pensmoore simply to chase after Wittentree's holdings? It's a wild thrashing move and I don't like that I can't see what is behind us. But two things are certain.

"First, that we would be fools not to rush down the west coast of Aayadmoore and secure it in his wake. Second, that we must help Rouranmoore to hold. Wittentree has offered me a bargain to work together and with her close on our eastern shore, we cannot afford to make an enemy of her. With the blessing of my wise council, I must make that alliance."

He tucked the hair back behind my ear and leaned over the cards to kiss my forehead almost reverently. I felt flushed by the attention.

"Why do you trust the heads so much when you defeated them?" I asked with my mind, laying my next card out carefully. He was distracted and I took the trick with a small self-satisfied smile of my own.

"A man knows himself best through the eyes of his enemies. They see the things I cannot." He laid his card swiftly as if he already knew what I would play next and then caught one of my hands in his, making it harder to play.

"But why would they help you when you are the one who killed them?" I pressed as he opened my hand, tracing each finger with his and then pressing a kiss into my palm and then my wrist and then the crook f my elbow. The blush in my cheeks was growing hotter and it was getting hard to think straight. *"It does not seem reasonable to put so much faith in the bitter dead."*

"I don't know why they are so compliant, so willing to work with me when I ended their lives. Perhaps, it is merely familiarity – a face they know when all others have passed away. Perhaps they were better people than I acknowledged. What I do know is this, they have only once misled me."

I cocked my head as I took yet another trick from him. He must be truly distracted. His next kiss was in the crook of my neck and it did dizzying things to my midsection. I swallowed.

"It was in the matter of the Sword," he said musingly.

"*Was it?*" I pressed. I nearly had this game won even with my struggle to think straight. I placed my card with seeming indifference.

He swept the cards aside and settled where they had been between us.

"It was," he said, lifting an eyebrow and grinning at my breathlessness. I cared not that I'd been prevented from winning the trick. "They told me his doom would come from the tides of his heart. But the Sword loves nothing. I have searched and searched for a thing he might love and found there is nothing but himself." He smiled ruefully as he spun his fingers through my hair again. "Perhaps that was what they meant. That his doom lies within." He seemed to shake himself. "But we were discussing strategy. We must move an army down the west to seize the coastline as we also rise to the defense of Rouranmoore along the east coast."

"Leaving our middle unguarded?" I was barely holding onto my wits well enough to discuss this. His fingers tangling in my hair lit up every nerve in my scalp.

His mouth twisted sourly. "I do not like that part. It leaves Pensmoore vulnerable. But with the Sword occupied on both fronts, will he be able to spare troops for such an assault? I do not think so. The only other person who could drive a force in between ours while we were distracted is Coppertomb and one might think that this is why he has allowed the Sword on his land, but that little display at the end of the Petal Ball tonight was proof of the rumors I have been hearing – that Coppertomb has set his sights on Ilkanmoore and will be much occupied with the taking of that land and happy to let the Sword watch his back as he finishes off Lady Tanglecott's thin army."

I opened my mouth to tell him how wrong he was, how they were allies, but the ghastly hand was there at once, blocking my mouth again.

Bluebeard tugged the hand free, irritation on his face as he flung the wraith aside a second time.

"Don't bother, wife," he said with a sigh. "I know you can confirm that Coppertomb and the Sword are working together. I know they are tied up with Vireo and his betrayal. No need to make yourself uncomfortable just to tell me such."

My gut felt heavy as if I had eaten a meal of stones. There was a wide flaw in his plan – right down the middle – and I could save him from grief if only I could tell him. The ghast shook her finger in my face as if she could guess what I wanted to say.

"But we will need to prepare you. As my advisors said, you must lead one of the armies."

I shook my head. I was not born to lead. I did not know battle. Nothing could spell failure faster than this.

"Fire of my eyes."

I wasn't looking at him. I was looking away in the distance, trying not to cry, thinking of leading men into a battle where they cried and screamed and died beside me. Where I could not stop it or save them. Where I died, too, mangled and broken in the snow.

"Izolda." His tone was kind, but I would not look at him.

Why should I have to do such a thing just because a wall of heads said so? They were dead already, and past the grief of this life. I felt tears sting my eyes and I blinked them away. Besides, this was ridiculous. Putting a young woman with no experience or skill at the head of an army wasn't reasonable. It wasn't sensible. It was the opposite of useful.

"Wife." He took my face between gentle fingers as if lifting a goblet so he could drink.

This time I reluctantly met his eyes.

"As a figurehead, wife," he said gently. "You will not fight. You will be protected."

From what? I wanted to scream. But I held my mind back.

Would he protect me from watching them all die right in front of me? Because it wasn't my body that I was afraid to see ripped apart – well, there was some of that, too – but mostly it was the horror of watching it happen before me and being powerless to stop it. How could I do that? How could I ask someone to die for me and for Pensmoore? And how could Bluebeard ask this of me?

"Would you rather see your people die for nothing because you would not sit a pretty horse and hold a rippling banner at their head?" he asked gently.

I shook my head within the hold of his fingers, but not because I agreed but because this was utterly ridiculous. Prophecies. Ha. Dead heads talking. It was my own fault for hauling Grosbeak around and increasing people's confidence in that. I wanted no part in any of this.

"I think that by their words 'Battle of the Bairn' they mean the fight against the son of the Aayaadmoore king. He will have the scrap of army on the west coast of the sea. So, you will be needed to sit your pretty horse and hold your banner there." There was teasing in his voice as if he thought he could get me to smile over this. "And I will be needed in the thick of the fighting on the east."

My eyes held his with all the intensity I felt.

"Yes, wife, I will be a slave to your efforts. I cannot watch over your shoulder, so I must trust you to do this without me."

I felt sick. This was madness.

"*What about Sparrow?*" I asked in my mind.

I felt like kicking myself, because *of course* everything was madness here and I was a fool to have expected otherwise. This was the Wittenhame, wasn't it?

"Sparrow is my right hand now, and the leader of my mortal armies. But she was not the one prophesied by the Wall of Wisdom. I will lend her to you if you wish it."

I nodded. That would certainly be more sensible, but what would she think of being saddled to me – a mortal girl with no value but the length of her days and a weak prophecy that may be no more accurate than this prediction about the Sword and the tides of his black, black heart.

Bluebeard kissed my forehead chastely as if sealing the conversation.

"As always, the thing we lack is time. But you must rest now, wife of mine."

"*If we lack time, wouldn't it make more sense to leave now and begin our work?*" I asked with my mind, but the yawn I covered with my hand spoke to the lie. I needed my sleep.

He chuckled but his chuckle had an iron core. "You are the land now, bride of my heart. Would you see it fade and suffer because you would not rest? No. Sleep now, and rest Pensmoore with your dreams, you devilish sensibility."

And to my utter shock, he leaned in, his fingers sliding from my face to tangle in my hair, and he kissed me as if he was drinking from a stream after a long ride, deep and long and wanting. My eyes shut against too many feelings, too much emotion, and to my surprise, for the very first time, I was parting my lips to let him in and kissing him back, wondering if I could fall in love with a man so hard, so unfathomable, so utterly impractical. If my racing heart was any judge, perhaps I could.

I tangled my hands into his shirt, feeling the warmth of his skin under it and I let myself fall into his kiss, embracing him back with all the hope I had in my heart.

His lips ripped away and my eyes shot open, shocked. Had I done something wrong?

"Oh. Oh no. You're kissing me back," he said, looking like he'd been caught stealing something. His hands fall from my hair and he leapt backward off the bed, his lower lip caught between his teeth. His eyes locked on mine and the boyishly guilty look he gave me was utterly incongruous with his slight beard and scarred body. He was breathless when he spoke and I thought maybe he was shaking a little. I certainly was. Everything inside me felt like it had been lit on fire and then the fire blown out. "Before this is over, fire of my eyes, they'll have snatched my heart, still bleeding, from within my breast. I would not have your heart risked, too."

He swallowed and then slowly the look of aching vulnerability on his face shifted into hardness and he spun, slinking across the room like a cat sauntering into the night. The latch on the door clicked shut behind him.

I slid, confused and a little embarrassed, under the warm blankets and let myself watch tonight's view from the room – the sight of a woodland glen in moonlight, dappled with white blossoms made periwinkle by the darkness. I'd spoiled the first kiss I'd fully enjoyed. That was the problem with letting yourself go. It never ended well.

I chewed on the edge of the blanket, trying to pretend I wasn't a little hurt. And I thought about kisses and why lips seemed to crave them like the body craved water. I thought of vanishing Wittenbrand with boyish smiles. I wondered if it really was so very dangerous to risk my heart on a man I'd already married, and I thought of what it would mean to lead an army into battle. I didn't like any of the answers my mind offered to me.

Around me, the fragrant black blossoms surrounding the bed waved and within me, doubts were soon overcome with a blanket of sleep.

Chapter Twenty-Seven

I WOKE to Bluebeard sprawled across the bed beside me, face down, arms and legs spread to their full extent, snoring. Of course. If I had to guess how he would sleep, this is what I would have guessed. There was nothing practical, nothing demure, or restrained, or tame in him. He was boldness and power, enthusiasm and full-commitment in everything – even sleep.

One of his out-flung arms was draped over me as if I were a drinking companion he was offering a friendly piece of advice to. My wry expression was wasted on him, and the flush on my cheeks at how nice it felt to have someone who cared about you sleeping so close was fortunately hidden. I hadn't thought before about what kind of comfort that might bring. I hadn't thought about how good it would feel to wake to the sound of someone else breathing. It was probably best that I didn't dwell on that. Not now with everything so unsettled. But I couldn't help but wonder what would come after when the game was over and the days used up. Would I have any left? And if I did, would I spend them with him? Would he sleep next to me, making that terrible sawing sound?

Would he be dead as he feared and leave me as a widow. Would he leap away and reject me as he had last night?

Thinking like that could only lead to trouble, so I took myself to the steaming black pool, drank the ever-present cup of hot tea, and then gave the gargoyle above the mirror a scathing look when it offered me a flowing velvet dress with a neckline down to my waist.

"I'm going to fight a battle, not try to cause one."

The gargoyle screwed up his face, making his eyes bulge, but I refused to be terrified.

"Not all battles are fought on battlefields," he huffed when I didn't bend.

"This one is," I said grimly.

"Fine," he said, and I could have sworn he rolled his eyes, but he spat out a pair of thick-woven leggings, tall riding boots, and a high-collared jacket embroidered with overflowing bowls of tears and – fortunately – enough room to move in. There were puffs at the top of the sleeves. There was also a small cape, and two short-sword scabbards on a belt. And every item from cape to boot was made with fabric or leather of a shade of blue ranging from the glimmer of dawn to midnight dark.

The pile of clothing was an intimidating sight but just when I was reaching for it, almost as an afterthought, he threw out a thing that might have been a silver circlet with a bit of netting behind it to catch my hair.

I dressed with care, but I lingered over the circlet and in the end, I left it on the floor beside the mirror, not sure of myself enough to throw it back, but not ready to wear it either. What was I queen of? Days, perhaps. And I had not nearly enough of them.

Bluebeard snored on, and so I took that moment to return to the Room of Wives with the little key he'd given me. I tidied it up from our stay within, straightening rugs, cleaning up chunks of mud that had dried in place, and letting my gaze trail over the women who had come before me.

Had any of them been warriors? Or better yet, strategists? Could they have led an assault down the west coast of Aayadmoore? I thought perhaps the one who had been so bent on tripping Bluebeard into her bed might have made a good warrior. She'd come at that problem from every angle before she'd been forced to stop. Idly, I picked up the journal of a girl even more wispy than I was – one with translucent skin so fair I could see the blue veins under her skin – and bright red tangled hair.

"Givanna" her nameplate read. Her book was filled with poetry, mostly. I skimmed through it. She would have been as poor at this as I, though toward the end of her book she'd written some verse for our shared husband that made me blush, and there, a few pages back she'd tried her hand at a poetic recounting of one of the ceremonies she'd heard was attended. I knew she hadn't been there herself. Bluebeard said he'd taken all the rest and kept them away from the court here.

Her verse read:

... and gossiped here to me:
"The Lords and Ladies have, I'd guess,
a pretty thing or two.
Coppertomb a silver sword,
Wittentree a marble shrew,
When asked where'pon they'd found these things,
The answers varied were.
'I found it on a rainbow swing'
'I gathered up a burr.'
But t'was Lord Towerrock's decry
that left me squint-eyed sure,
'A siren gave herself to me
and I, myself to her.'

She was a talented poet, but I had no time to read the rest of the gossip she'd accumulated. I shut the book and sighed, trying another one from a bride with silky brown skin and long black hair. Her skirt was wide and puffed out like a bell around her but there was something fierce about the way she held her chin. The plaque under her read "Tigrane."

I picked up her book, flipping through it, my eyes catching on the words "border raid."

I stopped for a moment and read.

"The Ayadmoore were raiding our borders that spring, in parties of twenty or thirty. My father allowed me to ride along to the Duke of Diasa's castle with him when he brought reinforcements to them. I found the journey educational and wish it was of some use to me now that I am stolen away as bride to this Wittenbrand prince."

There might be something to learn from this. I tucked it into my pocket. After all, I was headed into a battle. Maybe Tigrane learned something interesting that might be helpful.

I patted the lectern in front of her and said, "I'll return it undamaged," before turning to face why I'd really come. The hourglass.

I waited beside it a long moment until a single gem fell into the lower bulb.

My days. Dwindling far too quickly.

But the sight of them steeled me and gave me the courage for what would come. My husband was right. If I only had so many days to spend, I must spend each one with care.

I turned and strode from the room, leaving my sisters-in-fate behind me. If they were alive, maybe they would have wished me well. But if they were alive, then I wouldn't be here, and neither would they. I tried not to look at the empty pedestal. I didn't want to stand there frozen forever in whatever dress the gargoyle gave me. I didn't want someone to look at my empty book and wonder if there was just nothing to say.

I should write something. It had seemed a monstrosity before, but now it felt like a blasphemy not to write. Because though Bluebeard had told me I was the last, I didn't fully believe it. He had a big plan he refused to tell me about and that meant he'd need every scrap of magic he could get. My days would not be enough.

So, what should I tell my successor? What should I leave as a record? A warning? A message of hope? A note like Margaretta had left for me?

Maybe I'd think of something after this battle – if I lived to see the end of the Sword's dance with the Arrow. If I survived to see them change partners. Then, maybe, I would have something valuable to say.

It would probably be "Feed Grosbeak for me and don't talk to ravens."

Had I known then what would pass before I next entered that room, I might have paused to leave that note. But we are none of us privileged with the full truth of what is to come. Not even men with Vaults of Fallen Enemies.

Chapter Twenty-Eight

I RETURNED to our room to find Bluebeard fully dressed – mostly in weapons. Two short swords were laid out beside him on the bed as well as the many knives and swords he wore strapped to his body. But he was not sharpening them or pouring over maps. Instead, he was playing an instrument that looked like a balalaika, a dark look in his eye and a scowl as if the instrument had displeased him.

Through the window, dawn lit the sky bathing him in golden light at odds with his devilish glower. It was my turn to speak again. Finally.

"What do you mean by that behaviour?" I asked my most pressing question, crossing my arms over my chest and giving him my darkest glower. "You've kissed me many times. Mostly without permission. As I am your wife, I have not objected. But the one time that I kiss you back, you run away."

His glower grew deeper to match mine, and he set the instrument aside, standing and gathering the short swords from the bed.

"And now you won't reply?" I pressed. "You, who bids me lead armies though I am but a girl with no training in military things. You, who speaks lightly of leading your own charge against the Sword. You would run after kissing me? You're not a coward, so there is something else at work here – something more than risking my heart. I would have that knowledge, Arrow."

Still, he did not look at me, but he did reply with his mind. *"I would risk all myself for you, fire of my eyes. I would risk my body in your service."*

"So I see," I said boldly, crossing the room and parting his jacket so I could look at the blood blossoming already across his fresh shirt. He submitted to my work, letting me lift his shirt and look under it to check the wound. It looked no better. It was still crusted at the edges, but the center of the wound was open and oozing blood. My stomach flip-flopped.

"I would risk my very soul in this gamble to save you."

"Save me from what, exactly?" I asked coolly, but my mind was not on his grand words, but on his wound. He spoke like a god but bled like a man. I shook my head and glanced at the mirror.

To my surprise, it spat out a long bandage with only one rude expression on the face of the gargoyle. I scooped it up and brought it to Bluebeard, gently wrapping his wound.

"This shouldn't be left to fester. Surely there is some cure for it," I scolded him gently.

"Death cures all ills." His expression was maudlin. *"It will not pass me by."*

"Short of that," I said dryly, "let's at least keep this dry and bandaged."

My fingers grazed his skin as I worked to bandage his wound. It was absolutely shocking that he acted like it wasn't there. A mortal man would be dead of this by now. From the ill humors, if not the wound itself. I shivered.

"I would risk my heart, laid at your feet," he said in my mind and when I looked up, I froze. His expression was no longer a glower. It was caught midway between hard determination and a soft tenderness.

A tiny gasp escaped my throat, but he held my eye as he said in my mind, *"But I did not mean to risk yours with it. Your heart is mine to guard. Mine to ward. It will not be stolen, not by me or any man."*

"I think that's up to me to decide, don't you?" I said, trying to be gentle. He was ridiculous. "It is, after all, my heart."

His half-smile told me he didn't think that was true. A blush crept into my cheeks, hot as midsummer and I bit my lip.

"Well," I said, a little defensively. "If you're claiming my heart as your own, then it's only fair that you give me yours. After all, everyone else seems to be taking pieces of you."

His smile widened.

"Though I would prefer if you left it in your chest, running its long race at a steady beat."

I thought that perhaps he would kiss me again. Those were, after all, the most affectionate words I'd offered him. And he did step in so that my fumbling hands which had just finished tying his bandage were now pressed between us. But he shifted and the short swords that had been on the bed were jammed abruptly into the sheaths hanging empty on my belt.

"Angstbite you know," he said, *"and the other is Dreadtang. Use them well. Protect my heart."*

Perhaps this was how the Wittenbrand expressed affection. 'You melt my heart. Have a sword' or some such nonsense.

"I'm not adept in the sword," I said wryly, "but if someone comes to me bringing nonsense, they're in for a biting lecture and a strong glare of judgment."

"I suppose that will have to do. And now we must be off, wife of mine. We have a war to fight, a Sword to bring down, and a people to save."

He looked as if he might kiss me, but to my surprise – and an empty feeling that turned out to be disappointment – he did not.

Instead, he took my hand in his lovely callused one, and led me down the stairs to collect Grosbeak and his bow and quiver. I felt myself frowning when the specter returned to sit over my shoulder. I'd almost forgotten about her. I wished I could banish her the way Bluebeard did, but it seemed I was stuck with her until someone broke the "pact" from the Isle of Burning Guilt. She waved her finger in front of my face as if she suspected what I was thinking.

"There's something different about you two," Grosbeak said as I lifted his pole. His cruel snicker morphed into a yawn. I was not the only one who was tired this morning. "Are you making heirs now, by any chance?"

"I have too many who wish to inherit my lands and wealth already, traitor," Bluebeard said lightly. "I need not add to their number just yet."

He pulled a tiny knife from his pocket and made the slash of his mark on his cheek before raising an eyebrow to me and at my nod, offering me the same. We wore twin scarlet teardrops now. His sign to the world. I could only hope it would lend us victory.

But there was no time for more storms of doubt. And no time to wonder if I should have tried to kiss him again if he wasn't going to do it anymore.

Bluebeard led us to the fire where he leaned an arm against the mantle, and then his forehead against his arm as if surrendering to the exhaustion and anxiety I was still feeling even after a night of sleep.

"My fire," he sighed, his shoulders slumping slightly.

"My master," the fire replied warmly.

And then Bluebeard pulled the key from the chain around his neck, turned the key, and drew me into the flames.

I would never grow used to the madness that crashed into my soul from this kind of traveling between worlds. Never grow used to how it bored through my brain like a drill, how it left sticky trails of darkness through my thoughts and hopes.

When we emerged, it was all I could do not to vomit. I leaned over, hands on knees, coughing, gasping, trying to catch my breath.

Bluebeard did not pause to help me stand. He was already striding forward. I pulled myself together and began to follow and then froze.

We had emerged from a campfire along a bluff, looking out over miles and miles of land below. We were standing in a stone shrine built up on the cliff edge – a cut-stone floor smoothed to perfect levelness and surrounded by four pillars on each side leading up to a steepled stone roof. Green moss wreathed the pillars and edged the steps surrounding the shrine and black lichen clung to the stone everywhere I could see. If this shrine were in honor of a god or man, I did not know who it was. I stepped out from under the roof and looked back at the shrine. The only identifying feature was a weathervane set on the peak of the steepled roof, high, high above – a single arrow showing the wind was blowing due east.

"Nice place you have here. Well maintained," Grosbeak said muzzily. A fly took off from his head, buzzing madly before being snatched from the sky by a dragonfly. "Fabulous fauna."

A tent was pitched inside the shrine and beside it burned the indecently large fire we'd emerged from.

Sparrow rose from her vigil beside the fire, but it was not to the fire that I was looking. It was to the land. I had thought we were going to Pensmoore, but this was not the Pensmoore I knew. The land below the bluffs rose in a strange ridge as if it were made of two plates that had been jammed together by giant hands, roughening the edges of each, and leaving a long hillock of heaved rocks and earth in a scar across the land.

A scar that matched the wound on my face precisely.

I gasped and touched my cheek.

"You need to feed her more," Sparrow said wearily by way of greeting. "And she needs to sleep. You tied her to this land. Do you think it will survive if you burn her like a candle?"

"I know my business," Bluebeard said shortly – it seemed they would not bother with greetings. "And I bear a prophecy from the Vault of Wisdom."

"Our pleasure at your company once again, Sparrow," Grosbeak said as if he were a parent reminding them of their manners. His voice took on a higher pitch. "Oh no, it's my pleasure to serve *you*, oh great prince of the Wittenhame."

Sparrow ignored him. "Prophecies are well and good, but these are things you need to know, my prince. The harvest failed. The drought was too great. We have lost some to starvation and some to the ravages of this war, and those who remain healthy and strong fear for their children at home."

"Pensmoore is starving?" I asked Sparrow, my voice thick. Pensmoore had never starved in the memory of my father or his father. We were a northern country, cold and with harsh winters, but there was always food to be found in our rich forests and rivers.

"Mortals," Grosbeak scoffed. "Always dying of something. It's hardly worth it to try to keep them alive."

"Shush," I told him mildly, though I did not feel placid at his words. Which mortals were dying?

My own belly grumbled, and I felt my cheeks heat. I was *not* starving, and it was embarrassing to call such attention to myself.

Sparrow cursed and stormed away into her tent. I tried to catch Bluebeard's eye, but he was distracted, admiring a songbird that had landed on his finger. Three more stood on his head and several others were clustered on his shoulders. These were rose-breasted with blunt beaks. I would have said there was no practical use to an army of songbirds at your disposal, but that would have been foolish since they had carried him to my rescue.

When Sparrow emerged she shoved bread and fruit into my hands. "Eat. Eat it all. No crumbs now."

"Oh, but I couldn't," I said, horrified. "Not when people are starving."

Sparrow took a long breath as if she were summoning patience. "I heard a report that the Arrow mixed your blood with the land, did I not?"

"Yes, he did."

"He made you and the land one. Did you not see the scar rent upon the ground here when you received that wound on your face?"

I gasped, cupping my cheek.

"Yes, that one," she said, looking older somehow as her shoulders drooped. "Every night you don't sleep, every meal you don't eat, every pain you feel and every kiss offered you," here she shot a furtive look at Bluebeard, "are felt by the land and received into it, for good or ill. So, eat, that the land might produce food and your people might not starve."

"Cute. That's not at all risky, is it?" Grosbeak said. "She's tied to the land. He's tied to her. They're all tied up in the Game of Crowns. And here I am, more tied than all of them together. It's one big rat king of a tale from beginning to end."

I ate. I ate like one on a mission, since that was what I was, and as I ate, they talked. Bluebeard laid out his plan – the two fronts, the prophecy, his hope that she would lead the second army with me as it swept down the west coast and wrenched the Sword's land from him. I wondered idly if Svetgin were fighting with Pensmoore, or if the Sword had kept him close in Aayadmoore – as bait for me.

"You spoke to Wittentree?" Bluebeard asked Sparrow.

"Almost a moon ago now," Sparrow said with a nod, and I looked back and forth between them worriedly.

"And she was in earnest?" Bluebeard pressed.

"Three moons have passed since Vireo took you from our camp," Sparrow told me helpfully before turning back to her master. Grosbeak whistled as if he was astonished, but I knew it was only drama for my benefit. He neither cared nor was surprised by this. Sparrow went on as if he hadn't spoken at all. She hadn't liked him in life and that seemed to carry over into death. "In earnest, yes. Desperate, even. I didn't like the look in her eye. Like a cornered wolf. Whatever has passed between our opponents, she has not been invited into anyone else's councils. That I am certain of. She tried to keep it from me, but it was obvious in every too-quick word and every too-generous offering."

"You did not think it deception?"

She shook her head. "If I am wrong, we will know soon enough. But I am not wrong."

"Even a star-reader can be wrong from time to time and you are no star-reader," Grosbeak reminded her. "I recall speaking to one once who told me I would one day see my heart tied to the tides, and look at me now? No heart and no tied."

"She was close," Sparrow said a little poisonously. "Your head is tied to a pole. But as for the star reader, she was speaking of sirens. You know the old song that says, '*Oft the siren sings again, tying up the hearts of men, within her silken tides.*' Perhaps you should have spent more time at the sea if you wanted that fate."

I wasn't listening to their bickering. I was too horrified by what I had heard.

Three moons. It had felt like only days. Fear flooded through me, leaving jagged pains in my bowels and belly. Where would Svetgin be now? Did he still live? What about the people we'd seen when we rode from the river to the camps of soldiers? All those villagers and townspeople. Did they still live?

"Casualties?" Bluebeard said plainly, as if seeing my expression.

"As expected. Most of the border towns are gone. We moved what citizenry we could into the inner landholdings. But not all were spared. There are places along the border where the Aayadmoore have dug in past Pensmoore's borders and places where we hold defenses past theirs. The shape of the border changes with the day. I have maps marked for you. But if you really wish to lead this offensive, you need to ride immediately. Our forces are prepared to march by nightfall. An army four thousand strong. Two hundred light cavalry. Three hundred mounted bowmen. Five hundred longbowmen. Three hundred heavy cavalry. Ten catapults and their crews. The rest are officers and pikemen." She rattled off the numbers like they were written on the inside of her eyelids. "The supply lines and defenses are rigged as you requested. There are barges for the rivers with oxen to pull them. Teams to go with each one. The men are outfitted and ready."

"And the reserve army? The one you will lead with Izolda?"

"The one *Izolda* will lead with the help of Sparrow, or are you forgetting what the head said, big man?" Grosbeak snickered rudely and made a face.

Sparrow looked uncomfortable. "Skirmishers and scouts as you requested – six hundred. And two hundred light cavalry. No pikemen. No heavy cavalry. No catapults."

"And none should be needed. Had we spared more, he certainly would have guessed our purpose," Bluebeard said firmly. "And the banner? It is ready?"

She shrugged.

"You have it with you?" His tone brooked no argument.

"Of course."

"Aren't you going to show him?" Grosbeak pressed again. I didn't shush him this time. I felt like they were leaving me out of this planning, even though they expected me to play a role. I didn't like that. I didn't like the green-eyed monster that clawed up in my throat – a close match for his sister sitting on my shoulder. But while one monster bid me silent, this monster bid me speak and prove I was just as valuable as Sparrow, just as capable and strong. My cheeks flared hot because though my jealousy might boast of my assets, I was well aware that I brought none of those things with me. Swallowing down that bitter truth was no easy matter.

"Does she have to bring that rotten head with her?" Sparrow asked, shooting a poisonous look at Grosbeak.

"Yes," I answered before Bluebeard could. And I didn't know if I was keeping him because I wanted the company and felt responsible for him or just because it irritated her and not knowing that bothered me even more. I was known for my practicality, not my spite. Vindictiveness did not suit me.

"Then you'll both leave now, too," Bluebeard said, ignoring our side conversation. "Travel the path I laid out. Do not move from it or our timing will not stay true."

He was still looking at Sparrow. He didn't even glance at me. I felt that deep in the pit of my stomach.

She nodded. "All has been done as you specified, Arrow. All of it. I'll strike camp now. I have a horse for your lady wife – the dappled grey. And yours is the roan gelding."

"Excellent work, Sparrow. Your efforts will see fruit yet," my husband said with a warm smile for her. Something in my heart went icy cold.

He turned without so much as a goodbye and strode for his horse, leaving me standing there wide-eyed and slack-jawed. At least Sparrow was too busy hurrying to obey to notice.

No goodbye? After all those words of dedication and all those kisses, he wouldn't so much as kiss me goodbye? I remembered a little late that I hadn't offered any such words in return and that my only kiss had resulted in his sudden flight. Perhaps his words and kisses had only been about demonstrating ownership of me, not about true affection. Perhaps the tiniest sign that I might feel affection for him in return had ruined that and sent him running.

Belatedly, I remembered that I didn't need him. That I was my own woman. That I hadn't married for love, and I wouldn't love him even if he wanted me to because he was a villain from a storybook who I'd only allied myself with because the alternative was so much worse.

It was good to remember those things.

"You're disappointed," Grosbeak whispered, narrowing his eyes in delight. "Everyone can see it."

I looked sharply away and came face to face with the specter on my shoulder. She nodded gravely.

Both of them could go suck horse apples for all I cared.

I felt my hands trembling and my face flushing with humiliation, but when I turned, planning to go and examine the horse meant for me, I looked up into the eyes of Bluebeard. His horse was trotting up to me – made soundless because none of its hooves touched the ground.

Our eyes met for but a moment and then he pulled the horse up. He could not speak to me here and he would not speak in my mind and possibly use up my days. He did not break his rule, but he leaned down and seized me, kissing me swift and hard – so swift that the songbirds leapt from his shoulders to the branches above, piercing the air with loud shrieks.

And then he wrenched his lips away and my hand clawed at the empty air where he had been and in the blink of an eye he really was gone, riding off into the morning sun as his brightly colored bird entourage hurried to catch up.

"Really?" I said out loud.

"Really," Grosbeak said with a bubbling laugh. "This story is just too good, and I get a front-chain seat to all of it."

Chapter Twenty-Nine

AS THINGS so often are in fairytales, the world seemed to order itself to our story, so that our pounding hooves echoed under clear, azure skies and gentle breezes tossed out horses' manes in picturesque curls and ripples. It was almost as if the dew encrusted leaves and grasses and the heady scent of wildflowers were all singing the same song. "Victory," they sang. "Victory."

And I was a fool because part of me was beguiled by their song, and I believed it. I was a fool because when Sparrow finally produced the banner in her hand, I agreed to carry it.

It was a flowing white banner of silk showing a single blue arrow buried into the ground upon its field – the arrow from the Wittenhame that had been stuck in the stone and would someday show to them all their great king. I remembered the story, and while I doubted any mortal would notice the symbol, you could not be Wittenbrand without noticing it.

"Tell me again what I must do," I'd said nervously as we approached the camped army, our horses' hooves ringing out loudly on a road that had morphed from hard-packed dirt to cobbles as it entered what had once been a small seaside town – and probably a charming one – but was now filled past overflowing with armed soldiers and their mounts.

"Keep the veil over your face," Sparrow said grimly.

At her advice, I had agreed to wear a light veil of white that covered my face from below the eyes. It hung from an odd helmet ringed at the top with groping metal branches, so it looked almost like a woodland wreath. The center of the wreath held a small citrine gem with a cloudy surface, so it only glowed yellow when the sun hit it directly. The veil was of a light enough material not to hinder breathing, but it felt odd and awkward though it was trimmed in silver and tied to hang delicately from the temples of the branch helm.

"Despite what he thinks, no one is going to trust a woman so young and unblooded as you to lead them," Sparrow had said. "Confidence is key. If you speak, speak with authority and I will go along with it, only please do not order me to do anything I have not already told you we've planned. This can go very well or very poorly, and now that you're being handed the visible reins, you can be the source of chaos that sinks us. So, be silent as much as possible. Speak with authority when you cannot. The veil will hide your age and inexperience and the expressions on your face that might give you away. You are to be a symbol – a figurehead – a reminder of why they fight. You are not to actually lead charges or swing those swords. You'll hold the banner with one hand, the pole fixed in the pocket on this saddle. You'll hold Grosbeak in the other – and fortunately for you, I had a second pocket made because it will be a long day indeed with two of these heavy poles to keep raised. Keep them high and straight, ride with a straight back and your chin up, and your very presence will inspire and add confidence to this whole proceeding."

It was a practical solution to the problem of being saddled with me, to be sure, and I approved of it for that reason. This was not my world. This was not my expertise. If I was being fair, I had no expertise. I had been raised to be an adequate wife for a nobleman of middling success – to manage money and purchasing of supplies, to keep tradespeople from cheating me, to settle small disputes, to be frugal but generous, hard-working but not ambitious. I had, on my own, learned the ways of horses, but I had no list of skills or attributes to credit me. There was nothing I was qualified to do except sit my mare as I was told.

At least I could say with confidence that Sparrow had chosen a mare who was very well matched for me in terms of size – she was strong but delicate with an arching neck and graceful feet – as well as temperament, for while I was no high-spirited lass, I appreciated high spirits, and this mare danced and pulled a little, longing to be about her work. I admired that.

I balked at the dress and cloak, though. "I'm dressed already."

"Not like this," she had said, holding up a filmy white dress and cloak that looked more like a living cloud than anything that might protect you from a breeze, never mind battle. It was translucent. I'd hate to wear it with the sun behind me. There'd be no hiding my shape at all.

"That's entirely the point," I said crisply, pursing my lips. "I am wearing as practical an outfit as can be contrived in the Wittenhame. *That* looks more like a bridal gown for a faerie queen."

Sparrow shook it out and looked again. "Hides too much for that. Faerie queens show more skin. This is the dress of a virginal bride, a symbol of innocence and purity. It's a dress for you."

My eyes felt dry they were open so wide. "It's the most impractical thing I've ever seen."

"Do you want to win this battle, or do you want to argue fashion with me?" she'd said, leaning forward with a grim expression and I was reminded that while she might be my sex, she was entirely different in species and just as likely to rip out my throat if she didn't like the words coming out of it as any other Wittenbrand was.

I wore the wispy dress, rode the majestic horse, and bore the heavy branch crown with the white veil and I felt less myself than I'd ever been, even when I was stolen away for the first time by my strange Wittenbrand husband. Even when my hands were dirty with his betrayal. Even when I'd listened to my own king sell my life away. I felt like I was completely invisible.

And so, invisible and a stranger in my own skin, I found myself led to a council where the plan was laid out and the captains introduced to me. It turned out that I had become an expert in something at least – remaining silent. Sparrow spoke for me, explaining that I was the wife of their patron, the mortal woman Izolda of Savataz. This raised some eyebrows for every face gathered was of a Pensmoore set and I recognized more than one of them. And when she said I would lead the battle, their eyes narrowed, and their fists clenched. But as she spread the maps and spoke about positionings and which villages would be quickly taken and which bypassed entirely, what route would be used, where prisoners would be housed, and who would defend our flanks, they seemed to relax. As I remained silent, never interjecting, never adding my own opinion, they seemed to relax even more, occasionally catching my eye when they looked nervously in my direction but smiling nervously if they did instead of looking angry.

Very well, if my job was stoic silence, it was a thing I was at least well prepared for. I comforted myself with little peeks into Tigrane's book. It was written in an old form of the language, but with concentration I could make out what she was saying.

"This is the written account of the short life of Tigrane Hussanafe, Princess of Ptolemoore. I have written this account in the hopes that one day my family will find it and know I did not suffer and that those who follow me might gain wisdom from my words."

Wisdom would be nice. I could use that. I'd flipped past the poem at the beginning of every book and flipped past her early childhood and found her later accounts more interesting. Her father had been preparing her to rule, and it seemed he had taken pains to teach her his business.

"We were busy fortifying our northern border. Though we had stemmed many raids, they were continuing in waves. It was the famine that drove them – drove all of us. Desperate men do desperate things and opportunists seek to profit without working themselves."

Like us in this raid. We were being opportunists.

"I was assessing the arrow stores at the tower beside the Fountspring River when a band of raiders made it through the line and attacked. The Sergeant stationed with me was quick to act, gathering in his troops and furnishing the line. They were scattered, but his quick action focused them. After the tumult he told me that if a group of warriors is scattered, concentrating them again should be your first thought. Strung out, they are vulnerable. A leader doesn't leave his men vulnerable. I am sad when I think of Sergeant Quistide. I will miss his pearls of wisdom."

I'd have to remember that.

Grosbeak was not so well prepared for silence and reading didn't interest him, but I found it easy to silence him before the council, for as they served refreshments, they laid out fruit, and just as he opened his mouth to speak – and I was sure he'd say something I would regret – I snatched up a bright orange and jammed it into his open jaw so that throughout the council he could do nothing but make muffled noises that sounded like curses. If those seated thought he was demonic or mad, I cared not at all. It only lent to my air of mystery.

I was glad when – at last – the council was over and we rode, the troops falling in behind and before.

That was three days ago. Three days of hard riding are enough to soil a white dress, though I'd done all I could to keep it clean. Enough to leave me wrung out like a rag so my stiff spine was more of a bending willow than a strong oak. Enough to make that veil feel like it was smothering me.

The first assault had been easy. We'd taken the seaside village with hardly an effort. And I'd certainly played my part. I'd ridden in at the head of the army when the defenders were slain. I looked the part of the leader of the conquerors.

Shortly after, I'd emptied my stomach along the side of the road, barely saving the veil from the mess.

The people in the little village had been close to starving. I'd never seen so many pale, drawn faces. So many too-deep sunken eyes. And then there had been the children. Those adults still left clung to them with hopeless, empty faces. And there were so few men and women left that I did not know how they would feed those little ones. Every able-bodied man and woman had fought us. And they were now nothing more than corpses on either side of the smooth road.

I wiped my palms often on my dress, feeling the stickiness of blood on them even when they were perfectly clean.

My white dress was nothing more than a mockery. My crown a disgrace.

I kept the orange shoved in Grosbeak's mouth for the entire day for I did not dare listen to what he would surely tell me – that I ought to have worn red and borne a crown of flames.

Guilt sawed through me at the next town, but at Sparrow's insistence, I rode ahead of the victors. This time I kept my eyes forward, hoping the veil hid most of my tears. I could hear the sobs and cries of the survivors on either side of the road. I thought that, perhaps, I had more in common with them than those I rode with.

Is this what my husband had in mind when he sent me on an "easy" campaign to sweep up the rear of the Sword's territory? If it was, then it changed how I saw him. I changed whether I could trust him. How could he be so gentle and kind when his hands bandaged me and yet order his troops to sweep over this land like wolves over a pack of caribou.

"It's not that bad as wars go," Sparrow had said in our tent that night. She'd not said anything else to me and since I'd been silent all day, no one was suspicious when I took my meal to my tent and did not leave it, spending my time reading Tigrane's memoirs instead of socializing with them. "Hardly any casualties. None of children or the elderly. We can't help it if they choose to fight."

"If they choose to defend their homes and livelihoods, you mean?" I asked, and even to me, my tone was more bitter than ginger root.

"You've been gone three turnings of the moon," she said carefully. "Which is why you don't know that your own homeland looks the same. The people are hungry. They lack necessities. The sooner this war is over, the sooner they can prosper again. The sooner the sick can be cared for and the hungry fed. We do them a favor by making it short and fast."

"We do them a favor by twisting them into wars there would be none without us?"

"What do you mean?" her words were cold now.

"I mean that I watched as they tossed the tiles and pulled out war. And there was no war before that. I was there as they plucked the little figurines from the molten lead. They did not have nations assigned to them before then. The Wittenbrand made this war. Without them – without you – it wouldn't have happened at all."

"Mayhap," she said, her voice still colder than the mountains of my homeland. "Or mayhap it would have happened anyway. What do you know of courts or kings? You were a minor noble of a minor house in a minor nation and at his first opportunity, your king sold your life away."

"Where is he anyway?"

"He reviled you when the Arrow brought you to his court."

"Yes," I said. "Is he with my husband on the other front or cowering in his castle?"

She barked a laugh. "Neither. Your Wittenbrand husband heard his words and took his head as the price of his ignorance. He'll brook no insult to you, bride of bloodshed. You'll never see that poxy man again."

I gasped.

"Did you think this was a simple game?" she hissed, nastily as she pinched the candle out. "Did you think it would be carved pieces on a board or cards laid out precisely with a bid? It's a game of lives. A game of nations. And if you care about your own, you'll have to be willing to sacrifice theirs. Your squeamishness will ruin the men's morale, so I thank you to keep it to yourself and trust the Arrow to know best."

"If these are his actions, then I'm not sure that I do trust him," I said. "I'm not sure he's worth trusting after all."

The sound she made was of utter disgust. "Don't even talk to me, wretched mortal. I have married my fate to your husband, and you won't even marry your trust to him."

I felt my face flushing, but I would not back down. Not with those children's faces etched into my heart.

"Trust is a thing earned by honor, not demanded by might."

"Says the betrayer," she'd muttered and that was the last thing she spoke to me until dawn.

I lay in the dark alone, calling in my mind to Bluebeard.

"*Husband? Are you there? If you're there, please explain yourself. Tell me why I should trust a man who sent me to slaughter my kind. Tell me why I should keep leading these men to make orphans and widows multiply and lay ruin across the earth. Tell me, if you can.*"

But whether he could not hear me, or whether he would not answer, I did not know, only that he remained as silent as the many, many graves trailing in my wake.

Chapter Thirty

ON THE SECOND DAY, I removed the orange from Grosbeak's mouth. If I was going to be miserable, I might as well have company. Besides, Tigrane's sergeant had told her to show mercy wherever she could even to the worst of men because mercy always triumphs in the end. I thought I might give it a try.

"I shall never forgive you for muzzling me," Grosbeak growled when I removed the orange. I was mounted on my pretty mare, my arms already burning from keeping both the flag and Grosbeak in place. I'd rigged them to be held entirely in the pockets when we were motionless, but if we moved, I had to hold them steady. And we always seemed to be moving. I preferred that. It distracted me from the knowledge that I was on my own in a living nightmare with no help from the distant husband who had condemned me to this role.

"It's going well," Sparrow said a little breathlessly when she rode up at the end of the second day. We had driven all the way down to the seaport of Dhayyad and found it defenseless. To my enormous relief, the port had surrendered without a fight. Unlike the dozen or so towns and villages we'd taken, the citizenry seemed to understand the penalty for defiance. After Dhayyad, the city of Gren-ayad had sent word that they accepted our rule of the region and would meet with us to discuss terms when it was convenient. A surrender without even the need to pose as conquerors. "You should be more cheerful. This is as bloodless as war gets."

And it was still too bloody for me.

We'd run into a shepherd on the road two hours ago, butchered with his sheep. I had just looked at Sparrow. Just looked and nothing more.

"You could exhort the men if you like," she said with a sigh. "You can remind them that mercy is golden. But if you do that, they will have doubts. And look what doubt is doing to you."

"I had no doubts," Grosbeak said from where he swayed on his chain. He was undisturbed by grisly news or sights. "Not even one up until the very end. Assurance is a delicious thing, worth any price."

"Misleading, in your case, I would think," I said absently. This was not his fault.

"Oh, certainly. But you can't go through life always torn up – not in days of war and trouble. You have to do the job in front of you and worry about it later."

"Killing me was the job in front of you," I said dryly.

"Exactly," he agreed happily. "And if I'd managed to get on with it without being caught, I wouldn't be here now second-guessing my choices. See? I'm not wrong. Doubts and second-guesses are best left for the dead. We have nothing else to do."

"You don't know what gift you've been given," Sparrow had told me with disgust. "It's wasted on you."

And she'd ridden off to talk to the captains and arrange the next day's excursions. Our line was thinning, stretched as it was across such a swath of land. I'd been watching that, noting how we had to leave soldiers at each important junction and with them, supplies. How we'd had to leave too few to really guard those areas so we could keep the bulk of the troop together. If we continued our streak of success, it shouldn't matter. We'd be reaching the southernmost tip of Aayadmoore before the end of another day, and from there we'd establish a head and start shipping supplies and reinforcements in. But if we saw even the slightest turnabout of success, we could find ourselves stretched out too thin and easy to gobble up.

On top of that, I sensed the captains were restless. There had been no true glory yet and, unlike me, they craved the kind of action that would fill their drinking stories and garnish boasts of prowess. They wanted to take a large target that fought back so they could earn their victory. They almost needed it, they craved it so much. The thought of that sat poorly with me.

It was these moody thoughts that were upon me when we were surprised on the plain just outside of Cataayad, the southernmost port city of Aayadmoore.

I was positioned – at Sparrow's order – on a hill looking over the plain, a forest at my back, taking a quick break as the troops passed by on the plain, row upon row upon row. She had set me up like a statue to inspire them more than once and I was used to this routine. If I was careful to disguise my book, I could read it as they passed.

Tigrane had proved a very interesting writer, full of wit, practicalities and an interesting perspective on her father's never-ending wars. I thought we could have been friends had we known each other. She had been twenty-three when Bluebeard took her – old enough that her mother despaired of her ever marrying and her father rejoiced in her ability to run his kingdom at his side. She had no siblings, no cousins, none to replace her. And I had never heard of her family line. I was frequently saddened by that. All memory of her was in this book and her lifeless body frozen in time on its pedestal. But I would remember. And I was learning much about ruling a kingdom and leading people. And with every sentence I read I watched Sparrow and the other officers and compared their actions to Tigrane's words and found myself wishing it was Tigrane leading these troops and not me. She would not have been roped into a war she wanted no part of or dressed up like a strange doll and paraded around for morale and nothing more. She would have done better than this.

Though the soldiers were traveling to battle, they seemed in good spirits and looked often toward me as they passed, their chins lifting and spines stiffening when they saw me. If I inspired them with pride, it was only because of who Sparrow had made me – the perfect, faceless figurehead. They could imagine me looking back over them with pride or with hope or with admiration or any other emotion they wanted to imagine because my face was hidden from them, my true heart buried deep within.

The last of the troops were passing by, and in a moment, Sparrow would send a rider from the front to come back and retrieve me as she always did. Her disgust at my lack of enthusiasm for bloodshed never prevented her from using me perfectly as her foil.

"Something is amiss," Grosbeak said as a cloud shifted in the sky. In the distance, to the west, the sky looked almost red, made more apparent with the rays of the sun hidden away.

The sight of it made my stomach twist.

"The battle will come in red," I whispered, putting my book away.

"So they said," Grosbeak agreed. "But in your case, I think the battle will come in moping and moaning."

"Just because you have no compassion doesn't mean I should smother mine," I argued.

"Then don't smother it, but also don't use it as an excuse to shut your eyes and stop your ears. You could have been using this time to win over the captains of Pensmoore's army and endear yourself to the troops."

"Sparrow wants me to be a distant figurehead."

"And is that what the Arrow demanded when he left you here? No. He told you to lead. But instead, you're sulking like a nineteen-year-old girl."

"I *am* a nineteen-year-old girl, in case you haven't noticed."

"Ah, but there lies the trick of it, for you've been one now for nigh on thirty years and you should know better."

"I know the names of the captains," I objected. Was that red I saw on the field now, too, and coming down that nearby hill? Or was I imagining things? "And I know what they want – glory and honor and bloodshed. And what they'll do to get it – anything. And I've decided I want no part of my people. I want no part of their war. I just want to live a quiet life."

"Oh, isn't that so nice," Grosbeak said nastily. "And then someone else can go fight and die so you can have your nice life of peace. And he can get his hands bloody, and his conscience stained, while you sit in your superior white dress."

"I didn't choose this dress," I said sharply.

"But you chose that attitude and isn't it an unflattering thing. Everything worth having has a price. And the price of peace is sometimes war. What do you think the Sword will do to this place if he's left alone for a hundred years to do as he likes? What was he willing to do to you?"

I flinched from his words.

"You aren't a passive, useless person, Izolda. You are not a decoration to act as a living statue. Why do you think Bluebeard sent you to this battle?"

"Because of a prophecy," I said grimly. "And because I was bound on – "

The specter wrapped a hand around my mouth, and I rolled my eyes. Grosbeak had been there. Who was she protecting my words from?

"I think he sent you because you have skills that Sparrow doesn't have. Look."

And as he said that, a tide of red rolled over the hill and into our troops. It was like watching an arrow fly through the air and puncture plate armor. Like watching a mist lion leap and bear a deer down to the ground. Our line flinched and then shuddered as the impact of red-coated bodies slammed into them.

Stunned, I watched as a second group poured out of the city walls ahead, blocking off that way of escape for our lead-most troops. That left only the ocean and the way back, but the line was crumpling where the hammer of their forces had hit us, buckling and bending, and then – in the space of heartbeat – we were two groups cut off from one another.

Retreat. We had to retreat. And *I* had to sound the retreat.

I spun my horse to see if anyone was behind me. There were only the last few lines of soldiers who hadn't marched past me yet, but they weren't running forward to help their fellows, they were forming a line, pulling in cooks and porters and the others that usually made up the rear of the line and forcing them into position as a third wave of red rolled in from the rear.

I realized without having to be told that these weren't local forces. I'd looked at the maps and heard the captains as their spies reported and then they discussed what they would do. I'd listened as Sparrow rattled off estimates of manpower and horses and how far off lords and their house guards were located. These were none of those groups. This was the Sword and his army – those I had thought my husband went to fight in the east. They had laid a clever trap and we'd fallen into it like a duckling into the jaws of a shark.

It only took a heartbeat to realize this. One more to watch as Sparrow tried to form up her group on the other side of that red river to join us. A third to know what I had to do.

I lifted the banner, rode to the line trying to form beside me, and roared in my best imitation of my father, "Up Pensmoore, up! To me!"

Ready or not, this battle had come for me.

Chapter Thirty-One

"THIS IS NOT the front seat that I paid for!" Grosbeak protested choppily as his head swung back and forth on the end of the chain. My very pretty horse was capable of fancy footwork – a boon in our present situation. I danced her to the center of the men forming and grabbed the flag from the pocket, lifting it to wave it back and forth. "They should have left you with a guard!"

"They dressed me in white, Grosbeak. Clearly, I was meant to be the sacrificial lamb."

Behind us, screams mingled in the air with the clash of steel, a hymn to death and fury, a song to melting ambitions. I clenched my teeth against it, trying to stop my ears to individual cries lest I ache for each voice. My belly felt like water and my legs trembled where they gripped the dappled mare.

The soldiers needed a rallying point. With forces on every side pressing in and cut off from the front of the formation, they needed some shared goal. That's what flags were for. That's what *I* was for.

I tried to focus on that and what I could remember from Tigrane's beloved Sergeant, instead of on the clash of steel and the cries of fear and panic. These were men of Pensmoore, and while I'd spent the last three days furious with them, appalled by their success, aching at the misery of even an easy war, they were still my people, of my homeland, raised on my land.

The battle wasn't here yet, but it was quickly forming up. It seemed almost incongruous with the soft breeze and dappled sunlight in this wildflower field, but we were preparing to wash it in blood.

Three rows of fighters formed up in front of me. They would not be enough against our enemy. Those who had come up from behind us were running down the road in an effort to meet us here – our cooks and farriers with their weapons clenched in trembling hands and determination etched in every face.

But they weren't the only threat. In the center of what had been our formation, more ambushers slammed into our men on the forest side, gaining ground.

Our defenses there were little knots of men – threes or four here, a dozen there – trying to fight from horseback as they faced an equal number of light cavalry riding from the forest and rushing along the side of our formation – if you could call this ragged grouping that – in a sweeping maneuver meant to drive us back.

A sudden memory of my childhood overtook me. Svetgin setting up his rows of toy soldiers. Rolgrin laughing as he made horse noises and pretended to draw two of his horses along the side of the neat soldier ranks.

"You can't do that! There's only two of them!" Svetgin had protested.

"It's a sweep. It's meant to keep them in place until my heavy forces pin them down."

They'd learned that in the strategy classes my father's arms man taught them. I was suddenly wishing I'd been included, too. Tigrane's recorded memories were not enough to teach me battle.

"You should get down off the horse, lady," a man wearing a sergeant's baldric suggested as he trotted past me. "You make a pretty figurehead on a hillside but you're a target for archers now."

He didn't stop to watch if I obeyed. He and his group of ten reached the line drawing up at what had been our rear and was about to become the front of our fight. The sight of them arriving put a new strength in the faces of the bluff workers around me. I could almost hear them thinking, "ah, real soldiers."

I wasn't so optimistic. We were armed haphazardly, caught out unprepared. Meanwhile, the group surging up the road we'd just traveled were heavily armored and carried heavy maces. The armor made them slower, explaining the need for the light cavalry to pin us.

Cold sweat broke out across my brow. I could see it all from where I sat, the sergeant and others like him hastily setting up the line, the groups of our own light cavalry being forced back where they were stretched out in small groups between here and at what had been the center of our line but was now a river of death. We were spread out too thin. And that line at what was now our backs had crumpled. It was only the chaos of fighting individuals and the distance between us and them that gave us even a breath of safety from that bulge that cut our rear contingent off from the front of the army.

Worse, the front army had the captains and Sparrow in it. How had we not planned for this? How had *I* not noticed it? I, whose only skill was noticing things other people missed. I'd been too emotionally tumultuous to pay attention to the details, too torn up by the horror of war. And I wouldn't apologize for that, though now I might reap the whirlwind consequence.

In a flash of insight, I realized another truth, Sparrow and her captains had positioned themselves all in the front to stay as far away from me as possible. The men who died now died because I had been so miserable that my attitude had pushed the officers away. I felt a flash of cold, harsh guilt, harsher than any specter sitting on my shoulder. In mourning lost lives, I may have doomed more.

Biting my lip, I peered at the faraway group of officers and their part of the army, trying to judge if they were holding. They were locked into a smaller space than we were – not spread out but balled up in a churning huddle as they fought attackers on every side, weapons flashing as they moved with lightning speed.

Grosbeak cursed and I tasted blood as my tooth went right through the flesh of my lip as I finally saw a detail no one else was noticing.

"Trust mortals to botch a perfect battle," he muttered. "At least they have the colors right, red versus blue."

I urged my horse forward to where the sergeant who had warned me off was dressing the line.

"Sergeant," I called.

"Not now, lady. We are preparing to meet the attack coming down the road."

"Sergeant," I tried again. "You're forming up in the wrong place."

"Lady, you form where you stand, or you fall. And I told you to get off that horse."

I looked up, judged the distance between the heavy infantry marching toward us, judged the forming line, looked back over my shoulder at the harried cavalry drawing inward toward the sea, at the crumpled line, at the knot of trapped officers.

And the words of Tigrane's journal came to mind.

"My tutors tell me that if you find yourself facing foes in multiple sides, reduce the number of sides which you must defend."

Right, then.

I'd been sent to lead. If I was going to die, then I would die leading.

I wrenched the veil off my face with one hand and threw it to the ground.

"Form your line, Sergeant," I ordered, energized by the feeling of air on my sheltered face, "and then we will retreat, slowly, backing up to join our spread-out forces and increase our numbers."

"You don't know war, lady," he said, still moving down the line, working as he spoke. My horse followed, dodging rushing men as they worked. The wagons had been cut loose from the supply horses. Carts had been overturned across the road. They were making quick work, but by my estimate, we had minutes until the tide of men hit us.

"She doesn't know defeat, either," Grosbeak said flippantly.

There was a roar from behind us. The last of our men fighting on foot in the middle space had been overwhelmed.

The tide from behind was roaring forward. We would find ourselves in the middle between them both. We needed one less side to defend.

"We'll gather up what cavalry we can as we retreat and try to sweep to position our backs to the ocean."

"A losing proposition. Do you not know that tides change?" the sergeant replied.

"Do they change in an hour?" I asked. "I'm asking you to hold just that long."

That made him pause. "Just an hour? Ha! Do you know how long an hour is on a battlefield?"

"Every hour of my life is weighed and measured," I said through gritted teeth. I could see this in my mind. It was the right solution. "Every day of mine is being spent. I can count them as they pass, and I know their futility. I know also what I ask of you. Now, form the line, set a steady retreat, and sweep to the ocean while I round up the light cavalry scattered from here to the enemy."

"While you what?" he asked, aghast. Pausing for the first time to actually look at me. "While you *what*?"

I didn't answer, taking my inspiration from my taciturn husband who never answered those kinds of questions from me. Instead, I turned my horse and kicked her up to a trot. The sergeant knew his orders. I could only hope he'd follow them.

"Look at you, ordering military men around like you think you know what you're doing," Grosbeak snickered.

"I can see more because I'm on horseback," I said shortly. I had to hold both the banner and his head pole to keep them steady as I rode.

"Maybe this slaughter agrees with you after all."

"I assure you, it does not."

"And yet your orders were exactly what I would have given when I was one of Bluebeard's war leaders."

I'd forgotten that he was ever more than a talking head.

"It was the practical suggestion," I deflected.

He laughed again, this time with seeming enjoyment. "Oh, war is a practical thing, mistress. It's all about cold calculations and weighing what cost you'll pay for what return. Like a cart merchant with a barrel of apples to sell, but the apples you're selling are men's lives."

"They're giving them no matter what," I said tightly. "I'm just trying to increase the cost to the buyer."

"And if you'd thought that way from the start, maybe we wouldn't be selling so many apples," he said.

His insight cut to the quick. I could see the truth of it, and I hated myself for it. Hated that my very compassion had tripped me up and made me useless.

"You were never meant to be ornamental, Izolda. You've not the face for it, nor the temperament."

He was right about that, too.

I reached the first group of riders as they were ending a bloody skirmish. Their attackers had ridden on, leaving them broken and splintered. Three horses were down, kicking in their own blood as one of the riders stumbled from one to the next, ending their misery with his blade. His coat was torn and bloody, his face streaked with sweat and dirt. I found my stomach flipping at the sight.

"Pensmoore," I said in greeting as the survivors turned their exhausted eyes to me. I straightened, trying to look confident. "Have you mounts for the wounded?"

The man who had been killing the horses looked around him, devastation on his face. He was counting.

"Aye, lady," he said after a moment. "I'm sergeant here."

"Take your men and join the foot. They're retreating to make a stand with the ocean against their backs. You can meet them halfway if you hurry," I ordered him.

He looked helplessly at the trees. "Orders are to hold in line if attacked. This is my spot in line."

"I'm changing those orders," I said grimly.

"No offense lady, but pretty crown or no, this isn't your field. This isn't your army." He sounded tired. Too tired to argue, though he was making a try of it.

"Ooooh. Big sergeant," Grosbeak hooted.

I wrenched off the crown of branches and threw it at him, pitching my voice to make it loud enough for his men to hear, too. He caught it, astonished, as I spoke.

"I don't care about crowns. I don't care about captains. But I care about Pensmoore. It's why I carry her banner. It's why I lead this army, whether you believe it or not. And it's why I'm going to get as many of your tattered hides home to your wives and sweethearts as I can, even if I have to hang a dozen more heads from my lantern pole to accomplish it.

A lone soldier gave a half-hearted cheer before a friend hushed him.

The sergeant was motionless for a full breath, staring at me, his own chest heaving as he tried to catch his breath, but whatever he saw in his face was what he needed to say because when he did speak, he nodded, dropping the glittering crown to the ground, fluttering veil and all.

"Hashek, Roirden, ride with the lady to enforce her will. You'll be gathering the whole line, lady?"

"Yes."

He nodded again. "Aye then, we'll take our wounded where you've sent them, and god send our foot are still there when we arrive."

I glanced over my shoulder and clenched my jaw in time to see the first of the enemy slam into the lines I'd left with the sergeant. I could only hope he really would lead them to where they could get the ocean behind their backs before they were flanked.

"Hurry," I said, but there was no time for more, so I rode.

The two men he'd called off fell in behind me.

I gathered up two more knots of men – these without any surviving officers – and sent them to assist the foot without any more argument. Maybe it was the men at my back. Maybe it was the lack of veil and crown. With it gone, all eyes looked to my banner and every now and then, one of the men would touch his cheek as if in honor of my husband's sign. Their patron saint. The one who had sent his wife to fight this battle.

And fight this battle, I would, though he'd be hearing about it from me later.

It was at the fourth knot that we encountered the enemy. There were little unpredictable dips in these plains, and the fourth knot of men and wounded horses were situated right beside one of those. I pulled up beside them just as the enemy charged out of that dip, howling and waving their swords as if their sheer noise might slay us where we stood. I checked that the flag was secure and grabbed Grosbeak's pole.

"I am not a weapon. I am not a weapon. I am not a weapon," he chanted, but he need hardly have bothered. I didn't get a single swipe in. Hashek and Roirden cut the enemy down before they could touch me or the four surviving men. They had only two horses between them, but they didn't hesitate to mount up and ride in the direction I pointed.

"You need to get back to the foot," Grosbeak said from where he swung on the chain. "Look."

I did look, cursing when I saw what he had.

Our foot had obeyed my orders, angling so their backs were to the ocean, but the reinforcements I was sending were not enough.

The enemy army who had attacked our line in the center were rushing toward the men I'd gathered, abandoning their search of the wounded and dying. One glance showed their red-coated masses splitting us so far from the front of what had once been our line that the thought of rejoining again seemed nearly impossible.

I swallowed down a knot of fear. There was no time for that now.

I scanned everything, assessing it quickly. There were a few more scattered groups out here, but the time it would take to gather them was too valuable. I looked to them and then back to the foot.

"I'll ride to them," Roirden offered, and at my nod, he whipped his horse into a gallop.

It was the best we could do.

We spun and turned back to the lines of foot I'd left to fight, riding hard to meet them. My hair was loose from its braid and streaming behind me like a second flag and with it, my fears and hopes streamed out, too. It was ridiculous that I was here at all, ridiculous that I was trying to lead where I should have just held my tongue and left this to those who were responsible to act. But how could I have remained silent when I could *see* what was coming?

I tried one more time to call my husband. *Please,* I said with my mental voice. *Please listen to me. Please come to me. I will not rage or yell if only you will come to me. I will not throw recriminations at you, if only you will save me.*

He did not come. He did not answer.

I clenched my teeth and rode towards the men I had positioned to fight a final battle. The first wave of attack had been quelled, but our enemy was drawing together and preparing for another thrust. I would live or die with these men I'd gathered. They could not escape the enemy now that they were pinned on one side, soon to be savaged on the other, with their only guarded side held by the sea. It was an impossible situation. And one I'd thrust them into.

I scanned their eyes and faces as we drew closer. I noted the determination swirling with fear and fury. And I saw how their eyes lifted to me, painful hope flashing there.

"If you'd ordered them to the trees, they'd be slaughtered one at a time. Like carrots in a row ready to be picked," Grosbeak reminded me. "It was better this way."

Even so, I couldn't be so confident. And it was on my word that they'd amassed there. I needed a plan to save them, and I needed it now. I tried to see what was obvious that I might be missing. I tried to think about what Tigrane had written.

But nothing came to me, not even when we reached the edge of the line, trampling fallen bodies in the mud under my horse's feet – remains of the last wave of fighting. I held tightly to my churning belly and tried not to think of the horror of their desecration and how damned my soul must be at the indifference of my action.

The moment we joined our diminished army, Hashek spun to join the defense. I touched him lightly on the arm in thanks and to my surprise, he saluted.

"Whenever you call, lady, I shall listen."

I felt my eyebrows raising but I couldn't seem to straighten them as his words were echoed down the line.

"Whenever you call!" the men said.

A little shudder went through me. I'd better figure out how to call. And fast.

I rode to the back of the line, my dapple's hooves splashing in the tide.

There were just under fifty or sixty defenders here. Someone cried out. The enemy reforming on the road side of us was moving again, ready to come in a second wave. I quickly assessed what we had to fight.

Rallying the spread-out light cavalry had added maybe another thirty men on horse trying to harry the flanks, but with the second force closing in things were grim. Would it be enough?

I reached the sergeant as he was passing orders about the care of the wounded at the back of the line.

"We're here, banner lady," he said, looking up from his work. His tone was wry with disbelief. "I hope there's a second half to this plan of yours."

There wasn't.

I closed my eyes and hoped.

Chapter Thirty-Two

A RALLYING CRY from the enemy sounded. They must have seen the second force waiting to join them. My heart pounded in the cage of my ribs. I felt like I couldn't take a breath.

"Breathe, Izolda," Grosbeak said. "Think. What do you have that no one else has? What can you use?"

I had common sense. A bodiless friend. A specter that shut my mouth for me if I mentioned certain things. A missing husband who had dropped me right into this mess. A room of secrets that opened with a key. Nothing that would help. Even the room could only provide temporary relief and delay the inevitable – and that was assuming my army would fit in it.

My teeth set on edge. My head was ringing as the next wave of attack crashed into our fighters. The sounds of fighting ripped through my concentration. Shouts and battle cries and the clash of steel and screams of death blocked out everything else.

We were pushed back until my dappled mare's feet were half-sunk in foaming seawater. It licked green against her grey legs.

There had to be something I hadn't thought of yet.

I clenched my palms tightly closed and felt one sting just a little – a stinging feeling I had gotten so used to that I'd forgotten it had existed at all. It was the sting from the cut on my palm when Bluebeard bound me to the earth. That might have proved useful had we been in Pensmoore. It might have led to some kind of magical connection to the land that could save us all. But we were not in Pensmoore and this land was not tied to me.

A soldier fell beside me, and I leaned down to grab his arm and haul him to his feet. Our eyes met, locked in desperate fear. A blade slid into his chest and blood bubbled up to his lips. I gasped, letting his arm go as my dapple danced to the side.

Another man took his place, pushing the enemy back while I was still staring at the man I'd tried to help, but we were losing ground. Someone was yelling that we couldn't bring the injured into the water. I hadn't even noticed that my dapple was knee-deep. When had we given so much ground?

I rubbed a hand over my weary face, flinching at the pull in my wounded shoulder. No time for that, Izolda. No time for pain or "could-have-beens." There was only me and these brothers of my blood, stranded out here in a strange land where we should never have come. We'd be buried far from home on foreign shores. Maybe even this beach. But we weren't part of this place. We were part of one far distant, one that filled my lungs with sweet air and my heart with gladness when I thought of it. Pensmoore. The land itself – the hills and trees and brooks in spring, the snow in early winter, drifting down like a gift, and later winter, driving like the angry hand of a vengeful god.

My last thoughts would be of home. Maybe theirs would be, too.

A clash beside me distracted me again and I lashed out with Grosbeak's pole, shoving an enemy in the back as he battled a soldier I recognized. Hashek. He plunged his sword through the man and twisted to drive a second enemy backward, their red coats disguising the mortal wounds he dealt.

I swallowed, scanning the line. Everywhere I looked men fell and bled and died. We were losing ground too quickly, being swallowed by the sea, and yet still my army fought.

I let my eyes cling to them for a moment, an acknowledgment that they were fighting and dying just because we'd asked them to, and I wondered if Bluebeard's story were true about the god who made the world in his chest so that the very tides were his breathing. I reached out with my mind as if I could feel it, too, and as I reached, I felt the earth beneath me shake – though that must be my imagination – at the strength of my love for another place far from here.

I could almost feel it on my palms, taste the snow, hear the whinny of horses, see the dawn staining the snow pink. I closed my eyes just for a moment – maybe my last moment – and breathed it in.

I wouldn't think of regrets or of what a terrible idea this had been. I would think only of love. May my last breaths be laden with it.

"I told you I had a front-chain seat," Grosbeak said. "Look."

I opened my eyes.

A gasp caught in my throat. I'd done something after all.

The men of Pensmoore glowed slightly.

They pushed up from the sea like the tide reaching for the earth, made faster somehow, larger, stronger. When they dodged, blows seemed to slow. When they moved, they sped so fast they blurred before my eyes. When they struck, their blows had the force of thunderclaps. They drove our enemy back, their ragged defense turning suddenly into a forceful counterattack.

White froth churned up as we pressed from sea to sand and then sand to rocky shore.

"Toward your fellows, Pensmoore," I called, realizing they were pushing out in every direction. If we lost focus, we'd be separated and slaughtered, even with this mystical strength and speed. "Fight for your home."

I lifted the banner from its pocket and raised it as high as it would go, kicking the dapple forward to lead the charge. My people joined me, their eyes bright, hope in their faces and power in their hands, their strikes fast and sure.

"I love a good charge," Grosbeak shrieked as we rode, and I couldn't tell if he was serious or mocking us all. "Forward! For honor! For glory! Forward!"

It was like some unbelievable ballad. The story of seventy beaten down, huddled on the beach, almost lost to the waves and the foe and then rising up against hundreds – and winning. A girl on a dappled horse leading, her banner filled with the wind.

I caught the eye of a nearby soldier and at our shared glance he roared, a smile tingeing his face. The next gaze I caught was the same and the next. We rode on a wave of renewed hope and we rode together.

I could barely contain my giddy relief.

We pressed toward the other half of our people, pushing hard. My mouth fell open in wonder as the enemy parted before us, slain or scattered, and turning around in confused circles as if they, too, could not believe what was happening.

"To me, to me!" I called, riding at the forward edge of our rising wave, watching as the enemies before me were pulled down at the last moment before they could impede the dapple or me. It was like I was the hull of a ship parting the water. It was as if I was the figurehead on her bow, leading the charge.

I didn't fight it. I leaned into it hard, letting it carry me along.

An enemy blade struck toward me. I swiped him aside with Grosbeak's pole. It shouldn't have been possible. He was too large and experienced, I too small and too green. And yet, he was swept aside as if by forces great than me.

And I realized that when my husband bound me to the land, he'd bound me to every person who had grown up upon it, fed by its bounty, loved by its kindness, nourished by its rain. We were one in this. One with each other, one with our forebears, and one with the land.

I threw a man from my path with a single snap of Grosbeak's pole. I was more than a slim girl riding a horse. I was Pensmoore.

"If you're going to keep using me as a weapon you could at least let me carry a dagger in my teeth!" Grosbeak protested.

We burst through our enemy, emerging suddenly in the ranks of the other half of our army, all of us heaving and gasping with the force of that charge. Behind us, a trail of shattered bodies, clad in red, lay ruined on the beach. We ringed our compatriots eagerly, looking for familiar faces.

I'd expected someone to seize my authority back the moment we joined them. I'd expected a harsh demand to know what I was doing. What I saw instead were white faces and trembling hands. In the center, a group of pale-faced soldiers was a ring of dead and the only one of the captains not in that ring was cradling Sparrow on his lap, his face like that of a ghost. And I would know since I had one who was ever with me. I glanced at the specter and she raised an eyebrow at me.

Sparrow had a dozen arrows in her chest. I swallowed at the sight of them and then searched her face for life.

Her eyes met mine, rolling slightly as they moved.

"Orders, lady?" the sergeant asked me, running up to the side of the dapple. He gave Sparrow a single glance before turning his full attention to me. "They're turning. I think they're running. Should we pursue?"

"Hold fast!" I called out so everyone could hear. We couldn't afford to be scattered again. "Gather in our wounded and shore up the line," I told the sergeant in a quieter voice, and then I leapt from the horse, bringing Grosbeak with me.

I hurried to Sparrow's side, my face set in a grim cast.

She coughed, spitting blood.

"Day," she gasped.

"What's that?" I asked, almost choking on the words. My throat was rough from shouting. My hands were trembling. I thought Wittenbrand didn't die easily. But she looked like a pincushion. Who would even waste that many arrows on one person? My mouth felt stuffed with wool at the sight of it.

"They're running," the captain said, his eyes burning with intensity. "Now is the time to pursue. Get some of our own back."

"Just one day," Sparrow begged, her voice so faint I could barely hear it. "Get it for me and I will live."

I looked from the captain to her and back and the key tingled around my neck. What should I do?

"She's delusional with pain," the captain said firmly. "Pursue our enemies or we may find ourselves mired here a second time."

I bit my lip.

"Last time you took a day he overreacted," Grosbeak reminded me. "Took it very personally. Is Sparrow worth that? Is she worth a single day of your life?"

"If we don't move now, they can rally. Pin us here. We need to pursue or retreat," the captain said again.

"If you want my opinion," Grosbeak said, "you'll leave them all and ride as hard as you can for the border of Pensmoore."

"No one is asking you," I said sharply as I sucked in a deep breath and drew the key from around my neck, and turned it in the air. The room opened with an audible gasp from the onlookers. "Hold this position," I ordered them. "I'm going to get the war leader her day."

Chapter Thirty-Three

"YOU SHOULD REDECORATE IN HERE," Grosbeak said as we entered the room I was beginning to think of as the Room of Wives. He was peering back and forth, swaying on his chain as I ran up the aisle of other women. "Tell them who is wife now. You know, put your personal touch on things – something somber in black and forest green with just a hint of red for all the blood you make the Arrow shed."

"If these other women are any judge, I won't be wife for long," I huffed dryly, skidding as I reached the hourglass and its falling garnets. Good thing I'd lost that helm and veil, or I wouldn't be able to run like this.

"Oh, I don't know. You just survived your first campaign, that has to count for something."

"So did Tigrane. That didn't keep her from losing all her days."

"Ah, but he married her and these others in the mortal way, not the Wittenbrand way. It's not the same."

"So, everyone keeps saying," I muttered, seizing a gem from the garnets gathered in the top bulb. It was just a day, right? Just one day that might be full of sunshine and walking through waist-high fields of grass under a blue sky with my horse nickering beside me. I blinked back sharp tears.

Grosbeak seemed to realize what was going on in my head. "It could be the kind of day when you have the ague and you spend the whole day out of your mind shivering in your bed and moaning incoherently."

"Thank you," I said, patting him on the head. "That was shockingly kind coming from you."

I spun before he could answer, garnet clutched in my hand, shoulder on fire, and sprinted back down the aisle of wives.

"Everyone keeps bringing it up your marriage because no one does that," Grosbeak rambled as I ran. "No Wittenbrand would marry a mortal in that way. We seldom marry *each other* in that way. Did you hear how binding it is? 'As long as rivers run and moon shines, as long as the earth has bones and death has claws, as long as the ages pass and fail, so long shall I be husband to you.' That kind of vow is like magic. It's insane to do it. Madness. It's got all the force of reversing a siren cry."

"I don't even know what that is," I said breathlessly. Why was this room so long?

"Oh well, you know, if a siren catches you in her net, you're stuck for life even if you wiggle free, but the pull can be reversed if you can match the note. It will shift your binding to whoever played that note. Luckily, they're not regular notes or a person could end up a marionette dancing at the end of the strings of one master after another – but who am I to talk, right? I'm the king of marionettes."

He was very chatty for a bodiless head.

I reached the far side of the room, panting from my sprint. A stitch was forming in my side. I should have ridden instead of run. Why didn't I think of that?

"But I digress," Grosbeak said, clearly enjoying himself. "It's the curse at the end that makes the Wittenbrand vow so strong. 'If ever it be otherwise, may I waste away with sickness and may famine eat my strength..."

I turned the key in the lock and ran through the door while it was still opening, hardly listening as Grosbeak kept speaking the marriage vow.

"... may my enemies overtake me."

I burst out into the mortal world and drew up short.

"Done," a voice drawled out, answering Grosbeak's words. "I so like granting wishes. It makes me feel like a jhinn."

I looked up. And further up. Icy cold filled me, rushing down my legs and pulling my nerve with it.

The Sword's naked blade was inches from my throat, and he peered down at me in haughty delight from the back of a magnificent white charger – white, not grey, for nothing could be as white as this mount was, not even snow. The charger bore a sword of bone on its forehead as a diadem, much like the skeleton of a fish I saw on the wall of a tavern that time my father took me on the ill-advised trip by boat upon the heaving sea. The fish had been called a swordfish.

"A sword horse," I said dazedly.

The Sword laughed. "I shall immediately begin calling them that. It's a very fitting name. It's a shame you didn't consent to be my wife, mortal girl. You could have entertained me with little charms like that one."

But I wasn't listening. The Sword never had anything to say that was worth listening to. Instead, I was trying to edge around his sword horse – despite the wicked gleam in its rolling eye. Red coats surrounded the Sword and what had been the doorway to the room. And through the little gaps between them, I managed to catch just a glimpse of my own people. They looked down at their feet, shame their shared emotion.

"How long," I gasped.

"How long were you in your little closet?" the Sword asked dryly. "Maybe ten minutes. Not long. It could have been days. You mortals always seem to forget that any passage into our world risks the loss of what you're seeking to the ravages of time. But this little adventure cost you just enough of it to spring a tidy trap and snatch up your tender army. I do love playing War. It's my favorite of the games. It satisfies on an almost spiritual level, don't you think?"

I tried to lean around the sword horse.

"Sparrow?" I barely kept my voice from trembling.

The sword horse stepped forward, blocking my view again.

"Uh uh uh, my lady," the Sword warned me, preening his golden hair. "They're my hostages now. If you want them safe and returned to your lands, then you'll need to do as I ask."

"Where did you come from?" I asked tightly. "How were you hidden here? We'd won."

He laughed. "Well, of course you did. But you didn't think I wouldn't be watching, did you? You didn't think the Arrow was the only one who could weave pretty little doorways when he needed them? I always keep one eye on what's mine."

I swallowed at that. The way he was looking at me could suggest that he meant that he was watching his lands or that he was watching *me* and the thought of that tasted like a mouth full of maggots.

I tried to edge around the horse again and it leaned forward and bit at Grosbeak like an apple.

"Hey! No! Bad horse!" he yelled. And then his yell turned into an ear-piercing scream.

All my anger unfurled at once. I cuffed the horse in the nose – a thing I'd never do to such a magnificent animal under normal circumstances – and strode past it, chin held high.

I reached within, feeling the power of my land. I needed to give it back to my people so they could fight. I needed – I rounded the horse to see them penned by a ring of red, weaponless and defeated. A look of betrayal hunkered low and growling in every eye I saw. I swallowed.

They looked away, refusing to meet my eyes, and the power I'd felt in my blood – the power I could give to them – fizzled out like a flame in a harsh rain. I couldn't give them what they wouldn't accept.

In the center of their group, the captain still held a gasping Sparrow, blood trickling from her mouth.

"I offer you a bargain," the Sword drawled from behind me. "Their lives for yours. But no, I'm being dramatic. I don't plan to kill you. Let me be more precise. Their *freedom* for yours. Agree, and I'll weave them a little gate and send them off with all the fanfare of a conquering army. Refuse, and I'll kill them all. And either way, I get you."

"I need to speak to Sparrow," I said tightly. I needed to get her the day. Just one day to heal herself as she'd promised, and then she could lead them, and they could fight their way out.

"The bargain comes first," the Sword said, leaning down and out from his horse like a trick rider. The fearsome creature barely shifted to accommodate his weight. Impressive. "Accept, and they go free. Decline, and they die, but either way, I take you."

I shook my head. "There's no bargain there."

He smirked. "There is if you're one of *them*."

"She's barely holding on, lady," the captain called out, his voice raspy with something. Pain? Fear? "We might not be able to move her."

Grosbeak was oddly silent, his breath rasping as if he was trying to hold back a panic attack.

"Would you like to watch her die here?" the Sword asked, and he sounded more curious than threatening. "If they go free, she could be seen by a mortal wise woman or what have you, but perhaps this is not what you want. Perhaps she is your rival? I could imagine that. She has been close to the Arrow all these years. And now she is his right hand. Interesting, don't you think? He chose *her* for that and not you."

"I just need to speak to her," I said tightly. I had to get her the gem. I had done all this to give her my day and if I didn't do it now, then it had all been for nothing.

He sneered. "They tried to tell me you'd give yourself for them. Isn't that adorable. But I knew it would not be enough."

He snapped his fingers. and a horse was led forward from the back ranks of his people.

I gasped.

"But I remembered you had a weakness. A brother."

Svetgin was tied to the horse. On his shoulder perched a wraith identical to mine. She wrapped both her hands around his mouth while another wraith held him fast, like a squirrel gripping a tree – both arms and legs grasping his arms tightly to his sides. His eyes met mine. Hopeless. Despairing.

"He's not part of the bargain, of course, but if you don't bargain for all of the others to go free, I'll kill him with them," the Sword said. "And I'll enjoy it as I always do. We call that 'upping the ante.'"

"Release them," I said roughly. I knew he was needling me, knew he was manipulating me, and yet I couldn't help myself. The stakes had risen to be too high for me. "My freedom for theirs."

The Sword laughed, but he flicked a hand elegantly and said, "It is agreed."

And then, before I could gasp, the Sword reached out a hand and the men of Pensmoore began to flicker, winds whipping all around us so hard that Grosbeak's head suddenly flew out, pulled parallel against the chain.

"Captain!" I called and I threw the garnet – my single day – at him as hard as I could. It might not make it. It might fall short. The wind might catch it and pull it away. I'd never had much of an arm for throwing which was why I hadn't tried before. But Sparrow needed my day. It all had to be for a *reason*, right?

Something – something that looked like the ocean reaching up like a long curving arm, rose up beside us. No time to look.

The captain caught my garnet, his mouth opening with shock as he looked from me to the rising wave, and then – like magic, because that was what it was – the men of Pensmoore and Sparrow with them, disappeared.

I gasped, caught between relief that he had the day and panic that I didn't know what had happened to them.

And then something icy seized me in its grasp – something that smelled of brine and despair and the drowning of all hope.

Chapter Thirty-Four

THE DAY after my father took me to the sea, I woke in the night screaming. I had dreamed that the sea itself had risen and swallowed me up and I was drawn into a place where I could neither see nor hear and when I opened my mouth to scream, fish swam in and choked me.

My mother, sweet soul that she was, had sat up with me and made me honeyed tea and petted my hair and coaxed me back to my bed and down into the depths of sleep again, but for many moons after that, the act of falling asleep – of sinking unconscious into the darkness – had felt too much like that nightmare and I found myself up in the night, reading by candlelight until my eyelids could no longer stay open rather than surrendering to that heavy grip willingly.

And now, once again, the sea had a hold of me, and once again it bound me in its embrace and drew me down to its heart, filling my ears with the roar of its fathomless churnings.

I was tumbled and battered and beaten by the roar of the tide. It sucked me under and no fighting, no gasping, no surrender could free me. I clung to Grosbeak's lantern pole, hugging it to my chest like the last loaf of bread in a starving village, my eyes squeezed shut to keep my stomach from churning more than it already was.

By all rights, I ought to have drowned. And yet, somehow, I was breathing, and my lungs were not even aching, though I knew I was breathing water and that water, in turn, was chilling me inside like ice water sipped slowly on a teeth-achingly cold day.

Hours, or perhaps days passed before I bounced gently against something, bobbing up and bouncing again. I opened my eyes with reluctance fighting panic down as it clawed at my throat – as desperate as I was.

When my eyes opened, the world around me wavered unsteadily as if it was just as inebriated with misfortune as I was. My panic left jagged black lines across my eyes.

Breathe, Izolda, I told myself and then nearly laughed hysterically at the thought. I was underwater. I was telling myself to breathe. I was insane.

"I am not fond of the sea," Grosbeak said, wobbling bubbles coming out with his undulating voice.

And then hands were tangling in my hair and when I tried to spin to look, they shook me roughly and dragged me through the water by my hair, towing me behind. The world twisted and elongated, and I heard someone screaming just out of reach and I knew without needing to be told that I'd been dragged from the mortal sea to a sea in the Wittenbrand.

These moments of madness were getting worse and as I tilted along a line of dark thoughts it took everything inside me to pull me back from the brink and tell me to open my eyes – to keep living, keep fighting. Not to give in to the howling without and within.

When it finally abated, I found my feet, coughed and to my surprise, I could hear Grosbeak speak.

"There's just no creativity in the ocean. It's water and fish and a few sodden plants and then more water." His voice was slightly blurred as if the water masked some of the sound of it, but it was clear enough despite the wobbling bubbles that rippled up from his mouth.

We were surrounded by what I took to be waving grass. But as I peered at it, I realized there was not a plant in sight. I clenched my jaw as hard as I could to keep from screaming as the Sword let go of my hair enough that I could turn and see him. I kept my eyes locked on my enemy because I didn't want to look at *them* rippling where they stood at the bottom of the sea.

"I take it back, Izolda," Grosbeak said. "You shouldn't redecorate. There are much worse ways to store those who have run out of days."

And he was right, because we were surrounded by what must have once been living souls. Now, they looked a lot like the specter that guarded me – tall and wispy, pale and hollow-eyed. Their hair swirled upward in the water and their arms were above their heads, waving softly in the water as if they were hanging upside down instead of standing on the ground.

I refused to look. Refused to acknowledge that all their faces had turned to us.

"I am beneath the sea," I said calmly, trying to remind myself that in this utterly impractical world I was still sensible. My voice was just as warbling as Grosbeak's. It sounded as if another girl was speaking my words. "With my best friend who is a talking head, and my brother who is wrapped up in specters like sea kelpie, around us there is a thick lawn of dead souls and my worst enemy."

"Right, right, right, wrong and wrong," the Sword said with a laugh and there was a fey look to his eyes that made them more alive than I'd ever seen them. They shone with shivery delight and every breath of seawater he drew in was drawn in with shuddering ecstasy. "Those souls are not dead though they are not precisely living, and I, dear Izolda, am not your worst enemy. Not at all."

I gave him my most skeptical look. "Then prove it. Release my brother."

He laughed. "You're nothing if not predictable, mortal girl. But I need you compliant for this next part. And for that, we need your dear brother as your surety. Come, now. Time is something that you – of all people – should not want to waste."

He snapped his fingers and to my surprise, a half-clamshell lifted like a coracle bobbing to the surface of a river. A moment later, shapes lifted from the swaying souls ahead, shapes that were harnessed and tethered with cords of seaweed and gold, their reins studded with diamonds the size of my fists. Such heavy reins for such delicate creatures. They were the size of three carriages and soft as down pillows, but they ballooned out like pillow-cases, their blush-pink sides swelling as they opened up. Tiny streamers flowed behind them like too many forgotten tails. I was surprised to realize that I found them beautiful. Incongruous, utterly odd, ethereal, and yet lovely.

There were a half dozen of them and as they rippled upward, coming alive like a gladiola blooming in a row of blossoms. And as each joined the others they began to sing, a wreath of subtle, barely-heard, twisting melodies and harmonies that built and deepened with each addition made.

The coracle lifted, and the Sword tossed my brother onto it unceremoniously. He yanked me by the arm until I was settled in the front of the clamshell with him, and my brother tucked in beside me.

I tried to meet Svetgin's eyes but his were blank, staring off into the distance as if in a trance.

"Oh, you'll pay to use these, Sword," Grosbeak chortled. "The magic you're expending! I could animate an army of dolls with it!"

"And do what? Replace the legs you'll never have again?" the Sword sneered as our coracle rose and bobbed into the rolling depths of the frothy sea. "Replace the poor judgment that led you first into my pay and then into the power of the Arrow?"

"I need neither now," Grosbeak said glibly, "for my new mistress takes me places you could only dream of, Sword, and the tales I see – sweet sleep of death, they are good. Every twist a gem, every new character a ripe plum of juiciness. In fairness, I should thank you and offer you the same, though I fear I cannot wield a blade to lop your head off."

"Peace, beheaded one. Had I need of gossip I would have married for truth," the Sword said, but his heart hardly seemed in it.

A peace had come over him since we'd reached the sea that was so odd it tickled something in the back of my head. I tried to think. Did it have to do with the song of the strange empty creatures?

"Why are we here, Sword?" I asked carefully. "Are you here to sing for your sovereign?"

He laughed. "Hardly. I shall replace him."

"Replace him?" Grosbeak asked, shocked. But I was not shocked. I had figured out the riddle, too.

"I am the culmination of desire, the fruit of death. I am the summit of loss, the passing of weight. What am I?" I said. "It's the Bramble King's riddle."

I glanced over at Svetgin, to see if he was listening, but his eyes were still glazed over, either in pain or exhaustion. He neither moved, nor watched, nor struggled. I clenched my jaw, worried for him, but there was nothing I could do yet. I needed to focus and find a weakness. There was always a weakness if you knew where to look. I knew that before and Tigrane's book had reminded me of it. Her father had lectured her often on "chinks in the armor." "There's always one," he'd told her, and she'd written it down. "And it's usually where you don't expect you'll find it. It's usually at the strongest point."

"Inheritance," the Sword said, and there was hunger in his eyes that overwhelmed the peace that had been there before. "This year – this Game – is different. Whoever wins this one, wins everything. The whole world."

"What would you do with the whole world?" Grosbeak sneered. "You can't eat it."

"It's not about eating it," the Sword said, baring his teeth to my friend. "It's not about consuming or reforming or controlling. It's about mastering. I've always wanted to be the best. The very best." He looked at me then, his eyes so hungry that I shivered. Not hungry? He was the hungriest man I'd ever seen. "I want it so much I can taste it when I wake. It coats the back of my throat as I try to sleep, it taints every bite of food, every drop of drink, every stolen kiss. It works its way under my skin, itching, itching, itching until it's all I ever think about. I want it like the moon wants the tide. I want it like the plant wants the sun. I want it with all the heart I have left."

"Sorry, I think I drifted off," Grosbeak said. "What was it you wanted?"

I rolled my eyes.

The Sword's breath was almost like panting as he answered. "I want to be the best and I want everyone to know it. I want it to be undeniable." His voice calmed a little and he spoke now in a voice different than I'd ever heard from him. "When I was a young man, I had everything I could ever want. Affection, respect, my needs and wants met. I lacked for nothing. And I thought I would find happiness in it, but it was nothing but ashes in my mouth. I remember my mother gave me a pony made of sunbeams and sweetgrass and it was beautiful beyond compare and I rode it every day until one day I rode past a mirror being delivered to the house and I saw myself atop that golden pony and was struck so powerfully by the sight that I fell from his back and lay so still that they tucked me into my bed and nursed me for weeks until I could speak again. They thought me touched by some ill magic, but it was only the magic of understanding, for in that moment I saw that all around me was fair and good and noteworthy, but I was not. There was nothing intrinsic in me that gave me the same value. Do you understand that, mortal girl? Surely you must. You, alone in the Wittenhame, are plain and serviceable and utterly unremarkable. There is nothing of note in you from hat to shoe. Surely, you must understand what it is to see nothing in your reflection. To know you are born to nothing and will return to nothing and that nothing will be your bread and sup all your days.

"I rose up," he said, "and I said 'enough' and enough is what it will be, for I will *win* at this game. I do not care how or why, only give me the best opponents, the brightest, the cruelest, that I may make for myself a crown of their bones and show the world I am no longer that empty boy on an undeserved pony."

I glanced up to the crown he still wore – the one with my husband's rib woven into it – and my stomach flipped within me like a struggling fish.

"And how will you do that, Sword?" I asked.

"Oh easily," he said as he flicked the reins. "I'm taking you to the Vow Breaker who lives beneath the sea, and she will sever your ties to the Arrow, and leave him flapping like the end of a rope in a high wind and then I shall strike his heel and he shall tumble to the ground where he belongs. And when the Arrow is gone, there will be none to challenge me."

"And me?" I asked. "And my brother?"

He waved a hand. "You may go. You matter not to me. What are you anyways but empty shells beside a golden pony?"

I bit my lip, thinking furiously. He had to have a weakness. A chink in the armor. But what was it? What? Something practical that the impractical Sword wouldn't think to protect? Something so impractical that I'd never think of it?

We traveled for a very long time. So long that the bones of my seat began to ache. So long that my mouth became parched. So long that I eventually took Tigrane's journal out to read, unsurprised that it was not marred by the sea, for the Wittenbrand sea did not behave as I thought a sea ought.

I tried to read it, but it was hard to see anything that could help me figure out what to do when an insane man kidnaps you, drags you beneath the sea, and claims he will break your vows. The only thing written about vows was to avoid them and simply honor your word. Wise, practical advice. I would have liked Tigrane's father, I thought. There was also a comment she wrote about Bluebeard that seemed to be of note, though it would not help in this situation.

"He seems to always be waiting for something," she wrote. *"As if it might appear around the next corner at any time. He takes no joy from sup or drink or company but he spends what time he has to command, that which is not taken up with the troubles of his Wittenbrand affairs, in writing poetry. Sometimes I read it, and it seems to be for someone who is not me, though I've witnessed no lovers and if he has a lover, that one abuses him terribly by never giving him any time at all. I think sometimes that he is a man out of time with the world – even this odd world – as if he was born too soon and living only on time purchased or loaned, swindled or thieved from others."*

Incredibly insightful, but it had nothing to do with the Sword. I wished Bluebeard had introduced her to his rival so she could write a note about him, too, but then perhaps it would be her whisked away in an under-the-sea chariot and what good would that do.

I put the book back in my pocket and waited as the hours drifted away and my eyelids grew so heavy that they began to drift despite the danger I was in.

"Izolda?" Grosbeak hissed, waking me. "Izolda!"

"Mm?" I blinked awake, wondering if I'd missed something.

"You'll want to see this."

I looked up, rubbing my eyes to clear them, and gasped.

Our strange chariot had taken us to a cloud of creatures just like the ones pulling us and as they parted before us, we sailed out over what could be thought of as an ocean plain. Moonlight trickled down, filtered by silver and black brackish waves, and with every ripple and wave of the sea, I had a sensation that something was watching me.

And then, that sensation winked.

And I realized what I was looking at.

I had thought the Bramble King was impressive. I had thought he was huge and so much a part of the land as to hardly be man at all anymore. This woman was more so. She *was* the sea. I felt her flowing through my veins as the water of her person called to the water in mine. I felt the sharp pain of her coldness go up my spine as deep called to deep. I could only make her out in the occasional swell of water on water. She was of the sea and in the sea and she was the sea and she held us and surrounded us and breathed her current over us – her one winking eye the size of the Sword's whole palace.

And I felt like my throat had frozen closed when a single word fell from her lips and reverberated through the water like the boom of the ice when it swells over a lake.

"Well?" she asked.

"I am not well," Grosbeak muttered. "And I may never be again."

Chapter Thirty-Five

"BONDBREAKER, LADY OF SEA," the Sword said, addressing her with reverence, "Queen of Depths and Ruler of the Dark Below ..."

He went on, but I was not listening to her many titles. I was watching the ripples of the water that suggested the shape of a woman in these depths. I felt her – somehow – prodding at me, the ripples of her water lapping at my skin, and something deeper, something more insidious connecting with the water within my own body – with the blood that beat in my heart and pulsed through my arteries, with the water that cushioned my brain. And she was in that water somehow, measuring, reading, knowing me in ways I did not want to be known.

I shook my head. Ridiculous. She could see nothing of me that was not plain to all, and what was plain was not what mattered. I gathered myself inward and held on tight to my soul.

The Sword leapt down from his shell chariot as he was still speaking, pulling both me and Svetgin after him and as our feet cleared the chariot, the water ahead of us rippled and revealed a strange stone circle half-sunk into the sand. It leaned drunkenly to one side, the pillars ringing it reaching up like skeleton ribs from the wreck of a ship. From each one dangled a barnacle-encrusted cage large enough for a pair of eagles.

What was I going to do? If I tried to flee, the Sword would kill Svetgin – or do something worse like plant him among the grass of souls. If I tried to attack the Sword or hurt him, both Svetgin and I would die, for it was the Sword's magic that kept us safely breathing underwater and we were far too deep to swim up to the surface.

And if I did nothing at all, he claimed this ancient, goddess-like being could sever my marriage to Bluebeard. Of the three, one would think that would be the easiest outcome – the loss of a marriage I had not asked for and had not consummated – whatever could be the problem with that? And yet, I found the thought left me hollow and twisting with anxiety.

If the Sword succeeded and my vows to Bluebeard were severed, what then? Would I never see him return to me clothed in songbirds? Would I never again see that flash of understanding in his cat's eyes or watch him leap into action faster than I could take a breath? Would I go back to living a quiet life as a mortal girl, carefully managing a household, perhaps, or working as a servant in one now that my family was no more – using all the practical skills I possessed so well. I'd be incredibly useful and valuable to those around me as more than a hostage. Perhaps I'd even find a similarly useful husband and raise healthy children. I'd have everything I claimed I wanted.

I realized – with utter horror – horror that gripped my heart and twisted it until I felt sweat on my brow despite the cold of the sea and felt my stomach heave and gasp and reel – that I did not want my mortal life back – I didn't even want a better mortal life back.

I swallowed, terrified of what I was finding as I looked within. I was bound to Bluebeard – oh yes, but with more than vows of marriage and more than common purpose. For under it all, when I looked in my own mirror as the Sword had, what I saw was not a desperate desire for mastery. What I saw – what made me so ill that I dry heaved on it – were thick ties of loyalty and the first quickening of what could only be considered love. Perhaps, some other woman stronger than I might have welcomed these things in her heart. Perhaps, Tigrane would have. Perhaps, in her great courage, she would have embraced them with joy. But I stared them full in the face with the chill of understanding knowing that my doom was upon me.

The words of the little song that Sparrow had quoted bubbled up in my mind. *Oft the siren sings again, tying up the hearts of men, within her silken tides.* My siren husband had stolen my heart, it seemed, without me ever realizing it. Not in passion or infatuation, but by slowly, step by step, purchasing my loyalty with his blood.

And I was sick with the knowing of it.

Made sicker still by the thought that this great sea could swallow up my ties and break them apart and I would find myself suddenly bereft before I'd even realized what I had.

"Lady Vow Breaker," the Sword was saying, finally done his acknowledgments and salutations, "I beg of you aid. This woman was taken against her will, forced into a marriage neither asked for nor wanted. Break her bonds to the man who took her and set her free."

He wanted to break me free of Bluebeard but leave him with his eternal Wittenbrand vows so that he could not access my magic but could not take for himself another wife. Clever.

And if I had been the Izolda from just a half a moon ago, I might have said, "yes," but instead I whispered "no" and my whisper reverberated through the sea.

The sea's reply was deafening. It felt as if it originated within my own mind – but loud, far too loud, so that I clutched my head in my hands trying to protect it from something I couldn't keep out. "*The blood is yours, the red wide sea, but the tide is mine and the endless deep.*"

"Yes, Queen of Tides," the Sword agreed.

"*Only sacrifice of the empty shell, the heartless husk, or the endless well,*" she whispered, and the whisper made us stumble it was so powerful.

"Is it just me or is the rhyming getting old?" Grosbeak murmured in a cloud of bubbles. I was too frozen with worry to reply. "It's tacky, is all I'm saying. Sure, there's power in rhymes but you wouldn't catch me dead talking like that."

The Sword swayed but gathered himself. "An offering, I have already."

"*Then let us weigh this offering and come to know if you grasp the heart of what lies below,*" she whispered and the voice echoed through the sea once more, and I felt it in the blood of my veins and the water of my brain and I was sick with the intimacy of her words. Sicker still when she moved and for just a moment I caught a glimpse – almost a vision of a ship sinking beneath the waves, its occupants fighting and thrashing as they were dragged into the depths.

The Sword snapped his fingers – a hard thing to do under the sea – and the specters dragged my brother to the nearest cage, and though he twisted and kicked, they dumped him neatly inside it. There was a crunching sound as he tried to find his feet. The specters wrapped around his face and torso made that difficult. I peered into the other cages, squinting, and my heart sped up a pace when I realized that every cage was lined with bleached bones. Other offerings. That explained the crunch.

"Leave him alone," I whispered feebly, but I had no way to stop this, no way to know how to prevent it now that it had begun.

"The offering is made," the Sword said, and I lunged, wielding Grosbeak's pole like a spear. What cared I if I killed him and drowned for it? He was going to kill Svetgin anyway. At least if we got him first, we could try to swim for it.

"*One half is here and one apart, two halves must be close before we start,*" the Vow Breaker whispered but this time I didn't flinch. This time I struck out with the pole.

Grosbeak's chortling scream was mostly bubbles. It cut off when the sword caught his pole and wrenched it from my hands, tossing it into the nearest cage. I felt my face go pale.

"I don't count as an offering," Grosbeak protested. "I'm already dead. Suffering is for the living!"

"Let's test that theory, shall we?" the Sword said, flinging the cage door shut.

He drew his sword effortlessly despite the heaviness of the sea and how it hampered movement.

"And now we call your husband, mortal girl," the Sword said, stalking around me on the seafloor, his every footstep kicking up a cloud of sand and fleeing fish.

I stumbled backward, my pale skirts tangling my legs and my hair swirling around me in blinding ribbons.

"He can't hear me," I said, fighting to keep my voice steady. Even if he could hear me, mind to mind, I would not call him. I'd betrayed him once and twice – both by accident. I would not betray him a third time.

"This, he will hear," the Sword said. His blade jabbed through the ocean and though I could see it coming, though the water hindered it a little, it did not stop the thrust and I was not fast enough to dance aside.

The blade plunged into my side, and I gasped, crumpling over the blade, grasping at it, trying to keep it from going further, going deeper. My palms shredded and my side leaked red clouds into the seawater. I gasped, and choked, and gasped again. Pain shuttered across my mind, driving thought and reason away. The agony doubled as the Sword drew his blade slowly back out again.

I fell to my knees, pressing my shredded hands to my shredded side, my legs splayed out beside me.

"Izolda! Girl! Can you hear me!" Grosbeak's frantic voice, cloaked in bubbles, rippled through the sea to me. I clung to it with my mind. Someone was watching. I was not alone in this pain. He was cursing as he watched me look down at my ruined body. "What have you done, Sword? You terrible fool. What have you done?"

"You should be proud, Grosbeak," the Sword said calmly. "I finished what you started."

My eyes opened a crack – long enough to see his blade in the sea, my blood swirling around its length in a slender sheath-like cloud.

I gasped and my eyes shuttered closed again.

"I'll rip out your tongue," Grosbeak cursed. "I'll give your eyes to the bats and your hands to the dogs, and you don't even want to know where I'll put your feet."

"But spare my ears," the Sword said flippantly. "They've already suffered enough from having to look at you."

I heard a sound like the beat of a heart. Faint. But there.

I let my eyes drift open again, afraid to even breathe when every breath was pain. I'd fallen over into the sand. Everything was sideways.

And then there he was, stalking over the sand, short hair swirling in the water, sharp eyes glimmering, violence in every line of his face.

I was dreaming. And it was the best dream I'd ever had. I tingled all over with it, melting even though I was ice cold.

He came in cautiously, carefully, like he expected a trap. He shouldn't come at all. He should run and run and run. I opened my mouth to say that, but the words wouldn't come, and all I tasted was blood.

"Ah," the Sword said from somewhere above me and there was so much satisfaction in his voice. Satisfaction morphed to triumph. "You have found me, oh my enemy."

And then pain burst through me simultaneously with the sound of a stick breaking in half. I choked on a scream and my lungs protested with a feeling like something popping inside my chest. I drifted in a sea of pain.

"Do you like the bait with which I set my trap, little fish?" the Sword asked. He reached up, touching the rib slotted into his crown and seeming to twist it. "Does it lure you in? It's so hard to tell. Some fish like what's bright and shiny but some ... well, you have to chum the water with dead and dying things to get their interest."

A growl – muffled by bubbles – rolled out from where the heartbeat was, and my own heart leapt in response.

And then I was lifted up and for a moment, I thought that perhaps my husband was saving me, like he'd saved me so many times before, but when I was flung through the water, crashing into the bars of Grosbeak's cage and landing on the floor of it, I knew it was not he who had lifted me. I lay in a crumpled heap, fighting to lift my head enough to see and when I finally did see, I almost wished I could not.

Bluebeard's eyes met mine through the shifting water and the look of distinct agony in his eyes seared me to the core.

My wife, he said in my mind and my heart was chanting back, *my husband, my husband, my husband.*

Chapter Thirty-Six

"I'M HERE for what is mine," Bluebeard said, stalking toward me and with his mind, he said, *"And I am chilled to the core at what my tardiness has wrought, wife. Have you not heard me calling for you these past days? Why did you not answer my pleading? Why did you not bid me come?"*

"Heard. Nothing," I gasped, tasting blood in my mouth.

My husband's face was a stone, and I did not know if that was rage or pain in those eyes.

The Sword slipped between us, blocking his view, sword held out. "But I have taken up matters with the Sea and asked her to unbind what was bound, to unravel what has been woven. He is here, Lady Unweaver, Queen of the Ocean, Maiden of the Sea. The second one in the bond that I wish to see broken is here. And you can break that bond now, as you promised."

And to my surprise, the sea replied in prose instead of poetry.

"I sentence you thus, men of Wittenhame. Fight to the death. Throwing knives will be your weapon. Each of you will have one hand pinned to a pillar, your enemy pinned to the opposite pillar. You shall drive in the pin yourself. Dance all you want, dodge all you want, throw as you must, and may the fated winner win."

"And *if* I win?" the Sword was quick to ask. "What shall be my reward?"

"Then you take your prize – the girl, unbound from the Arrow."

"And if the Arrow wins?" he pressed. "What shall be my penalty?"

"Then he keeps her bound to himself."

"And if she dies before we do?" Bluebeard asked, his voice like a tiger in a parchment cage.

"She will not," the Sea said, and I felt more than saw her shift. "It is said the Sea has no mercy. It is said the Sea is heartless, the breaker of all ties, the unmoorer of all hopes, the queen of despair. And these are all true, but never let it be said that the Sea lies. By my word, so am I bound."

I closed my eyes – only for a moment. Just to breathe for a moment. Blackness shuttered over them.

I woke to eyes right in front of mine and a horrible nightmare of a face. A fish was sucking along the forehead, as if cleaning it of debris.

"Oh good, you're awake again. You didn't miss much. Roll me over a bit so we can both see," Grosbeak said and with effort, I moved my hand, slowly, slowly, and shifted him from in front of my face, turning him so we could both see out the closed door of the cage.

Thinking hurt. Everything hurt. Trying to hold onto thoughts was like grasping at my blood tainting the sea. But I had to think. I had to think. I couldn't just watch Bluebeard fight for my life. I had been around the Sword a lot. Surely, I must have noticed some kind of weakness.

While I'd been passed out, the pair of them had taken their places. They stood with one hand spiked to a stone pillar by a throwing knife stuck through the palm. I swallowed down bile at the sight of the knife in Bluebeard's hand. Red stained the water around the wound, just as red stained the water around his side, reminding me of his everbleeding wound.

"They're pinned with Wittenbrand blades," Grosbeak told me helpfully.

That meant the palm wound in Bluebeard's left hand was another wound inflicted by Wittenbrand steel. Another wound that would not heal. Another scar to bear forever just to save me, protect me, keep me from the siren call of death.

Sirens. There was something about that which tickled my mind but the thought wouldn't swim close enough to be grasped.

"Sing me the song, Grosbeak," I murmured. "The song."

We were in a swinging cage hanging from a pillar, equidistant between the competitors. Svetgin opposite us, was caged and bound in ropes of specter. He would watch me die here. Probably. Each breath certainly felt like death.

"Which song? I know many. One about victory, maybe? Or a cheerful ditty about a girl who was stabbed in the side and then cut off her attacker's head and kicked it around a field for fun?"

"Not that one," I gasped. Grosbeak and I had very different ideas about what was cheerful. "It sounds terrible. The one about the sirens."

I didn't hear his next objection, because my eyes met Bluebeard's and his look was a caress.

I tried to call to him with my mind, but I couldn't make it work, couldn't force the thoughts to come. I tried again.

"*You don't need to do this,*" I told him with my mind. *"Don't do it."*

His mental voice was sharp and clear as ever. "*I find you more beautiful and precious than all the jewels beneath the earth and sea.*"

And then, as if that was all there was to say, he tore his eyes from mine and nodded to the Sword and the Sword nodded back and to my shock, the water around me pressed down, hard, hard, hard.

It took a minute before I realized it was not just me struggling to breathe that made the water feel so heavy. We were rising. And as we rose, the pillars righted themselves, and the platform drew level, and our cages swung to hang perpendicular, as everything slowly rose upward from the ocean floor.

Beside me, Grosbeak sang – his voice marred by bubbles, but clear enough to hear. "Oft the siren sings again, tying up the hearts of men, within her silken tides."

It was something about that song. Something about tying up hearts of men. Something about being bound. And then, as the water began to grow lighter – blue now, rather than black – I realized what was bugging me so much. It was the comb. That mother-of-pearl comb that the Sword had used when he took me to his Petal Ball. He'd treated it with care and reverence like a treasured possession. The one with the emerald set into it.

And it could mean nothing. It could just be the way he treated all his personal items. Or it could be that he really did love it, but for other reasons – reasons I didn't know about like I hadn't known the story about the horse and the mirror. And yet. There was something about that – something that my practical side was screaming to me was important.

"Did it help?" Grosbeak asked when he was done.

"It didn't hurt," I gasped, the words wracking me with pain. "I fear I am fading, dear Grosbeak."

"Hold on," he said grimly. "You won't want to miss this however it plays out. I must say, I've never seen anyone mad enough to bargain with the sea. You can't win with her, you know. There was that king once who tried to flog her and you saw what happened to him."

"I did not," I gasped.

"Well, I mean you *could* see what happened if you like watching someone chained to the bottom of the ocean and eaten by fishes only to be reborn and live through it all again the next day. After the first few days, it gets boring. By then you've seen it all the different ways there is and there's no point watching again."

Sometimes I forgot how bloodthirsty my pet was.

"I don't want anyone to resurrect me when I die," I managed between gritted teeth.

"You say that now, but we'll see how you feel when it's over," Grosbeak said. "Try to hold onto that sweet innocence in the afterlife. It suits you."

"I can only do what's practical and possible," I murmured.

He laughed nastily. "In that case, I doubt you'll keep it for long."

The platform emerged from the frothing sea into the warm air. I gasped in my first breath of air after breathing sea and it tingled through my lungs and down to every nerve ending so that I did not know if I was grateful for it, or dying because of it.

Brackish water poured off the platform in a rush that soon turned to thick runnels and then to tinkling trickles until everything was completely above the surface of the water and under the Wittenbrand sky.

It was dawn above the surface, and we rose into it among rose-and-gold-tinted clouds of fluffy white. They were layered, cloud upon cloud, up and up, into a sky of the softest lavender. Soft golden rays branched and divided around the graceful pillars of this strange platform and were I not in so much agony, I might have been curious as to whether it had been put to similar purpose before and whether that time had also seen a morning more fit to a wedding than a slaughter.

In my mind, my husband's voice was clear as a sounding bell, "*Hold on, fire of my eyes. Do not fade from this world before I can tend to your wounds again.*"

And as if his words in my mind had rung a bell somewhere or blown a trumpet, the clouds parted, and tiny white petals began to rain down with a single note of angelic song. It sustained, wavering in the air like a butterfly not sure if it wanted to land – and then the voices split and wove into a canticle.

As if it were planned – and maybe it was, what did I know? Perhaps all of this was a fever dream, and I was drowning to death below merciless seas – the clouds parted again and this time they were edged with spectators looking down – Wittenbrand, one and all. They lounged on the fluffy clouds sipping steaming drinks or dipping pastries into them as if milk tea and blood sport were how they started every morning.

Glazed by waters still retreating, the stone platform reflected the audience back on themselves and in the center of the anticipation were the barnacle-encrusted cages and the two competitors – both of whom were still grand despite their soaking, still looking as if they'd stepped from oil paint works of themselves.

"*My husband,*" I managed with my mind, the rest of the thought stuttering and fading. But, like a hand placed over mine, I heard his mental words, strong and sure.

"*Hold fast, my heart.*"

Bluebeard bit his lower lip, the throwing blade perched between two fingers and that hand held up so that his smallest finger met his jaw as he considered his opponent. His eyes were not on mine any longer, even if his thoughts were.

I closed my eyes for a moment, gathering my strength and what shreds of hope I had left.

"Keep your eyes open," Grosbeak complained. "We're just getting to the good part."

I forced my eyes open again.

The Sword swept a grand bow to the crowd, dancing his first knife over the backs of his knuckles and then flipping it in the air only to snatch it back with perfect precision.

But it was the Sea who spoke, her words stark and pitiless, reaching into the depths of each of us where her waters thrummed and roared. I could not see her face anymore, and yet we were all cushioned on her breast like a sleeping infant.

"We play to the death. Begin."

Chapter Thirty-Seven

THE SINGING MORPHED at her words, and this time, the spectators joined in, as if this were a folk festival, as if these two were not squaring off for a throwing knife fight to the death.

"*Fly with the Arrow,*
Dance with the Sword,
Give your heart to the barrow,
Die with your Lord."

I forced my eyes open and looked up at the singing crowd. The pillars surrounding our platform had changed – subtly. They were topped with rippling banners and strings of bunting hung from one pillar to the next. The banners and bunting fluttered in the wind, and I gasped as I realized they were specters tied by spectral hands and feet so that their bodies rippled merrily in the wind.

"They say you can judge a society by how they treat their dead," I whispered as my eyes flickered from one ghastly face to the next. The expressions of the translucent dead flickered from agony to horror to terror and something inside me flickered with them.

"And how do you judge?" Grosbeak asked.

"I find the Wittenbrand wanting," I said as firmly as I could with my breath sawing so painfully inside my lungs.

"And how shall we bury your dear husband when he falls? Should he be a flag for the next duel?"

"He won't fall," I gasped.

"So much faith," he said, laughing nastily. Mist rose off his head in a cloud of soft pink as the dawn burnt the last drops of water from his hair and face. If not for that laugh – if not for being Grosbeak – he might almost look angelic.

"Are you dying, fire of my eyes?" Bluebeard's voice in my mind was sharp and focused.

I thought for a moment and decided on answering with the truth. *"I am not dead yet."*

"This battle is one I must fight. Hold yourself together a few more minutes and I will bring you to safety." His words in my mind were tense, coiled, like a snake waiting to strike. *"I found Sparrow. She told me of your battle. If pride had a name today, that name would be Riverbarrow."*

Sometimes, I forgot that was his name. I wanted to think of something meaningful to say. Something practical.

"He's blinded by ambition. If you rile him, you'll have an advantage," I said.

His half-smile twinkled as he caught my eye, as if he could grant me assurance and strength in a single look.

"Sing for your sovereign,
Bow to your Dream,
Make haste for the fallen,
Rise in esteem"

The choir was still singing when the first knife flew out from the Sword's hand. The singing cut off sharply.

Bluebeard shifted his weight in a manner that looked lazy, but the knife missed striking his shoulder by the tiniest hair's breadth, and I thought that perhaps the dodge had not been as easy as it had seemed. His return throw was immediate. While he was still shifting to dodge, he flicked his wrist like he was snapping a fan open, but rather than a fan, a dagger flicked from his fingers, gleaming as it spun through the air.

"Speak to my riddle, Sword. Who moved like a snake and like a fish? Who tried to rob wives from me before and paid the price? Whose head did I take with you watching on? Who stands as a warning of what is to come?" Bluebeard asked.

The Sword danced out of the way, graceful as a swan on a crystal lake. The soft petals raining down around him almost tricked my eye into thinking we were back at his Petal Ball.

"You want to speak of women you've killed, Arrow? You want to speak of breaking my heart and claiming the head of my lover for your collection? Then let us speak of what I will do to your current wife when this is done, and let us speak of your other wives, collected in a closet. There are things I can do to them, even now that their time is up. Things that would make you squirm. You, who thinks himself lily-white while he is drenched in scarlet."

The Sword whirled and spun into a kneel, graceful and smooth despite one hand pinned in place. His knife flew from his hand like a bird released from a cage.

Bluebeard didn't move this time and my heart seized in my chest. What was he thinking? He was going to –

He snatched the blade from the air, a look of concentration on his face, and then flung it back, but not before I saw the glimmer of sweat across his brow. His pinned hand was still leaking blood and his jacket had been pulled back as he moved, revealing the patch of red in his white shirt from his wounded side. He would weaken from all that loss of blood, wouldn't he? And then he'd be pinned here, an easy target. I chewed on my lip and tried to hold back my own pain enough to think.

"From a man's mouth comes the treasures of his heart, even as in his vaults his heart is seen," Bluebeard said as if he were quoting something. "What do you keep in your vaults, Sword? Is there anything within your empty heart?"

"I have no need to hide what matters to me, Arrow," the Sword said, waving a hand before him, palm up, as if demonstrating his innocence. "I am transparent to all, open to see and be seen. I wear your rib upon my brow and your wife upon my arm. What need have I of vaults or treasures?"

And I thought I detected a spark of fury in Bluebeard's next throw. It narrowly missed the Sword's face, leaving a streak of blood along his cheek where he'd narrowly dodged it.

Clapping from the audience masked any banter they might be throwing out with the knives.

"I did the right thing, trying to kill you," Grosbeak said happily to me.

"Look what it has achieved for me? I'm seeing the world – two worlds – and all the best events of the season."

"Well," I said through teeth clenched in pain. "The head wall did say to keep my token close."

He laughed. "And what? I'm your token now? Yes, do keep me close, Izolda."

He was still laughing as he sang the chorus to the folk song in his terrible, off-key voice. It was made even worse by enthusiasm.

"And if ever you be broken
And gasp on the ground,
Hold up your fine token
And join with the sound."

If he really was my token, I'd been holding him up this entire time on that lantern pole. I'd done that much at least. I clenched my teeth against a moan. I was feeling nauseated as the bleeding in my side made my head light. I should pack the wound. I just didn't seem to have the strength.

"*Speak to my riddle, wife of mine. What knits broken flesh, what salves all wounds, what will I give to you when all this is done?*"

"*Time,*" I answered, though there was little comfort in it since my days were numbered.

"*Wrong,*" he said in my mind, silky and smooth. "*Kisses. And I shall rain them on you like the tears of a spring sky.*"

The Sword danced away from another thrown knife, and this time I saw his strain as his hand pulled against the knife pinning it. Blood flowed down the pillar. How were these knives driven into stone pillars anyways? Pain flashed across his face and as if that pain had inspired him, his next three knives shot out one after another in a steady rain.

Without pausing to dodge, Bluebeard tossed his out, too. I couldn't keep track of how many had been thrown now. They were a blur of knives and dodges, dancing, dancing, ever closer to being struck.

A knife found its mark, blooming in Bluebeard's throwing shoulder. But his knife struck the Sword's thigh almost as quickly. The Sword wrenched the knife free with a wild look in his eye, sending it spinning back to my husband.

"If you like riddles so much," the Sword taunted, "then maybe you'd like to know what the Bramble King's riddle means. Maybe you'd like to know that this is my grand move that will cement my victory."

"What's not a riddle, Sword?" Bluebeard asked in a bored voice, pausing just long enough to wink at me. "What's so plain that it's not hidden at all?"

"Then you know I'll take his place when this is done. This whole Wittenhame will be mine to do with as I please. And I please a lot of things. With you gone, none of the others can stop me. It's a bold move, but I'm a bold man. What do you think our home will look like when it's made in my image?"

And then they were back to being a blur of movement. They both moved so fast that I couldn't keep up with every spin and dodge and throw.

I fought the pain wrapping its tight claws around me. It was getting worse. Not just the throbbing in my leg but the aching agony in my side that broke me with each shuddering breath. Was this what my husband felt all the time since giving his rib to me?

I could only squeeze my fists and clench my jaws and hope, hope, hope.

A voice in my mind broke through the pain. "*As long as rivers run and moon shines.*"

My eyes fluttered back open in time to see a second dagger strike Bluebeard – this time in his leg. I felt like I could feel the hit, too.

I trembled with the shock of it as the crowd cheered, little snatches of song lacing their cheers as if this was a beautiful event, a wedding or a name day, and not a sickening death sentence. I swallowed down a moan of despair.

Bluebeard shuddered at the wound and his voice in my mind was shakier. "*As long as the earth has bones and death has claws.*"

My eyes squeezed shut again.

I could feel those claws trying to close around me. I hated this helplessness. Hated that there was nothing I could do. I was the one lying broken on the ground just like the song said. I was the one who had kept her token close. If only I had the strength to lift it and wave it and then the song would come true and we would all be saved, wouldn't we?

Or maybe I was having fever dreams.

"*As long as the ages pass and fail – that long shall I be husband to you.*"

He was saying our Wittenbrand wedding vows again. He was making promises even as he fought for me. Promises that our bond would not be broken. Promises that he would find a way forward. And what had I to give to him in return?

I could promise something back, but the best promise was an action and I was beyond action.

"Yes!" Grosbeak crowed from beside me. "Such a good strike."

I lifted my heavy eyelids. One of Bluebeard's knives had hit the Sword directly in the chest. And then another. He stumbled slightly, his crown shifting to lean drunkenly to one side, Bluebeard's rib within it gleaming softly in the sunlit dawn.

The crowd roared again. They loved blood – whose seemed not to matter.

"*Flesh of my flesh and bone of my bone you will be.*"

Bluebeard's eyes met mine, pain and promise, agony and desperate determination. And the warmth in those eyes broke me.

"How can either of them survive?" I moaned feeling as if I would be ripped in two by the sweetness of my husband's silent vow and the agony of watching him bleeding and fighting for his life. "They'll never recover from so many wounds."

My breath sawed through my lungs. I clung to the look on Bluebeard's face, the calm certainty in his eyes as he spoke the next words, as if there were no one else here but him and me, as if he wasn't fighting at all.

"*Spirit of my spirit.*"

And I found I wanted that. For the first time, I couldn't help but wonder if we could be married, married. One in spirit. One in more than purpose. Living together, eating together, playing card games with those odd folk of his.

He bit his lip so hard that blood came when his eyes bored into mine.

"*Heart of my own heart.*"

But he *shouldn't* be looking at me and making sweet vows. He should be focused on his fight. It was almost as if he expected something from me – something that would help him somehow. But what? What could I give?

"Oh, it's not Wittenbrand steel they're throwing, so they'll likely recover from the knife wounds," Grosbeak gabbled, not realizing that in front of him the greatest drama of all was playing out silently between an ancient Wittenbrand and the broken mortal he had taken as a bride. "Just copper and silver. It's only Wittenbrand steel in the dagger pinning their palms. Dining out will be grisly after this, but then it always is, and at least it will make dinner party conversation interesting."

And then I realized what I could give. I could give my vow in return.

And my heart soared as I forced myself up on my elbows and said in my mind as clearly as I could through the fog of pain and fear.

"*Fall what may, we shall be one,*" I said in my mind.

And his eyes shuttered closed for just a beat, a tiny smile of absolute satisfaction on his face and when he breathed out, I felt almost as if he were right here, as if I could feel that very breath on my face.

He turned back to the Sword, steel in his eyes, his chin jutting out, flinty and unmoving, and when he leaned forward onto the balls of his feet for his next throw my heart seemed to stutter to life like it never had before.

"Izolda?" Grosbeak pressed.

"I don't care," I said with a shuddering gasp, "about dinner parties."

"Good. Tell yourself that. Tell yourself you're only focused on winning, like the Sword does. Though how he got so wound up about it, I don't know. It's almost like the power of a siren song with him."

Knives were flying again, fast and sharp, and I could hardly see them through my glassy tear-filled eyes. What I'd said – the vow I'd just made – it had shifted something in me that I didn't know was there to be shifted. If I were the sea, all my tides would be in time with Bluebeard's breathing like the earth in the story about the world and the god who had made it.

"Grosbeak," I said, panting as I heard the dull thunk, thunk, of more knives striking flesh. I could hardly breathe. "You're remarkably obsessed with sirens."

I was grateful for his rambling. I needed to clear my head before I was utterly swallowed up by this new thing – this overwhelming, alive thing inside me.

"I was hoping to fall in love with one while we were here. It seemed like convenient timing. After all, I can hardly chase her until I die when I have no feet, and I've always wondered what that kind of obsession would feel like. You know, the kind that keeps you going when all the odds are against you? The magic kind."

"It looks like *that*," I said, pointing vaguely to where the Sword tossed a knife from an arm that already had three blades sticking out of it. His blade struck true, and I flinched at the sight of another knife stuck onto my husband's shoulder. He swayed slightly and I bit my lip, blinked back the tears spilling onto my cheeks. This had to stop.

"If she sang courage into me, or charm, or anything else, it would never leave," Grosbeak went on, sounding like he was in a daydream. "Not even if she died. Did you know that? It would fill me up. It would make me whole without a body. Nothing could stop it."

I did know. It was how I felt right now.

I coughed, tasting blood, fighting for that practicality I prided myself for. "Except for the wrong note, right? Didn't you say before that you could change a siren song by matching the exact right note?"

"Of course. But who could ever do that?"

A chill came over me, tingling up my arms and down my legs until I shivered. My thoughts were stuttering, racing over each other in their hurry to drag me over the finish line and reach the conclusion they could see in the distance. A siren, filling you up with something that wouldn't change even after death. A head on my husband's wall. A matching mother-of-pearl comb. It was all suddenly so clear.

The Sword had been enchanted by a siren at some point. I would bet everything I had on it. A dead siren whose head my husband had taken and placed in his Vault. And that meant that the Sword could be weakened, or maybe even conquered, if someone, somewhere, sang precisely the right note. But there had been singing all around and in the Wittenbrand there always was, so surely, surely someone would stumble onto it, wouldn't they?

No, it couldn't be so easy.

The roar of the crowd was so loud now that I could barely hear Grosbeak though he was still speaking. They chanted both names, crowing with delight at every hit. If I knew the Wittenbrand, they were probably betting on the result.

"Sword!" someone called from the crowd, and it was Lady Tanglecott, dressed in a long, flowing white dress edged in pink by the rising sun. Her perfect blonde curls framed a face that would have inspired song in any mortal world.

She held in her hand a gleaming throwing knife that looked to be entirely of gold. She strode forward, flanked by her pair of four-winged striped lions, their bright cat's eyes – so like my husband's – searching the crowd and their pink tongues licking hungrily at their chops. When their eyes landed on me, I flinched. I was wounded prey. They knew it and I knew it. But her hold on them was flawless and they stayed close as she tossed the golden knife.

The Sword caught the underhand toss easily, his eyes gleaming with pleasure when he examined the blade. His breath gusted out in magenta-tinged clouds and sweat matted his golden curls. He was panting and worn just as my husband was, the jagged hole in his pinned hand stood out bright against the angry flesh around it as every dodge, every dance, every escape from death opened the wound further.

There was a gasp of delight from the crowd as Lady Tanglecott said, "I think I owe you a Wittenbrand steel throwing knife with a golden handle, don't I Sword? I'd hate to have you die without seeing my debt repaid."

Laughter rang out from the crowd, but my eyes narrowed because I knew this was no little jab at my husband. None of these regular blades could kill him easily – but any mark this blade made would last -and any mortal wound with *this* blade would surely kill him.

I held my breath as the Sword took careful aim.

My husband spread his hands apart, waiting, his body relaxed, mouth quirked in a mocking smile, but in his mind, he spoke to me.

"*My body, I dedicate to none other.*"

The Sword took aim and tossed and like the expert swordsman he was, my husband danced forward and caught the blade with his palm just seconds before it pierced his heart. It stuck through his hand, and I gasped. He would have matching wounds now, one on either palm.

He leaned down and plucked it free with his teeth but as he was drawing it out, Lady Tanglecott cried out again.

"I was mistaken, Sword! I believe, I owed you, two." And quick as a hummingbird, she tossed a second knife, twin to the first and the Sword snatched it from the air.

The breath gusted from my lungs. I could see it all unfolding before me as if time had slowed to a crawl.

My husband, one hand pinned, the other stuck through with a knife he was trying to pull free with his teeth, his eyes widening as he realized he was trapped.

The crowd, laughing, swaying together, and singing that damnable chorus again.

"And if ever you be broken
And gasp on the ground,
Hold up your fine token
And join with the sound."

Me, lying broken on the ground.

Broken.

On the ground.

And suddenly I remembered the grass egg I'd ripped open. The one that had sung that same chorus to me. And with my heart in my throat, I reached up into my hair and pulled out the little golden bell ornament I had fastened there, and lifting up my token, I rang the bell.

Chapter Thirty-Eight

THE BELL WAS SO quiet compared to the cheers and singing that I thought no one would hear it, but the Sword staggered, his head whipping around to look directly at the bell dangling from my fingers.

For a moment, confusion lit his face, and then he sagged like a bridge with too many horses in the middle. His hand lowered for a moment and the look of desolation in his eyes gutted me. I didn't even like him and it cored me out and left me empty. No one should look like that. No one should look like they were watching their hope thrashing in its own blood.

He gasped. And then he rallied, his shoulders straightening, his chin rising again.

All the compassion I'd felt a moment ago fled and fear seared through me. It hadn't worked. It had barely slowed him.

The gold-handled knife rose in his precise grip, and I saw Lady Tanglecott rise up on her toes in anticipation, her mouth forming a delighted "oh".

The crowd quieted, every breath held fast.

And my glorious husband raised his chin in defiance of fear and death, his cat's eyes narrowing to a slit and his jaw clenched against the blade sure to strike and leave a lasting mark.

"My days shall be yours and your happiness my own." My mental voice

was desperate. I couldn't help it. Why did he not seize my days? Why did he not spend each one to fight this?

"*The bounty of my wealth is yours,*" he said like a vow and then his eyes opened and met mine. And I fell into them, deep, deep, deep not bothering to catch my heart as it fell for there was no point guarding it now that we were both at the end.

How funny to come to the end of your life and find in that moment that you are already mortally wounded and this with the dart of love? I'd been married now for half a moon, but it felt like I'd just been married here and now as I spoke these words and meant them as a vow this time and not just a ward to stay alive.

And then someone screamed.

And the scream reverberated through the audience.

Our gazes wrenched apart, and I looked over to see the Sword jamming the Wittenbrand steel knife into his own throat and ripping it out with a brutal tearing motion. His head began to roll to the side before his hand stopped its grisly work.

"I love my afterlife," Grosbeak breathed reverently. "It's so much better than my before life."

This time, I did vomit, spilling what little was in my stomach all over the floor of the cage. The movement pulled at the wound in my side and made me vomit all over again. Darkness flooded over my vision. It was all I could do not to pass out. Only the reminder that I'd tumble into my own sick kept me together. That, and Grosbeak's cursing.

"Mortal hands and mortal bellies that's gross!" Grosbeak moaned, brought low from his moment of ecstatic revelry by a sensible reaction to what was going on. "Gods of rivers and thorns save me from mortals with vile constitutions."

He made a dramatic vomiting sound, spitting and choking as if he was going to die. It shook me from my own stupor, and I pressed myself up palms splayed across the barnacle-encrusted cage floor, watching in doleful fascination the thread of blood that poured from my side as I found my hands and knees and then forced myself to twist into a seated crouch.

When I finally pulled myself together enough to look up, I saw the spectators drawing back, the bunting and banners falling limp and morose. Even the rose and gold of the clouds had faded to a somber grey.

"*The moment this pin is removed, and my magic is restored to me, I will come to you, and I will repair every wound and bind every slash and heal you with kisses sweeter than honey. Only have faith in me, my wife,"* Bluebeard told me with his mind and this time when I met his eyes, the light of victory was in them. We'd won. We'd survived.

Tears of relief flooded my eyes, and I drew in a long, shuddering breath.

I drew it in too soon. I relaxed too soon.

My fate was like a girl in a tale, for always, I forgot that there were no happy endings for me, no moments of quiet after the monster was slain and the lady rescued. No cheer from the onlookers and a large banquet laid out and peace in the land that lasts for a thousand years. Oh no, not for me.

From that grey backdrop of life-drained clouds, a face emerged, and then a head, and then a throne, and the Bramble King opened his eyes and looked down on his shrieking, scrambling subjects. He paused for a moment, as if taking in the pandemonium below him, the broken corpse of the Sword, the pinned figure of the Arrow, the exultant Lady Tangledcott with her head thrown back and arms spread wide as if receiving a blessing – three of his players emerging from a deadly game. He blinked and then without a flicker of change to his features, he said in a voice of finality, "The death of the Second Move is upon us. And with it, the Third Move is born. His glory fades."

And then he sank back into the grey clouds, the rumble of thunder his herald, and the flash of lightning his trumpet, and we all held our breaths, frozen for a moment in our places as if we were afraid he might return and announce our punishments for being petty, squabbling children in a game that was meant to pull him down and plant another on his throne.

And it was there, into that frozen tableau that Lord Coppertomb emerged, walking to the center of the platform with a kind of casual disinterest as if nothing here met his standards. He paused to look Lady Tangledcott over and something I could not read passed between them, and then as he moved past her, she turned and swept her hands forward and her mist lions leapt into the clouds and her with them and they vanished as one.

And I did not know why, but their disappearance made my heart speed up because it knew what I could not – that this was a handing over of the reins, a changing of the guard. And my heart knew the face of treachery and shrank from it.

There was a sound like something shifting, and then something in my belly seemed to drop. The platform was lowering.

"The bargain, lady," Bluebeard said steadily and I realized he was speaking to the sea. And then his voice sounded a little less sure as he reached with his knife-crossed hand and tried to wrench the knife from his pinned hand to no avail. This time his voice was a growl, but I heard the desperation in it. "The bargain, Queen of Seas."

The sudden silence made me look up and my heart stuttered to a stop. The observers were gone. I watched as the last of them vanished into the clouds. Somewhere above, a single gull cried into the darkening sky – a cry of loss and desolation.

"Ohhhh!" Grosbeak said as if he'd just understood something. "It was a fight to *everyone's* death. I get it now. That makes so much more sense."

"It does?" I asked, breathlessly. I realized I didn't even know if the cage I was in was locked. I hadn't had the strength to even find my feet and try it.

"Of course! The sea has no mercy. It never made sense that she was going to let one of them live."

"A point to the reanimated head," Coppertomb said coolly. "And for your observation, a reward. I will not kill you today, Grosbeak."

Grosbeak smiled, but I could tell by the way his eyes were hooded that it was not a nice smile, though he was wise enough to keep his thoughts within.

Coppertomb turned to my husband as a sudden wind ripped the banners and bunting away so that they swirled for a moment in the air, and then were gone. Coppertomb's tidy, monochrome clothing swirled around him with that wind, but he did not seem to notice. Not even when the edge of the platform furthest from Bluebeard tipped and began to sink under the hungry waves.

Coppertomb stepped over delicately and snatched the Sword's crown from his brow before the waves could take it and to my shock – though how did anything shock me, now? – he pulled a penknife from a pocket and with a deft hand, extracted one of the Sword's molars and slotted it into the crown. How many bones would fit within its swirls and gaps?

He rose and faced my husband again.

"I see you've been investigating the four mysteries, Arrow. You should have stuck to the ship on the sea or the snake on the rock."

"I already know the way of the eagle," Bluebeard said, drawing himself up. There was no pleading in his voice, and he did not address the sea again. But I saw the burning in his eyes, the anger leashed only by the strongest of self-control, and whatever he was saying on the outside, he was saying something different to me with his mind.

"*If ever it be otherwise,*" he said with his mind and the vow felt like a caress.

"*Husband,*" I said with my own mind, and he shuddered at my word, his eyes half-closing in pleasure for just a moment.

Coppertomb, unaware of the love story playing out in our silences merely raised an eyebrow and said dryly, "May we all take such joy from small things."

"So, you were behind this somehow," Bluebeard said. The look of barely suppressed violence in his eyes was at odds with his knife-quilled figure. He did not slump or bow under the weight of the blades, not even the Wittenbrand ones stuck through his palms. "And here I thought it was Lady Tanglecott."

"*It's b –* " I tried to tell him it was both of them, but my specter reached her hand around to clamp my mouth, shaking her other finger under my nose. Not even now, not even with us sinking below the waves, would I be allowed to say anything.

The water rose as the platform tilted, dark bottle-green sea swirling with red blood and the Sword's viscera. It swallowed his corpse, dragging it below the waves unnaturally as Coppertomb opened Svetgin's cage and drew him out. My brother stumbled forward, empty-eyed, still bound by wraiths.

"What good is a trap if your prey sees it?" Coppertomb asked. "And who would suspect a first-time player of setting his opponents against each other. But fear not, Arrow. I am well aware it was a strange year. That had it been any other, you would have had no weakness to exploit." He was halfway to my cage, now. "I had to take the opportunity while I could, don't you think? What other time would you play into my hand so single-mindedly?"

"And now what? You let the sea serve you and take me to the depths?" Bluebeard challenged, but in his mind, he was still speaking the rest of his vows to me. "*If ever it be otherwise, may I waste away with sickness and may famine take my strength.*"

"My will alone, I solely enact," the sea's voice boomed out and I flinched as the platform shuddered. *"None binds it thus except by pact."*

"I'll make your pact, Vowbreaker," Coppertomb said quietly. He pulled a flat circle attached to a chain from his pocket and considered it before looking up again. "I'm no fool to come to the sea empty-handed. Take this enemy of mine and bury him deep and in exchange I give you the lives of fifteen Pensmoore ships in the North Sea. My agents await with orders to scuttle it on my signal."

"Agreed," the sea replied.

Coppertomb snapped his fingers.

I felt suddenly lightheaded and as if I was seeing a vision, I saw sudden snatches of ships tumbling down into the sea, in one a man held an axe, scuttling the ship under him. In another, a man snuck furtively into the hold, lighting a fire when he arrived. The rest were just glimpses of desperate men wailing as their ships were dragged under and they were trapped like flies in amber beneath the hungry waves.

"Don't faint," Grosbeak hissed. "You can't save them, and you'll fall on top of me and then I won't be able to see what comes next."

Which was a very sensible thing to say. I fought to control my horror.

"May my enemies overtake me," Bluebeard's voice rang in my mind, and it was heavy with sadness, thick with regrets unspoken and deeper than this angry sea in its fullness of commitment.

In my mind, I joined him as he finished our vow. *"And siphon from me the blood of my life."*

I put my hand to my side, and I held it up to him and our eyes met as he held out his wounded hand to show me, too.

"Done," the sea said, and it echoed through our bones. *"Your price is for one living Wittenbrand, and one I accept, the rest will leave and not be kept."*

The door of my cage squealed as it opened, torn by the wind. I knew Coppertomb was striding toward me, but I didn't look, my eyes were locked in goodbye with Bluebeard's and there was something about the farewell in his expression that was sweeter than honey, more comforting than a warm fire, and safer than my bed in the midst of a storm.

I clung to it as Coppertomb pulled me roughly from the cage. I could not stand on my own. I crumpled around the wound in my side, my crushed leg unable to bear my weight. Coppertomb supported that weight as he snatched up Grosbeak.

Still, I clung to Bluebeard's gaze as the Wittenbrand threw my bodiless friend at my husband's feet and then reached into my bodice, snatched away my golden key, and tossed it there, too. Clung to it even as Coppertomb held me up like a broken chair, wobbling unstably on one leg.

"Whoa! Wait! I wasn't a part of the deal," Grosbeak sounded panicked. "I stay with Izolda."

His head landed barely out of the water as the platform dipped wildly into the sea, leaving only the pillar where Bluebeard stood unsubmerged. Water swirled around my knees, dragging at my sacrificial white skirts. But it was not me being given as a sacrifice.

"I think not," Coppertomb said smoothly and though he turned to me, I did not look at him.

I was drinking in the last look of my husband, his short hair still slick with the sea's water, clinging to the curves of his head and curling slightly around his ears, his beard, a little longer than he usually kept it – enough that the blue of it was distinct – his bright eyes almost white they were such a light blue, and his crooked smile promising secrets revealed and knowledge unveiled. I would never know all those secrets now.

"I am not a wasteful man," Coppertomb said as he shoved me toward my brother and to my surprise, Svetgin caught me awkwardly as I moaned in pain. The specters were gone from his mouth and arms as if they had never been there – I saw them missing in the corners of my eyes, but I would not wrench my gaze away from Bluebeard's steady regard. Not when this was my last look, my last chance to fill myself with all that steadfast sureness. "I do not misplace tools. You've been very useful, my little tool, and now I will put you back where you belong, a surety against the day when I have need of you again."

The water climbed now to my waist and Grosbeak's protests were lost in bubbles as he dipped beneath the water.

Bluebeard watched me steadily as Coppertomb moved, putting a hand on my shoulder and one on Svetgin's.

"My husband," I gasped, desperately, feeling panicked. My heart was beating so loud, my breath sawing in my lungs so strongly that I almost missed the echo of his voice in my mind.

"*My wife.*"

My last glimpse was of his cat's eye winking at me and then everything was gone.

I blinked my eyes and there was no Coppertomb, there was no Wittenhame. We were on a mortal beach somewhere – a place where the colors had leached out of the land and the sky was an indifferent blue. And in between waves of pain so thick now that I couldn't keep conscious, I heard my brother sobbing those deep sobs that men try to hide when they are overwhelmed by them, and he was murmuring between their tempests, "Hold on, sister, I will find help. I'm sorry. I'm so, so sorry."

And then that, too, was gone.

GIVE your
HEART
TO THE
Barrow
SARAH K.L. WILSON

Fly with the Arrow
Dance with the Sword
Give your Heart to the Barrow
Die with your Lord

Chapter One

THE LAW of Greeting stole me away. The machinations of man brought me back, torn from the Wittenhame and dragged – ragged and bloody – back to the washed-out world of mortals. I had no say in the first and less in the second, caught as I was like a leaf tumbling on the surface of the river, swirling and bobbing in the grip of a mighty current. But so it is with the great stories. They create their own currents, forge their own streams, and we poor mortals are ever subject to them as the tide to her mistress moon.

"I'm so sorry, I'm so sorry," my brother's harsh sobs echoed, and faded, and then returned a long time later with other voices joining his. I was cold – so, so cold – as I lay shivering on the hard ground, but not nearly as chilled as my husband must be in his place beneath the greedy sea.

I saw him in my mind's eye, his blue beard and bright cat's eyes under the swirling depths, his flushed cheeks turning pale and then blue, his teardrop of blood washing from the planes of his lovely face, the fish snatching at his hair and clothes, as he was pinned to the pillar, immobile, trapped.

It was not for myself that I moaned when they lifted me into a carriage with concerned voices. Not for my own fate banished back to this plain mortal world that brought tears slowly leaking from my heavy eyes. They brought me to a close dark room filled with whispers and worry but it was not for my own self that I sought when my consciousness was snatched and returned and snatched again.

It was for him that I searched in every whisper of speech I heard, in every gentle touch, in every small glimpse of a face. It was for just one more glimmer of him, one more of his words passing like fine silk through the ring of my mind, one more sweetly bitter kiss searing my lips like fresh ginger.

But none of these attended me. Nothing at all tended me except the cold hands of mortals, the plain speech of plain people, thrall to the whims of nature and time. As I grew well again, it was only their faded faces and pale food that greeted me, seeded though it was by generosity and charity.

From the first, the sea called to me. Any open window meant the echoes of her moaning voice – so like the one echoing forever inside of me. I learned to listen for it beneath the sounds of the household around me. For if I could not touch my husband again, I could at least listen to that which touched him and caressed him daily in his grave.

Eventually, my broken body healed and grew strong again, to the great relief of Lady Greatspur who had graciously taken me into her home and ensconced me in the chambers of her long-deceased daughter. I pleased her with my quiet manner and my willingness to embroider every cloth she put before me as I convalesced in her home. I ate little, spoke less, and kept my hands very busy – a credit, she said, the sign of a good wife and lady, and didn't my brother need that right now in his sister, what with the chaos in the capital?

But though my hands worked busily, and my manners worked even harder, it was the sea I was listening for in every space where the good lady drew a breath and paused her musings. It was the sea I watched for in glimpses through the windows. I was as attuned to it as a mother with a new babe, noticing its every mood and whim and bending myself to it.

I waited patiently, biding my time until the first day that I could sit unaided and cross the room without assistance. That night, I crept from the lady's great house, passing the doors of those who slumbered with as much silence as the specter on my shoulder. No matter that I was in the mortal world, she lingered still, wrapped around my shoulders, waiting for the moment where she could morph from spectral collar to guardian and snatch the words from my mouth. For a wonder, none of the mortals around her seemed to see her there. It was just the two of us who knew she shared my silent vigil.

I stepped out onto the stones, my bare feet feeling every slippery surface, every snatching grassy caress of a dull empty land. I slipped toward the call of the sea, careless to how rocks bit my feet or cold stung my skin. The moment my toes met the freezing water, I ran over the glazed rocks and threw myself into the sea. What did I think I would find within? Did I think I would hear his voice? Did I think I would find some strange magic that would bear me to his side? Did I expect that the sea would bargain with me?

If I expected any of that, I was wrong. Gravely, sorely wrong. For nothing greeted me but *nothing* – a great raw roaring nothing as if my very life had been hollowed out as one hollows a wooden bowl and scraped down to the narrowest shape that can still hold a soul.

I returned to the grim estate eventually, hiding my misadventures with a hasty bath beside the well and hanging my clothing by the fire to dry. When questioned, I claimed a fever had taken me, soaking me in sweat. And after the chill of the night, I was just as feverish as I claimed, and worry filled the glances and words of those around me as they had when I first arrived.

The fever passed as all mortal things do, and when it did, I tried twice more. The first, in a small fishing boat I stole from the shore. I discovered nothing except that I was very bad with oars and not nearly as strong as I'd hoped.

Of my husband and my life, nothing was left to me.

On the last time that I slipped out to the sea in the night, I arrived with fury and acceptance and the words of a funeral on my lips.

The wind howled, blustering along the shore with the violence to stir clouds of sand and bursts of sea spray up into the air in swirling specters dancing over the landscape in murderous frenzy. There could be no more perfect atmosphere for what I was to do there.

I sank to my knees on the sand, the dark of midnight clinging to me like a second specter and with no one to witness what I did but the wailing wind, the sober moon, and my grim spectral companion.

"You loved drama and murder." I spoke my memorial to Grosbeak. If he were here, he'd be insisting on a better funeral than this. He'd be insisting that I do the impossible and find some way to go down to him in the depths and draw him back. "You were a friend both kind and terrible, and in your jests and screams I washed up on shoals of kindness."

There. It had been said.

I spread my fingers on the sand and sank my weight into my palms, wetting my lips to speak funereal words for my husband. It had been three weeks since we were found on the edge of the sea.

Three mortal weeks could be decades in the Wittenhame. He could be long dead, his tumbled bones half-hidden by sand and memory, his people scattered, and his lands razed.

Or, it could be mere minutes for them, and even now he could be gasping under the sea, his lungs filling with choking black water as the sea sucked his life from him and forced him unwillingly into her embrace. And even now when I spoke the words over him, I could be speaking his death when still he clawed for a last scrap of life.

And I couldn't do it.

I couldn't.

I broke down as I had not yet broken, wailing my sorrow in a terrible harmony to the crash of the waves and the cry of the wind. I cried and cried until I thought, perhaps, that I had cried an ocean large enough to fight the sea for him, a salty jhinn to champion my cause and rise up to bear my standard.

But in the end, dawn rose as my husband did not, mocking his submersion with her flagrant ascent, and no champion emerged but a battered fisherman troubled to find me not far from his nets and distraught beyond human ken. He put me on his donkey and rode me to the Lady's house where dark murmurings filled every corner and kind hands put a hot drink in my hands, tucked me in a warm bed, and whispered that the Lord Savataz's sister had lost her wits.

It was from that miserable stupor that I emerged the next morning to find the house in an uproar.

Lady Greatspur entered my room with trepidation just before noon, clutching a black gown to her chest and worrying at her lower lip as if I were the lady here and her the poor wretch dragged in by an ancient mariner.

"Lady Izolda," she said timidly. "Can you dress yourself, my girl?"

I could not have found a kinder hostess. I sank deeper into the blankets thinking of the night I had hidden in a ball from my new husband in just such a bed.

The lady crept to my bedside and if I had been more in possession of myself, I would have been shocked by how she – a lady of Pensmoore – sank to her knees so that her face was not far from mine, and she could whisper to me.

"We ladies have little power over ourselves, Izolda of Savataz." She paused, listening for a moment, and then shook her head and spoke again. "And you have clearly suffered a great loss. Doctor Ryvataz believes you to have lost your wits and he will tell your brother so – indeed he already has told him in the missive he sent, and you brother is riding here with great urgency – and this on the verge of his coronation."

Coronation? That made me sit up and push the hair from my face with heavy hands.

The lady was nodding. "Indeed. After a bloody struggle and a bloodier peace agreement, your brother is to be crowned king of Pensmoore. The wars have taken and taken, and to find a living lord of Pensmoore capable of managing the nation – well, the kingdom has rejoiced that he is returned to us. Surely, my girl, you must realize how desperate things are for us that we rejoice to have a second son of Northpeak to reign."

I nodded, my voice too thick to speak, but the nod seemed to encourage her.

"And that is why I am here. For I see before me not a deranged woman lost to sense, but a woman in deep grief as I was when my daughter was taken by the fever while not yet thirteen." Her lip trembled at that, and I reached out to take her vein-crossed hand in mine and the look in her eyes was steel and purpose. "So now, listen to me, and I will tell you what I would have told her if she had lived to lose all she loved. Grief honors our lost. The greater the flow of it, the greater the heart that once held love. And yet, you must take back possession of yourself, or find yourself locked away in a madhouse and what tiny freedom you have left stripped from you.

"So now, heed my words. Dry your eyes. Fix your hair. Put on this gown I have brought – one of my own. I have done you the dignity of choosing black. And when you are dressed, and coifed, and shut away inside, you will act the perfect lady again and you will embroider, and you will listen, and you will be a great boon to your brother and your nation, and whatever this great grief is, you will let it take you within, but never without, for if you do not learn to bridle it and force it to hand, then you will be ridden by it and lose what little hopes you still have."

And her words were sensible and wise and so I opened my swollen lips and spoke with my thick tongue.

"Thank you."

By midday, my brother was upon the household with a grand stamping retinue of men and horses. They arrived in the first squalling snowfall of the season, their breath and pride puffing out in white gusts.

Svetgin was pleased to see me well and dressed in muted black, my hair drawn back sharply from my face, and as unadorned as a proper widow ought to be. He praised Lady Greatspur and took me off with him immediately once his party was refreshed at her table.

"I'm to be crowned tomorrow," he confided in me in the carriage. "And I will be counting on you for your help, sister, in securing my reign."

And I had smiled a tiny, serene smile and kept my face and hands as calm as Lady Greatspur had advised me, but my heart rolled and broke as the sea within me, and the roar of the ocean filled my ears and mind and did not let me go.

Chapter Two

I CLAIMED VERY little from my royal brother after the coronation – only a room in his tiered castle, an occasional place at his table and in his counsels, and a royal horse.

He certainly received the best end of the bargain as I worked tirelessly to secure him the support of his military, to secure his borders, to reestablish trade, to calm impassioned nobles and impassion calm ones. I was for him everything a sister of a king could be and handy with a pen and ledger besides.

I ate with care, careful not to miss meals after those first few months. I dared not see the land starve for my grief, but the rain and snow never seemed to let up – changing what crops we grew and how we built. I could not prevent that, for though I could force myself to eat for the sake of the land tied to me, I could not dam my tears.

Despite my careful attention, I had grown to hate Pensmoore as one hates a sister who has stolen the affection of one's betrothed. I hated her success because it was bought with the death of my love. I hated her peace, for it was bought with my pain.

I was not a fool. I knew all this was only possible because the Game of Crowns had shifted. War was constant south of our borders. Constant and growing, encompassing everyone else – even Aayadmoore was overrun, and we shipped much of our surplus grain and meat to them in aid and compassion – or so we told the people. In actual fact, the longer she held out, the longer it would be before enemies crawled over our border like a swarm of grasshoppers eating all there was to consume as they had with her. We bought ourselves time with every barge of grain that sailed, with every lowing cow that was driven over the bridge, with every piece of gold sent to her relief.

I alone, of all Svetgin's counselors, saw what that meant. I, alone, understood our reprieve was temporary, that war would come when the powers that ruled from on high remembered we were here.

It mattered not. My brother, my fellows on his council, and even my own self would be dead long before the patterns I saw came to fruition. I fought now – against them and for Pensmoore – only for a memory. I fought for the memory of my mother's eyes and my father's smile and the thought that both would shatter if I did not keep safe what they had entrusted to me.

I did not forget those who had died for me in this faded mortal world, and I steered my brother toward patronage not only of Northpeak's stables – ensuring our cousin who stood now as landholder would have enough ready coin to keep up our parents' legacy, but also toward the stables of Lord Danske who had so nobly died in defense of my honor. His successor – his steward as no living relative could be found – honored me with the gift of a horse along with horses we purchased for the army.

The horse, I adored. He was a gorgeous black stallion pronounced unfit for riding, for he was too spirited and too nervous. A mere glance at him shot my heart through with pained nostalgia for he was precisely the horse my father would have chosen. He danced at the smallest sound, balked at orders, tried to throw anyone but me, and was altogether too large and too expensive for a stable in the city.

I doted on him, giving him apples when he bit the fingers of the stable hands, preparing his hot mash myself, and pressing my pale forehead to his dusky one. The people of Pensmoore City called me horse-mad and referred to him as my prince so much that I began to call him so, myself.

"And how are you today, Horse Prince?" I murmured to him, gratified that no one bothered us this morning.

To the dismay of Svetgin and his men alike, I – Princess of Pensmoore though I was – rode him to the sea every month. I would have ridden out more if I dared, but the journey was a three-day ride and though I stayed with Lady Greatspur, I spent one of those days and nights every month riding up and down the shore looking, looking, looking for my lost love until I thought my heart had grown numb from it. And yet, I could not stop. What if one day his body washed up with none but the old fishermen to find and bury him? That, I could not allow. What if I heard a cry and he still lived, clawing his way across the sand in need of succor and care? What if he perished after so long, due only to my failure to come to him?

The rumors among the people that Northpeak's sister was Wittenbrand-touched were only confirmed by my behavior, and there was much feigned pity for him, but only raised noses for me. I did not care. I was more than happy to be the Mad Princess. It suited me inside even if on the surface I was carefully composed, neat as a fresh-baked roll, and always draped in stainless black or forbidden blue.

"Please, Izolda, please," Svetgin begged me the first month. "Cease in this madness. Stay in the castle and help me. Marry well and help me forge an alliance."

"Twice you have married me off for the benefit of Pensmoore, and twice the choice has circled back and bitten you on the nose," I warned him in icy tones. I had not found renewed affection for my brother. Living with him was like wearing clothing from my girlhood – it did not fit anymore and did not suit me, king though he was.

He hissed at my words, but he could not declare my strike untrue. Eventually, he agreed. "Then I shall marry, and you must stay to help me tally the numbers, repair the fences, and keep this kingdom from falling into the brink."

For seven years it had been so. Svetgin married well and sired a pair of sons and a big-eyed daughter whose beauty and sly charm rivaled her mother's.

And for seven years, my heart beat only pain and my hands worked busily for the benefit of others. I scribed and tallied, scored and listed, inspected and ordered, investigated and counseled, and each month I rode out to the sea on my grand, foolish stallion with the blazing hooves.

Seven years was not enough time to make me forget. It was not enough time to dull the agony of my loss even a fraction. My brother's gifts – mink stoles, golden trinkets, and soft velvet cloaks which I gave to the orphanage as often as I was gifted them – did not ease the feeling of claws snagged in my soul. Not one bit. My place as a princess felt no more real nor meaningful than the games I played with Svetgin's small children, and if I had beauty of any kind, it had long fled as my eyes grew ringed in purple shadows.

"Time heals all wounds," Svetgin said sagely last year. Svetgin made a good king. The people all agreed on that, calling him Svetgin the Bountiful. But he was a terrible counselor. Time healed nothing, it only amplified everything as echoes amplify a noise until it was all I ever heard ringing in my heart.

And so, once more, I set out for the lonely shores of the coast of Pensmoore in my black riding habit, wrapped up against the bitter squalls that haunted the shores. My specter wrapped around my face, an ever-present reminder of the world I'd lost.

I'd tried once to access the Wittenhame through a colossus as Vireo had told me was possible. I'd tried to cajole the specter into helping me, but she had denied me any help and in the end, I left home emptyhanded and broken-hearted. There was no access there for mortals on their own. The only scrap of Wittenhame left to me was the specter on my shoulder and her mute judgment.

When we stopped in a village, I tried to tell a peddler on the road about the conspiracy between Coppertomb and Tanglecottt just to feel the ghostly hand grip my jaw and force me to swallow the words. It comforted me to have my spectral jailer with me – one tiny piece of the Wittenhame kept with me.

We left the village, turned off the road, and wended our way through the waist-high grasses that rimmed the well-worn trail to Yellow Squall Bay. Prince shook his head, jingling the reins, desperate for the freedom he'd come to expect, and I slipped from his back and pulled the well-oiled tack from his head, freeing him. He waited only long enough for me to mount again, our time-shaped practice. This time, I gripped his flowing black mane and clung tight, lying flat over his neck as he reared and then plunged down the path. The autumn air rushed through my lungs, spiced with an icy edge and fragrant with the death of leaves and the tang of mushrooms.

Anyone with sense would panic at a nervy stallion given his head and racing toward the cliffs along Yellow Squall Bay, but I never had and never would. Once you'd lost everything, losing your life seemed of little consequence. I loved the way the wind plucked and tore at my long hair as it became unraveled from its pins and streaked out behind me, long as my history. And as all proper decorum unwound around us, something tight unwound in my chest and flapped loose, trailing us, snapping and screaming in our passage. Sometimes I thought that our souls were like that, riding white-knuckled on the perilous ride our bodies forced upon them.

We galloped through the November winds, dancing through little whirlwinds carrying the lightest dusting of early snow – just enough to nip at our skins and remind us we would be soon assaulted by Lord Winter but not enough to freeze us. Until, at last, red-cheeked and winded, we settled into the dogged pace of those determined to cover ground.

I rode with my eyes on the shore, on the querulous bottle-green waves, on the white froth. I scanned the flotsam washed ashore – great viridescent weeds with bulbous boles, half-desiccated fish carcasses, shells and rocks that gleamed from a distance but would prove to be valueless upon inspection, and timbers that had been adrift so long they'd been leeched of color, kin to the mortal world adrift on the tides of fate.

The song of the sea that never let up in my heart erupted again, loud and long and aching. I wondered, for what must have been the thousandth time, why I combed this beach over and over when Coppertomb could have set us down anywhere. I might not be near where Bluebeard was drowned. I might not be where the confrontation had taken place. I might be on the other side of the world.

And yet, my heart was buried with my husband, drowned with him in his watery grave, buried with his body so certainly that if it had been sliced open, seawater would have flowed out with the blood.

True to my new nature, I hunted and sought and refused to bend even now, seven years from the time I'd last seen him.

No one else roamed along the ragged shore. Sometimes there were birds.

The first few times I went, Svetgin had irritably sent soldiers along to watch me. Occasionally, I saw a fisherman or clam digger from afar. Eventually, they all stopped taking notice of me. My comings and goings were of no more importance than the wax and wane of the moon.

Which was why Prince reared when the grass in front of us moved against the wind, as suddenly and uncertainly as if an uncanny hand shook it.

He neighed his horsey displeasure, coming down hard on the bank, front feet stomping like weapons, just in time to shy back from a pair of figures that emerged from the grass. They did not paw upward as if they had lain in wait but revealed themselves from the air, as if they had just been rendered visible. A third emerged a heartbeat later.

That was too much for Prince. He screamed, reared again, and this time I could not hold on and I was thrown into the grass while he tore away, shaking his equine head as if he could dislodge a spectral rider.

If my three visitors cared, they did not show it. The center one adjusted his ragged doublet and held out to me a small token in his palm.

"Frost! Yarrow!" he cried as if he'd forgotten they were right beside him. "She does not match her image!"

"I believe that is your token, Lord of the Wittenhame," I said, collecting myself and getting to my feet. My voluminous skirts rustled stiffly and the light widow's veil I usually wore was gone – blown away in the excitement.

"The ruler of Moravidmoore," one of the pair whispered to him and the Wittenbrand looked from me to the piece and back again.

My heart thundered harder than the sea as I took a step forward, drawn to them as a moth to the flame. For here, in front of me, were living people once more, bright and bonny – even the hoary Marshyellow – and alive as none of the mortals I lived my days with ever could be. The attraction of them drew me ever forward, even as I knew they were made of blades and poison rather than blood and flesh.

"But we came for her, we did," Marshyellow muttered to himself. "She is ... she lives. She is."

"She's the wife of the Arrow, now lover to the Sea," one of them whispered to him and I hoped that "lover to the sea" was a euphemism because jealousy rose in my heart as a fire rises when oil is thrown on its fury.

"Oh, yes!" Marshyellow said and his fey eyes lit with excitement. The little token vanished and if he'd used sleight-of-hand then I would do best not to underestimate him because his actions were firm and sure. "Bargain with me, mortal wife of the Arrow. That's why I'm here. To see if you'd like to taste a sweet bargain."

And, with all my heart, I found that I did.

Chapter Three

"A PLACE, A CIRCLE. FROST!" Marshyellow muttered. A bubble appeared in the corner of his mouth. Even the Wittenbrand could become disgusting when tossed upon the surf of ages, and yet this flotsam fae still commanded the respect and service of his men.

Grave in face and action, Frost and Yarrow trampled a neat circle in the waist-high, cream-colored grass. It lay down tidily for them, and once the perfect circle was crafted, they took up their places again on either side of the raving Lord of the Wittenhame – two halves of a whole, two mirror images. They wore their single braid on opposite sides of the head, the other side shaved. They wore their leather straps and buckles opposite to one another and their clothing was divided down the middle. One side fawn brown, the other pale cream, and these, too, were mirrored. What made a powerful creature like a Wittenbrand choose not only a life of service but to be formed so much to it that they styled themselves as pieces rather than as men?

I regarded them surreptitiously but when I caught the eye of Yarrow by accident, the pure murder in his eye chilled me, rippling through my body. My very fingertips vibrated until he released my gaze.

Well then. They were not playing pieces. More like tigers strolling along on twin pieces of string while a babe pointed and burbled. They were me with Svetgin – tolerant, dutiful, capable. They cared for the cause over the man. There was a lesson in that, if I could find it.

Marshyellow settled himself in the center of the flattened circle, sitting cross-legged, his worn palms held on his knees as if he were to soon receive a gift. He turned his face up, eyes closed, hoary eyebrows twisting into their own uncanny pattern.

Frost jerked his head to me, and I realized I was meant to sit opposite their Lord.

I took my time finding my place. It's not easy to sit cross-legged in skirts – not even wide ones – without getting insects inside them. The grasses crunched and hissed with my movements like little bones snapping under my weight instead of plant stalks.

Marshyellow's eyes snapped open the moment I was still.

"A bargain I offer, a pledge between souls, for the jockeying of position and the fanning of coals."

Whatever had taken his mind had not taken his poetic ability. But I had not spent these years as a mortal negotiator without learning a few things myself.

I spoke my own poem, and if it wasn't as fine as his, at least it had the benefit of rhyming. "A pact beneficial to both of us two, is what I'll consider, that neither will rue."

His laugh put me in mind of a raven. It screeched out between throaty coughs, leaving him swaying, smiling, a little breathless. His leashed tigers didn't so much as flinch.

Above us, snow clouds gathered in roiling charcoal and Prussian blue, an ominous sign if ever one could be.

"Make your offer, Prince of the Wittenhame," I said smoothly, and his grin turned toothy.

To my horror, I saw his teeth had been sharpened to points and they were stained – not the brown and yellow of age but a maroon as if he feasted regularly on uncooked flesh.

I kept my face blank and careful. It was impractical to bargain with the Wittenbrand and yet I found I could not prevent myself from leaping into his offer. I wanted nothing more than to return to their untamed world by any means I could find.

His devil grin widened further, and he spoke each word as if it were a boiled sweet he was turning over his tongue.

"For the winning of a key, a hazard for a watery captive's release, would you wager a season to your enemy, your hand to a friend?"

He winked when he was through and I prodded the offer carefully in my mind, twisting it one way and then the other looking for holes, for hooks, for what might turn and bite me.

I was thoroughly sick of being proposed to. I did not wish to marry again. But did he know that I would do anything to free my husband – even that? I did not know. I watched him guardedly, but he let nothing slip from behind his mask of madness.

Carefully, I countered.

"For the winning of a key, a hazard for the release of my heart's conqueror," I began.

He'd been right in guessing what might tempt me to bargain with him, but I wanted to be specific. I didn't want the key to *any* captive's release. I wanted the key to *this* one's release.

"I would give this hand of mine in its current form."

There. I wasn't available to marry but I'd submit to whatever ceremonies or transfers of wealth he desired if only for this. But I'd need to sweeten the pot for him to accept a variance in what he asked for.

"Binding to it now all that was bound to you and offering to you its many skills."

There. I offered him skills – I had some a Wittenbrand could use – and if I'd worded that correctly his two guardians would not be able to harm me because they would be bound due to their loyalty to him. I could smell my own fear sweat as I carefully wove my counter-offer. Negotiating with the Wittenbrand was more dangerous than walking over beds of burning embers or through halls of spitting snakes. A viper or a fire could only kill you once.

And now to make up for the season I would not give him, because never again would I give one of my days willingly to anyone other than my lord Bluebeard.

"And I will forswear all vengeance by my own hand on the taker – both now and always."

He snickered and it was so close to Grosbeak's snicker that it made my heart swell with pain.

"A clever counter. A clever..." His eyes went glassy. "Did I make a mortal again?"

Frost leaned down to whisper in his ear and Marshyellow's vision sharpened once more. I did not like the smile he turned on me – all hungry bright eyes, sharp red teeth, and wild, unkempt hair.

Little sizzling streaks of fear ran down my spine as he looked me up and down, winked, and said, "Done, done, and done. You'll find your key on the water's edge."

And then he snapped his finger and my left hand flared with such blinding pain that it took all my self-control to hold back the blackness that threatened to take me, as Marshyellow produced a single silver key, turned it in the air, and then vanished through the door he'd made to the Wittenhame with his tigers on his heel.

One of them looked back at me before the door had closed and the derisive glee in his eyes sent terror whooshing down my spine. I followed his gaze to my hand, resting on my lap.

What I was seeing wasn't possible.

Breathe, Izolda. Measured breaths. Controlled. One. Two. One more.

I blinked. And blinked again.

But still, when I looked at the hand in my lap, the flesh ended abruptly at my wrist, smooth, as if healed naturally, leaving a hand that wore no flesh at all. I lifted it, crooked a finger, and then had to catch my breath as my skeleton palm and finger responded exactly as a flesh and blood hand would.

My hand.

He hadn't meant marriage at all. He'd meant my actual hand.

I was still swallowing down bile when a watery cough sounded from the edge of the water.

I did not hesitate. I leapt to my feet, stumbling through the high grass, sliding when I reached the sandy bank, afraid to catch myself with my skeleton hand. What if it broke? How easy did finger bones snap?

But my mind was caught up in a dream of hope, soaring and bold, desperate in hope. Was it him? Could it be that he'd be returned to me with only the loss of a single hand needed to secure his release? Would I be in his arms in moments, kissing his lovely face and drawing him from the water?

He had promised to shower me in kisses like rain. No, Izolda. Don't get ahead of yourself. But I couldn't breathe. My thoughts snapped and sparked with excitement.

I scrambled over the dunes, following the sound of coughing, as confusion overtook me. I couldn't see him, couldn't find him. My breath came in sobs and gasps as excitement turned to panic. Twice, I fell, slipping in the sand and surf, recovered myself, and ran again, my heavy skirts wet and dragging. If my mangled hand was less effective, I did not notice.

I tore down the beach, tripping on my skirts as thunder cracked the sky in two. Lightning danced between banks of clouds like the laughter of the Wittenbrand.

The coughing was close, deep, echoing, and full of power. It sounded from behind that large, whitened drift log. I scrambled over it, heart in my throat.

There was no body. I clawed through the surf, a mad thing, as if I could drag something from nothing in the swell of the tide.

Something croaked from behind me.

"I'd expected madness and mortal foolishness, but this takes the cake, Lady Arrow."

I spun and he was there. Not *him*. Not my beloved husband. But rather the bodiless head who had been my friend for so long.

I threw myself to my knees, not giving a thought to the icy fingers of the November sea, and scooped him up, choking on a sob.

"Careful now, careful. I'm still made of flesh, rotting and poxy though this severed head may be!"

His skin was swollen and bleached, far too pale even for a dead thing, his lips so blue they were almost green, and something had chewed off one of his ears. Seaweed twisted through his tangled black hair – and there, amongst it, was a golden key on a chain. *My* golden key to the Room of Wives.

I yanked it free and threw the chain around my neck. A hand for a key. That had been the bargain. And yet this was both less and more than what was promised.

"My husband," I said through thick lips. When had my teeth started chattering like that?

"Him whose side was wounded, and hands pierced through?" Grosbeak's lip curled derisively.

"The very one," I agreed. "Does he yet live?"

His pause was filled with thunder. Above us, the storehouse of heaven opened. Snow fell heavy as goose down, melting as it touched water and land with equal abandon.

"He lives," Grosbeak said and something like hope burned through me, hot and quick and nauseating.

Hope is a torturous thing. It wrenches one from despair just long enough to allow one to take a breath before plunging her back beneath the icy waters. If it wasn't for those breaths, it would be easy to let ice claim the soul. Easy to let surrender swallow the struggle. But hope – cruel mistress that she is – is not satisfied with so neat an ending. Like a house cat with a tiny prisoner, she wants only to torment the soul again, and again, until it dies from a burst heart.

"He still dwells beneath the waves, though for how long he can stave off the advances of death, I do not know. He is to that old inevitability as a maiden in her first season of society – so desirable as to not be ignored," Grosbeak said, "I would have thanked you to leave me there at his side."

"You would?" I asked, surprised out of the terrible gnawing wretchedness that came at his word. I had not the return of a husband. I had only a key to it. And even the key was a puzzle.

"I told you I would fall in love with a mermaid and so I had," he said, sniffing.

"A mermaid who allowed half your ear to be eaten away?" I asked wryly.

But his nonsense had brought me back to my senses. I had a key. I had some way to free Bluebeard, if I could just figure out what it was. The first step was not to freeze to death on the shore.

"Who's to say she didn't nibble it herself?" Grosbeak asked coyly.

I stood, wrapping my skeletal fingers through his tangled hair and carrying him away from the sea.

"And what will you do now, mortal girl?" he asked through chattering teeth.

"I will take you home with me, tattered trophy," I said as I caught sight of a black stallion galloping toward us along the beach. "And you will tell me everything that has happened these past seven years that you have been at the feet of my husband."

"Seven years?" he asked, stunned.

"Yes."

Prince arrived in a flurry of hooves and snow. He stopped before me, snorting, head bent in apology.

"You should be sorry," I scolded him. "It was cruelly done to leave me with those creatures."

The horse snorted again and tried to take a bite out of Grosbeak's hair. I held my prize higher and off to one side and calmed my stallion with my other hand, leaning my forehead against his.

"No luck today, my friend," I whispered to him. "We must head back home."

"No luck? Is that what you say upon our reunion. I would have thought you would be starved for my company after seven long years. Seven! Why, you're old now!" Grosbeak looked horrified.

"I'm twenty-six," I said coolly, mounting Prince and grabbing a fistful of his mane as a handhold.

I very pointedly did not look at my left hand. How would I hide it? What excuse would I make for it in the Court of Pensmoore? I shivered at the thought of being caught with such a hand.

"Like I said, ancient," Grosbeak told me. "Meanwhile, I was only beneath the sea for two days."

"Two days?" my gaze snapped to his. "You fell in love in two days?"

He laughed, a terrible creaking laugh, arrested suddenly by a fit of coughing and then he spat out a bright silver minnow, crossed his eyes, and grew greener before finally saying, "Did you forget us, Izolda? Did you laugh at our demise? Your Bluebeard won't like the sound of that."

"Tell me everything about him," I demanded as I kicked Prince into a gallop and the snow puffed up around us in furious clouds. "Can he survive much longer? How can he be freed?"

"No," Grosbeak said coolly.

"No, he can't survive?" I asked, feeling colder than any snow could ever make me.

"No, I won't tell you," he said, instead, sounding irritable. "I promised I would not and some of us still keep our promises, you terrible solemn thing."

Chapter Four

OUR RIDE HOME was wild and woeful. The storm grew worse with each passing moment as if it had declared war on our very selves. I determined to declare war back.

I rode to where the tack had been left and awkwardly fitted Prince with it, cooing to him and calming him with my flesh hand while the skeletal one worked. He did not like the feel or scent of it and shied away if it touched his body. I didn't blame him. Twice, when I tried to brush my hair back with it, I froze at its cold touch against my face. The feeling left me ill and wretched.

"Lost a hand, did you?" Grosbeak asked. "And I missed seeing it. Tell me you traded it for something of equal value, at least."

"I'm beginning to suspect I did not," I said coolly.

I was almost grateful that the storm lent me little time to fuss over it. I needed a warmer cloak and gloves. I was soaked through and the wind bit with long teeth. And yet I felt a sense that I must return to the capital as soon as possible. If my Bluebeard lived, then I must formulate a plan to get him back. I had new tools – my Wittenbrand guide and a key to a single Wittenhame room. Perhaps it was not enough, but it was more than I'd had these past seven years. I would not waste this gift now that it had been granted.

"Where are we going?" Grosbeak asked as soon as I had Prince tacked again, my living knuckles red and fingers clumsy with cold.

"We'll ride to Lady Greatspur's home, where I will beg a fur cloak and gloves," I told him as I mounted, settling my skirts and balancing his head in front of me. "Did you shake that fly problem?"

"Even flies must fly the flag of defeat when presented with a league's depth of seawater," he grumbled. "But I was not ready for the enthusiasm of crabs. The creatures torment me yet."

I reached into his hair to remove a sand-colored crab the size of my thumbnail. I flicked it away with disgust. His sojourn – short though it may have felt to him – had left its mark.

"I'll have to leave you in a tree somewhere while I beg for clothing," I said grimly as Prince began to walk. "It will be hard enough to hide a ruined hand, never mind the head of a corpse."

"The hand is hideous. Were I offered such, I would have refused."

"At least I have a hand," I said tightly. Would my husband think the same when he saw it? Would he shudder at the sight of me and rear back from my touch?

I hadn't thought of that.

I held the imposter up before me and flexed the fingers. The sight sent shivers through my jaw and an uncomfortable feeling blossomed in my mouth like biting into meat only to find a sliver of arrowhead within.

"If you think to make me jealous with those diviner's tokens you now call fingers, think again. I'm perfectly happy to be free of hands if the alternative is *that.*"

"Tell the truth, at least," I scolded.

"I don't like trees and I won't be left in one," Grosbeak said miserably. "I have not been in good humors of late, Izolda. You ought to have turned your attentions much sooner to freeing me. Seven years! Teeth of the Gods, that's a long time. The sea does not agree with me."

"Clearly." My mind was absent, watching our trail. It was hard to see it in the swirling snow. My heart was also absent, drifting out across the turbulent waves, wondering if beneath their emerald furor my husband gulped and gasped in briny breaths.

"Besides which," Grosbeak continued, "the nattering of a lovelorn swain is hardly the type of entertainment I'd bargain for and yet I could not stop my ears to it. I tried coaxing the crabs into them, but you can see that was a disaster."

I paused, and Prince halted with me, his movements easily conforming to mine. "Lovelorn?"

My heart skipped a beat, warming in my chest. I couldn't breathe. Something was trapped in my throat.

"Don't you dare look like that," Grosbeak said darkly. "One of you is bad enough. If I must deal with two, I will need ichor smoke, a chest of cherry-pit brandy, and at least a dozen mermaids."

"What can you possibly offer mermaids when you're nothing more than a rotten head?"

"Your lack of imagination does you a disservice."

Lovelorn. His choice of word echoed in my mind all the way to Lady Greatspur's house.

I likely should have asked for the cloak and gloves. I was no natural-born thief. And I knew the lady well enough to be certain that I would have been given them with a generous smile and a reminder to mention her to the king. But as the gale grew louder, wailing all around me, blocking sight of the tree where I'd tied Prince and hung Grosbeak from a branch, I changed my mind. There was no certain way to hide the hand. Not without gloves. And I knew the layout of the house completely. I knew Lady Greatspur would be taking tea at this time in the afternoon and with the storm afoot, her servants would be hunkered down within, attending only to those chores that kept them inside.

Sneaking in and out through the kitchen door in the back proved to be as easy as I'd hoped and I was soon back with Grosbeak, hands tucked into leather gloves and a warm fur cloak wrapped around me. And if I felt guilt, it was nothing compared to the pressing need to be home with quill in hand and parchment before me to solve this mystery.

"Tell me how to free him," I begged my newly returned friend.

"I will not."

"Then tell me he can hold on a little longer." My jaw was tight.

"He'll likely expire before the next dawn. I will not mourn his passing."

"So cruel. You're sure it was only two days to you?"

"I'm sure of nothing. Perhaps it was two centuries, and I was too enamored of soft lips, sleek hair, and the iridescence of scales to know otherwise. And as for cruelty, it is my greatest asset, and I would no more abandon it than I would abandon this year's fashions if I were offered them. Which I have not been, I'll remind you."

The cloak kept the worst of the wind from biting me and was bulky enough to hide Grosbeak inside it and none would be the wiser. Perhaps I could make a sling and carry him like a child.

"You'll do nothing of the sort!" he said when I put it to him. "*That* is not fashion at all."

"Perhaps, I will anyway, if you do not tell me how to free my husband," I said tightly. Inside my thoughts buzzed like flies, untamable with excitement, while also edged with irritation. Everything conspired against me now that I had a tool to get him back. The hand. The storm. The one I'd called friend. Everything.

I turned Prince into the wind, found the road, and urged him to a gallop. He tossed his glorious head, arrogant in the face of driving snow and blinding wind, and ran as if his mind were kin to mine.

"I told you I made a promise. 'She'll try to come here,' he told me in one of his long monologues. 'I'll have your vow not to lead her here, Grosbeak.' I tried to ignore him. Trust me, I had affairs of my own to conduct." He paused and then snickered. "I said, I had affairs of my own – "

"It wasn't funny the first time you said it."

"If it isn't funny then why should I bother telling the rest?" He was almost more snappish than I was.

I made a sound of disgust, but I wasn't sure if he could even hear me over the rising wind and the pounding of Prince's dish-sized hooves striking the cobbled road. We were riding through the nearby village, the wind swirling at our backs, the tang of snow in our noses, and the church bells of the town clanging intermittently in a discordant rhythm to the thunder above.

Night had fallen, deep, luscious, and filled with broken dreams in the form of stars.

"Ha. Ha," I said eventually to get him talking again. It came out in a wooden imitation.

"I'll take that," Grosbeak said sourly. "At any rate, he pressed me. 'Your vow,' he said to me. 'Not a word spoken to her of how to free me or what she must do.'"

"What I must *do*? Then it's up to me somehow?" I pressed.

His answering snap was sharp. "I'd forgotten how witless mortal girls were, but it seems you'll remind me with every breath. Did you not hear I made a vow? Besides, forget the sea. There's no drama to be had there. We were awash in sea and fish and nothing of interest. Take me instead to where mortals sup and drink and we shall celebrate my return in proper style."

"Did the vow include gestures?"

"Had I hands, I'm sure it would. As it stands, it matters not. Is there no succor in this frozen land of yours?"

"Did it include winks, hints, or puzzles?"

"It did not. Words were the only thing ripped from my jaw. But though you seem enthusiastic, you should know that I know no language of winks, I mislike puzzles, and consider hints a fool's errand. And I did not much warm to the method used on me to extract this extraneous vow and I will have my revenge on it in this life or the next. So, enough of this ghastly talk and find me a stuffed pheasant and some oranges or it will be the worse for everyone."

"We can work with that," I said firmly, ignoring his request for food. We would have to work with it. Right now, it was all I had.

"I do not plan to work at all. We Wittenbrand are well known for toiling not nor spinning."

"When I'm through with you, old friend," I said, threateningly, "I'll have worked you so long and hard, you'll claim my firstborn as wages."

He sounded forlorn when he answered. "I fear I cannot. He bound me from that, too, when he heard me devising a trick with the help of my harem under the sea."

That closed my mouth with a click. We were riding through a second town already. Usually, I would stop to spend the night here, but Prince's feet were full of fire and my heart was galloping with him.

"A harem?"

"Indubitably."

The gates loomed ahead, we sped through, kicking up snow as the guards scattered, cursing us as we passed.

"As in, more than one?"

"It's impossible to have a harem of only one."

"More than one mermaid fell for your charms under the sea?"

The town was empty, the streets clear, the small diamond-paned windows of the homes and inns lit with dancing marigold light.

"Your lack of faith offends me." He sounded truly hurt.

"Your lack of charms should offend all. I do not believe a word you are telling me."

He clicked his tongue irritably. "You bring to the surface all the salt of the sea, mortal girl. Must I remind you that your imagination is insufficient?"

"Must I remind you that your bodily form is the same?"

And to my surprise, he laughed, a horrible throaty, chesty laugh that should be impossible for a man with no chest. It fell into wheezing as we thundered through the gate on the other side of the town, riding for the capital as if our heels were being dogged by mist lions.

"Did he know you were coming to me?"

"It would break my vow to tell you."

"Did he send a message?"

"Anything he would say would be whimsical nonsense and we both know how you hate that."

I clenched my jaw, clutched the reins to my chest with my living hand, and tried to keep from shattering as the memory of that first ride with my Bluebeard howled through me with more force than any winter storm, and this time, I let the loneliness and pain of his loss howl on and on and I did not try to gather it in. Not when it might fuel his return.

Chapter Five

RIDING through the night seemed like a fine thing to do and one would think it would shave a full day from a journey but that only worked in fairy-tales and stories. In actual fact, I had a flesh and blood horse, and while he was high in spirit and brim-full with energy, he was also a living thing.

By morning, Prince was slow and tired. I dismounted to lead him into Brackenstown, a hamlet just outside Pensmoore City. From this point, the roads would be filled with travelers and lined with hawkers, wayside stops, patrols, army posts, and any number of things that would slow a traveler and draw all eyes on her – especially when the one journeying was the King's mad sister.

I chose, instead, to stable Prince for the day, pay an exorbitant price to have him fed and rubbed down, and hurry to hide in the inn's best room before anyone would wonder why I was hunched inside a fur cloak and wearing gloves when the sun was bright in the sky as a new penny. There were some things I liked about being Svetgin's sister. Not needing to wait was certainly one of them.

My breath frosted the air as a yawning serving girl lit my fire, ignoring my protests that I could do it myself. Two men and three more maids filled a steaming bath and left a plate of breakfast, and not a word I said deterred them. Royalty must be treated a certain way, even royalty that everyone whispered was mad as a Wittenbrand and possibly just as dangerous.

I fought a maid off my cloak when she tried to take it to hang up for me.

"But Lady Princess, it needs to dry," she protested.

"I will keep the cloak on, thank you," I said coolly, clutching it closed with my flesh hand. I'd tucked the skeletal one inside the cloak and it was tangled around Grosbeak's drowned head. I could only imagine what any of these mortals might say if this poor girl succeeded in ripping the fur from me and saw what I clutched against my belly.

"But Princess, the –"

"I keep the cloak."

They fled before the fire in my eyes, likely to start more rumors about the ill-mannered wildness of the princess, and I bolted the door, stuck a chair under the handle, and set Grosbeak on it.

"Princess?" he asked in a drawl, eyebrow raised. "What a complicating occurrence. Do tell me it comes with perks."

"They made Svetgin king," I said, feeling my face flush as I hung the fur coat over another chair by the table to dry. My dress was a ruin. I had more in my saddlebags, but none so fine as this one.

"That quivering mortal? The weeping one? They made him king? You did not speak out against him, saying unto them how he had sold you twice and found the short end of the bargain each time?"

"If I had, they would have applauded him for it and made him king all the sooner," I said dryly, turning his head around so I could undress.

"I'll never understand mortals. A bad bargain made is all you need to besmirch you with the Wittenbrand."

"And an attempted murder gone awry is all that's needed to sever your head and leave you a mortal's pet."

"Touché. That hit strikes hard."

I was just as tired as my horse. My mind had bubbled all night with daydreams of riding to my husband's rescue and dragging him up from under the sea while he still lived. They had only been daydreams. Each plan I tried to concoct involved knowing where he was imprisoned. Marshyellow might know. But I'd have to get to him first. Grosbeak knew, but would not tell, and I doubted I could torture it from him since anything I might threaten to do had already been done to him.

I looked back and forth between him and the hot bath, considering.

"You can't drown information out of me," Grosbeak said snidely. "I've been underwater for so long it's made me twice the weight."

I made a moue of agreement.

Mixed generously with my new relief that my husband yet lived was the terrible, gnawing anxiety that he may die at any moment and my very mortal-ness – the slowness of my horse, the frailty of my body – was preventing his rescue.

"I don't know why you turn me around," Grosbeak grumbled as I spun him quickly in place. "It's hard to speak with my head facing the wrong way."

"Yes, but it's easier for me to bathe that way."

My ruined dress was off quickly, my flesh hand running over the long twisting red scar on my side before I dropped into the steaming bath and worked to clean my hair. My bone fingers tangled in the long strands, and I had to pick them free with my living hand as if I was cleaning a comb.

I shuddered as I regarded the foreign limb, dead and horrifying where the pink of my flesh ended suddenly at the wrist and gave way to ivory digits. It would be a very miserable life if I spent it blanching every time I saw my own hand. I should simply accustom myself to it and move on. I tried to do just that, focusing instead on cleaning myself. I smelled of sweat and horse and the sea.

If I arrived at the palace rumpled and unwashed, there would be questions and I must avoid questions until I decided what to do about Grosbeak.

I would be keeping him – of course. He was my one link to the Wittenhame and it was possible he would slip and let out a clue even if he was trying to avoid it. Perhaps the key was to find those mermaids – if they existed at all.

He was not easily disguised.

"Perhaps, I should keep you in a shrouded cage," I said, considering. "I could claim I had acquired a bird from afar. One that speaks."

"The indignity!" he hissed. "I won't stand for it."

"You don't stand at all, and that is the problem. Perhaps a large satchel."

"And breathe leather all day? What will you say next? A basket for bread? A barrel for fish? No, you must hang me from a pole as you did before, so I can see properly."

The warm bath was not soothing me, but rather making my stomach swim. I left it, dressing in a crumpled black dress from my saddlebags – the only other one I'd brought, and it was damp at the edges – and then turning him around.

"If I do that, they'll pack me away to a nunnery and I'll be imprisoned for the rest of my life with a bunch of chaste women nursing the sick and copying scrollwork."

"That's an option?" his eyes lit.

"It's not as fun as you seem to think. Scrollwork is very fiddly business," I said wryly. "I need a way to keep you hidden and I can't wear heavy furs forever. Perhaps your mermaids have a suggestion. We could ask them."

"Ha! You misjudge if you think me so easily fooled, mortal princess. I know a coy womanish plan when I hear one. Not winkling the secret out from me, you think to rob my oysters of the pearl."

I shook my head and fell silent. I had played my hand too early. Best to focus for now on how to get him into the palace. After that, I'd have time to work on his cooperation.

But when I'd eaten and fallen into the bed, I still had not come up with a solution that was not ridiculous. Sleep took me and I woke to sunset and the sound of drinking in the inn below.

"Time to ride, unworthy princess," Grosbeak said with a snicker. "Do you wear a crown?"

It took bare moments to gather my things and hide him in my cloak. "I do not wear a crown. I'm known as the Mad Princess."

He nodded sagely. "Then they won't mind when it seems you talk to yourself. Convenient."

"When we arrive at the palace, I will need to speak to my brother," I said coolly. "And then I will get to work discovering how I may return to the Wittenhame and how I will fetch my husband back. You'd best spend the ride considering how you'll help with that."

"Easy. I will not help you. I will, in fact, do everything to hinder you until he has breathed his last and no one but the Bramble King himself could bring him back to life."

Acid churned in my stomach.

"And if you were wondering, I would guess his time is measured in moments, not hours, so if you were thinking of taking a terrible risk, you shouldn't be wasting so much time."

My face flushed hot at that, heart pounding hard in my breast.

I took a last look in the mirror. My hair was settled and braided, my face and dress clean. The specter sat sadly on my shoulder as she always did, sending her mournful, shivery gaze over the room as if I might spill my confidences to it if not for her guardianship, and my huge fur cloak – bear, I thought – covered the drowned head of Grosbeak.

"You'd best consider if you'd like to spend the rest of your immortal life thrown down the hole of the castle garderobe. If you fail to help me rescue him, that is where I'll put you."

He was mercifully silent after that, even when I reached the common room of the inn and inspiration struck.

The Whiskeylamp Inn catered to a noble clientele and seated around a table to one side was Lady Sergaz of Cliffmeadow and her two daughters. In tune with the latest style, the lady had a leather satchel at her feet, the nose of a ferret peeking out of it.

He was silent for the brief conversation and negotiation. Silent, as I left the inn with one highly prized ferret and the extremely fashionable bag that held him slung over one shoulder. I could wear this bag in court, and no one would notice, provided I fed the ferret.

He was not silent when I turned the corner of the inn, slunk into the alley, and stuffed his head into the bag.

"You're mad!"

"So, they tell me."

"What is this thing in here with me? Oh, Bramble King above, it bites! Stop it! That's my nose. My nose! Izolda!"

I cuffed the bag. "Both of you make yourselves silent. We have a horse to mount and a night journey before us."

Fortunately, few nobles depart as the sun is setting, even though our roads are safe for travel. Prince was saddled and stamping almost before I finished requesting it. I sprang onto his back, stretched my fingers in my gloves – one hand fit them better than the other – and took up the reins before the grooms so much as blinked.

We trotted boldly from the stable, cantering onto the street, and galloping down the road, ignoring the icy blast of the wind and the slick frozen puddles in our path, as if we were the heart of winter freed upon the north.

"I hate the cold," Grosbeak said from within the bag. "If you think this will make me talk, you can think again."

I said nothing, giving Prince his head and reveling in the freedom of traveling at speed as we flew through the cold, morphing into one spiritual creature, horse and rider, purpose and action, two halves of one whole. Riding was the last joy afforded me, and I clung to it as a child clings to a beloved toy. This time, it was not enough. It could not ease the gnawing in the center of my belly.

Too late, the sound of hooves on cobbles told me. *Too late. Too late.*

"Ferrets are not a legal form of torture." Grosbeak's voice muffled for a moment. "And this one reeks of something terrible."

We cycled from a gallop to a trot and then a walk and then up to a gallop again, shifting from one to the next as Prince required it.

"At least tell me this creature has a name," Grosbeak said eventually.

"The lady called him 'Honey,'" I said, "for his sweet temperament."

"Sweet? She called this hellion sweet?"

"Oh, I think you'll find he's sweet compared to me if you continue to deny me what I most want," I said in my most honeyed tones. "I thought you said you were my pet and not the Arrow's and yet I see none of that sworn allegiance. But I will take pity on you and grant you one boon."

"Good. Let it be the death of this creature." His words were muffled, and the ferret yelped as if it had been bitten.

"I will not kill it. It has done far less to harm me than you have. I thought, rather, that I would let you rename it."

Grosbeak's yelp told me the ferret was giving as good as it got. Good. I'd hate to leave an innocent creature in that bag with him. Someone had carefully embroidered vines on the flap of the purse in a pattern known as a lover's knot.

"To name a thing gives it power," he muttered.

"To rename it puts it under your power," I countered.

"Wise," he said with a nasty twist to his words. "Perhaps that is how you wove your spell over your Bluebeard."

"Perhaps," I said lightly, but I hoped it was not true. I wanted nothing between my husband and me except what had grown up on its own. It would be a horrifying thing indeed to find your affections and loyalties were merely the product of glamor.

We rode some hours before he spoke again.

"Then I shall name it '*Look And Despair*' in hopes that it will do just that."

"I think it's a she," I said.

"You don't need to tell me."

We'd reached the gates of Pensmoore City and one of the guards held up a hand to me. I gently drew in the reins, bringing Prince up short.

"Princess Izolda Savataz of Northpeak now of Pensmoore City?" the guard asked though we both knew who I was.

"Is something urgent?" I asked instead.

"Your brother bid us give you this missive were you to arrive at this gate," the guard said with a hasty bow. It was just as cold for them as it was for me. My flesh hand was so numb from the cold that it couldn't have taken that slip of paper if it was required to save my life. To my surprise, the bone hand had no such trouble. I plucked the sealed note deftly from his hand, cracked the seal, and studied it.

My brother had been in a hurry when he penned it, but it was in his florid hand.

"*Izolda. Urgent we speak. Come to the hole when you get this.*"

Something was awry in our kingdom. I felt a stab of cold run through me, but it was not dread, just impatience. I had not the time for this, not when I finally had the key to free my husband and a desperate reminder that his life was nearly forfeit.

"Trouble?" Grosbeak hissed.

The guard looked up sharply.

Irritated, I gritted my teeth and repeated, "Trouble, I'm afraid. Please burn the note for me."

I handed it to the guard and his face glowed with pride as he placed it on the glowing brazier meant to warm him on this terrible night.

At least someone was pleased. I turned Prince to the palace, hissing to Grosbeak as we rode, "If you speak where someone else can hear you again, the garderobe will look like the happier fate."

"Keep threatening me and see where that gets you. You're toothless as a sapped snake and just as venomous and I do not give you one solitary tremble."

Chapter Six

I HAD THOUGHT to sneak up to the secret room my brother and I called “the hole” with little trouble, but the moment I rode through the palace gates I could smell the magic of the Wittenbrand. It clung to the frosted doorposts and rolled down the icy steps. It swept up in curls of temptation and trailed streamers of cinnamon-sugar desire down every cobbled path. It had not been there when I left this place five days ago.

My teeth set on edge, and I tasted metal as I dismounted a dancing Prince and offered him to the groom.

“Stallion seems wild tonight, princess,” he’d said, biting his lower lip and looking over his shoulder.

I didn’t answer him. He was just as edgy as the horse. All the staff I saw were, backs straight as pokers, movements jerky, eyes darting, dark Pensmoore uniforms pressed as if order could be restored by an iron. What in the world had happened here?

Whispers followed me – harsh and prickling.

I hurried up the steps, shushing Grosbeak as I went, and shedding the fur coat into the competence of a waiting maid. She flinched when the wet fur fell into her arms.

I could see why my brother had sent for me. Nothing short of renewed war could turn this well-oiled palace, this luxury of polished wood and woven fabrics, warm fires and the scent of pine, set amid snowy defensible rock, into the snappish threadbare place I'd returned to. Even the maid's bow was tight and shallow.

I didn't have time to so much as turn around, before my brother's wife swept down on me like a velvet and lace-clad hawk on a mouse.

"Sister," she said tightly, wrapping an arm around me. Her arm was shaking though her curls were tightly ironed.

My eyebrow rose without my intending it to. That she called me "sister" was a sign of deep distress.

"Has someone died?" I asked calmly. I bit the inside of my own lip. Could it be Svetgin? He had an heir in her son. She had no need to implore me for help. Her rule through him was secure.

"Not yet," she said ominously, and then she was hustling me down the hall so fast that my ferret bag smacked one of the corners. Grosbeak yelped and my sister by marriage hissed, "Quiet! You'll disturb the servants. They don't need to know that there is pain raining down on us, Izolda!"

I felt my eyebrows rising as a cold draft caught me from behind. My specter caught my eyes placing her silent finger to her chin, as curious as I was. Her eyes danced. Every denizen of the Wittenhame lived and breathed anticipation of violence. What terrified mortals was just the beginning of a fun evening for them.

"I think you should tell me what has happened, my queen," I said calmly. Seven years of this had at least taught me to keep myself under strict control.

The queen rolled her eyes at me. Another surprise. Usually, Emelina was the height of decorum in all situations. I had overheard her complaining that I was a disgrace with my direct words and informal addresses on more than one occasion. To have her throw that away was dire.

Again, I smelled the scent of the Wittenbrand in the air. Frost and cardamom and danger. I wanted more of it. I wanted to bury my face deep into it and never recover.

"I think we can dispense with titles today," Emelina said. Her eyes were red-rimmed. Had she been crying? "By tomorrow we may not have them. Or at least, I may not."

"Heaven forfend."

Her chin trembled, and now I really was worried.

Emelina hated me on principle. She had hated me from the moment her tiny feet touched our land and her perfect doll eyes had taken this country in and found only one thing wanting in it. She'd hated me from the moment her artful lips had formed their perfect smile and her slender finger its perfect crook as she drew my brother in and realized, to her chagrin, that it did not draw me in with him.

I did not care that she was lovely, fecund, rich, and of a royal bloodline. She was welcome to take the brother who had betrayed me and doomed my husband. Welcome to have the throne of the land that had sold me like cattle and shamed my parents despite it.

I thought, sometimes, that it might be my sanguine goodwill and indifference that bothered her most of all. She was the instigator of at least half the rumors of my madness. For my part, I contented myself with daydreams of her deposited in her royal robes and crown in the Wittenhame, shrieking at the horrors that awaited her.

But the more I refused to react to her jabs and barbs, the more she threw at me, whether in the service of close study or vent spleen, I could not have guessed.

That she was here now, crying where I could see it, was disturbing for both of us. It was the widow Princess Chasida, returned to us from Ptoolemoore where her royal husband died of a fever, who was usually in her confidence, not me. And yet here she was – on the verge of tears – sharing this with *me.*

The Wittenbrand. I forced myself to keep my face immobile. They must be at the root of this. The suspicion of it was enough to leave my senses tingling with a terrible mixture of fear and anticipation. There would be a riddle at the heart of this. There would be a way back *in.* If I was bold. If I recognized it.

It was no use. My heart was racing.

I tried to swallow down my hopes so they would not choke me but choke I did.

We hurried into a large reception room, empty of people but thick with trophies and the latest brocaded seating from Ptolemoore. Emelina had taken care to outfit every public room in the palace with the finest fashions of last season. It was I who had argued strenuously over the strain to our coffers, choked with more dust than gold after decades of war and deprivation. Now, Emelina slammed the inlaid door shut with no care at all for how the expensive carving shuddered and whirled to face me in the empty room.

"Izolda, you must save us. Please. If you care for me at all." My cold expression must have killed that speech before it finished. She changed tacks quick as a ship before a storm. "If you care for your brother, or his kingdom, and I know you must or why are you still here?" That was a point well taken. "You are the only one familiar with them and their whims."

It *was* the Wittenbrand. I knew it!

I could hardly catch my breath. Calm, Izolda. You must not rush in. You must wait for the opportunity.

But it was coming. I could feel it just on the edge of sight, coming to me. It left me aching with hunger.

"It must be you who settles them," Emelina said. "I don't know what I'll do. I just don't."

She dissolved into tears – ugly, gasping sobs that contorted her face like a gargoyle's – very much like the one she'd placed there in the corner, which had become a favorite of mine since it reminded me of a once-dear friend. The one currently muffling a giggle from within my leather satchel.

I found myself in the awkward position of having to allow her to weep on my shoulder while my specter pulled faces and leaned away. Drama, the creatures of the Wittenhame loved. Sentiment, they did not.

"What in all of Pensmoore and her many hills is going on, Emelina?" I asked as she wet the shoulder of my gown right through. But under my calm words, I was quivering.

"A lady of the Wittenbrand arrived tonight." She hiccupped between sentences. "She made demands. She says your brother must marry her."

"Ridiculous," I said, dryly. "He is married to you."

"She says he must put me away and disinherit our children, and if he doesn't –" Her wail swallowed the words.

"I'm afraid I didn't hear that."

Were those feet just outside the door? Was the time to act here already?

My mind was racing so fast it tripped over details.

Where had they put this Wittenbrand lady, and which one was it? This had to be about the Game of Crowns and Thrones. If one of them married Svetgin, then what? Would it rip the playing piece from my husband's grasp and disqualify him? If one of them was making a play to seize Pensmoore, then the game was still afoot, and my husband was still in it.

Still in it. My heart lurched and stuck.

Which meant we could still get him back. If I was just capable of finding and seizing the opportunity. I clenched my jaw and forced the words out.

"Explain, please, Emelina."

"She says that if he doesn't agree by tomorrow night, she will rip our children apart and feed them to her beasts," Emelina managed, choking on the words and on her sobs.

"Typical," Grosbeak muttered, no longer able to contain himself.

Emelina looked at my bag in alarm.

"What beasts?" I asked as if my bag had not spoken. But I already knew.

"The ones with four wings. Lions of the Mist, they were called."

Lady Tanglecott. I was warm right through with satisfaction.

This was her next move. And I was here to counter it.

"Take me to my brother," I ordered.

Like all palaces, the one in Pensmoore City had back stairs for servants and spies and so many hundreds of people that they were hardly secret, but the hidden ways were still faster than the main stairs where the nobility "chanced" upon one another day or night. It was to these passages that we fled, speeding up one set of steps and down another, through a series of turns, and then another, until we finally reached the hole.

Seven years ago, I would have been intimidated by Wittenbrand and bargains and royalty. Now, my mind was on what kind of bargain Lady Tanglecott might have offered, and whether there might be some way we could word it to trap her with her own schemes. I needed back into the Wittenhame. And she would be my way in.

My brother, it seemed, had found *his* solace in the jug. It was, all things considered, the worst place he could have gone to find it. We found him sprawled across a scarlet tufted chair, head thrown back and eyes glassy. On the table in the hidden room maps and documents were strewn with the haphazard look of a place that had been rifled for valuables. Doubtless, he had scoured them for a way out and found nothing.

My fingers twitched to touch the document in the center of it – one touching no other paper. It was written in gold script on a parchment so pale white as to be unnatural. A complicated, florid seal on gold wax with purple ribbons was fixed on the bottom of the page. That would be her proposal.

Not yet, Izolda, I told myself. Patience.

Volkov, Svetgin's general, sat opposite him, head in his hands. I did not think he was quite as drunk, but his eyes were just as red-rimmed, his breathing just as labored.

The merry tapestries hanging from the walls showing dryads dancing in the forest and great battles won mocked the desperate pair. Some of the candles around the room were still lit but the rest had burned to a stump and gone out hours ago. They must have started their hopeless vigil before night fell, and now they were still here when dawn was close to rapping on our doors.

There was more broken pottery in the corners and wet patches on the walls than I'd thought one raging man could make. Perhaps, I could still underestimate my brother in some things.

I did not judge them. I'd spent my share of nighttime vigils despairing of life. I'd bargained with myself back and forth and lost, just as he was doing now. But I didn't judge myself, either. Not when this might be my chance to be rid of all of that.

"You're drunk," Emelina cried. "Our family hangs in the scales and you're drunk!"

"What would you have me do, Lina?" Svetgin asked, his voice a pained croak. It sent me back to his sobs the night I'd lain cold and near death in his clutching arms on a lonely piece of coast. "I'll not watch our children ripped to pieces by beasts."

"Then you'll set us aside? Send us to the countryside without name or protection – to what? Starve? Be sold to men with ill intentions? Shall I sell myself to feed them?"

"Don't be so dramatic, woman," Volkov said, his head still in his hands.

He said it in the way men do, with the calm knowledge that the things spoken of will never be their lot. But I found myself sympathetic to Emelina. Any woman could find herself in the same position in the blink of an eye, queen or scrub girl or mad sister of a king.

Svetgin straightened, finally facing his wife, his red-rimmed bleary eyes meeting her tear-filled ones. He quivered with helpless rage as bitter words dripped from his tongue.

"What would you have me do? What? Were I to slit my own throat before you, it would not save you now, nor them. I may choose to watch you die fast or slow, but that's all the choice left me, woman. You heard what she told us, and it's written in golden script if you wish to read the particulars for yourself."

"I think *I* will," I said calmly, striding past their agonized tableau and drawing two of the guttering candles closer so I could read the parchment laid on the desk as one lays an execution warrant.

"Written in her own hand," Grosbeak whispered from the leather bag as the ferret's head popped up over the edge of it. How had he made a hole in the seam? It hadn't been there when we started out, but I saw one of his terrible gleaming eyes light up as he watched from the inside of the bag.

The script was elegant and elongated as if to draw out the pain of the words.

To the Royal Blood of Pensmoore, on this eighth day of Gray in Pensmoore City, capital of Pensmoore, from the great Lady Tanglecott of the Wittenbrand, Princess of the Oak, Patron Saint of Ilkanmoore.

I present to you this formal offer. You will make all preparations and present yourself to me at midnight of the next full moon on the roof of your palace, renouncing the mortal world and all within it. For three days, you shall live in my home in the Wittenhame, and for three nights you shall warm my bed.

Failure to present yourself as proposed will result in the death of your loved ones who I will feed to my mist lions as is a fitting consequence for such defiance.

Failure to formally disentangle yourself from your mortal ties will result in the same.

If you fail to live through our sojourn in my home, I will inherit your lands, title, and sovereignty, and I will use your land and people as I please.

If, however, against all odds, you survive these appointed days and nights, you shall be returned to the mortal world and be free to resume your ties and loyalties as you wish. In my magnanimous bounty, I shall even grant you one other soul – of your choice, excluding my magnificent person – to bring back with you to those lands.

The bargain is made, with or without you. Present yourself or suffer the consequences.

The parchment was signed in an illegible overly ornamented swirl that I assumed was her name.

Behind me, bitter words were being exchanged, but my heart was in my throat as I reread it twice. This. This was my opportunity.

"It's a Three Night Bind," Grosbeak whispered to me from in the bag.

He sounded gleeful. "A classic trap. It warms the heart to see her keeping up the traditions."

"Tradition?" I murmured.

"Certainly. Mortals have been offered the bargain many times before. Surely the tales remain of it in your world, too?"

"Has anyone survived to tell the tale?" I whispered back. I was only asking absently. My eyes were searching the letter for any detail I might be reading incorrectly. I couldn't afford a single misstep.

"One," Grosbeak said. "Luritan the Poet of Ilkansmoore saved his lover from the Wittenhame that way. She had been dragged away and hung in the lake upside down by her hair to drown endlessly for all eternity."

"How pleasant," I murmured.

"Marshyellow thought so. 'Twas he who placed her there. But when her lover was offered the Three Night Bind by Lady Wittentree, he took it in a heartbeat. Poet he was, but also prince, and she thought to snipe his lands from whoever was playing Ilkanmoore at the time – Antlerdale, I think – but in the end, she lost, and he fled the Wittenhame with his drowned lover."

I shivered. I was not sure that was a happy ending. For anyone.

"And the other times?" I asked.

"Mortals die easily. And then their lands are forfeit, and the Wittenbrand who thinks he is playing them as his pawn finds it gone and his game lost."

"Then I have guessed right," I murmured, "And if Tanglecott wins this Three Day Bind, then my husband loses this nation and his stake in the game. Which, I recall, is his very immortality."

"Yes," Grosbeak said, and he sounded so excited that I half expected his bag to quiver. Fortunately, the ferret was squirming around the top, disguising any movement. "Ouch! This must be her third move. And a very, very clever one at that. A classic. The Wittenhame will be abuzz with it."

"Why can she not just take the land without the Three Day Bind?" I whispered. Upon a fifth reading, I had found nothing in the letter I didn't see the first three times. My mind was nearly made up.

"Sovereignty can only pass by inheritance, the spoils of war, or marriage. She cannot inherit. Your Bluebeard beat them off in war – and though she can certainly go back to that and likely win, we both know she is allied to Coppertomb and his allotted lands for this game lie between hers and ours. Her best bet is to steal them by marriage."

"Marriage? This is not marriage. It's a brief kidnapping."

"In the Wittenhame, it amounts to the same."

"Your kind are very obsessed with marriage," I hissed. Behind me, my brother's wife had collapsed in a heap on the floor, sobbing hysterically.

"We like rules. They are fun to have because then you get to break them."

"What rules do you live by then, Severed Head?"

"Wouldn't you like to know?"

"My brother is already married," I pointed out, returning reluctantly to the point.

"But if he renounces all mortal bonds, he will not be." The nasty snickering began again. "Oh, I do so love drama. I wish I could watch this one play out in full. To be part of a Three Day Bind, ah could the afterlife truly be so good?"

"What if the person stolen were married to a Wittenbrand?" I asked him. I needed this last answer quickly. Things had devolved behind me. An earthen tankard crashed against the wall, and Svetgin was cursing so loudly it was a wonder I could hear Grosbeak at all.

"Well, it wouldn't count as a marriage then, that's understood. The rest of the bargain would still need to be fulfilled, and lands and lives still exchanged, but I do rather feel the audiences would find it a cheap trick. It's not as much fun as a marriage."

"Fun aside, it would still be binding?"

"I never put fun aside."

I shook the bag.

"Fine. Yes. Binding."

Well, then. I drew in a deep breath and turned just in time to step hastily aside and avoid a second flying tankard.

My brother cut off mid-curse, shocked to realize he'd almost hit me, and I took the opportunity to step forward and speak with an authority I did not feel.

"No one needs to be fed to lions or turned out to die of starvation. Not today, at least."

Chapter Seven

"NO, NOT TODAY," my brother said bitterly, collapsing back into his chair. He snatched a decorative egg from the table beside him – a gift from the court of Salamoore – tracing the gilding with a finger. "Tomorrow. Tomorrow she will return."

"Return? She is not here?" I asked and he finally met my eyes, and for just a moment there was a look of brotherhood there. No one in our land knew the Wittenhame nor the denizens within it the way we two did. Far from my tingling excitement, his eyes held only swirling horror.

"She will return when she comes for me on the roof tomorrow night. I'm not even to have your hasty wedding, Izolda. I'm to be snatched away like a callow youth stolen by a great monster." He ran a hand through his thinning hair. It was always strange to think he'd once been younger than me. Now, he was a man in his forties, and I was not yet thirty.

"You're of a dramatic turn tonight, Svetgin," I said coolly. On the floor, Emelina had collapsed into breathless sobs, trembling, but mercifully silent.

"I love it," Grosbeak hissed from his bag. "Drama. Misery. Risk. Mmmwaaa."

"Did your ferret speak?" Volkov asked, watching the creature frolic in the mouth of the bag with drunk wonder on his face. His blue eyes were alight, his mustache twitching.

I was spared having to answer when Svetgin cut him off.

"Of course, I'm dramatic, sister. I was there with you. I saw everything. I will not be pinned to a pole and made a target for throwing knives. I will not be wrapped again in dead spirits." He took a long drink. "I still feel their hands on me sometimes upon a night, still feel their whispers and corpse-like caresses." Emelina shuddered as if absorbing his words. He did not modulate them for her sake. "I will not be led around like a trophy on a leash for her pleasure. I will not be degraded." He was bright red now. "I'm a man, not a beast. And I will not give up my lands or my people. I see only one solution." He snatched up his stein, stared at it miserably when he realized it was shattered beyond use, and then simply drank straight from the jug. "I must fall upon my sword – tonight – before she can come to claim me."

Emelina stopped sobbing, turning her wide eyes on Svetgin.

"The loyal wife. How touching," Grosbeak whispered as if this were all entertainment for his amusement.

How interesting that this was what made her *stop* sobbing.

"I swear, the ferret spoke," Volkov said staring at me blearily. His hand felt for the sword hilt at his waist wrapped in white silk and red ribbon.

"I think you forget, brother of mine," I said calmly, "that there is more than one royal in this palace."

My brother's eyes flicked sharply to his wife and to his credit, drunk as he was, he straightened in his chair, puffed out his chest, and said, "I will defend my wife and children to the last drop of my blood."

"Very noble, I'm sure," I murmured before saying more clearly. "Shall I remind you, Svetgin, that I am also of your blood? Royal, though the court may not like to admit it. Available, despite my marriage to the Lord Riverbarrow."

Svetgin shivered at that. We did not speak of Bluebeard. The mention of him still left my brother trembling with rage and then spewing up his breakfast all day. Our time together in the Wittenbrand had left acid wells in his heart and mind that if touched at all, overflowed in ill humors.

I made my voice firm and steady. "There is nothing in the missive that would disqualify me from taking your place."

"No!" The muffled protest was from my bag. "That spoils the whole thing! It should be a three-day marriage, not an empty human puppet theatre. Why drag me from the depths only to corrupt the epic of the ages before my rotting eyes?"

"I'll bring the ferret with me, of course," I added dryly.

"Well. Well. Front row seats to a Three Day Bind? You mollify my fury. I accept."

It was all I could do to not roll my eyes.

"The ferret really did speak," Volkov said, pale as a ghost. He leapt up, lightning-fast, snatched the ferret from my bag, and dangled it before him by the scruff of its neck, peering into its eyes. "Speak, creature."

To Honey's credit – or what were we calling her now? Look and Despair. To Look and Despair's credit, she snarled and snapped at Volkov.

"If you don't mind, General," I said smoothly, "I'll keep my pet. I'll need him in the Wittenhame."

My blood hadn't pumped this fast in years. My cheeks flushed, blossoming of their own accord. My heart began to throb with song, building in my heart, layer on layer, as the familiar theme returned from the crypt it had been banished to. My feet itched to move. I was going back. Three Day Bind or Three Lifetime Doom, I did not care. I was going back. I could barely breathe.

"I should break the creature's neck," Volkov muttered. "It's witchcraft."

"It's so much worse than that. Trust me."

Volkov ran a hand over his face, ignoring my retort, and then thrust the ferret at me with a shake of his head as if he could shake away the memory. "The missive was addressed to the royal blood of Pensmoore, Savataz. I think she counts."

She. Like I was a breeding mare. Volkov always discounted my opinions and person. And no wonder. He was only a general because the good ones and the old ones were all dead. If they hadn't been, he'd still be a puppy of a lieutenant who only had his commission because his father was a minor noble and had bought it for him with a dozen good horses and a dozen bad.

He twisted his mustache between two fingers and watched me with glittering eyes, running a hand over his well-dressed chest as if to remind me of his rank. Most of the court was too dead to remember his past. The departure of my accurate memory would suit him perfectly.

I received Look and Despair back and dropped her into the bag. She popped up again, looking out. Beneath her, Grosbeak grunted.

Svetgin took the letter from my hand, his eyes not meeting mine. Shame burned hot in his cheeks. He read it – or looked like he was reading it. If I'd drunk as much as he had, I wouldn't be reading anything at all.

"It says the royal she takes will warm her bed," he said finally, miserably. "What do you say to that?"

"The wording is very specific. I must warm it. I could do that huddled in one corner with a knife in one hand and a cranky ferret in the other."

"It had better be me in the other hand or the deal is off," Grosbeak murmured. "It's front row seats or nothing."

"Witchcraft," Volkov whispered unsteadily. He reached for Svetgin's jug as if more alcohol would help his judgment.

"Your lands and title will be forfeit," Svetgin said, and I knew he was going to give in. He was just putting on a show for himself now.

"What lands?" I asked, spreading my hands.

He snorted.

I leaned forward, eyes steady. "And as to the title of Mad Princess, I have enjoyed it, but it does not well suit me. I don't gibber enough for the impressive role."

It was only in the silence that followed those words that I realized Emelina had quieted. She rose to her feet unsteadily.

"It says you'll renounce your mortal ties," she said, not hopefully, but challenging as if she didn't believe I'd do it.

"You keep assuming I will die in those three days," I said. But these words were making me nervous. It was my ties to Pensmoore that had made me doubly valuable to Bluebeard – more than anyone realized. That and my days. And I was gambling them both on my ability to survive the Wittenhame.

But either I took that gamble and found a way to free my husband before he died in the endless brine, or I lived out my moldering years here in the mortal world, slowly drying up until I snapped like old leather with the sure knowledge that I had been too late to save him.

I wasn't the self-sacrificing saint they thought I was. I wasn't doing this for my brother. I wasn't doing it in a fit of compassion for Emelina and her children. I was, very practically, killing a whole flock of birds with one arrow. If I could survive just three days – and nights, I should not forget the nights – in the home of Lady Tanglecott, then I could save my brother, his wife, their children, his kingdom, and so much more importantly, I could find a way to draw my husband back from the embrace of the sea. And I could go back to the Wittenhame.

If.

Svetgin blinked at me owlishly. Volkov's eyes were narrowed on the bag. I could barely keep my hands from trembling with excitement.

Emelina seemed the swiftest on the uptake – maybe because she was the most sober.

"Then we're saved." Her voice was small. Barely more than a whisper.

"I can't offer you up a third time," Svetgin said, his face crumpling. "What kind of a man would I be?"

"What kind were you when you gave me to the Sword?" I asked acerbically. He'd never actually apologized for that. I wasn't entirely sure he was sorry. It had been justified. He'd had the right of it. In his mind, at least.

"An honorable man," he gasped, and Emelina trod carefully over to him and put a hand on his shoulder.

"It's a practical solution," she said calmly, meeting my eyes a little fearfully as if she thought I might abandon this cause now that I saw it benefited her.

"You'll do this, then?" Svetgin asked me, his eyes thick with misery, as if even this salvation was worse than the original curse. And in a way it was, wasn't it? Would I not rob him of his manhood if I took this burden that was his to bear? "You'll take my place?"

And he looked like he was going to be ill. As if he both desperately wanted my assent, and also needed me to deny him.

"I will."

"Your oath on it. Double clasp."

I hesitated. If I took off my gloves, he would see my skeleton hand.

"No oath?" he asked, freezing now, his voice trembling.

I took a step back, carefully angling my body. "Come here and I'll give it."

I removed one glove, twisting just a little so his body would be between me and the other two. He joined me readily, hands already held out as I removed the second glove.

He froze at the sight of my skeleton hand, eyes wide with shock, I lifted a single eyebrow and he swallowed.

"Is something wrong?" Emelina's voice trembled.

"Nothing," Svetgin said hoarsely as he crossed his arms and I crossed mine and we clasped hands. He couldn't hide his wince at the feel of my bones between his flesh fingers.

"I swear on life and death to do what I have promised, to stand in your stead before Lady Tanglecott and the Wittenbrand," I said calmly.

"I accept your oath." His voice broke on the end and his eyes never left my hand until I'd covered it again.

His head hung like a whipped dog's when he turned from me, and Emeline wrapped an arm around him.

"You could build her a statue to honor her sacrifice," she said kindly.

"In the square?" he asked looking up at her with boyish hope.

I went ahead and rolled my eyes this time. "I won't require a statue."

"In silver?" Svetgin asked, leaning toward his wife. He looked exactly like a man who had spent the night drinking now that he was relieved of his burden.

"In any material you like, my love," Emelina said, leading him toward the door. He leaned heavily on her light frame, and I knew she couldn't help her satisfied smile. After all, she was getting everything she wanted – safety and position for herself and her children, no risk to her husband, and an annoying rival removed forever.

"Volkov." Svetgin's order was bleary as they reached the doorway. "See to my sister's well-being. We don't want anything to happen to her. Her sacrifice tomorrow will save us all. See to it she has whatever she wishes."

"Hold on!" I objected but he was already gone. Volkov took a step toward me, and I didn't like the calculated look in his eye. I seized the ferret from the bag and held it up toward him in the most threatening manner I could manage. "I think I'll be going to my rooms."

"Or we could chew his ears off." Grosbeak snickered nastily. "It's not fun feeling them ripped apart so slowly. Trust me."

Volkov swallowed three times and I was almost certain it was bile he was fighting down.

"I think that would be best," he said, when he could finally speak, staring at Look and Despair, his face green as my old enemy, the sea. "I'll place a pair of guards at your door and two more on the roof watching your window. You'll be safe until tomorrow night. Or tonight, I suppose, if dawn is already here. I can never tell in this accursed hidden room. Ask them for whatever you need, but please keep that demon in your bag. Pensmoore is cursed enough already."

I left with my heart in my throat. I was going to the Wittenhame. And all I had to do to win my husband back was just not die. I was reasonably sure I could manage that. I'd done it quite well for twenty-six years now. What were three more days?

Chapter Eight

IN THE INKY MIDNIGHT SKY, the moon hung as a brass sliver just over the edge of the horizon as if someone had carved free the edge from a button and then tried to tuck it behind the hills for safekeeping.

I'd watched a moon just like it once with my mother before the Everburn feast in the dead of winter, only then, the two of us had scraped frost from a small, glazed window instead of standing on the palace roof. We had looked out over the slumbering hills where the herds of horses slept, silent before the great silence of a sleeping world. Now, I stood overlooking sleeping Pensmoore, its shops and smithies, warehouses and taverns, and inns and homes spread out all around me like a rumpled blanket after sleep. They were frosted with snow and wreathed in hearth smoke and in every one of them dwelled a living being who was counting on me right now, though they did not know it. What would my mother have thought of that?

Likely, she would have had a story for this, too. Not one about catching the firebird or riding the ice dragon, but one about a girl with a savage heart who was about to wrestle a blizzard into submission. I wished, for what might be the thousandth time, that I could see her again. Of all that I had lost, I missed her most of all.

I'd slept most of the day away. A person did that when they were truly exhausted. The sleep had been fitful and left me raw and edgy, as it did that when you weren't quite exhausted enough to block out fear of what came next.

Grosbeak's loud snoring had not helped.

I had refused the many gifts Svetgin offered through the afternoon, taking only a large black wolf cloak trimmed with rabbit, an embroidered woolen overcoat, and a pair of thick black boots. If I had to wait on the palace roof at midnight, at least I was dressed for it.

"You should have killed the general before we left. You saw how he was watching you like a goat staked out for wolves. It's a fool who leaves a living enemy behind him," Grosbeak muttered for the ninetieth time. "Also, the ferret stinks."

I was resting against a parapet, grateful that while much of the roof was peaked and shingled in cedar to shed the snow, Pensmoore still had battlements.

"She said midnight," I hissed, though why I was whispering was anyone's guess. No one else was here. I'd refused the escort. Why should they freeze up here with me? If she even arrived this decade, she'd be on time for the Wittenbrand – and besides, I didn't want to give her options. She was bound to be upset when she realized it was me here. Best to leave her with no other mortal she could snatch in my place.

I clung to her too-pale missive as if it were a ticket of passage. It was, in a way. A ticket to opportunity.

"Did you know they stink?" Grosbeak pressed.

"Everyone knows that." I wiggled my frozen toes and focused again on the errant moon. Did it belong with the silver stars? They seemed an unmatched set. As unmatched as me and the elegant Tanglecott. How would she collect me from way up here? I'd made my way out onto this part of the parapet from a window, but we did not keep it clear in winter and with this ice and snow, one misstep would send a girl falling straight to her death in a way that even the encrusted snow and dancing lights of the city could not charm from my head.

Below, the sound of song drifted up. I did not begrudge Svetgin his merrymaking. But laughter and song did not fit my mood. Anxiety suited me more. Could I live three days in the Wittenbrand surrounded only by those most hostile to me? I'd barely survived last time and that was with help.

Grosbeak growled in his hiding spot. "Ferrets don't taste like food, either. I tried it. Nasty thing."

That explained some of the noises coming from the bag, but since neither of them was dead, I hoped they'd sorted out their differences.

"I know not why you have chosen to doom us both back to hell, Izolda, but I must admit I relish the thought. To be back in the action. To once more watch the princes fight and dance over mortal souls. Ah, but I have missed it."

Something fluttered in the air above me and I looked up to see a small bird battling the gusty wind. Was that an orange breast I saw? It was too late in the year for an oriole, and yet this one flew, battered and rolled by the wind, clutching something in one clawed foot that fluttered madly in the gusty wind.

"You act as though you were beneath the sea for an age, and yet you tell me it was a mere two days," I said wryly. My toes were so frozen I could not feel them and the skin on my cheeks was tight and sore. How was that summer bird flying in this weather?

"Yes," Grosbeak said as if it were a curse. "Days! Days out of the game. Who knows how many moves we've missed?"

The bird fell from the sky so suddenly that I gasped, certain he'd been shot with an arrow or died of the cold before my eyes. He fell, spiraling bonelessly, and I lunged forward to catch him in outstretched hands. My gasp caught in my throat as he looked up at me, his feathers ruffled by the icy blast of the wind. The bird chirped sharply and thrust its laden foot at me. Gently, I took the scrap of parchment from him and then cooing, tucked him into the large pocket of my overcoat under the fur cloak. He could warm up there. Though he might want to fly away before I went to the Wittenhame. No mortal creature could survive there long.

The oriole snuggled in, tucking his wings around his little body and his beak to his breast. I unrolled the parchment and read.

In falls of dew and howl of wind, there comes the cry of eagle grim,
Along the falls, the black bear waits, his sober eyes survey the brim,
But fiercer still, the visage of the one who stole my heart and love,
For only she can bid me die and bid me watch her steps above
This terrible monstrosity still echoes in the empty plot
Where once dwelt rib and heart. I grasp yet still she lingers though I rot.

I felt the last blood rush from my face and extremities. These words.

The voice behind them was as familiar as my own. I knew them though I knew not how I had received them. It was like receiving a letter from the dead.

Desperately, looking around as if I might be caught, I folded up the – what? Poem? Letter? Dare I say, *love letter*? – and tucked it inside my dress where it could sit next to my skin, my cheeks flaring hot.

"What's going on out there?" Grosbeak complained. "If there's drama unfolding I remind you that in my debt you are, and for that debt, you must pay."

"I'm not in your debt," I told him breathlessly as I coaxed the bird from my pocket and carefully set him in a nook at the base of the parapet. He shivered there, but better for him to shiver here than to die in the Wittenhame. Poor brave little soul to have brought this to me. But how had he found it? He was no sea creature, and he certainly was no diver. Could my drowned husband have sent him to bear this last present to me from some other place? And if he had, what did it mean? Was it a last goodbye?

I dared not dwell on it.

A sound like fabric being torn made my spine shiver and then the snow rose in a swirling gust, blocking out all sight of the roof and the city and even the brass sliver of moon.

As the snow settled silently, a carriage was revealed, hanging in the air as if it, too, were a moon and pulled by four harnessed snow lions, their wings extended and their eyes glittering with hatred. Rather than proper leather harnesses, the bonds holding them were merely wisps of smoky cloud. One of them snapped at me, barely held back by that meager binding. I danced to the side, almost losing my footing on the narrow battlement. Down at the end of the parapet was the carving of a cat just like that mist lion but without the wings – for all the help that good luck charm was providing now.

I swallowed my unease and gasped as the coachman bowed to me, revealing he had no head. His collar flapped around his absent neck like a tattered flag.

"I believe we've found your match, Grosbeak," I said, a little unsteadily.

His snicker was unsettling. "How rude. I'd rather eat a pair of golden scissors than be attached to *that*."

I felt my eyebrows rising, even more so as they trailed to the carriage.

It was a pumpkin.

Occasionally, the Pensmoore countryside will produce large pumpkins in strange oblong shapes, their bulk more fascinating than beautiful. As they grow, they seemed to pale, as if form and color could only be found in limited quantities and must be stretched and watered down to extend to the larger parts of the pumpkin. This pumpkin was not like those. Perfectly rotund, deeply, duskily orange, edged in frost and crusted snow, it was an imposing, ridged gourd. In the side of it, in lieu of windows, someone had carved a garish face that looked so much like Grosbeak that I almost pulled him free to compare the two.

A hand – lily-white, naked, bearing a single silver serpent ring – reached out the mouth of the pumpkin. I passed the letter to her, saying nothing.

"Ah," the cultured voice said, sounding satisfied as the hand withdrew into the pumpkin's mouth. The way she formed each word was sultry and seductive and I was utterly immune. "You've agreed, then? A Three Day Bind with a wager? Three enchanted nights and three spellbinding days – and if you still have your skin and your wits when you're through, you win your life back and one other besides. If you do not survive, then I gain your mortal fortunes."

Still, I remained silent. One false word and I might lose this chance.

"I bid your assent," she said, and there was hunger behind her cold words. "My oath is spoken, but now to bind us, you must speak your part. I will have it, royal. Do not forget the consequences if you do not agree to my generous terms."

My heart raced in my chest. This was it. My one chance. To take it, I would need all the cleverness and courage I'd ever possessed. I seized all my courage and held on tight.

"I assent," I said clearly. "Take me to your home, Lady Tanglecott."

"What is this?"

The carriage door was thrown open – the entire face of the pumpkin swinging outward to show the carved hollow of the interior where Lady Tanglecott sat. Strings of pumpkin flesh and smooth seeds the size of dinner plates swung from the coach ceiling.

She looked at me, aghast, her waterfall of golden hair seeming to stand almost on end and her eyes flashing bright. She hissed, her beautiful face turning viper-sharp.

"Wife of the Arrow. You were not the one sent for."

"Was I not?" I asked grimly. "Am I not a royal of this land? I'm the Mad

Princess of Pensmoore – as royal as I am odd. Specificity is the friend of legal documents."

Her curses were like black diamonds, perfect and cutting. Quickly then, before she could think of a way to wriggle out of her contract, I slipped into the carriage, dodged a swinging seed, and closed the pumpkin door behind me, my heart in my throat. This was my only chance, and I'd only get it if I rode in – white-knuckled though I might be! – and took it.

Pumpkin carriages are exactly as disgusting inside as one would think – even frozen ones. Strands of pumpkin flesh solidified in thick ropes where they ringed our seats, while the seats were constructed of rib cages shoved into the pumpkin flesh and frozen in place and then swathed in layers of deer hides, fur side up. To my relief, the rib cages also seemed like deer, though scraps of flesh still clung to them just like the scraps of flesh clinging to the pumpkin interior as if both were butchered by a careless hand – or possibly a hand wielded by a body with no head. I was more grateful than ever that everything was frozen.

Lady Tanglecott's mouth remained open at my boldness as I settled myself opposite her. The paleness of her face blushed the slightest dawn pink. She'd dressed to kill – if I was a man – in gossamer fabric so light I could see her every curve and valley under the folds of it. The edges shimmered when they caught the light and a cloak of sealskin sewn in luxurious strips cushioned her bottom and would hold back the cold if she but drew it around her. I did not want to know what my brother might have thought of this obvious enticement, were he here in my place.

Personally, I had no interest in the form of her body or what she was so obvious in offering with it – but I *was* interested in the key dangling from her neck on a golden chain. It was silver. I'd seen its kind before.

Lightning fast, I reached across from my bench, snaked my hand into her bodice, caught the key, and pulled it forth, twisting it in the air before she could open her mouth and scream.

The carriage juddered as if suddenly swept up in a blizzard, rolling hard to one side so we were thrown into the pumpkin walls. Thank goodness I had left the bird behind. The ferret shrieked with alarm. Half-rotted vegetable scent filled my nose despite the frost, and then we were righted as the nightmares seared across our minds, spinning us into madness, sifting us down to threads of persons, and reweaving madly like a grandmother intent on having completed gifts by Yearswatch Night.

"I'll wring your neck. I'll wring it!" I didn't know if the threat was Tanglecott or Grosbeak.

I was Izolda and not Izolda. My heart was buried in the sea. No, it was queen of the mountain. No, it was black as the night without stars. My family were there and then gone, dead a thousand ways and screaming in in my mind, on and on and on. My throat raced to catch up, my scream competing with the matching screams of Lady Tanglecott and Grosbeak, and then the carriage juddered again, and spun, end on end, so we were flung against opposite curved walls of thready vegetable. It struck something so hard we shuddered, spun, and then stopped abruptly.

When a pumpkin bursts, it falls into gory plant pieces and even a frozen one is no exception. Bits of orange flesh coated my face, hair, and wolf coat. More settled in wet pulp over Lady Tanglecott whose curses had grown more vicious.

My bag had spun away and sat now on its own shred of pumpkin as Look and Despair peeked out the top as if expecting a hail of arrows incoming. Beneath her, Grosbeak's string of curses melded in harmony with our lady kidnapper's.

I picked myself up from the tangle of rib cages and deer hide and pumpkin. The walls had fallen outward when the carriage burst apart and the roof with the long curling stem had fallen between Lady Tanglecott and I like a trophy for a game not yet played.

Who would win? I wondered.

We'd crashed into the sacred monument, the un-drawable arrow stuck into the rock before us. Only this time, there was no white marble altar – only a great lump of black, twinkling rock, and the white flames that once roared around the arrow were only caught by the corners of my eye when I turned my head, as if they had become specters.

This time, our arrival was not met with an unearthly chorus, but with the woeful beating of ominous drums, starting low and soft and slow so that I thought they were only the beating of my heart. Gradually, they gathered speed and sound until they produced in me a terrible foreboding.

And this was not the clearing in the forest where first I'd seen that arrow. I looked around me, bewildered by the clifftop we'd crashed upon. Scant grasses blew in the wind along a cliff's edge and in ragged patches nearby. Small tumbles of the same black rock were dotted across the grass, but the world below the cliff was naught but mist and treetops, and the world behind faded into fog in the same way.

"Three Days in my house," Lady Tanglecott said, spitting the words. "And Three Nights in my bed. This was the bargain."

"I read it," I said, boldly. And perhaps the madness had taken me this time because my heart was soaring. Every color was brighter, every sound clearer, every pain more focused. I was in the Wittenhame. It tasted like hot coffee after a night with no sleep.

"And you must survive each one," Tanglecott said, drawing herself to her feet, flicking a piece of pumpkin from her cheek, and then gathering her swirling seal cloak around her.

"My life is not my own," I told her steadily. "It was bought with a price, and I will repay the buyer."

His words echoed in my mind, *This terrible monstrosity still echoes in the empty plot, Where once dwelt rib and heart.*

She laughed then, condescending and waspish. "You'll have a hard time fulfilling that bargain, mortal woman. You have my invitation, but you'll have to find my door to enter my house, and find my room to enter my bed, and I wish you luck in doing what no mortal ever has."

She snapped her fingers, and her four harnessed lions were suddenly there, their feet kicking up pumpkin debris and their four heads snapping in four different directions. She took up their reins, snapped the spectral threads within her palms, and they sped away and into the fog, somehow drawing her along behind them as if her feet were shod with runners from a sleigh.

And this time it was my turn to look around me fruitlessly. I had assumed she would take me to her house. I had guessed wrong.

"I have never liked pumpkins," Grosbeak said miserably. "They feel like they should be combined with beans and cinnamon and steaming milk, but I can't for the life of me decide why."

"That sounds utterly terrible," I said, scooping up his bag.

"I saw it in a vision of hell once," he said dreamily. "Perhaps I will open my own ale cart and sell them to the folk."

"You'd need hands for that," I said absently, turning in a circle and looking for tracks. Lady Tanglecott had left none. I was on my own.

"You'll be my hands for me. After all, you'll need to pay someone to tell you where Lady Tanglecott lives. And you'll have to offer me something valuable to get me to tell."

"What if I offered you a continued adventure?"

He cursed. "I'd hoped for more, but we've already established that you have a poor imagination. And I did promise your drowned husband that I wouldn't intentionally kill you."

"How sweet."

"I thought so."

Chapter Nine

"THE QUESTION IS NOT how you'll find her house," Grosbeak said as I finished picking shreds of pumpkin pith from our faces and hair, "but how you'll get in. She would not have dared you to try if she thought it easy."

I picked up the bag again and slung it over my shoulder. It was not winter in the Wittenhame, though it was night. A dusky breeze blew the small flowers of the hilltop, tussling them like curls, and the warmth was already melting the frozen edges of the pumpkin. The fog should have paled everything around us, but the colors were sharp and vivid, and my heart sang with anticipation at the sight of them.

I paused, taking a moment to stare at the silver arrow plunged into the stone. It seemed too normal, too average to be a portent of disaster and yet it drew me toward it – my gaze, my thoughts, even my feet.

Without meaning to, I was already pacing toward it when Grosbeak said, "We have but a few hours until day and then you'll need to be in her house. Not long to solve a puzzle, mortal girl, and you'll need all the time you can get."

"Is it far from Bluebeard's home?" I asked, holding my breath as I climbed the jagged black stone and reached delicately toward the silver arrow. I ran my fingers up the shaft. It trembled at my touch – or perhaps I trembled at its touch – and for a bare moment the song that had been sung here for my prince of the Wittenhame seemed to echo in a perfect note in the air or perhaps in my heart, tuned in such a way that my whole self vibrated with it. The fletching under my fingers' touch felt almost real for all that it was silver. On a whim, I gripped the shaft of the arrow and pulled.

"What is near? What is far?" Grosbeak intoned.

I hadn't expected movement, but to my surprise, I felt the tiniest shift in the arrow. My imagination, of course. I was too excited not to be seeing things. I was strung like a ready violin now that I was within the Wittenhame. It was as if it had robbed me of all my brightness these past seven years, leaving me pale and desolate while it stored up that vibrant emotion here in storehouses already brimming.

Perhaps that was why I couldn't help myself any more than I could have stopped Grosbeak from spewing obscenities and insults. I tried to pull the arrow again, face flushing hot at my own temerity.

The arrow did not move. It was locked solidly in the rock. Whatever response I'd thought I'd felt was mist and ashes.

Grosbeak snickered. "I told you no one gets it out, but oh no, you thought to prove we immortals foolish with your mortal might. And you're not just any frail mortal but a prematurely elevated lesser noble who spends the only time she has weeping and haunting the barren shores like a sad scrap of ghost because the man who kidnapped her lies under the waves. Pathetic."

I drew in a patient breath. I needed Grosbeak to guide me, or if he would not, then I needed to seek Bluebeard's house and if I could get in, I might consult his Wall of Wisdom to get answers. That must be a last resort for me. It would take up valuable hours with no guarantee that the house would even let me in.

"How may I arrive at Lady Tanglecott's house, decapitated warrior?" I asked formally.

Grosbeak made a rude sound. "You've given your heart to the barrow, that's sure enough, but at least you kept your head. Get it? Kept your head?"

"It's not a very good joke," I said coldly. "And I asked you a question."

He looked away coldly, intoning as if he were speaking funereal rites, "Your head knows he's a bad bet, but your heart keeps saying otherwise."

"The way to the Lady's house," I demanded, refusing to acknowledge his japes.

This time he turned a look of vitriol to me. "You don't want to end up head-ed in the wrong direction."

"What I lack in imagination, you lack in a sense of humor," I said, crossing my arms. "Is there any end to this? Immortal, you may be, but who knows where you'll end up if I fail this Three Day Bind."

His tone turned to one of impatience as if I had interrupted his fun. "Just snap your fingers and think about what you love about Lady Tanglecott and you'll arrive immediately on her doorstep."

"And if there is nothing that quickens my heart about her?"

"Then you'll have to walk. There's a reason that almost no one uses that trick."

I screwed up my face and tried to think. I did love her sense of fashion. She looked gorgeous all the time. It was not a trait we shared. I concentrated on her pretty dresses and closed my eyes.

"Your efforts are pale as a twice-dead fish."

On the island of Burning Guilt, she'd been a fearsome thing as she made that secret contract to battle my Bluebeard. A hand snaked around my mouth – the specter, of course. But yes, I admired that about her. Maybe even loved it, because if I played my cards right and brought her down it would force a toppling of her whole alliance.

"Acceptable effort, mistress mine."

I opened my eyes to see we'd moved. We were deep in the Wittenhame under the canopy of massive trees that always made me feel like a toadstool or a mouse. Their leaves were too high to hear the rustle of the wind, and yet still, I fancied I heard it. Before us, a still lake lay, cloaked lightly in mist and in the moss of the bank facing it, I almost thought I saw the face of the Bramble King before it was suddenly gone, lost in the darkness of the fading night.

I shivered, but it was only half fear that made me shiver, the other half was still anticipation. Three days and three nights and if I played my hand well, I would have my husband in my arms. I swallowed against a dry throat, hands shaking with overexcitement.

A tiny bird chirped in a tree nearby – warbling in a way unfamiliar to me.

Someone had fixed a bill to a nearby tree where it depicted a pair of knights in full joust armor tilting at one another in what might be the most elaborate woodcut I'd seen. I could almost feel the roar of the crowd shown around them. I squinted in the darkness and made out the word "JOUST" decorated with flourishes – some of which looked a little too much like twisted bodies and tortured souls. Beneath the woodcut were the words, "Brave Fools Only. All Comers Unwelcome."

"What an expensive woodcut to make just to tell people not to come," I said grimly. "Where is the house?"

At the word, "house" a pair of doors appeared hovering over the edge of the lake where it met the shore – still as water in a drinking glass. The doors were made of mist, barely discernable in the moonlight, but one thing about them was certain. I'd never seen doors like this before.

The bird's long song trilled out a second time.

"Bellies of Mortals, you're stingy with the information. Are you looking at an invitation to a joust?" Grosbeak said from within his bag.

"It's hardly an invitation. It specifically said not to come."

I examined the doors. They each bore a half-ring pull but the pulls moved and were held in place by a complicated device in the shape of a swooping owl on one side and a leaping salmon on the other. Both hands were required to move the owl, though the piece slid easily like a well-greased geared lock. I moved the bird form with authority and pulled, but though I heard the snick of a latch opening, the other door still held this one in place.

"Well, that settles it," Grosbeak said firmly. "We are going to that joust one way or another."

"You wish to ride in the lists? I suppose you would make a target that was difficult to strike."

I released the owl and moved to the salmon. A ridiculous pair. An owl should be paired with a mouse or a songbird and an eagle or osprey with the salmon. Behind me, the visiting songbird sang his song as if to emphasize this. These two designs were not of the same kind at all. I placed my hands on the heavy salmon device, but as I shifted it to unlatch this side of the door, the owl shunted back down into a locked position.

A frustrated sound escaped my throat and I moved back to the owl, only to have the salmon slip back to its original spot.

"Ride? You mock me." Grosbeak sniffed. "But the spectacle! The grisly deaths and broken hearts! Perhaps, I will bargain with you, and you'll ride in my place for honor and the token of a lady."

"I care not for the tokens of ladies. I have plenty of my own handkerchiefs, thank you."

I stretched across the spirit door, accidentally slipping into the ankle-deep water as I tried to reach both handles at once. My arms were not wide enough. The arms of a grown man would not be.

A nasty chuckle rang out from my bag. "See? Not so easy, is it? I warned you, but no, for you it's all heart and no head."

"Don't tempt me to drown you in the lake."

"Don't think I wouldn't like it. I have a mermaid waiting for me still."

I ignored him and stepped back. There must be another door somewhere. With a sigh, I resigned myself to hiking around the shore looking for it.

A flutter of wings was my only warning and then soft feathers brushed my cheek as something settled on my unoccupied shoulder. A piece of parchment floated down, and then another brush of wings and as I turned to follow the motion, I saw a bird very much like a small chickadee bobbing through the trees.

I scooped up the missive. It smelled of brine and something like cloves.

That's my last wife watching you with granite
eyes and iron spine. I call her my late
wonder. Her dark suspicions my days lit
and then she was plucked out my arms by fate.
And so, I mourn. My plans hollow with her
Gone, my power lost in her spooled out days.
But love smolders hot in my soul and spurs
Me cling to her and treasure her strange ways.
Forget me not, sharp maiden of ordered
mind. Hold me in your heart as my last breath,
tickles the memory that once bordered
on the divine and shatters me in last rest.

I paused. If these were real and from his hand then it worried me that my husband was spending his last moments sending me these love letters by bird when he ought to be thinking about how he could escape his bonds before he drowned beneath the sea. Wouldn't that be the practical thing to do?

What worried me was that much like Prince, much like my dear mother, my husband was never practical. He may indeed end up drowning beneath the waves while finding a second rhyme for "bordered." I gritted my teeth together. It was up to me to go get him. I was the only one with any sense left to do it.

"What did you mean when you teased me that I'd given my heart to the barrow?" I asked Grosbeak as I made my way along the edge of the lake. I was starting to worry about that phrasing.

"A barrow is a grave," Grosbeak said as if I was a child.

"I know that." As I crept along the shore, the door vanished entirely. Panicked, I backtracked, and it appeared again. Well then. I'd need to be right on top of any alternate entrances for them to show themselves. And I only had a few hours.

"And your husband is a dead man."

A chill shot through me. "I thought you said he still lives."

Could the birds be bringing me messages from beyond the grave? My heart twinged at the thought.

"Well, he did when I saw him. And that was what ... days ago in the mortal world? Which could be years here. How long do you think he can live under the sea with his magic gone? You can't live on the echo of it forever. If I was a betting man – and oh, but I am – then I'd bet he is very, very dead and here you are pining for a dead man, risking your entire future on a splinter-thin chance at receiving his corpse back from the sea. Or perhaps only his bones. I'm sure they're lovely and white but hardly worth all this trouble."

My stomach suddenly felt sour. I wished I had not eaten before we left. The scent of pumpkins clung too heavily to us and every waft of it left my nose curling and lips twisting.

"So that's why I tease that you've given your heart to the barrow, for never has such a thing been so apparent. It could inspire a minstrel – if there were any looking for a miserable story about two fools."

"Silence yourself and help me find the door," I muttered. The Wittenhame seemed leached of color now and the sourness of my belly had crept up to my mouth.

"There won't be another door. More fool you are for looking for one with the moon sinking like all your hopes."

His voice rang too full of truth to deny him. Besides, I knew he wouldn't bother lying to me about this. His fate was sewn to mine. Sink me and he sank himself. Irritable, I tromped back around the edge of the lake, my wet foot bothering me. Each footstep was a *squelch* that only reminded me of my failure to open the ghost door. Flowers woke along the path I trod, their drowsy heads rising, opening – as if to look at me – and then tumbling back to slumber. Even they knew better than to get their hopes up about me.

"I can't open the door," I grumbled. "My arms are not wide enough."

"No matter how wide they were, the handles would simply move out of reach," Grosbeak said amiably. "'Tis a friendship door and can only be opened with the help of a friend, of whom you have precious few."

"I rather wonder that Lady Tanglecott is fit to open her own door, then," I said, letting a tinge of bitterness seep into my tone.

Grosbeak snickered. "It seems you're more friendless yet, but don't let me stop your salty chatter. I crave bitterness as the hummingbird craves nectar. I have sorely missed it."

"And here I thought you were already filled to overflowing with the draught. I should point out that despite your insults, you are my friend. Or at least I thought you were."

"If it is friendship you need from me, you have it already," Grosbeak grumbled. "If it's hands then I'm afraid you helped bury mine years ago. You'll need someone whose appendages are still unrotted – or at least attached."

Here he gave my gloved hand a pointed look. I flinched. I kept forgetting about it. It was easy to forget with the gloves cloaking my deformity.

"A friend," I said, wary. I glanced up at my shoulder but the specter drew back, hands raised defensively. She was not my friend, clearly.

The forest was of no assistance. No helpful fauns played pipes near this place. No dryads lingered near the water's edge. No strapping young shepherd boys. Less fancifully, none of the Wittenbrand could be seen or heard to be debauching themselves anywhere close or even snoring in the dead of the night.

Friends were in short supply.

I swallowed and looked down.

"I don't suppose you can help me?" I asked the ferret.

Under my questioning gaze, it chittered and disappeared into the bag.

"No, not there! That's my neck, you horrible rat! Izolda, what are my sins that you have judged and condemned me to be eaten a morsel at a time by the lowest of creatures?"

I bit my lip. Think, Izolda, think. What do you have that might work? Perhaps a bit of twine that could hold the latch in place?

"I can see you thinking about wedging the door with a stick or tying it with rope or some other mortal nonsense," Grosbeak said in a muffled voice. "Were it so that life in all her tangles be so simple, but this door is a magic portal, my *friend*," he spat that last word, "and it will only open when its eldritch conditions are met. Find a friend with hands, or risk dying nastily when you fail to enter this house by dawn. I'd say you have an hour, but what do I know?"

So, no mortal items. I still had a ferret and a talking head. The head was, clearly, worthless. I had made my way to the part of the shore where the door was visible. I looked now from the latch to the ferret. Even a highly trained ferret could not possibly manipulate those latches. They took two hands. I'd need a human helper and even a one-handed one would not be enough.

I bit my lip. I would not curse or cry with frustration. I would think. Despite Grosbeak's childish jokes, I always used my head first. Where could I find a friend in the Wittenbrand where I had no people, no home, not even a room to my name.

Wait.

A room.

The words of the poem I'd just read echoed in my head "*That's my last wife watching you.*"

Swallowing, I slipped the key for the Room of Wives from around my neck.

"Going to record your failures in your little book?"

I ignored Grosbeak and turned the key.

The room was *exactly* as I'd last left it seven years ago, bloodstains and all. The women who had once been married to my husband lined the hall, their faces lifeless, their perfect bodies posed like statues, their garb rich and vibrant as they no longer were.

"Your fascination with this place is revolting," Grosbeak muttered as I hurried within. I must be quick. There was no guarantee this crazy idea would work. "You should talk to someone. Perhaps a draught of poppy milk would help. Or the smoke of a cypher tree. Anything but all this lingering in a magic crypt."

"What would you say a friend *is* Grosbeak?" I asked as I ran down the hall to the hourglass full of garnets. There were so many more in the bottom than there had been before. Seven years more. It snatched my breath away like an ill-timed wind.

"Someone who doesn't kill you on sight," Grosbeak said with a grin that rivaled the jack-o-lantern carriage.

"Then all the mortal world is my friend," I said dryly. I snatched up a garnet from the hourglass, trembling at the feel of it in my palm, and gasping at the wall of nausea that hit me when I took the gem. The last time I'd done this, things had gone very poorly. But I had a possible hour – maybe less – to make a friend and very few candidates.

"Someone whose loyalty you can purchase for a sum within your means," he suggested.

"Ah, now we are closer," I agreed, hurrying down the line of Bluebeard's former wives. "Let us both hope I can pay the price."

I paused in front of Tigrane now, Bluebeard's war-like bride, and then reconsidered, circling back to where Princess Margaretta stood in her hourglass perfection.

I scrambled up onto her plinth, awkward with my bag of severed head and ferret and my heavy wolfskin cloak. She was a tiny little thing, delicate as spun glass.

"Take my day and be my friend," I muttered, trying to put the gem into her hand.

"Try the mouth," Grosbeak said unexpectedly. There was a strange tinge of anticipation in his voice as he realized what I was trying to do. "She could hold it there."

It felt wrong to force the gem between her lips, but not as wrong as a messy death and the loss of all hope would be.

I popped the garnet between her full pouting lips and held my breath.

I expected a slow awakening and possibly gratitude.

I did not expect the sudden scream that sent me flying from the plinth and landed me on my back.

Chapter Ten

I BLINKED up at the ceiling, the painted angels and demons on it leering down at me as if they might laugh with the same hoarse wheeze that Grosbeak was laughing.

"She startled you, oh well done, Arrow's wife!" he chortled.

I shook my head like a fighter trying to knock off the blow and forced my shaken body back to its feet. Who knew if she might try again?

Margaretta quivered before me, her deathly pale skin flushed bright rose and her tiny hand raised to cover a wide, open mouth. Shock led her eyebrows to climb higher than I thought possible.

Her voice was tiny as a mouse. "This is not what he promised me! Oh dear."

She sneezed and spat the garnet out and instantly froze in place.

I ran to where it rolled across the floor, picked it up, wiped it on my skirt – ugh, it was still wet – and placed it back between her lips.

This time, I caught her shoulders as she sneezed again.

"Dear me!" her squeak was so like something Princess Chasida might make. Though Chasida hated me, and I had some hope that Margaretta would not.

"Margaretta, Princess of Pensmoore," I said firmly. "I have given you one of my days. Spit it out again and it will not be offered a third time."

Her eyes were wide as a frightened hare as her lips shrank to a rosebud and both delicate hands moved to cover them.

"You can talk," I said, trying to be patient. "Just keep the garnet in your mouth."

"Mine were sapphires," she said, moving the garnet to her cheek in a way that only slightly disguised her speech. "But who are you? Is it time to wake?"

Her eyes danced around the room, little smiles lighting at each wife she saw. "Oh! You're a wife, too!" Everything she said sounded like an exclamation. I watched her, fascinated. "You are breaking the rules and the bargain if you're stealing your own days. You really shouldn't do that," she said shaking her head violently. "You really shouldn't. No."

"Could you pick one with a brain?" Grosbeak said. "Hands might not be enough if she can't think enough to operate them."

"It's for a good purpose," I said slowly as Grosbeak pulled an exaggerated bored face.

Margaretta was like a human butterfly. Utterly exquisite in looks, fluttering with every movement, and bumping up against the glass as if she didn't realize it was there.

"Oh. Well. I suppose you would know. Of what nation are you, Princess?"

"Pensmoore," I answered simply.

She gasped, wringing her hands. "But that's my country. You don't look like one of us! You don't."

"I am Izolda Savataz of Northpeak," I said calmly.

"Savataz? Mercy. Oh no. Mercy." She sat down hard on the ground, fanning her face.

"We really don't have time for hysterics," I said, watching her through the side of my eyes.

Grosbeak snickered so loudly I felt sure Margaretta would be insulted but she just kept fanning herself. "Next time, I pick which wife to wake. I, at least remember some of them."

"My family. My poor family. And all my friends. They must all have perished for so minor a house to have ascended." She looked up, horrified. "I mean no insult, of course."

I could probably tell her that her niece lived, but that might lead to more questions and more hysterics. Especially if she heard that our shared husband had killed Chasida's father. Who would be Margaretta's brother? Nephew? I couldn't remember. Best not to say.

"I require a friend," I said patiently. "Rather urgently."

"A friend." She drew in a long breath as if composing herself. "Yes. Of course."

She stood up, smiling again and curtseying to each wife. "I took such consolation from these dear girls. Each of them is just so precious."

She looked up at me docilely and I found I was without anything to say. What had Bluebeard thought of her? She was so ... sweet.

"Were you ... married long to the Arrow?" I tried, taking her hand and putting it on my arm as courtly ladies did in Pensmoore. She seemed to relax at the familiarity and allowed me to guide her toward the door.

"Oh, I don't know." She blushed prettily. "He sought neither my counsel nor my bed. I spent most of my time arranging flowers and embroidering. Perhaps you saw my hummingbird pillows?"

"Nevermind. I like this one," Grosbeak said as I walked her toward the door. "I could have danced her all across the Wittenhame and made her bend to my every whim if he'd let me near her. Imagine what she'd look like in a dress made of sewing needles and broken promises? I bet she'd still dance even through the pain. Just to be a nice girl."

"Then let's all be glad he did not," I said in a quelling tone. I needed to get Margaretta out the door and then back here as swiftly as possible. She was more delicate than I'd ever imagined.

"Who is that grim little voice?" Margaretta asked, quailing a bit at Grosbeak's leer through the tear in the bag.

"My pet, I'm afraid," I said.

"Oh dear." She looked at the mouth of the bag where Look and Despair had settled and then back down to the tear where Grosbeak's expression was visible and she bit her lip. "You're an animal lover, then?"

Grosbeak's chortle was disturbing.

"It would appear so," I said dryly.

I opened the top of it so she could see Grosbeak and the ferret. She blanched.

"I don't do well with *creatures.*" The last word was so faint I could barely make it out.

"Neither do I," Grosbeak said from the bag. "Not even fine ones with a perfectly turned ankle and a bosom as vast as the plains of Myygddo. Just so you know. They say you killed yourself, you know. Died by your own hand."

"I didn't mean to," Margaretta said, looking guilty. "The glass just broke."

We both looked over at the hourglass and I shuddered. I didn't want to hear more about that.

"Please," I pleaded. "I need your help. I must make haste."

"Yes. Yes, of course. I would love to help and after all," here she gave a very nervous titter. "I am living right now on borrowed time."

"Oh, good one," Grosbeak crowed from in the bag. "Not just a princess of Pensmoore but a princess of puns. Maybe she's the comedic character in this exciting narrative."

"I rather think you are." I leveled a disapproving gaze at him. "Though anyone who laughs at you must have a black, black heart."

"Do we really have to hurry? I'd love to stay and help the others," Margaretta asked, looking over her shoulder as I hustled her to the door.

"I'm doing this to save my brother," I said gravely. "And his wife and children."

Her face brightened. "They live still?"

"Yes," I said, face burning.

She nodded, looking very sober, and then she took my hand in her rose-petal soft ones. "He took that from all of us – family. Love. Devotion. If you still have a chance at it ..." She shook her head as her words drifted off. She looked around the room of wives as if memorizing each face. "I will help you. For them. For all of them."

"Thank you," I said, deflating a little in relief. "Can we hurry?'

"It seems we must. But can you ask your pet to be quiet? He worries me."

"I try, but no one listens to me, I'm afraid," I said, giving Grosbeak a pointed look.

"Oh dear," Margaretta said as I led her through the door.

We emerged onto the lakeshore, but we were no longer alone. A host of folk watched us in eerie silence. Antlered men with gaudy doublets and chains of goose-egg-sized jade beads stood beside winged women, pale and slender with hair like dandelions before they blow away, and these, in turn, were surrounded by men with deer legs or women sitting astride bullfrogs the size of carriages.

Every one of them was so still, so silent, that it made me bite my lip. It felt like the calm before the storm.

"Don't tell me your kind grows nervous when placed upon the stage," Grosbeak said with a cruel laugh.

"Stage?" I whispered.

"They've assembled to watch. Someone must have let slip there's a Three Day Bind. Every free soul in the Wittenhame will want a glimpse of it."

"There won't be much to see," I muttered. "Come on, Margaretta."

She moved to join me at the door, gripping the salmon where I held the owl, and I did not like the sensation that filled me as the silent crowd strained to watch and we disengaged the locks and opened the door together. I felt as though something slinking and slippery had crawled down my mouth and into my throat and lodged there and I did not like it. I did not want it there. I gasped and choked on my own breath as the doors opened and I stepped, unhurried, inside.

I could do this. I could do it for the chance to save the man with bird messengers and obscure verses.

"You don't want to be here," Margaretta said sympathetically as I tried to compose myself. "You feel trapped. Trust me. I know the feeling. It will pass."

"Thank you," I choked out. "Will you go back now to your pedestal?"

"I think you might need me for a bit longer. And we're practically sisters since we're both from Pensmoore."

She nodded gravely as if to impress on me the importance of our faux sisterhood while I tried to compose myself enough to breathe. I hadn't expected compassion. It was surprisingly touching. So much so that I hardly knew what to do with it.

Lady Tanglecott's entranceway was barely larger than a closet and completely dark. A door led further into her house – so close I could have reached out and touched both it and the front door at the same time. A light glowed around the edges of it, inviting me to move on. But I needed to breathe first.

In and out. Come on, Izolda. It wasn't practical to panic when I'd come so far already. It was just that now that I was in her house, I could see all the ways it might go wrong – and if I failed, I didn't just fail for me – I failed for him, too.

"The real entertainment is in here," Grosbeak said. "You saw the crowd wanting to get in. And I have front row seats! Ah, sweet afterlife, you have loved me well."

"Do you take him everywhere with you?" Margaretta asked, staring at my bag.

"He's less trouble when you keep him close."

Margaretta and Grosbeak snorted at the exact same moment.

"I've decided you need a friend very badly," Margaretta said, drawing her narrow shoulders back in a determined fashion. "And I think it will be me."

"I wouldn't get too attached. She'll only be here for a day," Grosbeak warned me and then turned to her. "You shouldn't get attached either. She's very hard on the rest of the cast in this little drama of hers."

I felt the beginning of the kind of smile that creeps up your face slowly like the dawn and I leaned into it, letting my gratitude for Margaretta wash over me, but before it had fully formed, the doors to the rest of the house were yanked open and golden light framed the silhouette of Lady Tanglecott in all her beauty.

She snapped her fingers and Margaretta disappeared.

Before I could even gasp, Lady Tanglecott intoned, "The Lord giveth and the Lady taketh away. I will not tolerate strays within my home. Come now, bound one, and receive your due."

After the silky sweetness of Princess Margaretta, her very presence was like a sharp slap. Like drinking vinegar after apple cider. Like biting into a heat pepper after a strawberry.

"I told you not to get too attached." Grosbeak snickered. He was getting his drama just like he'd hoped.

Chapter Eleven

"MY DUE?" The words were hardly out of my mouth before she threw something into my face – a powder, I thought. I sneezed and then the world went black.

I woke to the sound of lapping waves and the brightest sun I'd ever seen. It was as if a heavenly body had sprung to consciousness and arranged a personal vendetta against me.

I could not move, but I felt my limbs being kept in an awkward position. I was arranged so that I lay on my left side with my left shoulder and hip pressed against the ground. My right leg was bent so that it was standing on its foot, the knee in the air, my left leg sprawled where it had fallen on the ground. My right hand was turned upward, elbow slightly bent, palm flat, and my head was placed on top of something that pressed it up from the ground so I could see out toward rock and rolling waves and just a little above me up into the sky.

Something soft pressed against my left cheek. It groaned.

And if I could have screamed, I would have. The elongated horror my face was frozen into would have to suffice. Inside, my mind was screaming, "Get it off! Get it off!" My mouth made not a sound.

To my utter revulsion, the squishy thing under my cheek was Grosbeak. The softness was his tangled mass of drowned hair and the slow decay of his flesh. He'd said the flies were gone, hadn't he? But there were crabs. Had I felt one brush my cheek? Oh, no, no, no.

"Izolda?" he asked, and his voice sounded gritty. "Are you conscious?"

"Oh, she can hear you just fine," Lady Tanglecott drawled, setting a polished sheet of clear glass on my knee and hand. "Hmm, good but still a little bit unsteady."

She drew out Look and Despair from my bag. She was frozen standing completely straight on her hind legs. Tangecott wedged her under the glass to make a third leg. She looked as though a taxidermist had taken his job too figuratively and tried to impress upon the viewer not only the form of his stuffed animal skin, but also the last emotions and thoughts running through its head when it was caught.

I wished I could swallow down the terrible suspicion that I looked the same way.

"We agreed to three days and three nights, Izolda," Tangecott said, with a waspish smile. "We did not agree on how they would be spent. Today, you will serve as my table. You're not pretty enough to wait the table, and your left hand is a terrifying thing – what madness possessed you to strip it of flesh? – but you are perfectly capable of having drinks set upon you. If no one at this council grows so enraged that they smash the furniture, you should suffer through this with nothing but your dignity taken." She paused to laugh – a light tinkling laugh as one might expect from a fairy in a story. "A word of advice – you should close your mouth. Something might crawl into it."

I wanted to scream. I wanted to cry. I wanted to rage. Instead, I stayed completely frozen as Lady Tanglecott laid out drinks on the table above me.

"How disappointing," Grosbeak said from his place beneath my cheek. I felt his head vibrate as he spoke. "I'd hoped for better than this, Lady Tanglecott. Disabling your competitors is such a boring move."

"It serves more than one purpose today, revenant," she said calmly. "I won't be manipulated into changing it. Not by you, not by anyone."

"And yet you let me keep my voice. Perhaps, you couldn't take it. Perhaps, the dead are immune to your charms. Or perhaps you are struck with fear. This is the first game that has seen so many competitors removed from the board along with their pieces. I recall only one player losing his life in the past five games combined and now we have lost two. Are you afraid you might be next?"

Tanglecott crouched down low, still graceful even while her perfect oval face drew level with our ghoulish ones.

"My dear disgraced servant of the Arrow." Her voice was refined as a harp in perfect tune. "You suffer under the misapprehension that I care to hear your commentary. Silence yourself, or you will be returned to the sea. And I shall accommodate you with a swift kick of my pretty slippered foot."

She stood, straightening as easily as a willow freed from a heavy snow, and then lifted her translucent skirt and wiggled a foot set in a perfectly cut and faceted crystal slipper.

"Are you really wearing a glass slipper?" Grosbeak snickered. "Like from a Witenbrand tale told by mortals?"

A quick flick of her ankle and I felt the impact on his head below mine. A spike of fear shot through me at my proximity, helpless and trapped.

"Your point is taken," he said in a slightly muffled voice and then I heard him spit, and on the rock where I'd been placed a tooth bounced and tinkled, leaving a tiny trail of blackened blood.

"Keep it ever in your heart," she said charmingly and glided away.

She left nothing to look at but the glaring sun, the creamy rock, and beyond it a sea so azure, so perfect, so wreathed in rainbows that it hardly felt real at all.

"We still have front row seats," Grosbeak whispered. "That's worth a little indignity."

Front row seats to what? My humiliation and eventual death? I was as stuck as a fly in honey. As trapped as a mouse in a bucket. I wanted to scream.

"Did you know we aren't far from the place your husband stands vigil under the waves? I can almost see it from here."

And just like that, there was fire in my heart again.

Chapter Twelve

I WOULD HAVE THOUGHT that by now I was an expert in the briny humors of the sea. I'd watched more than one afternoon move from lazy doldrums to pounding breakers. The Wittenhame surpassed even the greatest transformation. In the space of a long breath, she transformed utterly.

I breathed in and a dozen mermaids leapt from the crystal-clear calm of the azure waves, their hair as tangled as Grosbeak's, their teeth snapping like attacking sharks, and their fish bodies flashing in the bright sun. A song, haunting and sharp all at once, four harmonies interweaving through it, burst out like a clap of thunder as if songs could be war trumpets.

In the time it took to let out that same breath, the siren mermaids had fallen back into the sea without a splash, their song gone, and in its place, the sky turned to a mulish grey, the clouds bubbling up along the horizon, thick and roiling as a pot boiling over. As if to mock the smooth surface I'd witnessed, the sea erupted into powerful waves, tossed one way and then the next as if by changeable childish hands, their roar unsettling in its power.

"A Storm Clock has been declared," Grosbeak said over the sound. He waited but he must have realized I couldn't answer. "That means the participants of the meeting must all arrive before the first rain drop falls or they are barred from attendance, and the meeting will be over the moment the storm clears. It's usually agreed upon beforehand. While the storm is in place, there can be no violence between participants. We, I fear, have no such sanctuary."

Of course.

In the distance, I felt like I could still hear the echo of the siren song calling to me. It seemed, almost, as if my very name was woven into the strands of the song and the beating waves of the sea. Perhaps sirens really could lure people to their deaths just with a song, because that echo seemed to touch every part of me from the inside out.

Light footsteps tapped along the rock and then someone peered down at me. It was Marshyellow. I shivered as I realized he was holding two things in his ancient papery hands. In one, he held a delicate piece of linen, sewn all over with flowers in the exact pattern my mother had taught me, and in the other, he held my flesh and blood hand, severed at the wrist, pinkie lifted as it danced a silver needle through the cloth.

Something like bile rose in my frozen throat. I fought it back, terrified of what vomiting would be like with my mouth frozen and pointing upward. I'd likely choke and die on my own revulsion.

"Lovely sampler, Marshyellow," Grosbeak snickered. "Think you to sell your needlework at fairs? You'd make a fine shop-mistress indeed. You have just the smile for merchantry. I'd watch that hand with care, though. Every part of its owner has drawn only trouble as shavings to a lodestone."

"A talking stump and a stumping talk," Marshyellow said absently before he withdrew. I heard a chair scrape somewhere behind my head and a whiff of ancient man came from that direction.

The words of our bargain came back to me: *Binding to it now all that was bound to you and offering to you its many skills.* He was a fool to have brought my hand with him, for though it showed off my skill with a needle, all I had to do was find a way to snatch it back and I would have all that was bound to him. My fingers itched to do just that. I'd crafted the bargain carefully to be double-edged – even though I'd thought it was about marriage and not about a physical hand. And despite his current mental state, he was a lord of the Wittenhame, and it should have occurred to him to keep it hidden.

I was startled out of my musings by a new voice. Lady Tanglecott's glass slippers tapped on the rock again as she led someone new to the table.

Lord Coppertomb looked down through the glass at my frozen face and if I could have cowered back further from his regular features and angular-cut plum doublet, I would have. He disguised deviousness under simplicity and a tangled mind under a blank face.

"You don't like my trophy wife?" Lady Tanglecott asked in a tinkling voice.

"I don't think you can call someone else's wife you've taken as a trophy a *trophy* wife," Coppertomb said dryly. "It's not an accurate use of idiom."

"Whyever not?" she asked coyly as he seated himself.

"Sooth. Be not insulted. I brought you a gift, Lady of Ilkanmoore." His tone was so dusty it could have made a frog sneeze.

"A gift? Your presence alone is a gift, Prince of Wittenbrand."

He lifted a narrow eyebrow, reached into his doublet, and produced a diamond the size of my ear, strung on three strands of braided black pearls.

"They call it the Heart of the Ocean and you know full well its true nature and provenance," he said, flicking it with a finger so that it spun. At the heart of the gem, a flaw ran down the center that made rainbows dance from its surface when it twisted like that.

"Why such a gift, my lord?" Tanglecott asked and to my surprise, I realized the emotion I saw in her eyes was fear.

"Why not?" he asked, boldly. "When you can best make use of it."

She swallowed and perhaps my angle was the best because I could see where a tiny bead of sweat had formed on her brow and was running down the side of her cheek. It smacked the glass and spread into a flat, wavering droplet. Tanglecott laughed falsely, took the rich gift in her hand, and tucked it into her skirts where a pocket must have been hidden.

"Well, since we are giving gifts, you're welcome to take the trophy wife's pet," she said gesturing.

Coppertomb ducked his head under the table and ran a finger down Look and Despair's chin and chest.

"Delightful though she is, I have rodents of my own already."

"I meant the other one."

"I do not collect heads. Unlike the Arrow, I need none but myself to advise me," he said in a clipped manner, his expression set with vexation.

"Do as you please," Lady Tanglecott said lightly, moving to greet a new guest, but I found the exchange interesting. These two who I had thought were fierce allies were riddled with tension and doubt. I could work with that, if I could just find a way.

"I see you down there, wife of the Arrow," Coppertomb said lightly, smiling out at the gathering storm. There was a yellow tinge to the sky I did not like. It stood out like a bruise against the dark clouds. "Did you enjoy watching your lord and master sink into the heart of the ocean? Does it thrill you to know he's been stolen to be the groom of the sea just as he stole you? Revenge, I have always thought, is a dish both sweet and bitter. Sweet in the tasting, bitter in the aftertaste."

I desperately wanted to ask what that meant. It was the second time it had been suggested that my husband was lover to the sea.

"Did it cheer you to see him offer up his days to another against his will just as you offered yours? Did you savor the vengeance?" He paused as if something had just occurred to him. "Or are you still his plaything even now? His tidy pet to display and direct? Yes, I see that look in your eyes and I know what it means. You're his creature yet. Hmm." He rubbed his chin and looked at me with speculation. "Do not think I am finished with you. Banishment was only the beginning. Your uses are numerous and I will wear you out like a well-worn rag."

A mental shiver rolled through me despite the fact my actual body was frozen.

"Ooooh, big words," Grosbeak crowed. "Challenge her then, Coppertomb! Set her a challenge or a riddle or offer her a bargain. Or maybe ride against her in this Joust. Wouldn't that be a delight to watch? I've heard rumors you're not much of a seat in the lists and upon speculation, I've not seen you ride. Mayhap you'd be only just a match for a mortal woman."

I did not care for Grosbeak cajoling further repercussions from my tormentor, but I could not prevent him. Instead, I focused on every word my enemies spoke. Who knew if there might be a key in one of them that might open my way to save my husband before it was too late?

"I will do none of those things, cadaver. She is a plaything – and a treacherous one, at that. She is such a fool that she bought her own doom with a day. So insidious, she wormed her way into the heart of my enemy and hollowed him as ants hollow a log. If she lives in hell now, she bought every second of it herself. Why would I offer her any relief? I'll give her not one drop of balm, not one ripple of sweet water. If I choose to use her, I will make her feet dance, whether she wills it or no. I need not puzzles, bargains, games, or riddles to make her my pawn. I need only my will and her weak mortal flesh."

The echo of the siren song grew louder as if it were – somehow – trying to dull the pain of his accusations, rising as they rose, rocking me gently in the song like a babe in the cradle.

"I think your fears outstrip your creativity. I could invent better vengeances than you claim to devise," Grosbeak said with a snicker. "But fear not, I'm sure creativity is not required to win your game and you have all the allies you need to conquer the whole of the world and eat it up like a round of rye."

Coppertomb snorted. "I see why they keep you, carrion. You're droll as a fifty-day-mummer. Perhaps I will take you as my party gift, after all. You can amuse the denizens of my dungeons and dull the pain of those trapped in amber beneath my floors."

Grosbeak's mouth shut with a snap.

Coppertomb looked away from us leisurely but then his gaze snapped back to me. "I see you loaned a hand to a friend, mortal girl. How revealing."

The raindrops were falling harder now, steaming whenever they hit Coppertomb. Someone came with drinks, placing Coppertomb's goblet in such a way that it hid most of his face from me.

My muscles were starting to cramp – never mind that I couldn't move them even if I wanted to. They screamed at me, agonized and painful. I tried to think of something else, anything else, and then – finally – Tanglecott's voice spoke again.

"We asked you here because we find ourselves short a fourth."

"A fourth?" The voice was unfamiliar. Masculine with a hint of nobility and an edge of an accent I did not know. "Were you three scheming with the Sword before he stepped on his own ear so painfully? Or was it the Arrow who chose to die for *love*?"

A note sounded as if someone had plucked the string of an instrument and the specter around my neck slid her dead hand up across my jaw and clamped over my open mouth. I felt far more of it than I ever wanted. My heart pounded with panic. What if she reached down my throat and …?

"Ah!" the newcomer said, and I strained my eyes trying to see, but he was over my shoulder entirely. I could see the edges of Tanglecott and Marshyellow but not a shred of this man. "I see you've sworn yourselves to secrecy and why wouldn't you – and yet even in this you have shown the edge of your slip. Have you not, lady and lords? For is that not the widow of the Arrow beneath the table and is her mouth not bound, too? I see you cannot speak of it, but it worries me that you would ally yourselves to the Arrow and yet allow him to slip beneath the waves to gain yourselves one less competitor. Would you not do the same to me?"

Widow? My heart sped up, my breathing gasping and hitching. He said it as if it were obvious. Was I too late, then? Had the sea made my husband her lover and then torn him apart as she did so many sailors in the mortal world?

"That's Lord Antlerdale, I would swear on it," Grosbeak hissed for my ear only.

"We may not disclose," Lady Tanglecott cut off, and though I could see no specter on her shoulder, one must even now be gagging her. Interesting. Perhaps they could not see my specter, either, unless they were searching for it.

Coppertomb seamlessly picked up from where Tanglecott had left off. "While there may be histories better left untouched, we know who we address. We are not strangers to your ways, Antlerdale."

"He's a serial monogamist," Grosbeak snickered to me – quietly enough that those above us could pretend they hadn't heard. "You'd think the old adage would be true, 'Who could ever learn to love a beast?' but in his case, they line up – still do when he's not occupied with this century's love of his life. Ghastly thing to do to women, keeping them locked up in an eternal library until they die, and you replace them all over again with that 'I'm under a curse, help me!' beast routine, but I suppose some people like thick beards and roaring."

There was so much I wanted to say to that.

Coppertomb's foot kicked out, seeming at random, and Grosbeak *ooffed* in pain.

"Consider," Grosbeak said through what sounded like thicker dead lips, "if anyone knows histories, it's him. He hoards books in that library the way your husband hoards severed heads. It's disgusting. Shelves and shelves of butchered trees shoved right up against each other and," here he gasped, "cataloged. I'll say this for your husband. He doesn't cataloge his trophies. He gives us that small dignity."

"The head has the right of it," Antlerdale said calmly from above. "I've read my share. And that's why you worry me. I hear reports that your people lay siege to Wittentree even as I sit here, Lady Tanglecott. They say her island is selling birds' nests and cat hearts for the price of a good estate, so starved are they. You'll have dragged down another of us before this treaty is whispered so much as signed. What do you need me for?"

The rain was coming down hard now, flowing around me so high that my left boot was full and tugging off and my skirts felt like they weighed a thousand pounds. Grosbeak's voice was muffled by water when he spoke.

"A faithful man, Lord Antlerdale and steady. When a thing works once, he never deviates. He won't join them," my advisor said through the streaming water.

"Won't he?" Tanglecott's voice sounded amused, pitched though it was over the torrent. "You'd be surprised who turns to our cause."

Behind everything, I still heard the siren song, but now the echo was only my name over and over and over forever.

"*Izolda, Izolda, Izolda, Izolda.*"

Perhaps that last crossing directly into the Wittenhame had hollowed my mind as surely as Marshyellow's.

"Tempt me then, lady," Antlerdale said. "And not with your flesh of which I have no need, nor of your goodwill of which there is none to be had."

"Pensmoore," she said softly. "I'll have it as my own by the end of this Three Day Bind. Surely you've heard of the bargain I've struck with the wife of the Arrow."

"Rumors reach even my ears, though they are mostly speculations about this coming joust. You'll be riding in it, of course. How will that influence this comradery?"

Coppertomb seemed unable to help interjecting. "You're as bound as we are, Antlerdale. We can't go where we aren't welcomed, can't steal the mortal nations unless it be by marriage, blood, or pact. You've only the nation you were dealt. What is it? Ptoolemoore? Soaking up the Sword's madness as his people flee in droves to your land. Rumors say you're close to taking Aayadmoore for yourself. It's a respectable conquest on a map, but in reality, we both know what it means – thousands of hungry mouths. Thousands of fatherless orphans. A hundred thousand headaches. More land, less army, drawn-out, weakened, and ripe for attack." I felt Antlerdale shift uncomfortably. Coppertomb's assessment was accurate. "But if you had Pensmoore – well, that's a well-fortified nation. One that came through years of war with a king and lands and prosperity of a kind. It could anchor your holdings in the north, feed the country south of it, and shore up a lace-woven land for you. What fool would turn his back on that?"

"What fool indeed," Antlerdale sounded sour but thoughtful. "And you will have the lands to offer me in three days."

"Two after this one and three nights. You could have it on the third morning," Lady Tanglecott said smoothly.

"I wouldn't bet on it," Grosbeak said darkly.

"I think *I* will," Antlerdale said steadily. "The price is only my part in this foul alliance?"

"Don't call what is fair foul, Antlerdale," Coppertomb scolded. "Not when together we can endure past the others."

"And then?" Antlerdale asked, a note of anticipation in his voice.

"And then the gloves will fall and each of us may use tooth or claw or a poisoned kiss to bring down the rest."

"Agree and we will bind you as we are bound," Lady Tanglecott said a little too quickly.

Antlerdale laughed. "When the three days are up, Tanglecott. Not before time. I'll make no move until I know your promise is certain."

The rain had slowed now, but the chant went on in my mind.

"*Izolda, Izolda, Izolda.*" In my madness, it had begun to sound like that voice most dear to me.

"Then we four shall meet again, three days hence," Coppertomb said formally.

"Three days porridge hot, three days porridge cold," Marshyellow agreed.

"*Izolda, Izolda, Izolda.*"

"Three days," Antlerdale and Tanglecott agreed in unison, and then as if a candle had been snuffed, the rain stopped, and the sun blazed through the clouds.

I heard the sound of feet as everyone rose, and then Coppertomb's mouth formed a look halfway between a cold sneer and an amused smirk as he looked through the glass table at me. He lifted his goblet and brought it down on the table with a crash and I couldn't even scream when a sliver of glass went into my mouth and another into my open eye as the rest rained down around me in a shattered shower of knife-like shards.

"Tsk, tsk," said Tanglecott. "No need to kill her right away, Coppertomb. We have days and days for that. Come when you're ready, Izolda. If you can."

And then their feet echoed on the stone path, but I was still frozen in place as the voice that had been chanting my name so steadily paused and said, "*Izolda?*"

And in desperation, I asked back, "*Bluebeard?*"

But there was no response except the agonizing emptiness in my chest where once my heart dwelled, matched only by the emptiness in his chest where once there was a rib he gave for me.

Chapter Thirteen

IT WAS hours before my frozen body finally loosened and collapsed. Hours in which I had been stuck with my open eyes streaming both tears and blood, my open mouth parched to sand, that sliver of glass balanced precariously on my tongue. Hours in which I still heard my name sung intermittently in the most mournful of tones. I clung to it. Mad or not, it was all I had.

I drifted. I dreamed. And in my dream, I heard my Bluebeard saying his vows to me once again, as if we were still on that platform as he confessed them and I swore them with him, each unable to move to the other's side.

"*As long as rivers run and moon shines, as long as the earth has bones and death has claws, as long as the ages pass and fail – that long shall I be husband to you. Flesh of my flesh and bone of my bone you will be. Spirit of my spirit. Heart of my own heart. Fall what may, we shall be one. My body, I dedicate to none other. My days shall be yours and your happiness my own. The bounty of my wealth is yours. If ever it be otherwise, may I waste away with sickness and may famine eat my strength and may my enemies overtake me, and siphon from me the blood of my life.*"

And my heart ached with the memory for he had broken no vows – not a single one. He had been nothing but true to me. He had given for me his rib and his future. And I was determined that it should end there. I was determined that he should not give his life.

I would lose my own flesh before I agreed to lose his. I felt a hot tear slide from my eye as I thought of my hand. I missed it yet – and still, it was no sacrifice if only I could draw him back from the depth. I would lose my own spirit before I agreed to lose his.

My heart I could not offer. It was already taken, conquered, occupied.

The sea and storm became placid as my mind raged as if it were somehow mollified by my misery.

And through all my revelations and internal passions, Grosbeak complained miserably beneath me.

"If she doesn't release you soon, you're sure to fail your tasks. You can't spend the night in her bed if you can't get to her bed. But she can't make it impossible. That would break the rules of the Three Day Bind. The spectators would revolt."

He went on to tell me of four other times he'd witnessed a Three Day Bind – all quasi-marriage-like, or quasi-kidnap-like depending on how one viewed it. I sympathized with the victims of these forced arrangements, but their stories gave me no hints on how to survive this. Grosbeak seemed much keener on the perpetrators. There was no surprise there. At the heart of him, Grosbeak was a crime waiting to happen.

"Antlerdale tried one before his current arrangement with mortals. It was with one of the Tanglecott folk – a lovely creature, mostly dryad. It's all in his book. They say she chose to root herself to one of his grandfather clocks and hide in the woodgrain there rather than suffer marriage to him." He started to laugh and then stopped. "Poor Antlerdale. He has more remnants of past wives around his house than your Bluebeard does. Love, is not for the Wittenbrand – not if you want to keep it for more than a fortnight. You should remember that, Izolda. Joint purpose, deadly cause, and pacts of murder are far more likely to last."

I had grown so weary of his voice that by the time my body finally collapsed, his sudden silence was relief. I clamped my tongue hard on the glass piece as I fell, and to my relief, I trapped it against the roof of my mouth.

The rest of my body was not spared. My living hand – raised all this time above my head – was lifeless and numb. My right leg was similarly asleep. My eyes had shut involuntarily as I plummeted and the one with the glass sliver in it screamed in pain – along with every muscle of my body and most of the bones. I was a living scream made flesh. Mercifully, I slipped from my balance atop Grosbeak's head and I lay sprawled on shattered glass, a discarded, broken doll.

A small squeak told me the ferret was in the same condition.

"Get up," Grosbeak demanded. "If you have an hour left, I'm a Neverwatch Eve goose."

I neither knew nor cared what that was. Awkwardly and with every bit of strength I still possessed, I rolled onto my back, flopping like a fish drawn from the water and left to suffocate in the emptiness of the sky.

Carefully, I drew my skeletal hand up to my lips and plucked the sliver of glass from my tongue. It is a complicated thing to extract a sliver of smooth glass with two smooth phalanges – more complicated than I had imagined. After the course of several desperate minutes, it was finally out, my tongue only slightly cut. I was left quivering as an agony of pins and needles flooded my right side.

This is good, I tried to remind myself. You need the feeling back.

"Izolda, Izolda, Izolda," the sea half-crooned and half-sobbed.

I looked out toward the horizon as I tried to catch my breath, wondering if I could simply walk beneath the waves and go to him. I could feel him in my heart – so close but so far away. So precious to me and so unattainable.

It was a childish fantasy. I was mortal. I breathed air. I had no business thinking otherwise. I was delirious, my brain looping and drifting when I needed it to focus.

And why was the sea so cloudy?

I lifted my skeletal hand and closed my left eye.

Oh no.

I could not see at all from the right eye – the one with the glass splinter.

Panicked, I scrambled up to sitting.

"Blood of Gods and Men! You're cutting yourself on the glass! Fool of a mortal!"

I crawled out from the glass, stunned as if I'd been knocked flat by a runaway cart, and kept crawling to where the rock overlooked the brackish water.

I peered down with my one good eye and watched my reflection in the calm sea as a drop of red blood rolled from my wounded eye into the water.

It struck like ink in a dish of clear water, spreading, muddying. That eye was white already. Didn't it take years for an eye to glass over like that? Even a dead eye? I had not the experience to know.

"Scars and sires, Izolda. Do you see how low the sun has slunk? Like a lover caught with another woman, it creeps away, head hung low."

"Poetic." My voice felt like it belonged to another.

From where the blood had dropped a torrid ripple spread.

As it spread, the chant of my voice faded away. No more song to sing me through.

I sighed and turned. There was no point in panicking about what had already happened.

Look and Despair lay on her back looking miserable but alive. She'd escaped the slivers of glass and as I watched she flipped over very slowly and crept to huddle beside Grosbeak. He looked none the worse for the latest episode. It was hard to get worse than long dead. There was a pearl clipped under a few layers of crusted hair. Had that been there before?

I swallowed, trying to work moisture back into my mouth. In a moment, I would have to stand and face the challenge of finding Lady Tanglecott's bedroom. No time for misery or self-pity. No time to mourn an eye. I gathered myself, preparing to stand, and then a hand slid from behind me and covered my mouth.

The spirit? What had I tried to say that she would censor me?

But no, this hand was cold and clammy. I reached up to fight the grasp and then it spun me, and I was face to face with something that seemed half-woman, half-monster. She smelled heavily of brine as she paused, half in the sea and half out. Her skin gleamed and flashed like a trout's, her eyes were large, round, and protruded too far and her hair hung in tangled skeins, decorated with debris that must have caught in it – a strand of sickly yellow seaweed here, a bit of blush shell there, a generous helping of sand and several skittering crabs so much like Grosbeak's that suspicions dawned.

"Uungantha!" he said, and his voice was worshipful. "Who are we that the most glorious maid of the sea should visit us?"

She didn't even look at him. Her mottled black and silver hand flew up and she put one finger to her lips. I barely had time to note that her fingers were shaped oddly before her other hand darted out and she snatched me, ripping me from the air into the sea. I struggled, thrashing in the brine, sucking in a mouthful of awful brackish water as she pawed at my face with her fishy hand, obscuring what vision I had left. Don't panic or you'll drown, I told myself. Don't panic.

I felt pain in my eye and saw a glimmer of something glittering and red-streaked between her grasping fingers. To my surprised horror, her fish lips brushed mine and then she hauled me from the water as if I weighed no more than today's catch and flung me onto the rocky shore. I crouched there, gasping in breath, as she turned, leapt as a salmon leaps, and re-entered the sea with a nearly silent splash.

I could see. In both eyes, I could see. I was coughing up half the sea, my lungs screaming, my hair dripping around me like weeds and my lovely dress ruined, but I could see.

Who would have imagined?

I swallowed hard, trying to herd my thoughts back like a goatherd with an unruly flock.

"Most glorious," Grosbeak said, longing thick in his voice. "What little sentiment still dwells within me reaches for her. You are honored above mortal women, wife of the Arrow. Honored more than you know."

I pulled myself unsteadily up the rock and to my feet, eyes locked on the ocean. I wanted to follow the violent mermaid to wherever she had gone. I knew a gift when I saw one. And I knew who had to have given it to me.

Even wrapped up in bonds of damning fate, his heart bent to mine. I could not save him from the worst agony and yet he saved me from the least.

I peered into the sea – calm again – but there was nothing there except my own reflection and it stared back at me with two good eyes and a streak of blood running down my right cheek. His sign. His red teardrop.

I gasped, pulled back, and with my flesh hand, I lifted the ferret to my shoulder where she slumped half-dead across it like a lazy stole. The specter peered at me from the other shoulder, misery running cold in her eyes. With my skeletal hand, I gathered up Grosbeak by the weeds he called hair and turned toward land.

"Let us find Lady Tanglecott's bedroom and let us best her at her own tricks, friends," I said.

"If you do either of those things, you'll do better than I expect," Grosbeak said. "But by all means, try not to die today. I'll just be here mourning my one true love."

"I thought you loved only yourself."

"Yes, that's who I'm mourning. You did know I was dead, did you not?"

Chapter Fourteen

I TURNED AROUND and around on the rock. There was no obvious way to leave it. On two sides, the waves crashed, spraying everything with brine. To one side a bog lay, thick with reeds and showing no obvious path, to the other side a forest – but this was a tangle of bushes, fallen trees, and driftwood driven high up past the rocks by storm waters and unpredictable tides. It looked like the sort of place a traveler might be lured into that they may be lost for a hundred years. Between the two, a sluggish yellow smoke rose from a tear in the moss cover of the forest floor. I could not see a fire making it.

A raven peered down from one of the trees, seeming almost familiar, though it paid me no mind.

To make matters worse, the occasional face appeared in the clouds or the knot of a tree and then vanished just as quickly. They sent icy spikes down my spine every time I caught sight of one of them.

"Anxiety doesn't suit you, Princess of Pensmoore," Grosbeak said after the third time. "You're jumping at the faces of spectators. They come only to watch your drama unfold."

"Perhaps they could offer some suggestions on how to get to Lady Tanglecott's house," I muttered.

"We're in her house already," he said, waggling his eyebrows.

I lifted his head and peered into his face grimly. "Listen to me, Grosbeak, you horrible dead corpse, you repulsive harbinger. If you know how to get out of this place and closer to where I need to be right now, you had best tell me."

I shook him, trying not to mind the small crabs that fell from his tangled locks. One skittered onto my bone hand, slipped, and fell to the ground.

"And spoil the fun?" he said between rattling teeth. "There are bets riding on this. I bet the specter a pair of crabs and a tertiary secret that you'd lose."

"The specter thinks I'll win?"

The specter leaned around so I could see her silent smile. She looked smug.

"I'm gratified I have someone's confidence, at least. But as to you, Grosbeak, I could throw you back into the sea," I said firmly. "No, even better. I could set you down in the swamp and leave you there. I hear there are interesting bugs in swamps. Would it give you joy to have a new infestation?"

He shivered. "Would you lose your guide to the Wittenhame so easily?"

"I would if he didn't guide me. You said you were my friend, but you acquit the post poorly."

He bit his lip. "Fine. Fine. Don't take such a look with me, Izolda. We each have to find our own way and I'm only trying to keep my path smooth, in a manner of speaking."

I poked his cheek with my skeletal finger, and he flinched.

"It's the smoke. I think," he said hurriedly. "Her house is likely sitting in a different dimension only accessed by scent and the smoke will likely take you there. You just inhale. But make sure I do as well, or we'll be in two different dimensions and that will be very, very uncomfortable."

I strode toward the smoke as Grosbeak began to sing the old song that saved me last time I was in the Wittenhame. For such a terrible singer, he certainly loved the sound of his own voice. He let it warble and wander and sang with the gusto of a tavern maid newly hired.

I was grateful for the distraction. An entirely different song kept on echoing through my mind, and it felt like base treachery to turn my back on the man in the sea and walk toward land.

"*Fly with the Arrow,*
Dance With the Sword,
Give your Heart to the Barrow,

Die With your Lord."

"*With* your Lord?" I asked, interrupting Grosbeak. I was inspecting the smoke. It was a black-laced yellow and I didn't like the way it shifted toward my face no matter where I stood or how I leaned. It was giving off the scent of cedar and gingerbread. "Not *for* your Lord? As in during a battle or trying to achieve his aims?"

"It's definitely *with*," Grosbeak said nastily. "And maybe you should get that part right since you've done the rest."

"Are you saying all I have to do now is die?"

"It's inevitable, wouldn't you say? One last piece of a puzzle."

I rather hoped he was wrong. I was not in the mood to die.

"You are mortal. Have you forgotten that? Brushing shoulders with your betters doesn't change your twilight life. It's over almost before it begins. I'll barely be finished introducing you to the Wittenhame and already you'll have withered and died and I'll have to find someone new to protect me from my fate as the Arrow's trinket."

"Are you sure we have to inhale this smoke?" I asked, wondering what might happen to me if I did. I didn't trust the Wittenhame or the tricks of the Wittenbrand. I'd have to if I accepted breathing in this smoke, but I'd rather know more about what awaited me.

"Lily-liver," he accused. "Callow heart."

I shook my head. He was more nuisance than a help.

I stepped into the smoke and inhaled long and hard. On my shoulders, the ferret and the specter both coughed and then the smoke cleared and we were at the foot of a glass staircase. Through the glass steps, the bog and forest could be seen, but if I followed them with my eyes, they opened up to a crystal balcony above and a wall filled with open windows and misty curtains waving in the wind.

"Ah," Grosbeak said, stopping his mockery for a moment to cough horribly as if he were going to die right there. "The mist dimension. You should have expected that with her affection for Mist Lions. Well, carry on, then."

He went back to his song.

"*Sing for your sovereign,*
Bow to your dream
Make haste for the fallen,
Rise in esteem."

The words "make haste for the fallen" skittered up my spine. What if I wasn't fast enough? What if I ruined everything?

"Perhaps we should try entering quietly," I hissed as I crept up the glass stairs. It was a terrible feeling to climb them. I kept feeling like each step would sink right through and I'd fall on the rocks beneath, which in turn was replaced with fear of falling into the trees beneath, and that in turn with the misty clouds beneath. It took all my nerve to mount them as the sun sank lower and lower toward the horizon, bleeding out across the Wittenhame like a fallen foe.

Even worse, I could see all the spectators peering up through the glass stairs, grinning, or leering, or licking their lips hungrily.

Worst of all was that never-ending feeling of betrayal with every step I took that propelled me further from the sea.

"Ignore me all you want," Grosbeak said primly, "But you'll be sorry you did if you forget the words to the song. After all, it helped you once. It might help you again."

"That's all well and good," I said, feeling a little dizzy now that I was so high up with nothing to hold onto but my drowned friend and nothing beneath me but invisible stairs. "But I don't exactly know how to sing for my sovereign or bow to my dream."

"You didn't know how to hold up your fine token and that still worked out," he said smugly.

We reached a door, but this one opened with a single touch, and I found myself in a glass room, with a glass floor over the clouds. Glass walls were barely discernable by their edges, glass decorations by the way the light bent around them. A glass grandfather clock filled the entrance, *tick, tick, tocking* away and glass doors decorated in glass scrollwork led from the hall to other rooms of the house.

"If you're so confident, then why are you betting against me?" I snapped at Grosbeak. All the glass was making my head ache. I couldn't tell where one thing ended and another began. I was going to walk into walls. And then they would shatter and I'd cut myself and fall to my death.

"What's the fun in only playing one side?"

My voice was tight with fear. "You are the worst of knaves and death has not succeeded in reforming you."

"And may it never succeed! I'd drink to that, but drinks are in short supply."

"I'd think that would be a pleasant turn of events after the last seven years of drinking the sea." But my heart was not in my words. I was rattled by this empty glass house.

"I think you'll find that closing your eyes helps," Grosbeak said blandly.

I closed my eyes, drew in a breath, and felt my way to the nearest door. I had no idea where I was going, but the red sun told me I didn't have much time to get there.

"Is the whole place like this?" My voice sounded small even to my own ears.

"Only in this dimension."

"How many dimensions are there?" I was feeling my way down a hall, door after door lined it and my heart was in my throat because I didn't know which one to try.

"How many do you want there to be?"

"One! I want there to be one clear, practical dimension."

"How utterly absurd. If you don't like this one, I'd inhale some more smoke, just be sure it's one where the house stays visible."

"How will I know?" And now I really did feel panicked. This was so far beyond me. Why had I thought I could trap the Wittenbrand when all they did was trap me again and again?

I smelled garlic and oranges and my eyes snapped open. I was standing in orange smoke. I must have blundered my way into another smoke pillar by mistake. Grosbeak was inhaling audibly beside me. I followed suit and reluctantly found myself in what felt like a rabbit warren inhabited by a human. Glowing silver footsteps that looked just like they might belong to glass slippers marked the hall, bypassing door after door.

I followed them, running now, until at last, I came to a door at the end of the hall. I opened the door and stepped right through a wave of pale pink smoke and then into a room with glass walls and a glass ceiling but a floor of wooden planks, a huge roaring fire, and a bed so high it should have been higher than any other ceiling could accommodate.

Through the glass walls, the sun had reduced to the merest red echo of light and darkness was swelling to fill the sky. And from the top of the bed, piled in mattresses, eiderdowns, furs, brocades, silks, and satins called a voice.

"Up here, Princess of Pensmoore. Up here on my bed of conquest by the time the last shadow reigns or you've lost your bargain."

I swallowed down a wave of worry and grabbed the side of the mountainous heap, jaw set and determined.

How hard could it be to climb up into a bed? I tied Grosbeak's hair to my belt, shuddering at how utterly disgusting he was. I was a practical girl. I could do what needed to be done. Even if it meant hanging severed heads from my belt.

I stood on tiptoe and reached up. My hand sank into something soft. A feather bed perhaps. I gripped it with my skeleton fingers and pulled, finding footing in the soft mattresses.

On my shoulder, the ferret squeaked weakly.

I pushed up a single step and checked the grip of my skeletal hand. It didn't tell me often enough what I was feeling.

My skeleton fingers were jammed in something soft, alright.

Someone's eye.

A beautiful, pale, pale man's staring white eye, his eyelashes frost white, tinged pink by the dying sun.

I screamed, lost my grip, and fell to the floor, rolling over just in time to projectile vomit across the wood floor and into the fire.

"Thank you," said the fire.

"You," I gasped, and it flared brightly.

"Teeth of the Gods that hurt," Grosbeak moaned. "What happened?"

"An eye," I gasped, wiping my mouth with the back of my living hand. The skeletal hand I held out far from the rest of me as if the simple touch might contaminate the rest of me. Perhaps I should scorch it in the fire to clean it. But would I feel that?

From my shoulder, the ferret chittered something and then climbed to balance on the top of my head. Her little claws dug into my scalp, making my skin crawl.

"I know," I muttered to her, "I don't like it either."

"On one of the dead men?" Grosbeak practically shrieked at me. "*That's* all? You'll need to be made of sterner stuff than that, my girl. Hurry! We're almost out of time!"

He was right. I could barely see the red thread of the sun anymore but the thing that worried me more was the phrase "one of."

I looked up at the bed a second time and this time, I saw what I had failed to see in the mess of drapery and blankets, quilts and coverlets, feather beds and mattresses. Squeezed between the layers lay open-eyed corpses. All male. All lovely, half-dressed, and all very, very, very dead.

Or at least, I hoped they were.

Because if they were not, then they might reach out and grasp me back as I climbed. Perhaps a wrist, or an ankle and then they might gobble me up.

The ferret chittered, claws tightening in my hair as if it had the same thought, and Grosbeak sighed.

"Don't tell me you're scared of a few dead men? A scrappy little thing like you? With the fate of your brother, your nation and that fool you call beloved all tied up in your success and failure?"

It was exactly the right thing to say. Heart in my throat, iron in my spine, I reached for the stack of mattresses again and began to climb. Who would do this? And why were none of the corpses rotting?

"They say these are her lovers," Grosbeak said, and I could hear the grin in his voice even though I couldn't see his face. "I dare say that the rumor is true. That looks very much the image of Cryptalis, and that poor fool mooned for Lady Tanglecott for all of the Moonless Fox Hunt before he went missing. Perhaps this is why. Perhaps she took him to her bed and decided to keep him forever."

"Surely someone would notice if all her lovers went missing," I said between gritted teeth.

"Notice? Of course. Care? I fear you have misjudged us yet again, Izolda. Why do you expect any of us to care about men unable to keep their own souls inside their bodies?"

"I care about you."

"Fool that you are, it seems that you do." His tone was dry as dust. "But don't blame me for that. I've done everything possible to disabuse you of any affection."

"Fool that I am," I agreed darkly. But it was not for him I was doing this but for my husband. It was for him and the possibility of freeing him. Three days. Three nights. And all I had to do was not die.

It had seemed easier before I was climbing past a steady stream of the corpses of those who had failed. Before I was looking into their dead, glassy eyes and taking in their states of dress or undress, now curled happily with face pillowed on a tangle of blanket, now sprawled half hanging from the morass with arms draped down like tree branches, now with only a single perfectly-formed arm sticking out of the mountain of soft covers. I shuddered.

"There's a tale in my land about a princess," I told Grosbeak as I climbed.

I felt something tickle the back of my mind, but I ignored it. I didn't dare lose my nerve now.

"Dead or living?"

"Living, in the tale."

He grunted as I ascended. The corpse nearest me held a golden dagger trimmed with gilt bees. A weapon that had not been enough to spare him. I swallowed back nausea at how much he looked like a perfect version of Svetgin. It could have been my brother tucked away in the last layer if not for me.

"A prince was thinking about marrying her, but he needed proof of her delicacy."

"That's not usually what they want proof of. Usually, mortals want childbearing hips. No scars from pox. Virginity. That sort of thing."

I coughed. "Anyways. He insisted on proof she was royal, so he insists she sleeps on ten mattresses without knowing why and secretly he placed a tooth from his childhood under the bottom mattress."

"That's dangerous magic there. You shouldn't waste childhood teeth on brides."

I kept climbing, face screwed up in concentration. How many layers were there? Did Lady Tanglecott just lay a new mattress over her last dead lover and start again?

"The next morning, she claims not to have been able to sleep all night and when they check she's bruised on her shoulder just from sleeping on the tooth, so he knows she's a true princess."

"Ha! No. She knows he's truly cursed because a single bone from his youth causes a malaise. She should stab him through the eye with a ruby dagger, or through the liver with a sapphire dagger, or if she only has iron, she could use it to pin his liver to a birch tree a one-mile distance from the rest of his body."

I was silent for a long moment, climbing. The man nearest me had a wing. It was broken in half, the bone jutting out in stark ivory and shrunken dried tendons between the black feathers. I retched, closing my eyes for a long moment.

"What would that achieve?" I asked at last.

"It would break the curse and eliminate it from haunting his descendants forever."

"I'm pretty sure that a basic murder would do the same thing."

I forced my eyes open and climbed further. Almost there. Almost. There.

"You never know, and you can't be too sure," Grosbeak said, knowingly. "What's the point of the tale?"

"I've forgotten. I just think that maybe Lady Tanglecott isn't a true princess since she sleeps every night on a lot more than teeth."

A hand reached over the edge and hauled me up to the top of the swaying bed.

"I never claimed to be a princess. I want so much more than that," my hostess said, and behind me, the last light of sunset winked out.

Chapter Fifteen

"BY THE TIME this Three Day Bind is complete, I plan to have doubled the kingdoms under my charge and be ready to crush my enemies, put them under the heel of my boot, and drag their miserable corpses through the slime of defeat." Lady Tanglecott's mouth formed a vicious bow.

"How lovely for you." My tone was dry as week-old bread.

All around us, through the glass walls and roof, the stars bloomed and flared, filling the sky so full they became a spill of froth across it, bright, pale, and unfurling. With them, the moon rose, silver, winking, and half full. I watched that sky warily. That was not the moon I'd left in the mortal world. How much time had passed?

A chilling *tick-tock, tick-tock* seemed to beat where my heart used to be.

"You do well to watch the heavens, Izolda. You must stay in this bed until the dawn breaks the night sky or our bargain is void." Tanglecott lay back against a wealth of pillows, her golden hair spilling around her like an unearned halo.

I took up a spot on the opposite corner of the mattress, legs crossed before me, back straight. I didn't dare sleep and I did not care for the uneven lumps beneath my straight spine.

"You should rest. The days will be eventful," she said, her eyes closing as she lay back.

"I have no certainty that, if I drift off, you will not fling me from this bed and into the fire."

"I hunger," roared the fire from below. A little spill of sparks emphasized his words.

Lady Tanglecott laughed, long and tinkling. "And spoil the fun? I think not. That fire has not visited me in two centuries and now he makes an appearance for your sake. Surely, you can see the delight in this charming pantomime. Besides, you're already destined to die of a broken heart. Why should I speed the process? I will plant my poison dart in your mind tonight and watch as it slowly takes you down. There is a wingless dragon in the southern isles – a miserable, unformed thing, slow as the mud of summer, ugly as your bodiless friend there," she pointed idly at Grosbeak. "But when this dragon bites, its poison lingers, slowing its prey, deadening its response, slowly draining the victim of life. I do so admire such an approach and I think to use it with you. Let us see how long you kick and thrash against the inevitable."

"How will you do that?" I asked, but my teeth were on edge, fear thick in the air around me. I caught the scent of oranges and fresh-washed linen. Had she filled the bed with more of her smoke to cloud my mind? Had she laced the sheets with poison – beyond the obvious poison of seeping corpses?

"With words, mortal girl. Are you not aware that is how we women fight? The jab of the insult aimed perfectly to strike the liver of your faults, the bludgeon of endless politeness barbed with the need to respond in kind, the twist of the compliment that shines false, the turn of the words that tilt your beloved out of your reach." Her smile was angelic. "It's been too long since I employed these well and now, I find myself surveying my arsenal and choosing the exact weapon required."

She tapped her chin.

"Is that what you did to these men in the mattresses?" I asked boldly.

She chuckled, low and sultry. "Ah, those lovely fools. Did you not enjoy observing their exquisite faces and sleek forms?"

"I prefer my men alive," I said pointedly.

She quirked an eyebrow. "As do I, but once I'm through, I hate to share. I'll not allow what's no longer needed to be claimed by another. Not with men. Not with nations. Not with anything."

Her hand hung idly from one wrist, and she plucked a golden curl from her bed, twirling it around her finger.

A chill flooded my senses. What would she do with me when this Three Day Bind was past? I was her plaything. She wouldn't want to share that.

She lounged, smiling like a cat watching a bird in a cage, her eyes bright and large.

"While you sleep here, perhaps you can be of some use to me. You seem good at riddles. See if you can learn the answer to this one. It's the latest from our sovereign, the Bramble King."

"You think I'll answer riddles for you?" I asked in disbelief.

"I think you're a practical girl. Answer this for me and perhaps I'll spare you."

"How can you spare me?" I asked, unable to keep the wryness from my tone.

"I can offer the antidote to the poison I'll give you next." She raised a single brow, shifting to spread her arms and legs wide as if she was enjoying every moment of her time resting in bed. "So, set your mind to this riddle, *From stone to feather, from stillness to motion, from stagnant to shift – the time has come. Sing the song of genuflection, bow ye to your broken dream."*

"I'll work on that," I said, but it was hard not to betray my excitement. I had the clue that Bluebeard had missed while under the water and he'd need it when I finally rescued him. I could be helpful. All I had to do was remember.

"Don't look too happy, because now comes your barb," she said, winking as she sat up, as if she was doing something playful rather than trying to kill me with words. "You thought that by taking this Three Day Bind you could save your husband from beneath the waves. You thought your bargain with me would give you a safe release back to the mortal world with one other." She held up a hand. "Don't interrupt. I am not going back on the bargain. You can have whoever you want – whoever I can access. You can have that horrible rotting head, or the half-dead weasel draped over your shoulder. Strength of men and beasts, but that thing stinks. You do realize it smells, yes? Your mortal nose is not too dull to smell it? I digress." She waved a hand. "Know ye this – you cannot have your drowned husband. The bargain for him was with the Sea, and to get him back, there can only be a strict exchange – Wittenbrand for Wittenbrand, body for body, soul for soul. In order to get him back, you'd have to trap one of *us* -

one of those better, stronger, more magical, more beautiful, and more clever than you. And you would have to give *their* life to the Sea in exchange for your husband. And you have no chance of that, whether you survive my home or not. You can't even cheat and give up your own mayfly life. You aren't Wittenbrand and your life does not count."

And then she was gone, slipping over the side of the bed. From the floor, she called up, "The words of the bargain said you'd spend three nights in my bed. They never said I had to spend them with you or with your repulsive pets."

She left through the door, and though it was glass, she was gone the moment she shut it behind her.

Frustrated, I threw myself back across the blankets, trying with all my will not to think of the corpses layered beneath the mattresses and blankets. Trying not to think about what it might do to a person to spend a night of repose over the dead – even the unrotted dead. Wondering if, perhaps, we all did that as there was only so much earth in the world and so, so many bodies to have buried over the years.

My Bluebeard had wives sealed in a room – carefully preserved and tended, frozen in time and space, like preserved flowers. I'd thought that a horror before. Upon seeing what Tanglecott did to her beloved, I saw it from a new perspective. There was a least some faint sliver of honor and respect in his methods. He had not layered over them to cavort with his next victim over their unfinished remains.

Who would have thought I'd consider as honorable what had once held me in claws of fear? The heart was an odd winding path, dark and tangled even to its mistress.

I sighed.

"She's going to win," Grosbeak said very sincerely.

I ignored him, my eyes stinging with tears of frustration.

"She's going to win because she's right. Her poison will break your heart. Mortals aren't very strong. She must have seen – as I did – how your heart is as a wrecked ship on the teeth of an island's rocks. You have not simply given your heart to the barrow, you have cut it from your breast, butterflied it, and forced it through the barrow's teeth and into its maw."

"Your metaphors disgust me," I muttered, but my heart was not in it. I would not cry. I would not bend.

"And you won't be able to do it. We both know you're no murderess.

You nearly killed yourself in Aayadmoore to keep those lily-white hands clean. To plot, to plan, to execute the extinction of another? You haven't the liver for it."

How in the world could I trap a Wittenbrand? How could I do it while I was trapped here in Lady Tanglecott's bed? I was of no more use than those poor dead fools who shared this bed with me. Despair grasped for me and I barely held it back.

I turned to Grosbeak. "Are there spectators here? Is anyone watching us?"

He snickered. "They can't come into her bedroom. The only ones listening now are the specter and the fire."

"I hunger," said the fire.

I checked carefully under the pillows and the top two layers of blankets. There was nothing dead under them.

"Is it just me, or are these riddles from the Bramble King too easy?" I asked.

"You call that one easy?" He scoffed.

"Clearly he means that it's time to take the arrow from the stone." I poked around on the mattress, investigating any lumps or bumps. I did not want to sleep here, but if I did, I definitely did not want to sleep on something dead. Or at least, I didn't want to sleep too closely on top of something dead.

Grosbeak snickered. "It can't be that. *That's* impossible."

"Nevertheless," I said dryly. "The Bramble King plans to die and pass on this realm to the winner of the game. He wants that one to take the arrow first. It's all very transparent."

"Or you're wrong."

"Or I'm wrong." I massaged my own forehead with my living hand. All these sacrifices. All this striving. I was farther away than I had been before.

"Why would you tell me the answer to the riddle?" Grosbeak asked warily.

"You're my ally, aren't you? My one friend in this deadly game?"

I flopped back on the pillows, confident that the dead were at least a mattress-length from myself.

"What about the song part?" Grosbeak pressed.

"That I must still consider," I replied but my mind drifted back to when I'd touched the arrow only hours ago. Something in it had sung to me. Perhaps it was related.

The fire flared extra bright, making a sound not unlike a belch and then a scrap of flame drifted upward and while I was still too surprised to think beyond the unthinkable thing my eyes were seeing, it transformed into a bird of flame, bearing a flaming parchment in its fiery grip. It flapped twice to me and offered the conflagrant note. I took it in a trembling hand, huffing to blow out the flames before they consumed the entire piece. The bird blew out with the flames, leaving nothing behind him but a puff of smoke that smelled like the intoxicating scent of the smoke of a birch fire.

"Thank you," I said stupidly.

"You are welcome," intoned the fire.

Feeling foolish, I unfolded the note and read what was written on it.

I waste.
I fade.
I am borne below.
She lingers.
Lasts.
Against the foe.
Live now my heart
Live now for me.
I gasp.
I die.
I ache for thee.

I crumpled the letter to my breast, crumpled myself around it, and I thought of how different Bluebeard's bed with the night flowers, and the window to nature, and the disgruntled mirror were to this monstrosity I was trapped in tonight and how the Wittenhame shaped itself to its princes and princesses it was dominated by. And I wondered – not for the first time – why my husband allowed himself to be so misjudged when he had a heart that loved beauty and kept all it could pristine.

And then I couldn't help the silent sobs that shook me like a rag doll in the mouth of a mastiff. Because he was drifting away, and I was still here and I didn't think I could murder someone to bring him back.

"What will you do?" Grosbeak asked me, breaking into my misery.

"I'm going to try to sleep," I said miserably. "It's been a long day."

The ferret crept wretchedly from my shoulder and curled up against me as I settled on my side, my skin crawling at the act of relaxing on *this* bed. My heart heaved up great miseries at every thought that surfaced. I pulled Look and Despair close to my chest. She reeked of musk, but her chest went up and down when she breathed, and her small body was warm. I appreciated the life there. I appreciated that she was still so solidly real in this land of nightmares.

"And what about me?" Grosbeak complained, sounding put out.

"You should sleep, too," I said in a small voice.

His mumbled curses were the last thing I heard as I sank into the pillow – and I would have been shocked if I were still awake, suspicious of magical influence at the very least, for I fell immediately into sleep without dreams.

I woke abruptly, blinking in the darkness. I'd sunk into the thick blankets and soft mattresses of that terrible grave of a bed. So deep was I between soft layers that it felt as if I were being slowly digested by a terrible cloth-layered beast.

I swallowed down bile and clawed myself up. The ferret chittered sleepily, clawing to drag itself up my shoulder and under my braid. I heard a squawk and a squeal as it fought with the specter for pride of place, but I ignored them both.

I peered around the star-lit bed, over the rumpled tangles of blanket and sheets, and to my horror, I could find no sign of Grosbeak.

"Grosbeak?" I whispered and then a little hoarser, "Grosbeak!"

Had he rolled off the side?

The bed leaned precariously when I tried to look. Carefully, I lowered myself to my belly, so only my head was over the edge as I checked on every side. He was not on the ground. He was not dangling from a hand or foot of a corpse.

"Grosbeak!" I called louder.

The only sound in the darkness was the sound of the fire snoring.

I did not need him here to tell me that I could not climb down and get him. Not with the dawn not yet arrived.

I made my way to the center of the mattress, drew my belt knife, and sat with my arms clasped around my knees, shivering in the cold.

My only friend was gone.

The ferret chittered.

My only friend who *could talk* was gone.

In the back of my mind, the mournful sound of the chant returned.

"Izolda, Izolda, Izolda."

"I love you, Bluebeard," I tried to say. *"I will save you if I can."*

I thought I heard a reply – only a breath of a mental sound. *"I come."*

I gasped, clinging to those two small words as a man clings to the last scrap of bread he has.

But the voice could only be my imagination because no one was coming for me. No one was staying with me. Not among my friends. Not even the dead.

I squeezed my eyes tight and clenched my fists, flinching at the grinding bone-on-bone sound of my skeletal phalanges forming a fist.

"I will not let her poison kill me," I whispered to myself. "I will not let this bring me down. If I need a captive Wittenbrand to feed to the ocean, I will capture one. I will force one beneath the waves. If I need to solve a riddle, I will solve it. I am not helpless, and I am not yet dead."

And those words gave me strength as I thought long and hard about which Wittenbrand I had a chance to trap, how I might trap them, and whether I would ever see my bodiless friend again.

Chapter Sixteen

WHEN DAWN finally lit the sky, creeping in like an embarrassed friend, I gathered Look and Despair into my arms, looked her in her black eyes, and said firmly, "Today, we find a way to get some of our own back, ferret."

Her chitter could have meant anything. I took it as support. With precious few on my side, I had to take what allies I could get.

The way down the side of the bed was worse than the way up. I had to find my footing blindly, unsure if what I stepped on was blanket or corpse until I drew level with it. By the time I reached the bottom, I felt both overwhelmingly nauseated and in need of a priest.

I searched fruitlessly for Grosbeak, but there was no sign of my severed head friend, no trail of crabs or streak of briny rot.

The fire burned so low it was barely a smolder, but I approached it anyway, crouching low beside it to warm my hands.

"I wish I could take you with me," I told it. "You, at least, are a friend."

"Thank you," said the fire – somewhat predictably.

"If Grosbeak were here, he would have some kind of advice for me." My voice sounded lost even to myself. There was no way to bathe in the room – though I badly needed a bath. No way to change my clothing nor any clothing to change into – though I also needed that. My wolf cloak was long gone. My black dress dirty and torn.

I made my way to a small dressing table to one side of the glass room, hoping for a glass comb or a faint mirror to fix myself with. There was nothing on the glass table except for glass bottles – nearly transparent. Something to drink, perhaps? I took one up at random and removed the stopper, sniffing it with my eyes closed. It did not smell potable. It did not smell of liquor. Rather, the scent of moss and musk and something almost like melting snow filled my nostrils and when I opened my eyes again, the house had changed again.

Now, the bottle I held was a rich emerald green, and the others on the oaken table were of various colors and shapes. A mirror rimmed in oak leaves showed me myself – rumpled and worn, my hair out of place. I tidied it hastily before turning around.

The bed remained the same, though the corpses in it looked paler and deader and more ... human ... than they had before. Everything else had morphed into wood and rich cloth, to carved lintels and mantels and heavy baseboards and wainscotting. Pine boughs hung with red ribbon formed a garland over doors and across the walls. The room smelled of pine.

That it had four tangible walls and a firm floor, decided me. I put the bottle of scent in my pocket. If I breathed something worse, I'd like to return to this reality at will. It was one I was more able to navigate.

Without my bodiless friend, I had no one to provide a dry monologue as I slipped out of the room and crossed a narrow wooden bridge between steep-peaked wooden buildings. There was no way out of this tiny outdoor space. Wood buildings surrounded it on every side, without gaps between them but lined with clinging ivy. On the other side of the bridge, a door was open and glowing with warm light, so I made my way across the bridge, pausing in the middle to look down in the water.

To my horror, there was something in the calm water – many somethings. They were skeletons, I realized after a moment. I flexed my skeletal hand and swallowed. The skeletons of six – yes, I counted a second time, there were six – moose, their antlers hopelessly tangled, were submerged in the still water of the pool. They had died – or settled, with their heads low on the ground, their front legs kneeling, but their back legs still standing, pelvises at the highest point. It made the horrifying sight look like a six-pointed star. Green algae coated the edges of their bones and even in the faint light of dawn, they seemed a stark white against the black pond water.

I shuddered and hurried the rest of the way across the small bridge.

That couldn't be natural. But who would do such a thing to such massive creatures?

The sound of cutlery on dishes and the murmur of voices came from the open door and the scent of bacon and something sweet and cinnamon met my nose. I was drawn forward, hungry despite myself.

The door opened into a grand hall, lined with taxidermy – moose, elk, leaping cats, beavers complete with a fully reconstructed beaver house, so many fish of every kind on every wall that any angler would be put to shame. I stared at one near me, trying to determine the species – some kind of trout, I thought – and then it moved. Just the tiniest flicker of struggle.

I froze. The eye of the moose nearest me rolled in its head.

Revulsion rose.

Between these creatures – frozen in place, but not dead – lay a massive fireplace in which a dancing fire seemed to wink at me, and in the center of the room a long live-edge cedar table had been laid with hot steaming silver pitchers and silver trays stacked with glistening bacon, gleaming rolls generously frosted, candied fruits, bowls of creamy yogurt, and tiny delicacies crafted in star-like perfection.

At one end of the table, Marshyellow drooped over his food, a squirrel eating the same food he did from its place on the crown of his head.

At the other end, Coppertomb drank from a pewter mug while reading a book of which something had taken a large bite. He was as precisely neat as always, but today his cheekbones and eyelids were dusted with gold and his jacket was a rich violet. He did not look up when I entered.

To the side, Tanglecott ate, one hand draped on a sleeping winged snow lion at her side. The other occasionally offering a tidbit to a head on a silver platter beside her. The head of my friend, Grosbeak, who leered at me as I entered – not a captive at all, but an invited guest.

I felt the blood rush from my face.

Something dripped onto the cedar table. I followed the path upward and gasped at the chandelier built from a hundred elk antlers and filled with a thousand lit candles. Below it, spreadeagled, belly down, arms and legs arching up painfully above her from the chains suspending them, was Sparrow. Her entire back was encased with wax drippings. They formed strange runnels where they found paths downward from her long hair. But her underside was wet with red patches and as I watched both wax and blood dripped to fall on the table and the food with equal disregard for where it landed.

I gasped, choking on my own horror. I felt not unlike the fish mounted live upon the wall, left to breathe forever the air they were not meant for.

"Try a sticky bun," Grosbeak said with a snicker. "They have a little extra something. For flavor." He made a sucking sound as if he were licking a non-existent finger. "I think they call this spice, 'Sparrow.'"

"I see you've had a little extra something, too," I said, touching the side of my face where he had a smear of white frosting. "Though I suspect the flavor is 'treachery.'"

"I did tell you I was betting against you," he said dryly. "It's not my fault you didn't account for it."

"He told you he was going to betray you, and you trusted him?" Sparrow's voice was barely audible, more a raven's croak than the voice of a woman. "And to think the Arrow placed his faith in you. He bet his life on you, worthless rag. For what?"

I swallowed, feeling the blood rush to my face as I looked up and met her eyes. She screwed up her face and spat down at me, but she didn't have the strength to aim it right. It fell instead in a quivering gob on top of a shiny orange.

"Mayhap I'll even ride in the joust," Grosbeak said merrily as if Sparrow were not even there. "Or at least have a front-row seat from the end of a pike. I'll take either at this point."

My mind was racing. There was something significant about Sparrow being alive, wasn't there? Because she had taken that message from the Bramble King in Bluebeard's place. It meant their fates were bound together. And that meant that if she lived, then he was still in the game, didn't it? Which was why Lady Tanglecott was trying to get his lands by other means. Did that mean she was forbidden from killing Sparrow outright just as she was forbidden doing that to the other players? I wished I could ask Grosbeak. Judging by the gleam of satisfaction in his eye, he knew what I wished for.

My head whipped up and met the eyes of the golden-haired beauty who had arranged all of this, my bottom lip quivering with something betwixt horror and rage.

"Felicitations," Lady Tanglecott said with an arched eyebrow. "I see you've figured it out at last. But you can't prevent my conquest. I'll take every shred from him, and every ally, and I'll hang them up and cut them to bits like I have that fool woman decorating my chandelier. Did you see the lovely tanglecott in the pond? A rare piece, that. It's what I'm named for. And it's what I plan to do to all of the Wittenhame."

"A bit presumptuous of you," Coppertomb said mildly, licking his finger and turning a page. "But I do like your stirring attitude."

She smiled tolerantly at him. "No great deed is truly done unless it is observed, Coppertomb. You should be pleased that I chose you as my observer."

"And the head?" he asked, flicking a finger at Grosbeak with tolerant amusement as one might do when a child explains the governing of a state in a fanciful daydream.

"Him, I need. I can't let the girl use him to her ends anymore. Not now that she knows a painful little secret."

I gasped. Did she mean that I could have put Grosbeak into the water as an offering on Bluebeard's stead? He was, after all, another Wittenbrand, dead though he was. I had not thought of that.

"I told you she wouldn't figure it out unless you said it plainly," Grosbeak drawled. "You could have left me in her possession, and she would never have thought to use me as her sacrifice."

"Better fortified than ravaged, I always say." Tanglecott plucked up the orange Sparrow had spat upon, saluted her with it, and tossed it at me.

My skeletal hand flew up and caught it before it smacked me in the face. I bounced the fruit on my bones, the fires in my heart flaring hot and fierce.

They were all terrible people – terrible in power, terrible in kind.

"The sun at dusk," Marshyellow said, lifting his pale eyes to stare at me. "The brilliant orb. In the sky. Lived its time. Time to die."

"I think he wants your orange," Tanglecott said with her mouth curling in disdain.

Carefully, I crossed the room, edged past Marshyellow's stony keepers, and dropped the tainted fruit into his hand.

He laughed, his chuckle starting as barely more than a wheeze and then spiraling upward. What would a realm be like with him as ruler? What would a mortal kingdom be like with him at the helm? I shuddered, unable to help myself.

"A curse on you," Sparrow breathed from just above my head. "As he loved you, may our home hate you. As you have failed to rise up for him, let it rise up against you."

I shivered. I would rise up for him if I could. I would do anything for him.

"Izolda, Izolda, Izolda," the echo said, melting me inside until I was nothing but hot wax in an Izolda shell.

I forced it from my mind and forced myself to study Marshyellow before backing away. He was using my hand to prepare morsels to eat. The sight of it made me ill.

"Do you always eat breakfast together?" I asked Lady Tanglecott mildly.

Her laughter tinkled.

"Only when I have weekend parties. These other Wittenbrand are my guests. Even Sparrow, though she does not know how to show her gratitude."

"You won't live for him," Sparrow grated out, still accusing me. "You won't die for him. You won't kill for him. You only drag him further into the depths. His enemies have become your friends because you have not the heart to stand against them."

Harsh.

"Yes, yes, Sparrow." Lady Tanglecott flicked a bored hand. "You're bitter. We know. Let us at least enjoy breaking our fast without needing to sweeten it with honey."

My mind was racing. I needed a way to get a Wittenbrand into the sea. And it couldn't be Grosbeak. Because if he really was the key, they wouldn't be waving him in front of my nose like that. It was clear enough that he was meant to be a false lead to draw me away from real possibilities. I also needed a way to get Sparrow free. As soon as I might.

My eyes flicked to Marshyellow. He had taken out my hand and was letting it cut his sticky bun for him.

"Go dress yourself, mortal woman. You're dressed disgracefully for a party. I told my denizens to put something in my room for you," Lady Tanglecott said and there was an edge to her voice that left shivers up my spine. "Run along now and be quick about it. You have ten minutes. Longer, and I will release the lions to take out my wrath on your Sparrow. I won't have you sneaking around my house like a mouse searching for cracks and crumbs while I win this Three Day Bind. Which I will, of course."

Coppertomb clicked his tongue.

"Don't censure me, Coppertomb," Lady Tanglecott said dramatically. "I have more than one chandelier in this house."

"But not more than one tongue," he enunciated clearly. "Don't tempt me to take it."

I was out of the room before they'd finished their banter. I didn't know when the ten minutes started, and I didn't want to guess wrong or what might happen to Sparrow? Would Tanglecott really allow her to be ripped apart by lions?

I sprinted over the wood bridge, trying so hard not to see the tanglecott in the pond. Avoiding it only made it more apparent and I was green-faced and stumbling by the time I reached her room again.

A dress dummy had been set in front of the bed while I was gone, and on it was a dress that clothed from chin to toe and with sleeves that pointed over the hand to cover as much of it as possible. It was a light dove grey and tailored to hair-breadth fit and precision, pieced in such a way that it seemed more like armor than a gown. Tiny onyx buttons ran right up the front to just under the chin. It was so utterly practical that I was shocked Tanglecott had provided it for me.

But there was no time for shock. The longer I left Sparrow in their hands, the longer they had to torment her. I must dress quickly and return. I owed that Wittenbrand, whether she despised me or not. She belonged to the Arrow, and I was the Arrow's wife which meant she belonged to me and it was my responsibility to rescue her and get her to safety.

I donned my dress armor, tied my hair back, and steeled myself for battle.

Chapter Seventeen

THIS TIME, when I returned over the bridge, I strode like a woman preparing to enter a battle, each footstep stark and echoing. I held my head high. I wasn't sure yet how I would get Sparrow down from that chandelier, only that I would. I would bargain. I would trick. I would beat them at their own game.

I flexed my skeletal hand, reminding myself that I still had power in this strange Wittenhame world. It was a power that should not be discounted – the power to make sacrifices.

Look and Despair shot down my shoulder and back into the bag, huddling in the bottom of it as if the rough leather could shield her from the nightmares without.

"I miss him, too," I whispered. But that was all the remorse I would spare for Grosbeak. He was an untrustworthy bow, shattering at the very moment the enemy came pouring over the hills, useless before he ever truly was useful at all.

By the time I reached the breakfast room door, my mouth was a grim line and my blood thundered in my ears with each clench of my fists. A tiny qualm swam to the surface of my mind at seeing it closed. It had not been closed before. Gargoyles were carved in relief on its surface, making indecent gestures insulting faces at whoever dared enter.

Smoked glass was inset around them and through it, I could see the orange glow of the room beyond.

"Wish for me that all the turnings of fate land in my favor," I whispered to Look and Despair, and then I wrenched the door open.

Some doors squeal on their hinges. This one seemed to give off an eerie laugh-like screech. With it echoing in my ears, I reentered the breakfast room.

Perhaps, if one has never seen a poorly kept slaughterhouse or the aftermath of a battle then one would not know how to picture what I saw. I had seen both and still, I stumbled, gasping as I took in what was before me.

The Wittenbrand had departed, leaving their half-finished breakfasts still spread across the cedar table. Marshyellow – mad as he was – had even forgotten to take my hand. It lay in the center of a tray of oranges, trying to peel one on its own and sliding miserably over the tough fruit hide.

One chair lay on its back to the side. Another was slung over a moose antler as if a scuffle had broken out.

It was none of these things that made the breath freeze in my throat.

It was, instead, the head in the middle of the table.

In gruesome drama, they had severed Sparrow's head and set it directly in the middle of the table. Her corpse still hung from the chandelier coated in its turtle shell of wax, trailing its lifeblood onto the table below, while the head sat pale and pristine in the center of the breakfast table as if it were a match to Grosbeak – salt to his pepper, oil to his vinegar.

I stumbled, reaching for the nearest thing to gain support.

The nearest thing turned out to be a massive two-handed sword with a bloody blade. I swayed, gripping the pommel to keep myself upright, my vision jittering in and out.

The sword pinned a note to the ground, but I did not have the wherewithal to retrieve it just yet.

Sparrow. Dead. She who was right hand to my husband. His most loyal supporter and the link to his fiefdom here in the Wittenhame. I still did not know him well enough, despite how we two had been bound by vow these past seven years, but this I knew – this act would scour him to the bones and wring the marrow out of them.

Unsteadily, I stumbled forward, my mind numb. I'd need to find a place to bury her. Not the tanglecott or the bed. I shuddered at the thought of those two places. No, somewhere respectful. Perhaps I could place her in the Room of Wives until a proper resting place could be found. I could wrap her body and head. I could ...

My mind jumped and skittered and I was surprised to find tears on my cheeks. I was not fond of Sparrow. She had been harsh with me when we two led Bluebeard's troops into battle as if she'd lost patience with my mortal heart. Harsh, when I cried over the travesty of war. And yet, she had been faithful. And of all his band she'd been the most welcoming. She did not deserve this.

I crept forward, hesitant, and yet certain. I owed her this and I would give it – ritual, respect, kindness.

Her eyes shot open and an uncalled-for shriek tore from my lips. I stumbled backward, my feet skidding uncertainly.

She blinked and seemed to stretch the muscles of her face before her baleful eyes turned to me.

"Izolda." She said my name like a curse and no wonder.

My hand flew to my heart, and I fought to get my breathing back under control. No need to panic. It was not as if I hadn't seen this before. I'd carried Grosbeak around with me everywhere and he in a state just like this. It was only that ... how to explain? With Grosbeak it had seemed almost a natural state for him, as if he had been born for the indignity of life without a body, whereas for Sparrow it seemed the worst of travesties. It did not seem real.

"Sparrow," I forced the trembling word through my dry throat. I could be practical about this. She was an animate severed head. This was nothing new. No need to panic. Had I said that already?

I straightened my shoulders consciously and stepped forward. She deserved better than revulsion. That much, at least, I could give.

"This is your fault, mortal wife of my prince."

"Of course it is," I said briskly. "In the end, everything seems to be."

"Don't be flippant with me," she said, raising an eyebrow threateningly. "Again, you bear blood guilt. Again, you have brought disaster upon all of the Arrow's dealings. You are the one fly in his ointment, the one rotten apple in the cart, the one glass bauble in a chest of gems."

"The one weed in his garden of flowers?" I asked. I found, suddenly, that I had no patience for this. "If your only purpose here is to fling insults, I fear I must inform you that I have become inured to their sting. They seem to be all the hospitality anyone has for me anymore."

"Don't pout, it doesn't suit you. You're not the one who just lost her head."

I strode forward, scooped up my living hand from where it fumbled, and struggled with the orange. I held it up in front of her face with the skeletal one.

"We've all lost things that can't be recovered," I said grimly.

The hand still moved. Without my control. Without my request. That fact alone left my stomach crawling. I tried not to vomit as I stuffed it into the bag with Look and Despair. That I'd found it again was a stroke of favor in this game. I – alone, perhaps – knew what a great stroke it was for if Marshyellow had suspected the trap I'd laid in our bargain he would have held onto it better.

"I've lost my life and my body because of you. A hand is nothing in comparison."

"Because of me?" I asked, but I hardly cared what reason she had for saying that. I was guilty in the minds of others for all the ills in this world and the mortal one. Why bother disabusing them of their prejudice? I strode to the note on the floor and tore it from where it was pinned, my back to Sparrow.

"It occurred to Lady Tanglecott that you might decide to trade me for my master, and so she eliminated me promptly."

At that I spun around, searching her face.

"Oh yes," she said bitterly. "It was a possible move, though I can see you did not think of it. I am Wittenbrand. I *was* alive. Had you drowned me in the ocean, you could have traded me for your husband."

I felt the blood draining from my face. That, I would never have done.

"Don't look at me in that lily-livered way," she spat. For a severed head, she was very animated. Perhaps everyone gained a dose of spite and two doses of drama when their head was removed from the body. "You'll have to do it to someone, or had it not occurred to you?"

I swallowed. Because it *had* occurred to me. And yet, despite my many flaws, I had not yet reconciled myself to murder.

She rolled her eyes. "What does your note say?"

I turned my regard to the missive. It was written in Lady Tanglecott's elongated hand. I read it aloud for Sparrow's edification.

"Izolda, Wife of Arrow,

Let us adjoin ourselves to the sea where we can spend a pleasant day in the part of my home that hears the echoes of your husband's wasted life, for what is so thrilling as to taste tears and relive sorrows and what shall bind us together more than that?

Distinguished Above All Others,

Herself, Lady Tanglecott"

Perhaps, murder was not unimaginable.

"You really weren't going to trade me for the Arrow, were you?" Her words were said in a strange way, like she wasn't sure what to make of my responses. She'd never known what to make of me – mortal, but married to her prince in the Wittenbrand way. Mourning for the deaths of innocent mortals, yet willing to sell myself to her kind. I was a mystery to her.

Good.

Perhaps I could be a mystery to all of them.

"Should we … bury your remains?" I asked gently, not bothering to answer her question when the answer was so obvious.

Sparrow barked a bitter laugh. "And what? You'll say words over me and then I'll say words over myself? Spare me your mortal sentimentality."

I nodded calmly. "I plan to attend Lady Tanglecott's invitation. Will you join me?"

"You ask as if you want me to attend a ball with you, rather than a death trap along the shore."

"In the Wittenhame, those things seem very much the same," I said with a sigh and then paused. "Why do you hate me so?"

"Is it not obvious?" she asked bitterly. "Since my prince married you, you have ruined his plans, ruined his dominance in the Wittenhame, led to the death of my two trusted compatriots and now my own death, stolen the hearts of his folk and his fire, and twisted up all his well-laid plans so terribly that I fear they may never unwind again and despite it all, he is so devoted to you that he has given himself again and again for you. I hate you for who you have made him – that he has stooped to condescend to you – a mayfly mortal. And I hate you for what you have made me – lackey to a failed lord, dead before my time."

"Fair enough," I said boldly. And her accusations were very fair. My face flamed hot at the shame of it, but there was no use reveling in shame when there was work to be done. "That was the life and death you lived and it's yours to tell as you please. Now, it seems, you have an afterlife just like Grosbeak and, like him, you have the chance to change and live it new or to fall back into old ways and habits. So, what is your will, Sparrow? Do you will me to take you to Bluebeard's Vault or would you be pleased to come with me to see if we can yet pluck your prince from the surf?"

She snorted. "Had I any choice in companions, I would not choose you."

I forced iron into my words, but it was not too hard. I'd been pushed and pushed and now when all was lost, I would not be pushed any further.

"It's absurd to wish for what cannot be. Deal with what is or revel in your despair. But choose quickly, for time is short."

Her tone was bitter. "Don't you know we Wittenbrand are dreamers? Can't you see it in our homes and clothing, in our delights and vagaries? Asking for us to be practical is like asking the wind to sing or the birds to snow."

"I've seen stranger here," I said coldly. "Choose."

I could appreciate that she was bitter toward me – and perhaps with good reason. I could appreciate that her life had just been stolen, and she must feel quite at odds with her new position. But I was not her priest, and I had no time to counsel her. In the back of my mind, the *tick-tick-tocking* was growing more and more urgent. And though I flinched from my own internal honesty, I could admit something to myself now – I *would* give Sparrow's life to get Bluebeard back. I would give a thousand Sparrows for just one of him. And I would not even regret the choice.

"Take me with you," she spat.

Without waiting for anything else, I seized her by the waxy-coated braid, held her head up like a torch, and commanded, "Show me the way to Tanglecott's ocean, bitter ally. And perhaps together we can turn these tides."

Chapter Eighteen

IT WAS NOT difficult to trace the way back to the ocean, though the *tick-tick-tock* in my head sped faster as we wended our way through the halls of Tanglecott's house. I'd brought the two-handed sword slick with Sparrow's blood, even though I could hardly lift both it and her. I let the tip drag on the ground behind me as I hurried, bumping over stones and occasionally smacking into door frames like a toddler tearing through the house dragging a broom.

"You're breaking the cardinal rule of weaponry," Sparrow said miserably.

"And what is that?" I asked her gravely. I did not care. I would break all the rules. I would burn the Wittenbrand down if I must.

"Never choose a weapon you can't handle."

"I'll let you in on a little secret, Sparrow," I said dryly. "It can be just between you, me, the ferret I acquired, and the specter set on my shoulder without my permission. What do you say?"

She grunted. Afterlife was making her grumpier.

"My entire life is a weapon I cannot handle. I was born to a happy family full of laughter and hard work. I spent my days tending our horses with the ostlers, running the errands the household sent a young occupationless girl on when there weren't enough hands for work, listening to my mother's fanciful stories as I helped her with her stitches and embroidery, and with cleaning up after my brothers and father. I was of noble blood in a far-flung holding where we were more like a big rambling rural family than masters and servants.

"I can cook a little because I've helped Cook when she needed it. I can garden a little because I've helped bring in harvests on rainy autumns when every hand was needed and I've helped tend when brown worm comes out of nowhere or drought is upon us. I can hunt because I've been in the party when they were short hunters.

"My whole life before the Arrow came was family – love and loyalty for them bending all my choices to service and kindness, claiming my weary moments, and lighting up my spare ones. And then this came. Snatched from it all, brought to a world where love and loyalty seem as rare in the Wittenhame as magic in the mortal world, where my death is desired and sought by almost all, where my happiness is constantly thwarted, where it has taken time for me to discover who my new family is, only to see them turn on me later. A girlhood of love and hard work and sober sensibility does not prepare one for the Wittenhame.

"And in the seven years I returned to the mortal world, I tasted only bitterness and ashes. My family gone – long dead. My home passed on. My duties changed. My life shattered like a dropped mirror. And no husband or children to console me. I was just as ill-equipped to be princess as I was to be wife, but I dragged a sword through those halls, too, and I learned to wield it – to use it well enough to forge a path back to this mad world to save the last scraps of family I have.

"I don't care that you think me weak and unskilled. I don't care that you despise me. I will do whatever I must, wield any weapon I can find, and I will not stop until there's not a scrap left of me to keep fighting."

I paused for breath and Sparrow said, "Your brother. You came to save him. Lady Tanglecott told me."

I laughed, bitterly. "My brother was the excuse and yes, I will save him with this act too, if all goes as I hope. But there is no guarantee that any of it will."

"You said you came to save the last scraps of your family. Is that not him?" Now she sounded wary.

We exited a last door and stepped out into bright sunlight and the gleam of dew on leaves and grass, and light mist across the murky sea.

I snorted. "You think my brother is the family who has my loyalty now?"

Sparrow frowned. "Who else could there be?"

I lifted her braid so I could look her in the eye and make myself very clear with my furious scowl. "I am loyal to the last family I have – my husband."

She gasped.

I had expected mockery – as Grosbeak surely would have offered. I had not expected sincerity. Her reaction made me suddenly mortified at having revealed my heart.

I lowered her head immediately and began to walk along the shore. Of Lady Tanglecott, there was no sign but as I walked, patches of mist cleared, revealing another Wittenbrand waist-deep in the surf. I gasped at the sight of Marshyellow bathing in the sea, his two guards standing to either side of him, arms crossed over their chests.

In the back of my mind, I could still hear the tick-tock-tick of time running out. And here he was – ready to be forced into the sea. A life for a life. I had said I would not hesitate or regret – so why did I suddenly feel so heavy?

"Tell me about Marshyellow," I whispered as I crept along the shore through the mist. They had not yet seen me – Wittenbrand though they were – but still, my heart was drumming in my chest. Not because I was afraid of being seen, but because what I planned to do next made every pore of my body break out in sweat. The sword grip slid in my clammy hand and my head felt light at the thoughts buzzing so swiftly inside it.

He was my enemy. He would use me and kill me as he saw fit. And if I did not do the same there would be nothing left for me to bother living for.

"Do you want me to recite his misdeeds?" she hissed. "The widows and orphans he crafted and how he tormented them? The women he debauched, the children he desecrated, the spoils he took from the poor, and the agony he inflicted on the innocent? Would that make it easier for you to kill him?"

"It would, rather."

"Justify your actions? Salve your conscience?" She mocked me in her whispered tones.

"Yes!" I hissed back.

"Then I will tell you none of it. Act. Do it dispassionately. A decision made. A balance in the scales. Make your choice, and don't pretend for even a second that it's not murder because you found some reason to make that murder holy in the eyes of others."

I swallowed. She was right. There was no justifying what I would do next. It would be murder and I would be as stained and guilty as all of them.

In the back of my mind, I heard the echo again, *Izolda, Izolda, Izolda.* But it did not seem real like before. It seemed to only be an echo of what I wished. Perhaps, the lips that once spoke those words were too far gone now to speak them still. Perhaps, the mind too far down death's path to hold them. I grasped for them, and they slid further away. I was about to commit murder and it may very well be for nothing.

How could hollowness feel heavy? My chest felt like it was both.

I set the sword gently on the sand. I was no fool. It could not help me in this.

"That's right. Put the sword down. The question of whether you'd be morally culpable for murder is moot. You have not the capacity to do it at all." Sparrow seemed miserable at this declaration as if she'd hoped beyond hope that I could surprise her in this.

I didn't have the strength for her hopes. My own were pressing so hard on me that they may very well snap my spine.

I crept down the beach trembling so hard I could barely hold onto Sparrow's waxy braid.

"You *can* kill him, you know," she whispered to me. "You aren't a player in the game. It's not forbidden to you. You're a loophole and no doubt one that Lady Tanglecott planned to use to rid herself of a competitor. Did you know that in the other games almost no one was killed? This one is determined to be different."

"I'm aware," I murmured. I should have asked her why she hadn't tried this. I should have asked her about how she had been caught and how Bluebeard's people fared. I should have done that rather than ramble to her about my past and life. Selfish. I was so selfish.

I set her head down on a rock, high enough that if I failed and the tide came in, she would not be swept away, and then I peeled the ferret from my hair to place her on top of Sparrow.

"Keep her company," I whispered and still the stark trio had not moved, though the eyes of Marshyellow's guards were on me now, tracing my movements.

"Don't leave me here," Sparrow gasped, but I could not take her with me. Not for this. I could barely take myself.

I stepped to the edge of the water holding my stolen hand before me in both my living hand and my skeletal one as if I were making an offering. I kicked off my boots in the sand, flexing my toes as they let the sun-warmed sand cup their form. Courage ebbed and flowed within me, one moment certain, the next flown. I did not dare let its whim determine my actions.

I stepped into the brackish water, boldly. Small creatures fled from my path through the water and the waves lapped up, caressing first my foot and then my ankle and slowly wetting my hem as tears wet a handkerchief.

Murderous intent made me heavy. Heavy in heart, heavy in spirit. Even my tongue was heavy, the words like lead, refusing to be spoken lightly.

"Marshyellow," I said eventually, and even that was like rolling a boulder upstream.

He paused in his bathing and turned to me, his shriveled flesh truly yellow as he bathed in the sea. He looked almost innocent as he cradled a handful of crabs in a mirror to how I held my own living hand. The water was up to his waist, and I could not tell what garments he wore beneath it, only that he wore nothing on the top and I could count every rib between his liver spots.

"I've made another mortal," he burbled happily. "Bargain with me, mortal. Bargain for your life."

"I've already bargained with you," I said, slow and heavy, my whole body tingling. "Do you remember the words?"

His guards looked back and forth between them and one put his hand on the hilt at his side. Wittenbrand weapons must be different from ours if they risked bringing them into the sea.

The water surged up to my knees now – or perhaps I had stepped that far into the waves. The heavy skirt of my dress grew heavier as if it, too, would slow my hand.

"We agreed on these ones: *For the winning of a key, a hazard for the release of my heart's conqueror, I would give this hand of mine in its current form, binding to it now all that was bound to you and offering to you it's many skills. And I will forswear all vengeance on the taker – both now and always.*"

I paused. No one ran screaming. No one lunged with a bare blade.

"I fear a harm has come to you, Lord Marshyellow, for this hand has come back into my possession. Now I, and not you, are the taker and with its return are returned to me the skills of my hand and all that was bound to you. Is that not so?"

He laughed and he seemed actually delighted, but Frost and Yarrow exchanged a look of anxiety and then lunged as one toward me in the water. Frost's sword left the scabbard with a *shing*.

"I suppose it is so," Marshyellow agreed. "But will not my companions simply take the trinket back?"

The looks on their determined faces agreed with his guess as they waded through waist-high water toward me. Frost tilted his head back and forth, stretching his neck. Yarrow's expression had turned dark, his mouth forming a slash-like grin in anticipation of the violence to come.

If I hadn't been sweating before, I was now. My dress clung to my spine, stuck fast to the skin. They were only paces away.

"But were not your companions bound to you before our bargain?" I asked lightly but the words did not feel light. They fell from my lips like heavy marble. "And does that not mean that in my retrieval of this hand, I have taken possession of their bonds?"

Frost and Yarrow froze, horror in their eyes as realization rose in them like the tide rises in the sea. Their eyes met and the sword fell from Frost's fingers and sank into the surf.

A look of keen understanding flashed into Marshyellow's face as he gasped, "No."

"Yes," I said gravely, sorrowfully. "And I bid them – I bid you, Frost and Yarrow – draw Lord Marshyellow under the sea until the Sea takes him for her lover in place of my dear husband, the Arrow of the Wittenbrand, and looses him to fly to me again."

"No," Marshyellow said, his voice trembling so I could barely grasp it.

His two protectors looked down at their own bodies as they pushed through the water back to their master and the twin looks of horror on their faces told me that even they had missed the barb I'd laid in that bargain. But their bodies did exactly as they had been told, bound by geas and honor.

This was worth a hand. Worth so much more than that. Worth even the terrible sick feeling that seized me as they reached Marshyellow in the foaming surf, took him by either spindly arm, and dragged him between them, deeper and deeper into the sea. Unstopping. Unrelenting. Unable to stop their own hands and feet.

Marshyellow's gaze stayed over his shoulder, never leaving mine as his mouth shaped again and again the word "No" until it filled up with saltwater and only bubbles remained. A moment later, his burning eyes were swallowed up by the very thing that had swallowed my heart and hope. And a moment after that, they all vanished beneath the inexorable waves.

I couldn't move. I couldn't so much as shift my weight. Guilt roared through my ears, drowning out thought, dragging me down so that I wondered if I, too, might sink beneath the waves.

My hands were clean. I'd done no violent act. And yet I was a murderess. An unseen brand had touched my heart.

Worth it? I could not tell. I did not have room in my soul for anything now except the burning knowledge that I was innocent no more. I was tainted by destruction, stained by iniquity. There were still bubbles coming up from the place where my victim was sent. I could bring him back. I could take back the sin I'd done. It was not too late.

But worse than the deed itself was the knowledge that I would not call it back to me. I would not purge my own shame.

I was still trembling when laughter drifted to me from the shore, dancing through the air in tinkling threads as if woven of wedding days and safe births. That was not Sparrow.

I whirled, the sea lapping all around me – the water was nearly to my waist now.

"Do you think that will be enough?" Lady Tanglecott asked from the shore. Her perfect face smiled serenely. She was holding something up, studying it in the light of the sun as if she hadn't just witnessed a murder. "How naïve of you, mortal girl. How delectably tawdry. As if you could defeat such a curse with so small an offering."

Chapter Nineteen

"WHAT ARE YOU SAYING?" I asked, "Are you saying this exchange is not enough?"

I could hear the panic rising in my voice. The bubbles weren't rising anymore. It was too late to take back what I'd done.

I'd killed. I'd murdered. Marshyellow's eyes were seared into mine. I still saw them being dragged inexorably under the water again and again and again in my mind's eye. I shivered – that kind of full-body shiver that left nothing out. And still the clock *tick tick tocked* in the back of my mind as if the great hourglass of my life had been shattered and the garnets were pouring out.

The specter on my shoulder shifted as if my despair was contagious.

Lady Tanglecott's smile blossomed like a snake slowly unfurling from its coil on the rock. "Your husband's life was given to the ocean, and he was borne down to the ocean floor pinned to a pillar by an iron dagger. You saw this just the same as I. You've bought his life back – very cleverly, I might add, if predictably. But he's still pinned there. He needs someone to go beneath the waves and pluck the dagger free. Surely, you must realize this, mortal though you are."

"If that was true, you wouldn't tell me so," I said grimly.

The tide was rising, the water very slowly lapping higher and higher up my skirts, soaking my feet and echoing the cold dread in every bone of my body. I had murdered a man for nothing. I had stained my soul and for what?

No Bluebeard emerged triumphant from the waves. No Arrow soared upward in a roar of waters. Only an empty wind howled around us.

My gaze darted to Sparrow on the shore. She was watching, silent, her expression as worried and confused as my own must be. Beside her, Lady Tanglecott had set Grosbeak's head. His mouth had been sewn closed by three thick stitches of something that looked like twine. If she were lying to me and he knew it and he wanted to tell me about it – and none of those things were certain – then he could not help me now.

"And why would I not?" Lady Tanglecott asked. A ray of sunlight pierced through the mist, lighting her golden locks as tinder lights a set fire. They glowed and burned like burnished gold – like a good faerie from a story, like a godmother who grants wishes, like the heroine the prince rides to save. I was surprised the truth of her essence didn't ooze from her pores like black tar. "It suits me to tell you, Princess of Pensmoore. But don't offer your trust to me if the time is not yet come. Let us wait together and see if your husband delivers himself from the embrace of his lover. Let us wait together. Who knows? Mayhap this one time, I am wrong."

We waited for hours, her smug, me desolate.

The sun crept slowly across the sky, an indolent fool, not hurrying, not working, sauntering as though there was nothing of import hanging in the balance. We did not eat. We did not drink. I moved up the shore as the tide began to come in, collecting the two heads and the ferret and carrying them further up the rocks to keep them from washing away.

Despair swept away my senses so that my vision grew dull, my mouth dry and my thoughts sluggish.

Gone. All my chances gone and not one way to get them back.

Tears flowed from Sparrow's eyes, but she did not speak to me, and though Grosbeak's expression wiggled and he tried to tell me something with his eyes, I would not look or acknowledge him. He had betrayed me to my enemy. None of his japes could change that.

It was when the tide began to recede again and all my hopes with it and a low moan of defeat ripped from my throat against my will, that Lady Tanglecott spoke again. The wind had loosened both our hair and hers swirled around her like golden ribbons, catching the sun and rippling bright.

"It suits me to bargain with you, mortal child, for I have precisely what you need. Even now, your husband languishes, trapped forever even though you bought him back, for to purchase and to collect are two different things entirely. You are seeing this now, I think. You might wait here all your life and never see him emerge. Or – you could go to him. I have the means of this. You saw Lord Coppertomb give it to me himself – the Heart of the Ocean."

My eyes darted to the necklace she'd been toying with all this time. It was the very one Coppertomb had offered her. A flawed diamond the size of my ear strung on three strands of pearls. I remembered it very clearly, just as I remembered that Tanglecott had paled when he'd given it to her. She was not pale now. Her cheeks were bright and rose-tinted, and her eyes were liquid and swirling with mystery.

"Wearing this, a mortal could journey beneath the waves on a single breath. She could saunter down into the depths and retrieve a wayward husband. Would you like that, daughter of dust? Would you like to rescue your drowned half? To haul him up like a deep-water thing and watch his insides swell from the relief of the sea's grasp as he's drawn again to the land of the living?"

I shuddered at the metaphor. I'd heard of such phenomena but my experience with fishing was relegated to streams and lakeshores. I would not venture on a boat again. Not after the first time. The sick feeling in my belly was not just from the memory of that. I had failed. I had given everything I had and used all my ingenuity and I had failed.

"I have nothing to offer you in return," I said grimly.

And it was true. I'd been stripped down to the bone, the last remaining flesh teased from my soul just as my flesh hand had been stripped from its skeletal remains. I'd been pilfered and paupered and betrayed. To my name, I had left one ferret, the head of a woman whose hatred for me fed her afterlife, one silent spirit stuck guarding my words, and one soaking wet dress. I did not count Grosbeak who was no longer mine.

That I had one blackened conscience, rotting and mangled, would not interest her. That, too, had been wrecked upon the shoals of the Wittenhame. I paused at that thought, for it was not true. I was no victim of chance. I had made a choice. I had broken myself on the shoals of my own volition as surely as if I had held my own spine between my hands and snapped it over my knee.

Tanglecott laughed her tinkling, horrible laugh like sugar added to a wound. "You have your beauty, mortal princess, little of it though there may be. It was enough to trap a prince of the Wittenhame, and I would have it for myself."

"My beauty?" I asked, stunned for who would bargain for a thing I'd been told again and again I did not possess.

Her grin matched the snow lions she favored.

"A thing sometimes is worth the pain its owner will feel at its loss more than its objective worth, don't you think? For while you are not very fair at all, I think you will be ever conscious that you have forfeited what little scrap you once possessed. And with that in your mind, you will sink beneath the sea, set your husband free, and see for yourself the horror in his eyes at what has been stripped away from you. And then you'll be nothing but an ugly little murderess, discarded by a husband she gave everything to possess, and all for the one thing she can no longer claim. What a delicious story. I would so like to see it play out, wouldn't you?"

"Will the necklace truly let me find him under the sea?"

My heart was pounding. It was a terrible bargain. Terrible in every sense. But I did not hear his voice calling my name, not even the echo of it anymore. And it had been hours since his last bird arrived. His last poem had been a dirge. If there was any time left at all, it was nearly gone. I had waited hours and he had not surfaced. I had been patient and tenacious. So, what did it matter if I was fair or foul? What did it matter if I gave the last thing I had, paltry though it may be?

"The Heart of the Ocean will bind you to the ocean, so you may breathe the waves and see beneath their darkness for as long as you wear it. And for as long as that may be, your beauty is mine," Tanglecott said. "But know this – for I would have you make the choice with open eyes," she widened her eyes as she said this – the picture of innocence. "You will not be able to remove the necklace with your own hands. It will be yours forever just as your fairness will be added to mine forever."

"Agreed," I said, almost too quickly – for I had given my innocence and my future, my family and my sanity. What more was the one thing I'd never really had at all? But my agreement sounded like a death knell even in my own ears and from the shore, I heard muffled sounds of protest from behind Grosbeak's sewn lips. Who he was arguing for and what he was protesting? No. I did not care what he thought anymore. I would not spare the traitor a single glance.

"Agreed," Lady Tanglecott said with a smug smile. "Hold out your hands."

I held them out, cupped before me, expecting her to place the jewelry within them.

Instead, she tossed the necklace like a horse wrangler tosses a rope and the heavy loop opened and fell through the air and over my head to land with a thump against my chest. I stumbled under the weight of it as I felt my features shift and change.

To my surprise, Lady Tanglecott shifted before my eyes just as dramatically, like the shifting of a sunset – from one glory to the next, so that by a small degree she was more beautiful than she had been moments before.

In my hands, I held ashes, white and chalky, laced with grey.

I gasped and tried to step forward, but my feet could not leave the water. It was just as we'd agreed. I was the ocean's now, with the means to chase after my husband. It was only occurring to me now that there was much ocean and only one of me.

"Where is the place the platform sank?" I asked, and my voice was small in my ears.

Her only reply was laughter as she took a step back from the waves.

"Where?" I asked even knowing she would not answer, and that Sparrow and Grosbeak could not answer.

"You're like a rabbit in a trap," she said, and the light shifted and suddenly the angles of her face stood out more intensely and the shadows deepened and the viciousness of her was seen in every line. "You're chewing your own leg off and you still think you might get free. Enjoy your journey little rabbit. Enjoy rotting alive beneath the sea. At least the brine won't ravish your fair face, for it has not a scrap of beauty remaining, not even in those bright eyes, which I swear were almost charming once. Oh, and I ought to note that you've doomed your land, too, for how can you spend another night and day in my bed and home when your feet are trapped in the blue?"

I felt the blood begin to drain from my face, and I couldn't breathe. My heart was racing so fast it was all I could hear. I thought that Sparrow might be trying to say something, but I couldn't hear it, couldn't think, couldn't do so much as lift my eyes from the white ashes in my hands – the ashes not just of my beauty but of all my hopes and ambitions, of all the Izolda that ever was. I'd never been enough to save him – not at my brightest, not at my darkest, not as an innocent or a murderess, a princess or a wife. It was all just ashes in my hands, ashes in my mouth, ashes in my heart.

I closed my eyes, certain now that my heart was going to explode and hoping it would happen soon because I wasn't sure I could take one more blow.

The backs of my eyes flared bright red and I opened them to see the clouds parting, the sun blazing bright and full in its last golden hours before it died in scarlet. The ocean shone back brightness to brightness, and then in a spray of droplets, a figure emerged clad in seafoam, water, and rainbows, and garlanded in black seaweed. A flight of white birds shot up with him, made entirely of pale seafoam. They flew in all directions, singing a soaring aria as they spun through the breeze and then burst into foam flecks and fell back to the sea.

And the face that emerged from the rainbow brightness bore a blue beard on his cheek and vengeance in his eyes.

And it was at that moment that my heart chose to burst.

Chapter Twenty

IT COULD NOT BE HIM. And yet it was.

I drank in the sight of him, tracing every line, watching every flicker of expression as if I could make up for seven years in one long drink of sight.

At the edge of my vision, Lady Tanglecott's mouth opened, and she swiveled as if she meant to flee, panic strong in her eyes. I did not care. Who cared about her with *him* here?

Pawing and snorting like a beast cornered, a frothing wave of the sea rose, its crest and rivulets forming the image of a watery stallion for the barest blink of an eye, and then it raced around Lady Tanglecott, flinging up sprays of water as it ran. The spray wrapped around her – a silver net of water and fury. It drew her until she was standing ankle-deep in the lapping sea.

"What nefarious bargain have I stumbled upon?" Bluebeard asked and his face was cold and terrible, his cat's eyes flashing, and his fists clenched until the knuckles were white. And the sight of him was balm to the soul, was water for the thirsty. "Have I arrived just as it is being sealed?"

Even now that he had drawn up level with us, he was still wreathed in rainbows, they danced and frolicked around him, hard to see if you looked directly at them, but filling the edges of my vision. Black, tangled seaweeds clung to him, barely keeping him decent where his clothing was rotted to almost nothing. The seaweed tangled fecund and grasping where the rainbows were light and ethereal and through them all, I saw the jagged, unhealed tear in his side and the open wounds on each palm, peeking between this garb that painted him caught betwixt the heavens and the pit, half angel and half denizen of the deep.

"You're free," Lady Tanglecott gasped, a horror in her voice that jarred against the swelling joy in my heart. "But her actions could not possibly have –"

She swallowed whatever she was about to say and smiled, trying again. And in that moment, my own horror dawned.

Oh no.

She did not think my actions had anything to do with his release. She had led me here, taken my beauty, and watched me murder her opponent knowing all along that my actions could not free him. My stomach fell out from under me so hard that I could have sworn it hit the sea. Something where it used to be twisted into a tangled knot. Murderess, it told me. Guilty murderess.

The world swayed. And still, he had not looked at me – as if he knew that my hands were stained with blood not my own.

Lady Tanglecott tried a smile. "How pleasant that you return to the Game, Arrow."

"The bargain, Termagant."

"It's no affair of yours, Arrow," Lady Tanglecott said, drawing herself up in radiant dignity, her beauty so powerful it hurt to look at her. "While it warms the heart to see you restored to land, whatever has transpired between me and this mortal bound to you is between us two and no other."

He looked at me and it felt as if lightning had struck me. My heart seized. I could not breathe.

Something lit in his eyes behind his immobile mask – something hot and deep, something that burned and judged while eating me up.

I had the terrible sensation that I was shrinking, fading into the background, melting into the sea, and my emotions inside raged like two rams fighting on the mountains, crashing into one another only to fall together down the slope.

Half my heart sang with his return, the colors grew brighter, the light shone fiercer, the world tilted back to turn on the correct axis again.

But the other half asked, how dare I to even look at him? I, whose beauty was stolen, whose innocence had been offered up for nothing, who stood here now with soiled hands and a conscience seared with shame. I was thief and murderess, sullied, soiled, and ruined and I should flee before he discovered all I had become.

I looked away, miserable with guilt, my stomach tilting and teetering with it. I was going to be ill. I was going to fall into my own sick and drown forever.

Bluebeard made a sound at the back of his throat and the water seemed to part before him as he lunged toward me, seized the Heart of the Ocean, ripped it from my neck, tearing out hair with it in his haste. He flung it out as one tosses a ring neatly over a post and it landed square over the head and onto the shoulders of Lady Tanglecott.

"*You traded beauty for ashes, wife, and sealed yourself to the sea?*" he asked me grimly with his mental voice, and still, I could not meet his gaze. "*And this fork-tongued adder led you to it.*"

Behind him, I heard Lady Tanglecott wail. The ashes in my hands vanished, leaving only the faintest trace of smudge on my fingers. I gasped and without meaning to, I looked up. She regarded me from over his shoulder, and I barely recognized her. That was not her face.

"I turn the bargain back on the bargainers." Bluebeard's voice held a sting.

Lady Tanglecott had lost not just the beauty she'd stolen from me, but *all* her beauty, and in her cupped hand was a heap of grey. She threw it furiously into the sea, took a wobbling step toward land, and stopped, leg raised halfway to the shore.

"As you tried to bind my wife, so I bind you," Bluebeard said, not even looking at her. His eyes were on me, hot and burning and I caught them only with the edges of mine lest I be burned by their intensity. "The terms of her imprisonment are yours – trapped in the sea until such a time as other hands save you. Your beauty plundered and given to another. Your home and lands forfeit. A fitting judgment, I think."

The sound Lady Tanglecott made was not human. It was something between a howl and a roar, but before she'd even finished making it, a gleaming hand reached out from the waves and drew her under, and I saw the trout-skinned mermaid under a blanket of water for only a flash before they were both gone beneath the waves. Tanglecott's last look to me had been one of utter devastation, as though what waited for her beneath the waves was worse than just water and fish and a drowned Marshyellow held under the waves by those who had once been his faithful guard.

The breath caught in my throat.

"*Look at me, wife.*"

I dared not look. It was enough that he was restored to the world. Even if it was not by my hand. Even if all my paltry efforts had been of no more use than the ashes in my hand. It was enough that he was free. I would return to the mortal world, out of his way, out of his life.

I felt the sudden urge to cover myself and my dripping dress. But wrapping my arms around my waist did nothing to hide my guilt.

"*Look at me,*" he thundered in my mind and this time my gaze snapped up to him. I could no more disobey his voice than I could disobey the ache of my lungs to breathe.

My legs trembled, the knees no longer strong enough to hold me.

His side still bore its wound, open and ragged. His hands bore twin piercings, red with his blood, but it was his gaze I was drawn to as the tide draws the water from the land.

What did he see when he looked into my eyes? I knew what I saw when I looked into his. It made seven years feel like no more than an hour. It made everything I'd given up feel like rags and dust. It made the seams of the world seal themselves together again. I did not have to be worthy to acknowledge it was so, to find deep, searing delight in its certainty. I did not need to be clean to know all was right again with the world – even if it could no longer be right for me.

To my shock, there were tears in his eyes, swimming, unspilt.

He reached out – quick as a cat – and drew me fiercely into his embrace. I gasped at the shock of it, clinging instinctively to him. The warmth of his breath gusted over my hair and the way his bare wet flesh fit against my cheek when he pressed me to his breast pushed aside all other thought. If I only had this one, unworthy moment, I would take it entirely.

I closed my eyes and let all my feeling go to my cheek pressed against him, the feather-light touch of his hands holding me, the gust of his breath, the beat of his heart.

"*How could you doubt that I would come to you? Me, who would move heavens and earth for you? Why did you think I required murder at your hands? Foolish bargains made in haste? Excess? Wife, what madness has possessed you? You who has been order to my chaos. You who has aced this world with grim sensibility. From whence came this madness?"*

And how could I bear such accusations, steeped as they were in truth?

My lips trembled as I held back seven years of tears. To my astonishment, he caught them in his own, gentle at first, feeling their way, imparting to me the softness at the core of his heart and then blossoming into something fiercer. It was wholeness and fire. It filled me like food did not, and seared me at the same time, pain and desire all tangled into a healer's draught.

I was the one who pulled away with a gasp, long, long before I wanted to.

"I don't dare kiss you," I said, aching. "I don't dare touch you." Even though I was still touching him. "I'm stained with blood. I'm ruined in my soul."

His nod of agreement as I spoke hurt more than the cut of a dagger. I knew. I had felt both.

"I have little strength right now, I fear, but what shreds I have of it are still yours, fire of my eyes."

I could not bear to look at anything other than him. I kept my eyes fixed on his, as if setting my course to the north star. He took something from my grasp – my hand, I thought, and flung it to shore, not watching it, but watching me. So intent were we on one another that I only heard the sound of wings when they beat around us and lifted us into the air. I did not watch it but kept my eyes fixed steadily on him. But I was not surprised by them, for they were at his command and had done this once before.

"I must spend three days in her home and three nights in her bed or Pensmoore is lost," I gasped, sudden fear bubbling up in my throat. Was it already too late? "And I have only spent one of each."

He blew air from his nose as a bull snorts in irritation and then opened his palm and in it were two garnets. He flung them at her beach.

"Did it not occur to you, wife of mine, that you could have done the same, and rid yourself of that grasping gull in one flick of the wrist?"

It had not occurred to me – fool that I was. Nor had it occurred to me to bear us on the wings of white seabirds to a nearby island off the coast – which is what he did. It took only moments and I spent them with my head cradled against his chest and my body snuggled up against his and I tried not to think about how much of him was exposed to my touch and how little right I had to touch any of it. Or how quickly this moment might fade if he changed his mind and held against me all my sins.

"Is this still her home?" I asked with a trembling voice as we set down upon the rocky shore.

"*It is no one's place but ours,*" he answered as he seized my hand and in that strange almost pounce-like way of his, led me to a place where the rocks of the shore had formed a natural cave and the tide had gone out and left only small pools and soft white sand behind it. Sunlight dappled the darkness, filtering down through holes in the rock above.

He leapt into the mouth of it and with only his touch, he led me to sit on a slab of worn stone and he knelt before me, so we were eye to eye, knee to knee, hand to hand. I dared not speak. I hardly dared to breathe. I could drown in those eyes. How could he look at me like that, when I had traded away my beauty and bartered away my innocent soul?

"*What is this, wife?*" he asked me threading his fingers between my skeletal ones and lifting my hand between us to inspect it.

"I traded my hand to Marshyellow for a key to free you. He gave me the key to your Room of Wives and also Grosbeak."

He nodded.

"*And Grosbeak gave you my message.*"

"He told me not to come to you."

"*Not that. The message.*"

"Message?" my words felt foolish, they seemed to stumble as they fell from my lips. "He gave me no message."

The fire in Bluebeard's eyes deepened. "*He did not bid you wait only a little longer? He did not tell you I would soon be free and come to you?*"

"He did not," I gasped. "But the birds brought your words. They seemed to me the last words of a dying man."

He watched me gravely, his eyes deep and full of things I could not know and they drew from me a full confession though my voice shook with it.

"I thought I could free you if I were just brave enough to try. I bartered with Marshyellow and I bargained with Tanglecott. I thought I could trade Marshyellow for you and come down and draw you from the waves."

He clicked his tongue in a way that seemed both censure and pity.

"I gave up my hand and I ... I killed a man. Not by accident. Not because he attacked me. On purpose."

I looked down miserably, but after a moment I glance back at him still watching me as if waiting for me to say more. So I forced out my next stumbling words.

"And they say you are lover to the ocean now, consort of the sea."

At that, he smirked.

"And I woke Margaretta to help me open Lady Tanglecott's door even though I promised you I wouldn't steal any more of my days."

"*You woke my wives?*" I could not discern why his gaze was suddenly so wary.

"Just one of them."

"Did you put her back?"

Back? As if she were a dish I borrowed? My brows furrowed.

"Yes."

But now my tears were spilling out because laying it all out before him made me feel so foolish. It had made complete and total practical sense in the moment. I had done exactly what I'd had to do to save my beloved from the sea. But with him here, restored to me *despite* my actions instead of because of them – with him here in front of me, it felt like my hands were still full of ashes.

"I ruined everything," I whispered.

Silently, he drew me into his embrace. Without a sound, his powerful arms encircled me, and his chin rested upon my head and his chest heaved.

"I can never go back." My voice was small against his chest and my tears spilled over my cheeks and ran down his skin.

Something hot and wet ran down my hair, my face, mingling with my tears and dripping from my chin to slip down my neck. To my surprise, he drew back and gripped the collar of my dress and I saw by the red rims to his eyes that he had been crying, too.

He tore my high-necked dress straight down the front, exposing me to below the collarbone. The small black buttons popped off, flying in every direction. Here it was – what I'd been anticipating all along. The judgment. The rejection. I braced myself for it. Apparently, it would start by taking back my ill-gotten clothing.

His eyes met mine, swimming with sorrow mixed with something that looked so much like devotion that it broke my heart. And he wavered in my vision as my matching tears disguised his form so that I could not tell what he was planning next. My cheeks flared hot with shame.

"*Would you be healed, wife?*"

"Healed? I am not wounded. I am the one who made wounds."

"*Would you be washed of guilt?*"

"Yes," I said, my voice so small it was barely there at all. "But such things cannot be."

"*You say this to me who has bought you with blood? You say to me that you cannot be whole again? I will show you otherwise.*"

I gasped when he drew me in again, shocked that his touch was gentle and loving when I'd expected the opposite. His tears bathed my bare skin and my tears mingled with his, and when my chest heaved with a suppressed sob, I thought that maybe his did, too.

His pierced hands came up and caressed my neck, my shoulders, tracing the curve of flesh and bone and the wounds were still fresh, for trails of pink blood mixed with the saltwater of his tears and mine.

"*With sorrow and blood, I wash you, wife.*" And now his mental voice was a whisper. "*To me, your guilt is washed away. To me, you are clean. Speak to my riddle, fire of my eyes. Who may condemn she I have called clean? Who may accuse she who I have found worthy?*"

"But Marshyellow," I stammered as he shocked me by placing a kiss in the curve of my neck, hot on my naked flesh. I felt my cheeks flare hot.

"*Is no more dead than I was,*" he said against my skin. "*Is no more trapped than I was.*"

He kissed the column of my neck and then just under my ear and then my temple – a trail of soft kisses, slightly roughened by his blue beard. And I shivered at every one of them – for their tenderness, for their fleeting sweetness, for the sharpness of how little I deserved any of them.

He drew back and he was smiling very faintly when he met my eyes.

"*Let us see if he has the power to return. Let us see if he can rise from the depths with healing in his palms as I have done. I rather doubt it, but I will not tolerate any more self-flagellation from you, wife. You are washed in my tears and heart's blood. That should be enough for you since it is for me.*"

I did not wait for him to reach for me. Shyly, I slid one hand around his mostly naked waist, feeling the shreds of ancient cloth crumble at my touch, and the other to clasp the muscles tensed at the back of his neck, and – slowly, still not sure if he might reject me and toss me aside – I found his lips with my own and drew them into the welcome of my mouth.

We were occupied in welcoming each other in that way for enough time that he probably could have done a great act of magic if he had spent that part of my day on something else. But is it not magic to tangle futures and limbs? To soften your heart and your body to shelter another? To open your arms and your generosity to them? It felt like magic to me.

"*You will need another dress,*" he said ruefully when we paused our kisses – for even the most ardent of lovers need air from time to time. He traced the edge of my face with a finger. *"The last I remember of you was the repeating of your vows to me – marrying me in the Wittenbrand way with your heart and your bargains just as I had married you. The days I waited to see you again were long, fire of my eyes."*

"The years for me were far longer," I said wryly.

He smirked. *"I would not place that bet. You may find yourself lighter of whatever you wager."*

I turned to kiss him again, my hands drifting lower than his waist but he arrested the motion with a gentle touch. My heart was in my temples and somewhere lower than my belly as he caught my wrists – one flesh and one bone – and drew my hands up to tangle in his and sit between us.

"*Not yet, fire of my eyes.*"

And I felt hollow and aching at his "not yet."

"For I have made my vows to you, yes, but I have made other vows I must honor first."

"And what vows are those?" I asked and I could not keep the edge from my voice. Disappointment will do that.

"*I have vowed celibacy until the day I can free my wives and give them back their days and lives. This I told you.*"

At that, I sat up tall. He could not have surprised me more if he had flung cold water in my face. "What? I thought you told me you were waiting for your true wife."

"*And so I was, but there is more. Why think you that I keep them in that room?*" he asked me with furrowed brow. *"Did you think me a gruesome collector to take from them their lives and then set them one after another upon pedestals as trophies to my wickedness?"*

"Yes?" My cheeks were hot, but I didn't know why *I* was blushing.

He laughed wickedly, reminding me he was still Wittenbrand and still delighted in my misunderstanding of his ways.

"I plan to give them their lives back – every single one. But not until my

plans have turned from flower to fruit and their days and place in life can be returned in all their fullness."

"But how can that be possible?"

"I will make it possible. And when that is accomplished, on that day, I may seek my own pleasure and not until."

So, never then.

"Has it not been difficult to be celibate all this time?" I asked. I had spent the last seven years in the king's home, listening to his warriors and ladies bragging about their conquests. The idea that a man would be celibate for hundreds of years would have been more impossible to them than that he would fly across the ocean on the backs of birds.

He tilted his head to one side in contemplation. *"I find it much more difficult to restrain myself from killing every soul that irritates me and collecting their heads. Is there a word for murderous chastity? Murity? Chasterous?"*

"I think not," I said, grimly.

"I was afraid that was so."

I turned to kiss him again and he laughed and took my hand instead, guiding me to my feet.

"Even so, you try me hard, wife. Let us return home where clothing and food awaits and where the delicious tangles of your dark hair and the smoothness of your skin stop tempting me to roam to the edge of my vows."

"Must we?" I pressed and his husky laugh told me he was finding the notion as difficult as I was.

Chapter Twenty-One

WE STEPPED from the cave and the sun struck my skin where my ruined dress fell over my naked shoulder. I tried to capture the hanging cloth. Bluebeard took one look at it and tore it off entirely.

"Off the shoulder is always fashionable," he said absently. There was a depth of something in his strange eyes that looked like both joy and deep sorrow swilling together into one draught. *"It looks particularly well on you, wife. Who would have thought a woman could look so hale when one of her hands is nothing but stripped bones."*

I held up my skeletal hand ruefully and he laughed. It was one of those laughs that was heavy and meaningful rather than light.

"We shall find a ring to set it off and remind your enemies you are no stranger to pain or sacrifice. That matters far more than a complete flesh hand does." He paused and bit his lip as his gaze raked up and down me and my cheeks heated hot because I'd never had a man dressed in only the barest amount of clinging seaweed and rotted silk look at me quite like that. *"Yes, I rather think the gauche hand sets off the beauty of the rest. You must keep it, wife."*

"It's not very practical," I protested, but why was I protesting? There was no way to change it. My hand was my hand.

"Speak to my riddle, wife. What keeps the foe at bay and the fool from trying his luck? What precaution ends a fight before it begins?"

"Intimidation?" I asked and he smiled.

From her perch on my shoulder, my specter hissed and I startled. I had forgotten she was there. Had she been there the whole time we were ... I looked back at Bluebeard, my eyes wide and he winked, seemingly unconcerned by her presence as his hand came up to stroke his chin, consideringly, and I was reminded again of the open wounds on his hands and in his side. He acted as if they did not bother him at all.

"Do your wounds hurt?" I asked him.

"They're no matter."

"But do they pain you?" I pressed.

"*Wounds to the body are always painful. We bear them. Or would you have me writhe at so small a thing?*"

"And will they heal? Eventually? Can you use some kind of magic or prophesy or something to mend them?"

He looked at his palm, flexed his hand so that blood welled in his hand, and then looked me in the eye as his mind spoke to mine. *"No."*

He took my hand as if defying me to object, and then, to my utter surprise he leapt into the waves with me in tow – no. Not into them. On top of them, striding with the soles of his feet cupped in the wave like they were stepping on the lightest coating of snow, sinking in just enough to shape the water to his foot, only to have it smooth back to perfection when he lifted his foot to step again. And I was right there with him, my feet skimming over the surface as he tugged me along at an impatient lope.

"No boots," he explained, "*this requires the touch of flesh."*

But I'd already lost my boots back on the beach. I glided with him on the buoyant surface of the waves, bobbing very slightly with each step in a way that reminded me a little too precisely of the boats of my past.

"*Think not of the waves,*" he said in a voice so low it let like a caress. "*Think only of your hand in mine. Who makes the waves bend to his will? Who commands the brine of the Sea and forces her submission? Who holds your hand in his?*"

He did, apparently. A mad prince to suit a mad princess.

The ragged edge of his wound tickled my palm and I swallowed, but I believed him. I trusted his power right down to the marrow of my bones.

"All my enemies live beneath these waves," I said. "It's only sensible to be nervous that one might surface and drag me under the water."

"*If they appear, wife of mine, we shall dance hand in hand and cast them back to the depths from which they rise. Have no fear of revenants when I am with you. But we must hurry, wife of mine, I can feel the movements of the Wittenhame calling me toward the fourth move and I know not where it might be announced."*

"Could it be at a joust?" I asked. "The Wittenhame speaks of nothing else."

"I jousted often as a younger man. I have a scar somewhere from one particular ride ... hmmm."

He paused, pulling the waistband of his trousers back and twisting to look back at himself. I kept my gaze fixed steadily forward, not daring to look with him. He couldn't do that and then talk to me about years of chastity.

"Mayhap you'll show me at a later date," I suggested, gaze held steadily forward and cheeks flaring hot.

"Mayhap I will." There was laughter echoing in his mental voice.

"Perhaps you can explain to me how birds bore your messages when you were beneath the sea," I said, trying desperately to distract myself.

The wind rippled his hair and tore at his meager clothing and we hurried forward again, his eyes drifting constantly to any bird in the sky and then occasionally to me as if I were a bird, also, and just as likely to surprise him as they were.

"I wrote them for you," he said, watching a gull as it shrieked above us. *"After seeing a vision of myself beneath the sea on the first night we met. The fire offered it as a wedding gift to me."*

"The fire did," I said tonelessly.

"A noble gift, was it not?"

"But how did they know to deliver them?" I pressed.

"Speak to my riddle wife. Who knows the twisting of the mind and every echo of the heart? Who guides the hand and marks the path and speaks the night to naught?"

"Honestly, I have no idea. But it can't be birds."

That seemed to be all the explanation I was going to get because just then a dark raven fell from the sky and landed on my husband's shoulder and at his keening call, Bluebeard gripped my hand harder and broke into a trot and it took all my speed to keep up.

My whole world, for a time, was brilliant sunlight and flashing waves, dancing rainbows, the tearing and wailing of the wind that drowned out all speech, the warmth of my husband's hands and gaze, and the wickedness of his teasing smile.

"I think we'd better get home at once," I said firmly, pitching my voice over the wind, as we drew near to shore. "Someone might see you like this."

To which he only smirked more, and my face went crimson hot.

"*Fear you that another might steal me from you, fire of my eyes?*"

"I fear, rather, that your dignity will be marred by striding about in mostly your skin," I said. "Besides which, a wind is picking up and you can hardly expect seaweed to shield you from its bite."

And his smirk turned into a twinkle and his twinkle into a laugh.

"*Indeed, my sober monstrosity. Your words ring with accuracy. Let us hie us home. The time has alighted and it sings to me that it is time to tell you my secret, the terrible cause that I hold so close to my bosom.*"

And even more than his torrid kisses and feverish touches, this promise made my heart race and my breath catch for if there was anything I longed for it was to know what plan had led him on this strange, twisted path and how it could possibly turn certain defeat into some manner of victory.

We paused on the shore to retrieve our friends.

The ferret ran up my arm with relief in her eyes and promptly fell asleep slung over my shoulder and dead to all else but sleep.

Bluebeard crouched to lift Sparrow's head in both his hands and hold her up to meet his eyes, and the look on his face as he lifted her was torn with regret.

"What shall I do for you, loyal Sparrow. Speak the words and I will make them so. Shall I shelter you with my wives until you can be bought back? Shall I set you on my wall with my advisors, or would you ride with me as my wife's pet rides with her?"

"As you please, Arrow," Sparrow said respectfully – a tone I still found surprising seeing as she never granted such a thing to me.

"I please to keep you safe and then to return you to your glory," he said gravely. "Your body is near?"

At her assent, he turned to me.

"*Unlock for me the vault of my wives. We shall set my faithful servant within that she may partake in their fate with them.*"

Grosbeak made a muffled sound from the ground.

"*Do not bring the traitor within. He deserves his gnat infestation, the crabs, the stitches, and whatever else has been inflicted upon his unworthy form for he did not deliver my vital message to you, nor did he stay by your side as even the most inadequate pet might do."*

I did not argue, because I found I quite agreed.

I twisted my key in the lock and Bluebeard disappeared within. I gathered up my living hand and shoved it – wriggling like a dew worm – into my leather bag.

Bluebeard emerged a moment later without Sparrow's head.

"*Wait here but a moment for me,*" he said and there was an edge to his voice that made me frown, but he was gone before I could ask him why he sounded so torn.

I leaned down and regarded Grosbeak.

"You horrible little monster," I told him and his eyes flashed as if he were speaking back and by the spark in them, I could only assume he was speaking entirely in curses. "You were not my pet. You were my friend. What shall I do with you now? I dare not trust you. Did we not have a bargain, you and me?"

His face turned a terrible puce and the muffled sounds only grew worse.

I could kick him back into the sea. I could leave him here.

I could leave his mouth stitched up, which surely, he would find torturous.

He deserved it all. He was a traitor to his only friend and an accomplice to Sparrow's murder. And if Bluebeard hadn't rescued me, he would have been an accomplice to seeing me trapped forever beneath the sea.

But was I not all those things, too? And had not I been forgiven for them.

I sighed, leaned down, and picked the knot tying his stitches in place. Tanglecott had used a wide thread – almost a butcher's string – and it was easy enough to loosen the knot and then draw the string through the running stitch that held his rotting lips together.

"A curse on you and all your house," was the first thing he said.

I stared balefully at him. A less worthy recipient of my generosity would be impossible to find.

"If you think this one act of mercy somehow makes you better than me, you can think again," he said, spittle flying as he put all the force of his fury behind his words.

"I think that simply not being you makes me better than you," I said coolly. "Perhaps I should seal you to the same fate to which you sealed me.

Would you like to be sent back to the sea? Unless I misremember, there was a mermaid waiting for you."

"Mermaids! A pox on them all! She chose the Lady over me, and she with her beauty lost entirely!"

I thought back to the lashing figure that had dragged Lady Tanglecott beneath the waves and I laughed.

"She did, didn't she? Perhaps she prefers an uncouth face, for she chose both you and the besmirched Tanglecott – though of the two I still find you least fair."

He rolled his eyes dramatically.

"Would you like to explain your treachery?" I asked and I couldn't keep the frost from my voice entirely.

"No."

"Not even if it might earn you a place again at my side?"

"I am unrepentant. Badgering me will not alter what has been wrought within my heart. "

"I thought you no longer possessed one of those."

In the distance, a trail of smoke was rising into the sky. I watched it, worriedly. Was that not the direction of Tanglecott's breakfast room?

I heard the sound of something dragging and turned to find Bluebeard shuffling forward with Sparrow's wax-coated body slung over one shoulder.

My mouth fell open and beside me, Grobeak snickered.

"Are you collecting wives still, Arrow? I thought you had put that childishness away."

Bluebeard ignored him, stepping into the Room of Wives silently, and then returning so quickly that it seemed he hadn't left at all.

"A geas I place on you, corpse," Bluebeard said the moment he returned, taking Grosbeak's head up and shaking it as if to dislodge something from him. The slit-pupils of his eyes had expanded and his face held the mournful look of a man who had seen too many things. "Every curse you seek to set upon my wife will be set on you. Any twisting of your loyalty against her will be felt in pain within you. Any lasting insult to her person will be turned on you as an image is shown in a mirror. The arrow may fly toward her sent by your purpose, but the sting of it will be caught in your own soul. The blow may fall toward her, but the blade will cleave your flesh. I bind you now, revenant. I curse you with the twist of your own evil and corruption of your own cursed mind."

"Indignity! Cruelty beyond the pale!" Grosbeak shrieked.

I lifted him by his tangled hair. I'd lost his bag entirely.

"*You ought to leave him here,*" Bluebeard said idly. "*He's of no use to you and of considerable harm.*"

"I'm afraid I've grown used to him. Have you set Lady Tanglecott's home ablaze?"

"*I told her I was stripping her of her home. If she did not wish it so, she should not have tortured and killed my most loyal lieutenant. A millennium of collected curios is too small a price to pay for what she wrought here.*"

I thought of the bed and its layers and shuddered in agreement, but I was still worried. "Won't the fire spread?"

"*It will only add brilliant reds to our Wittenbrand dance of purple and gold,*" he said easily, offering me an arm. "*Come to my nest, my paragon. Let us line it with the ashes of our enemies.*"

I took his arm and to my surprise, he led me from the beach and toward the blaze of Tanglecott's house.

"My master," the fire said, blazing violently, and leaping at our arrival as a dog leaps to greet its master.

"My fire," Bluebeard said, satisfaction in his voice. "Take us home old friend."

We stepped into the fire, and once again I felt the pain of burning while not burning at all and the world whirled around me in smoke and rushing flame, and then we were in the main room of his home, stepping out of the hearth, just as we had all those years ago after the petal ball. My heart leapt with joy.

The ferret on my shoulder screamed, leaping from me as if she had been stung and then shrieking in a way that sounded like curses as she rolled across an intricately tufted rug, leaving a trail of soot behind her. Her coat was patched with frizzled hair and her expression was pure murder. Before I could catch her to see if she needed help, she was racing up the mantle, leaping to the antler-and-bone chandelier, lunging at the cat sleeping there, and then tearing up the chain and into the starry sky above. I lost sight of her somewhere near the north star.

"Oh dear," I said.

Bluebeard strode into the room, letting go of my hand and sweeping up a tumble of parchments that had fallen through a hole in his door, making a neat heap.

"Have you considered not making unwilling creatures your pets?" Grosbeak asked me dryly as I moved to join my husband.

I lifted him to look him dead in the eye and said, "You can go down to my husband's wall, or I could throw you into this fire or out the door. I do not require you at my side. If you wish to leave, it can be arranged. I am so deeply wounded by you that I'd be entirely in my rights to abandon you."

"We made a bargain," he growled. "Is your mortal word so thin you'd wrench it apart over hurt feelings?"

"Our bargain was that I would keep you near and give you revenge on the Sword if you would advise me about the Wittenhame," I reminded him. "The Sword is no more."

"And I have advised you! It is not my fault that you ignored my worthy advice, mortal woman. Must I remind you that I tried to murder you in life? Is it truly a shock that I tried to do so again in death?"

Bluebeard didn't even look up at our squabble, his eyes flashing as he raced through one missive after another, setting them on a cluttered side table as he read. They balanced precariously there on something that looked like a snow lion jawbone.

"I thought we were friends," I told Grosbeak, and this time I couldn't keep the hurt from my tone.

"We're friends *now*," he spat bitterly. "Your husband has seen to that with his cursed geas. There's not a thing I can do to move against you."

"And is that so bitter a thing?"

"It is, rather. I deeply enjoyed making your life miserable and it will be a terrible deprivation to give you nothing but joy. And I know you won't throw me away. You have that strange mortal magic you call practicality. It will bind me to you, for you shall know it is wise to keep my unwilling council near, and so with this sorcery of insight and frugality, you will be bound to maintain me."

I frowned, but he was right. It made sense not to lose him as a resource and Bluebeard had pulled his teeth. He could not bite me, bound as he was.

Bluebeard broke the seal on a larger missive and as he opened it the smell of fresh-cut grass and something like clover poured out. He smiled and turned to me.

"We are not too late to join the fourth move. Set your pet aside, fire of my eyes, and let us array ourselves for what comes next." His eyes glittered with some perception I did not understand. "Night has fallen. I will remind you that you are bound once more not to speak until morning, but there are many preparations we can make mind to mind, and I would seek your counsel, for my other counselors have given up their heads or their loyalties and you are my last confidant."

"*Besides,*" I said with my mind. "*I was promised a rain of kisses.*"

He leapt suddenly to my side, leaning forward so that his lips brushed the shell of my ear and made me shiver as he whispered, "So you were."

Grosbeak snickered. "Serves you right to lose your counselors. That's what you get for being so single-minded. Anyone else would have indulged in a little pleasure now and again. Do you think I would have rebelled if you hadn't married her in the Wittenbrand way? Do you think Vireo would have?"

I ignored the head and set him on the ground among the roots of the spreading tree from which hung capes and hats and in his place I took up my husband's wounded hand.

To my surprise, Bluebeard, ignoring Grosbeak entirely, leaned down, scooped me up in his arms, and though for a moment there was sorrow in his eyes, still his grin turned boyish as he burst into a run and took the stairs two at a time, bearing me to our bedchamber.

"*I can walk, you know,*" I said practically with my mental voice as Grosbeak's protests faded behind us.

He said nothing, only held me closer as if he were afraid of losing me. When we reached the door to the room, Bluebeard flung it open and stepped inside.

I sighed, sinking into the feeling of being home again.

The fire leapt in the grate as if to welcome us, the gargoyle over the mirror opened its eyes, and the black flowers around the bed bloomed, opening a little more with every breath we took as if drinking in our presence. The open wall was a snow-coated forest, thick and full and heavy but not at all cold, and I was still staring at it when he set me on the bed, drew down my torn sleeve and gentle as the rain of the spring, set one soft kiss after another from the spot just under my ear, slowly down my neck, across my shoulder and down the arc of my arm.

"Rains of kisses, as promised," he murmured and then straightened, looking at me in the reflection of the gargoyle mirror.

"I recall telling you a story when first you came to my home, wife of mine," he said in a burred voice, thick with some emotion I could not discern. It made my belly do flips, but even as I was sinking into his words, something else caught me. My reflection in the mirror was not right.

I stood up and stumbled forward as he spoke.

"I told you of a fox and raven, doomed to love one another forever but only to be one and the same for the blink of an eye at twilight. Remember you, this?"

I gasped, my hands flying up to trace my features as I looked at myself in the gargoyle mirror.

"I think perhaps that we two are like those ancient lovers – apart for days or years, only to intersect for precious moments before we are ripped apart again. Before we plan, I wish to give you assurances, wife, that these stolen moments are as precious to me as the moments in that tale. I live and breathe for the warmth of your skin against mine and the way your hard face softens when you catch sight of me."

He bit his lip a little awkwardly as if feeling exposed by his confession, rather than by the tattered shreds of clothing barely clinging to him.

Sweet as his words were, and scandalous as his apparel, I could not focus on either. I felt ill. My face – my face was all wrong.

I beheld it in the mirror with rising horror.

Those were still my eyes – still a little too large and slate grey. That, at least, was comforting. But the rest – my too-thin face was slightly more heart-shaped, my overly-high forehead softened, my cheekbones a more pleasing shape, my nose and lips slightly fuller. My hair was still dark and long, but its lustrous thickness fell in perfect waves.

I did not like it. Not even a bit.

"Izolda?" he asked and my name on his lips swelled like music reaching a climax.

I tore my gaze from the mirror.

"Do not weep, wife of mine," he said huskily, raising one hand awkwardly as if to forestall emotion. "One day these will not be stolen moments. Like your flesh hand is to the skeletal one, so will our lives be then to what they are now. We taste only the beginning, only the sparest structure. Then, we shall feast on the fullness." He paused. "Still, you mourn. I bid you tell me why."

I laughed bitterly. "*This is not my face.*"

He shook his head, eyes narrowing confusedly. "Is it not?"

I laughed again, but my laughter was close to a sob. "*Obviously, it is not! It's perfect, don't you see?*"

His smile was smug, and he drew back to cross his arms over his chest. "I do see, and if this is your attempt to seduce me from my vows, it is a valiant one, but I fear my mind is firmly set."

My eyes widened with horror. "*I… No. I'm not trying to seduce you!*"

He raised a solitary eyebrow, his smile shifting to a smirk.

"*I'm upset because I am not this beautiful.*"

"You seem to be exactly this beautiful."

His eyes raked me and I looked down. To my horror, it was not just my face that had changed. My plain figure had – shifted. My waist had narrowed, my hips widened. I was still slender, but now I was a slender hourglass. I could be full of garnets and it would only make sense.

"*Speak to my riddle, husband.*" If it was possible to wail mentally, I was wailing. "*What steals a woman's form and face, and her husband cannot see it?*"

And he – he choked on a laugh, and it took all my willpower not to strike him in his laughter.

"You heard me turn Lady Tanglecott's curse back on her. She is tied now to the sea, bereft of beauty and you are here with me, full with the same."

"*I want to go back!*"

"You wish to be trapped in the sea?" he looked surprised. "Trust me, wife, it is no pleasant thing. The sea would rend you apart, shredding your lungs with her waves and rotting your flesh beneath her weight."

I opened my mouth and shut it twice and the last time was a clash of frustration. This entire – costume. Yes. That was what it was, a costume disguising me! This entire costume was not *me* and I did not feel like myself in it and he was saying it was who I would be forever? My head swam with the impossibility of it.

"Don't look so dour wife, you've not the face for it anymore. Though the hand gives you an eldritch touch. Your pet will also help with that. There is no one so lovely that carrying a severed head does not mar their beauty somewhat."

I blinked at him, too stunned to reply, trying to shoot arrows with my eyes where my words would not express my frustration.

His features turned melancholy. "You tempt me too sorely, wife. How am I to keep my vows with you so near and looking at me so fiercely?"

"Maybe you should have left me ugly and then it wouldn't be a problem," I said dryly.

He leaned forward, eyes narrowing and hands clenched and I could not tell if it was violence or desire that made his every line so sharp.

"I fear it would not help. Ugly or beautiful, skeletal hand or whole, all I see is you, wife of my heart. I am drawn to you as birds are drawn to the south in autumn, pulled by invisible cords, and then driven back to northern climes come the first blush of spring. Where you are, there must I go and where you go, there, ever, I am."

He paused for a beat and then pounced forward, reminding me yet again of a cat, and with one quick movement he plucked a hasty kiss from my lips, scooped me up, ignoring my gasp, and flung me in the hot spring off to the side of the room. The ferret shrieked, clawing her way out of the pool and running from the room.

"Romance aside, you need a bath," Bluebeard said as I gaped at him from the water. "You smell of long-dead lovers and candle wax."

And before I could object, he dropped into the pool with me.

Chapter Twenty-Two

IF I'D BEEN EMBARRASSED by his frank nudity when the Sword took his rib, I was doubly embarrassed to be bathing in this pool just feet away from him – and not even in my own body but in this altered one. My face was hot as I squirmed out of the remains of my dress and shift while staying submerged. I was so preoccupied with it that I didn't even notice him clean himself and leave the pool until I glanced up to be sure that he couldn't see me and found him standing in front of the gargoyle mirror, dressed in breeches and a light shirt and pulling on a heavily embroidered midnight-blue doublet. The cut of the doublet made his hips look narrower and his shoulders wider and it was covered in stitched birds in every shade of blue imaginable and done so precisely that they seemed almost alive. One of them chirped and I startled.

My husband laughed, his gaze flicking in my direction before returning to his task.

"I'll ask the mirror to give you something just as decorative, wife of mine. And then I'll ask the ravens for repast while you finish in the pool."

"I thought you said you'd grow that beard to your knees," I said with my mind when he scratched at the stubble on his cheek.

"I've not yet had the time, though I cultivate it with full readiness."

Now I regretted teasing him. I was not a lover of beards. Of any length.

He left with only half his laces tied, swaggering from the room like a victorious general. The moment he was gone, I seized the chance to duck under the water, scrub my face and hair fiercely and then hop out of the pool, streaming water as I hurried to the mirror.

"Do you have a drying cloth?" I asked it and then had to lunge to catch the cloth it spat my way.

I dried off furiously, trying not to tangle my skeletal hand in the cloth or look too closely at the rest of my body. I wasn't even close to done when the mirror spat again, and this time, it sent out a bunch of light underthings and a dress of such a dark blue it looked almost black with a pair of red foxes peeking out from under the skirts, a boned bodice, and a swooping neckline. I dressed in the underthings and struggled into the dress, fighting my wider hips through the skirts, and huffing as I tightened the laces. I wasn't finished with the back before Bluebeard sauntered back in, pausing to bite his lip at me from the door.

"You're a tumble of hair and skirts, wife of mine," he said before setting down the pewter tray and hurrying over to cinch the laces up my back and tie them for me. I was fairly certain I ended up with far more knots than were required. There was something about him and string. He couldn't help putting snarls and tangles into everything.

He ran his hand through my hair and seven years had not been enough time for me to forget how much he loved playing with it. He set the wet strands into a braid, taking far longer than efficiency demanded as he played with the strands, weaving a seven-stranded braid, and then he reached into his pocket – for a ribbon, perhaps? – and a songbird flew out, cheeping loudly before settling on the gargoyle mirror. I startled, and his breathy laugh was hot on my neck.

I shivered at the caress of his breath. I was starting to resent his vows. Were they really so sacred?

"Peace, woman, your milky neck could be the spill of stars in the night sky," he murmured and then he dropped the braid over my shoulder where it slid to follow the curve of my very new cleavage.

Before I could blink, he had released me and was busily pulling a pair of tufted chairs from their places to sit beside the spill of snow where the wall opened into the frozen forest. He pounced on a small table next, flipping it into place between the chairs, and then set the food he'd brought on the table. There were hot biscuits and hotter tea, two kinds of cheese, four kinds of pickles, and sliced peaches. The ravens, I remembered, did not do meat or eggs.

My mouth was instantly watering even before he invited me to sit.

"Eat, wife of mine, or Pensmoore is famished – as we both are," he said, pouring the tea as if he sat every day and poured from a delicate pot rather than ripping off the heads of his enemies. The look he gave me when he looked up again put an entirely different spin on the word, 'famished.' He swallowed visibly before continuing, "but we have the Wittenhame to conquer, revenge to be wrought, fortunes to be made, and magic to coax to our side, so we must set aside our better judgment for now and attend to our work."

"Don't you mean that we must set aside pleasure because of *our better judgment?"*

"I mean precisely what I said. It would be going with my better judgment to take you as my wife right now and here and in this bed of mine."

Was that me who made the strangled sound? I thought I might have swallowed my own tongue. The look in his eyes when he said *'take you'* made the fire look tame.

"Unfortunately, I must work *against* my better judgment today and take care of these other necessary things instead."

"Of course," I said weakly, while my better judgment screamed to me that he was right and there were things I should be focused on that were most definitely not the bed he'd just mentioned. My better judgment was growing very difficult to hear. All the worse judgments were reminding me that I'd been married to him for seven years and really, why not be married all the way. Perhaps, there were some loopholes in these vows he claimed to have made. And hadn't he made some vows to me, too? It was all I could do to force my thoughts back into line. *"Where should we start?"*

"With the joust," he said enthusiastically – maybe too enthusiastically, as if he, too, were struggling – flinging the invitation I'd seen him reading onto the table so that it sat on the cheese plate. "Tell me, wife, does your iron expression extend to an iron spine and iron skin when it comes to racing toward an opponent armed only with a long silver needle?"

"I fear it does not," I said dryly, lifting up the invitation and examining it.

"A pity."

The invitation said very little – only that a Springtide Joust was planned, Buebeard's magnificence was requested at it, and the time stated – but since I knew not the hour or day in the Wittenhame, it was no help to me.

"*When is the first day of Springtide?*" I asked.

Bluebeard licked a finger and lifted it in the air, his eyes seeming to cross for a moment, and then he smiled. "Tomorrow night."

I drank my tea to avoid looking worried. That did not give us much time.

"*I think that perhaps you should give me a list of the vows and promises you've made, my husband – the ones that must be fulfilled during this game and with my remaining time.*"

He nodded. "A sensible path for your thoughts, wife. I would expect no less from you, young as you are. We who are older know that sensible plans crumble as do our days."

He was so grave, that I couldn't help myself.

"*Have you not noticed that I have aged seven years, husband?*"

He looked me over and then snatched up a small silver fish from the platter and tossed it in the air before catching it in his mouth and gulping it down. "No."

I blinked. "*Perhaps the new beauty I wear disguises it.*"

He waved a hand dismissively. "Are you not sitting there fretting over practical things? Then you are my Izolda. We all wear flesh – well or awkwardly, with dignity or without it – it is the one living under the mantle that sears the heart and whose soul I cling to as to a rock in a storm. What flesh you wear means no more to me than what dress you don. Which reminds me, your foxes hunger."

I looked down and one of them whined plaintively while the other licked his chops. Living dresses were a lot of work. Carefully, I fed them smoked cheese from the platter. He did not notice. I had feared he would tire of me and my aging mortal body and plain mortal mind. I had been a fool. He did not seem to notice, never mind care.

"My vows are many, wife of mine but only a few will affect our cause. First, I have made a vow to my folk – that I will renew their lands and glory. That I will bring to them an age of peace and protection from all their enemies."

I nodded at that, slipping a bite of fruit between my lips.

"That vow is graven on my bones. But there are others. My wives, for instance." At this, I forced my eyes to meet his. I would not be jealous. I would not be. I was, all the same. "I have spent their days wantonly on all I required to get this far, but I fear, fire of my eyes, that in marrying you in the Wittenbrand way, I can marry no others."

"*Such a terrible restriction,*" I said wryly.

"Speak to my riddle, wife of mine. Who must win or see his immortality stripped away? Who has but one chance or fail forever?"

"*You do,*" I said grimly.

"Worse than that, heart's beloved. If I lose, I will not only forfeit my immortality but with it my place as Prince of this land. My holdings will go to another, along with all my possessions and even you, love of mine."

"*Wait. What?*" I froze. "*How could I go to another?*"

"By laws of inheritance."

"*You can't inherit a wife.*"

"We balance on the very teeth of the monster of death."

That was not an answer.

He drank his tea and it felt too common a thing to do after announcing that our fate was so grim and staring us straight in the face.

"*So. You have vowed safety and prosperity to your people,*" I said. "*Which can only be acquired by winning this game.*" He nodded. "*And to your wives, you have promised ...*"

"The full return of their days. Which is why I bid you leave them on their pedestals and do not take them down to play with them again, or if one is broken, my vow to her will fail."

My eyes narrowed. He sounded as if he were discussing dolls.

"*But how could you possibly give them back their days?*" I did not have the stomach to eat more, now.

His eyebrows rose. "By winning, of course. Surely, you must have figured out the clues by now. If I win, then I will inherit the title of Bramble King, and nothing will be too difficult for me."

I pinched the bridge of my nose, rubbing it. "*The current Bramble King could return their days to them?*"

He hesitated. "The Bramble King fades."

"*Then, he cannot.*"

"He may, perhaps. But what he is now is as the waning of the moon. Whoever replaces him will be as the waxing of it – swelling in power and potential."

I paused, thinking. "*The Bramble King holds this Wittenhame together, doesn't he? I see his face in the sand, the sky, the trees, the rock.*"

"You do."

"*If you take his position, will you take that place?*"

"I must."

A rush of cold filled me and without realizing what I was doing, I reached across our small table and took his hand in mine. The skin was warm under his firm callouses.

"*Will you still be a man?*"

He seemed wary as he answered. "That is a riddle I have not solved."

Dread weighed heavy in my belly. "*Will you be as he is?*"

"Yes."

His word was like a heavy nail shutting up a door. Whether he won or lost, I would lose him. If he lost, he would fade away, his vows unfulfilled and his spirit hollowed for the rest of what would be a short mortal life. If he won, he would become something completely other, fulfilling his vows to all but me.

I fought against something that had me in its grip. It shook me and tore at my chest and I couldn't draw in a deep breath. I would not have him as a whole husband whether he won or lost. Just thinking it shattered me, broke me in a way these seven years had not. Then, I had hopes of saving him from death. Now, I could see there would be no saving him. He would die a failure, or give his life a victor, but one way or another he would burn it up on this and me with it.

"*There is no third option?*" I asked weakly. I smelled smoke but when I looked up there was no fire, and yet the scent of it made me dizzy.

I was being foolish. Wives gave up husbands to duty every day. They gave them to war. They gave them to work so long and vast that they only saw them in barest snatches before the man collapsed on his bed and a snatch again before he was gone into the dawn to toil again. They gave them to months and years away in merchant trade or conquest. I was not unique in this.

I set my tea down heavily and the cup clattered on the saucer.

"There is no third way. Win or lose are my only options. And where I must go, you cannot follow."

I struggled to fight my breath in place.

What he said made perfect sense. It was absolutely practical – so utterly unlike him. I was only rejecting it because I hated it with all my heart, not because it wasn't the prudent thing to do.

I closed my eyes, breathed out through my nose, and was properly composed when I said in my firmest tone, *"Then I will follow as long as I can."*

"You will fight at my side?" Hope sparked bright in his eyes, mixed with a kind of burning pain. It ached to look at it.

"Until my last breath."

He nodded, grim and beautiful.

"Are you sure you must fulfill all your vows?" I asked, looking longingly at his bed.

His voice was iron, but he took up my hand again as he spoke, and his gentle touch took some of the sting with it. "I will fulfill each one to the letter, heart of my own heart."

I took a great breath and then I said with admirable calm, *"Then let us consider how we might win."*

Chapter Twenty-Three

"TO WIN," Bluebeard had explained, "We must chisel away our competitors. We must make them flee before us."

To my surprise, he pulled his playing piece from his pocket and set it on the table. It moved, peering up at us, and to my horror, the former King of Pensmoore was now the new King of Pensmoore – my brother Svetgin. The tiny figurine Svetgin looked old, though. His miniature shoulders slumped under the burden of rule.

The specter peered around my shoulder to get a better look.

"Traditionally, we've made them bleed through their human realms."

"*How marvelous,*" I deadpanned.

"Do you know your mortal historics?" Bluebeard asked, so taken with his explanation that he didn't seem to notice when yet another bird tumbled from one of his pockets. It startled, making a *tee taw, tee tee taw* call before hopping up his sleeve and lodging itself on his shoulder where it stared down critically at us. "Was there any reference to one called Romanovich?"

"*Romanovich the rampager?*" I asked, eyebrows raised.

"Perhaps. He would have been from Elkanmoore?"

I shivered. I'd read the histories. The towns put to the flame, the inhabitants savagely brutalized and killed. Whole nations swallowed up in a single bite. He'd campaigned for fifty years by most accounts, destroying the continent, setting everyone back to the dark ages and seeming no more bothered by the fact that every cloth weaver was gone, or that there was no longer a herd of cattle to be found, than most people would be over waking to discover it had rained in the night.

"*There are none who have not heard that name,*" I acknowledged grimly.

"That was the name Lord Antlerdale went by in a previous game."

He stared out into the snowy woods, eyes lost in thought, his fingers tangled around a loose strand of my hair he was tying into knots. My eyes felt dry they were open so wide.

"And that is how he won the game," Bluebeard said grimly, his hand in my hair tightening to a fist. "He was granted ... concessions ... as a result."

"Concessions?" I did not mind him playing with my hair. I only wished his fingers would creep up the strand and tangle in the rest of it and –

"Mortal slaves who serve him eternally. Serve him however he pleases. If we beat him at this game, they'll go free, too. Any winnings of a previous game revert back to nil if that type of game comes around again and the reigning champion fails to achieve victory."

As if we didn't have enough motivation already.

"*Where does he keep these poor souls?*" Even mentally, my voice trembled.

"In his home. But let us not dwell on such right now." Bluebeard poured more tea and poked at the invitation. "This game is running a different course – a deadlier one."

Maybe for the Wittenbrand. From my view of it, watching a few Wittenbrand rip each other to shreds was less awful on the whole than the death of tens of thousands and the destructions of civilizations.

"We cripple and wound," he gestured at his side where the blood had soaked through his blue coat once more. "And if a player is so disabled that they fail to attend a move, they are eliminated. Sparrow saved me elimination by standing in my place. If some other Wittenbrand feels such loyalty to Lady Tanglecott in this next move, then she will remain among us. If not, then she will be removed just as the Sword was. The same trap is set for Marshyellow."

"*Won't his people stand for him? They seem very loyal.*"

Bluebeard tapped my skeletal hand. "They are indeed very loyal. Loyal to you, I would think. Is that not how you executed him? By means of the loyalty of his folk?"

I swallowed.

"What will you do with Marshyellow's people and holdings, my practical horror?"

"Should I not set them free?"

He snorted, leaping to his feet and moving to the bookshelf. He grabbed a book, thumbed through the pages, and then set it aside.

It was called, *Negotiation: The Subtle Art of Sticking a Dagger in a Belly.*

I shuddered.

"Speak to my riddle, wife of mine. Does the rope wish to flap in the wind? Does the ship sail with no anchor? Does the horse handler rejoice when there is no stable and the merchant when there is no market?"

I tapped my chin. I had enough to do already without bringing order to the chaos of Marshyellow's people.

"I leave that puzzle to your sensible mind." He drew another book out and flipped through it. The title read, *War: A Romantic's Guide to Conquest.* "We must plan for war on the mortal plane. Too long was I beneath the sea. Our armies will be ragged-edged and slack. We must send you to your brother to give him my orders."

"What makes you think he'll listen to me? I am not of much standing in Pensmoore."

He frowned now, throwing various items from his shelf as if he were not the one who would need to clean them up later. There seemed to be more items than could possibly fit on so few shelves. Titles flashed by, but only one caught my eye, *Keep Your Head: How to Avoid Panic and Beheadings.* Grosbeak should have read that one.

"Pensmoore is yet one more thing that we must not lose, fire of my eyes. I would not see my mortals slaughtered or ravished. But I fear your lands once more need the steering hand of a patron. I feel the feet of her enemies edging over her borders and if we do not guide her hand, they may soon storm her gates. More than that, the moves of the game dwindle and our armies must attend the last battle or watch Pensmoore overrun."

"The last battle?"

"You must have rumors of the Plains of Myygddo even in mortal stories and song." His eyes met mine and narrowed as he said. "It always comes to a battle there in the end – a great assemblage of armies. Fail, and the barbarians crash over the land. Succeed, and you may ride home, broken, battered, missing a limb, a friend, an eye – and your nation lives. There are none who escape war unscathed and the winners suffer with the dead, drinking a double portion of the bitter draught until the end of their days."

"*So we will ride to this last battle?*" I swallowed uncomfortably. So much was at stake in two different realms and war was not a thing I had ever wanted to see again. "*I still don't know why you set my hand to fighting Aayadmoore in the last battle. I was not best pleased to ride as their figurehead and watch the innocent slain with the guilty.*"

His burning blue eyes seemed to bore through me. "You would rather another suffered that pain? Who would you set it on? Name the substitute."

I ran a tired hand through my hair, but it was the bone one and it tangled in the locks. I stopped, frustrated, to try to free it with my other hand.

Bluebeard sighed. "Our armies are not the only ones who drink bitter draughts. We, too, must drink this to the dregs. I would spare you if I could – I will spare you from the rest. But you are a woman full-grown and strong, and you must bear this mortal burden. I will treat once more with Wittentree. She will be your ally."

"*Why choose her so often?*" I asked, surprised by the burst of jealousy in my chest. Hadn't he been fighting alongside her and coming to her land's aid when the Sword dragged me into the sea?

He laughed then, snatching something from a small wooden box and throwing the box to the floor in triumph.

"I treat with those who will treat with me, my wife."

And then, in a single motion, he'd moved to kneel before me, and he took my skeletal hand in his and placed on it a bright ring. It was oval-shaped and long so that it covered half of my third phalange from one knuckle to the next. The face of it was split in two – one half in silver depicted a moon crossed by a soaring bird picked out in sapphire. The other half depicted a leaping fox laid out in rubies on the face of a blazing golden sun.

"I thought it fitting," he said and then he kissed my bone fingers one by one, looked up at me with a boyish half-smile and leapt back to his feet before I could so much as move.

"*Thank you –* " I began, but he was already shaking his head before his words slipped out.

"Maps are below. I must study them now, but you are mortal and must rest."

I looked around at the ruined room and shook my head. "*The planning. The joust –* "

"Will wait. Rest now. Do not fear that I will leave you in ignorance, for you are now my compatriot in all things."

He scooped me up, my foxes snapping at him, and carried me to the bed where he tucked me forcefully into the eiderdown and clamped the foxes' yipping mouths shut with his fingers before settling them down around me.

"Darkness, my fire," he ordered, and the fire dimmed. The mess grew less bothersome in the encroaching darkness while the moon in the forest beyond grew more full.

"Slake now your mortal need for sleep, fire of my eyes," Bluebeard whispered and I did not know how he possibly thought I could sleep when he punctuated his words by trailing kisses across my brow, down my jaw, along the column of my neck, and ending only just barely over the rise and fall of my heaving chest. He lingered there for a moment and I thought his resolve might finally fail him but instead, he shook himself, grinned ruefully in the moonlight, and – as if admonishing himself – said, "Sleep."

And then he was gone, the door closing with a *snick* behind him, and I was left there in his bed that smelled so richly of him, trying very, very hard to fall asleep when all of me was suddenly awake, alert, and unsatisfied.

One of the foxes snapped her jaws and I buried my face in my pillow and tried to pretend I was not so desperately in love with my own husband that it was making me feel a little ill.

Chapter Twenty-Four

I WOKE, blinking in the darkness to an arm draped heavily over my waist and another slipped under my hip as if I had been lifted sideways into someone's lap.

Someone, in this case, was my husband. His breath purred in my ear, his lips so close that I could feel them shuddering on my skin.

I knew I should get up. I should see to preparations for the all-out battle we were planning. I should learn to joust, or I should scold Grosbeak, or find the ferret, or change out of this dress with the foxes who were currently yawning dramatically and wiggling their way out of the covers to study the wall which had opened up into a dark desert. It was filled with the looming shapes of dried-out bushes, the uncanny pattern of sand formed only by the wind and never the rain, and the strangely effervescent scent of creosote.

I did none of those things. Instead, I let my breathing match Bluebeard's, and I soaked him up as the thirsty ground soaks up rain after a drought. I had missed him for seven years. I'd pined for his presence, ached for his arms. And I wanted this moment, right now, to go on forever.

I wanted the sweet stillness of him resting safe and well beside me. I wanted him, and only him, forever and ever, and I realized – only with a little bitterness to mix into all this depth of rich sweetness – that I would take whatever he would give. If his vows allowed only this, then this was enough. I would treasure it. I would keep it close to my heart in the stark days to come. I'd honor his word. I'd honor his sacrifice.

I'd woken like this twice before in this very bed, and the echoes of those times added depth to this moment, like seeing a field from three different sides. I liked this vantage best.

I rolled over slowly, so as not to wake him, reveling in the way his arms trailed over my waist as I moved. His face was peaceful in sleep – unlined, relieved of its usual ambition and intensity, and despite his blue shadow of a beard, he looked younger in sleep, sweeter.

I could not help myself. I caught his lips between my own in a butterfly kiss and just as I started to wonder what he would think if he were awake, I felt them curve. Startled, I pulled back to find him grinning sleepily at me.

His voice was husky with sleep. "Your affection, unearned though it is, wakes the fires within."

He drew me in close and tucked my head under his chin so that my cheek was cradled in the warmth of his breast and his powerful arms formed a basket around me. Just as I was once swept away by grief, I was now consumed with contentment. It stole into my heart so unexpectedly that tears formed, and I gasped at the relief I felt as if a burden had been taken onto other shoulders.

"Not yet, wife of mine. Do not surrender yet. This is but a reprieve in our war, a breath between battles."

He drew back to prop himself up on one elbow, keeping his other hand idly on my hip while he yawned.

"Tonight, we attend the Springtide Joust. I will ride in the lists. You will collect valuable information on our rivals – their holdings, their lands, their weaknesses, their mortal allies."

I nodded my agreement. It had worked before, hadn't it? I'd read the Sword's copy of Antlerdale's book and discovered how his army was equipped.

"When we are done," Bluebeard continued, and he seemed tense. "You will ride to the mortal lands – and this is key, wife of mine – and I stress it now in case I am injured in the lists and cannot remind you of it after. You must take my key and go immediately to your brother's house and there you must have him lead his armies to the Plains of Myygddo. You must send this missive I have addressed to the loyal lords of the Aayadsmoore who will join his armies with their own under his command. They must stand and fight on the plains there in the last battle, and you must see that they do."

"*Myygddo is far to the south in hostile lands,*" I objected.

"Even so," Bluebeard said, reaching to find the letter he'd written the night before. It was sealed and tied with ribbons. I found myself more distracted by how the muscles bunch and lengthened in his arms and bare chest as he moved. I did not like my gaze drifting to the open wounds in his palms and his side – did not dare touch them unless I must – but they were there, too, just as much a part of him as his beauty. "Myygddo is where this battle for the mortal lands must come to a head and so that is where we shall bring it to meet us. If we can manage to disable Antlerdale in the lists, then Ptolemoore will be vulnerable and your brother may march his troops through their lands with only mortal resistance, Moravidmoore and Ilkanmoore being crippled by their loss of patrons."

"Mortal resistance is still resistance," I said wryly, *"and we mortals find it daunting."*

"Hmm." That sound was the same as before – an acknowledgment of what I'd said while being unmoving on the point. "Time to prove, then, that he is made of royal stuff. He seized a throne. Let him earn it."

I hated how miserable my mental voice sounded when I said, *"I do not wish to be parted from you."*

He squared his shoulders in a way that made me anxious. "Where I go next, you cannot follow. I would save you from tasting my fate, for it is bitter indeed."

"Then is this the last?" I asked, catching his hand despite the wound in it and weaving my fingers through his. *"The last night? The last kisses?"*

He caught my chin in a tender pinch, his thumb grazing my lower lip. "Still, I hope for more. Still, I hope for a triumph that exceeds expectations. Am I a fool to hope for the unhopeable? To look for the unseeable?"

"*Don't speak to me in riddles.*"

"Then I cannot speak at all."

His kiss was as fierce as it was sudden, and it fractured with fear and knit itself back together with the intensity of commitment. We broke apart, gasping.

"With my vows, I bound you to death. With my choice of you as my one true bride, I turned the key in the lock of the crypt and bound you there with me."

"I don't understand."

But it wasn't entirely true, was it. I did understand. He was planning to be heir to the Bramble King, to be there and not there, sleeping, drifting, no longer a man. Was that not a death? And even the cords of our love could not take me there with him. I was bound just as he, but I would be bound to a dead man.

The look in his eyes made my heart ache. "Forgive me, if you dare. Forgive me for the doom I've brought on you. You fell in love with the bird, little fox, and now we have only this tiny splinter of time to love a lifetime in. Better, when it is through, that you fight at the head of your people and watch your innocents plucked from the arms of death and saved – better that, than that you stand beside your husband and watch him dragged down into hell."

A trembling cry escaped my lips, but he had already leapt from the bed with his usual energy, tugging his high boots on and strapping a sword to his waist as if he hadn't just told me he was going to send me away again so he could pass on to another kind of life without me.

"I think, perhaps, it's time to show you Riverbarrow, wife, and what I first set out to defend. It will do both our hearts good. And then we'll choose a mount for the joust. What say you?"

I smiled tremulously, keeping my emotions in check by will alone, but his answering smile warmed my heart as I rose, and tidied myself. If I had only this day, I must not waste it in tears or misery.

The mirror offered me a crown that I refused and a back-less fur-lined jacket that I accepted. It would sit over a practical dark blue dress – Bluebeard had declared the foxes unwelcome in Riverbarrow – and warm my neck with a collar so high that the fur fringe caressed my chin, while still showing off the scars on my back. They had not left when I donned my new, unwanted beauty. The dress was worked with weeping figures sewn onto the cloth in onyx and ivory beads, their heads cradled in their hands and shoulders hunched with sorrow. How fitting.

To Bluebeard, it offered a short cape in a dazzling blue and a blue-worked black doublet. He looked as dashing as ever. He'd even made the red slit on his cheek that was his mark.

"*Can you change me back?*" I asked him as I braided my hair before the mirror. My too-beautiful face looked back miserably at me, and he paused in his preparations to look over my shoulder and study my face in the mirror.

"I think not," he said, a calculating look in his eye. "Keep it as a bargaining chip but be clever in how you word your vows when you trade it away."

My eyebrows rose with his words, and he shrugged mischievously. "I would say all things have a price, fire of my eyes. I would say all things can be bartered. Except that I have won you and I would never gamble you away. Meet me below."

He was gone before I'd thought to tell him that I loved him, too.

I finished the braid and drew in a steadying breath, following him down to the hall below, and feeling nostalgic as the nightingale stairs sang my descent. Everything about this place echoed of birds and wings and distant flight.

I found Bluebeard attaching Grosbeak to a new lantern pole.

"Would that I might leave him behind, but I fear you would miss him," my husband said dryly. And I couldn't help the relief I felt at that, for betrayal or no betrayal, Grosbeak was my friend and I had missed him those long years that he lay beneath the sea.

And perhaps, I would at least get to keep him when I lost my husband to his victory.

"He fears there will be no wit to guide either of you unless you bring the brains of this adventure," Grosbeak said scornfully.

"And that's you?" I asked him dryly, but I was fighting a smile.

"It's certainly not her." He scowled as the ferret ran up the pole, down the chain, and settled in a curled-up heap on his head like the worst possible fashion in fur hats. "Tell her I would appreciate it if she did not nest in my hair. I will never get the smell out."

"I prefer your more recent pet," Bluebeard said, running a finger over the ferret's head. She preened to his caress. "She very sensibly has not tried to kill either of us yet. Besides, the fire likes her, and he likes so few people."

"Thank you," said the fire.

"This may remain here," Bluebeard said, holding up my living hand before placing it on the hearth above his fire. "It is less likely to betray us than the corpse is."

"I take deep offense at that comment, Arrow," Grosbeak said with a terrible sneer.

"As you should, damned one." Bluebeard finished his work, passed me the pole, and set a hand lightly on my shoulder. "Dawn waxes, I fear, wife of mine, so with these words, I grow silent, but in my silence, find my duty a delight for it flows ever to your sea." He paused, and in his pause, I felt all the words we wanted to say and couldn't find. "Come, let me show you my lands and holdings in all their aching glory."

"This is what I had to put up with for *seven years,*" Grosbeak complained.

"I thought you said it was only days for you," I said, meeting my husband's eyes and his very gaze was a caress. Something in me melted in its warmth.

"I remember it as centuries," Grosbeak moaned.

And then Bluebeard seized my hand, grinned, and suddenly the room around us grew monstrously large and I jumped as a mouse squeaked beside us as it skittered away, its bare tail as long as a cedar tree.

I clung to Bluebeard's hand, small as a bug for the second time in my life. I just managed to throttle back a scream, when I was knocked off my feet only to find myself bobbing and weaving through the air erratically.

"Don't drop me! That grip is not firm enough!" Grosbeak wailed.

Bluebeard's grip on my hand guided me to a proper seat behind him, as I realized – to my utter surprise – that we were mounted on a dragonfly. I clutched his waist with my free hand and found a better grip on Grosbeak's pole with the other.

"You are going to have to do exercises to get a stronger grip. I mean it. I absolutely refuse to be dropped in these mad adventures."

My eyes were wide as they could go. I looked out to my side to see the zipping rainbow wings spread out to one side and then, quickly, I looked out to the other side to watch the matching set scissoring on the other side. Under us, the carapace of the insect was bright as a gem, blue as the sky, and iridescent.

Dragonflies were beautiful when caught in glimpses on the side of a sulky river, darting between tall reeds. They were more glorious yet when they were large as a pair of team horses and vibrating under your seat.

I was so involved in admiring him that when I finally looked up again, I had to cut off a yelp as the dragonfly sped right toward the wall.

"I hate this part," Grosbeak muttered. "Only the Arrow would hide his land in so diminished a manner."

We were aimed directly at the dramatic painting of a riverbank at dawn. The reeds and weeping willow on the bank were so carefully depicted they almost looked real. I could nearly smell the scent of fecund earth and flowering grasses as we plunged toward the painting, my heart in my throat, my lungs caught in that moment of breathless terror, and then I realized we were no longer in Bluebeard's home for when I looked over my shoulder, I saw only the river and the reeds and the sway of the wind and the bright baby gold of the rising sun.

Riverbarrow, it seemed, lay within a painting on my husband's wall.

Chapter Twenty-Five

THAT MY HUSBAND loved this land was apparent in his every aspect as we skimmed over and through the heart of Riverbarrow. It was just as apparent in the land herself and I felt an ache of almost-jealousy as it reached out to him, every blade of grass and wisp of breeze trying to caress him, to embrace him, to entangle him forever and love him to the end of time.

Mine, I thought viciously at them all, and had to shake myself because I was sounding a bit too much like Grosbeak for my liking.

I had not realized how far and fast a dragonfly might speed and when I finally grew as used to such movement as one could grow – for I was still sitting on the hard, slick, jointed back of a beautiful insect and it was no comfortable ride, nor did I feel secure as we hovered and leapt, sped and dodged – the landscape seemed to rise up and meet us.

Birds dashed in every direction in flights of one or two or two hundred. White and grey, blue and palest pink, black and white flecked or barn-owl brown and eagle gold, they were everywhere, and far from flying away from us, they often flew toward, welcoming their miniature prince on the back of their insect kin.

We dipped down through a flight of birds and while we were still dodging waving grasses too tall and deep that my eye could not find both the dark stalks where they met the roots and the waving tassels high in the sky, we were already rising up above the field again, impossibly fast.

My palms were sweaty, and I clung to Bluebeard's back a little too tightly in my fright. I had never flown. I was not one of his beloved birds darting and swooping along the breeze to be near him, and I did not enjoy the experience of flight even though the practical part of my mind was reminding me that this was a very economical, quick, and effective way to travel and if it had been possible to reproduce in Pensmoore, the trade and political advantages would be numerous.

We skimmed up through oak leaves, their massive proportions sheltering us in dappled shade for moments before we burst back into the golden heaviness of the morning, rising so we could see the next four bends of the river and the reeds on either side. A small family was huddled on the riverbank. At first, I thought them beavers, but as we drew closer, I realized they were some kind of living rock with heavy carved faces and limbs and the parent stones were gently showing the smaller stone children how to cross the still water.

There was no wind this morning, and a peachy haze hung gentle over the calm silver river, its mottled surface intermittently broken by fallen logs or clumps of rock or spreading river flowers.

Drowsy, over-large blooms nodded gently on the banks and then perked up when we passed and opened their tumbled burrows for figures that seemed half-human and yet woven of willow and furze to stumble out and lift a hand of greeting to us.

Small insects buzzed over the surface of the river while below fish broke the surface, their questing mouths braving the dangers of air to lip at the bugs.

A clump of gnarled men in clothing too big for them fished along the bank, smoking cob pipes, eyes closed, as they soaked in the sun's warmth. As I watched, one snapped his fingers, and a trout as large as he was leapt from the water to land with a tumbling flop right in the basket set on the bank. The man closed his eyes again, drowsing as his supper smothered to death in the open air.

One of the smaller of the speckled birds darting around us swept down upon the remaining insects in twin beauty and violence – so very like the husband whose waist I was gripping as if that grip were my life.

And he *was* my life. He was my whole life in a way that felt terribly sacrilegious – blasphemous, as if I may very well be struck down for the temerity to have hitched all my hopes to just one mortal man. And yet he was not mortal. Perhaps, one part of my heart suggested, small and timorous – perhaps, he *can* bear so deep a loyalty, so devastating a love. And yet he'd told me himself that he was passing from this world of birds and pastoral scenes and on to some place where I could not join him.

Pensmoore, his wives, and this Riverbarrow had given the futures of all their thousands to him. Their lives and livelihoods rested entirely on his moves in this game. I dare not step between him and them.

My breath hitched in my throat, and I pressed my cheek against his shoulder, letting myself hold on for this one lone day.

We flew higher as the trees multiplied below, and the river became but the barest ribbon beneath, and his wild folk faded from view. Up we flew, up, up, to where I saw the faint purple peaks of mountains to the east and the periwinkle haze of sea far to the west. The only sound up here was the whooshing of the wing pairs on either side of me as their gossamer thinness was all that was between us and plunging to our deaths.

Small hamlets speckled the landscapes and a bare few towers thrust upward, but no dusty roads or open-pit mines were to be seen.

"What of this is Riverbarrow?" I whispered to my husband over the buzz of the wings of the dragonfly.

"It's all Riverbarrow," Grosbeak said from where he hung on the pole, saving Bluebeard from exercising magic to speak to me in the day. "As far as your eye sees and beyond. There are small villages and the tangled homes of those who live below and above, but it's mostly a wild, untamed place. Nothing like the crypt city of Coppertomb, or the stag hills of Antlerdale, or the populated fortresses of Towerrock. Your husband's people are a plain, peaceful folk – un-regarded, unwanted, non-useful in any conflict. There are no orcs, minotaurs, or tridents here. Not even unicorns as the Sword bred for hundreds of horsey generations. I'll miss that braggart. He was always good for a laugh." My memories of my would-be 'husband' were not so fond. "Oh, there are halls and fortresses of a kind and the food they make here is the best of the Wittenhame," Grosbeak continued. "There are some wise practitioners of this or that, and bold noble souls in strange old-folk bodies, but look not to them for an army."

But it was not an army I wanted to see here. That was not why I'd come. I'd come to see his heart and despite the tranquility of this day, I saw it here in the tangled way the forest grew – inviting and yet terribly wild and fierce. I saw it in the warm smoke curls from villages built on chicken legs that roamed between the trees while beneath them long creatures with longer jaws bit and snapped. I felt it in the way the wind wasn't howling right now but seemed to be suggesting that it might begin to at any moment, and in the way every rock was jagged, every pool held dark shadows, and every tree was the keeper of secrets so aged and ripe that no outsider would be granted them. I saw hints in the smiles of the leaf children we passed, tumbling together in a game – but I saw them just as well in a clump of trees we shot past that held a dangling ghost on the end of a noose from every branch and twig of it. This place was lovely, but not safe; warm, but not tame; sweet as the sweetest nectar, but with a stain of bitterness. It was him, all him in every echo of every strain.

My husband turned his face so he could press his rough stubble cheek to mine, and I felt the muscles in it tighten with a smile. An army was not what he was looking for either, for I saw what he saw. I saw a folk vulnerable and beautiful and ancient in a land wilder than anyone knew, and I knew why he loved them, why he kept them safe with every beat of his heart, and why he'd had to see them one last time before the end.

"They've diminished," Grosbeak said dismissively. "You should have seen this place in its glory – absolutely stunning. The dragons alone were worth the price of admission. I thought back then that he had a point in trying to preserve it. It drains his magic, you know. He sustains this whole place with his power. That's why he has to use your days for extras. He's all tapped out just keeping this rustic haven untouched by the world beyond."

I felt my eyes grow wide at Grosbeak's words. I was looking at a place larger than Pensmoore in size and scope. Seeing this – all of this – added a depth to all that had gone before. I could imagine these folks as they must have slowly gathered to arrive at his home with their plea. I could imagine them stealing away to slip me the note when I was kidnapped. Those things had felt commonplace. I'd scarce known the sacrifice and toil to accomplish them. What other things was my husband gathering together and tying fast in his efforts to fulfill all vows and recompense all people?

We sped toward a waterfall, dipping down from our height to draw toward it.

Someone had built a tall, spiked tower at the peak of the falls. It rose like a singular mountain, but the stonemasonry was nothing I'd seen before in the courts of Pensmoore or Aayadmoore. It was carved as if by inhuman hands – and likely it was – carved almost as if it had been grown of earth. It was intricate in its every delicate detail, woven rather than chiseled from stone.

A pavilion of stone extended from the roots of the tower to look out over the bright falls, and even this pavilion was woven of twisting strands of stone rather than carved from a block. It curled up as tree roots might and the platform it produced seemed almost more by accident than design.

It was to that pavilion that the dragonfly shot.

I clutched my husband tightly as we descended.

"He guards the entrances to this place as a miser hoards his wealth," Grosbeak said. "It makes for an insular society. I do not envy him his wealth in it."

"Don't you?" I asked, annoyed by his scorn. "You who have no body do not envy a man with a whole realm?"

Grosbeak snickered. "I who have no responsibilities nor ambitions, do not envy him who is eaten moment by moment with his. I do envy you, Izolda. Would that Tanglecott's spell had reversed and made me the beautiful one."

"We could bargain for my beauty," I suggested, eager to be rid of it. "Have you anything to offer?"

Bluebeard squeezed my hand in rebuke.

"Undying bitterness and a penchant for evil. Tempting, isn't it?"

I snorted. "Hardly."

"You've grown dull, Izolda. Women in love are always dull because what they want is so predictable. I much prefer women in hate."

"A predictable penchant, as you inspire the emotion so effortlessly."

He snorted, and to my surprise, Bluebeard chuckled with him as he set us down on the massive platform and then gripped my hand. The platform shrunk and the world around us wobbled for a moment and then we were normal-sized again.

I did not see what happened to the dragonfly. I was too distracted when Bluebeard took me in his arms and kissed me long and deep and lingering.

"*Welcome to my lands, fire of my eyes. They know you now as mine.*"

"Oh, ewww. Save it for the bedroom. Some of us don't have legs to walk away."

I could almost have believed that Bluebeard lengthened our kiss just to annoy my friend further. His mental voice was a caress in my mind.

"With so few prospects left to us, let us seize every one we may."

And then he kissed me a second time and pulled back only long enough to bury his face in my hair for a moment before stepping away.

"If you don't want your revenant eaten we might need to leave him here. I must settle a thing or two now that Sparrow is in the Realm of Patience. I owe her that at the very last for all she's done in my name. Wait for me?"

"Of course," I replied and to my surprise, he leapt off the platform in a swan dive and slid into the river without making a splash. I would never get used to that man.

"If this is a romance story, the pair of you should stay together more," Grosbeak said. "One of you is always running off to save the world and it makes it hard for your story to progress."

"When I mean to betray my friends and wreak general evil upon the world, I shall consult you. In matters of the heart, I fear you will only lead me astray."

"I told you before that you ought to follow your head and not your heart," he scolded. "If you had listened, you'd be ruling Pensmoore as a new patron saint right now rather than shackled to the Arrow."

"I'd be drowned beneath the sea," I said dryly.

"Perhaps. Or perhaps not. I don't know why you insist on seeing me as your betrayer when what I did just moved the story along. Someone has to do the heavy lifting so you can swan around in fox dresses kissing pretty men."

Bluebeard surfaced a little way up the river and to my shock, a creature rose from the silver water with him, a creature black but dappled just as the river was dappled, not entirely solid, and yet not entirely spirit. It seemed more made of water than made of flesh, its lines and curves made fluid by the water of its equine form. The edges of it flashed in the sun, growing opaque with bubbles around nose and mouth as it pawed ripples into the water.

"That's what I do," I said distractedly. "Swan around."

The horse towered over Bluebeard, three times his height. Its neck curved nobly down so that its wet nose could touch his head, and when it drew back rivulets of water ran down my husband's forehead and dripped through his beard as if he'd been baptized by a roan priest into a church of flowing water and living stone.

"What," I asked, awe in my voice, "is that?"

"The river?" Grosbeak asked, sounding bored.

"The horse!"

"That's the river. Or the kelpie, I suppose, but it's the same thing. The spirit of the river, more real than the water that people name 'river.' He serves as the steward to Lord Riverbarrow when he is absent and a more sober and bromidic a being I have never met, yourself perhaps being the exception."

They were deep in conversation, my husband and the river, their heads close together.

"Your insults warm my heart," I said, but I wasn't paying attention, every part of me was leaning over the edge of the pavilion, trying to see as much of the kelpie as I could. His crystal edged flanks flexed as he stomped and a wave splashed back and forth behind him in a long tail. Now *that* was a mount. Would Bluebeard ride such in the lists?

"Don't even think about it," Grosbeak said, snickering. I forced myself to look at him, but I only wanted to look at the kelpie. What would it be like to run my hands over his sleek coat? "He'd never take his river from the land. It would be robbery and the good Arrow is far too great a Wittenbrand prince for that. Fool that he is. No, if you're thinking about how he'll ride in the jousts, its more likely to be a mist lion as his mount or perhaps another dragonfly, but this one made large instead of him being made small."

"I was thinking a toad, perhaps," Bluebeard replied, and I spun to see him smiling there behind me, drenched in water, leaning forward in that way he had that suggested he might pounce at any moment. My face went hot as I saw how the cloth clung to his shape and I looked at the river abruptly trying to both drag my eyes from his cunning form and to catch a glimpse of the kelpie as he left.

"I would have liked to meet him," I said wistfully.

Bluebeard ran a hand through his wet hair awkwardly.

Grosbeak laughed. "The kelpie *is* the Arrow. And he is the kelpie. And he is the river, and the river and the land together are him. It's all a terribly crisscrossed tangle."

"I don't understand," I said as Bluebeard blushed under his beard. My eyes were only for him, not my tutoring head.

"No one does, but that's how it works for the princes of the Wittenhame. Their lands and holdings *are* them and so is the converse. You won't be fighting the Sword anymore, since he lost the Game, but you might see his heir strutting around learning roughly how to embody Towerrock, and if these folk of the Arrow's were not fools and cravens and we went to war with their folk, then if he came and put this land to the fire, your husband would burn alive from the inside out. When he is weak, his land produces no food and his river sinks into the ground, when he is happy it dances and flowers. And when – as appears to be the case today – he is utterly at peace the place takes on a story-book cast that seems almost impossible to believe. I swear, I've never seen it so."

"I think you've waxed poetic enough, you craven monster," Bluebeard said, flicking Grosbeak's cheek. "Let us hie us to the pastures to find a mount for the lists."

And with my mouth still open, I followed the man who was also a river, who was also a land and a horse and a bird and the most intriguing, heart-stopping, pulse throbbing being in all of the many worlds I'd tasted.

Chapter Twenty-Six

"ANOTHER DRAGONFLY, perhaps. What say you, Grosbeak," Bluebeard had said as we slipped along a path only as wide as we were. The branches reached in to snatch at us from trees that towered far above and Look and Despair snarled and snapped when they threatened to dislodge her from her place on Grosbeak's head.

"Not a stalking cat?" Grosbeak asked. "Not a unicorn? That's what the Sword would have used."

"And likely what his heir will ride."

"Won't you only have to joust against the current competitors?" I asked, worriedly, shivering in the shadows of the narrow way. Bluebeard reached a hand back to take mine in his, warming it.

Bluebeard's eyes were tight, but they softened when his gaze met mine.

"Oh no," Grosbeak said, and I could tell he was coming back into his own by the sound of vicious glee in his voice. "The joust is for any who might wish to test their mettle. There will be prizes for various categories and there will be other bouts of fighting, but the competitors in the Game who ride in the lists and do not fall will have advantages in the Game and that is why they will ride. Additionally, either the players or their representatives *must* ride or forfeit their seats in the Game."

"What types of advantages?" I asked, nervously. This path was bringing back memories from my childhood – stories of children losing themselves in tangled paths in the woods.

"Luck, mostly. Turns of fate. Maybe your mortal land's food stores don't rot and last longer than they ought. Maybe they lose fewer of their people to stillbirth or have cleaner water or an artisan who crafts for them better weapons."

I inhaled sharply. Their game had such power over our lives? It didn't seem right.

"Who knows if perhaps your very grandparents might have had stronger foal seasons on a year I won, or if your family might have taken the crown sooner had not some other player lost?"

I swallowed. Sometimes it was easy to forget that there had been many games just like this in past ages and that this man I was married to had played in them – gambling with the fates of people just like me. But Bluebeard hadn't needed to win those like he did now – both because he'd married me in the Wittenbrand way and now could not take another wife to try again, and because the stakes were so high with the inheritance of the title of Bramble King.

"Then we must not fail," I'd agreed as we slipped into the sun-dappled pastures. We came out on a hill from which we could see trampled fields dotted with low stone walls and the occasional spreading oak standing alone as shelter from the weather. "Perhaps you should ride a grand horse, my husband. Something like that which you rode in the races."

"Nonsense," Grosbeak laughed. "There are points awarded for the difficulty of the mount."

"A dragon, then," I said. He shouldn't choose something as delicate as an insect if he was going to win this – and we needed to win. "Something fierce and large. Something like those long-mouthed things snapping at the houses on chicken's feet."

"Admire you those, fire of my eyes? I shall offer a dozen to you as pets."

"More pets would not be practical," I said. "Some sense of what I should watch for at the event would be more useful."

I couldn't help my tight tone. Now that we were getting closer I couldn't help but think about how if he won I'd lose as much as if he lost.

Below us, the pastures showed a streak of antelope running far in the distance, deer and horses closer by but wary of one another. Something huge and shambling like a draft horse made of vines occupied a place under the nearest tree. A winged bear – a terrifying sight – pawed at an anthill halfway across the rippled fields. And was that a leopard with four heads? I shuddered at the sight. There would be a mount here for him somewhere. And then he would ride in the lists and I would lose him forever.

"If you want to watch, then watch for treachery," Grosbeak suggested. "Tanglecott isn't the only one who might want me to turn on you."

I shot him a suspicious look.

"And would you turn again? Even after all this?" I asked him.

"For the right price, I would."

I gritted my teeth angrily.

"Or, you could bribe me."

"Stop trying to deal for my wife's excess beauty you gnarled corpse," Bluebeard growled. "She must save it to deal with others. It would be entirely wasted on you."

"I don't see why." Grosbeak sounded truculent.

"'Twould be a waste as I've already set a geas on you, splinter in my heel. You can no more turn on her than you can dance a jig."

"I dance well from the end of this chain."

"Then, by all means, do dance and do not let me inhibit you." Bluebeard sneered, but his eyes were wandering over the field at the various animals and birds that wandered through it.

"I would think you would take a bird," I suggested but I did not care. I only wanted him to look at me again so I could see the thoughts deep in his eyes. "It would suit your temperament and inclinations."

"*So it would,*" he said, brushing a lock of hair behind my ear as he bit his lip. "*But sometimes one must bring a surprise to gain an advantage.*"

"The four-headed jaguar, then?" I asked and his smile told me it would not be that creature. I did not care. I could lose myself in the depths layered upon layer beneath the surface of his gaze. "The winged bear? He looks to be a terror."

"*Ah. I spot my quarry close by. Wait for me, fire of my eyes.*"

"I have waited these seven years. What is one more moment?"

He kissed my forehead reverentially. "*Jar up that feeling. You will need it often as you grow into being my wife.*"

I gave him a wry look – after all, patience went both ways, didn't it? – but it was hard to hide the satisfied smile that kept wanting to break through. I liked it when he kissed me. I liked it when he suggested that we'd be together long enough that I would need stores of patience. Even if we both feared it was not true.

"Round and round and round it goes," Grosbeak muttered to himself. "And where it stops, nobody knows." He pivoted on his chain in a way that gave me the creeps. "That's life in the Wittenhame, mortal woman. It was you who thirsted so mightily to return. You can't say now that you don't like it, complain when your husband abandons you for his fun, or object when the head you thought was your pet turns around and bites you."

"It's not your bites that sting, Grosbeak," I said firmly, watching the grass rustle where Bluebeard slipped through it. "Your teeth are half moldered away. It's that I can no longer trust you."

"You never could. Now you know it. You ought to be thanking me for opening your eyes. And all kisses and sweet murmurs aside, you ought not to trust that husband of yours either. Sparrow trusted him and what happened to her?"

"You betrayed her."

"And he didn't stop me. Vireo trusted him for a long time and then he watched you rise while he descended. I trusted him for most of my life and then he married you the Wittenbrand way and sealed our doom. He made you the last chance we had and a grim, miserable one at that. Do you like his folk? Are you fond of this land of his? Care you for his home and fire? Then it should pain you as much as it pains me to know you'll undo it all. If you were one of us, you'd jump ship, too. It's only your mortal frailty that leaves you without options."

"Why would I want an option I'd never take?" I asked coldly.

Bluebeard stalked something in the tall reeds near a pond. I thought I'd seen a tiger with six legs walk into the reeds there and that seemed a likely prospect for a mount for this joust where they rode everything but horses.

"If you wouldn't take it then you're three times the fool," Grosbeak said scornfully. His head was vibrating on the end of his chain. "Love will only bear you while it lasts – which for you will be short. He's loved you for a pair of weeks in our time. And for the Wittenhame even that is an aged love, so close to death that one might as well measure it for a shelf in the crypt. If he loves you the rest of the week out, you shall indeed be a lucky mortal."

"He's vowed to love me forever," I said, and I was proud that my voice did not tremble.

"And how miserable will he be when he's bound by vow while his heart strays and tarries with every passing Wittenbrand lady."

"He wouldn't," I said and this time I sounded just slightly less sure because time really was different to the Wittenbrand.

Grosbeak snickered nastily. "Or, perhaps he wouldn't. Perhaps he'll merely wither and fade from loving something so beneath him as a mere mortal. Don't think your unnatural beauty will bridge that gap – it can't. You are rotting as fast as I am, but I'll still outlive your mayfly span, even now that I'm dead. Or perhaps he'll spend himself for love of you – fast and hot as a candle burns, and he'll die knowing he lost everything for a mere slip of a woman with only forty more blinks of an eye left to her span of years. It matters not how you make his vow chafe – only that it will, as sure as the tide turns and the moon wanes."

I didn't expect to feel so heavy. I'd thought he'd lost the ability to wound me.

I couldn't even seem to shake the melancholy that descended when Look and Despair rose on her hind legs and Bluebeard landed suddenly beside us on the back of a knobbly cane toad larger than even the winged bear had been.

I gasped as he reached down for my hand from his seat.

"Speak to my riddle, wife? What rides the wings of surprise? What sends shivers of shock down the spine and tingles of anticipation along the fingers?"

"You do," I said wryly, and he seemed pleased.

I found my seat behind him. It's surprisingly easy to steady oneself on the back of a toad because of the knobs that hold one in place, but a toad this large made my legs spread so wide to straddle him that the muscles were aching before I'd even arranged my skirts and I did not like how his juices dampened my skirts.

"A truly terrible choice," Grosbeak opined. "No one has ever won a joust on the back of a cane toad."

"Then I shall be the first," Bluebeard said idly, but when his eyes caught mine, he switched to his mental voice. "*As you are* my *first, fire of my eyes. First that I've loved. First who I've given such vows. First I think of in the morning. First in my heart forever.*"

And just as my heart swelled and my cheeks flamed the toad leapt and a shriek tore from my lips.

Chapter Twenty-Seven

"HAVE you any fears surrounding this joust? Will there be trickery?" I asked as we made our final preparations. We ate a small feast of foods – once again, courtesy of the ravens – and changed our clothing. Bluebeard, into light-weight garb that could slip under plate mail for the jousting, his tabard worn over it all, though he'd put that over the plate mail later. It bore his sigil – a black arrow with a red streak of blood behind it and a black bird above on a field of blue.

He wore a matching red streak down his cheek where he'd nicked it – as he'd nicked mine immediately afterward – to make his mark.

The spirit on my shoulder eyed the sigil suspiciously as if she thought I might spill the secret I was bound with now that I saw the glory of his standard.

He shot a glance over at me in his too-quick way that always reminded me he was more than human. "*Would it smirch my script to admit I paw the earth at the mention of a joust? That my lance arm tenses and my knuckles go white in the hunger of anticipation? That already I see my opponents behind the lids of my eyes, and they fall one by one? That the wind in my face and my shoulder – aching from bracing against the blow of toppling them, ignites in me a thirst for more? Trickery is the road I ride and treachery is ever waiting for me in the shadows.*"

"So, you're excited?"

His bright eyes lit, and he paused to dart over and place his forehead against mine. *"Only you thrill me more than the expectancy of battle. And it is a near thing."*

He stalked away, cat-like, and began to pull the plate mail from an innocent cupboard. His readiness was dulling his attempt at moving and behaving more like a human, and the edges of his inhuman speed and inhumanly bright eyes were peeping through in every movement and glance. He was more than a man right now. He was a force of something greater and he reared in the thrill of the battle. I wondered if that swiftness and brightness were the river part of him, swelling with spring melt and glittering in the sun.

Grosbeak sneered.

"Not much of a knight if you keep your armor in the cupboard. It shows a lack of fighting readiness."

"Or perhaps it shows I'm so ready I will not stand for laborious lacings and bucklings when I could leap across the room and carve my claws through my opponent's throat."

"Why are you called the Arrow?" I asked, admiring his inherent speed and precision.

I was adjusting my own matching tabard between bites and offering tiny tidbits to Look and Despair who had planted herself back onto my other shoulder.

Bluebeard – to my surprise – and his conspiring mirror, had dressed me for the event. My jerkin, unlike his loose one, fell halfway to my knees in imitation of a tidy skirt and was cut to arrange itself around my borrowed curves. He'd provided an overcoat for warmth. It was plain dark blue and pleated and starched to hold a stiff shape that gave me a very martial feeling but even with a long jerkin and overcoat – fitted as they were to my female form, I still felt too naked in only tight hose and high boots to cover my legs. The one thing that cheered me was that the severe tailoring of the clothing and the long tabard carved away the curves of my overly pretty body making me look more like my old self.

"I've seen you use bow and arrow to great effect," I continued, "but I've seen the same with throwing knives and with the sword. You're capable in all weapons so why are you named for just this one?

"He's so dubbed for his role in the court of the Bramble King," Grosbeak said. "Did I not tell you this before? He's meant to fly true to the heart of what the King would seek. Just as his fellow, the Sword was meant to strike as the Bramble King desired."

"Then the Sword failed that most incredibly."

Grosbeak laughed a terrible, half-gurgling laugh. "Do you think so, fool of a mortal? Think you that he failed simply because he pitted himself against you? What if I told you they both served their purpose and served it well? What if I opened your mind to the fact that the purposes of the Bramble King are not your purposes, and his ways are so beyond mortals as to be incomprehensible to you. His left hand deals a strike and his right hand tends a wound and who are you to say otherwise? Who are you to step in the way of that?"

"Who are *you*?" I shot back. "You are the one who lost his head. It must mean something that we have not yet lost ours."

"Not *yet*," Grosbeak agreed. "Throwing that against me in endless mockery is growing stale. You need fresh insults if you wish to sting me. But rest assured, this game is always satisfying and I'm certain there are twists and turns yet to come. You should know by now that I will cheer your husband's demise as hard and as merrily as I cheered the Sword's."

Bluebeard walked by, idly flicking his hand out to cuff Grosbeak and set him swinging on his chain.

"That hurts, you know!"

My husband didn't deign to respond. He was fumbling through a cluttered cupboard, tossing everything onto the ground until he found a tangle of leather and knife sheaths. He strapped one to his thigh and another on his forearm, checking the knives within for sharpness by shaving the hair on the back of his hand and making small noises of satisfaction when he found them sharp enough.

Those little noises made my blood tingle and I swallowed, trying to concentrate on my moldering head friend.

"You bring all this on yourself, Grosbeak," I told him. "I offered you friendship and you discounted it. If we're truly in a grand dance before the Bramble King then you should pick a side, or you might find yourself abandoned far from the action while others are showing their mettle."

He sputtered at that making incoherent noises and then calmed, his eyes far away as if he were really considering my words.

Bluebeard strode to me and gestured for me to sit and to my surprise, he knelt before me and paused on one knee looking up into my eyes with a gaze of such devotion that my knees felt weak. He could look at me like that forever and that would be enough. He could melt me for an eternity just with those eyes.

I swallowed hard.

He cocked his head to the side as if in question and my answer came out a little breathless.

"Whatever you are asking, the answer is most certainly yes."

I swallowed down a lump of nervousness and then his knuckles grazed my thigh as he felt his way gently upward and I bit my lip before I realized his purpose. He gently fitted the leather of the knife strap in just the right place and cinched it tight around my thigh, over the snug hose, tight – but not too tight.

But his touch when he handled me – his every movement around me – was so fluid and gentle, so utterly different than his violent purpose with everything else, that my heart tumbled further toward him. I was hopelessly devoted. I did not think there was anything he could do now to shake my allegiance.

"*I fear we lost your swords – Angstbite and Dreadtang – during our battle with the Sword. I will need to replace them. May this dagger serve for now. I still have possession of Edgeworthy – the token you gave me, but I will keep it within my home, I think, and not risk it today.*"

I barely had time to catch my breath before he was pulling me to my feet and guiding me from the breakfast table.

He passed me Grosbeak's pole, speaking to his former friend as he did so, "Come, rat of a Wittenbrand and watch the joust you so crave. Revel in the drama and hatred, the small cruelties and massive shifts in fortune, for you shall find them all, and with them the intoxication of senses they call the Springtide Joust."

"That's what I'm asking for! Is it really so much?"

And then we were away, leaving the warm familiarity of his home and heading out into the gloaming on the stinking back of the biggest toad I'd never wanted to discover.

As darkness fell, I reminded myself grimly that I must not speak to Bluebeard and I pressed my lips tight together to remind me.

I did not know if the house on grouse feet had borne us closer to the event while we were traveling in Riverbarrow or if the toad was simply covering so much ground with every stride that it felt close, but in two great leaps, the lights appeared and in three more we were sailing between poles strung with bunting made – once again, because who doesn't love to terrify the spectators? – with the howling spirits of the departed, tied up on a string of glowing spirit, and jeering those who arrived between their despairing wails.

I swallowed, feeling small at the sight of them, but Bluebeard seemed to worry not at all.

The Springtide Joust seemed to be equally joust and fair. The entrance had been laid out for grand effect and as we entered the grounds, everything we might indulge in was spread before us. At the lowest point, where it could be seen from every surrounding hillside, was a long flat field separated by a meridian of wooden rail along the center. Someone had taken their time with the rail, carving a series of severed heads pulling terrible grimaces all down its length that I later realized would move to turn their eyes so they could watch the competitors.

Everything was well-lit though it was night, poles lined the sides of the joust field and were spaced all through the hillsides, and at their crests fire danced, lighting everything with the flicker of flames and shadows. Huge bonfires had been lit at the entrance, down by the stands where spectators watched the festivities, and throughout the grounds.

Pavilions had been set in clusters at either end of the field and they glowed from within though they were no mortal pavilions. They were decorated with banners of old man's beard and rosettes of twisting ribbons as if the decorator cared not at all whether he used made or found materials to fit them. And the actual shelters were not of fabric made but woven of leafless vines that appeared dead and yet flowered with bowing, bell-shaped, white flowers.

On the other side of the field was a stand of boxes woven and decorated in the same manner – for the more formal spectators, I thought, and in their center, almost obscured by dead vines, was the sleeping Bramble King.

And all of it was washed in the flickering there-and-not-there light of dancing flames and cast shadows that made even mortal things appear haunted and brought a fresh shiver and twist to those things of the Wittenhame.

We wove our way through the gathered spectators on the surrounding hills who were attending the booths set up all around. There were fair games that at first, I thought I recognized until I realized that nearly every one contained a violent twist to an old favorite and I learned to quickly look away after a shooting contest that awarded points for how many live foxes weren't alive anymore when the shooter was done and another one where competitors faced each other and drank poison until one succumbed to paralysis and the other was declared victor. A heap of staring-eyed losers was shoved off to one side and when one of them twitched madly, I almost lost the quick dinner I'd eaten at our home.

The Wittenbrand celebrating were always terrifying to me. A group of Wittenbrand in elaborate matching costumes that made them look like birds of prey decorated with golden coins over their eyes and long beak-like masks, formed what I first took to be a terrifying group of torturers, but were in fact a musical group. They beat long lines of varied skulls as drums, and played upon flutes made of bones.

As Bluebeard hustled us around them, we nearly tipped over a knee-high table surrounded by rabbits with antlers who had been enjoying a mug of something green and frothy. They squeaked their protests, baring pointed teeth before we passed them, too.

The hillsides were alive with tableaus like this.

People gathered to sit and drink their choice of bubbling, foaming, melting, or fermented drinks, or to eat pastries and delicacies of an odd variety. One woman wearing a dress entirely made of living squirrels, who churned and tussled over her so thickly they served as a cloak, was eating something that looked like an upside-down silverfish full of pastry cream. A man with the horns of a bull ate a large pastry horn and with every bite he tore from it a cloud of bees whirled into the air. I turned my gaze away promptly.

Those who weren't eating fought, or gamed, or kissed with abandon and everywhere I looked there were bodies and more bodies behind those bodies as if we'd been set into a stew of life at a roiling boil.

I clung to the toad, and to Grosbeak's pole, as Bluebeard's lance and plate armor bumped against me. I was glad to not to be on the ground. Glad to be well out of this madness even if the toad had slowed to short, delicate hops so as not to squash anyone under his stout body.

We were just around a corner between two booths taking a quick breath before plunging into the fray again, when a white elk rode into the same tight spot and I gasped as the rider pulled down her hood to show the face of Lady Wittentree, patron saint of Rouranmoore. Her single yellow eye glittered and she leaned out over her majestic elk's back to whisper, lowering her voice enough for us to hear.

"Arrow." She said it as if she were giving a command.

"Wittentree," he responded idly, as if her sudden presence were of no matter.

"I'm glad I caught you in an eddy from the storm."

"I see only blue skies," Bluebeard said which was certainly a metaphor as the night sky was black as ever and pierced through with starlight.

"I wanted to tell you face to face. Always, you have treated me with honor. Now, I do the same." She drew a blue feather from her pocket and promptly broke it, tossing him the pieces. "Thus, I break our alliance."

"So soon?" Bluebeard asked.

"Too late, perhaps."

"You're a losing prospect, Arrow. You were battered and overwhelmed by the Sword and then nearly lost all to that clever play by Tanglecott."

"Sometimes you must appear to lose in order that you may win," Bluebeard said, but his muscles against mine were stiff.

"With you, it is more than appearance." She gave me a significant look that I could read quite well. I was a liability, in her eyes, as in the eyes of all others, and he was the fool who chose me instead of victory. And what did they expect him to do about it now? He could not un-marry me after marrying me in the Wittenbrand way. There was no going back, only forward.

"And then what? Will you fight Coppertomb yourself, head to head, when he's beaten the rest?"

"Yes," she said, her mouth thinning firmly. "When he's weak from his battles and my hopes are less grim. He has what it will take to vanquish you, Arrow – newcomer though he may be – and I do not. If I aid you to the end, and then we turn on each other, I will surely lose."

"And when do you begin to aid him?" Bluebeard asked, raising an eyebrow.

There was a chill in the air that had nothing to do with night.

A tick beside her grim mouth made the chill worse and then she shook her head and began to ride past us with the words, "I already have."

Bluebeard cursed viciously and I was forced to cling to him as he spurred the toad, uncaring now, as we leapt out into the fray. We came down on something – someone – who screamed, and I clutched at him, barely remembering not to speak to him now that it was night.

"*You're going to kill someone!*" I protested.

"Do I look like I care?" he snarled, glancing at me over his shoulder and his eyes were bright and vicious. He did not look like he had even a hair of compassion. I felt my own eyes going very wide as we leapt forward again, and my belly lurched and churned.

We flew through the air, Grosbeak shrieking like a ghoul as he bounced madly on his chain with every landing.

I did not look down. I did not want to know who was being trampled by the toad. At one point, I heard a horrifying *pop* that could not be good, and the frog's leap seemed to slide slightly as if he were launching from a wet surface.

Don't think about it, Izolda, I told myself sternly. That can only lead to trouble.

And then we were all breathing hard – even the toad – and Grosbeak was cursing so loudly that I thought he might turn the air blue.

"Silence your creature, wife," Bluebeard said, and his voice was so cold that I felt ice shoot all the way through me. Could this still be the man who played with my tresses and dressed me to his tastes?

"Be quiet, Grosbeak," I managed breathlessly.

We'd landed directly beside Coppertomb. He sat upon a proud jaguar whose inky pelt contrasted perfectly with his citrine eyes and the white teeth revealed when he curled back his lips.

The Bramble King was before us, his eyes half-lidded as he looked out from the mass of dead vines speckled in spring drop flowers at the heart of the stands of watchers. He blinked slowly at us, unconcerned by our sudden arrival.

Behind us, I heard the drum of hooves as if someone was bearing down on us, but when I shifted to look, I saw that I had misjudged. The joust field was directly behind us, and even as I twisted to look, a pair of hooved creatures thudded by – one a stag with tattered white skin barely clinging to it as its rider – a wild-eyed Wittenbrand with bone wings jutting from its back – angled his lance toward the other rider, a figure so swathed in plate mail that I could discern nothing about them except that they rode on an over-sized warthog.

I yanked my gaze away. This was not the main concern. At that moment, the competitors crashed behind me and the crowd roared.

Coppertomb's gold-lashed eyes caught mine for a brief moment, glanced down to catch on the ring decorating my bone finger, and then his eyes tightened into something that looked very much like cruelty before they dragged past me.

"Ah, Arrow," he said silkily. He was perfectly groomed, his cheeks highlighted again with gold and his plum coat embroidered with crowns. "What excellent timing. You can listen to the Bramble King rule on my case. I've requested the armies of Aayadmoore to be given to me. As well as Ilkanmoore and Moravidmoore. Fitting, don't you think?

Chapter Twenty-Eight

"AFTER ALL," Coppertomb said, with a secretive smile, "it was I who pitted you against the Sword, causing his downfall."

I couldn't breathe. My spirit was covering my mouth with both her hands, wailing as if someone she loved had died, but it was not me giving his secret away and it should not be me suffering for it.

I fought her with all my strength.

"Is this so?" Bluebeard said with dangerous frost in his tone.

"Of course," Coppertomb said with an arrogant tilt to his chin – how he'd changed from that first move when he'd tossed the tokens so officiously for the others. He was wearing the crown the Sword had made – the one that held my husband's rib within it – now bleached white. The sight of it made all the blood drain from my head until I saw spots of black dancing in my vision.

And I realized his spirit was gone from his shoulder and no one was gagging him even as I was being choked to death for his words. I needed air. I needed it now.

The hands released and I gasped in relief, my throat agonized and raw. On my shoulder, I heard a chitter and felt a scuffle and my relief turned to gratitude. Look and Despair had driven the spirit from its attempt at murdering me.

Behind us, there were shouts and the sound of something heavy being dragged away. I risked a glance, nervous as a new-broke stallion. It was the plate mail figure who had ridden the warthog – or what was left of him. Four people were dragging him away ... in three pieces.

Heavens above! That was not normal for jousts. Or at least, not in the mortal world. A scream caught my ear and now my gaze darted to see the crowd desperately trying to catch the reins of the warthog as it trampled through the edge of the spectators, its head tossing to catch them on its cutters. That was also not normal for human jousts.

I gasped and returned my gaze to Coppertomb who was speaking again. Neither he nor my Arrow, nor the Bramble King seemed to care about what had happened behind us. Even Grosbeak, lover of drama that he was, seemed to lean forward as if this exchange before the King was more riveting than the death – or deaths – of the jousters and crowd.

Bluebeard leaned forward, a grim expression on his face. "Speak to my – "

"No." Coppertomb cut him off. "No riddles. Just facts. It was I who gave Tanglecott the Heart of the Sea." His delivery was grand as any speaking minister before the court, "Which she so foolishly used to her own downfall. And it was I who pushed Marshyellow to deal with your hideous wife, Arrow. Each tiny win you think you've managed has been a gift from my hand – well, not a gift. A gift implies that you get to keep it. Call it a temporary reprieve. And now, I come to receive my due. To lift the reprieve. To once more ride forth in the great Game of Crowns."

There was a shifting sound as all the dead vines seemed to move like crawling snakes, white drop-like flowers trembling, their petals falling like snow.

"Stand before me as men alone," the Bramble King intoned.

Bluebeard stiffened and Coppertomb clenched his jaw. Neither man spoke, but they gave each other a hard look before turning. Coppertomb set his jaguar into a loping run toward the end of the field where the warthog had rampaged, just as the toad leapt in the opposite direction and I had to grab at its knobbed back to catch my seat.

"Wait in this pavilion for me," Bluebeard ordered breathlessly, as we reached one of the glowing vine-covered pavilions.

He coaxed the toad within and turned him around so that he faced the entrance. The large amphibian took up most of the space within. Anyone wishing to don plate in here would be very cramped.

Bluebeard dropped the plate armor on the ground, but shoved the long black lance into my free hand so that I was stuck holding the lance in one hand and Grosbeak's pole in the other.

"Stay calm! Stay calm." He kept saying it as he worked – loudly, as if he were scolding me.

"*I* am *calm,*" I said with my mind after the third time, and he glanced up at me with a peculiar blend of perplexed fury. The words were not for me.

"Stay calm," he said through gritted teeth, closing his eyes and balling his fists for a moment before he spun to me with sharp orders on his lips. "Stay here with the toad. Don't leave the tent. Don't drop the lance."

I'd never seen him so shaken. Not when the sea was taking him. Not when I betrayed him with that stolen gem.

And then he was gone, his muttered "stay calm's" trailing him as he loped down the field. My belly felt like that fish full of cream.

If Coppertomb found the favor of the Bramble King, we'd lose all our gains up to this point – all the armies of the defeated players we'd brought down together would be his and not ours or even off the playing field. Without an ally left, what would we do? All our many sacrifices made for nothing. Seven years of misery for nothing. My skeletal hand, for nothing.

I bit my lip until I tasted blood and shifted to move the lance across the toad so he could bear some of the weight. My arms were tired.

"Don't even think about dropping me," Grosbeak growled. "You're in enough trouble as it is, don't you think?"

"Yes," I agreed, my face pale and drawn. Maybe I should chant "stay calm" at myself, too.

The toad rocked back and forth under me.

"You'd better stay calm, too, toad," I muttered.

"You realize you're ruined, don't you? Both of you are," Grosbeak said delightedly. "Both of you are. The Arrow thought he was so clever, but Coppertomb has out-plotted him, out-maneuvered him, out-done him. And I get to be here to watch it all. Do you think I'll get to watch him rip out the Arrow's heart?"

"Why would he do that?" I asked, but my voice was trembling.

"Well, your precious Bluebeard bid his immortality. If he loses, that's what they'll do to him. Rip it out while he's still alive – though he won't be that for long."

I leaned to the side. If I vomited, I shouldn't do it on the toad. My head was swimming. I couldn't hear what they were saying in front of the Bramble King, but I could hear Grosbeak's wheezing laugh going on and on.

"Serves you right for being fool enough to fall in love with a prince of the Wittenbrand. I thought your strength was in your common sense. Wasn't that your bid for relevance? And you threw it all away on a man." He snickered a nasty, rattling snicker. "I love it! It's a perfect star-crossed-lovers tragedy, better than the theatre because it's all real and I get to taste your every ache of despair."

"I tire of you, Grosbeak," I murmured, but I was seeing stars. I felt like I needed to be sick.

"But you won't leave me. I've learned that now. I can say anything and do anything and there's no real threat because you won't leave me. You need me to tell you what's what even if I turn the screws when I do it. And I adore your torture. I thrive in your pain. I love to ache, watching your doomed romance flower and fall. It's the absolute most delicious drama and I get to be here for all of it. I must have pleased some far-flung god in my last life to be treated so well in the hereafter."

He sighed and in the distance, a horn sounded and then Grosbeak made a strange hiccupping bleat.

The toad under us leapt forward in a leap so massive that my head crashed into the dead vines over me. I bit my tongue, tasting blood as the vines ripped away, and we were flying through the air as I clung desperately to the lance and the pole Grosbeak was hanging from and hoped that my legs could grip hard enough as they sank into the toad's wide, soft sides.

The lance rattled against Grosbeak's chain as he screamed, "Stop it! Stop! Oh, teeth of gods and men, I'm going to die! I'm going to die!"

I felt small feet running back and forth across my shoulders and neck as the ferret panicked with him.

We'd reached the top of the toad's leap and now, as he leaned forward and I frantically shifted my seat to stay on his back, the scene before me spread out.

"Stay calm," I wanted to say to myself, but it only came out as a muffled moan. Everything unfolded slowly, but slow as it was, I could no more stop it than I could stop an avalanche.

Everything was below me – the crowd amidst the leaping bonfires and horrifying bone music unfurling on every side, the sleepy gaze of the Bramble King regarding me from in front of the twin looks of horror and glee on Bluebeard's and Coppertomb's faces to the right, the meridian and a charging grey lizard to the left.

The rider of the lizard had his lance trained toward where the toad was about to drop.

I did not scream. I got that much right.

But I definitely fumbled as Grosbeak's head chain tangled on my lance, driving it from the resting place I'd had it in and pushing it forward. I dropped his pole, clutched the lance with both hands, and braced myself with gritted teeth.

We dropped and I couldn't tell if the rider was past me, or under me, but the lance was pointing down and I was afraid it would rip my arms off if we all hit at once. I tried to bring it up and at first, it moved and then it hit something hard as rock and was torn from my hands. The frog turned sharply to the left, his rear skidding to the right. I grabbed him under the front legs with both hands, my face pressed against his knobby back.

I sucked in a desperate inhale and then sat up.

There were no lances in me though I was trembling from head to toe. I looked over the head of my toad just as he opened his mouth and a tongue that was far, far too long to all fit inside this huge toad flicked out, unfurled, and grabbed the fallen rider *and* his mount from over the other side of the meridian and lifted them into the air.

I had just enough time to see my lance skewered through both of them before the whole lot were drawn into the mouth of my mount and with a terrible shudder that I felt right up through my pelvis and into my spine, he swallowed them whole.

The seat under me shifted, bulged, shifted again, and was now at a different angle.

I couldn't move. It had all happened in seconds. Just seconds and I'd accidentally ... oh, sweet heavens ... I'd jousted. I'd killed a man. Or a woman. Or a something. And some kind of grey beast.

I couldn't quite draw in my shuddering breath. It kept escaping me.

Something moaned nearby.

"Is that how you treat a friend?" Grosbeak moaned. "I thought better of you mortals."

The tongue shot out a second time and I reached out, mouth open in a protest that would not come, as the toad snatched up the pole with my dangling friend hanging from it.

"No! Down, frog! Down toad! I taste as terrible as I look!" Grosbeak pled.

But to both of our surprise, the toad reached his tongue back and let me pry the sticky bar from the curl of it before he tucked the appendage away again.

"Well," I said, with nothing else to say.

"Beautifully played, Lady Arrow," a voice pierced the silence. "Who knew you were so keen to enter the lists."

I turned to see a smug Coppertomb adjusting his rib crown.

"I haven't entered the lists," I said in a small voice.

Beside Coppertomb, Bluebeard's face was completely ashen as if he'd seen – well, not a ghost – those are everywhere here. As if he'd seen his own ghost. Or mine.

"A man is dead. A Komodo dragon eaten. It seems like you've entered to me," Coppertomb said silkily. "And you're doing so well. I congratulate you, Arrow," he clapped Bluebeard on the back in a way that would seem jovial, were he not wearing one of my husband's ribs on his brow. As if on cue, the damp patch in Bluebeard's shirt widened. "You've picked a fine substitute for this game. I'd never considered running a mortal in such a deadly joust, but then again, I've not your gift for stratagem."

The last was said with such venom that I flinched, and then as if he'd been there all along, Bluebeard was at the toad's head, leaping onto the mount in front of me. He made a sound in the back of his throat that sounded an awful lot like the one Grosbeak had made in the pavilion, and then the toad leapt, and we were in the air, sailing toward the vine tent while my husband muttered as if he were praying, "Stay calm. Stay calm."

Chapter Twenty-Nine

THE MOMENT we were in the tent, he spun the toad around, leapt from its back, grabbed Grosbeak's pole from my hand, and hurled him across the room.

"A pox on you!" Grosbeak yelled as he smacked a clump of vines and tumbled to the ground, bouncing off Bluebeard's plate armor before rolling to a stop on the floor, his eyes seeming to roll in two different directions at once and the pallor of his skin looking deader than ever.

"Don't speak, revenant, lest I strike you in my anger and you never speak again."

There was cheering outside and the sound of metal hitting metal. There must be another joust taking place.

"Stay calm. Stay calm," Bluebeard chanted, running a hand over his face before looking up at me, his expression agonized. "What have you done? What were you thinking? Why would you do that?"

His hands shook, his normal tight control flapping in the wind like a torn flag.

"I wasn't thinking anything. The frog just leapt!" I pled with my mind.

It had only been seconds. There had been nothing I could have done to stop it.

"Your lance was pointing at the opponent! If you'd dropped it, then it wouldn't have counted as a run!" his voice was growing louder but he sounded like he was pleading with the past to change. He pressed his palm to his side, and it came away scarlet but he didn't seem to notice. He ran the hand over his face, streaking blood through his short beard.

I couldn't stop the trembling of my hands. I slid down from the toad.

"I didn't know! You said not to drop the lance."

"Because I didn't want the point chipped! Not because I wanted you to joust in my place!" He sounded frantic.

I didn't know what to say. I was starting to worry that this was worse than killing the person I'd ridden against – and the horror of that still hadn't hit me.

"It was an accident," was the best I could do.

I fumbled with my clothing and found a handkerchief too small to be much use. I tried to use it anyway, reaching to pad his wound. He shrugged my hands away.

"You've ruined it all. All of it. It's gone. It's just gone, Izolda."

He reached for me, and I froze, not sure what he was going to do. He tugged off my belt with a single movement and threw it aside. I gasped, as he yanked the tabard over my head to the angry chittering of the ferret and the wagging finger of my haunting specter. He threw it over the back of the toad, and I didn't know what he was doing or why he was undressing me but I didn't like it. Not here. Not like this. I stumbled back a step, my hands rising to hold him off.

"Would you calm down?" he asked, not sounding calm at all. "I'm just trying to put the plate mail on you before you have to ride again."

"Again? I'm never doing that again!" My thoughts came out with a very physical snort of disbelief.

He took two steps away from me, hands clenched into fists. "Stay calm. Stay calm."

He snatched the plate armor from the ground violently and I didn't think he needed to kick Grosbeak's head away like he did.

"Ooof. Would you do me the courtesy of *not* kicking me?"

"You didn't warn her, bodiless refuse," he snarled. Whatever trick he was using to stay calm with me wasn't keeping his frustration with Grosbaeak at bay. "It's your only job. The only one."

"This makes a better story," Grosbeak said thickly. His face was pressed into the mud too much to speak clearly from the place he'd landed. "You're such an accomplished jouster that none could be expected to give you pause. Her, on the other hand, she's inexperienced, frail, mortal. The true underdog. I didn't make her do it, but I'm delighted that she did."

"I don't understand," I said, barely holding back tears as Bluebeard fitted his breastplate roughly around me and cinched the straps. It was too large by half. *"It was all just a terrible accident. It happened so quickly."*

"Stay calm," Bluebeard told himself and I was starting to hate hearing him say that. He turned to me, and I'd never heard this kind of despair in his voice. "You're going to die. You're going to be killed and there's nothing I can do to stop it."

"I didn't mean to!" I said again. Could he not hear my mental voice? *"It was not a conscious choice. It all happened by accident, even the lance in my enemy."* And now I was crying despite all my work to hold tears back. *"There has to be some way to fix it. There has to be."*

He cinched armor onto me with rough movements and at such an alarming rate that I couldn't quite catch my breath. One hand was jammed into a gauntlet. He didn't bother with the skeletal one – wise, since I could barely keep the metal on with my flesh hand. It slipped if I didn't curl my fingers.

"That you rode, weapon in hand," he said grimly, "means you rode in my stead. That you won, confirms it, and makes you my substitute. You must ride thrice more. If you die, all is lost, and I will become mortal and any hope for Riverbarrow, or Pensmoore, or my former wives, or Sparrow, or any of those I have made promises to is gone with us. If you refuse to ride again, the same. If I try to flee with you, the same."

"And if I lose?" My mental voice sounded small and hollow. I *felt* small and hollow.

"A loss is permissible. But if you die or show coward, there is no quarter given."

"I don't have a lance." My teeth were chattering. I didn't mean for them to do that.

He picked up Grosbeak's pole and shoved it into my hand so roughly that my skeletal bones hurt as he jammed it against them.

"Try not to lose this one."

"I am not a weapon!" Grosbeak protested.

"No, you're a schemer and you stepped tidily around that geas I set on you since you did nothing directly against my wife, so consider this your fit punishment."

"They'll break me like a melon!" he protested.

"Good riddance, then."

Bluebeard knelt, buckling the greaves over my legs.

"I'm sorry," I said. *"I'm so sorry."*

"So am I." But he didn't sound sorry. He sounded furious.

"Do I have to win?"

"You have to not die. It's harder than it sounds."

"Any tips?"

He lifted me, armor, Grosbeak, and all, onto the back of the toad. It burped loudly – which only proved it was a Wittenbrand creature and nothing like the toads of the mortal world.

"Couldn't you have picked a horse? Or a dragon? Or anything classier than a toad?" Grosbeak complained.

"No," Bluebeard said, but then he leaned in close to me, his gaze so heavy it could have sunk a ship. And without warning, he took my face gently between his hands and kissed me, long and slow, as if he were kissing me for the last time and he tasted of bitterness and honey and the salt of my tears and his sticky blood all rolled together.

"Enough tears now," he said when he pulled back. "Aim the lance low and then bring it up to the center mass of your opponent as you leap. Cling tightly to the toad and try to let the opponent's lance skim off the plate mail rather than skewering you."

Well, that didn't sound so bad.

"And when you die and you go to the next life, you'd do well to forget me and move on into the glory of that place alone."

"As a failure who ruined everything?" I asked bitterly.

"As a beloved wife, loved no less for failing, but free now of her deadly vows to me." And then he jammed the jousting helm over my head and my world shrank to what could be seen through the narrow window.

"I'm pretty sure the rivers will still be running and the moon rising even when I'm dead. I won't be free of my vows to you. And what if I don't want to be free?" I asked him, my heart feeling like it was ripping inside me.

Grosbeak interrupted, "Stop with the sweet talk, we're up!"

"What if I waited seven years for this and I'm owed at least a little time with you?" I pressed.

The frog shuffled forward, peeking its head outside the pavilion.

"A three-headed grizzly bear!" Grosbeak hooted. "At least I'll be crushed in a glorious tilt for the ages!"

"Then live," Bluebeard said, his voice harsh with emotion. He slapped the toad on the rump, it leapt, and he fell behind me with everything else.

Chapter Thirty

LAST TIME, we'd just leapt into the fray. Not so, this time. We leapt only a little way and then paused and on the other end of the field, I saw that Grosbeak was wrong. The three-headed bear that had stood there was being led away and another mount was being led up in his place. It was a grey stallion with a swirling horn jutting from the center of his skull and with only the faintest look at him, my breath caught in my chest.

Someone's voice rang out over the field, and I spared the narrowest glance to look at him. He was a man with goat feet and goat horns, holding a horn in his hand that looked very much like the one on the unicorn's head, but when he spoke into it all the crowd could hear his voice.

"Qualifications are completed! The first round will now commence, the competitors are ..." he paused and glanced us over to check who we were, but my eyes were back to the unicorn, my heart frozen in my chest.

The unicorn was white, white, white with only the faintest taffy hints at tail and mane and the man sitting astride him was helmless, his light golden hair picked up in the wind, brighter than hair should be, the collar of his red coat edged in gold peeked up from his plate armor and the tabard he wore matched it, crested with crossed swords and a wicked-bladed knife cross-wise below them.

The Sword.

I couldn't breathe. I couldn't tear my eyes from him.

"Ferna din Brayen, now named the Sword, Lord Towerrock!"

The crowd cheered and over them, I could hear Grosbeak whistling his appreciation. "Ferna is a fine figure of a Wittenbrand. You're honored to be jousting him."

I was going to die.

"And his opponent, standing for Lord Riverbarrow, a mortal woman of no consequence!"

There were confused murmurs and when I glanced over at the announcer, Coppertomb was leaning over him, a calculating look in his eye.

He lifted the horn again. "I apologize. Riding for the Arrow, Lord Riverbarrow is Lady Arrow!"

For no reason I could discern, the crowd cheered for me, too. Maybe they were all Grosbeaks. Maybe they were just here to watch someone die in an interesting way and it mattered not to them which of us it were.

I swallowed, made sure of my seat and then a burst of red and gold sparks went off in the center of the field and my mount must have known them for he immediately leapt.

The world sank behind me and all that existed now were my mount, my grip on Grosbeak's short pole, and my tattered courage. I held to them all with the strength I had.

On my shoulder, Look and Despair shrieked her ferret battlecry.

Just like we had before, the toad crested his leap and then turned to plummet forward. We were still descending as the unicorn bore down on us, forehead thrust forward as if that were the only lance he needed, feet churning the mud of the course.

My eyes narrowed on the new Sword's lance as it began to rise toward me. I was no warrior. I knew not when to dodge, but to my surprise, the toad dipped at just the right moment, belly to the ground and I fell as the lance struck over my shoulder and past it, the wind of its passing grazing my cheek. Something seemed to tear as it passed, but I had no time to look to see if cloth or skin or even mail had been scored. The unicorn had closed the rest of the distance, and now we rose just in time for me to flail at it with Grosbeak's pole.

I missed the horse entirely, though the roll of its eye would haunt my dreams forever, but Grosbeak struck the new Sword hard in the head and to my utter surprise his teeth bit down on the man's ear and he bore him off his horse and to the ground, ripping the pole from my grasp.

The new Sword screamed as he fell and his unicorn spun, front hooves churning the air before him for only a moment before slamming down on his rider. I gasped as the horse reared again, slamming a second time and a third, narrowly missing Grosbeak who rolled to the end of his chain and was stuck there screaming a combination of the vilest curses and terrible derision as you'd expect to hear from a damned soul.

"Try again, equine maladroit!"

Before I could do more than rip off my helm with my skeletal hand, the new bearer of the name that had haunted me for so long was nothing but pummeled flesh and a rag that had once been a gold and crimson tabard.

I was still on the toad. I clung to him as I vomited over the side, clutching the helm to my chest.

"A draw!" the announcer declared.

Confused, I looked from him to my dead opponent. Had losing my lance lost me the match?

But then I saw it. The Sword's lance had killed, too. Just not me.

Stunned, I stumbled from the toad's back and across the field to where the specter who had sat so faithfully upon my shoulder these seven years was pinned to the ground by the Sword's lance. I fell to my knees beside her. The plate mail – awkward and overlarge – was not inhibition enough to keep me from ripping the lance from her poor tattered spirit body. She smiled – the first time I'd seen a real smile from her – and then she was gone.

To my surprise, I felt as if I'd been kicked in the belly. She had not been my friend but my warden – and yet, she'd bet on my side when Grosbeak took wagers. She'd seen all I'd seen these seven years. I would miss her always there, always reminding me of what had happened that terrible day she was affixed to me.

"I didn't know you could kill spirits," I said sadly.

"You can kill anything you want if you just know how," Grosbeak said miserably.

I turned to see the toad bearing him to me, pole in his mouth. Around us, the crowd cheered, and I was starting to suspect they'd cheer anything at this point.

"You need to make your bow to the Bramble King so that the next set may ride," he advised me.

Miserably, I donned the helm again. Gathered up both Grosbeak and the lance – the new Sword wouldn't need it now – and found my seat on the toad again.

"They'll need to find a new Sword. Three in almost as many days." Grosbeak chortled with apparent amusement. "I wonder if they'd consider a severed head."

"By all means ask," I said bitterly. "Then when the Lord and Lady Riverbarrow must dispatch yet another Sword we'll know the best way to do it."

The toad – a truly well-trained mount – hopped in front of the Bramble King for long enough for me to bow and tip my lance. From the corner of my eye, I watched Coppertomb staying right beside him and watching me with that slitted gaze.

"Oh, and how would you kill me?" Grosbeak asked me as we leapt back to the pavilion.

"I'd drown you in a chamber pot. It's the only fitting end to one such as you."

He was still laughing when we entered the tent again. Still laughing when, to my utter shock, Bluebeard ripped the helm from my head, caught me in his arms, lifted me from the toad and dipped me backward to kiss me like a prince from a fairytale.

Well, then. Perhaps he wasn't furious after all.

Chapter Thirty-One

AFTER THAT KISS, I'd expected an apology of some kind – but I had forgotten that Bluebeard didn't apologize. The kiss was, perhaps, the closest I would get.

"I commend you for taking the lance, fire of my eyes," he told me with a wink, taking it from my hand and examining it. "It will serve you for the next round."

"Does that mean I may see a reprieve for the next round?" Grosbeak asked, sounding almost too hopeful. "It draws near."

"How soon?" I gasped.

"There are sixteen qualified competitors of which one has now departed this living realm," Bluebeard said, stripping the armor from me as quickly as he'd put it on originally. "We have the time of the other fourteen clashes to check you over for hidden wounds, check the integrity of your armor, check your mount and spear, and talk about your strategy, though truth be told, accident has served you well so far."

"*What happened to the Sword?*" I asked, still reeling from his death.

"One shouldn't ride a unicorn if one is not ready for the risks," Bluebeard growled, checking each piece of plate as he stripped it from me. "They will trample any unhorsed rider – foe, or in this case, friend, indiscriminately. You think I chose the toad at random? His reliability in the fray is unparalleled. Not the proud stallion too arrogant to serve, not the vicious cat, or the violent buck who put their lives before the rider, no give me the stability and hunger of the mighty toad."

"You're going to inspect me, too, right?" Grosbeak asked. "This right eye definitely feels wrong, and I think I've lost all my crabs."

Bluebeard ignored him, moving to inspect my mount as I drank water from the beaded pitcher at the side of the pavilion. While I was gone, someone had brought refreshment and while my belly could not take food, I was parched from the effort so far.

"*How did the Bramble King rule?*" I asked carefully, worried at how Bluebeard might react to the question after his outburst from my accident.

Bluebeard froze in his work and looked up at me with his mouth set in a grim line.

"Against. He ruled against. Coppertomb is to have the mortal kingdoms of all those we have felled."

"*All?*" I couldn't believe it.

Grosbeak hooted and this time, I did the honors. I lifted him by his pole and set him outside the pavilion.

"Wait! I won't be able to hear from out here!" he complained.

"Or laugh."

"You'd rob me of the succor of lightheartedness?"

I ignored him and went back in to see Bluebeard cleaning his hands in a basin before he turned to me.

"Now you. You were hit?"

"Only my specter."

He examined my shoulder, running his hands through my hair and over my neck and shoulders.

"Is there pain anywhere?" he asked, his hands continuing in their search as they carefully felt down my back and arms, his fingers swift but kind. He seemed to be looking for lumps or wounds or breaks.

"*No pain.*"

"This ruling makes our plans more urgent," he said as he skimmed my waist and ribs, still searching me for injury. "If you live twice more, then the moment you are victorious we will send you through to your brother. He must gather those he can and proceed immediately to the Plains of Myygddo."

"*But without allies,*" I said, horrified. "*Without our help, he'll be marching Pensmoore to their deaths.*"

"He's a king. He can handle this."

"*He must cross other nations – territories who have no good will for him. Why must he go at all?*"

Bluebeard was finished examining me. He stood, his eyes boring into mine.

"Any who survive this fifth move must gather their mortal armies to the Plains for the last battle. Fail to do so, and their nation falters and they have lost. I had thought to bring him there with two or even three more armies under his belt through the lands of Aayadmoore. Such hopes are dashed now."

My mouth was dry. Svetgin could lose his whole force just trying to drive through to the Plains. We could all be ruined.

"*And if he doesn't?*" I asked in a weak mental voice.

"Then the horrors we have discussed will befall Pensmoore and all the mortal realms."

I swallowed. Years of starvation and grinding poverty after Pensmoore was ravaged by an unanticipated force. Darkness sweeping across the world, knowledge lost, cultures eaten as by vermin.

"He must attend with his armies or see another age come and pass as that one did. And you will tell him so, if you survive this."

I was nodding.

"*Surely we must have some allies, though,*" I suggested. "*Surely someone must have freed you from the iron knife that pinned you to the pillar. You never did say who.*"

He lifted my chin with a finger so he could look me directly in the eye as he said, "Recall that I told you that time is different in the Wittenhame?"

I nodded.

"Then know, too, that there are ripples and wells in this realm that change the experience of it. You say you waited seven years for me in the mortal world."

"*I did. Though Grosbeak says it was only two days for him.*"

"It was three days for me. And also three centuries and three eternities and in time, the rock pillar broke apart and released me and I scraped the dagger from the wound and freed myself."

I gasped. That sounded like torture.

"I suffered every moment of it in the firm knowledge that it was for the good. And we will suffer what comes next in the same spirit. Come, let us arm you again."

"Shouldn't we see to your wound?" I asked pointing to his bleeding side.

"That wound will not fade until all my work is accomplished. We shall not waste our efforts upon it. You are fit. The mount is fit. Let us armor you once more and then to the battle."

"You'd better hurry!" I heard Grosbeak call from outside. "They're going through the lists awfully quickly! It would be a shame to forfeit, don't you think?"

"I may yet take more than his life," Bluebeard muttered but he was hurrying now, dressing me as swiftly the second time as the first. He cinched the straps a little more gently, though, and when he was down to just the helmet left, he surprised me by leaning his forehead against mine. "I would shelter you from this if I could, but you do me proud. I have not before – nor am I likely to again – put the gamble of my plans on the shoulders of another. I am better suited to take heads and destroy all those who stand against me than I am to bind myself to the sidelines while another rides out for me. And yet, I have married you in the Wittenbrand way and you are heart of my heart, and bones of my bones, so now you will be the hands of my hands. Strike hard, and true, and without remorse, and know you have my heart."

And then, so sudden that he surprised me, he thrust the helm over my head and lifted me – armor and all – onto the toad, pushing the black lance into my hands.

"You shouldn't be lifting me when you're wounded. You're going to tear something," I scolded.

"I shall lift all the world," he said fiercely. "And I shall smash it in the hearth flames like a crystal glass brought in tribute to a king and drunk to his health."

"Well, if that's the way it is, don't expect such tribute from me," I teased, trying to distract from my fear.

Bluebeard led the toad to edge out of the pavilion.

"Finally!" Grosbeak croaked from the side. "You've been missing everything! It's glorious! Tanglecott's heir won her ride from the back of a golden gryphon. She'll suit as heir, oh yes! Almost made me miss the original Tanglecott. Oh, the glory! And Bluffroll slew an upstart from his own ranks who dared to ride against him. He does not have your macabre habit of taking heads, but I did see him snatch a tooth. What a joy to see."

His voice drew closer and then to my surprise, Bluebeard set the severed head in front of me, removed from its hook on the end of the chain but positioned so that Grosbeak could ride just ahead of me, facing outward. Balance, it seemed, was not a concern for him.

"This time, you'll suffer her fate, betrayer," Bluebeard said lightly.

Behind us, the crowd had burst into their favorite chorus once again.

"*Fly with the Arrow,*
Dance with the Sword,
Give your heart to the barrow,
Die with your Lord.

The lights flared as their voices came together in a sound both merry and haunting, otherworldly and slightly vicious.

"*And if ever you be broken*
And gasp on the ground,
Hold up your fine token
And join with the sound,

I shivered at those words. I'd already felt their truth. I dreaded where else this song my lead.

"*Sing for your sovereign,*
Bow to your Dream,
Make haste for the fallen,
Rise in esteem,

There were definitely going to be fallen again. I watched as a Wittenbrand clad in nothing but a loincloth, his own antlers, and his wild, thistle-strewn beard settle his mount at one end of the field. He rode a creature with curling rich brown hair and a pair of curved horns. Its head and shoulders were heavy and its beady eye glittered as it watched the crowd.

"*And if ever you be broken,*
And gasp on the ground,
The word may be spoken
And salvation found."

On the other end, a woman with silky moonbeam hair sat astride a white tiger and both she and the tiger were strung with silver bells.

"Close your eyes," Bluebeard whispered to me as the song faded out and the competitors were announced.

"Riding for himself, Lord Antlerdale!"

The cheers chilled me. I opened my eyes for a moment to scan the crowd and what I saw there chilled me more. Their eyes were alight, fists raised, faces twisted into uncanny hunger. They loved this. Loved the death and violence. Loved pitting their own against one another and watching them fall and die.

"Riding as an independent, Lady Moonshine!"

I snapped my eyelids shut. What future had I in such a place? None, perhaps. Perhaps these were my last days, lived with my wild husband in his wild world and trying alongside him to shift the tides of fate and time. Even tasting the edges of my own death, I knew I wanted no other end.

"Keep them closed," Bluebeard whispered.

"No, keep them open," Grosbeak said, naked bloodlust in his tone. "Watch a life end before you. It's more powerful than any other thing you can witness. It changes the world, plucking a soul away forever."

"What about birth?" I protested. "Is that not just as powerful?"

He snickered. "Your naivety is sweet to the palate. Never lose it, Izolda."

"Keep them closed," Bluebeard murmured and then the sound of the feet of large animals moving and the sound of a thousand pairs of lungs gasping in a breath ending in a piercing, high pitched scream that went on and on and my imagination was too much for me. I couldn't take the suspense.

I opened my eyes and immediately wished I had not. Lord Antlerdale rode right past us on his fierce, snorting beast. Dangling from his lance – and how could something as slender as a lance hold such weight? – was the crumpled corpse of the moonlight lady, her silver bells still tinkling even after her spirit fled. She waved raggedly from where she was pierced through like a bedraggled banner. I felt ill.

"Why do you Wittenbrand bathe in death when you could live as immortals in peace and security?"

The question ripped from me almost unwittingly.

"Peace wears thin beside power," Grosbeak scorned.

"It is for this that I have entered the fray," Bluebeard said in a low voice. "It is to upend what has been and forge it new, to wash all in seas of my own blood and paint it back in the colors of peace. You see as I do, wife. But peace is never bought by inactivity and the plant does not thrive from neglect. You see now why the path is fraught and painful – for nothing short of pain and death will save us now."

I didn't entirely understand him. I did know I didn't like the idea of washing everything in seas of his blood. That couldn't be right.

"You're up," Grosbeak said. "Ready to die on the end of a spear?"

I swallowed. "I fear I am not ready, Grosbeak. How fortunate that I have you as my vanguard."

Bluebeard caught my shoulder in a last firm grip. I found it oddly steadying. My name was being announced again – this time with less derision and a bigger cheer from the crowd.

"Do not die. A thousand centuries would not be enough to ease the pain I'd feel at your passing."

Still not an apology. But I would take it.

He slapped the toad's rump and it leapt to the starting place, my stomach lurching up at even this small hop.

Look and Despair chittered into my ear, joining me in the helmet. The stink of her musk filled my nose and mouth, and I would have protested, but in a way I was grateful. It was hard to be properly afraid when you were gagging on a gross smell.

The announcer was declaring my opponent.

"Riding for his own glory and the fifth move of the game, Lord Bluffroll!"

My heart was in my throat as he burst forward, mounted on some terrible creature twice the size of my frog. It had five legs – no – four legs and one was its nose. It curled upward, trumpeting from the strange feature, as ears the size of ship sails waved in the breeze. Clumps of thick hair hung from its sides and back and formed a thick curtain over whatever eyes it might have. The hair billowed behind it like witch's hair moss hanging from the branches of trees in a wind storm.

Bluffroll sat the back of the enormous shaggy creature, lance held in a hand and braced over the shoulder so it pointed downward where his foe must be. His wide grin and the green skin of his face made my belly roll wildly.

I just had to live. I just had to live.

"Any advice?" I asked Grosbeak.

"Try to die in an interesting way."

"I loathe how you plot against me," I told him. "I'd give you all this beauty of mine if you'd but return to my side as friend."

He snorted. "That's exactly what your husband didn't want."

The sparks shot and my toad leapt forward. I gripped the lance in both hands, but even as we reached the peak of our leap, we still weren't as tall as the massive creature. Bluffroll, confident in his height, wore no helm and his grin was yellow and wide.

"No beauty necessary," Grosbeak wailed. "Throw me over the side and I'll be your man for life."

"Promise?" I gritted out.

"I do! I promise!"

I let go of my lance with one hand, dashed Grosbeak over the side, and then returned my grip to the lance, aiming it up as my frog leapt a second time.

At the peak of our leap, I brought my lance as hard as I could, and to my surprise, the toad veered hard to the meridian, smashing into the massive creature and crushing my leg between the bodies of both mounts. I had no time to register more than pain as musk filled my nostrils, my vision was obscured, and then a dark shape shot down my lance as my weapon found its target while at the same time that something slammed into my shoulder.

I caught a last glimpse of my ferret leaping from where my lance had struck to the face of my opponent and then I was flying from the toad, through the air, and falling in a burst of pain to the ground.

A roar rose from the crowd and behind the roar, a scream pierced the air, but my head was spinning, everything numb. I thought I found my way to all fours, my head ringing. I pulled my single gauntlet off and removed my helmet, but the world was whirling far too quickly.

I vomited again, my whole body heaving and curling on itself.

"Seriously? I only just promised to be your creature and already you are splashing your filth near me? Can you not survive a single tilt without showing your mortal underbelly?"

Grosbeak. I knew that voice.

I scrambled forward – or tried to. I couldn't tell which way was up, couldn't tell which way was down. Something in my right side hurt so much and I couldn't feel enough of my arm to know what was injured.

And then I stumbled and fell face-first into the mud.

My last thought was that so many different creatures sure let a variety of terrible manure smells. And then everything went black.

Chapter Thirty-Two

I WOKE to something cold on my face and a pair of cat's eyes close to mine. Curses turned the air bluer than my husband's blue eyes and blue beard.

"Well, now you've gone and woken her," Grosbeak complained. "You shouldn't have done that. She'll have to ride again."

"And who would you have put in her place, revenant? You? You can't hold a lance. Besides, both our fates are tied to her now."

"Both?" Grosbeak sounded disbelieving.

"My magic sustains your life, you fraction of a man," Bluebeard said. "If I die, you wink out with me and what's left of you will rot where it sits or feed the birds."

"Ugh. You can't be in earnest."

"Believe as you wish, it changes nothing. If she does not ride, I do not live, and you do not get to keep watching the world like a favorite drama."

"Then you'd better work fast," Grosbeak said, and I realized that – true to his word – he was on my side again. "They've decided she's at a draw for that one since her ferret chewed Bluffroll's face half off. A pity the stinking creature didn't survive its encounter. It was finally making itself useful. There are only two more jousts before her name is called again."

Poor Look and Despair. She was no more made for this Wittenbrand world than I was but she'd fought as hard and intently as any ferret ever could – tenacious to the end.

"Don't look at me like that," Grosbeak said. "It's not my fault you're madly in love with her."

"I am not."

"There's no point bluffing me. I've been here the whole time."

"'Madly in love' is too weak an expression. It is mild as a sun shower to my howling winter storm."

I could hear Grosbeak's eye roll in his voice. "Oh, forgive me then for underestimating your madness."

"I forgive the trespass."

A wave of pain washed over me, and I moaned.

"Fire of my eyes? Can you hear me?"

I nodded, struggling to try to sit. A sharp pain flared in my shoulder and collarbone and I fell back gasping in agony. I wouldn't be sitting up yet.

"I have to strip this armor from you and heal you. Will you take a day?" he asked, briskly. "You have refused them before – to your credit – but heal you we must or you will not ride again, and we'll have lost all your days in a moment."

I nodded again, feeling too thick-headed to speak with my mind.

He bent over me, and I realized he was loosening the straps on my breastplate. He pulled at something, and I couldn't hold back the scream that tore from my lips.

"Hold fast," he said, gripping my flesh hand as if to comfort me and then trying again.

I would like to be someone who screamed less, but today was not the day to begin that.

There was a rustle from behind us as I fell back against the cloak spread on the ground, gasping wetly.

Bluebeard cursed, running a hand over his face. It left trails of blood and dirt on his nose and cheek that were more dramatic than even the tiny decorative cut he gave himself. They mingled with the anxious sweat on his face to make him look as if he'd just left a battlefield.

"Whoever has entered this pavilion," he growled, "Will be made to eat their own toes one at a time unless they give me a good reason for their presence here."

"It's stuck on bone," a crystal voice replied. "Dented in so deep that the broken edges can't come loose."

"I'm well aware," he snarled. "Why have you crawled into my fold, serpent? Once you've bit me, will you bite again while I am occupied?"

He turned to address her, and I saw a flash of Lady Wittentree's scarred face. She peered past him.

"That I'm tied by hands clasped and words spoken to your enemy does not make me a threat to your wife, Arrow. I came to lend you a pair of hands. Your only other helpers," here she shot a look at Grosbeak and the toad, "seem bereft of them, and it's impossible to heal her while she's still full of the earth's ore. Tell me you don't require the aid and I shall leave."

Bluebeard said nothing, but the lines of his face were tight. He moved slightly to the side so she could join him in watching me struggle to breathe.

"Where's the javelin?" Wittentree asked, her slender fingers tracing something on my chest as her single eye roved over the mess of armor and Izolda.

"I don't know," he snapped.

"Tip is likely still in the wound."

"I thank you for the observation," he growled.

Their words washed over me through waves of pain and I was too occupied with riding the swells and ebbs of it to do more than listen.

"Don't act the wolf with the sore paw, Arrow," Wittentree said firmly. "It is not I who bid you risk your immortality on this venture. It's not my responsibility to guarantee you win over me when I set a wager, too."

"A light one, if I recall. A winter palace," Bluebeard growled.

"I am very fond of that palace. The fishing in the nearby lake is beyond compare. Some of us do not hold our immortality so lightly."

"I have aims of which you know nothing."

"Hold her down and I will wrest the armor from her," Wittentree said in a clipped voice. "And do not think I don't guess your aims, Arrow. You think you can set all right by taking the Bramble King's place. Don't look at me like that. I can parse riddles, too. But there is no reason that the Bramble King couldn't be the Bramble Queen. Why should I roll over and offer the seat to you simply because you have so many wrongs to atone for and I have only a missing eye and a few missing fingers on the tally?"

I felt pressure on my shoulders and then my scream ripped through the air again as Wittentree pulled. It felt as though I was being torn in half while still alive. I could feel all the bones of my chest flexing and levering apart in ways they shouldn't. I couldn't breathe – as if someone had banded my chest in iron like a barrel newly hooped – and my scream choked off to wet gurgles. I collapsed against the ground – but still, my breath wouldn't come. My heart stuttered. My vision was whirling.

Their voices had faded over me to nothing but scraps. My mind could not hold them. I fell in and out of a blurry consciousness.

I woke to something soft on my lips and I opened them wider, trying to suck in a breath.

"Kissing her like that is going to make it harder for her to breathe," Wittentree commented.

My eyes flew open and met the blue cat's eyes so close that I found them only after his nose grazed mine as he pulled away from the light kiss.

His face was clean or at least somewhat clean, as if someone had swiped a wet cloth over it as an afterthought. There was still grit and dried blood between the hairs of his beard.

I blinked back sudden tears, not able to form clear thoughts to define the soaring relief shuddering through me.

I could breathe.

I sucked in a clear, trembling breath, letting it fill me enough to sit up.

Wittentree smirked when she met my eyes.

"Truly you've found devotion and undying faithfulness," she said ironically. "How tragic that it is with a man so other than you, that he cannot enter your world or you his."

Nothing in my body hurt anymore and the release of that gave me boldness that perhaps I should have inhibited. I lifted my skeletal hand and held it up to her palm forward. Her eyes caught on the ring Bluebeard had placed on it and they narrowed in consideration.

She thought I could not enter his world? I had paid a hand for the privilege.

She snorted. "Oh, I see your entry fee well enough, but now look to your left."

To my left was my husband looking like a rag rung out. His side had bled so much that his entire front was soaked in blood. His doublet and shirt were crumpled, his hair mussed, and face smeared with dirt and blood.

"There's your real price and if you love the man, you'll stop paying it and go stay in whatever crypt or closet he's stashed the other mortal wives he took," she said grimly.

"Your words on this are not welcome," Bluebeard said grimly. He was trembling head to toe, but I could read his expression enough to see he was torn between fury and gratitude.

"I thought the Wittenbrand did not give gifts," I said hoarsely, sitting up. Gingerly, I felt my chest and shoulder. I was whole. I took in a deep breath and let it out. My body felt completely well – in utter contrast to my heart. Ready, I supposed, to go and possibly die one more time.

"I'm most generous," Lady Wittentree said, collecting herself to her feet.

"It was not a gift," Bluebeard objected. "You owed me a debt."

"Consider it paid," Lady Wittentree said. "And think again about this mad plan of yours. You can only lose and lose badly. Why not accept your fate? You have lost. You are not the prince you thought you were. So be it. Go live what mortal life you may with your mortal wife. They say that mortals enjoy marriage sometimes. They raise children, and I know not what else – horses, perhaps, or goats. Tame mortal creatures so solid and substantial that they are always themselves. And the mortals who raise them grow old and see some manner of dignity in it. Go, and do that, and trouble us no more with grand schemes meant to upend the world."

She took my skeletal hand in both of hers, ignoring the ring most pointedly, and said, "You, at least, ought to hear the wisdom of my words, Lady Arrow. Return to Pensmoore and haunt our lands no more."

And then she dropped my hand and was gone, and I did not know why I hid it, but I stashed the tiny object she'd pressed into my grasp in a pocket for something about her furtive gift felt ... different. It felt like dull colors and food without taste. It felt mortal and it sang to my mortal bones.

"One more, then?" Grosbeak called cheerily. "One more ride for the win?"

"Or the draw," I said grimly, pulling myself to my feet to face my demons one more time.

Chapter Thirty-Three

MY CLOTHING, it turned out, was ruined. So ruined, that my simple shirt and doublet would not be able to hold themselves up. To my surprise, my husband stripped his own off and offered them to me, soaked down the front with his own blood.

I wasn't excited to wear bloody clothes. My own were ruined with the same but it was *my* blood and that made it somewhat less revolting. The hopeful look in his eyes and the fact that one side of my shirt almost fell off entirely, exposing my shift underneath was what eventually swayed me and I changed quickly, glad that at least my flimsy shift was still mostly intact. His doublet was far too large, and his shirt so bulky and wet that I didn't want to tuck it.

Even without his proper raiment, he looked all the prince as he helped me onto the toad. There would be no helm or breastplate this time. Both had been ruined past any saving. One greave had been bent clean in half – suggesting that Bluebeard must have fixed a break in my leg when he was healing me from my other wounds. I wore the remaining gauntlet on my flesh hand. My too-big clothing with my hair all tumbled around me untidily made me look more like a wild Wittenbrand than ever before.

I'd lost my lance. Bluebeard was rigging my lantern pole to stand in its stead one more time.

"Usually there are more weapons available, but you can only ride with what you carried in the qualifiers, or you take from your enemies. Don't think for a second that you can sacrifice me as you did your other companions," Grosbeak lectured. He seemed happier now that we were at peace once more. "I'll not go quietly into anyone's dread night."

Bluebeard set him on my lap.

"We're at a clear disadvantage," Grosbeak said, slightly muffled until I set him straight. Bluebeard had not been gentle. "We haven't been watching the others. We don't know who you'll be riding against, and we don't know how he's behaved in the past."

"It will hardly matter," I said grimly. "I've only made it this far through chance and pure nerve."

"Skill would be better," Grosbeak said, sagely.

I didn't bother to answer such an unnecessary remark. Instead, I leaned down, not waiting for him to initiate, and kissed Bluebeard gently.

"You've done what you can for me." I made sure to keep any tremble from my voice. I must be brave now. "*Do not mourn if I die here. Make what you can of your mortal life. Find an understanding wife and make babies with blue cat eyes and an undying thirst for adventure – just like you.*"

I forced myself to smile my goodbye. I'd been lucky three times. There could not possibly be a fourth.

"If you're saying goodbye, you'd better hurry," Grosbeak warned. "The crowd grows boisterous. This must be the last tilt of the main tournament."

"I'll do none of those things, wife of mine," Bluebeard growled, leaning in so he was close enough that his lips brushed the shell of my ear, and his scruff tickled the sensitive skin along my jaw. "I planned all this to be done alone – a solitaire knight errant set to right all wrongs, but you have bent me and made me half a double. I can no more conquer without you than I can breathe if you do not breathe, too."

And then he stepped back, and without giving me a chance to say anything he swatted my toad on the rump, and we leapt from the pavilion and into the field of gore and offal beyond.

The faces along the meridian mocked me and the crowd looked no more civilized than the carved horrors as they offered insouciant leers and wild hoots of excitement.

I did not do this for them. I did not care if they so much as noticed.

Grosbeak did. He hooted loudly, trumpeting his excitement to the excited waves of anyone who caught his eye. One winged woman winked and a girl with double pairs of swan wings made a moue with her mouth at him

In the stands, the announcer lifted his horn.

"The final tilt of the day will be watched and judged by our good lord, the Bramble King!" The crowd went wild at that, and the Bramble King's eyes opened enough that he almost looked interested. "Make your bows to him, competitors!"

"You need to hop up there!" Grosbeak instructed and I quickly whirled my toad to obey. "When you get there, bow."

I was aware of a figure swathed head to toe in a black velvet cape, the hood of which hung low over the face, but I did not focus on who I was fighting. I made my obeisance focused instead on what I was fighting *for* or rather who, my eyes drifting to where the Arrow stood with his arms crossed over his bare chest, the gaping wound in his ribs exposed for all to see.

I couldn't tear my eyes from him, not when we were told to rise, not when we made our way back to our opposite sides of the run, not when the announcer gave my name. I managed it, though, when he gave my competitor's name and my eyes went wide as the black cloak fell, revealing the man I feared most, the man who had slowly conspired against me and everything I did from the moment I met him.

Coppertomb.

He saluted.

I tried to imitate his motion.

But all I felt was boiling fury.

Of course, it was him. Of course, he was here to force me to fall. He'd take back those few things I had left. And he'd love doing it. He was rot in solid oak, mold in the crust of good bread, stink in a cut of meat. And here he was, prepared to take my life, to spill out all my hopes and future over the mud.

He'd been planning it all along from the day he bid me steal my own garnet and give it to him and I'd played into his hand again and again. If you want to change an outcome, you have to change one of the decisions that brought you to the result – right? Was there anything left that I could change? Anything he hadn't thought of first?

"A wager," I called out to Coppertomb, my voice stuttering slightly with nerves. "A wager to you on this tilt!"

The crowd cheered. Added drama was always their favorite thing.

Coppertomb paled under his gold highlights.

He was wearing the crown with my husband's rib in it like a badge of violence, but if he was wearing armor I could not see it. Perhaps he was being a sportsman since I'd lost mine – though that didn't sound like him. Perhaps he'd lost his own in the earlier tilts. Or perhaps, this was his arrogance, his strong assurance that no mortal could touch him.

"You've nothing to offer me, mortal woman," he called back to the hushed boos of the crowd. They seemed as disappointed as I was.

"It's bad form not to take a wager when offered," Grosbeak grumped. "Bad luck, too. It could doom him."

Coppertomb must have felt the same. "Why take a wager for dust? Why judge as precious what is worthless?"

"Why run from a child with a sling?" Bluebeard asked and suddenly he was at my side, shoulders bent forward as he slung his verbal insults. I was surprised to see him there. I'd have thought he'd be upset that I'd offered anything to my opponent – especially when anything I might wager was his. "Why flee in terror at the dawn?"

"Hear, hear!" someone from the crowd yelled back and there was jeering laughter amidst the cheers.

"If you think her so like to win, Arrow," Coppertomb called, "then you should make the wager with me. Wager something I want and cannot get with the sheer expediency of removing her head from her body."

He shook his hand and the lance in it – while short – shivered up and down with bluish-white light.

"The Lightning lance," Grosbeak hissed. "I hadn't realized he'd brought that. With that, he could blow you into the next world, Izolda. If I could pee myself, I'd be doing it right now. Just a suggestion."

"And what good would that do?" I hissed.

"Maybe he'd let you wear your skin to the grave if he thought it too much trouble to take from you?"

I shivered at the terrible thought he'd put in my mind and then squared my shoulders. There'd be no signs of terror from me. I could do that much. And I would.

"Is it real lightning?" I asked calmly, my question hidden by the mad jeers of the crowd.

"It will turn living human flesh to marble on touch," Grosbeak replied, his tone bordering on awe.

I shuddered.

"A venture then, Coppertomb – all the mortal kingdoms you possess shall be mine if you fall in this joust – those you've won, those you've negotiated for, and that whose token you carry."

The crowd fell quiet, ears perking up and with them the corners of their lascivious mouths. There was nothing the Wittenhame liked more than a wager. But my heart was heavy. I could not deliver. My husband would never get what he bargained for.

"A hazard it is," Coppertomb said, and his careful expression cracked into an unstoppable grin. A smile on his face looked as wrong as a dead talking head. "I will take your bet and match it – if your substitute falls to me, she will give me her heart."

Fear sweat slicked my brow and trickled down my spine.

"I carry that," Bluebeard said easily. "And it is from me you would have to collect it."

"Then make it so," Coppertomb said.

"It is agreed," Bluebeard confirmed.

And before I could even think of what that wager could possibly mean – was it literal? Was it metaphorical? Was it something somehow worse? – the sparks burst in the center of the field and like it or not, my toad leapt to the line.

Chapter Thirty-Four

COPPERTOMB HAD CHOSEN to make his passes on a horse made entirely of bone. Wisps of glowing purple mist held it together as it raced toward me.

"This is bad," Grosbeak whispered fervently – as if I didn't know. "This is terribly bad."

My heart was in my throat. I clutched my lantern pole in both hands, knowing it could never possibly be enough.

"Do not fail, fire of my eyes. Use all that good sense you so embody and carve me a path so I may ride over him and grind his bones to dust." He sounded so certain, like he knew I could save all this when there was just no way that I could.

My toad leapt into the air once again, and my belly lurched. I fought the nausea of the lurch, so preoccupied with it that I didn't realize until too late that my pole had jammed into the meridian as we leapt. It ripped from my grip, tearing away.

No weapon. What would I do now? How could I possibly pit myself against a weapon that froze living flesh if I had none of my own? Not even a lantern pole?

"Lost!" Grosbeak wailed from in front of me. "Lost, lost, lost!"

My heart hammered in my ears. I opened my mouth in a gasp at the same moment the crowd roared, and we reached the apex of the leap.

I looked down at what could easily have been the last thing I ever saw. Wild-eyed and bloodthirsty, the crowd pushed in, eyes bright, mouths snarling, or open to shout their support. Coppertomb's lance was aimed perfectly to catch me in the un-armored torso. His clever eyes narrowed in concentration.

The lance gleamed a bright copper in the moonlight as if it were a living thing, craving my blood, longing to turn the softness of my living flesh to stone. Perhaps it really was as alive as I was.

As alive as ... I ... was.

I flexed the bones of my skeletal hand in thought. A simple problem required a simple solution.

I saw it all in the space of a heartbeat. I forgot my fear, forgot my nausea, and angled sharply to my right and forward, twisting so that as we landed, I could reach out and grab the lightning lance with my skeletal hand. Coppertomb had braced it against a pocket of leather in his belt – wise, if you were planning to use the full force of your charge to plow your opponent off their mount. Unwise if their hands were free and they could grab it. I used it against him, leaping from the frog's back, ignoring Grosbeak's scream as I shoved all my strength into forcing that lance back and to the left.

Grosbeak's cry faded and cut off in a stream of curses, but I didn't dare look at where he might have tumbled. I was off the back of the toad and hanging – for one impossible second – in the air, as the full force of my downward, leftward trajectory combined with the force of Coppertomb's forward trajectory angling the opposite direction. The combined force spun us both, toppling him from the saddle as we flew out from the lance pinned between us.

For one terrible heartbeat, we both hung in the air, and I knew from the shock on his face that his lance should have frozen my flesh and stopped any movement. But he hadn't bet on my skeletal hand. He hadn't bet that I had a way to touch this terrifying weapon without being burned by it, for I thought that perhaps metal gauntlets would be just as affected as human flesh, drawing that heat into their metal surface and searing a person right through.

My triumph lasted barely a flash of thought, and then I fell heavily – belly-first – on the stone meridian and the air was knocked from my body. I pitched over it, head-first, and fell in a crumpled heap.

The crowd gasped.

I blinked hard against pain and the black and white flashes popping across my vision. Perhaps my head had been injured.

I heard nothing.

I shoved a hand under me and forced myself up from the mud. Something in my ribs screamed. It would have to go on screaming. I could do nothing for it now.

"Heart of my heart, your victory will be sung in the Halls of Riverbarrow for a generation hence." Bluebeard sounded shockingly proud.

I was barely up to all fours when a roar – like a fire when the door of a furnace opens – rolled over me, leaving me lightheaded and disoriented.

Up, my mind urged me. Get up.

Or maybe it was the voice in my head that was pleading with me, *"Get up."*

I found my feet and the cry redoubled. In the fog of my surroundings, I made out the wide-mouthed faces of the crowd as they bayed their approval.

And then Bluebeard was beside me, landing lightly on his feet, head thrown back and arms wide, the ultimate showman.

"My surrogate has unhorsed her opponent. I claim this victory for Riverbarrow."

With another roar, the crowd closed in further – too close – their faces alight with frenetic enthusiasm. Between them and us, a dazed Coppertomb found his feet. He seemed uninjured, though he favored his right leg. His cloak and lance were gone – sunk in the mud somewhere. And his expression was one of absolute fury.

I didn't see why. We'd both lost. Or we'd both won. Surely, there could be no forfeits from wagers that no one had won.

"The mortal woman was unhorsed just as I," he bellowed. "And just as I have been laid flat before you, so has she been. There is no victory here."

"No victory?" Bluebeard asked, dramatically, physically recoiling. "Can such a thing be so?"

He was clearly playing to his audience. His eyes were still spread wide and then he snapped his fingers, and something belched behind me. I spun to see the toad, squatting happily before the spectators surrounding the Bramble King in the boxes. He opened his mouth and his ridiculously long tongue flicked out, caught something from the ground, and flicked it toward us.

I dodged on principal and shooting pain froze my chest in place as well as any lance could do. I couldn't breathe. I couldn't ... I leaned on the meridian for support, losing my chance to watch Bluebeard catch the missile. I didn't miss what happened next. He held the head of Grosbeak high, considering it with a thumb and forefinger to his chin – for all the world a Master of Ceremonies playing to the crowd.

"What say you, Traitor Grosbeak? Surely a fine connoisseur of drama and intrigue such as yourself might have an opinion. Is it victory to snatch an opponent's lance from his hand? To leap like the pouncing puma and tear out his throat? Or is that defeat?"

"Oh, a fine victory," Grosbeak intoned, laughing cruelly. "For to add insult to injury, the green Lord Coppertomb found himself bested by a mortal with no battle training. As like to see a knight unhorsed by a white rose as to see the Lord of all Coppertomb unhorsed by so dainty a blossom. And her riding a toad of the mud, while he barreled forth on fine horseflesh!"

"What say you, Wittenhame?" Bluebeard asked, looking out at the crowd as if in need of advice.

The response was half cheer and half laughter, but Coppertomb's growl of annoyance was met only by snickers. He swallowed, brushed himself off, and tried another tack.

"I appeal to the Sovereign," he said coolly, turning his back on them and toward his lord.

"Speak to my riddle, Grosbeak," Bluebeard said, but his voice was pitched to carry. "What cries as a seagull when there are entrails to eat but hides as a sand crab when challenged?"

"Is it a yellow-streaked coward, m'lord?" Grosbeak asked and then paused and melodramatically squinted. "Or is it this so-called prince of our malevolent Wittenhame, begging for adjudication when all who watch know him whipped like a cur?"

"Silence your pet, Arrow, or I shall silence both him and you," Coppertomb hissed and this was *not* for the crowd though they hung on his words, eyes fastened to every movement, however small it be.

"DRAW," the Bramble King's voice boomed out.

"Then shall we ride again, Lord Coppertomb?" Bluebeard asked with a mild smile. "But I find myself so inflamed by the desire to sport against you, that I must ride for myself this time."

"I think not." Coppertomb's words were clipped. "I think rather that the joust is done, the players secure. And you and I must collect our bets."

Was I the only one who saw my husband pale? His eyes flicked directly to mine and then to the Bramble King. He drew his arm close and whispered something into Grosbeak's ear. My friend snickered.

"PRESENT YOURSELVES TO ME," the Bramble King said, his rumbling voice shaking the field and jarring my painful ribs against one another. "AND THE TERMS OF SURRENDER OF PROPERTY WILL BE DICTATED."

I caught the look of triumph in Coppertomb's eyes and the slight smile as he looked at me and then Bluebeard eclipsed him, jamming Grosbeak's head into my skeletal hand and twisting the silver key from around his neck to hang around my neck.

"We've no time to waste, fire of my eyes," he said, tucking his head down close to mine so it looked as if he were wooing me rather than desperately spilling all I needed to know into my ear. "Coppertomb has made a pretty bargain and I must pay it full. But you, sweet fire of my heart, bright light of my eyes – I gift to you Pensmoore – yours already and tied to your blood – and with it, I gift you the kingdoms I have won in my wager today. Take Aayadmoore, Ilkanmoore, Moravidmoore, and Salamoore, and march them fast as you dare to the Plains of Myygddo. Dare they flinch at your command, you need only spill your own blood and seal your orders with it and they will be bound to obey. Go, now, while still I live, for the Last Battle comes and your five nations must hold off the other three or see themselves sunk, their land ravaged, and their people destitute. Do not return to this place having failed. Promise me."

"*I promise,*" I agreed. But I was afraid. What did it mean that Coppertomb had won my beating heart? "*Tell me they aren't going to kill you.*"

He pulled back enough to look in my eyes and tangle his hand in my long hair and the look on his face was agony and then he shook his head as if dislodging a thought and whispered.

"I know this, if nothing else. You must flee this place. You must save your mortal world. We dare not fail in that. And if any breath of me remains when all this has passed, know it breathes only and always for you."

My heart stuttered and my breath hitched then.

"I wanted a life with you as wife," I admitted as his fingers tangled so tight in my hair that it stung. *"I wanted all your tomorrows, to touch you with tenderness, and care for your heart as if it were a precious gem, a field of good crops, a stallion of perfect bloodlines."*

"I would wish all that and more," he said, his voice a harsh pain. "But it was always running this course, always galloping to this cliff, from the moment I saw your grey eyes and determined ferocity and knew I must not sacrifice you as I had all those before but must take you to wife by blood and vow. Promise me this, fire of my heart. Promise me you will think of me at the last."

"Who else would I think of? Who else has my heart?"

He looked wistful for a moment, and then his fingers untangled from my hair, and he wrapped my fingers around the silver key, pressed his lips on mine, and turned the key.

I was ripped from his arms and into the instant hell of the passing from the mortal world to the Wittenbrand and as my spirit screamed, I howled with it.

I was not ready to go.

I needed to stay to help him, to save him, but I could no more save him from this, than I could save him from the sea and as I was dragged through a living hell, every imagined horror I feared for him was played out before my eyes, until I was left a sobbing, howling mad woman, screaming into the blackest night in a world robbed of color and warmth.

"I always hate that passage," Grosbeak said glibly. "They really ought to build a less traumatic way back and forth."

His words grated on my bare soul until I opened my eyes.

"Done sulking?" he asked brutally. "Because I thought you had some work to do and since I promised to stay with you, I suppose I'm along for the ride. You'd better make it worth my while."

Chapter Thirty-Five

LUCKILY FOR ME – I returned to Pensmoore exactly where I'd left it – the battlements of the palace. Unluckily for me, it seemed some time had passed since I'd been there last.

"She says she's who?" the Captain of the Guard asked the pair escorting me as if I wasn't right there to ask in the flesh. A nervous wen appeared between his eyebrows.

"The mad princess!" the first guard said. "Our lord the king's sister, Izolda Savataz."

The captain peered at me and then at Grosbeak, gagged a little, held down his dinner manfully, and then looked at me again. He looked green. Green and slightly terrified. The lantern he held up flickered as everyone shifted uncomfortably. That I didn't recognize any of them was worrisome.

"Can't be," the captain said grimly, white around the mouth. "She must be a witch."

"I am no witch," I said calmly and with as much authority as I could muster. "And I request an audience with my lord the king."

"If you were really his sister," the captain said gravely, "you would know he lies even now on the verge between death and life."

"All the more reason to permit me an audience. But if he is in no state to receive a sister, then I will speak to General Volkov."

The captain snorted. "Shall I raise him from his drunken grave to receive you?"

Volkov dead. My brother ill. I shook my head in wonder as Grosbeak cleared his throat, reminding them that even a corpse was not past being bothered by me.

"Emelina, then. Your queen," I replied, not put off by his derision. "Tell her that her 'sister' has returned and comes to collect on her debt." I paused. All they saw was a defenseless woman. What could I say to shift that balance? "Remind her of what grave threat she avoided when I offered to take my brother's place with the Wittenbrand."

The captain of the guard snorted, but the white spots and green wash were gone, and his color was coming back.

"Keep her here until I return," he said before leaving us in the small guard room adjacent to the battlement. I hadn't made it very far from where I'd been found.

"Do any of you play cards?" Grosbeak asked brightly.

"We don't play with familiars," the first guard spat.

"What would you even bet?" the second countered.

I took a seat and set Grosbeak on the small table. This tower had been fitted as a place for the guards on the battlement to warm up, complete with a fire, a small table, three chairs, and a light repast laid out – cheese and bread and water, simple food for simple men.

I ate, not caring at the annoyed looks they sent my way. I hadn't eaten in a full day and in that time, I'd been battered pretty badly. My ribs still twinged with pain when I sat down or stood up or moved at all.

"How about ears?" Grosbeak suggested. "We each have two of them. Well, I have one and a solid half, but the whole one is twice the size of yours, so I say it evens out. 'Twould make for a lively challenge!"

"You're seriously asking us to bet our ears?" one of the guards asked, his eyes goggling. "You can't be serious."

"I am very serious, and also in earnest," Grosbeak said. "Whist, perhaps? Or do you play Nine Men's Knuckles? Merels? Copper flutes?"

The guards looked at each other and then back at him in horror. "We need our ears. We aren't deformed corpses set alive by the black incantations of a witch."

"Neither am I," Grosbeak said darkly, "And why do you maintain she is a witch when she has denied it? There's not the slightest whiff of magic on her person."

I ignored them, trying to think of what I would say if Emelina denied me access. I didn't like being here any longer than absolutely necessary. What might be happening to Bluebeard even now? Were they sentencing him to some terrible torture? Killing him? Was he imprisoned or thrown once more into the depths? My stomach knotted around the bread and cheese at the thought, wishing I had not eaten at all.

"She is too beautiful to be a normal woman, mad princess or otherwise," the guard said knowingly. "Surely such charms are only the result of the blackest of magic."

"Surely," Grosbeak said wryly. "I never see a beautiful woman without thinking, 'Now, that's some black magic right there!'"

I shifted my position to take the pressure off my screaming ribs and something poked me in the leg. Irritably, I reached into my pocket and pulled out the token Lady Wittentree had offered me – a carved mermaid set on a round base, made entirely of jade. It looked like a piece in a game of strategy. I played with it between my fingers.

"And you," the guards were telling Grosbeak, "must be her familiar, the source of great power."

"I tell women that all the time and they never believe me," Grosbeak said sadly.

I was surprised by how quickly the Captain of the Guard returned. Grosbeak and the others were still wrangling the details of their possible game of chance when he entered the room, another man hot on his heels.

He spoke, but it was to the younger man that held my attention. He was maybe twenty and one. Blond. Well dressed. Average in height. He had my brother Svetgin's exact eyes and the bearing he once had when he was a younger man.

"Queen Emelina will not see you," the Captain of the Guard said to me, "and she has made it clear that the mad princess died fifteen years ago and will never again grace us with her presence."

"Not her, then?" I said grimly. "And not Volkov and not my brother. Do any of his counselors from his early reign yet live?"

"I told you already that Volkov was dead of drink these six years and more," the captain said grimly. "And any other counselors from that time are only memories now."

I sighed. "That's the problem with mortals. They all die almost as soon as you get to know them."

"What then," the young man asked, taking one of the seats across from me with a flourish, "are you, if you are not a mortal?"

"Your aunt, if I'm not mistaken, Rolgrin," I replied, meeting his eyes, "and as mortal as the next woman. You're named for the brother who was born between myself and your father."

He swallowed, his eyes drifting to my hands, seeming to widen at the sight of the mermaid I was playing with even more than at the skeletal hand.

"I told you she was a witch," the captain of the guard muttered.

"Who gave you that?" Rolgrin asked hoarsely.

"Does it matter?" I let my eyes narrow. Better to make him think I knew more than I did.

"It does. To me."

"Hmm." I tapped it against the table. "Tell me, then, Rolgrin," I said. "Do you know a lady with one eye and eight fingers?"

He flinched. "That sounds like a riddle. Are you really in a position to be telling riddles?"

"You want a riddle?" I asked, my eyes narrowing and my skeletal hand reaching to set itself on top of Grosbeak's disgusting mass of tangled hair. Predictably, he snickered right on cue. "I can oblige. What has a crown waiting for him and a lady love in Rouranmoore?"

This time his flinch included a swift look at the Captain of the Guard who cleared his throat noisily.

"I think the prince has this in hand," he said loudly to the room. "Best we get back to patrolling."

As if the Captain of the Guard did any patrolling. I didn't watch them leave. I didn't care. All mortals were as wildflowers – here for a day or a week and then blown away on the winds of time. And I knew that I was one of them, of no more value or significance than they. Despite that, I held the means to prevent deprivation and death for my people.

I didn't want to be here. I wanted to be with my husband, standing by his side as he faced – whatever it was that he had lost in that bet. But this was his will for me, and it was my will to save as many as I could from the fires to come.

When they left, my nephew's eyes met mine. He was young and he looked younger with that pleading in his eyes and the scant beard covering the trembling in his jaw.

"What do you know of the Lady Hazinth?" he asked as if his words weren't confirming what I'd guessed.

I placed the mermaid deliberately on the table between us.

"I know she has powerful friends. I know they threaten her future."

The second part could be said about any living mortal, but he didn't seem to notice that.

"And?" he pushed.

"And if you do exactly what I tell you to, we can save her, and your sister and brother, and all of Pensmoore."

The combination of bitter and desperate in his eyes was far too familiar to me these days.

"Nothing can be saved. Even now, my father lies prostrate on his death bed. Soon the crown will fall to me, and I will have to marry for peace. Aayadsmoore, perhaps, which has overcome its chaos to amass on our border, or Salamoore which has been raiding the border since my grandfather's time and now congregates armies in the determination to take us once and or all. Rouranmoore has turned away our diplomats, but that's a new bitterness and we have no call for a state marriage there."

I looked at the green mermaid and I thought of Wittentree giving it to me. She must have known about this secret romance.

"How long have you been in love?" I asked him quietly.

He snorted a laugh, looking at the fire but not seeing it.

"When I was a child, Lindra would come and visit the former princess, Lady Chasida. They are cousins by marriage. I've known her all my life. We started to write when she was twelve, nigh on seven years ago now. I do not think I've disguised my interest as well as I would like, but it is not well known. Who gave you her token? It would not have been her. I gave her that chessa set and she has treasured it since the day she received it direct from my hands. We play by mail."

"Rouranmoore's patron saint gave it me," I said, watching him closely.

"The Lady?" he gasped, eyes wide.

"I am married to Pensmoore's corresponding saint, as you might have been told."

"I thought your husband was dead. I thought that was why you went mad. That's what father always said."

"We were merely ... parted," I said carefully. "And now I have returned on his behalf. And I would see my brother before I carry out the tasks I must do for Pensmoore."

"What tasks are those?" he looked almost excited.

I steeled my jaw. Despite my promises, I had hoped to deliver my messages and then hurry back to my husband, but here I was faced with an un-bearded youth and a kingdom on the cusp of change. My stomach rolled at what I must say.

"I shall lead the armies of Pensmoore along with Salamoore, Ilkanmoore, Aayadmoore, and Moravidmoore to the Plains of Myygddo for the Last Battle."

He laughed long, hard, and disbelieving. Until Grosbeak began to laugh with him. My bodiless friend's dry laughter sounded like snapping sticks and harrowing calls in the night. Rolgrin paled, straightened, and regarded my bodiless friend with revolted horror.

"Is that thing really alive?" Now he was the one who looked green.

"Yes," I said crisply.

"I'm alive enough to know a chalk-faced rat-eater when I encounter one," Grosbeak complained.

"And the hand?" my nephew pressed, turning his ill expression to me.

I lifted my skeletal hand, wiggling the metacarpals so he could see them move. Bluebeard's ring rattled against them.

"Also alive."

His throat bobbed. "This is why they call you the Mad Princess. Though your portrait doesn't do you justice, and neither does my memory. Were you always so beautiful?"

"No."

"Then how did it happen that you grew lovelier?"

"In the same way that I lost the hand." Had young people always been so exhausting? I grew tired of his prodding.

"Then I should take you to your brother," he said, at last, his eyes brightening shyly. "Do you really think I could marry Lindra?"

"I think there will be trouble if you don't," I said grimly, able to read a hint when one was shoved into my hand.

I found Svetgin exactly as my nephew had suggested I would. Unconscious. Hot with fever. Wasted away. I felt – to my surprise – a twinge of nostalgia for when we two had been children together, a quick memory of my mother running her hand over our hair and whispering sweet words as she tucked us into blankets on a pallet beside the fire during a fierce winter storm.

He was the last of my direct family still living and he would not be living for long. His room smelled of illness and death, the bed curtains heavy, the fire built up hot, the curtains closed over the narrow windows. I left as quickly as was polite.

I did not speak to my sister-in-law. If she had no time for me, then I had none for her. Some debts, it seemed, were easily forgotten. Her debt to me was weighed by the worth of her life. Perhaps, her indication that she owed me nothing was a confirmation of her worth.

Duty done, I begged parchment from Rolgrin, and to my surprise, he brought me to my brother's secret room – the hole – and offered me the desk there and as I wrote missives to the rulers of distant lands, sealed them with my own blood to ensure obedience, and bid him send them by messenger. His advisors came and went with excited glances at me, hopeful whispers, and at last, when I was done, one brave man dared to speak.

"You're truly the M- the Princess Izolda?" he asked.

"I am," I said firmly.

"Our Lord the King had a statue of you made in the Grand Hall and a feast is celebrated in your honor every year to mark a time you took – as he told us – death in his place. Is it true that you did?"

"I am very much alive," I said, skirting the question.

"But did you take a desperate penalty for his sake?"

"Yes," I agreed, finally turning to look the man in the eyes. He was older than I expected. Old enough to be my father.

"I remember that day in court that you spoke and came under the Law of Greeting," he said – which meant the Captain of the Guard had lied and this man could have been called to confirm my identity. There was wonder in his eyes and pain in mine for while I would not give up my husband for anything in all the world, that day had stolen much for me – much that ought to have been here in Pensmoore when I returned to it. "I remember the day you returned with your brother, dressed in black. Our Lord the King managed his holdings very well while you were his secretary. If a princess may be called such."

I lifted a brow.

Interesting.

He knew, then, that I had been the brains behind Svetgin's early rule.

"And you've come now to help Prince Rolgrin as he gains the throne?" he asked hopefully.

"It would seem so," I agreed.

And whatever it was that he heard must have pleased him, for after that, there were no doors barred to me, and I moved through the days with willful purpose and found every branch bending to my breeze, every trail twisting to my inclination, and every road made straight for my feet.

It was less than a week before we rode out to the border of Pensmoore but even such a precipitous departure was not brisk enough for me. I did not sleep – or did not sleep well. Food was as dust in my mouth and wine of no comfort. When Svetgin the Bountiful died on the third day and was laid in state for the court to view, my dour spirits were attributed to grief and seen with strong approval. It was a sharp lie.

Every moment, my nerves jangled like bells. The need to be moving filled my every limb. Who knew how much time would pass in the Wittenhame? Who knew what measure of torture Coppertomb might set to my husband? And all that time I was here, sleeping in a royal bed, eating royal food, and being griped at by a royal annoyance.

"It does no one any good to watch you play-act the widow with your husband not even dead," Grosbeak complained.

Another time he said, "All that beauty is wasted on a frown."

But we were both happier when – at long last – Rolgrin was crowned, and we rode out to the south, fully anticipating the armies of Salamoore and Aayadmoore to join us in peace.

It seemed a fool thing to expect when they had long been enemies, but I could feel their lands as I felt Pensmoore. I could feel deep in my bones that they had been given to my husband exactly as was his right and that they were now connected to me. They must have been able to feel it, too.

Each message was returned with a rider from that land, and I felt the pull of their earth from each of them. They seemed as tied to me as strands of web around a spider. The wager had been honored. They were my people now.

Rolgrin's only regret was that he could not wed before he launched this campaign.

My regret was that we had to ride forward blind, not truly certain of our allies or enemies.

We met the first of our new compatriots at the southern border. The men of Aayadsmoore wore a mismatch of ancient armaments and refurbished uniforms, their soldiers all too old or too young – those of fighting age cut down during the long wars. I watched them with a heavy heart full of memories of slicing through their country alongside Sparrow as she led Pensmoore to victory after victory like pearls on a string.

The men of Salamoore – whose land we must march through to reach the Plains of Myyggdo at the northern portion of the Ilkanmoore desert, reflected their patron in a precise manner, aping his simple dress and economical speech. Allies or not, I felt ill at ease with them – with all of them, really, until we stepped over the border into Salamoore, and to my shock, the land rose and reached for me, greeting me like hounds to the hunter. Blossoms and green grass swirled out from my feet and swept across the ground, consuming the dead weeds of spring and musty bogs of old-melted snow.

After that, I was regarded in such awe that none dared speak to me except in low respectful murmurs.

"You've snuffed out all the fun," Grossbeak complained three days past the Salamoore border. "There's no amusement in riding to everyone's deaths if we don't get to take part in the last revelries."

And revelries there were. One would think we were the largest band of traveling mummers ever to be seen and not a group of diverse armies.

I did nothing to stop the armies at their sport, though I left Rolgrin with strict instructions that the locals were to be paid and unmolested, and camp followers were to be strictly prohibited. All the thrown axes and darts, all the feats of acrobatics and strength, and all the drink they wanted to consume bothered me not at all. I kept my own counsel and tended my own worries, which grew until they echoed from moment to moment in my hollow heart.

What if I returned and they'd taken his heart? He'd said he held mine, but mine was clearly fine. And hadn't he said something once about how they'd take the living heart from his body? They had meant to take something. Clearly, we had his bet in hand or the land of Salamoore would not welcome me. What, then, could be assumed in the other direction?

The birds did not help my worries.

Everywhere I went, songbirds appeared, singing to greet me, alighting on head or shoulder or outstretched arms. My horse – not Prince who was long gone, but one of his line, which had grown a reputation as fierce and were known as Mad Princes in our honor – grew weary of shaking his head to dislodge them, and instead bore them on his long neck with dour stillness. But not a one of them bore a letter to me. Not a line of poetry, not a scrap of parchment.

One morning, I woke to find a nest woven into Grosbeak's hair and three speckled eggs laid within it. I refused to remove it or its occupants, simply carrying them with him as I went.

"It's a disgrace, Izolda. An embarrassment!" he protested to my deaf ears.

What the armies thought of him, I did not know. I heard the words "witch," and "saint," and "revenant," and "power of the dead" as I drifted through the camps, but I did not quell them. It bound them together, these three great enemies.

And then, at last, we reached the Plains of Myygddo, and the echoes in my mind turned to the roar of a fast-approaching storm the moment my horse's hooves hit the hard-packed white sand.

"*And lo, the armies gathered and at their head was death and despair traveled alongside,*" Grosbeak quoted as we stood and looked out over it.

"I suppose that makes you 'despair' then," I said, taking comfort in his grim snicker.

I'd done it. I'd done exactly as I was bid.

Why, then, did I feel so hollow?

Chapter Thirty-Six

"WHAT ARE WE WAITING FOR?" Rolgrin asked me once we had our camp set up and our defenses dug in.

"*You*," I said with emphasis, "are waiting for the arrival of our allies and enemies to fight what some will call the Last Battle. *You* are waiting to be either the greatest hero-king Pensmoore has ever known or very, very dead."

He straightened at that, back and chin stiff with the starch of resolution.

"The two aren't mutually exclusive," Grosbeak interjected. "I've been dead now for quite some time – decades, by your standards, and yet I find I am more heroic than ever."

"A multiple of zero is still zero," I said dryly.

"How did you die?" Rolgrin asked him. I snorted. Rolgrin was so grave and dignified that he seemed too noble to even be told the answer. "Was it in the execution of an act both brave and true?"

We were seated in his kingly pavilion and the servants he'd brought had made the place light and almost cheerful. His armor was polished and hung over a stand in one corner. A pallet was hidden in another corner behind a curtain, and we sat in the main area where a brazier burned lazily to scare away the late spring chill and folding three-legged leather seats had been placed around a low table.

"I was trying to kill *her*," Grosbeak said, sneering in my direction. I had not yet removed the bird's nest from his hair, and the bird was nestled down in it, sitting on her eggs. "And her husband took my head for my insult."

Rolgrin's eyes widened but he said nothing. He was surprisingly practical for a mortal, much more than his father had been. Instead, he turned his gaze to me.

"And what are you waiting for? Have you reconsidered leading our armies into battle, Aunt? I would not resist your hold over us. But I think you are eager to be off."

I offered a grim half-smile. "You see clearly. I have other troubles that must be met. I wait only to treat with your allies when they arrive. As Salamoore and Aayadmoore were persuaded to see that your causes are one, so it must be with the other nations that join us."

He nodded. We'd been over this.

"And then?"

"And then I must go to the Wittenhame," I said grimly. "And face whatever awaits me."

"Must you?" he asked easily. At the rise of my eyebrow, he shrugged. "You aren't saying it but if you are here carrying your husband's authority and in his stead, then something terrible must have happened to him. Some grim fate you fear to share. There, your life may be forfeit. Here, you are a valuable advisor to our court. We would even endure the black magic of your companion."

"It's not black magic. It's called living the life you're given not the one you asked for," Grosbeak complained.

We both ignored him.

"You could stay," Rolgrin offered. "You could have your own lonely tower to live in like a proper widowed aunt." He smiled, teasing me. "Or, if you prefer, a suite of rooms in the palace. Another husband perhaps." He must have seen the hardening of my face. "Or not. You would be under no obligations except the ties of family and the vows of loyalty to Pensmoore."

"It is ties and vows that bid me leave you," I said. "Ties to the man who has become closer than blood to me. Vows to him."

Rolgrin tapped his fingers on the table. He was playing with the jade mermaid in his other hand as he often did when he thought no one knew he was pining for his lady love.

"You love him, then, your kidnapper?"

"He's not that anymore. Maybe he never was."

"He stole you away. You missed the lives and deaths of your family. I'm named for the brother you barely knew." His words were bald and cold.

I swallowed. "I did lose that."

"They said he'd been here before – that you were not his first bride. How many more were there?"

When I did not answer Grosbeak answered for me. "Fifteen and all of them dead as doornails. He keeps their hollow shells lined up in a hidden room."

"It's not like that," I said carefully.

"It's not like what?" Rolgrin said with the kind of calm that spoke of violence.

"He has been working for centuries toward one goal – to change all the violence and trickery into a place that is safe for his folk and that shields and guards Pensmoore. He plans to give the lives of his other wives back to them someday."

"You can't draw back death," Rolgrin said grimly. His lower lip shook slightly as he said it. He'd been manful about his father's death, but still, it stung him. "And it sounds as if your husband demands much and gives little."

"He went under the sea for me," I said. "To save my life. He drowned under the tide for seven of our years."

"It was only a few days," Grosbeak said scornfully.

"He gave a rib for me when I was kidnapped from his arms," I continue, not mentioning that it was Rolgrin's father who had stolen me away. "His wound doesn't heal. Even now he lives with the bleeding wound in his side and two matching holes in his hands – all wounds he took for me."

"Mmm," Rolgrin said, but he was not convinced. "And what is so valuable that he spends you and fifteen others and the life of this horrifying creature." Here he flicked Grosbeak's ear, ignoring his *Ow!* "And all his resources to pursue it?"

"He would be king of it all," I said grimly. "Sovereign to the Wittenhame. The one who sets the rules and makes the land flourish. The one who ends these predations on mortals."

"Would he now?" Grosbeak hooted. "And no one told me?"

"I thought it obvious," I said tightly.

"And this king he would replace," Rolgrin asked "What is he like?"

"Remote," I said. "We barely see him and yet he is everywhere speaking cryptic words, watching from afar, never getting his hands dirty in the affairs before him."

"You say that with censure. Perhaps, though, it is the only way to rule such a land. What if your husband succeeds? What if you find that in replacing the sovereign, this husband of yours becomes identical to him – far away, other-worldly, hardly a man at all?"

I swallowed hard on my first response, silent as something twisted inside me.

"What happens to you then?" Rolgrin asked. "Are you set aside like a ceremonial garment, used for a short time and no longer needed?"

"He loves me," I said in a small voice.

"Can immortals love as we do? Can they grasp tightly to every moment knowing it may be their last? Can they multiply, and delight deeply, and throw all their passion into a few short decades when for them that is but a breath?"

"Yes." My voice was too small.

"No." Grosbeak's voice was much firmer. "And it's a lie to say otherwise. We live as immortals do – tasting every flavor, sweet or bitter, with equal passion. Having no attachments for those who fade and fall."

"The death head's words ring true," Rolgrin said grimly. "Think on it, Aunt. Stay with us mortals. Live out the rest of your life in peace and away from the menace of the unfathomable. I will not use you as my father did. I will not demand marriages. I will not give you in sacrifice. I will give you a home and work if you want it. I will tolerate your hideous pet, and I will leave you to live your life in what peace you might find for yourself. Abandon this immortal world you keep reaching for. It eats up your humanity as the flame eats the grass."

I looked away. I did not like how he saw my life and choices. From his view, they were not noble sacrifices at all, but the desperate grasping of a foolish girl. A tear fell and I dashed it aside.

"Think on it," he repeated and then stood up and left his own tent and his shaken aunt behind.

I sat there a long time, ignoring Grosbeak's occasional comments.

"Mortals," he sneered. "No better than dirt. Always wrapped up in morals and ideals. Nearly as bad as the Arrow. You'd think dwelling beneath the sea with a love-lorn captive would be the worst that could happen, but oh no, it's twice as awful to watch his heart-sick wife not even able to shepherd mortal armies without having some sort of crisis of conscience."

His grumbling went on and on. My thoughts were elsewhere.

Eventually, I left the tent and stepped out to join my nephew, lifting my skirts daintily. I was dressed again in embroidered wool with a modest headpiece as befitted my station in Pensmoore. It made me feel small as a wood mouse and just as plain.

Rolgrin stood looking out over his resting camp, a goblet in one hand and the other at his hip just over his sword belt.

"All men are as grass and their glory fades," I told him as I joined him. He didn't look at me and I joined him in gazing out over the thousands settling in before us. "Those of this separate race of Wittenbrand, this seemingly immortal kin not held by time or aging – they may seem as if they've slipped the noose of all that binds our days. But their glory is just as fading, just as passing, their years merely measured differently."

"All things pass," my nephew agreed.

"All but love and loyalty," I said grimly. "That echoes on and on past life. Still, I feel my mother's smile on my shoulders. Still, I feel the kindness in my father's gaze. And if our priests and wise men tell true, and we find ourselves in a life beyond this one when all else passes, I think it will be the love we wove here that greets us in that beyond."

He said nothing, but he took the mermaid out from his pocket and turned it over and over in his hand.

"Maybe you'll fall here in the battle. Maybe I will fall returning to my husband's side," I said gently. "But I can no more shirk my place beside him than you can shirk your place as king of Pensmoore. And his sacrifices, while twisted in your eyes, have cost him everything and all for the love of a wife his peers judge valueless. Can any love be purer than a love that gains nothing from the beloved except a return of affection?"

"I suppose not," he said, and now his eyes strayed to his mermaid again.

"Hold fast," I told him, and I left him there and went to retrieve Grosbeak.

I had planned to stay to bring Moravidmoore and Ilkanmoore tightly into our alliance, to exert on them whatever pull bound Salamoore and Aayadmoore to me. But our conversation had swayed me. I must leave Rolgrin to fulfill his vows and stand firm in his role.

And I must leave to fulfill my own.

I took out my key.

"Not now!" Grosbeak squeaked. "Your timing is horrid. The battle is going to start in the next few days, and we'll miss all the good bits! The brave charges! The terrible defeats. Bodies stacked toward the heavens like monuments raised to catch the eye of the gods!"

Gently, I took the bird's nest from his hair and set it in a dry desert bush. Hopefully, the bird would adapt. She would have to.

"And now you rob me even of my souvenirs!"

I turned the key in the air and gritted my teeth as the madness swept me away.

Chapter Thirty-Seven

MADNESS IS NOT something one grows used to. Perhaps, the truly insane forget they are insane and drift into it as a rock is buried beneath drifts and blankets of snow. Perhaps, they take comfort in the strange simplicity that finds itself on the other side of sanity. I was not so deep into it. I was only insane enough to know sanity had slipped away, and that all my fears and horrors were being realized.

When, teeth chattering and hands flexing and clawing like talons, I finally came to awareness of myself again, Grosbeak was moaning beside me and a small bird – such a bright yellow that I would have thought his coloring impossible – was plucking at my braid as if trying to drag me after it.

I coughed, choked, finally caught a breath, and pawed blindly for Grosbeak's head. He screamed, startling me for a moment, as his scream echoed and reverberated back to us. I blinked hollowly before I realized it wasn't an echo at all. Someone not far off was also screaming. Perhaps they, too, had just made the passage. Or perhaps not.

A second bird joined the first – this one a brilliant sky blue – knocking my Pensmoore headdress away and tugging insistently at my ear.

I found my feet, swaying, skeletal fingers tangling in Grosbeak's hair.

I needed to get my wits back.

A scarlet red bird descended on us like a falling stone and this one grabbed Grosbeak's hair and pulled.

"I'm coming," I said.

Already a second yellow bird had arrived, joined by a whole flock of his kind.

I stumbled along behind them, my ears full of faraway screams and the insistent chatter of an army of songbirds. They plucked at me, drawing me through the trees until we came, at last, to a twisting path.

White light – too white for daylight, too pure – burned through the trees, making the shadows stand out blacker than black.

I swallowed, for it seemed inevitable that this path would lead me to the place Bluebeard had spoken of when he said:

"One day, blood will be spilled on the Wittenbrand, the brand will turn gold, and on that day a great hero will arise, and he will pluck that arrow from the stone and he will be marked with white and chosen by the Wittenbrand to lead the people to an age of glory."

I shivered and it was not just for the haunting laughter coming from between the trees, it was with a sense that this prophecy, so long in the coming, was now about to be fulfilled before my eyes. I could feel it in the same way that I could feel Grosbeak's hair despite having no flesh on my fingers and in the same way that I could sense my husband was somewhere ahead and that these resolute songbirds were drawing me to him.

The path turned suddenly and I forced my reluctant feet down it, emerging to where a surprisingly reverent crowd of folk – each one bearing a blossom in their hands – walked up a stairway made of granite steps and edged with dark openings. Each opening bore a symbol and name over it and I realized with a stabbing sense of horror that I was walking up to a great tor burial mound.

At the top of the mound, the heather grew and the graves turned from tombs to marker stones and on the tallest of them, I saw the familiar arrow burning with the white heat of the Wittenhame. To one side of it, the Bramble King's face formed a faint outline in a stand of three ancient oak trees. His face reconfigured itself when they shivered in the wind, his eyes closing and lips moving as if in strangled speech though no sound emerged.

Before him, to one side of the arrow stuck in the stone, the remaining players were arranged, looking ill at ease – Bluffroll, Antlerdale, and Wittentree.

To the other side, someone had erected a standing pole – like a grave marker of its own – and carved into its full length the images of birds and beasts, angels and demons, one atop the other. I thought – perhaps – that I saw Marshyellow's face in the spire and guilt bit hard into the flesh of my heart.

It was not the pole that froze me in my tracks, however, but he who stood lashed to it, the wound in his side gaping open. At his feet, blossoms heaped in a fragrant pile that crowned as high as his waist. My husband, the Arrow of the Wittenhame.

Beside him, Coppertomb lounged, wearing the Rib Crown he'd taken from the Sword, arms crossed over his stark white doublet. He watched the crowd as if they were his servants, performing a task to his specifications.

To my horror, I realized that as each person passed, they dropped their posey and spoke funeral words over Bluebeard. They were half dressed in mud and blood-caked clothing and half dressed as if going to a grand gala as if they'd been called to it so quickly that no one had time to dress properly and had just thrown on whatever they had that was best atop or around what they'd worn to the joust.

One woman had thick leather boots and mud-caked hose but over it, she'd put a coat made of living snakes, sewn together lengthwise but still hissing and rippling as they tried to move. Her hair was pulled half up into a similar gold net and half falling down in a tangled mess as if she had been too hurried to dress it. Likewise, a gentleman nearby was shirtless but had found for himself a small cape and baldric of black velvet speckled with diamonds which he'd jammed over leather breeches and hooved feet. Their state of dress or undress bothered them not at all as they paraded past.

"He once turned an apple silver and gave it me at the faire," a mousy woman with the tail of a rat said as she passed, dropping a dandelion on the pile.

I mounted the first step, losing sight now of the top of the hill as I pushed in and through the procession.

"He was quick in his movements as a fisher cat," another intoned, and I could not see what she laid down in tribute.

I rushed up the steps, using elbows and Grosbeak in equal measure to clear a path, meeting cries of pain and husky laughter both.

When I crested the top of the burial tor, I caught sight of him again.

I bit my lip hard, tasting blood. My husband's gaze was on the arrow in the flame, but as my feet touched the hilltop, his head whipped to mine and his gaze met my own from under a floppy crown of flowers someone had woven and placed on his head. The flowers were speckled with blood as if they had bit the weaver, thorns their swords, and spines their daggers.

There must be some way to get him away from here, but how did you steal the grand spectacle from an event where every eye was on him?

His voice as it dipped into my mind was honey and incense, cedar and cinnamon.

"Are your armies in place, wife of mine?"

"Yes," I gasped, my mental voice stuttering in horror.

He smiled and my heart lurched. *"You've done well, then."*

His eyes closed as if in satisfaction.

"Is this your funeral?" I asked, creeping forward.

"Of course," he sounded somewhat amused. *"They send me off in style. I told you once that they would pluck from me my still-beating heart. I did not lie."*

He could not mean that.

I bit my lip, glancing quickly around the crowd to see if my suspicions were correct. Coppertomb was dressed exactly as he'd been when I left except for that bright white doublet. Wittentree too, I thought. The players I recognized were styled in dust and sweat with the occasional splash of blood. There had been no time or them to hastily don finery, not even scraps of it. So, it had been ... what? An hour or two since I left them? If that? Certainly, it was early the next morning. No later than that.

"Ah, what a great honor," Grosbeak sighed happily. "To be present at your own funeral. To hear all that others would say about you before you are gone." He raised his voice. "You were violent, Arrow, and purposeful. You took my head fairly from my shoulders and planted in me a seed of hatred I have nurtured every day since. Without you, I would have a working body and a future, half my load of bitterness, and a way to plant a posey on your grave."

"That sounded more like an accusation," I said between clenched teeth as I made my way slowly through the crowd, not shy about using a quick kick to the back of a knee to force the crowd to part.

There were a few ragged cheers for Grosbeak's loud pronouncement.

"Me? Accuse a man unfairly here at the Great Barrow? I think not!" Grosbeak protested.

"Great Barrow?" I murmured, sliding past a woman whose collar was a snake as thick as my thigh wrapped around her waist and then up her back, so its head draped over her shoulder. It smelled exactly as I expected it would.

"The silver arrow is buried here within the Wittenbrand – the White Flame. I told you this."

"I don't think you did."

"It changes the form of the landscape around it. You've seen it thrice before."

"I would have remembered this."

"Well, you crashed a pumpkin beside it. It's not my fault if you don't remember that. The poets call it the Great Barrow. And certainly, there are many whose ashes were spread here, or bodies secreted into the surrounding earth or buried under turned soil or in caverns dug for the purpose. As your husband's will be. Will you remarry? It might be convenient for you to take me as husband since we spend so much time at each other's sides."

"A woeful necessity," I muttered. "Not a thing I'd wish on myself perpetually."

"You say that, and yet here we are, together as always."

We had been making our way through the crowd, forcing a place between one knot of Wittenbrand and the next around the grisly marker poles that seemed to depict the faces of the dead and those they killed while alive.

In fairness to Grosbeak, he'd done his part, biting anyone foolish enough to get near his teeth. But now, we were nearly through, and I saw my husband's eyes open to watch me as Coppertomb moved to stand in front of the marker bearing the arrow and the white flames. He leaned on a copper cane. The long grey beards of moss hanging from the oak trees swayed woefully behind him.

He'd prepared for this. The way he stood told me it had been his plan all along.

My heart stuttered wildly at the thought. How many steps ahead of me was he?

"With a bold heart, I welcome you, folk of the Wittenhame!" Coppertomb said, his voice echoing across the field and cutting through every other conversation.

The Wittenbrand woman eulogizing my husband dropped her pansy and skipped back and around me all the remaining flowers drifted to the ground as the Wittenbrand reconfigured themselves to listen.

"And here, just in time, comes the mortal wife of our friend the Arrow. Welcome to our Gathering, mortal woman. Welcome to our Feast of Hearts, our Spring Crowning, our Opening of the Barrow."

Chapter Thirty-Eight

"ALL THOSE THINGS AT ONCE?" I asked, surprised by the boldness in my voice. "You do know how to satisfy a social schedule."

Grosbeak snickered from his place dangling from my skeletal digits and a few others joined in. There was no one like the Wittenbrand for enjoying a bit of mockery at someone else's expense.

Coppertomb's lip curled. "I also know how to satisfy prophecy. A talent your fool husband thought he was singular in."

"*What holds you here?*" I asked Bluebeard in my mind. "*Can it be broken?*"

"*I am held by my own vow.*" His eyes met mine. Resolute. Determined. "*And as such, that bond cannot be broken.*"

I shivered, feeling the weight of his words here on this burial tor with the long green moss waving a farewell and his people offering a last tribute. Fate marched toward me, uncaring, inevitable. I gritted my teeth in the face of it. What was not yet final could still be undone.

"Does our song not say," Coppertomb asked, and his voice took on an orator's quality, arresting the crowd so there was not a murmur as all fell quiet to listen. "'Fly with the arrow, Dance with the sword, Give your heart to the barrow, Die for your Lord'? Perhaps, like the Arrow here, you thought he could confidently say it spoke of him. And did I not sweat, as I watched him fulfill it step by step. Perhaps you noted it, denizens of Wittenhame?"

There was a murmur of appreciation and a few nasty snickers, but I could tell even those who derided him hung on his words.

"Lord Riverbarrow flies as like an arrow, indeed. And he brings with him this mortal wife to whom – or so my spies in Ayyadgaard tell me – he gave the gift of flight that she might escape his rival's attentions."

He held up a single finger as if making a list and the eyes around me lit with appreciation. *Tell us,* they seemed to say. *Tell us a story.*

"He danced long and hard, back and forth, in his scheming and posturing against the Sword. You saw that yourselves at the Petal Ball and later when he sank to his temporary death in the arms of the Sea."

A second finger flicked up and the crowd sighed. I edged closer to my husband, but it was harder to move between all these still, watching people.

"And perhaps," Coppertomb said, lifting a third finger, "Perhaps, giving one's heart to a mortal – who is as much dead as alive so short are their lives – may indeed constitute giving your heart to the barrow. What say you, noble Wittenbrand?"

There was a cheer. But it was not wild celebration rather it was subdued as everybody leaned forward, hanging on his words. They could tell this was all building to something. And it was certainly not building to the glory of the man tied to a stake to witness his own memorial.

I glanced around me and saw the same knowledge in every eye. And the crowd had grown, the edges thickening and filling as more Wittenbrand hurried to join what might be the spectacle of the season.

"Draw back now from this prince of the Wittenhame," Coppertomb said, and his voice was low with the threat. "Draw back now or share his fate."

Around me, the crowd receded like a tide.

I did not recede.

And perhaps I was my impractical mother's daughter after all. For as they drew back, I marched forward until I stood at the side of my captive husband.

"What do I do?" I asked him.

"Walk with me into the darkness?" His gaze was intense, but there was something else behind it. Some grim anticipation I did not know, and it chilled me to my core.

Something had changed in those eyes. When they had sought to guard me, they had been firm and impenetrable. Now, a softness filled them, a surrender that shook me to the marrow. When he had sunk beneath the sea for me, he had been so full of words. He'd recited vow on vow. His silence now was eerie.

"*Where you go, I will go,*" I told him firmly.

"Listen now to another story," Coppertomb said, and as he leaned forward, I saw his allies whispering to one another. Wittentree looked pale and Bluffroll as ill as a man with already green skin can look. "Listen to how I flew with the Arrow, racing beside him as he shot out, snatching his certainty with a word in his wife's ear and bending his flight back toward the mortal world. I set him on his course as surely as if I drew the string."

A single finger was held up again, but this time higher, like a proclamation.

"Watch as I bargained with the Sword, dancing him to his death at the hands of another. Watch as I sank both these competitors beneath the clawing waves."

A second finger snapped up and it was met with silence. Not the owlish silence of disbelief, but the tingling silence of anticipation.

"And think now of how I have won, by barter, the Arrow's heart – the heart he gave his love and which I won in the tilts. Watch how in just moments, I will offer his heart to the barrow." He spread his hands wide to illustrate where we stood. "Two can play at games of prophecy. Two can fulfill them." He raised three fingers high over his head. "Who is anyone to say whose story is the right one?"

He waited a beat as all were silent.

"Who?" he said again, echoing himself rhetorically.

But I know drama when I see it. I'd been friends with Grosbeak long enough. And I know the best way to ruin someone's grand speech is to reply.

"The Bramble King," I said, just loud enough that it echoed across the field and was whispered to those who did not hear from the lips of those who did.

All eyes turned to the shifting face in the oak trees and to our collective horror, it flickered, formed a face of screaming agony, flickered again and then faded until there was nothing left but the waving branches of the trees and a sick feeling deep in my core.

"The Bramble King," Coppertomb repeated in a low, menacing voice, and now he laughed and laughed in his carefully clipped, sophisticated way. "He and his grim riddles. 'Their glory fades,' he said. And then '*From stone to feather, from stillness to motion, from stagnant to shift – the time has come. Sing the song of genuflection, bow ye to your broken dream.*' All his riddles bent in the same direction. Did you earnestly believe, mortal fool, that you comprehended what we did not? This is and has always been about succession. And when I finish here today, I will take the place of the Bramble King and reign Sovereign over the Wittenhame. And will not all the Wittenhame honor me then?"

He looked out over the crowd, and they answered with a loud cheer, but still, it did not break into giddy majesty. Still, it was held on a leash. There was not one here who did not know drama inside and out. Not one who did not love the theatre of life and death, and all their instincts told them the best was yet to come.

"The game is not yet won," Bluebeard said, his first words since this began. "Nor is it likely you will win with your pieces forfeited."

And this time, Coppertomb's smile widened so far that I thought it might split his face.

"Ah. Your point is taken, Arrow. But while you – ancient even in this world – thought only of the game given us, I winkled out a different game and set it in motion. I care not what happens to the mortals. This will be over long before they set steel to steel."

Behind him, his allies shuffled uncomfortably.

"But even when that battle arrives, I have laid plans that have sown the dandelions into the fields of my friends. Their armies will be gripped in blood lust and shall wash over your showing – larger though it might be – with heedless abandon."

"That wasn't the plan," Wittentree said testily.

Coppertomb turned to sneer gently at her. "Plans change."

She flinched, but I saw her take hold of herself and stiffen. Surely, she could see, just as I could, that Coppertomb had command of the people right now.

"I don't need to win the Game of Crowns and Houses," Coppertomb said. "Not when I can negotiate a better victory. I see you are not shaken by my declarations, Arrow. And that is because you know a secret, do you not? A secret you planned to keep to yourself to the very end?"

And for the first time ever, I saw my husband's face go blank and pale.

"The secret of the Wittenbrand – the White Flame. How many of us have spilled our blood hoping to collect the Arrow? How many of us have done so in vain? But do you know what I have just discovered? When I use the knowledge we two have, I will claim the Arrow, and it will make me Bramble King beyond all dispute."

"What is this knowledge you claim to have?" Antlerdale asked without inflection. He must be as furious as Wittentree and just as controlled.

"Ah," Coppertomb said. "You are upset you were not told. But why would I tell you? Why would I open the door for another to take it first? You still have your life, and your pieces in the game you care so much about. What do you care if I take this? Do you really want to rule these lands?"

Antlerdale said nothing, his face an immovable mask.

"I didn't think you would."

I didn't care about their interplay. I was thinking – perhaps too hard – about Rolgrin waiting to do battle against the three armies coming to him on the Plains of Myygddo. Was it a drug Coppertomb had given his opponents? Or some kind of magic? I'd sent my nephew to that battle. I'd sent them all.

"What is this secret, then?" Wittentree asked, her tone bored. She wasn't fooling me.

"That sacrifice is powerful," Coppertomb said. "I wouldn't have realized this on my own, not being one to so foolishly give another what is manifestly mine. But my opponent winkled it out and by the process of deduction, I found what he was hiding. He was planning all along to carve out his own heart and place it here on the root of the ancient arrow, were you not, Lord Riverbarrow? And with that sacrifice, he planned to buy for his people a future. For as Bramble King – made so by winning the game – the worth of his life's blood given freely would be enough to work any wonder he chose."

"Is this so?" I asked, horrified.

"Speak to my riddle wife, how do you mend the unmendable and fix the unfixable? How do you roll back time and give back days? How do you unravel wickedness to the very root and burn the place where it dwelled?"

"Surely, the answer does not need to be your death." My mental voice sounded small.

"Answer this riddle another way, if you can, for I cannot."

I felt as if I'd been hit in the head with a branch. Or shot between the eyes with a stone. All this time when he said he had a plan, his plan was to die. My knees felt like water.

"Will you still walk with me, wife?"

The question hung in the air as Coppertomb, smiling smugly at his own cleverness, continued. "Since the heart was offered, the heart I will take, and it will win for me the arrow, the crown, and my right as Sovereign. And we shall all savor how it kills my rival – a delight I shall enjoy both now and in cherished memory all my days."

My heart stuttered, hardly believing this was real.

"I will walk with you," I told Bluebeard while I still had the chance. It was a vow and a choice all in one. A firm commitment despite my bubbling fear. *"I will walk with you wherever you go."*

But I could not keep the tears from my eyes as they tumbled hot down my face. I was not ready to die yet. There were so many things I'd hoped for with him. So many things I would never do with him or see with him or share with him now – we'd share only death instead – and the taste of disappointment was bitter on my tongue.

"No tears now, fire of my eyes," Bluebeard said grimly. *"No tears."*

"I want to save you," I told him, because this couldn't possibly be the answer. Not from a man who commanded birds and freed himself from the sea. Not from the man who led troops into battle and took the heads of his enemies as trophies. This man did not submit to death without a qualm ... did he? *"What can I do?"*

"Only stay with me. Do not let go of me. No matter what happens, don't let go."

"Or you die?" I asked, still desperate for someone to tell me that this wasn't really going to happen.

"No. Or you *do,"* he said and before I could ask what he meant, Coppertomb raised his hands wide, and I saw a knife the length of my palm flash in the morning sun. Such a small thing for what he was threatening, but I'd seen deer gutted with knives no longer than my forefinger and I knew that small does not mean ineffective.

"What say you, Wittenbrand?" Coppertomb roared. "Shall we see if I am to be your King?"

And this time, the roar was deafening.

Chapter Thirty-Nine

"THIS COULD NOT POSSIBLY BE your plan," Grosbeak hissed, furious. I'd almost forgotten I was carrying him. Quickly, I tied his long hair to my belt, trying not to gag as I worked. I needed both hands free for whatever came next. "You kept saying it was all in service of a grand plan – my death, Vireo's death, Sparrow's death – and your plan was to *die*? Don't talk to me of betrayal when you've betrayed us all."

His whisper was becoming a whine.

"My plan, revenant, was to free the world and preserve my bride. And my plan *will* go forward," Bluebeard said through clenched teeth.

"*Now, fire of my eyes, I plead with you.*" His eyes met mine and I shivered at the contact. "*Keep your hands on me. Let me feel the warmth of your touch. For you are one with your mortal land and one with those given to me. I have bound you together, but I must draw now on that tie.*"

I put my flesh hand on him, and he shivered, his eyes rolling in pain or relief – I knew not which.

Coppertomb had been busy laying the rib crown on the marker before the silver arrow in a formal manner with elaborate gestures and ceremonial words that meant nothing to me but terror.

"*I meant to spare you this,*" Bluebeard gasped in my mind, "*but it seems that you must walk this path with me.*" His words felt the same way a door does when one pokes one's head without and feels the howl of the wind rushing by. They echoed as if they came from a long way off – or a long way down – as if he were already buried beneath our feet with those who came before him. "*So let us walk this path side by side, then, for I cannot shelter you and yet I am loathe to give you up, here at the end.*"

I shuddered at his words in my mind my teeth chattering harshly together.

Last time we faced our deaths together it had been with triumphant vows – a blossoming of a love we had not yet realized.

This time, we spoke with terse simplicity, as if words could not hold all the meaning we must wring from them. This time, we faced the tempering, the beating on the anvil of suffering that would shape this love for which we'd dared to hope. He must know this more than I did, for his trepidation seemed even greater than my own.

I looked out across the crowd for any hint of an ally and saw only a thirst for what came next. The Wittenhame was united in one purpose – to taste the drama Coppertomb had offered to serve up. Their anticipation was palpable, their delight building up like water behind a beaver's dam, just waiting for the moment that a log was torn loose, and it could spill over into revelry.

I clung to my husband's side, heart in my throat. Perhaps, I could take the knife from Coppertomb. Perhaps, I could fight them off. Maybe it if I took the key from around my neck and opened up the Room of Wives or took us to the mortal world.

"*Wife.*"

I met his eyes – his strange, slash-pupiled, cats' eyes so pale a blue that they were almost white. Within their unnatural form I saw only familiar affection and devotion.

"*Flee if you must. Go where you will. I will not hold you with me unless you choose it. But do not think to fight off my accuser or steal me away from this place. I am bound by vow and word to see this through.*"

"*I won't.*" My mental voice was too small. I wished it could roar like a lion.

"*To be married to me is to be wed to death. I can offer you only this – I will not abandon you, nay, though death drag me deeper than the sea did dare.*"

I swallowed and let go of the keys at the same moment that Coppertomb finished his intoned words and stepped across the stone toward my husband.

Behind him, the three remaining competitors watched, still silent, still stone-faced. Were they as bound as the Arrow was? Were they, too, surprised by how this newcomer to their ranks had twisted the game around and was seizing the keys to their kingdom?

If they were, they showed me nothing in their expressions. Their eyes would not meet mine. There would be no help coming from them.

Coppertomb strode forward and a hush fell again on the crowd as he called out to them.

"With full right and before you all, I claim the heart that was promised to me."

He leapt, his arms striking out toward my husband.

I clung to Bluebeard, feeling my mortal feebleness in the face of this strike, hoping not to let go, as my husband's body heaved and jerked under my hands. Bluebeard gave a strangled cry – but I could see nothing. The force of the action had thrust me backward, stumbling, and the only way to keep my hold on him was to fall slightly behind him. I kept my hands on his side as a terrible wet sound met my ears and then Bluebeard slumped suddenly forward, and the crowd roared.

His mental voice was faint. *"Walk with me, wife, through these gates of death."*

And if this was his last request then he would have it.

I shifted my grip on him so that I could lay his slumped head upon my shoulder and hold him up with my insufficient mortal arms, tucking him into the feeble warmth of my mortal embrace. The wound in his side gaped wide – twice as wide as it had been and ragged around the edges, as blood flowed from it. I shuddered, barely keeping down my gorge.

All he asked was the last shreds of my broken heart and they were his, all his.

Many wives watch their beloveds die, I told myself firmly. Your father watched your mother die, though you were not there to see it. Just be glad you get to be here for his last breath. Just hold onto that.

But my wisdom was hollow, breaking between my fingers like poor-fired clay. And I could not help the way I flinched as the crowd roared behind me like surf breaking over a rock – and if I were a rock then I was limestone, wearing away. No, if I were a rock, then I was a heap of sand piled by children, decimated by each wave until I was nothing more than a memory.

I risked a glance over my shoulder to see Coppertomb holding something up to them. Something dark and wet. The sight of it both revolted me and drew me as if a thread ran from it to me.

I was too stunned to cry. Too stunned to think.

It felt as though this terrible thing had happened to someone else. It could not be happening to me. Not after everything. All the pain, all the patience, all the sacrifice, and this was what I'd earned? Hollowness? Brokeness? An ending that fizzled to nothing but the same death everyone had in the end. My mouth smarted at the bitter taste within. Would that I could spit it away. I could not sweeten it with hope. There was no hope now.

I must be sensible. I forced my traitor thoughts aside.

Bluebeard should be cut down.

With his head still on my shoulder, and my arm wrapped around his waist, I pulled his shattered body to me. I reached into my belt and produced a small knife, reached up, and severed the cords that held him. He fell heavily onto me, driving me to my knees with a gasp. We slumped into the heap of flowers, their sickly sweetness drifting up and mixing with the smell of blood and bile. By sheer force of will, I kept him upright, still leaning against my strength as I hugged him to myself.

And even if I hadn't promised to stay with him, I would have. I could not possibly have let him go now. Not even when his body as it pressed against mine had not a single beat of his missing heart. Not when this may be the last real embrace of my life, the last time my heart was ever full and ripe with love. The last time.

"I love you," I whispered. "I love you. I love you."

He trembled beneath me, but was that him trembling, or only the heaving of my chest as I clutched him to me?

The Wittenhame had paled when I looked up, washed of color, shaded in tones of copper and gold.

As Coppertomb laid my husband's heart at the base of the silver arrow, the flames flared a rich gold and then went dull. And as he drew the Arrow from the flame – just as he said he would – he seemed flimsier in my vision, frailer, as if he were the one turned mortal and I the immortal.

The white flame which was now gold – the Wittenbrand they were all named for – shot up to three times the height, the wet heart disappeared in a burst of flame, and its vanishing quenched the fire so that all that was left was an afterimage against my lids.

Coppertomb lifted his chin arrogantly as he held the arrow aloft in the view of the crowd and blasphemous cheers swelled around us. He retrieved the Rib Crown and placed it once more upon his head, this time it was printed by his fingers with blood, a permanent reminder of what had been done.

In the oak trees, the Bramble King's face formed, deformed, and then ripped to shreds, disappearing like clouds when the wind shifts. I needed no one to tell me he would not be back.

"And thus, I defeat all competitors," Coppertomb intoned, barely masking his overwhelming emotions at this final triumph. Tears and joy swelled equally in his voice. "And I crown myself the Bramble King, Conqueror of the Wittenhame."

And the roar of the crowd should have drowned out all else. It should have drowned out my very thoughts. But instead, I heard an echo on the cusp of hearing, whispering in my mind.

"Hold me in your heart as my last breath,
tickles the memory that once bordered
on the divine and shatters me in last rest."

I clung to the writer of that poem as my hot tears finally released into sobs, heaving like the sea, under the crash of cheers and applause. Sorrow clung like the tide, rising ever higher. And it seemed that the Sea and I had two things in common – neither of us would willingly give up my beloved and both of us wanted revenge.

Chapter Forty

I STROKED his hair and his sweet face, pressed my cheek against the top of his head, let my tears flow down his neck, and let the last echoes of his life wash over me. My future flapping free like a flag torn in the storm, loose, and then carried aloft never to be seen again.

"*I waste. I fade. I am borne below.*" His mind rambled to mine. I recognized one of his poems to me.

And I hoped he wasn't in pain.

And I hoped he wasn't longing for release even as I could not loosen my hold, would not lessen it by so much as a twitch. He was mine. These last moments of his were mine, and I would not give up the last of my treasure. Not to anyone.

Around us, the ghoulish celebration had started. Lines formed as the folk of the Wittenhame lined up to kiss the hand of their new sovereign. He exulted in their praise, head thrown back, arms raised high, glory sweeping across his features as happiness or sorrow might do and cloaking him in gold.

My stomach soured at the very sight of him.

"She lingers. Lasts. Against the foe." My Arrow's voice had lost it's surety, drifting now as the voice a dreamy child.

How long could a person hold on while his life drained away? Even an immortal Wittenbrand? It couldn't be long. No wonder he'd asked me not to let him go. No wonder he'd asked me to walk through the dark with him. No wonder he'd been so quiet. He'd known.

And what was there to say when all had been said already?

Someone was making a pitiful sound, miserable as a newborn kitten. Me. I was making that sound. The last sound he'd ever hear.

I cut it abruptly, sucking in a shuddering breath and forcing myself back under control. It would not be the last. He deserved better. He did. Even if his plan had failed, was it not valiant to have tried or so much? A holy ambition. A righteous hope.

I could not fault him for reaching for more than he could grasp.

"Live now my heart, Live now for me." His mental voice sputtered and broke and then gasped out the last, "I gasp. I die. I ache for thee."

My vision was blurry from too many tears and something in my chest ached in raw pain as if I were the one who had felt her living heart torn away. I clutched him to my breast as tight as I could and let his last thoughts flow through my mind like molten gold. They seared into me, leaving indelible marks – scars, some might say – but these scars would be my last remnants of him. I wanted every slash and sear.

His fingers tightened on me and then fell away, and then tightened again as if finding one last spurt of strength.

"I love you," I whispered one last time my voice trembling badly, stretched thin with sorrow. "How can you die when I love you?"

His touch fell away.

The absence roared like pain through nerve of my physical body and tightened round and round my heart until I thought it could not possibly manage a beat.

They were singing that awful song again. The one I'd thought would be my salvation. The one that never could be.

"Sing for your sovereign,
Bow to your Dream,
Make haste for the fallen,
Rise in esteem,
And if ever you be broken,
And gasp on the ground,
The word may be spoken
And salvation found."

There would be no salvation for me. Not from a song. Not from anywhere else.

And yet I couldn't help myself.

"Mercy," I whispered through my chattering teeth, and I did not know who I whispered it to, but for a moment, I thought I saw something. It was probably the haze of my tears making me see ghosts, but for the blink of an eye, I thought I saw the Bramble King's face in the strewn flowers heaped around us and I thought I saw him wink.

I blinked hard, and when I opened my eyes there was a face there, level with mine. I bit back a yelp.

Wittentree leaned back on her heels, squatting in front of me, Bluebeard between us. Her one good eye bored into mine.

"I'll give you mercy if that's what you want," she said grimly, holding up a curved knife the length of my forearm and making a subtle slicing motion with it to emphasize her point. "But I don't think you do. I think what you want is to keep suffering. I'll give that to you, too, if you bargain for it. But it will cost you."

"I won't give him up," I said raggedly, my voice torn by tears, the hands holding his warm body trembling so hard that he shook.

Someone laughed close by, merry and bright in contrast to all my black shadows. Murder filled my heart.

She snorted a laugh. "I don't want him. And I wouldn't be Saint Wittentree, Boon to Lovers – which is what they're calling me in the mortal world, by the way – if I kept taking one half of the couple as my own. No. I want what Tanglecott gave you. Not all of it. I'm not as cruel as my looks suggest. I just want the extra – what wasn't yours to begin with."

"You want my beauty?" I asked, shocked that the price was so small. I would give anything – everything – what was so fool a thing as looks right now?

"Don't sound so aghast." Her eyebrows rose. "You think the price too steep? He gave his heart and all his plans to protect you – the one fly in the ointment of his perfect scheme – and you won't give up a heart-breaking face?"

"What will you give me in return?" I asked, not willing to waste time disabusing her.

"What do you want?"

"I want him to live." My voice broke on the last word.

"He stays alive while you are touching him," she said.

Dancing had begun behind us, and someone called for a roasted pig. I'd kill them all. Rain fire from the sky. Carve out their ... oh sweet mercy.

"That seems a poor bargain." I managed with trembling lips. But I'd take it. I'd take it and be glad.

She barked a laugh. "That's not the bargain. That's already a fact. Or it might be. These things are dangerously slippery to work out. Didn't you know it? Isn't that why you cling to him as you do? As long as your flesh is in contact, he can siphon your days to keep him alive. Maybe. It's a shock to his body that his heart is gone, but he lives still until you abandon him, or until you run out of time. So, that's not the bargain. I couldn't bring back the dead, anyway. That's not where my talents lie."

"Can you keep us bound, flesh on flesh so that I do not lose touch with him unless I wish it?" I asked. "You said that might keep him alive."

She looked at us pityingly. "Think you that he'd want that? A ghost half-life stuck forever with you? Lingering in agony on the edge of sweet relief?"

"I think he wouldn't want to die until he'd won," I said fiercely, practically spitting the words as I blinked back hot tears. Would they not stop?

She shook her head. "There's not much chance of that now, not even if you meet all the requirements."

There was certainty in my voice. "I'll do whatever I must do. I'll walk this darkness with him to the very end. I'll die if I must."

"Then tell me, what do you want?"

I must stick to the practical. I knew nothing else.

"Can you make it possible that if he falls, as he has fallen now, that I may have the strength to carry him? Will you bind us that I may not fail him by losing my grip."

She looked at me long and hard.

"So, it's to be suffering then. Long, hard suffering. What strange creatures you mortals prove to be. So close to death that you seem almost to call to it, as if the great leap is no more than the hop over a mud puddle."

Some kind of dark longing swam in her single eye.

I jutted out my chin. "Once you make it possible, I will be no concern of yours."

She laughed at that, and I thought I saw approval in her eyes. "Fair enough, mortal girl. Consider this our bargain then, your excess beauty, above what you had before you met Tanglecott, will be transferred to me and in exchange I will bind to you the strength to carry your husband when he falls, and I will bind your flesh with his so that you will not lose that touch unless you ask it. And if you ask it, you must say these words, 'I beg release from this binding and I beg it sincerely.' Are we agreed?"

"Agreed," I said.

I felt the narrowing of my hips and bust, felt my dress hang looser, and my center of balance shift slightly while at the same time, I watched Wittentree's scars vanish, her hollow cheeks fill, her thin lips grow plump, and her hardened eyes brighten.

"Enjoy your suffering," she said.

"Wait," I said, and she turned halfway back toward me as if reluctant to say more. Around her the carousing was intensifying. Colored sparks flew into the air above her head. I forced the plea from my lips. "What do I do now? How can I save him?"

She snickered, proving she was Wittenbrand after all.

"I don't know if it will be more fun to watch you flounder at this or to watch Coppertomb squirm, so I'll tell you for a price."

"What price?" I gasped.

"That living hand of yours will do. I have heard interesting things about it from those who call themselves my allies." She raised an eyebrow.

"I don't know where it is," I said, truthfully. We'd left it on Bluebeard's mantle, but where might it have gone since?

"No matter." She snapped her fingers and my living hand appeared in her palm. She cocked a lovely eyebrow at me and then ripped off her eyepatch to reveal the other eye perfectly beautiful, though white as a pearl.

"The hand is yours," I agreed, unnerved by her eye of fog.

Her smile was smug. "You should have bargained, mortal girl. Never make deals when you are desperate. It blinds the eye and dazzles the mind. But here you have it: a riddle to guide, a path for the mind. Attend me." She paused, took a deep breath, and then spoke her riddle as I clutched my beloved to me like a lost doll newly found. "What once stood in a line, but now is missing a brother? What was taken for wealth and refined by another? What holds death or life in the gap left behind? What holds endless damnation in similar kind?"

And then she was gone, disappearing into the mass of dancing, drinking, hooting bodies.

And I was left in a heap on the ground, holding my slumped beloved.

Carefully, hoping I'd not been tricked, I stood, dragging him up with me. I angled my arm under his knees, the other still clutching his back, and I lifted him. He was no heavier to me than a small child.

From somewhere at my side, there was a spitting sound.

"Drown me in flowers, why don't you? What a terrible way to be buried. In gold? Of course! Under stone? Acceptable. Beneath the waves? If I must. But in rotting plants? The indignity!"

Grosbeak, it seemed, was still with us – unwanted though he may be. I should have traded him away and been double the winner.

I turned, my husband in my arms, to see the Wittenhame celebrating on the barrow of their dead.

Not a single eye glanced toward us.

Not a single hand turned to help.

Long tables had been brought and heaped with food. Casks of ale flowed. A band of musicians played instruments made entirely of bone for a crowd that danced with the fervor of slaves freed. Coppertomb sat in their midst on a throne made of heaped bones, his stolen arrow in one hand like a scepter, and his crown sitting very precisely on his grave brow. Courtiers were still trailing up to kiss his ring as I took a step backward, and he set a benevolent hand on the head of each one.

But to my eye, every Wittenbrand here was dull and grim, a parody of people, and all the Wittenhame had lost its taste and color. It was dead and faded and lost to me.

Dust in my hand.

Sand in my mouth.

And I wanted not a mote of it to stay with me.

I turned on my heels and fled as fast as my feet would take me, clutching my beloved to me as I ran madcap and trembling down the back of the tor and out into the deadly Wittenhame with a riddle in my mind, a sob in my throat, and the love of my life and death cradled to my chest, the ashes of all my wished-for future fluttering behind me.

DIE WITH YOUR Lord

SARAH K. L. WILSON

Fly with the Arrow
Dance with the Sword
Give your Heart to the Barrow
Die with your Lord

Chapter One

THE LAW of Greeting bound me to him. The Law of Unravelling stole me away. But it was the Law of my own heart that set me now on this careening course toward fate and death and the barest glimmer of hope.

When I was a little girl my mother would cuddle me and my two brothers on her lap before the fire and tell us Wittentales — tales too fantastic and grisly for the mortal world. Tales of creatures who chewed children's bones to dust and belched out nightmares. Tales of oaths pledged that ruined lives and of bargains made which brought fortune beyond imagining and of lovers and fathers and kings who knew not which they were making before fate forced them to dance to the terms set until their feet were bloody. She told tales of trickery so twisty and horrible that it spun the threads of man and changed the entire tapestry, nation falling upon nation, whole kingdoms swallowed in madness or sickness or storm.

When I became a woman, I no longer needed such stories, for despite all my attempts at practicality, I myself, became ensnared within such a tale. And as the weaver of the warp and weft of history brought together the tangled threads of this saga, she wove it with me at the core. Try as I might to buck the pattern, she had only woven my thread back in, and back in, and back in again until there was no untangling it from the course of fate.

I fled through the Wittenhame with my husband clutched to my chest and my heart in my throat. He was no lighter in my arms than a feather, though he was a full-grown man. I held him clutched to my chest, for he made an awkward burden despite his light weight, and even with Wittentree's magic binding us, I was terrified of losing my grip on him.

Ashes fell around us like rain.

At first, I thought they were my imagination, but soon they floated down as thick as leaves falling from the trees in autumn, great black, fluttery ashes with soft filmy edges. And they coated my hair and my tongue and filled the air with the scent of smoke.

"Cataclysm," Grosbeak muttered from where his severed head was tied at my belt, and it sounded as if he were arguing with himself. "But no, it cannot be. T'was to be succession, not the end of all things."

I paused in a sudden clearing on the edge of the tor, my breath sawing through my lungs, my legs trembling as I turned first one way and then another, my long hair whipping into my face and obscuring my vision as I searched for pursuit. They would be just behind me. They would be on my heels.

I was breathless, heart racing, mind hot with fear. If only I could have just one sip of water to cool me. But though I searched the shadows, there was none following. The clearing was empty.

Though I had run for only minutes — fleeing the celebration of Coppertomb's coronation, the festivities and drinking, the dancing and merry-making — there was no sound behind me. The faint screams and distant laughter had melted away, leaving nothing but the chirping of insects, and the soft fall of ash, and a loud ringing in my ears that was, perhaps, my own fear echoing back to me. It blurred and blinded my senses to such a degree that a figure rode out almost upon me before I saw him there.

He was a pale, pale Wittenbrand in a flowing white robe that folded in a fan across his torso. His white hair reached his waist and then fell further still, dry and hoary as it fluttered in the wind. It blew in a different direction than the ash fell, as if he were not subject to the laws of moving air or gravity, though it was peppered in grey and black and melting white from the blowing ashes.

He rode upon a bone horse so pale that it occasionally disappeared altogether and his hands were skeletal bones just as one of mine was. As I watched he flicked his white sword and a pale flame white ran up and down the edge of the blade.

I swallowed, looking up to his face. His cheeks were sunken and his eyes ghastly white pearls. They rolled as he regarded me, his mouth falling open and his tongue quivering there like a living slug.

There was a long moment of silence as we looked at each other and then Grosbeak screamed, terrible and ear-piercing.

I watched myself freeze as if I were watching someone else, as the figure reached to point a single digit toward me, and just as I was about to scream, too, I remembered something — Bluebeard, whispering poetry to me as he faded, his heart snatched away, his words only for me. I clung tightly to the memory and to the cry that wanted to escape me. He would take neither from me.

I closed my eyes and held my husband's corpse tightly to my chest and thought about that moment and my roaring love for him.

I took a shuddering breath and then opened my eyes.

The white Wittenbrand was gone, and we had been transported to the doorstep of Bluebeard's home. It stood there, bent and odd, squatting on grouse feet in amongst a group of other Wittenhame homes. Here, too, everything was abandoned, ashes falling so fast and silent that they created a blanket of white and grey and black.

Grosbeak's scream cut off and I heard him gasp, panting with exertion.

"Death. Death has come for us. But how did we escape? What manner of monstrosity are you, Izolda, that you can turn back the avatar of death?"

"That couldn't have been death," I said, swallowing down the emotions churning within me. I felt oddly disturbed by the sight of that terrible Wittenbrand. I could not quite name the emotion seizing me and making my hands shake like leaves in the high wind. It was something that combined fear and horror, something that rolled despair and dread all into the mix leaving me sizzling and snapping like fat thrown into the fire. "Were it he, we would not still be here."

In the distance, a horn sounded, biting into my ears and mind. I jumped. The sound seemed to come from every direction at once. It was long and soulful, eerie and spine-tingling, like the cry of an elk in the forest. It made my mouth dry with renewed fear, as if the sound alone had found and tapped a spring within me. My heart sped, blood pulsing in my ears.

Grosbeak responded with a moan of despair as I reached for Bluebeard's door.

"The Wild Hunt, the Wild Hunt! Our doom falls upon us!"

"That's very dramatic of you," I said grimly as I tried to shuffle Bluebeard in my arms so I could open the door of his home. I'd forgotten about the magic that took you to the door of someone in the Wittenhame if you thought hard about what you loved about them. It had certainly been a boon to us. Bluebeard's head lolled on my shoulder, both precious and terribly tragic. I pillowed it with one hand as one does with a newborn infant.

A good widow would bury her dead husband. I was not good, for I planned to carry him with me.

"Dramatic? I state only the truth, fool mortal girl, so plain as to be nearly gauche. The end has come. Our doom has come upon us. Saw you not the ashes of the sky burning up? Heard you not the horns of heaven?"

"I doubt that was the sky. There's likely a forest fire nearby," I said calmly. "And by the time it reaches us, we'll be elsewhere."

"Indeed," he said with a bite, "For if you have any sense you'll run. We're about to be hunted by the Hounds of Heaven."

"I thought the Wild Hunt took place in the Mists of Memory," I said, trying to find logic in these prophecies of doom.

"That's only the memory of it from another age, and 'tis bad enough! The real thing will harrow us to our bones. Did you not see Death himself on his pale horse?"

I paused as the door creaked open.

"That was Death?"

"Who did you think it was?" his voice was shrill with fear and drew up higher and higher with every word.

"I thought he was one of the Wittenbrand to whom I had not yet been introduced," I replied smoothly. "There are a great many of you, each more bloodthirsty than the last, I find. But if it was Death, then perhaps we ought to find him again."

"Find Death? Find him on purpose?" Grosbeak was practically squealing. "To what end? Do you think he will be swayed by compassion for your mortal bones as I am? He's not so soft. He's not tainted by an ungainly affection for a mortal. You're too mad for this world, Izolda. You should have stayed with the other mortals and fought their Last Battle with them."

I frowned. "Perhaps I fled from Death too quickly. If we'd followed him, could he take us to where Bluebeard has gone?"

I realized after a heartbeat that the keening sound I heard was Grosbeak. It finally dissolved into words.

"To the Barrow? Are you so lost to sense that you would die with your husband?"

I barked a laugh as I stepped through the door. "Isn't that what the poem says? 'Die with your lord?'"

"It meant with the Bramble King, obviously. And Coppertomb twisted it so that he could take your husband's heart and offer it to the Barrow and watch him die alongside his lord while the great Lord Coppertomb was crowned the new Bramble King." Grosbeak's words almost tumbled together he was speaking so quickly. "Were you not paying attention? We can't live it twice like a play we enjoyed. You have to sink into these things and soak them up or you'll miss them entirely. Sometimes I despair that you have learned nothing from me."

"You think I should have soaked up my husband's death?" I couldn't keep the censure from my voice. "Coppertomb reached within his chest and ripped out his beating heart."

"And wasn't it wonderful? Didn't it give you a thrill? Lord Coppertomb — or maybe I should say, the new-crowned Bramble King — is a great master of drama and portents and I applaud his excellent ascension. We will be singing the tale of it for centuries to come."

"I thought you said the sky was falling and we were all caught in a cataclysm?" I said wryly, still caught on the threshold just inside Bluebeard's door as my eyes adjusted to the darkness. I was afraid to enter. Afraid of what might greet me within. Would his friends and servants within reject me? Would the fire burn me up or the rooms shift and swallow me?

"I'll admit," Grosbeak said glibly, "a reign shadowed with such portents as Death walking amongst the living and the sky falling in ash is sure to be a short one." He paused, considering, and the fear in his voice was suddenly replaced by speculation and something that sounded very much like delight. "A short but entertaining one. Perhaps I will enjoy it after all."

I gasped as my eyes finally adjusted to the darkness of Bluebeard's home. There was no fire burning. I saw no cats or other creatures moving in the heights above. No raven. No folk. No smells of food or drink. The door swung closed behind me and slammed shut.

I gasped, feeling my way to the mantle. Hollowness rung in every corner of my husband's home. It felt as though the heart of this house had been removed just as his physical heart had been, plucked away by an enemy. I choked on a swell of that swirling emotion I could not name.

"Ooof. Take a care! You are bumping me into furniture!"

I found the tinderbox and a candle one-handed and then sank to the ground, cradling Bluebeard on my lap so that I could work with the tinderbox to light the candle. It took four tries and even then my shaking hands barely managed it.

"Where is the fire?" I asked, my voice forlorn. I had hoped the fire could help to transport us to somewhere safer than this. But beyond that hope, his loss was even greater, for Bluebeard's home felt dead without its blazing heart.

I looked down at my husband's lovely face, flickering in the pale candlelight. Had I bargained for the wrong thing? Was I merely spinning out his torment by dragging his near-corpse everywhere with me? I'd heard once of a mother whose child had been snatched by fever. It had taken four men to hold her as they wrested the child's body from her sobbing grasp. She could not bear to set his tiny form down.

"Dead, I'd wager," Grosbeak's words sliced into my thoughts. "Rotting now like the rest of this mausoleum, if fires can rot. It cannot live now that he is dead. Perhaps the same is true of you. After all, of what use are you in the Wittenhame when you are flesh and mortal bones without a single breath of magic to sustain you."

"And yet, if these mortal bones did not carry you, you'd soon find the Wittenhame considerably less entertaining," I reminded him.

I stood, carefully drawing Bluebeard up with me, and the candle also, so that I could scoop up the silver thread and needle and with great care, I carried my husband to the settee where once we caressed one another and set him upon the plush brocade.

He looked so vulnerable here, beautiful but broken, once-strong, now nothing but a wisp that was once a powerful man. I remembered yet how he came to me from the sea, how he strode over the water and divided out punishments upon his enemies. Now, he was vulnerable as a newborn lamb and cold as one stillborn.

The candle lit nothing more than a tiny pool around us, so that I felt as though I dwelt only in this small patch of lonely house. Perhaps, all that remained was this one settee with this single dead man lain across it. I hitched up my skirts and set his palm on my bare leg so that I could work with both hands. I must keep his flesh pressed to mine or he would flee this life entirely.

With care, I threaded the silver thread into the eye of the needle and then drew his shredded coat and shirt apart so I could see his ruined chest sagging inward where once a heart and rib were found. Nausea washed over me at the sight of his torn flesh and pale skin. I had to take a moment to look away and take deep breaths of stale air to compose myself. When I felt strong enough, I turned back and I drew in a shuddering breath at how very, very dead my beloved appeared.

"The view from here is ghastly. I'll have you know that I am in no mind to help you when you abandon me to the flights of chance," Grosbeak complained in a muffled voice. "You should consider that right now I can see nothing but your skirts and the cloth is not so fine as to require a close study."

"I have to mend my husband's rent breast. Is it too much to ask for a small dose of mercy from you?" I asked him.

"Indeed, it is, for I have none to spare, nor would I be of a mind to offer it to you. You bargained very badly just now and you are without beauty or living hand," he said nastily as I gripped the needle between my thin skeletal fingers and carefully set it through my husband's cooling flesh.

I watched his slitted eyes as I stitched, pulling flesh to flesh with each draw of my needle, bringing back together what was torn apart just as he had done for my back so long ago. I felt those scars from time to time when I bent or stretched. Bluebeard's face, ever lovely, had taken on a bluish cast, the sacred color of the Wittenbrand, and I felt my chest seize as I watched him, the breath freezing within and becoming awkward and tight.

"I fear you fail to realize your predicament," Grosbeak said and I could tell he was loving this, even with his face pressed into the hem of my skirt. "Let me reveal it to you. You are cast from the Court of the Wittenhame and into this dying house with your almost-corpse husband. He is spending your remaining days on this half-life of his with reckless abandon. The result of which will cost you dear and deny benefit to him. Unless you abandon him, you must drag him with you wherever you go for no gain but the possibility that he may someday serve a purpose once more."

"I find I am very skilled in carrying about dead weight," I murmured as I set the last stitch and tied a careful knot. The wound was bleeding still around the edges. That was not something that the truly dead did. "I have been practicing and practicing with you."

I cut the thread with deft hands — even if one was entirely skeletal — and then lifted my husband up and into my arms again, gathering the up the candle, and marching to the nightingale stairs. They did not sing as I ascended. The house was truly dying with its lord.

If only that were enough to fulfill prophecy and snatch victory from Coppertomb's hand. I huffed an ironic laugh but it was hollow and grim.

I was numb, I thought, above that mystery swell within. Numb to pain, numb to feeling, numb to thought. I stumbled along as if in a dream, hardly caring that I had seen Death face to face, or that some terrible horn had been sounded, or that the sky might be falling, or burning, or something about a cataclysm. I had set my feet and hands to a task and they carried me capably even as my heart and mind were locked to greater thought or feeling. They felt as inaccessible as my husband and just as lost to me as he was.

I had a list. I would follow it. That would have to be enough.

First, see to my husband's care.

Second, gather help.

Third, form a plan to bring him back. I had all of him except his heart. In the Wittenbrand, in this wide land of magic and mystery where bodiless heads prattled on and on, and specters sat for years on your shoulder, neither eating nor drinking, couldn't I find some way to restore my beloved missing only a single heart?

When I reached our bedroom at the top of the stairs, the bed had crumbled to dust, and the flowering vines desiccated. The window to another world was simply gone. In its place was nothing but tumbled stone in a heap. The spring and the warm bath were dry and cracked, the books on the shelves nothing but dust.

This time, I couldn't escape the gasp that dashed from my lips.

"You'll find no succor here!" Grosbeak said, delighted by my misery.

I swallowed, trying to work moisture back into my dry lips. Where could I go now? Even the few resources left to me were crumbling. How could I fight against Death himself and the new king of the the Wittenhame when I had not even that?

I set my jaw firmly. I was being impractical. I still had my husband — as much of him as there was. I still had my health and my mind. I could figure this out.

"Is this destruction only happening to us or to all the Wittenhame?" I asked my Wittenhame guide.

"That, my darling keeper, is the million crown question," Grosbeak said gleefully. "For if it is only you, then you are on a clock, are you not? Mere hours perhaps before you lose any chance of defeating Death and somehow wresting your beloved prince from the grasp of hell. Already his magic crumbles around you, his personality — upon which both house and fire were built — fades and molders in a way that even the sea could not achieve when he languished in her embrace. But if ... and wouldn't this be golden? Or perhaps diamond? What is more valuable in this age?"

"Get to the point," I hissed.

"If all of the Wittenhame is falling, then Coppertomb has lost with his win, and you have won with his loss, tearing down the roof of heaven with your ruination, and collapsing this world and everything in it with your downfall. It is a sleek blow to take your enemy down with you. I did not take you for the type to charge honorably to your own death, but I find it favors you. Perhaps, we can line you and Coppertomb up and let the masses cheer for which of you wears it better."

"I was not me who wrought this, but my husband," I said and my voice was strained with emotion, which was strange since I felt nothing but emptiness.

"Even so, to drag your enemies with you into death is a masterful move. Worthy of the greatest of princes."

"Do you call him such when your camaraderie has faded into animosity?" I asked

"Burdened though I am with a bitterness heaped on me by the likes of your prince, still I am servant of the truth and bearer of the obvious," he said sorrowfully.

"As am I," a thready voice agreed, and I gasped in relief as the gargoyle on top of the mirror stirred himself.

"Can you help me, mirror?" I begged as it pulled a horrific face at me. "I need fresh clothing for both myself and the Arrow —useful, hard-wearing clothing for our journey — and a sling with which I might carry him skin to skin against me."

The mirror coughed. "Skin to skin is it? How scandalous! I love it!"

"Please," I begged, worried he'd give me nothing useful now. "We must chase after death and go down into the grave."

The mirror laughed. "Usually, I would spit your wardrobe at you, but my power is weakening. Step through me and I will dress you, but come to me naked, for I have only one last gasp of magic within."

Grosbeak laughed, a horrible, cackling laugh. "Yes, put on a show for the gargoyle, Izolda. It's not like you have anything better to do."

"I can't run in these skirts, Grosbeak," I said coolly. "Not while effectively carrying the Arrow."

Carefully, I untied Grosbeak and turned his head to face away as he snickered.

"The virgin bride, undressing her husband for the first time."

"I've seen him naked before," I said acerbically. "I am no blushing bride."

"Ah, but have you undressed him with your own hands?" He asked me as I quickly stripped my own things off. I left my small clothes on. The mirror would just have to leave them as they were.

I was a mess of blood and gore. It would have been nice to clean myself in the ever-warm pool, but with it gone, I would have to settle for fresh clothing. At least the worst of it was on my clothes, though it made for an awkward dance to undress while still remaining skin-to-skin with my husband.

"I'm his wife," I told Grosbeak shortly. "His body is mine as much as his heart is, and I have just as much a right to tend it and care for it."

"You miss my point quite intentionally, virgin Izolda." Grosbeak chuckled grimly.

I found my cheeks growing hot as I began to strip my husband of clothing. It was awkward to undress him while keeping our bare flesh skin against skin but his clothing was ruined and torn. He needed better or he'd catch a chill. I laid a leg against the side of his torso as I wrestled his boots and trousers off. Even so, I was huffing with effort as I cast them aside.

There was no way to easily maintain this position while removing his shredded shirt and jacket. That would take great care to avoid injuring his ruined chest. There was only one way to manage it, and it was while straddling him. I felt grateful both that he was unconscious and could not see my disregard for his privacy over his health, and equally grateful that I'd had the foresight to turn Grosbeak around. I tried to keep my eyes to myself, and I mostly succeeded, but I could not keep them shut tight when, at last, I lifted him to carry him through the mirror.

He was beautiful in my arms despite his grisly wounds — the palms and side which never healed and the ragged tear I'd stitched together. Beautiful and far too pale. As blue as his holy color, as bloodless as a specter, as gloriously beautiful as a marble statue. I hoped I could find a way to breathe life back into his chest and keep his soul in this beautiful, ruined body.

I stumbled when an emotion returned to me — a deep, aching, sadness that swelled as the swell of the tide brings in the sea and washed over me with just as much kindness as the crashing waves of the vengeful ocean. And just like the hulls men sail out on the sea, so I was smashed to splinters beneath the rage of it.

I shook as I shifted him to my back as one would carry a large child, and bore him through the mirror, my spine straightening only in response to Grosbeak's continued snickers. I would not give him the satisfaction of breaking now.

We emerged through the other side fully clothed and shod. I looked in the mirror and to my relief, Bluebeard was clothed from head to foot in his usual blue coat and shirt, trousers, and boots, but these were clean, warm, and dry, and his shirt and coat had been left unbuttoned. I, on the other hand, had been fitted in a backless jacket and shirt so that his bare torso was pressed directly to my back and a wide band of blue cloth had been slung under his bottom, around my waist, and then crossed over his back and down my shoulders to tie to itself, keeping him harnessed to me. My own feet were buckled into knee-high boots and my legs fitted with fine leather trousers, ready for trouble.

"Thank you, mirror," I said and he winked but the wink was too much. The mirror cracked from side to side and the gargoyle above it froze in place, his mouth forever caught in a taunting twist.

"And now, Grosbeak," I said with careful calm, "we will find your lantern pole and begin."

"Begin what?" he huffed. "More dress up? More wasting time?"

"The beginning of the end," I said.

Chapter Two

IN THE MAIN ROOM, a lantern pole was hard to find now that I'd taken so many, but I did find a strange one with a hooked crook at the top like a shepherd's staff. This one was shaped like the head of a hissing rooster — a creature both intimidating and somewhat ridiculous. It held two hooks for lanterns in tandem across a wide bar. I hung Grosbeak's head from one of the hooks, ignoring his gnawed ear and the comb in his hair that a mermaid lover wove within the greasy dark tangles. I was used to his putrescence by now. Just one head hanging from the double tree made it swing so that the rooster stared off to the side as if to guard me against trouble on my right side.

"I do not care for this pole," Grosbeak complained. "I am not feed for a wild cockerel. If you ever prove worthy enough to stop running for your life, I demand a better option. A gilded pole perhaps, or a plush cushion on which you shall bear me."

"Do keep dreaming. I hear that hope keeps you looking young and you could use the help," I said absently.

Bluebeard was positioned so that his head rested on my shoulder and almost, I thought I could feel his breath, faint, yet there, against the curve of my neck. I clung to that. We would find a way to retrieve him. Nothing was so lost that it could not be brought back. I had been assured that he was not yet fully dead, even if his heart had been given to the grave and while there was life, there was hope. If he'd had a plan to restore his wives, then we could have a plan to restore him.

"I hope you are not planning something foolhardy, mortal woman," Grosbeak murmured as I lifted my candle and adjusted my grip on the pole. The candle barely lit further than his face and he was wreathed in the kind of shadows that heightened the otherworldliness of his visage. "If you chase after Death, my fun will be over."

"I make all my plans with the sole aim of amusing you," I said dryly, looking around Bluebeard's home for anything else that could help us. I was finding nothing. When I touched most objects, they turned immediately to dust or ash.

It was a strange thing to walk with the limp body of my husband strapped to my back. The weight was so light I barely felt it, but I had to move with care to avoid hitting his limp limbs on the furniture or turning too swiftly and knocking his lolling head to one side. I was learning — however slowly — to move with slow care, as one might when tending an infant.

"If you wish to amuse me, then keep me alive. This dying house will not keep out the Hounds of Heaven now that they are loose in the Wittenhame, and you must run like all the rest, or form a hunting party to hunt the creatures back. There are only two paths in this game. And as you have no vassals except me, running is the only option for you. I'll have you know that while I was the handiest in all the Wittenhame with arrow and spear, that option has been taken from me. It's run or die today, my mortal conveyor."

"Noted," I said, but it was not toward the outer door that I strode, for I was not fleeing Hounds nor chasing specters. I had a clear plan in mind.

I crept through the darkened, dreary house, the scent of mildew in my lungs, and then made my way down the stairs, and heaved open the heavy oak door there.

"Not the Wall of Wisdom!" Grosbeak protested, but I ignored him. It was not his counsel I sought. He'd made it very plain that he was only along for the ride. "There's nothing they can give you that I cannot! Nothing."

"Wise," the word whispered in my ear.

My breath caught. Had that been my imagination, or was it my husband barely whispering to me?

"Wise, stone-faced certainty."

I twisted my head to look at his face and saw only his slitted eyes and parted lips. It seemed that I had his approval — if that had been him whispering to me, and who else would it be? — and the notion put strength into my limbs and heart.

Husband? I asked within my mind. *Can you hear me?*

There was no reply, but for a moment I thought I felt a flash of emotion that was not mine. Tenderness, I thought. Like watching a new foal take to its feet.

I shook my head. That was not the right emotion for dealing with Bluebeard's advisors.

I made my way into the musty gloom below. Without the fire leaping to join us, the room full of the heads of my husband's enemies was a horror. The chair on which he had sat and dandled me on his knee was threadbare and collapsed. The shelves leaned at awkward angles, and for a moment I thought I might be too late — that the heads also would be gone, rotted away to nothing but empty-eyed skulls.

"You should be running," Grosbeak complained. "Do you want to be backed into a corner when the Hounds arrive? Perhaps we can leap into Riverbarrow."

I'd never endanger my husband's home that way. Grosbeak should know better. It was to be the mortal realm for us, or the Wittenhame, or nothing.

"Who disturbs our imprisonment?" The voice that came from the darkness of the shelves was the firm voice of Vireo.

I lifted my candle high so that he could see me.

He began to smile a gleeful, wicked smile when his eyes set on me, but it collapsed when his gaze shifted to my shoulder.

"The Arrow," he gasped. "What has come to pass?"

"Only the beginning of a cataclysm, Death riding a pale horse, the sky turned to ash, the moon to blood, and all that," Grosbeak said, and he seemed to be gloating that he knew this and Vireo did not. I leaned his pole against the shelves and he scowled but kept talking. "Oh, and now Coppertomb is the Bramble King." Vireo hissed at that. "His coronation was scarce an hour ago. And for the confirmation of it, the Arrow had his heart plucked from him and shoved into the grave."

"His heart?" Was I mistaken or did Vireo's eye turn to me for a bare second before returning to Grosbeak?

All up and down the wall, the severed heads stored there murmured their appreciation or apprehension, excitement passing over the faces of those I could see in my candle's light.

"It's all precisely as it was prophesied!" Grosbeak crowed, "and I got to be there for all of it! I was there to watch his heart feed the barrow and watch the triumph of Coppertomb. And now I will get to watch the mortal bride run with the slathering jaws of the Hounds of Heaven snapping at her heels, her bright shrieks painting the midnight with sparkles of terror, and her wet mortal life running out like water from a spring. Do you not envy me?"

"Mortal wife of Lord Riverbarrow," Vireo said very precisely. "As the only one here with hands, you would do us all a favor, if you were to cuff Grosbeak for his insolence. Your pet is terribly ill-mannered."

I cleared my throat. I was not in the habit of cuffing people. That wasn't what I'd come for.

"I'm here to consult with you, Wall of Wisdom, Vault of the Fallen Enemies of the Arrow. Will you hear my question? Will you consult on my riddle?"

"Only if you strike your pet," Vireo said. "Payment for services rendered."

"Hear, hear!" someone else said and I thought it might be Grosbeak's father.

Grosbeak snickered. "She'd never, weak mortal that she —"

Fast as lightning, my hand shot out and I slapped Grosbeak.

"Enough," I said and let my voice ring with authority. "I have no time for more stipulations. Either hear my riddle or ignore my plea but do not waste what little time I have."

"Speak then, mortal," the woman who looked like a mermaid said, her tongue coming out forked and green. Her tangled seafoam hair curled around her. "Tell us this conundrum and we will advise you if we see fit."

"We will?" Grosbeak's green-faced father snickered nastily. "We owe the mortal nothing."

"We owe her for a slap," Vireo said, considering. And his face now, after life had passed, held none of the ill will he had bourn me while he lived.

"She wears his blood," the head with the silver crown said. Her eyes were still closed, her mouth a perfect cupid's bow. "We can deny her nothing while she is sealed with that."

The murmurs quieted. Interesting.

"This is the riddle given to me by Lady Wittentree," I said, speaking clearly so that all of them would hear. "*What once stood in a line, now missing a brother. What was taken for wealth but refined by another? What holds death or life in the gap left behind? What holds endless damnation in similar kind.*"

"We've seen how well you do with puzzles, mortal wife," Vireo said easily. "Who can answer where you see not the solution?"

He was taunting me, I knew. And yet, he was partially right because I recognized a part of the riddle. It was tickling something in the back of my mind that I could not quite remember.

A head spoke, interrupting my thoughts and I recognized the square jaw and red curly hair of the seer who had prophesied for Bluebeard. Her glassy eyes were white as snow.

"A tangled path lies now before you, mortal wife of the Arrow, and only one way endures to the end. Turn to the left or the right and the ground will slip out from under you and drag you to your death."

I shuddered but then paused at the wide smiles on the faces of the advisors. They loved this as much as Grosbeak did, reveling in whatever suffering might come to me.

"Have you nothing more useful to say to me?" I asked. "I know already that the way is precarious."

"Nothing," the Seer said. "Any words might steer your course and any steering might take you from the solid path."

"It doesn't sound solid at all, I'll bet you three flies and a gnat she chooses wrong before she leaves this house," Grosbeak's father said.

"I raise you by a tooth that she makes it to the Hound's chase," Grosbeak countered. "She's cleverer than you think."

"But not clever enough to win?" his father pressed.

"Is anyone?" Grosbeak asked. "I once thought the Arrow capable of winning the game, but look at him now? He's a rag doll in the hands of a mortal woman."

"Mmmm."

I clenched my jaw, frustration filling me. I'd counted on this wall of heads to tell me something — anything, that I could find to point the way. I understood Wittentree's riddle to a certain extent. After all, Bluebeard had told me the story about the rib of the sovereign, there in the ground, mined out by evil men. If that wasn't the thing that used to stand in a row then I didn't know what was.

A loud cracking sound startled me and I swallowed, looking up at the dust spilling from the ceiling.

Mayhap, I should have listened to Grosbeak and run. I clutched at my heart with one hand, certain the whole structure was about to fall on us, when I realized it was laughter I was hearing, not the collapse of the house. Not the laughter of the heads, though some were certainly laughing in their cruel way.

When I raised my candle, it lit a flickering pattern of dancing shadow over a face as large as I was tall, jutting from the wall to one side of the shelf of heads. It was almost entirely hidden by tangled roots and squirming beetles, but I still made it out. The old Bramble King was here. It was he who was mocking me with his laugh. He seemed barely there, he was missing his crown, and he gasped between his chuckles, fading a little more with each gasp and then he spoke and he almost spat the words, he ejected them so harshly and intensely.

"*Mist and Memories,"* he spat and the words were echoed by the heads with confusion in their voices.

"Has he gone mad?" one particularly shrill one asked.

"He's nearly dead, of course he's mad. Coppertomb's replaced him. Do you know what you call a replaced king?"

"Has there ever been a replaced king?

"You call him past, you call him refuse, you call him boring, for that is what he is." I was pretty sure that was Grosbeak's father.

The Bramble King flickered again and then there was a strangled sound and one of the heads fell to the ground gurgling horribly and then suddenly still.

It *was* Grosbeak's father. I raised a single eyebrow. So typical.

"I'd wager that more respect might be due the Bramble King," I said calmly and the great king's eyes flickered to mine for a bare moment. Unlike the others, I knew what his words had meant for I remembered stealing a glance into the Sword's copy of that very book. "Mist and Memories: The Memoir of Lord Antlerdale." My heart was racing. I had an answer from the Bramble King himself.

"Chapter Ten," he said very clearly, a dozen beetles scuttling into his curving lips as he spoke. "Paragraph Thirteen."

And then he was gone and I was left repeating his words again and again in my mind so I would not forget. Chapter ten, paragraph thirteen. Chapter ten, paragraph thirteen.

"Well," Grosbeak drawled. "This has been enlightening. It's not every day you watch your father killed a second time, and this time by no less than the former sovereign of the Wittenhame."

"Is he *former?"* one of the heads asked. "He seemed anything but."

I shivered. Death and life had different meanings here. But I had my clue and it was time to move.

"A word of caution," one of the heads said in a thin reedy voice. I had to lift the candle very high to see a man ancient, with sallow cheeks. "I saw a man living with no heart once, surviving only on magic. Has he spoken to you?"

"Hardly," Grosbeak snickered. "He's decorative now, nothing more. Izolda's trophy husband."

"I'd not discount him yet," the voice said, "and I'd not leave us here when you'll need his advisors."

"She can hardly carry you all around on poles," Grosbeak said dismissively.

But the head was right. I should take them with me.

"The man I saw," the querulous head said, "was as if in a dream, living again other times of his life and unable to grasp what time or space he found himself in at the present. If you speak to him, I caution you to watch for signs of that."

"Thank you," I said.

"You're thanking him for that nonsense?" Grosbeak objected. "Where is my thank you? When have I failed to be useful? And yet I receive no thanks."

"Your thanks is your continued life," I warned him. "And now, I must hurry. We have little time."

"Finally, she understands!" he said with a dramatic eye roll, but his drama was cut off when I took out my golden key, turned it to open the Room of Wives, and marched to the shelves, scooping up heads by the hair, four to a fist, and hurrying to stack them inside the room around the pillar meant for me.

"What are you doing?" he objected. "You're wasting time."

But he had to speak loudly over the screaming protests of the heads.

"This is not what we agreed to!" they shrieked. "We are not prizes for the taking!"

"I have few resources," I huffed, not stopping in my task. "Best not to waste them."

"I would like to file an official complaint," Grosbeak called after me as I disappeared with the rest of the heads. "This is not an egalitarian society! Everyone does not have equal value. I am your pet. *Me!*"

I ignored him, as I ignored the many protests of my husband's defeated enemies and when they were all secured, I marched to where Bluebeard had left Sparrow's head and body, her arms crossed respectfully over her chest. I leaned down and snatched up her head.

Her eyes snapped open. "What is this?"

I ignored her and marched out of the room, trying my best not to listen to the hiss of the garnets as they ran out faster than I could spend days, locked the room behind me, and tied her head by its hair to the other hook on the pole.

"No, you can't do this!" she screamed.

"You are too mad for even the Wittenhame!" Grosbeak agreed, his voice a ringing shout.

"On the contrary. Only the sanest person can deal with complete insanity," I said coolly. "She neutralizes it, removing the poison by her mere presence. Heed me and be wise." I paused. "Also, though you both hate me, I believe I'll find your counsel useful, so it's both of you or neither."

"Neither," they said in unison.

"Both it is," I said firmly, scooping up the lantern pole, and I left the empty room with my candle held high and my jaw set with determination.

Chapter Three

I HURRIED UP THE STAIRS, balancing my double-headed lantern pole in one hand and my single candle in the other. Human heads are very heavy. Two at once would make me strong as a knight in the king of Pensmoore's training if I kept this up. A memory of Svetgin's proud grin when my father told me he'd been accepted as a knight seared through my mind and with it came a sudden vision of the knights of Pensmoore charging onto a dust-worn battlefield with my nephew Rolgrin at their head, a flag unfurling behind his foaming horse — a black horse sigil over a field of green proudly displayed upon it. Blood was splashed over his dark tunic and flashing sword. I blinked away the memory. It was not mine.

Grosbeak muttered a steady stream of curses and I clung to them to steady me. I wasn't in the mortal world right now. I was here in the Witten-hame, fighting for my husband's life and more than just my happiness rode on his slumped shoulders. Fail, and Pensmoore would fail with me. If she had not already.

"Teeth of the Gods! The indignity. Blights and barnacles!"

Sparrow maintained a dignified silence as my old friend painted the air bright blue with his words. She looked the worse for being dead, but her eyes were sharp and she seemed to be thinking very hard. I could only hope she was thinking to our advantage and not to trip me up. What would she give more weight to? Her love of Lord Riverbarrow, the Arrow, my Bluebeard, or her disdain that he'd married me, a mere mortal, in the Wittenbrand way?

My candle guttered as the air shifted and the boards squeaked under my feet. I swallowed down tremors of worry. What I was about to undertake would be an enormous task for one of the Wittenbrand, never mind a mere mortal. And this time, there would be no magical husband swooping in to pluck me free of a trap I'd sprung. Instead, he was counting on me for success.

I must summon all my practicality and common sense for this. I would need every shred of it.

I opened the wooden door at the top of the stairs, running a hand over Bluebeard's crest etched upon it. An arrow with a streak of blood behind it and a bird flying above. It squealed in protest, binding on the floorboards so that I had to carefully thread the lantern pole through the gap and then adjust Bluebeard on my back to squeeze the pair of us through. The house was shifting, falling apart at the seams. It made something uncomfortable lurch in my belly. I had begun to think of this place as home, but like all my homes from the past, this too would fade and fail and leave me without anchor or place once more.

"*Riverbarrow.*" This time, I did not imagine the whisper in my mind. I smelled the mint on the edges of it as I stumbled into the main room, heart in my throat. I paused, lifting the candle as I turned so I could see his face.

"The pearl," he whispered, his short beard tickling my neck and his words making my mouth suddenly dry. He could speak. He still had that much life.

His pale blue cat's eyes met mine, and for a moment I was almost nauseated by the powerful emotions that tore through me from my numb lips, through my aching chest, and down through vibrating thighs to my toes. Need, desire, hope, absolute obsession — how could I disentangle one from the other when they wove themselves all through every root and branch of me with just one shared glance eye to eye?

He wet his lips with a bloody tongue. "Please, sun of my world. Please.
"

I could never say no to that "please" and I did not try. Hope galloped in my chest as I hurried to where the painting hung on his wall — the door to Riverbarrow. I saw that yes, there was a pearl hanging from the frame, strung on a single cord of something that looked like hair twisted and braided into a narrow rope. It was a strange hair, indigo in color and rough in texture as if it were made from a blueish green horse. Or perhaps a kelpie? Was this hair from the water creature he both was and wasn't? My eyebrows were rising even as I reached for it.

This pearl? I asked with my mind and he gasped, almost inaudibly, and then with a look of enormous concentration, his hand lifted slow, slow as honey in the depths of winter, causing little flutters of emotion in my chest. He snapped his fingers and the painting vanished. His hand fell and his face sagged once more into my shoulder, his eyelids falling shut, and his cheek going limp against my shoulder.

I shuddered into the feeling of his heavy-eyed self resting entirely on me. It was like watching something precious as it dropped from a ship into the sea. One could not tear one's eyes away from the fall, but the moment it plunged into the water all would be lost.

I paused for a breath — refusing to give up the fall, if that was all I had left. And for that breath, I savored the press of his cheek into my shoulder, the sensation of his bare, cooling flesh against my back, the way his fallen hand was slung around my narrow hip. And when I breathed in, I breathed in his scent and I brought his air into me, and it was heady as good wine and it swirled in my heart and body in a way that made me gasp. Was that a tear I blinked back? Surely not.

"Put it around your neck you fool girl," Sparrow said in a tight voice that suggested her patience had thinned to a thread. "Don't you see he put Riverbarrow into it?"

The pearl was as large as the end of my thumb and a hole had been bored through it to take the binding of the hair rope. When I held the pearl up, I saw in its depths the same scene that had been in the painting a moment ago — one of the tranquil river and the blowing willows, with tiny golden fairies floating between them — as if the opaque surface were reflecting back what had been wrought in oil and skill. I swallowed and slung it around my neck, tucking the pearl into my jacket and shirt to keep it safe.

"Wouldn't that take an enormous amount of magic, to transfer a whole world like that?" I asked, in awe.

"Were I you," Sparrow said acidly, "I would not make my estimates of the Arrow so low. He always rises to exceed expectation."

I felt my face heat at that and grow even hotter at the knowing look in her eye as if she knew him better than I ever could. I did not like the splinter of jade jealousy that pierced me with her expression. It did not suit me or aid my efforts.

"Oh, yes, this is excellent. Ignore the end of the world to thrash out which of you is Queen Hen," Grosbeak mocked. "Will it be a battle of devil looks or sharp silences? Have no thought to whether you will hurt me in the crossfire. For I am unaffected by the evil eye and I can fill any silence. Have I told you about the writings of Mistress Le Pen? I was indulging in them not long before my head was taken."

His rambling shook me back to the present. He was right. What we had to do was urgent and there was no time for me to worry about where and how my husband's loyalties might be been entangled.

I strode to the frigid fireplace, searching among the stacks of books as Grosbeak rambled on. Antlerdale's memoir must be here somewhere.

"She writes the most scandalous truths, Sparrow. You really should have read them while you could. Delightful, flagrant, violent, and absolutely addictive," Grosbeak said, warming to his tale as I sifted through books in the light of my flickering candle.

These volumes looked intact and solid but they fell to pieces in my hands, bindings splitting apart and pages streaming out and spreading across the floor. In vain, I took up one after another only for them to slide through my fingers and disintegrate. But even so, I could read the titles and none were *Mist and Memory*.

All at once, the tangled roots of the tree that held coats by the entrance gave a terrible creak, and then with a shudder, the tree toppled, cracked, and split into two halves. The top half crashed downward, pulling with it the chandeliers, the candle ends, and the yowling cat that lived within them. He did not look right, his hair falling out in clumps and his tail dragging as he moved.

He hissed at us and then fled through the front door which had been knocked open and left ajar.

We were running out of time.

I lifted the lantern pole and scrambled over the tree when I heard the stones of the fireplace begin to crumble. I was through the door when a terrible crack split the air. My nose filled with the scent of dust and earth, I leapt from the doorway and away, as the house on grouse feet collapsed in on itself in a heap.

"The end of an age," Grosbeak whispered sadly.

"The end of a lot of things," Sparrow agreed, but her voice was more than sad. It sounded like resigned despair.

I stood for a moment, working my dry mouth, shock and worry filling every inch of me.

"I suppose I'll have to find the book somewhere else," I said, returning to common sense and trying to stay hopeful. We could find this book. Just not here. There was no point fussing about it. I needed to get to work to fix it.

From somewhere nearby, a dog barked and then the horn sounded again, long and eerie, and I bit my lip and tasted blood.

"Run, run, the hunt has come! The Hounds of Heaven flush the prey!" Grosbeak warned, delight in every syllable.

"I need to find Antlerdale's book," I gasped, but I heard the loud dogs baying not far from here and their barks sounded hungry and violent.

The sound stabbed directly into my heart, making it gallop with fear. It was not only myself I was risking here. It was my beloved husband and his entire world slung around my neck.

"And how do you plan to do that?" Sparrow asked coolly, the only one of us unaffected by the baying of the Hounds. She merely seemed merely impatient at not being informed of my plan.

"They should be everywhere," I said, my words laced with anxiety. "Grosbeak said that Antlerdale gave them out like candy. Everyone should have copies, and all I need to do is find the tenth chapter and the thirteenth paragraph."

"I see your predicament," Sparrow said with a lifted brow. Shouldn't she be screaming at me to run, too, or was it normal for her to discuss literature while listening to Grosbeak chant a song that either repelled dogs or drew them in, I wasn't sure which? "And it's a bad one because you can't just grab any copy of the book and look."

"Why not?"

"Because Antlerdale is constantly rereading the book and every time he does, he changes something and reissues the book. 'Each correction brings us closer to perfection,' I believe he said. So you'll need the original."

"And where is that?" I asked. Was that a snuffling I heard? It was getting closer.

"At his home," Sparrow said calmly.

"So we'll go there, then," I agreed.

"Now. We go now, right?" Grosbeak whined. "Now!"

And then a loud bark made me jump and down the row of collapsed houses, through the ashes filtering down from — yes, Grosbeak had been right — a crescent moon that had turned to blood and was dripping in the sky, leapt a three-headed Hound so large it made me wonder if we were accidentally dragon-fly sized again.

I spun in every direction looking for escape. Not Bluebeard's house. It had collapsed. As had every house we could see. Not the mushrooms, they had fallen, leaving black smears the size of army barracks where they had been.

I could try to run, but I couldn't outrun a normal-sized dog when I was utterly unburdened. I had no hope of outrunning this one.

Before the barking, slathering, short-haired Hound, denizens of the Wittenhame fled. A pair of figures mounted on an oversized fox flung arrows behind them at the beast, but the arrows were the size of pine needles compared to the spittle-flecked dog, and it didn't seem to notice them even when one stuck into one of its six eyes.

No fighting, then.

A group of tiny flying fairies kicked up like a swarm of sand flies, fluttering panicked in every direction. Someone screamed. Some others started to cry out but were cut off.

I spun again and caught sight of a toad the size of a horse leaping past. To my shock, Grosbeak whistled to it and it paused. It was my toad. The one from the joust.

I didn't stop to think, I just leapt onto its back, hoping that Bluebeard would stay tied to me and that I could hold onto the lantern with one hand as I tossed the candle behind my back and grabbed for one of the knobs on the back of the toad. He was leaping before I could steady myself, careening wildly from side to side as the barking grew louder.

There was a crack as something snapped its jaws beside me. I didn't look back, just gritted my teeth and held on for dear life as droplets of moisture that smelled like wet dog and old meat misted over us.

"Teeth of the Gods! Lords have mercy! Saints and scepters!" Grosbeak screamed.

A doggy foot landed right in front of the toad and he froze as a wet nose snuffled down, down. I caught a single glimpse of it and screamed just as the toad suddenly hopped again, brushing against fur edged in flame, and then coming down close to a towering tree and burrowing into a dank hole under a root. The roots ripped at my hair as soft earth cascaded around us. Behind us, the dogs howled their excitement and I heard the distinctive sound of a canine digging.

There was no time to dwell as the toad burrowed deeper and deeper, pressing fresh earth around me so tight and close that I could barely breathe, never mind hear the garbled screams of Grosbeak and Sparrow.

"Use the key, my mad folly," a breathy voice whispered in my ear.

Wordlessly, I fumbled for the key around my neck. I had two. One for the Wittenhame. One for the Room of Wives and in the darkness, I could not tell one from the other, but I pulled out the first one I could find and twisted it in the air.

Chapter Four

WE LEAPT out into the mist-filled, washed-out passage between worlds. The toad perched half within a steaming swamp, half on a tuft of grass, as the sounds of the terrorized Wittenhame disappeared and were replaced by the cloying silence of the mist.

The light filtering into this strange half-place was so grey that I could hardly tell whether it was a dark afternoon or a very bright night. I only knew by the whisper at my ear. Bluebeard would never speak to me in the day, lest the curse fall on us all. A curse, I might add, that he had never explained to me in full.

"Let my captains guide the toad, jewel of the Wittenhame," he whispered. I shivered at the feeling of his breath on my neck and then his thoughts hit mine in a jumble again. A sudden memory, as vivid as if it were my own, of a young Vireo and a young Grosbeak laughing together as they rode on bundles of straw that had been lashed together with glittering bands of what I could only think was magic to form the figures of horses. The straw animals ran and whinnied just like real horses and I felt a burst of delight that must have been young Blubebeard's, just before young Grosbeak's straw horse leapt over the river and suddenly burst into chaff, the lashings falling apart and dumping him into the water.

I swallowed and my husband's shared memory faded.

"Tell the toad how to get to Antlerdale's house, Grosbeak," I told my friend a little roughly, keeping my voice firm to anchor me. I dared not wander in the past with my husband's slipping mind, no matter how bewitching his memories may be.

"Am I now your carriage driver that you order me about?" Grosbeak protested but in the same moment, Sparrow rolled her eyes and delivered a very passable croak and the toad spun and hopped onto what almost seemed like a beaten trail.

My husband, I said in my mind and the words were sweet on my mental tongue. He was that still.

"I fade," he whispered softly, and his whisper was precious to me. "But I have a memory of a word upon your lips. You spoke to me of love."

I love you, I said in my mind and the words ripped at my heart, shredding the last bits of me and I did not care that it was my responsibility to keep us all on this hopping toad. I shifted so that I could hold the lantern pole wedged under my seat and use my free hand to cup my precious Bluebeard's cheek. *With all my heart I do. If this world no longer holds you then I want no part of it either.*

And in my mind his memories tumbled and fluttered and I saw myself as he did that day that I greeted him, only while that was most certainly my carefully remade dress and long pale face, and while that was the golden bell in my hand, I looked different in his mind's eye — powerful, vibrant, alive in a way I did not recognize from any mirror. And his emotions in this memory were a sharp combination of shock, hope, and dread.

"My true bride," he whispered but his eyes were glassy and his words stumbled and then stuttered. "True. True. Bride."

And then they faded away and in their place his mental channel opened, but it was not words he gave me but rather a strange soaring emotion and with it, the memory of flying on the back of a dragonfly, my arms wrapped around him and the air streaming through our hair. With it came a burst of such true contentment that it made me ache.

My long-dead mother had wanted me to be married and happy. What would she think now if she looked down at me and at my collection of friendly corpses fleeing for our lives, and discovered that this is what a happy marriage looked like for me? Perhaps I was, indeed, never made for the mortal world, ill-suited for good or wholesomeness, as fit for grim adventure as my skeletal hand.

I let my Bluebeard drift, and did not try to wake him. If this was that of which he dreamed, then who would deny him? Certainly not me. Certainly not now. Let him dream. And if I could not call him back to life, then at least he would go to death knowing he was beloved.

It was bare minutes before Sparrow asked me acerbically, "Are you going to sit there all day like a love-lorn girl, or are you going to dismount and take us to the book?"

I blinked back surprise. The toad had stopped in a clearing and when I slid from its back there was nothing here but pale, waving grass.

"Where is it?" I asked, carefully.

"Turn the key and we'll see if it still stands," she said impatiently.

I took out the silver key and turned it, and madness hit us hard as an axe blow. This was not my first time leaping between worlds, but the terrible feeling of being ripped apart and stitched back in a different way, tore through my mind and I was left reeling and sobbing, gibbering into my fist, one hand wrapped behind me to cling to what was left of my husband. I missed him. I feared for him. I was pressed beyond what one heart ought to suffer in this terrible lingering death of his.

I shook myself. I dare not let the madness break me.

The others recovered sooner. I knew because I could hear their voices as though through water and then, when I finally surfaced, they grew clear.

"Different, but still standing," Sparrow was saying. "I always told the Arrow that a few crenelated towers give a place a better martial look than those ridiculous bird's feet. At least his invisible mortals keep the place up nicely."

"Is that what he did with his winnings? Set them to gardening?" Grosbeak snickered. "I hadn't heard that. Waste of slaves, if you ask me."

"I don't even want to know what you'd do with mortal slaves, Grosbeak, invisible or not."

"You really don't. But we should hurry. If he finds us here he'll be furious, especially when he's keeping *her* here. Did you know he had a new captive?"

"When doesn't he? He's a serial monogamist. What happened to the last one?"

"Maybe she didn't fall in love by the time the last petal fell," Grosbeak snickered. "Don't ask me. I think it's a needlessly cruel game and I'm the one who *likes* needless cruelty. It was fun to watch the first five or six times but now it's too predictable. He should shake it up. Pick an older woman maybe. One with some experience with men who can see through his stories. That would make it harder."

"Well, he couldn't guarantee winning then," Sparrow replied. "Besides, few older women have cleavage so firm you could use it to hold the extra copies of your books. Where does he even find these mortals?"

"Could yours? When you had a body, I mean?" Grosbeak sounded speculative.

"Wouldn't you like to know."

"I do. It's why I'm asking."

I cleared my throat. "Discussions about lost bodies aside, I think we have a book to find."

"Sane again, grim mortal?" Grosbeak asked, a strange tone to his voice that sounded both mocking and ... was that actually concern behind his teasing?

A small brown bird circled us and then settled on my husband's shoulder and began to sing.

"As sane as I'll ever be when I'm dealing with you," I said as I surveyed the castle before us.

It was so large that I felt my heart sinking. Sheer walls rose to ridiculous heights topped by crenelated towers at various distances. I counted seven and more could be hidden by our limited perspective. Every inch of the place was disguised by tangled thorny vines and heavy red roses. Someone had taken care to trim wide swaths of tidy grass in every direction leading out from the castle. This lawn was dotted with topiaries clipped into couples dancing or kissing or engaging in other romantic pursuits ... and yet I did not fail to notice the sinister twist to the topiaries. Was I wrong or did that branch twist in such a way that it could be a supportive hand or it could be a dagger in his lover's back? Or how about that one where the two figures could be bathing in a river together — or he could be in the act of drowning her beneath the waves?

"This place makes my skin crawl," I said just as a woman stepped out from behind one of the topiaries wearing a scarlet cloak with a wide red hood and bearing a basket of long-stemmed red roses.

"You don't know the half of it," Sparrow muttered as I strode toward the woman. Perhaps she would know where the book was.

The roses woman was beautiful in the way of Bluebeard's other wives

— mortal, but one of those rare mortals of which no flaw could be found beyond their mere mortality.

"Why are all the mortals in the Wittenhame so lovely?" I asked.

"All? I rather think you're the exception to that," Grosbeak snickered while Sparrow spoke over him, "Physical beauty is the only way to disguise the stink of death you all carry. You embrace Death so tightly that you might as well be the specter himself come to call."

I flushed at her description but there had been none of that stink in my husband's memories of me. I could no more help being mortal than they could help being bodiless heads. We could none of us help what we were.

The other woman smiled blankly at me when I finally reached speaking distance.

"Good lady," I addressed her, "I beg you, please lend me your help."

"The castle is not open to visitors," she told me with glassy eyes. She was maybe eighteen or nineteen years old, just the right age to be married in my world.

"Can you help me find a book written by Lord Antlerdale?" I asked politely.

"The castle is not open to visitors." Was she looking over my shoulder? I glanced behind me but no one else was there, just me, my dead husband, and my two bodiless advisors. Nothing to see here.

"They're always like this," Grosbeak said dismissively. "Just ignore her and go into the castle."

"That has the taste of terrible rudeness," I objected, but I walked past her to where the castle doors were wide open. "And how will I enter? Do I not need the permission of the owner to cross? I thought that was true for Wittenhame homes."

"For most homes," Grosbeak chuckled, "But Anterdale's pride opens him up to invasion. He's opened this home to his invisible mortal slaves to come and go and to this beauty to slip in and out and that makes it open to us, too. A terrible flaw and one I expect he did not consider. Look you at the runes carved into the threshold. They bar the feet of other Wittenbrand but allow the feet of mortals."

"And we have no feet," Sparrow growled in agreement.

The gravel of the path crunched behind me and I looked over my shoulder to find the girl following me. At least the Hounds of Heaven had not made it to this place yet, but I dare not linger. They could not be far behind.

"Is this your home?" I asked her, but I did not let up my speed, increasing it instead. The girl kept pace with me.

"It is the home of my beloved beast," she said with a swooning look in her eyes — eyes that still did not meet mine.

"There's a beast in there?" I hissed to Grosbeak. "We should have brought a weapon."

"You can't wield one," Grosbeak said dismissively. "Do you remember the joust? What a disaster. Never in my days have I seen so disgraceful a showing."

"I believe I won," I said coolly but it was not him I was watching in fascination, it was Sparrow who was sputtering through a suppressed laugh.

"You have been in the Wittenhame too long, Izolda," she said once she had control of herself. "How would you describe Lord Antlerdale?"

"Aloof. A detached Lord of the Wittenhame who seems happy to work in the background of things," I said as we passed over his threshold. This place was massive. How would we find one book within it quickly enough? I wanted to shake the Bramble King — figuratively, I'd seen what happened to those who *actually* defied him. Why couldn't he have told us the key instead of giving us this riddle?

Sparrow was still snickering as we stepped into a grand entrance. "Lord Antlerdale has antlers, wife of the Arrow. Though that is no uncommon thing in the Wittenhame, I believe he would qualify as a "beast" to a true mortal."

The ceiling of the entrance was so high that it rivaled the ceiling in Bluebeard's home. Gilded chandeliers hung in clusters of five or six at various heights, all fitted with hundreds of unlit candles. Tall, narrow stained glass windows lit the room and the light was reflected and amplified by the walls which were made entirely of polished golden mirrors in gilded frames. The floor was a golden-toned wood polished and waxed until it reflected as brightly as they did.

One wall bore a larger stained glass window that clearly featured Antlerdale wearing a crown of red roses and dancing with a faceless woman in a flowing red dress. The place certainly had a theme. And like the others in the Wittenhame, the Lord of Antlerdale seemed glad to lean into it.

I caught a glimpse of myself in one of the golden mirrors, my braid wild and undone, little locks of hair escaping everywhere to wave around my face. There was a streak of blood across my jaw and chin and a smear of fresh earth on my forehead. The grisly lantern pole I held bore two twisted faces, tangled hair failing to disguise the ragged necks where once a body could be found, and on my back was slung a fully grown man who wore a short beard and dead, dead, pale-as-death skin. The mirror had dressed me in a high-necked jacket with a stiff collar and frogging that made me look like a conquering general — if conquering generals wore tightly fitted leather trousers and thigh-high buckled boots.

I was surprised to realize that I looked more Wittenbrand than mortal — more like a conquering power than the wisp of a girl who had been stolen away as an unwilling bride. I looked as though I was here to do the stealing. Good. That was exactly what I was here to do.

Behind me, in the reflection, the mortal girl drew down her hood to reveal her perfect heart-shaped face and rosebud mouth.

"The castle is not open to visitors," she said, her huge dreamy eyes still not meeting mine.

"I'm not a visitor," I said coldly. "I'm the wife of Lord Riverbarrow, the Arrow, and I will have what I have come for and then I will leave, and I think it might be best if we fetch you back to the mortal world when I go."

"We don't have time to save strays," Sparrow reminded me.

"The castle is not open to visitors," the girl said, and what in the world was wrong with her eyes? Now that she was close I could have sworn there was a red hourglass in her pupils.

I shook my head at the incongruity of it.

"The Library is down the hall to the left," Grosbeak said, helpfully. "I was here once for the most delightful party. Antlerdale made visible an entire staff of mortals to serve dinner and between courses he made them fight to the death. The food was less than spectacular, but by the end of the night you could barely dance, the floor was so slippery."

Nausea rolled over me. Would I never stop being horrified by the things Grosbeak had done in life?

"I was at that party," Sparrow remarked casually. "I lost two hundred gold crowns when my mortal fell in the last duel. Slipped on someone's intestines. Lost his footing. Terrible luck."

"You bet on that fight?" I asked, horror in my voice.

"He looked strong," she said defensively. "And his reflexes made him nearly Wittenbrand fast. If Antlerdale hadn't made them fight that round blindfolded, he'd never have made such a disaster of it. He was a prince among mortals I think. Very pretty."

"Ptolemoore," Grosbeak added. "A prince of Ptolemoore. Beautiful for a mortal. A war was launched for his twin sister's hand. I remember the drama of it. Antlerdale wanted the girl for himself but her brother took her place as a sacrifice to him, and Antlerdale put him in the entertainment as punishment for the insolence. Terrible waste, I thought."

"Mmm," Sparrow agreed.

I clenched my jaw, sealing my lips in censure.

"And to think I've felt pity for both of you being nothing more than severed heads now," I said, chastising them. "You deserve no pity at all when you have none for others."

"They were only mortals," Grosbeak said, snickering. "Hardly worth noticing until Antlerdale immortalized them in death."

"The same could be said of you," I snapped. "For your life was nothing before my husband animated your severed head."

I glanced over my shoulder to see how the mortal woman following us was taking all this, but she smiled calmly as she followed me, her eyes never meeting mine, as if hearing that her master made people die in grisly ways was of no more consequence than discussing the weather.

The hall to the library was lined from the polished floor to the high ceiling with skulls. They ranged from skulls so tiny they could only belong to a mouse to one the size of a fishing vessel that could easily have been the skull of a dragon. In that skull, the needle-like teeth were as long as my legs and laid out in three rows and the nose and brow bore bony ridges. I shuddered at the human skulls that accompanied them. Quite possibly one belonged to that poor twin prince of Ptolemoore.

The skulls were bleached and pale, mounted on walls of glittering gold, but I found I could not meet their empty eyes because when I did, it felt as if they were moving to watch me, as if they were as alive as Grosbeak or Sparrow. I had been too long in the Wittenhame to soothe myself with the idea that such a thing was impossible. Instead, the further down the long hall that I went, the more I was sure that it wasn't only possible, it was certain.

"Do these skulls speak?" I asked calmly.

"Not that I've heard," Sparrow said. "But they sing. One night,

Antlerdale wrote his own arrangement for their choir. A strange piece that. It involved a great deal of rattling and crashing. I did not find it particularly harmonious."

"He should stick to the written word," Grosbeak agreed. "It's not fair to be terrible at two forms of art at once."

"Not fair to the audience," Sparrow sniffed.

I glanced over my shoulder at my unconscious husband. I did not like bringing him to this terrible place when he was so vulnerable. I kept feeling a prickling in the skin of my nape, as though something terrible was about to happen to him. But what choice did I have? I must follow the clue or give up and I would not surrender for anything less than death itself.

We reached the towering doors of the library and I was grateful to have something else to focus on. I did not care for my friends' grisly stories. They felt entirely too real in this Wittentale of a place.

If the library was anything to judge by, Antlerdale adored books.

The doors to it were heavy wood set with stained glass that depicted roses climbing through the panes as if they were living things rather than fanciful glass creations.

Those doors were open already, standing as high as five of me tall. But I barely glanced at them. My attention was entirely absorbed in what was beyond them — at the swollen library ten of me tall, set with enormous shelves around its circular perimeter, winding ladders and stairs, and stacks of books so mountainous one could never hope to catalog them all, much less read them. As I watched, books took flight — sometimes solitary, sometimes in flocks — fluttering across the library and arranging themselves as they pleased, as if they were caged birds rather than tomes.

And there in the center, in pride of place, was a pedestal. On it, under glass, was a single red rose floating in the air with only one petal left hanging from its sorry stem. Under the rose, heaped in dead petals, was a bound red leather book with its golden title emblazoned across the cover.

Mist and Memories: A Memoir of Lord Antlerdale

I began to smile. We'd found it. That wasn't so bad.

But my smile was cut off when a door at the other end of the library was flung open so hard that the stained glass shattered and rained down and a voice boomed out, "Who in the fires of hell are you?"

Chapter Five

"I'M the wife of the Arrow," I said coolly, gesturing to the man himself who was passed out against my shoulder. He woke enough to murmur something.

"Tantalizing creature," Bluebeard whispered his breath tickling my neck. I shivered but dared not linger on his sweet epigraph.

Antlerdale paused in the entrance to his own library, gaze flicking from me to the girl trailing me, to the heads on my pole. I had considered antler racks like his to be unwieldy and strange on the heads of bucks. On the head of a man, they seemed like a terrible curse, and maybe they were. One of these curses or geases everyone in the Wittenhame seemed to have, like an annoying skin condition shared by villagers in the same glen. If the antlers were a curse, it was half broken. Or perhaps doubled. Was it more of a curse to have half an antler crown?

I froze. Wait. That had been his bet, hadn't it? His northern estate and one antler if he lost in the game of Crowns. I felt a chill of cold rush through me at the memory of what my husband had bid. His immortality.

If Antlerdale had lost his antler when Coppertomb won the game and claimed the crown of the Bramble King, then hadn't my husband lost his immortality with it?

It seemed a silly thing to be upset about. After all, he was half-dead and strapped to my back, but I found I was still shaken by the idea that the bids had been paid and collected.

"Antlerdale, Antlerdale lost him a crown," Grosbeak chortled. "Antlerdale, Antlerdale on his way down."

Antlerdale glared at Grosbeak. The crown of antlers only seemed to enhance the width of his shoulders and the fierce beauty of his face as he strode into the room, fury in his eyes.

"Another man's wife has no claim on my library. And her pets have no excuse to mock me within my own walls."

"And a lord of the Wittenhame should not bring a mortal woman to his home," I said, gesturing to the woman behind me. When I caught a glimpse of her, though, my stomach flipped and I felt a little ill. Her gaze was locked on Antlerdale, a look of such admiration in her eyes that I thought she might be forgetting to breathe.

"She's here of her own volition," Antlerdale said, a twisting smile curving the cruel set of his mouth. "And you're a hypocritical little creature to mention it, don't you think? Are you not a mortal standing where you have no right to stand, and speaking to those too high for you to address, and perhaps even ... loving those no mortal ought dare to love?"

His eyebrow rose at that and my cheeks flared hot. This was different. Different and not different at all and the comparison was humiliating. But it wasn't practical to be embarrassed about bare facts. Facts were cold and hard and did not change and I would not make them different if I had the choice. There was no point in letting my emotions run wild in doubting my choices.

"Is this love, then?" Sparrow asked acidly. "I'm glad I've never partaken of it. It agrees with none of you. You should all see a herb witch and have it purged."

"Talk of love aside," I said in my most courtly fashion. I'd better get on his good side and quickly. "I had heard you wrote a book of memoirs and I had hoped for a glimpse of it."

He barked a laugh, circling me slowly as if he thought I were some kind of threat. Was that because I was standing beside his mortal prize and the glass dome over the rose and book? He could just cross the room to us, and yet he rounded me, looking for an opening. I turned my body to stay facing him as he moved. I had my own talisman to protect. One who was muttering into my ear unintelligibly, his lips occasionally grazing my flesh in drowsy kisses.

"My memoirs are very popular and found in every home. There was no need to come to the source."

"Ah, but I am told that the original is unparalleled."

"Death walks among us. The Hounds of Heaven hunt, and you are here to read about my life?" His cynical snort mocked me.

"You are here, too," I reminded him.

"To retrieve my prize," he said calmly and then turned to the mortal girl. "Why did you let a stranger into our home?"

I edged toward the rose and book while he was distracted.

"Antlerdale, Antlerdale, half man, half beast," Grosbeak murmured, seeming to be enjoying himself enormously. "Antlerdale, Antlerdale, beg for release."

"The castle is closed to visitors," the other mortal girl said to Antlerdale, a tremble in her lower lip. Was she in love with him? She sounded afraid. Was I as pathetic as she looked right now? It made me frown in humiliation.

"Yes, that's what I told you," Antlerdale said in a low voice just as my hand hovered over the glass. "And what do I do when you break one of my rules?"

My gaze snapped back to him. I wouldn't be having this.

"Try to harm her and I'll take her back to the mortal world," I said coolly. "I have the power to —"

My words cut off as a fist crashed across my face, catching my cheekbone and making me stumble back.

"Hit her back! Quickly now!" Grosbeak shouted.

"To your left!" Sparrow agreed, but before I could comprehend that it had been Antlerdale's mortal love who hit me, she was already on me again, trying to swing for my face. I grabbed her wrist with one of mine.

I'm a thin slip of a girl but I've been carrying a human head around for ages now and that builds muscle. I caught her fist easily.

"If you took her back, you'd kill her, didn't you see the Wittenmark in her eye?" Antlerdale said easily, as if he were enjoying watching us struggle. He lounged against a bookshelf, his eyes darkening in a way that made me enormously uncomfortable. "It's the hourglass. In the eye?"

"I see it," I gritted out as I wrenched her wrist, forcing her to turn, and shoving it up her back. Wow. If I only ever had to fight people my own size I might actually resort to physical violence more often. It was effective.

"All the same, I do tire of her." Antlerdale said, lifting the glass dome at the same moment that I said, "Pardon?"

He flicked the last petal off of the rose and with a hissing sound like sand in an hourglass the woman in my grip turned to dust and drifted to the floor.

I sneezed.

That had been a woman. A flesh and blood woman who had been in love with Antlerdale and he'd ended her life with a flick of his finger like she was a beetle.

"Problem solved," Antlerdale said.

"I guess she wasn't properly in love with you," Grosbeak snickered.

"Oh, she most certainly was," Antlerdale said easily. "But it was me who had to fall in love with her before the last petal fell, and honestly, I never do. I think the game is rigged against me."

"That's what I was telling Sparrow," Grosbeak said as if they weren't discussing the deaths of mortal women brought here to play a sinister game they could never win. "I think you should switch up who you take."

"Should I?" Antlerdale asked, eyes fixed on Grosbeak. "What sort of mortal would you recommend? I've taken the most delectable ones, and yet they never seem to tempt me to lose myself."

He was so engrossed in their conversation that he didn't see me move.

I shoved the lantern pole at him, ignoring the startled cries of its passengers. Antlerdale caught it by reflex, his expression startled. I grabbed the book, flipping quickly through the pages.

Chapter ten, paragraph thirteen.

I flipped like mad to find it. Running a finger down as I counted.

Chapter ten, paragraph thirteen.

I distantly heard the crash and Antlerdale cursing. Distantly heard Grosbeak's loud complaints.

Ten. Thirteen.

The moment I had it, I read it aloud. Maybe if it didn't stick in my brain before Antlerdale ripped it away, then Grosbeak or Sparrow might remember.

"I spoke to the Bramble King and he put a geas on me which seems a cruel demand on a vassal. I will not mention the particulars here," I read aloud.

That was it. The whole paragraph. Frustrated, I ground my teeth.

"Izolda! Izolda?" Grosbeak called. "My view is very poor from here and it's all your fault."

I looked over at him dully and to my surprise, I found Antlerdale frozen and my friends face-first on the ground. Feeling guilty, I snatched up the pole again.

"I find myself impressed," Grosbeak said as I lifted him again and he caught sight of Antlerdale.

"The Bramble King really must have set a geas on him and you've triggered it," Sparrow agreed, but at the words "Bramble King" Antlerdale shook himself and then spoke slowly, clearly, as if the words he said were of utmost importance.

"Sixteen locks with sixteen keys,
From grip of death, vict'ry seize,
Silent brides of silent lord,
Unravel back Time's cord,
Bought by blood and claimed by oath,
Only one holds bitter troth,
One hand living, one hand dead,
She finds the place where hope has fled
Now let her choose what comes last,
Freedom now or holding fast."

And as the last words escaped his mouth something in his eyes turned back on. Released from the geas, he charged at me, his bright, feral gaze locked on mine, teeth in a harsh rictus.

I stumbled backward as his snarl echoed through his body as if this one theft of his will for a few seconds offended him to the very bones, never mind the years and lives and hearts he'd stolen from mortal girls along the way.

The book fell from my hands, tumbling into the glass dome that had guarded both it and rose before I removed them from the pedestal. Dome and book crashed to the ground with a loud crunch as Antlerdale's foot came down on the glass.

"Your mortal life is mine now, child of dust," he said, mouth twisting. "But since you're in my home, let's have a little fun first. I've done some truly villainous deeds within the walls of this castle. I wager a pretty little thing like you comes with an imagination." His smile was terrifyingly lascivious. "Let's play a game. I call it 'Guess the Villainy.' We go to each room of the castle. If you can accurately pinpoint the cruelty I inflicted there, you will be spared experiencing the same, but miss your guess and I'll enact that memory upon your flesh, and drag you by the ear to the next room and the next until you're nothing but a tattered rag that my invisible servants must dispose of in the waste pile. Deal?"

"Grosbeak," my husband's whisper in my ear barely registered and I did not know if it were a plea to my bodiless friend or a command to me.

I cowered back from Antlerdale, a step, two steps, fumbling for my belt knife while I held the two heads angled away from me as if they could save me from his plans to torture me to death. They hovered over the broken glass as I slid back a third step, hands trembling, heart in my throat.

I couldn't outrun the Wittenbrand. I was not fool enough to think I could. And I couldn't outfight him. But I hadn't forgotten the key. Maybe a leap between worlds would be fast enough. I fumbled for it in my neckline.

"Just a little to the right, Izolda," Grosbeak hissed, and he did not sound afraid, not even as Antlerdale backhanded Sparrow, sending her crashing into Grosbeak with a cry, which in turn tumbled him to the right just as he'd asked me to place him.

Elegantly, as if he'd practiced the move a dozen times, he dove with the momentum, and caught the empty rose stem — still hovering there over the pedestal — in his mouth, chomped down hard on it, and sucked it into his mouth with a thick, black tongue.

"No!" Antlerdale shouted, swiveling from me to Grosbeak, hand outstretched, mouth twisting in agony. He froze in midair.

I leapt backward just in time to pull my two advisors out of harm's way as the great Wittenbrand crashed, his heavy shoulders and chest toppling the pillar. He curled in on himself, twitching and shuddering as Grosbeak chewed noisily. And I watched in horror as his ageless face and immaculate body suddenly aged, passing through middle age, and then old age, and then into something ancient and shriveled and not at all human. With a last scream of anguish, he exploded into a burst of ashes.

I gasped.

"I think I could do with fewer people dissolving into the air," I said firmly, trying to get a grip on my sawing breath and jellified knees.

Grosbeak belched loudly and then made a considering face. "Tastes like … misery."

"I would have thought he'd taste like roses," Sparrow commented, unruffled by the violence and magic swirling all around her.

"No, it's definitely misery. I've tasted it before."

"What does misery taste like?" I asked, but I didn't get a response. A loud howling filled the air, reverberating the library with such force that books fell from the shelves in a rain of pages and then a great head stuck its nose through the door, snuffling.

Chapter Six

"SHHHH," Grosbeak murmured. "Shhhh."

I slid slowly backward through the other door, hoping the Hound did not enter the library before I had disappeared out the other side. I misliked being hunted like prey. Terror aside, it was slowing me, keeping me from running directly toward my goals. With trembling hands, I fumbled for the key around my neck, ready to flee into the half-world between the Wittenhame and the mortal world.

"I wouldn't," Sparrow whispered. "You don't have finesse with that. You might miss the inbetween and land us in the mortal world and who knows what might happen then. The Arrow might not have enough magic left to carry you out. Hide, instead."

The Hound snuffled again and snorted. My heart skipped a beat, freezing within my chest. Don't lose your head, Izolda. Don't.

Sparrow made a good point. Whatever was going to save my Bluebeard wouldn't be found in the lands of my people — or at least I didn't think so.

"Wives," Bluebeard murmured in my ear, following the same train of thought I was, or at least, I thought he was. "Wives, my mad folly."

I fumbled in my dress for the other key — the little golden one Bluebeard had given me as wedding present. I turned it in the air just as the dog leapt into the room, landing on Antlerdale's ashes, barking madly with two heads while the third sniffed the air.

I leapt, too, straight into the open door of the Room of Wives, turning the key desperately in the lock behind me. The rip in the air began to close, but the Hound was fast, leaping for the gap, mouths open and slathering. One jaw managed a bite inside the door, snapping shut inches from Grosbeak's face.

Grosbeak screamed and Sparrow cursed as I stumbled backward and the door shut on the Hound, closing him off from us, and leaving us alone with a pile of cackling dead advisors and a ring of sleeping wives looking on.

"Well," I said. "That could have gone better."

"Could it, though?" Sparrow asked. "From where I'm sitting, it went the very best way it possibly could. Grosbeak rather valiantly saved your life and you left with the poem. She repeated it as if to help me remember. And as she spoke the words, I looked around the room at the occupants waiting for us.

"Sixteen locks with sixteen keys."

There they were, fifteen dead wives ... and me. Sixteen keys. But where were the locks they fit into? Hadn't Vireo called me a key once? And hadn't Bluebeard called me his last wife long before he ever fell in love with me? Did he know about this poem? This prophecy or riddle or whatever it was? Had he known it before the Bramble King locked it inside Antlerdale's head to be revealed when the right phrase was read to him?

"From grip of death, vict'ry seize."

I felt cold at that line and I licked my lips because it was exactly, precisely what I wanted.

I have not yet lost, Bluebeard whispered in my mind, suddenly. Surprised, I turned to him but his eyes were closed, his lips forming little almost-kisses when they touched my shoulder like a newborn baby dreaming. *I have won but not won. Victorious but still fighting.*

"What could he mean," I ask, "If he says he's won but not won?"

"Don't ask me," Grosbeak sniffed. "I only live in this world."

"Silent brides of silent lord," Sparrow went on.

And that had been his one demand of me — that we remain in silence, him in the day and me in the night. So small a thing. And yet, if it were part of the key to return him to me, if he had known all along ... I shivered.

"Unravel back Time's cord," Sparrow whispered. She was really getting into this now.

I had no idea what that line meant.

"Bought by blood and claimed by oath,
Only one holds bitter troth,
One hand living, one hand dead,"

Clearly, this was me. Unless there was someone else wandering around with a dead hand.

She finds the place where hope has fled
Now let her choose what comes last,
Freedom now or holding fast."

Well, that seemed simple enough. There would be a choice eventually and anyone with sense would choose freedom. No one wanted to be locked up, enslaved, or tied to a failing cause.

But these things were never so simple.

"I need a moment," I said a little breathlessly. "A chance to catch up to all my thoughts."

"And to solve this riddle," Sparrow said dryly. "In case you've forgotten that the world is ending."

But I hadn't forgotten. I carried her and Grosbeak to where I could set them down to face the other heads piled by the entrance.

"Converse among yourselves," I said. "After all, that's why you're all here. To talk together and find us answers."

"I like the part about one hand living and one dead," one of the heads said. "Perhaps she has a hand in midwifery and another in undertaking."

"Or perhaps one of her hands is skeletal," I suggested, lifting mine and wiggling my fingers. "Do better than that."

"You can't leave us here," Grosbeak protested.

"I can for now." I was already striding toward the other end of the room.

"But we'll miss the romantic part where you two are alone!"

"Yes. Alone is the key to that," I agreed and then I was hustling my husband to the far end of the room and easing myself behind the hourglass of garnets. There were so many in the bottom bulb now that it really was effective cover.

I sat carefully on the ground, making sure both of Bluebeard's legs were facing the right way and then — with great care — I untied the cloth binding us together and gently eased him to the ground, keeping my bare back pressed to his chest until I could replace it with a palm instead, and lie down facing him.

We couldn't stay here long. Things happened very quickly in the Wittenhame. But we needed this rest, if only for a moment. I had not slept in a long time, and Bluebeard seemed to recover more of his faculties when he had been resting.

Husband, can you hear me? I asked him with my mind. *Remember you may not speak to me in the day, only with your mind.*

Fire of my eyes, his words were strong in my mind, though his eyes remained closed.

Bluebeard, I sighed with my mind as a ghost of a smile raised the corners of his lips.

Your name for me thrills me yet.

It's not your true name, which I remind you I have the right to as your wife, I teased him. I should be talking to him about where to go and what to do. *Can you help me know what to do next? Where do I go to find this rib in the earth?*

But he was still hung up on the request for his name.

What shall you call me? Call *me victor, for I have triumphed.*

It would not seem so, husband, I said tightly with my mind. *It would seem, instead, that we hover on the verge of ultimate failure. If I lose touch with you, then you will die forever and likely, I will die with you.*

As will all those who depend on me, he agreed, his eyes opening then, and his cat's pupils widening slightly as they beheld me. *And yet, I have indeed prevailed. It just is not yet apparent to all who observe, and we must see you fulfill your task to realize it.*

I thought that when you won you would fix everything — the lives of the wives you took, the heads on your wall, Riverbarrow. You told me a story about the Divine Sovereign and how the word was set into his chest. Do you remember it? I must find the site where they extracted that rib.

You and you alone, light of my eyes, make my heart glad and my chest swell with pride. He seemed to be drifting again.

Now is not the time to wax poetic, I told him, but my hands had begun to move on their own at his words, they skimmed along his chest and up his neck, cupping his face. *I need direction on how to get there and what I must bring with me.*

I must walk when we go from here. Our hands can be bound together, but I must keep to my feet for this next part. It will take all my energy. I fear I may be incoherent. Do not forget that this heart of mine, absent though it is, belongs to you.

Then let me carry you, I pled. Things were hard enough without making them harder.

It cannot be.

At least tell me where to go. Please.

That also cannot be, for I must remain silent to you in this as well as in truth.

A hint then, a clue. Anything.

The blood of nations. His eyes flickered open, locked on my face as if he was drinking in life just by looking at me. He reached out, but his hand fell between us, unable to go farther.

The blood of the nations? What is that?

I had not wagered that I would love. He sounded like he was drifting again. *I sought a true bride and married her in our way and I knew this would be best, but I did not wager for these tangles around my heart. I can explain them if I must by speaking of your love of your people and your monstrous way of looking at all things in light of their utility, but I fear my precious bride that words cannot contain the whole of it for I love you in a way that mocks the love of all others, dwarfs their empty promises of commitment and hollows the storehouses of affection they claim to possess, for I love you with a fullness, a depth, a circumference that is too great for mortal mind to comprehend.*

I wasn't going to get a clear answer. He'd fallen off into dreams and rambling.

Then I won't try to comprehend it, I returned dryly. *I'll simply get to work.*

One last boon.

I felt my heart melt at his plea. *Whatever you wish, my Lord of the Wittenhame.*

A single kiss.

I leaned forward so that now my body was flush with his, my heart beating where his ruined chest held no match, and I pressed my lips to his and then parted them, deepening our kiss, and he hummed with pleasure in my mouth and roared with it in my mind. My husband. My precious, dying husband. I did not dare rest much longer. I had to get up and find what he needed so we could bring him back to fullness.

Our kiss took the last of his strength and his eyes fluttered shut, and his breathing grew long and even.

Well, then. I supposed I had a task to perform immediately.

I helped him stumble to his feet and lean on me before binding both of our left wrists together. That way I could still hold the lantern pole in one hand while the other arm supported him. He swayed in my support, but he did not fall, and he did not speak again or open his eyes.

I missed my Bluebeard's wild competence. His flashes of genius and surprise. I swallowed down a wave of hopelessness. I did not dare give in to that. I'd read many Whittentales in my day and how many times had I marveled, awestruck by the bravery of the mortals in the tales who were doomed to perform great tasks for love and home? And we'd all claimed that we, too, would act with such courage if our time came. So why did I now, when I found myself in one, seem so reluctant to rise to the challenge?

Stories are different when they are your life. They sting and press and the discomforts that seem small in a story loom great in life. It took all my courage to stride across the room and approach my bodiless advisors.

"If you were looking for the blood of nations, where would you go," I asked.

"If we're going to leave here, then you'd better disguise the Arrow," Sparrow warned me. "No one likes to see a defeated enemy still walking around."

"Enemy?" I asked aghast.

"He was Coppertomb's enemy," she said and if she still had shoulders I would have guessed that she would shrug. "And now Coppertomb *is* the Wittenhame because he is its king. So yes, the Arrow is their enemy."

I guided my shuffling husband to one of his wives who wore a thick scarlet cloak, loosened the tie around her shoulders, and brought it down one-handed to drape over his shoulders and head. I tied it in place, though the cloak only went to his knees.

"Happy?" I huffed.

"You will be," Sparrow said with a side-long glance.

"And can someone tell me where to find the blood of nations now?"

"Do not taunt us with such simple queries, Izolda," Grosbeak drawled.

"Where else but the place you left your mortal nephew? The field of the last battle? For if there the nations battle, then there their blood will be spilled."

And it seemed so obvious when he said it that I gathered up his pole and pulled out the key and before he or Sparrow could even protest, I was opening the door back out into the Wittenhame.

Chapter Seven

THE WITTENHAME HAD a way of making the everyday seem impossible and the impossible seem everyday. Just when you believed you understood the rules by which it operated it swiveled and spun out new rules and laws. Perhaps there had been no Law of Greeting before Bluebeard needed to acquire sixteen wives in a hurry — well, a Wittenbrand hurry which can be five years or five hundred.

For the first time, a hand reached through the still-widening door, fisted into my hair, and ripped me through the door.

I gasped. I had thought that impossible, but the hand had me now and it drew me inexorably out through the door and into the open.

I was yanked, not into Antlerdale's library, but — to my utter surprise — into the heart of the Wittenhame where the ice and mushroom palace had stood.

I gazed in horror at the dripping icon. It had been reduced already by at least half, water pouring down the sides and flooding out from it to saturate the ground and create standing pools. And where there had once been creatures — human, Wittenbrand, and otherwise, frozen into the glass-like surface, there was now a stinking heap of corpses jutting out from the ice.

Before I could even grasp what I was seeing, an iron fist forced me to my knees, and I lost my grip on the lantern pole as it pressed me downward into a bow. I did *not* lose my grip on Bluebeard's hand, though he fell heavily to his knees beside me into the tainted water at our feet that now soaked through our clothing. His cloaked head leaned heavily against me and I was glad he had not fallen face-first.

I looked up to the hand holding my hair, stomach lurching in horror as around me little scraps of midnight floated down, speckled with bright white lights the size of berries.

Coppertomb stood above me, gloved hand tangled in my hair, a naked sword bared in the other hand, and for a heartbeat, my bowels froze and I trembled, shaking like a leaf in the wind, certain he was about to dash my head from my body and there would be no friendly mortal to carry me around on a lantern pole as Grosbeak had. My story would end right here, on my knees before my enemy.

But no, Coppertomb gripped his sword and shouted, "To me, Wittenhame! Feast your eyes on the prowess of your king!"

He was not looking at me at all, but rather past me as a Hound of Heaven bore down upon him.

A growling snap split the air and then a howl, and Coppertomb released my hair as spittle flicked across my face. I flinched, stumbling backward onto my seat, desperately gripping Bluebeard's hand as I tried to think fast enough.

From the place where I'd dropped the lantern pole, I heard a bubbling sound of submerged heads trying to shout. I couldn't leave them there.

I clawed myself back to my feet, dragging Bluebeard up with me and snatching up my lantern pole. I could live a thousand years and never want to see one of those again. But even as I found my feet, one of the massive heads bore down on me, snapping its mighty jaws.

This was not a time to panic. I braced my feet, twisted my hold on the lantern pole, and then deftly thrust it forward at the same time the Hound opened his mouth wide to swallow me down. I wedged the pole in his gaping mouth, dancing backward. He howled, shaking that head in a very doggy attempt to loosen the pole stuck in the sensitive parts of his mouth.

I leapt backward, drawing my shuffling husband with me, panting in relief, as the swinging heads on the pole screamed at me.

"Have you no care for the dead?" Sparrow hissed while Grosbeak yowled, "A curse on you, Izolda! A curse and four demi-curses! May your toenails blacken and curl for putting me in this thing's jaws!"

I spun, searching for a new weapon, sure I'd be attacked again, but at that moment there was a mighty howl from one of the heads and then it fell, crashing in front of me, as large as a horse, the flesh of its neck severed and blood fountaining out. To say this was the most grisly thing I'd ever seen would be an understatement and I was holding proof in my arms that I was not squeamish.

I barely had time to gasp before a second head joined it and then the third, and this time I leapt forward, set a boot against the creature's black lips, and yanked my wedged lantern pole free.

Huffing and gasping for breath, I balanced it, wrapped an arm around my husband, and surveyed the damage.

Coppertomb stood on the body of the dead Hound, his sword stuck into the corpse like a walking stick and his other hand on his hip as if he were a gentleman surveying his estate rather than a king who had just slain a monster. On his head was the rib crown and on his face was a cruel smile.

"Don't move, Arrow's wife. I have business with you," he said, pointing at me, and then he hopped down from the beast, strode forward, and tangled his fist back into my hair, bloody though it was.

"A manful victory, Bramble King!" Grosbeak congratulated him.

"Is that rose I see around your lips?" Coppertomb asked, a baleful look in his eyes.

Grosbeak licked his lips as if in confirmation. "I may be dead, but I can still bring down the mighty."

"I will not speak to the dead, revenant," Coppertomb said grimly. "If life has no more business with you, then neither do I."

Coppertomb began to move then, driving me before him with his fist as he strode through a crowd of gaping Wittenbrand, his steps proud and firm and his head held high. He was not a tall man, I realized. He was barely taller than me, but he seemed a span higher with the way he carried himself.

I clutched my ruined husband to me, tucked in his scarlet cloak, too concentrated on not losing him or the lantern pole to do anything about the pain of Coppertomb's twisting gloved hand in my hair.

I swallowed down a burst of fear as he marched me forward. "What would you have of me?"

"I will get to that."

The scraps of midnight still rained down over us and between the scraps, Wittenbrand ran and surged, forming shouting groups and chanting hordes. A ragged cheer went up as Coppertomb passed through them. And he flicked the viscous blood from his sword blade in salute as the Wittenbrand crowded around him, calling out their congratulations.

It appeared that they had already been busy here before their king slew the Hound. Banners were lashed to fresh poles and thrust into the sky, mounts were being chivvied into place, armor donned, and weapons displayed.

"Our great king has slain for us a Hound of Heaven! Whosoever doth choose to ride for the Bramble King to dispatch the rest must form a party and swear the oath!" A voice bellowed out and when I looked toward the crier, I saw a Wittenbrand man with long red hair and a cloak woven of nettles standing astride a pyramid made from the bodies of living rats. They did not stand still, but rather roiled and bubbled, churning beneath him even as he spoke to the Wittenbrand gathering at the place that had once been a festival location.

"What manner of madness is this?" I whispered, tucking the lantern pole under one arm so I could reach out to snatch up one of the midnight scraps floating down from the sky. They coated the ground and the shoulders and heads of those around me, and the bright glowing berry clung to this scrap.

"The sky is falling. And I'd say those are stars," Grosbeak said. "Taste one, Izolda, and tell us if they're stars."

"How in the world would tasting one tell you?" I asked.

"If it tastes like a star, then you'll know it's a star," Sparrow said impatiently. "How else will you know if the sky is falling?"

"And the world is dissolving as snow," Grosbeak agreed.

I was reluctant to put something glowing like an ember in my mouth. I offered it to Grosbeak who gobbled it up and then hissed, steam screaming out of his ears.

"Yes," he panted, face turning cherry red. "It is a star. Tastes just like one."

"Would that have happened to me if I'd eaten it?" I asked in horror.

"Probably worse," Sparrow said dryly. "Because it just fell through his neck. It would have passed into your digestive system."

"I think I'll avoid your food recommendations," I said sourly as Coppertomb dragged me onward. He paid our interaction no mind, but I noticed he refused to focus his eyes anywhere that the small stars twinkled as if their presence bothered him.

She shivers and my skin alights, butterfly tissue, burning bright, Bluebeard muttered in my mind. It worried me that he'd moved to verse. He sounded delirious.

A tiny blue bird landed on his cloaked head and began to trill.

Can you help me find a fast way to flee your enemy? I whispered to him with my mind, glancing at his face beside me. He frowned but did not reply.

"Why is the Wittenhame suddenly falling to pieces?" I hissed and Sparrow and Grossbeak met each other's gaze, eyes wide, lips tightly closed as if they didn't want to tell me.

"Were I you, I'd keep such observations to myself," Grosbeak murmured eventually.

"Why?" I pressed. "Is it not obvious to everyone?"

He made a hmm sound and then Coppertomb leaned in close, "I, also, would not make observations on the state of the Wittenhame were I you, mortal woman. The Wittenhame is mine now as I am her king. Blood of my blood, flesh of my flesh."

I paused.

"Then speak to my riddle, Bramble King," I said boldly. "Was not the Wittenhame whole and merry, fat and flourishing under the former Bramble King."

"It began to fade as he did. Everyone could sense it," Grosbeak replied hurriedly, as if trying to head me off. "Why think you he sought a successor?"

But Coppertomb said nothing, merely setting his jaw and forcing me forward. We were coming toward where the ruins of the ice castle formed a platform of sorts that was ringed with dark-garbed Wittenbrand I assumed were his guards. They were mounted on large black lizards with blunt noses and glittering eyes.

"Speak further to my riddle, Bramble King," I pressed. "Are you not hale as a young warrior and strong as a buck in season? Are you not healthy as a prize bull and more clever besides?"

He stopped, suddenly, turning me to look in his face and his black eyes held a look of death and I remembered, in that moment, that among his kind he was very young and that young men have easily bruised pride.

"You flatter me," he murmured.

"And yet, I speak only the truth," I said as my severed head advisors gasped and then pinned their lips tightly together as if afraid he would punish them for what I said.

"What are you saying?" he asked in a low voice just for me, and his face drew very close to mine.

"Victor but not yet won," I murmured but I did not mean the man in front of me, because if the Wittenhame echoed the life of its ruler and Coppertomb was hale and hearty, what did it say that the sky was falling and the laws of the place dissolving? Could it be that he was not the ruler of this place at all?

Could it be that another ruled? One who faded as I clung to his hand.

"Keep your poison words in your swollen mouth, daughter of dust," he hissed, and then he dragged me up on the platform surrounded by his lizard-riding guards and I swallowed down a burst of horror as something squished under my foot.

Don't look down, Izolda. Don't look down.

"I do love the pomp you've managed, Bramble King," Grosbeak said in a honeyed way that made me sneer. He was ever the bootlick.

Coppertomb ignored him, but he tilted his chin up as an announcement was made.

"Gather before your King!" the crier called at the same moment and there was the sound of blaring horns, that were half-trumpet and half-scream, and then the rat pyramid dissolved, and the crier fell from the sky, and there was another ragged cheer as they pressed in toward the platform. Bare bone woven into breastplate stood side by side with bronze scale and boiled leather painted to look like a creature of flame. A spirit of festivity surrounded the martial crowd.

"In a moment, I will address my people," Coppertomb said, leaning over now to look me in the eye. "But first I will deal with you. Right now, before them, so they may witness how those who defy me are humbled. You have stuck in my craw as your pole stuck in the mouth of the Hound and I will have you out one way or another."

He paused and then his hand moved lightning fast and he yanked the silver key from around my neck, snapping the chain and pocketing it.

"No more leaping between worlds for you, mortal woman. None but a lord or lady of the Wittenhame is granted this key, and none but a lord or lady is fit to use it. Two days I grant you." And now his eyes skimmed the scarlet cloak covering my husband's huddled form for the first time since he grabbed hold of me. "Two days to raise your dead, or bury him, for I will not have revenants walking this plane. A geas I place on you now."

My skin tingled as if I could already feel the magic and I shivered with the cold touch of it. But I would not beg for mercy. I would not ask for leniency. I knew Coppertomb too well to think he'd grant me either.

"Strike a deal with Death. Raise your dead. Or, in two days' time, your hands will bury him under the power of my geas and you will present yourself to me here as my bride for my Coronation Ball."

"Tell me this," I whispered, holding his gaze with mine. "The Wittenhame is thick with women so lovely they could break your heart in twain. Why do so many of you then find the need to steal an ugly mortal as your wife?"

Coppertomb's gaze flicked to my barely conscious husband. "He takes nothing without purpose and treasures nothing without value. If he found you desirable as his bride, then so will I. If he claimed your heart, then I will claim it doubly. If he laid possession to your flesh, then I will mark it as my own."

"I think you have a kingdom to rule," I countered. I did not like how he made my skin crawl or how certain he sounded that he could take whatever he wanted.

Coppertomb watched me, considering. "I will not marry. Nor will I be given in marriage. But you will come here in wedding clothes and surrender yourself to me and all my appetites, and I will see the heart I gave the barrow broken in twain and shattered forever."

He leaned forward, menace in his eye, and said. "Two days," before turning his back to me and addressing the growing crowd.

"Subjects!" Coppertomb called out. "Denizens of the Wittenhame!"

It was exactly the factual precision I expected from him. And yet, watching him address the Wittenhame, I felt almost as if he were falling apart, too. His eyes were too empty. His gestures overly dramatic. He was a parody of himself.

"The Hounds of Heaven have been called. Death walks among us! The sky falls to the earth and the earth dissolves beneath the fires of heaven!"

There was a cheer. Practically everything in the Wittenhame resulted in a cheer, even the announcement that the world was crumbling.

"What do we do now?" Grosbeak whispered. "Two days is not long enough!"

Fear crept into my bones. How powerful was this geas? Would it truly force me to bury my still living husband under the ground? I felt something tighten within me but I did not know if it was the magic, or merely fear, gripping my heart.

"Our time now has come! We ride against the Hounds of Heaven in the Great Hunt! Boons will be granted to the party that succeeds! Geases placed and the tax of a finger levied on all who fail!"

A finger is too great a tax. Perhaps my husband was more lucid than I thought. *But he would know, for he had to forfeit his.*

Husband, I gasped in relief in my mind. But I couldn't help glancing at Coppertomb's hand caught in a single glove. Did one of the fingers look stiff? Immobile? Like the finger of the glove might be stuffed with wool? I shook my head. It did not matter.

Can you free me from this geas? I must flee Coppertomb.

Patience, wife of mine, Bluebeard whispered in my mind.

There was a great cheer and the Wittenbrand began to chant, "Coppertomb! Coppertomb!"

Hold your patience.

Coppertomb turned and smiled his wicked twist of a smile and in his smile, I felt the barb of the geas on me. "Two days, little mortal. You'd better run."

With the suddenness of lightning, a murder of ravens rose up from around the platform in a roar of flapping wings so loud that they drowned out everything else. They rose over Coppertomb, buffeting him, the rearing mounts, and the startled Wittenbrand as they went. A pale unicorn reared, screaming horsily while a double-headed panther swore and snapped, batting a paw at the black mass. They cawed and flapped, obscuring faces, and figures, and voices, and then all at once they swirled around us.

Stand your ground.

I planted my feet, braced myself, ready to be bowled over by the surging avian bodies … and was lifted suddenly, into the air in a flurry of squawks and a rain of feathers.

Chapter Eight

"WELL, THAT WAS TERRIBLY INFORMATIVE," Sparrow said, considering, as we rose into the shredded sky on the shifting backs of the ravens. "Two days, is it?"

Bluebeard reached out and clung to me like a small child clutching a parent in sleep and I leaned into the softness of his embrace, sad because he was not warm and could not guide me. He had carried me far and fast in this Wittenhame, and now soon I must carry him again with my slow mortal feet. He had rescued me again and again, and now I must find a way to rescue him, and I only had two nights in which to do it.

"I believe my husband is the true Bramble King," I said quietly to myself, my thoughts turning inward. Coppertomb was missing the finger he'd bet. He wasn't in a woven cage … unless it was woven of something I could not see. Disaster, perhaps?

I prodded at the thought and finally spoke in my mind, *Are you the true king of this land, husband of mine?*

I was surprised when he answered. *Did I not gift my heart to the barrow? Am I not a corpse in your arms?*

He had indeed, though Coppertomb had claimed the victory.

Words and claims are powerful geases. And I have set all of my claims on you, heart of my own heart.

I was warmed by that. He had claimed me again and again and I was claiming him, but that aside, he might have given his heart to the barrow, and yet, the Wittenhame was collapsing around us as if it were tied to the man slowly ebbing out in my arms. I drew him in close to rest his head better on my shoulder.

I shifted on the backs of the ravens, feeling their feathery forms bump and lift, fall away and lift again, as they distributed my weight over their small bodies, providing just enough lift to keep me from tumbling to the ground. That I accepted this without balking showed how deeply the Wittenhame had crept into my bones.

"And based on what Coppertomb said," I continued. "I have barely two days to draw back his life."

And if I did not, what would happen? Would this world and my husband with it be gone forever? There was no place left for me in the mortal world. If there was no place here, either, then I was adrift.

"And what? You think that you, a mortal, can wrest the Wittenhame from the grip of Coppertomb, restore life to a dead man, and then dismiss the Hounds of Heaven and Death himself from our midst?" Sparrow asked wryly.

"She's done odder things before," Grosbeak mused.

"Name them."

"Well, she chose to take you along for this journey," he sniped. "That takes more intestinal fortitude than dismissing Death, I'd say. Surely, you know you're a horror to behold. Your pretty face frozen in the rictus of death and your once fine locks bedraggled."

Sparrow sniffed dismissively.

"I need to work this out," I muttered to myself as Bluebeard slumped further into my arms, pressing his cheek to mine as he shifted so that his chest was to my back again. "The blood of nations, the rib. It's all one big puzzle."

I tapped my lip in thought.

I keep my heart in your chest now, Bluebeard murmured, as though trying to help, but his thoughts were drifting again. *When I was a boy in Riverbarrow, I would fold tiny birchbark boats for the small people and set them to sail. I once folded one hundred in a single day. Can you build me a boat of birchbark for the river of death, Izolda, my heart?*

I am hoping it will not come to that, I said wryly. I shivered. It was cold up here in the winds.

Or perhaps, I will build one for you, and when the world washes away we will float in it together.

Yes, us and a pair of severed heads, what a terribly romantic prospect.

You should speak to Death, he whispered in my mind, seeming to be fading again. *He is not bound as I am. He could speak to you more plainly.*

Husband?

His mind drifted away and he was gone.

I sighed.

"Is it just me, or is this place getting more confusing as it falls apart?" I asked as the ravens bore us further up. Oddly, a warm breeze met us there, easing the cold from my bones.

I could see between the ravens' backs to the ground below as Coppertomb's subjects formed hunting parties, some hundreds of people thick, but others with as few as four or five people, and began to disperse across the darkened terrain, searching for the Hounds of Heaven.

Sparrow coughed and then swung to look at me.

"Do you truly think your husband is the Bramble King?" She asked me and to my surprise, her tone was reverent.

"I see no other answer to why your world is falling apart," I said plainly.

"Perhaps Coppertomb is merely an epically bad king," Grosbeak countered. "We've had bad kings in the past. Remember the Blood Rains, Sparrow?"

"They were before my time," she said, but her expression was thoughtful.

"It rained blood for three years when the Bramble King was wounded in a joust. A terrible time. Everything was red and slick. I hated it. And then there was the Plague of Frogs. Frogs everywhere. You could barely sleep for them hopping all over you. That was when the Mad Bramble was Lord of the Wittenhame. Is it all that surprising that the world is disintegrating under Coppertomb?"

"This is worse than frogs," I said as I watched one of the Hounds rush into sight beneath us. I wished I could cling to the ravens holding us up and beg them to keep us in the air. If we fell now, we would be torn to pieces.

"Aren't you supposed to have inherited Marshyellow?" Grosbeak asked. "Could you not command them?"

"How would I go about that?" I asked. It would be convenient to have someone, anyone, to command right now.

Instead, I clung to my husband as beneath us, the Hound fell upon one of the hunting parties, savaging its members and flinging them in every direction to break on the rocks and trees, as a dog savages its favorite fetching stick. My belly churned with horror and I barely managed to swallow down my bile.

Grosbeak seemed utterly unaffected by the screams and wails below as he launched into a lecture."Traditionally to claim a place as prince in the Wittenhame, there's a seven-day trial of combat and wit followed by five days of feasting. Or, if you are named directly by your predecessor, then just the feasting. At the end of the five days, if the feast was enjoyed, your people come and bow before you, you eat a handful of earth, and it's done. You're sealed to the land and the land to you."

"I don't have five days."

"Then I suppose you don't have Marshyellow."

I shrugged. "I don't have the hand anymore. Marshyellow was tied to the hand, not to me."

There was certainly no time for things like that right now. I was far more occupied with trying not to be ill as I watched immortal beings torn asunder beneath us. That could have been me if Coppertomb had not neatly severed the three heads of the one he'd destroyed.

"We mortals think you are immortal," I breathed, "and yet never have I seen such death as in the Wittenhame."

"We enjoy ourselves more," Grosbeak agreed. "Not everyone can handle our level of passion and pleasure."

"I don't think it's that."

"Perhaps it's the jokes then. I think they go over your head."

"Should I be trying to make the ravens take us somewhere?" I asked, searching for any distraction from the horror below.

"Make them!" Grosbeak hooted. "The arrogance of the mortal wife to think she can harness the birds. They came for their lord, the Arrow. They'll not leave until he dismisses them."

I swallowed. That might be a while. Or it might be immediately. Bluebeard was drifting and fading too much to be conscious of where he was and what he was doing.

"If we only have two days then we must be clever in our next move. I am done with being tossed about on waves made by others. No more fleeing from Heaven's Hounds or angry Lords and Ladies of the Wittenhame," I said firmly. "We can't afford to waste any more time."

"Yes, no more slow kisses when you think you can't be seen behind the hourglass," Sparrow agreed dryly.

Grosbeak laughed. "No more flirting with Coppertomb and getting geases placed on you."

"You can hardly fault *me* for the actions of a lunatic," I said stiffly.

Grosbeak snickered. "Don't play coy maiden with me, Izolda. You know how this land works."

I swallowed. I did know. And that was why my heart was racing. Two days was not enough time. And our ravens were already fading in strength.

Can you ask your ravens to take us to Wittentree, beloved? I asked my husband with my mind.

In reply, he sent me a memory again. This time of him in a cloud of birds laughing and leaping with them. When he jumped, they jumped with him, carrying him down, borne on their wings. When he called, they came in a rush of song and then he sang with them and the sound of his singing shattered my heart.

I was still gasping when he sent me another image — but this was no memory. This time, he drew me with him, taking me by the hand and I was in the gown I wore when he married me and carrying my marriage sword and I looked twice as lovely and twice as terrible as I'd ever been in life.

I sighed as the image dissolved. If he'd caught my message, he was too delirious to respond. His mind, it seemed, strayed wide and far. I was touched that it seemed to swirl around me, drawing me into his dreams and memories as flawlessly as if I were really there. I wished I had the time to sit with him in these fancies, to see the world through his stained-glass view, to imagine with him what a future for us could look like if he were not mostly dead and I were not limited by mortal restraints.

"There's another one," Sparrow said tensely, and I ripped my attention back to what was happening below us.

A skirmish was unfolding across a bare, rocky hillside dotted with moss. Five Wittenbrand — mounted on what looked like over-sized mountain sheep — were circling a single Hound of Heaven, but though they charged with barb-tipped lances, they were no match for the Hound. As we watched, the Hound scooped up one attacker in his jaws— ignoring the lance that plunged into his eye and stuck there — and flung the screaming

Wittenbrand over the side of the hill where he fell and fell, splashing into a lake below.

"Is he dead?" I whispered.

"Hard to tell," Grosbeak said, invigorated by the display. "Look, Sparrow! It's Klopfen the Bold! He's circling for the flank. And is that Wittentree I see preparing a charge?"

"It is," Sparrow said tensely. "Something is odd about this. The Hound that Coppertomb fought was not so wild."

I opened my mouth to ask her to clarify but my stomach pitched forward as our flock of ravens suddenly began to descend, at first slowly, and then quicker and quicker, little caws of exhaustion escaping them as those holding us flew away, delivering us to the backs of others, and still others, and then fewer and fewer, until we landed on a clump of moss with nothing but a single floating feather still remaining of what had been our escort and a pitched battle playing out barely a half-dozen steps from where we'd been set on the rock.

Wittentree, Bluebeard murmured in my mind.

Yes, very good, I agreed but inside something was gibbering.

Chapter Nine

I FOUND MY FEET, gasping, Bluebeard still pressed to my back, an arm of his wrapped around my waist. His head pillowed on my shoulder. He pressed deliriously against me, his mouth making little kisses along my shoulder blade as his mind wheeled free, either quoting poetry or making it up on the spot.

A terror to the Wittenhame, one mortal girl by oath claimed, she careth not that they be lords or ladies famed, and so I draw my eyes to her and tuck her deep within my breast, why find me now my wandering heart when I have hers to make a nest?

If I had the time, I'd sit and record it and gaze into his strange, beloved eyes as he told it me, but we had been dropped just steps from a battle and that had me somewhat preoccupied.

I focused my eyes and tried to take in what was happening, bracing the lantern pole in front of me.

"If, in the cockles of your limited mind you have conceived of a plan to plant us in the jaws of one of those things again," Grosbeak snarled at me, "then I am compelled to remind you that not only am I your last living friend, but I also saved your life by macerating the rose that held Antlerdale's curse, taking the death of a prince of the Wittenhame upon myself on your behalf."

"Did you inherit Antlerdale, then?" I asked but I was only paying them half a mind.

I was counting. Four remaining warriors. One was Wittentree, one was a Wittenbrand warrior I did not know, though her fierce demeanor and multiple braids made her look like kin to Wittentree. The other two were very familiar to me. No longer dressed as mirror images, they were still Frost and Yarrow, the pair that once guarded Marshyellow and who I commanded to drown him in the sea. I had thought them dead with him, but I was wrong, it would seem.

"Only the living may inherit, though were I alive, I would make Antlerdale so strong that I could challenge the Bramble King himself."

"Your bragging does not benefit you," Sparrow huffed. "And you are not her only friend."

"Are you calling yourself my friend now, Sparrow," I said absently. "I had not thought you would stoop so low."

The Hound was not faring well against these five. It took a snapping leap at Wittentree, only for her relative to chop its hamstring with her double-headed axe. The dog let out something that sounded like both scream and whine before attempting to leap forward again, its hamstrung foot dragging behind it.

I edged backward, trying to keep an eye on my footing and the battle both at once.

Sweet torment close yet far away, her voice would still my longing. But it's her silence I must crave, or spoil all our hoping. Attend your ears and bend your lips and place on me a blessing, then tangle me in strings of love, hark to my song confessing.

Bluebeard, shhh, I begged him with my mind. He was distracting me too much. And who raved in verse, anyway?

The way my breath seemed to tumble at his soft, soft kisses and the knowing that as he slipped in and out of consciousness it was ever me on his mind, was just too much. I had a battle to keep out of and a talking head to verbally spar with and I couldn't do that when I could barely think — which was what his poems did to me.

Shhh, he agreed in my mind and I rolled my eyes. He was going to be the death of me, too.

"You will admit I am friend to you in action if not in heart," Sparrow said coolly.

"I will," I agreed, still watching the battle. I thought it best to remain out of it. I was no warrior, but as I watched, I wondered if these were allies working together, or enemies forced into partnership. They did not seem too concerned with the safety of one another.

"Also, you should take two steps back and one to the left. Right now, I would wager." Her voice was so clipped that I scrambled to do as she said, and we stepped out of the way of a sudden swing of one of the Hound's heads, neat as you please.

I panted a heavy breath. "Should I be fighting, too?"

"Spare us that!" Sparrow spat. "Leave it to those who are good at it."

"And there's Yarrow with a strike!" Grosbeak said happily. "Klopfen rounds to the flank again, and yes! Another heel chop! Excellent, excellent work!"

"Grosbeak's always enjoyed a good gladiator match," Sparrow said to me, as if confiding. "He served as the Bramble King's champion for a season of entertainment once. I did not care for his loose form or dramatics, but everyone said his costuming was the best."

"What is a gladiator match?" I asked as Wittentree dove under one of the snapping heads and deftly slit one of the Hound's throats while her kin — Klopfen? Ran up its back and hacked at the place where the spine met the shoulders.

"A fight to disfigurement between two competitors for the amusement of the crowd," Sparrow said.

"And how is that different from everyday life in the Wittenhame?"

"There are more attentive spectators," Grosbeak grinned. He was preening. "And we dress up."

"What did Grosbeak wear?" I asked as Frost and Yarrow rode circles around the flailing Hound, keeping it pinned. I wasn't worried now about the outcome of this battle. The Wittenbrand were winning easily and when they were finished, I would beg an audience with Wittentree. I simply had to be patient.

Patience, Bluebeard agreed.

"Why do you ask what he wore?" Sparrow seemed to be suppressing amusement.

"I wore the greatest costume the world has ever seen," Grosbeak said. "It fit me to perfection, flawless in every way, unblemished, unmarred, perfectly balanced, and colored."

I rolled my eyes but I was following the fight still, waiting to time my greeting until the last head fell. "Of course it was. Tell me, did you dress as a creature of the sea, or as a pouncing lion?"

And then, out of nowhere, one of the Hound's heads snapped, catching Wittentree in its jaws and shaking her savagely. I felt the air whoosh from my lungs as I froze, unable to do anything to stop it. Klopfen smashed her axe one final time, severing the spine, and the creature collapsed, a broken Wittentree still in one jaw. I could not seem to close my mouth or to swallow the horror of what I was seeing.

"I was entirely in my own skin, obviously," Grosbeak said. "No other costume could be so lovely."

"Pity you lost it, then," I quipped quietly, but horror was rushing through me. Wittentree could have helped. Wittentree could have told me where to go!

I scrambled forward over the rocks, rushing toward where she lay torn and bloody, still half pinned by the jaws of the mighty Hound. Klopfen collapsed, exhausted, on its neck, her breath heaving in her lungs. As I drew near to Wittentree, Frost and Yarrow continued to circle, as if they thought the threat was not yet passed. I hoped they were wrong. I hoped that this was safe, because safe or not I was going in.

I hurried forward, careful of my footing on the rocks. Before me, the Hound of Heaven stank of death and wet dog. Its heavy jowls were thick with bloody fur and when I edged by its paw — as large as a small cow — I trembled.

The Hound bled out across the stone and who would have thought one creature could have so much steaming blood in it? That was three of them I'd seen killed now. How many more could there be?

"Why do they call them Heaven's Hounds," I muttered, "when they seem like denizens of hell?"

"I thought you knew, mortal menace." Grosbeak snickered. "The Wittenhame *is* hell. Anything that comes here to rip us apart must be heaven-sent."

"Then I suppose I am an angel," I said.

Drift from heaven, fall to ground, make my breath catch, my heart pound.

You should have been a poet, husband. I say in my mind, with a sigh. *When they cut you, you bleed poetry.*

"An angel of death, perhaps," Grosbeak said, his voice thick with scorn. "Where you go, misery follows. Dismemberment, terror, and death are your vanguard, and a sickening sense of misery your rearguard."

"Always with the flattery," I murmured, but I did not mind. His verbal sparing kept me sharp as I eased myself down around the still twitching corpse of the massive Hound to where Wittentree was pinned.

The teeth of the Hound clamped firmly around her torso, impaling her three times across the waist and hip. The jaw was locked in death, pinning her in place. Blood swelled in blackening bubbles from around the teeth embedded in her. She drew in a pained breath and the blood bubbled more, seeming almost to boil.

"I find my body loathes this trap and pains me as consequence," she said, her breath rattling in her chest.

That was unsurprising.

She still had the beauty she'd bargained for from me and it softened her lips and cheeks, but could not soften the sharp knowing in her golden eye or the glassy blindness of the pearl one. Her face was so pale it nearly matched that iridescent orb, and blood leaked harsh and scarlet from her ears.

"I do not favor death by dog bite. It has little to recommend it."

I crouched down beside her and she held out a hand to me. I took it before I realized it was my hand she was offering me — my living, flesh hand.

"Bargain with me, now at the end," she said grimly.

"How is this the end?" I asked, taking the wiggling hand in my skeletal one. It felt so foreign that it was strange to think it had ever been mine. "Are you not Wittenbrand? Can you not heal from this as you heal from all else."

She snorted. "Your perspective is wrong. Look up over your shoulder."

I turned and looked behind me just in time to see Yarrow skewer Klopfen on the end of his lance. Her mouth formed a silent scream as Frost took her head with a single swipe of his razor-sharp sword. Oh. So they *were* enemies, then.

"Treachery," I hissed and Wittentree laughed.

"Of course. Dear Coppertomb does not bear rivals well. It was only a matter of time before he set his Hounds on us — literal and figurative. I find it only shocking that he acted before we could witness the final glory of his Coronation Ball. I predict it will be poorly attended."

"He betrayed you. He broke the rules of the game." I felt breathless as I stated the obvious. Behind me, Frost and Yarrow were very thoroughly ensuring that Klopfen was completely dead.

"It's nice to know I was worth a betrayal in the end. But I have matters to set right so listen now to me, mortal girl, before they come for us. A bargain I would make with you for that hand you hold in yours."

"I don't want it back," I said firmly.

"I think you do," she countered. "And I require a boon from you."

"What do you want?" I asked, but Yarrow and Frost were carefully sliding down the back of the Hound and circling toward us and I could feel them closing in.

"Rouranmoore," she gasped, reaching out her other hand and opening it so I could see her token pressed within her palm. "Take the token."

I took it and stashed it in my belt pouch. I did not have enough hands, not even — ha, ha — now that my living hand was returned to me. I put it in the belt pouch, too.

"I have given my heart to that place in a way I did not think possible for an immortal Wittenbrand. Almost, I understand your specter husband and his fool plan of marrying himself to the land. Almost."

I made a humming sound that I hoped would tell her to get to the point. Yarrow whispered in Frost's ear and they both grinned wickedly at us, as if savoring the moment before they struck. Did Wittentree know she had the power to stop them because she possessed my old hand? Or, at least, I thought she did. I must indeed bargain with her for the hand and fast.

"All the nations crumble — all but Pensmoore now, and I have considered why that may be and made some inquiries."

"All that in mere hours?" I asked dryly.

She waved a hand, "It's been longer in that mayfly world. I have come to know that you are one with the land of Pensmoore. Now, take on Rouranmoore, too, that she may thrive when I am past."

I cleared my throat. "You love Rouranmoore so well?"

"Make the bargain with me. Your original hand back in exchange for a tie between you and the mortal land of Rouranmoore. What you do for

Pensmoore you do for Rouranmoore. How you anchor one, you anchor the other."

"The hand I'll take, and I will give you as you wish, but you must give me one thing more," I said in a hurry as the circling pair drew in closer to us. Frost shook the blood from his blade as if preparing to take more and Yarrow tossed his lance aside and drew out two daggers. I must be quick. "I must know how to find the place from which the Sovereign's rib was mined."

"A fairy story. A tale for mortals." She coughed and blood bubbled up, red and bright, almost pink as it foamed at the corner of her lips.

"Give it to me anyway," I demanded. "I must find the place at once."

She gasped, barely able to get her words out. "A bargain is struck."

"A bargain is struck," I agreed and then I tapped my living hand in the belt pouch, about to use it to dismiss Frost and Yarrow but before my mouth had opened to order them back, something beside me shifted.

I glanced down to see that Wittentree had used her silver key to open a door to somewhere else — the mortal world? — and with a power I didn't expect, she grabbed my coat, yanked me forward, and threw me — from a flat back and using only her arms! — through the doorway. I barely held on to the lantern pole, grateful that Bluebeard was clutching me with his own strength as I tumbled through the door.

Her words were nearly swallowed up as madness struck me, bowling me over, and sweeping me away, but I caught the edges of them as I reached for the hand of my husband and clung to the pole that carried my two bodiless friends.

"Look to Death."

And then she was gone from my mind, shattered into fragments as I fought against the tug of madness and a harsh gibbering in my mind. My eyes rolled back in my head, sounds faded into hysterical shrieks, and I struggled against the tide of insanity to keep a grip on myself.

I am Izolda, I reminded myself. I am not insane. I am merely traveling between worlds.

And then I caught a glimpse of something, maybe something my mind conjured in the throes of madness, or maybe something real. It was hard to tell and either way, I did not like it, because the image I saw was of Wittentree dying, ripped to pieces by the teeth of Frost and Yarrow.

Chapter Ten

"NO!" I gasped as my mind emerged from the madness of the gate between worlds. "No, no, no!"

Had Wittentree thrown me into the mortal world? After years spent in that place, I felt as though I should be able to identify it at a glance, but I was indoors, which made it hard to tell. Or at least, I thought I was indoors. The high vault of the ceiling was dark, the walls carved in precise lines and angles. There were no furnishings in the room we were in except for a single dark-wood chair such as you might find in a banqueting hall. Though lamps had been lit on great stands around the room, they flickered slowly as if afraid of dancing too wildly, and made it difficult for my eyes to adjust enough to see what lined the walls. Something trickled in a divot along the center of the rocky floor. A drain, perhaps?

"I hate this place," Grosbeak complained.

"So do I," I gasped and then I turned around and vomited, barely missing Bluebeard's boots.

"See?" Grosbeak said triumphantly. "It even makes mortals ill to have to be here."

"It's over," I said piteously. "It's done. There's no hope for any of it now!"

Sparrow stared at me with a line between her eyes. "Is she always like this or has the way through broken her?"

"I like this pitiful Izolda," Grosbeak said, not seeming overly concerned. "I have heard rumors that mad mortals are almost as clever as the Wittenbrand. It might be an improvement."

"Or, she might give up and then I'll never get my body back," Sparrow said grimly. "Your attention, Izolda Savataz," she demanded. "Look at me and end this piteous moaning."

I snapped my mouth shut and looked at her.

"That's a beginning," she said firmly. "All is not lost."

"There's no way we can get to the coronation in time now," I gasped. "Too much time passes here! It could be years that we've been gone already."

"Get back where?" Sparrow asked curiously.

"Or ..." Grosbeak let the word hang in the air.

"Or only a few days," I admitted, "But I do not have a few days. I do not have even a few hours! And all this for the most cryptic and useless of answers."

"Well," Sparrow said. "Not entirely cryptic."

"I hopped once from the mortal world and when I returned to the Wittenhame, I was two days in the past," Grosbeak said easily. "I bought myself drinks in the *Hop and Tarry.* Talked for hours."

"How is that possible?" I gasped.

"I'm an excellent conversationalist."

"We're not in the mortal world, Izolda Savataz," Sparrow said grimly as my eyes adjusted to the light. "Tell me, what do you see in those alcoves?"

I took a step forward, and then another, and then I was walking toward the vaults cut into the wall with horror in my belly. On the shelf nearest me, was a collection of tiny bones stacked in tidy rows right up to the top of the shelf.

"Phalanges" was engraved on a bronze plate under them.

Someone had labeled the shelf beneath it "Prussian Blue" on another bronze plate, and that shelf was entirely full of paint chips that looked as if they had been meticulously removed from something.

The next bore the engraving "Poisons" and had a collection of bottles and jars of various shapes and sizes, arranged by size and place on the spectrum of colors.

I shivered. I was already afraid to meet whoever had made this vault. What kind of mind would take the world apart like this?

The next shelf was labeled "Hearts of my Enemies" and here there were, indeed, dried and preserved hearts ranging from one smaller than the last knuckle on my pinky to one the size of my head. They were arranged, again, by size and someone had neatly pinned a note with an inked date to each one.

I swallowed.

Another shelf was labeled "Small Ceremonial Daggers." The blades were no larger than my hand and as small as my fingernail. Small indeed. I did not bother availing myself of any of them. With both my hands occupied, a weapon would be of little use to me.

"What are you doing here?" a voice asked menacingly.

I jumped with a barely cut-off squeal, as a hand clamped on my shoulder and spun me around.

"As I was saying," Sparrow said dryly. "This is not the mortal world. This is Coppertomb's home."

And it was the master of the house I was facing eye-to-eye.

"I give you two days and you plan to spend them in my vault?" he asked me in a dry tone. One eyebrow rose and the low light made the golden dust on his cheekbones stand out brighter than it normally was.

"I thought you were hunting the Hounds of Heaven."

He waved a hand. "I have vassals for that. I find that you are growing to be more trouble than the worth of your prize."

"Will you put my heart on a shelf, then?" I asked him, boldly.

"It's rather less cruel than a shelf of animated heads, don't you think?" he asked me. "Isn't that what your beloved husband has? A shelf of his conquered enemies, still there to consult at will?"

How did he know that? His eyes sharpened as if he'd seen the confirmation in my eyes.

"Everywhere I go, there you are. In my way. In my business. Do you not yet see how it is you and you alone who has brought the Arrow of the Wittenhame to his knees and to his final end?" I risked a glance over my shoulder at Bluebeard. His eyes were shut, lips slightly parted, and squished against my shoulder. "His weakness for you left him open to my blow. And all your meanderings enmeshed him in the plots that sought his life. And now, when it is all over, you desecrate his corpse by dragging him ever onward."

Coppertomb clicked his tongue in censure.

"Then why don't you kill me?" I pressed. Because why hadn't he? He was always here accusing, thwarting, placing geases on me, but never directly acting. "Why don't you dry my heart for your shelf? Why don't you take my husband from me." He was silent, and my eyebrows rose of their own accord as I pressed. "He protects me yet, does he not? You cannot touch me with more than your accusations."

"That doesn't mean that I can't hurt you," he said, and he reached out and plucked Sparrow's head from my lantern pole. "Will you bury your husband and bow to me if I take from you your friends and advisors?"

"No," I whispered.

"Really?" He tilted his head to one side. "What if I threaten their after-lives? There's no returning from fire," he said, striding over to one of the bright lamp holders.

"There's no need for that!" Grosbeak said shrilly.

Sparrow, on the other hand, had her jaw set in a grim line.

"I thought you had a kingdom to rule," I said sharply. "Have you nothing better to employ you than taunting me?"

He raised a single brow. "Have you not seen how the sky falls? The rotting husk of your husband rots my reign. I must see him buried and his works burned to ash or risk watching the Wittenhame rot with him."

And then with a flick of his wrist, the lamp beside him flared up to bright flame and he tossed Sparrow's head within it like he was tossing a bean bag for a harvest game. Her scream echoed through his vault and then she hit the flame and went up like a dry field put to the torch.

A cry ripped from my lungs, too, and I stumbled forward, only to feel hands dragging me back. Bluebeard's eyes were still shut, his head still resting on my shoulder, but somehow, he restrained me as Coppertomb flicked imaginary lint off his clothing.

"A reminder that I am the Bramble King and I have told you to bury your dead. Do it now, or see more losses."

I couldn't tear my eyes away from the remains of Sparrow's flaming head. Sweat broke out on my brow and tears stung my eyes. I hadn't liked Sparrow much, but she was owed so much more than this.

Trembling, I turned to Coppertomb. I still had enough strength to spit in his direction.

"If you were truly the Bramble King, then you wouldn't need to keep reminding us of it."

"Ooooh ... direct hit!" Grosbeak crowed but Coppertomb strode forward two steps, tilted my chin up, met my eyes, and said coolly.

"Two days. There's a shovel in the corner. You can bury him here in my crypt if you must. You won't be going anywhere else. When I leave here, I will bar the entrance to you. Think on what I've said. I could spare you. I could return you to the mortal world when the coronation is complete, if only you do as I request. And my request is so very reasonable."

"I think that you make promises you have no power to keep and threats you have no ability to carry out," I said but even to my own ears, my voice was weak and terrified.

He snapped his fingers and left in a burst of smoke.

"Needless dramatics," I muttered.

"Coppertomb is a delight," Grosbeak purred. "He never misses an opportunity to puff and display. Puts a peacock to shame. And to think he was not even a lord in the last game and now he is Bramble King." He sighed happily. "The Wittenhame is the best place imaginable."

"Tell that to Sparrow," I said bitterly.

"Fortunately, I won't have to," Grosbeak said easily. "I no longer have a rival for your ear and affections, and I find that is exactly as I prefer it."

With a sigh, I made my way to the lamp, but there was no sign of Sparrow within the dancing flames. Not even the ashes or the dust of her passing. It was as if she never was at all. And I would be the same unless I could solve this last puzzle.

Chapter Eleven

THERE WAS ONLY one door to Coppertomb's vault and when I tried it, it was locked just as he'd promised me. I looked at every shelf, at the strange drain in the floor, at the items cataloged, and behind them, I even examined the plain chair. There was no way out.

"Trapped, trapped, trapped," Grosbeak said, laughing wildly, and then every so often he would murmur another "trapped!"

If Tanglecott was the fairy godmother in a Wittentale and Bluebeard was the tortured lord, and Antlerdale the monster-turned-lover, then Coppertomb was the witch who tricked children into ovens and gnawed on their bones. The careful linear way he'd laid things out and the horribly specific way he labeled them, made me feel like I was inside the mind of someone who did not see living organic things at all, but only parts held together by muscle as a model is held together by wire. I could see a mind like this taking us apart and putting us back together again and the idea of it rattled me.

I was searching a shelf of rib cages looking for a door behind them, when I noted they were sorted differently.

"Why catalog two sets of rib cages?" I murmured to Grosbeak. I needn't have spoken. The bronze plaques spelled it out.

"Human Rib Cages" one said and the other "Wittenbrand Rib Cages."

"Because they're different, but noting that won't help you out of your trap, trap, trap," he sang.

Different?

I looked from one to the other and then back. They looked much the same. I counted on the human side. Twenty true ribs and four floating ribs. That was normal. Even I, a lower noblewoman, had enough learning to know that.

I turned to the Wittenbrand rib cage and paused. Oh. Sixteen true ribs and eight floating ribs. How odd. But something about it bothered me and kept on bothering me as we searched.

"There's no way out. You might as well bury him and see what happens," Grosbeak reminded me.

"I thought you were my ally now," I told him.

"Your ally. Not his."

With a huff, I set him on the chair and then crossed to the other end of the vault and eased my stumbling husband down so he could lay with his head pillowed in my lap. Maybe if he could recover enough energy, he could focus and help me figure this out. I had considered myself a clever puzzle solver, but I was stumped. I needed a hint. And his hint about the blood of nations was not enough.

Why was everything blood for these people? It was too much.

Blood and phalanges, hearts and ribs.

Ribs.

Sixteen ribs.

I froze.

We had to go to the place where the rib had been mined, right? And the poem was related to that. Sixteen locks and sixteen keys. Sixteen ribs. Sixteen wives.

My husband, can you hear my mind? I whispered to Bluebeard as I stroked his hair. He nestled in closer so that his face was pillowed against my belly.

Mmmm.

You cannot tell me what to do.

Mmmm.

But perhaps you can listen and tell me if I am right.

My beloved Izolda. I wasn't sure if that was encouragement to go on, or a sigh of despair. *Spirit of my spirit, heart of my own heart, fall what may.*

I licked my lips and drew little circles on his back and shoulders, flooded with an overwhelming sense of affection for him as I whispered with my mind.

It's all connected, isn't it? I asked him. *The Legend of the Sovereign and the world existing within his breast, the rib the people stole and the sixteen ribs of the Wittenbrand ... and your wives. Sixteen, right? Fifteen for the unmarred ribs and one more for the stolen rib. That's why all the rhymes and prophecies keep coming back to the one wife, the one of sixteen, the one rib. You're repairing the sovereign somehow. Is he also the Bramble King?*

My clever, sweet love, my one true wife, he murmured in his mind as his free hand found my waist and clung to me.

I held him close, my mind racing, my heart all in tangles.

What will happen to us? I asked him plaintively. *Are we to be sacrifices to the earth?*

Never. It was always my plan that my fifteen wives be restored to their time and place.

Fifteen ribs from all different lands. I paused. *The blood of nations, am I right? These wives of yours are the blood of nations.*

I wanted to ask "but what about me?" But I was too afraid to think the words. Because what if I was to be the sacrifice? What if I were to somehow take the place of that final rib?

The poem had left a choice to the last wife. A choice of freedom or ... something else. Maybe I was supposed to choose that something else.

Worse yet, what if he meant to dial back time and return *me* to my original time and place? Would I marry Lord Danske and care for horses? Would I be happy in that simpler, firmer, happier life? Or would part of me always remember this wild nightmare that had become a dream, that had become my home?

I was just like my father. I loved wild things. I loved them too much. I loved them so much I was spending my life away for glimmers of them.

"I choose you," I whispered to Bluebeard. "If there's a choice, then you are my choice."

I was your stolen true bride, I whisper in his mind. *But I mean all the vows. I find I cannot be Izolda without her Bluebeard. I cannot thrive while you languish. I cannot be hale while you are apart from me. Does it diminish me that I am only whole when you hold my heart? Then I will be diminished. Does it pauper me to give my whole heart to you, dead though you are? Then make me a pauper, spend every waver of my fool heart. For I am ever yours and I refuse any choice that does not have you at the end of it.*

He shuddered, an intense, powerful shudder, and then with an act that seemed to take all his strength and will, with jaw clenched and teeth gritted, he pulled himself up onto his knees, and his wild cat's eyes opened and his gaze met mine as he murmured in my mind.

Never have I loved until I loved you. I have sought you through lands and worlds, looked for you through the rush of time, bought you with my blood, delivered you with my pain, and I will put my mark on you, and claim you forever. There is no time to come where I am not Izolda's, or where she is not mine, and I say it by the power of my true name.

And then he whispered his name in my mind and I gasped at the gift of such an intimacy. I would tell it to no other. I would keep it forever as my most precious secret held tight to my heart. And in the moment of my gasp, he leaned forward, and his soft lips fluttered against mine for just a moment.

Hold fast, my clever wife. This is your battle to be braved.

And then he slumped once more to my lap, falling like a tree cut by an axe, and left me sighing and hungry for more as I broke his fall.

Well then.

There was only one thing to do. I must bring all his wives out and together we must find the source of the rib, unlock the sixteen locks, and free my Bluebeard from death.

Chapter Twelve

I URGED my beloved back onto his feet before I could change my mind. His dark eyes shuttered closed, but his muscles flexed as I drew him up. I twined my bone hand through his hair, as I positioned him against my back again.

Stay strong, my husband, I whispered to him in my mind. *I will not abandon you. Do not abandon me.*

I opened the door to the Room of Wives before I could talk myself out of it — Coppertomb could not snatch this key. I felt certain that was true. Had he the ability to take it, he would have stripped me of it, too.

I stepped inside even as I heard Grosbeak calling out, "You'd better not be going where I think you are! You'd better not be leaving me here!"

With a sigh, I went back for him. "If you insist on coming along, you'd best be helpful."

He sounded appalled. "Name for me, oh mortal soul, whence I have been anything but helpful."

I marched into the Room of Wives and past the heads I left in a circle, ignoring them and their curses and snarls. Some of them had rolled over and I wondered if that was intentional or if I had somehow damaged them.

Grosbeak stuck out a tongue at one of them and I shook my head. I should have left him.

"Cursed mortal, return us to our last resting place!" the one with the silver coronet said. "You have no right to own us or make us your slaves."

"I have the right of marriage," I disagreed. I held my head high with determination. It would take more than the objections of a few corpses to stop me now.

"Do not think you can treat us thusly and yet still our council keep!" another cried.

"Then to whom else would you pour all your acid words?" I shot back. I was used to talking heads spouting lies. I carried one around with me daily.

I thought I might need them, and despite their barbed words, I thought that they might need me, too. Bluebeard kept them for a reason. If the wives were the blood of mortal nations, could these advisors be the blood of the Wittenbrand, too? I did not know, but even if I hadn't yet worked out the reason for keeping them, that didn't mean there wasn't one.

There were exactly thirty heads there by my count. That was two for every wife but me. I had two, but only one of mine yet survived.

With my jaw gritted determinedly, I made my way to the hourglass at the end of the room and reached inside for a fist of garnets. It was hard to take them with my bone hand, though, and in the end, I was forced to pluck them one by one, and hold them in my jacket pocket. Thirty. Two for each wife. If we didn't succeed in two days, we wouldn't succeed at all. Strange to think that I held a month of my life in my pocket.

Strange, but not worth wasting time to consider. I marched to the first of Bluebeard's wives. Margaretta.

Because we had worked as partners before, I chose her first. I wanted someone who wasn't crazy and who probably wouldn't try to kill me. I needed her to be on my side before the others awoke.

"Oh! Oh, dear! It's you!" she squeaked when the two garnets were in her mouth. "So. you survived!"

"I'm good at that. To date, it's my only specialty," I replied. "I need your help."

"We're not opening another door, are we?" she asked me primly. "Oh dear!" She suddenly seemed to notice our mutual husband draped across my back. His scarlet hood was down and his beautiful face easy to see, though his eyes were closed in restless sleep. "That's not ... ? Oh dear. It's the very Lord of the Wittenhame who stole me away as his bride!"

"Yes, thank you for recounting that," I said dryly.

"Well, what is he doing here?"

"He needs our help," I said simply and I let her look for a long moment into my eyes before she grudgingly screwed up her face into a determined scrunch.

"I don't think the others will like it much. Their journals were not happy ones. You're waking them, right? I see you have more garnets between your fingers."

"I was hoping you could help me explain this to them," I told her, licking my lips nervously. "I'm not sure if you've noticed, but I'm not really a people person. Most of the people I knew in life are dead now. And my only remaining friend is hideous."

I shook Grosbeak's pole.

"Excuse me? Hideous? That is not how you speak to one you call friend."

"See?" I said.

"All of my friends are dead now, too," Margaretta said sadly.

"And yet you remain enormously likable," I said dryly. "Come, let's wake this next bride."

"I don't know about likable," Grosbeak groused. "Edible, perhaps. She's very edible looking."

The next bride was Tigraine. I stood well back. If she was going to slap someone in the face I wanted it to be Margaretta and not me. I'd already received my slap last time I woke a bride. But to my surprise, when Tigraine woke, her eyes snapped open but then quickly narrowed and she looked carefully around the room without so much as moving.

"Now that is the face of a mortal queen," Grosbeak said delightedly.

"Princess Tigraine," Margaretta began, a little breathless but Tigraine held up a single finger, still assessing until her eyes met mine and she nodded in understanding.

She pointed at me.

"You're the current bride."

"I prefer true bride," I said calmly.

"Apt." She tilted her head to one side. "I always wondered what manner of woman he might choose were he choosing simply for himself. I did not anticipate you."

I clenched my jaw. No one did. They saw only what they wanted to see. The exterior.

"Nor did I," Grosbeak confided. "I would have expected someone more like *you*."

"That's why you're dead," Tigraine said scathingly. "Clearly, you were not one of nature's thinkers."

I liked her already.

"Likely, you'll live to reassess that, mortal princess," Grosbeak said in a threatening voice.

"I rarely find the need to reassess," Tigraine said. "And yet, this true bride has finally done what I did not have the fortitude to try, and what I secretly hoped one of us would do."

"Kill her husband?" Margaretta asked wide-eyed.

But Tigraine was shaking her head. "She's waking us, isn't she? You're clearly a princess of Pensmoore, Princess …?"

"Margaretta?" Margaretta squeaked and then added a hurried, "Yes!"

"You're going to help her end this nonsense?" Tigraine pressed, her eyes locked on mine.

I nodded.

"Oh, yes!" Margaretta enthused.

"Who better to finish this than his wives? It's always women who have to clean up the messes, is it not?" Tigraine said, hopping down from her plinth. "Tell me, bride of Lord Riverbarrow …"

"Izolda," Grosbeak said. "Her name is Izolda Savataz of Pensmoore, though she also goes as the 'Mad Princess'."

Tigraine nodded gravely. "Tell me, Mad Princess. What would you have me do?"

"I want you to help me unlock the door to death."

She nodded grimly. "A worthy goal. I will ride with you."

"Great," Grosbeak said, rolling his eyes, "Now, let's repeat this nonsense another fourteen times, shall we?"

We woke the wives, one by one, explaining the need to keep the garnets in their mouths. We started with Coriannian, the bride who had first intimidated me with her majestic demeanor and powerful figure. She turned out to be incredibly meek, following Margaretta around like a very large lost puppy.

Ki'e'iren was the last — the bride with the snow-white hair and the thick golden belt. She watched me with suspicious eyes and she was not the only one who threw constant worried glances at Bluebeard where he was drooped on my shoulder.

"Is he really dead?" she asked me, eventually.

"Mostly," I said. "His spirit lingers."

"There is a wound in his side that is crusted and ugly," she said calmly. "He did not have that when last I saw him."

"He received that for me," I said with bright cheeks.

"What else did he receive for you?" she asked. "Has he lost his ability to restore us to our rightful places as he promised?"

"I ... don't know," I said and her lips thinned in censure. "But we will restore him and then he can fulfill all his promises."

"What promises has he made you?" she asked me. "Are you to be restored to your time and land?"

I swallowed, but I was saved from answering by the cackling of Grosbeak.

"You may well ask what promises she has received, for he has poured promises into her ear as an advisor pours honeyed wine for a king. He has strewn her path with promises as a maiden throws flowers before the bride. He has laid them like cobbles and woven them like reeds, built them up like stones in a wall and —"

"I rather think that is enough," I said grimly. "We hear your words, revenant."

But as if Grosbeak's words had provoked a memory in him, Bluebeard mumbled into my neck, "As long as rivers run and moon shines."

With a gasp, the brides drew back.

"Yes, it's somewhat unsettling to watch the dead speak," I told them grimly. "But he is not so dead that we cannot restore him. So, work with me. Join my cause. And then you will receive all he promised you."

"We weren't told we would have to do more than lend our patience and I find I have no depths in me which long to give," Ki'e'iren said, putting her hands on her hips, but to my surprise, Tigraine slapped her hard across the face.

Ki'e'iren froze, mouth open, eyes lit with inner fire.

"You aren't the only princess here, so stop acting like you are," Tigraine said, leaning in close to make her words more threatening. "Would you risk the futures of the fifteen of us for your own pettiness?"

"It is possible that I would," Ki'e'iren said, snapping her mouth shut and flexing her hand as if she would slap Tigraine back.

I felt as though I was back on my parent's holdings, keeping the mares from biting. I shook Grosbeak's pole between them.

"Nnnnrggh," he muttered.

"Enough, I beg you," I said before forcing my gaze to run over all the wives as I spoke. There was Givanna, the poet, and the lovely redhead I'd so admired, and Margaretta's hopeful face. "Think carefully on what you will do. I know not what perils may lie along the way or what will happen to your bodies, or chances of returning to your lives, if harm befalls you. But if we fail, you'll remain here, cold and untouched, insensible until time fades away or the magic unravels."

"How will you bring a man back from death?" Tigraine asked, making her way to my bodiless advisors. "And what will we do with these?"

"I thought we might take them with us," I said grimly. "Why should I be the only wife with a Wittenbrand advisor?"

"We do not wish to go anywhere," the head that looked like a mermaid spat.

"All the more reason to take you," Tigraine said, picking her up by the hair and inspecting her.

"Ewww, they're all dead!" Margaretta said, scrubbing her hands on her dress even though she hadn't touched any of them. "I don't like touching dead things."

"You say that now," Grosbeak purred. Was this him being charming? "But you'd sing another tune if you tried it."

"No," Margaretta said primly. "I do not think so."

"And can these advisors advise?" Ki'e'iren asked. "Do they know how to find this place where a rib is missing and broker a deal with Death?"

"If we knew, we would have mentioned it by now," the head with the crown said.

"Perhaps you can bargain with Death for the knowledge." Tigraine's eyes were on me as if watching to see what I might do. It was a practical suggestion, though I would have no idea how to go about doing it.

"He *does* walk among us now," Grosbeak said with a leer for Tigraine. "Why not try the princess's suggestion."

"You do not amuse me, revenant. Keep your charms to Margaretta," Tigraine circled the heads.

"Oh please, no!" Margaretta said, her hand clasping her own throat.

I cleared my throat. "Is there a way, advisors of my husband, to call Death to you? I cannot bargain with what is not here."

"The dead see him," one of the heads said in a bored tone.

"Can you see him, then? Dead as you are?"

"The *newly* dead," that head corrected.

"Or those dying," the head with crown agreed. "Not possibly dying, but dying in truth. The man who lingers long on a gut wound may indeed see Death. I've witnessed that myself. Or the woman bleeding out after childbirth may hear his footsteps, or the victim of a poison with no antidote may converse with him. All these might earn the chance to bargain with Death while still living."

"Well, I'm hardly going to kill someone just to draw Death near," I said wryly. "Perhaps there is another way?"

There were murmurs but they sounded discouraging and I looked from face to face. The head with the crown sniffed, and Margaretta crouched in front of her, staring, eyes wide.

"Back up, girl-child. I can see right up your skirts."

"Eee!" Margaretta skittered backward, kicking one of the heads in her haste. It, in turn, knocked over the next and the next, and it took me a moment of scrambling with the help of the wives to set them all straight again and calm down a frantic Margaretta.

"I think that maybe you should stay here with me," I told her grimly, but as she made her way to me, something pricked my side under the arm where I held Grosbeak.

I startled, heart racing. It felt as if a hot poker had been driven under my skin for just a moment, and now uncomfortable heat spread out from that spot like the fingers of a fire.

"What —?" I started to say and I turned to see Ki'e'iren holding one of those tiny pinprick daggers in one hand and a bottle in the other. I had been too distracted by Margaretta's antics to see that she had swiped them from the shelves of Coppertomb's home.

"Neverseed, isn't it?" she said, sniffing the bottle. "Smells like aniseed and lemon bore a love child together."

I swallowed. I wasn't sure if it was panic or the poison she'd stabbed me with, but my head was suddenly swimming. Everyone froze, silent, eyes wide.

"Fool," Grosbeak breathed.

"Doubly fool since all our fates ride with her," Tigraine said and it was her face — suddenly dead pale that made me panic more. She straightened slowly.

I was poisoned.

"It's a long-acting poison," Ki'e'iren said breezily. "She gave us two days. I'm giving her the same. If she's careful, and doesn't overexert herself, she might even make it to three days. Wouldn't that be nice?" Her smile was saccharine. "And she was the one who wanted to see Death. I've granted her wish, have I not?"

And as she gestured, I saw that she was right, for a pale figure on a pale horse was riding through the wall of Coppertomb's vault and straight toward me.

Chapter Thirteen

"BARGAIN WITH ME, DEATH," I said through lips made thick with fear as I walked through the open door and out of the Room of Wives into the Coppertomb's vault.

They were arguing behind me, but I dare not let that distract me, just as I dare not let fear control me. I had asked to bargain with death. I had received my wish. Later, I could dwell on the terrible consequences of this wish.

"I really wouldn't bargain with Death, Izolda," Grosbeak hissed. "You don't know what you're getting into. Other Wittenbrand might take a hand, or a few years of your life, or your free will, but Death always plays for keeps."

I planned to play for keeps. I would be a hypocrite if I thought he wasn't playing the same game.

"BARGAIN?" Death asked, the words sliding over his white slug-tongue. He sniffed the air as if he could smell something about me in it. And his words were strange in my mind, seeming to be both there and not there at the same time. Final, and yet ephemeral. "WITH ME THERE ARE NO BARGAINS."

A little shiver of fear ran up my spine. Death smelled like a grave and his very nearness turned my stomach.

"Good, no bargains," Grosbeak said hastily. "No need to catch the eye of Death."

Terror made his voice quiver. It made my blood sing with possibility. Finally, I was talking with someone who might get me nearer to what I needed. Finally.

"Are you not of the Wittenhame then?" I asked. Sweat was beginning to form on my brow. "Do you no longer take joy in bedevilment, or set your heart on the trickery and trappings of the great ones?"

He paused and his long filmy hair swirled around him like the head of a blown dandelion. He looked around the room with pearlescent eyes and then back to me and he seemed transfixed by something over my shoulder — my husband, I thought.

"DEATH BOWS TO NO MAN."

"No one is asking you to bow."

He backed up a step as if threatened.

"DEATH HAS BUT ONE SOVEREIGN."

My heart was beating in my ears. He was going to flee. I could feel it.

"No one is asking to rule you. I would only bargain with you, Lord of Death. "

A cold wind blew from him and he swayed with it, his horrific scent tangling through the breeze. I had to clench my jaw firmly to keep from gagging.

As he swayed, he rattled a little, and I realized his long white robe was sewn all over with tiny skulls like beads, and so were the reigns of his bone horse which stamped now, pawing Coppertomb's floor and casting its dead gaze to me as it flickered in and out of sight.

"WHAT DO YOU ASK OF ME, DYING MORTAL?"

"I would have my husband's life back," I said boldly. Best to ask for what I really wanted first.

"THAT I CANNOT GIVE YOU."

"Then I would that I could reach the place from which the first sovereign's rib was plucked and through the door into your realms, that I might go and retrieve him myself."

"YOU WILL COME TO ME WHETHER YOU BARGAIN OR NOT. THE DRAUGHT OF THE NEVERSEED STEALS YOUR LIFE A BREATH AT A TIME, AND THOUGH YOU TARRY, YOU WILL COME."

I shifted, swallowing uncomfortably. I did not have time right now to deal with the knowledge that I had been poisoned. And yet, a little butterfly of panic burst free each time I thought of it.

"I wish to enter your lands while still living."

"THE PRICE I WOULD ASK FOR SUCH IS SO MUCH MORE THAN YOU CAN BEAR."

"Name it."

"A PIECE OF YOUR FLESH GIVEN WILLINGLY. AND YOU WILL WALK THE PATH OF PRINCES. FAIL AT ANY POINT, AND THE BARGAIN IS STRUCK DOWN."

"What is the Path of Princes?" I asked, nervous now.

"Don't do it," Grosbeak whispered. "You can't succeed at that."

I heard feet behind me. The wives had not stayed put. They had followed me out into the vault.

"The Path of Princes is the way of the song," one of the heads said imperiously. "You know the one."

And then she began to sing and the chorus was taken up by the others.

Fly with the Arrow,
Dance with the Sword,
Give Your Heart to the Barrow,
Die with your Lord

And if ever you be broken,
And gasp on the ground,
Hold up your fine token,
And join with the sound.

Sing for your Sovereign,
Bow to your Dream,
Make Haste for the Fallen,
Rise in Esteem.

And if ever you be broken
And gasp on the ground,

The word may be spoken,
And salvation found.

"I've done half those things already," I said boldly.

"I rather expect he'll want you to do the rest of them then," the head said, sounding bored. "Not that we care, really. Many have tried to follow the Path of Princes, but who can follow it utterly?"

I cleared my throat, trying to ignore the murmurs behind me.

"I will need you to lead me as my guide," I told Death.

"YOU WISH TO FOLLOW WHERE DEATH HAS TROD?"

"You don't!" Grosbeak shrieked. "You don't. There will be no bargain with the mortal, Death. I am sworn by blood and honor to defend her and I will not fail in my charge. Stop this insanity, Mad Princess!"

"I must make this bargain," I said firmly. "I must, if I am to succeed. So that is the bargain then? I will give willingly a piece of my flesh and follow the Path of Princes but if you betray me, then I will receive back my flesh and be restored to my life. And for your part in this, you will guide me on the Path of Princes and bring me to the gates of your kingdom and to the place where the first sovereign's rib was snatched and if I fail to do all you have required, then you may leave me with no obligation remaining and you shall have my companions with me, for there will be no way out for any of us then."

Grosbeak cursed quietly and the murmurs behind me were unhappy.

Death seemed to pause a very long time before he finally said, "A BARGAIN IS STRUCK."

"What parts have you already fulfilled?" Tigraine whispered over my shoulder and I saw that behind her, the wives followed in a line, each carrying the heads of the fallen, though Margaretta looked like she might have been struck by a cruel Wittenbrand and then frozen that way, her face was so horrified. And Givanna was pale as Death himself.

"I have flown with the Arrow out of the tower of Ayyadgaard," I said and I made it a declaration for Death to hear, too. "I have Danced with the Sword at the Petal Ball. I gave my heart to the barrow when I declared my love to my dying husband and it is to my own heart that I choose to journey, for there my Bluebeard must be. And now, with the backstab of Ki'e'rien, I am now dying with my Lord. I called for Mercy to Wittentree, when I was broken and gasping on the ground, and she gave it to me. And salvation was found in the sound of my token when the sea set my husband to war against the Sword."

"Yes!" Grosbeak agreed. "Yes, she has!" And then he paused. "But I thought that poem was for the finding of the Bramble King."

"It's the Path of Princes. Of course it gives us a king," one of the heads whispered noisily.

"But she's not the Bramble King," Grosbeak hissed back.

"Maybe it has more than one use," the head whispered.

They were making me even more nervous. Or maybe it was the poison running through my blood that made me feel like my heart was rushing too quickly.

Death bowed to me, an acknowledgment of what had transpired, but I heard Tigraine whispering behind me and I had to bite my own lip to remain calm as she listed what I had yet to accomplish.

"Sing for your Sovereign,
Bow to your Dream,
Make Haste for the Fallen,
Rise in Esteem."

"But how do you do any of that?" she asked in a whisper. I really did think she was on my side. She sounded invested and ambitious, as if it were she and not me who must accomplish this.

Death, on the other hand, was smiling, his pointed teeth forming a terrifying grimace. He was too pale. Even his lips and the rims of his eyes were white as snow. He held out his hand and brandished a dagger in the other and I knew exactly what he wanted. A pound of my flesh.

"No! Not more of her!" Grosbeak said in horror.

"Now you're on my side?" I asked wryly.

"I have always been on my own side, but you won't be able to carry me if he takes another hand," Grosbeak said miserably.

"He won't have to." I made my voice hard as flint. "Your flesh," I said, and I reached into my pocket, produced my living hand, and offered it to Death.

It made an independent rude gesture, but Death took it and bit it. I did not know how to feel about the blood that stained his teeth when he smiled again, or how he snapped his fingers and the hand rose up and floated near his shoulder, following him as he turned and began to ride toward the locked door.

And I heard my husband's voice in my mind again, *For as long as earth has bones and death has teeth, that long will I be husband to you.*

This time, when I shivered, it was with more than just fear. There was a preciousness mixed in that shiver that I dared not deny.

"Time to march, little army," I said over my shoulder to the other wives, and then I turned the golden key in the air, closed the empty Room of Wives, and followed Death through the now open door of Coppertomb's home.

No doors, it seemed, were barred to Death.

Chapter Fourteen

IF I HAD BEEN ASKED to guess at what Coppertomb's home would look like, I could not have guessed it would look like this. The vault, odd as it might be, was in keeping with the rest of his home. We passed in silence up a long, drafty, stone staircase made entirely of hard stone lines and copper edges. Ever-dancing lamps burned in bronze cages, giving off the feeling that something alive was inside each one and suffering.

Margaretta began to cry somewhere midway up the steps and I heard Corinnian trying to comfort her with kind shushes as the heads they carried mocked them.

"You're not made for the Wittenhame, softlings."

"We most certainly are not," Corinnian agreed with a scold in her tone. "No one should be made for this terrible world."

"Your leader is. Her who married your husband last. She has a skeletal hand, a head for bargains, and a will of iron," the head replied loftily and I marveled that it would describe me in such glowing terms when I was no Wittenbrand.

"Yes, she's awful. Just like her horrific husband," one of the other brides said and there was something hot in her voice that I could not identify. "I'd like to know how she tripped him into her bed. None of my tricks worked on him." Ohhhh. That's who she was. The one with the scandalous journal. "But she might get us out of here and besides Ki'e'iren already poisoned her, so she won't be around for long."

"She's going to just die when she hears what you're saying," Grosbeak said, trying to twist on his chain so he could look back at them. "Aren't you Izolda? Just die. How ever will you live under the criticism of such fine specimens of womanhood?"

"I suppose I won't," I said dryly. "One of my sister brides has made sure of that."

"Well, you can hardly expect me to fault her for taking proper advantage of a situation," he agreed. "I only wish Sparrow had lived to see it happen. She always appreciated a good twist."

"Mmm," I agreed.

We'd reached the top of the long staircase now and found ourselves in the open air in a strange depression in the earth. A long, shallow-grade spiral began at the edge of the depression and slowly looped round and around to the top. The edge of the step was hammered with copper so that the line was easy to see, and all along the wall edge of the ramp were the figures of Wittenbrand carved of stone in a never-ending line. They had tortured, twisted features, each face a different mask of pain, and they carried stone torches. Their bodies were completely identical and I had the most terrible feeling that they might come alive at any moment and attack us.

"That was his home?" I asked, confused. "But where does he sleep?"

"Perhaps on one of the shelves," Grosbeak snickered. "Did you see one labeled 'Coppertomb?'"

I shook my head. "How does he eat?"

"He eats the hopes and dreams of others."

"Where does he keep his fine-pressed clothing? He always dresses to the most exacting standards. I expected libraries and luxuries."

"And no doubt they are here — somewhere — but also knowing Coppertomb, you likely have to find the right horrible face among these five hundred and twist its ear, and then go extinguish the right torch, and then the whole depression rises a thousand spans into the air, and a palace is beneath, and we discover we only ever saw the attic, or some such," Grosbeak said, unconcerned. "He's hardly the type to keep his secrets where anyone can see them. There are likely a thousand mortal slaves in there keeping his copper-thread clothing pressed and clean, and the finest morsels on his plates, but he'd never reveal that to you. He's a Wittenbrand of secrets deep as the earth."

As we reached the bottom of the spiral of earth, Death turned and beckoned me, and then his horse stepped as though it was planning to walk up into the sky rather than up the spiral. One hoof rose, and then a second, and by the time a third flickering hoof stepped up, I realized it was — indeed — stepping into the sky and as we followed, our feet stepped up with him.

The murmurs of fear behind me made my spine stiffen as if their fear granted me courage. I would not be weak when my husband needed strength. I would not let nerves or fright from heights make me whimper or waver. I was grateful for these others for existing, for they showed me how I could be and how I must not allow myself to be.

I followed resolutely, my hand firm on my husband's, my skeletal hand still gripping Grosbeak's pole. And if I paid more mind to my husband's sleepy breath upon my neck than I should, who could blame me? These moments of stolen intimacy were all I had, and though I was willing to die for him, I was not willing any longer to live without him.

"You're sweating, Izolda," Grosbeak said, a little flicker of excitement in his eyes. "It may well be that I shall watch you die with my own eyes."

"You seem unnaturally excited by the prospect," I said grimly and he was not wrong. My heart was acting strangely, fluttering in ways it should not, and the world felt too hot.

"You were privileged to be there for *my* death. It is only fair that I be there for yours. I am already preparing your funeral speech."

"How prudent," I murmured. "You'd hate to be caught without a quip."

We marched up into the sky and for the first time, I saw the Wittenhame spread out below and around me. It was night — I thought — though the moon hung very low and was the rich, deep color of clotting blood. What stars remained, clung to the lower edges of the dome of the sky, as if it had begun to crumble from the center and had worked its way lower and lower until soon it would reach the land. Beneath me, the trees and lakes, hills and streams, and estates all trembled slightly. Not as an earthquake might shake the ground, but as if it were breathing just as in the tale Bluebeard had told me.

It did not breathe evenly. The breath that moved it fluttered and snatched in an untidy rhythm and it took a few moments before I realized it was perfectly in time with the uneven rhythm gusting onto my neck.

I swallowed. Coincidence? Or was my husband the Bramble King and was the Bramble King also the sovereign who held the whole world within his chest?

I felt — small — beside the incomprehensible feeling of that. Small, and grateful to be small. What would it be like to bear all the world upon your chest? What would it be like to be more than a man, to have nothing to shelter you, but to be the shelter for others, to have nothing to succor you, but to be the dwindling succor for both your friends and your enemies?

The very thought was too great for me. It made my mouth dry and my brow glisten.

Or, perhaps, that was the poison working through me.

Death marched us lower, and as the ground rose to meet us, all I saw in every direction were Wittenbrand dressed for battle. I blinked, remembering the Hounds, and sure enough, there were twelve heads laid out around a throne on a dais, but though the crowd was battered and bloody, they were forming up once more into ranks and types. This time, I saw more types of Wittenbrand than ever before — winged and with hooves, with vines tangled around eyes, and thorns jutting from faces, with strange bark-like skin and hollow luminescent eyes. The very smallest rode on great creatures made of twisted moss or grasses, and the mermaids and men clung awkwardly to shambling sea-weed beasts.

"Underfolk," Grosbeak muttered dismissively.

The underfolk — if that was truly what they were — carried little cages with strange flickering or swimming or screeching creatures. They had upon their backs great packs of bright silk or tough leather, stuffed and crammed full and tight. And hanging from belts were trinkets and tools I could not name. Strung in antlers or around necks or over shambling backs, were chains of gold and diamonds, of rubies and drilled coins, of tiny glowing butterfly wings — thousands of them — or dried hearts, or locks of hair tagged and cataloged.

This did not look like a hunt so much as ... what?

This reminded me of something.

I gasped. It reminded me of the countryside of Ayyadmoore when war raged there and her citizens poured out of towns and cities and flowed out to the countryside in puddles of refugees that became streams, and streams that became rivers, until every last one who did not fight was fleeing on foot with whatever they could carry.

I looked back up at the moon … or was it the sun? I could no longer tell. And that explained it.

They were fleeing the Wittenhame. Even I could see that. But where would they go and why were so many of them bristling with weapons and armor?

Death led us down and into the midst of the loud horde and as we arrived, those around us stilled, eyes widening as they beheld Death walking in their midst and then widening again as they saw the procession behind him.

I glanced over my shoulder to see my fellow brides following with eyes set forward, faces pale and drawn, the severed heads they'd brought with them were raised like talismans. I liked to think that even the Wittenbrand would find them a terrifying marvel.

Silence swelled out from us as we slowly passed through the ranks and many of those we passed made signs of warding with their hands. How strange. To be the horror to horrors. To be the monstrosity to monstrosities.

I found I rather liked it, dying though I was. I had never hoped to be well-esteemed, but I had hoped for a little respect. I was being granted it to a degree I could not have imagined.

"I thought I caged you, little mouse," I heard Coppertomb say, and the ground under us rolled with a growl that I also heard faintly in my ear as my husband's breath gusted over my neck.

"Your cages have holes in them, Coppertomb," I said calmly, locating him and then watching as he moved to pace beside us. He was on a horse. A regular, mortal horse. No big cat for him or strange shambling seaweed creature. Not even a skeletal horse from a different plane like Death's. Coppertomb's horse was plain and brown and smelled of the stable. A nice palfrey I would have chosen for myself were I to take a pleasure ride. She snorted at me, a big horsey snort, and my heart lurched a little with a wave of sadness. I was dying. I would not give my affections and time to a horse again. I thought of Prince, long dead now, and how I loved to feed and care for him. This mortal horse with the big earthy eyes was warm and strong as he had been, and I missed the feeling of warm mortal flesh and warm mortal dreams pale as they were.

Coppertomb laughed — a sound that was more fit for the barrow than the dance floor when it came from him. "It will matter not. This world passes away and without the key I took from you, you will pass with it."

"And how will I meet you at your Coronation Ball if this world is passing?" I asked him coolly.

He leaned down so I could see the twist of cruelty in his mouth and smell the strange spice of him — a little too like the poison I'd been nicked with — and his black eyes narrowed.

This close to him, my breath felt like it was sucked from my body. My mortal mind could never get over the intense beauty of the Wittenbrand. Even Coppertomb, cold and lifeless as both copper and the tomb, was utterly gorgeous, his copper-tinged short curls clinging around his slightly-pointed ears, his cheeks sunken which only made his bone structure more noticeable, his rich, full lips pouty even when he wanted to be firm and his eyes glittering black gems you could lose yourself in while he laughed pitilessly and ensured you never found yourself again.

He was still wearing that single glove on his left hand. Was it only my own wishes that made me think he was disguising a missing finger?

"There is a very rich world waiting for us to pluck it like a berry," he said in a voice smooth as wine. "And pluck it we shall. We wait only for Bluffroll's army before we breach the gap and pour over your poor mortal cousins, seize their homes, snatch their children to serve us, their fields to feed us, their estates to house us, and their courts to entertain us. I could go to Salamoore, of course, where I am honored as a saint, but seeing you here getting so friendly with my home, makes me think I'd be happier learning the intimacies of yours. If you manage to escape this world, you might find me in the Court of Pensmoore ... or Rouranmoore? I feel that place in you, too. How odd. From whatever court I choose, I shall reign over all the mortal world, and if I find any living that share your blood, I will use them as human footstools — and no, that is not figurative. Scurry, scurry, little mouse."

And then he was back up in the saddle and wheeling his palfrey with a haunting laugh.

"You should be honored," Grosbeak said with a tone of delight. "The Bramble King himself has chosen you as an enemy. You could rise no higher than that!"

"I rather think I could," I mused. "I think I could be married to the Bramble King."

"You'd have a time of it," Grosbeak said, watching Coppertomb go. "If I had to guess I'd say he plays as cruelly in the bedroom as he does anywhere else."

"I'm not referring to Lord Coppertomb. I speak, rather, of the true Bramble King."

"Keep telling yourself that. Poison, they say, makes one lose all sense as it kills. I don't know if that's a blessing or curse for you Mad Princess."

"You'll have to advise me on how to navigate insanity, Grosbeak. You've been doing it so barely-adequately ever since I met you."

"I'll take that as a compliment, however it was meant," he said with a toss of his head. "Lords of Viscera," he cursed suddenly. "Are some of your fellow wives crying? How disgusting."

I glanced over my shoulder to see that most of the brides of Bluebeard were, indeed, silently crying. And why would they not be? I had just walked them through a living nightmare, and it was only the beginning. The exceptions were Tigraine and Ki'e'iren. One of whom was watching the Wittenbrand as if she might leap and rip their throats out at any moment, and the other was watching them with what looked somewhat like jealousy. My husband, it seemed, was no judge of women, or he would not have selected such a viper to put in his vault.

I would have to be very careful with these two at my back.

"Well, if you aren't motivated to succeed yet, there's no helping you," Grosbeak said happily. "Your husband is nearly gone for all eternity, you will soon follow him, and Coppertomb will dance on the backs of your kin. Improbable as any win for you would be, it is your only chance now."

"And yours," I said acidly. "As you have been grafted to my fate."

"It's a sacrifice indeed. Never say I have not been for you the most excellent of friends."

"You have certainly not been the most excellent of friends," I replied.

"Oh, well, it doesn't count if you add unnecessary words. That's just deflecting from the meaning, which proves you cannot resist my charms."

"Tell yourself whatever you must to get through the next two days," I said. "And then you will see, one way or the other."

"So much hope," he said, smacking his lips. "I like this look on you, Izolda. It's nearly brilliant. Do keep it up."

Chapter Fifteen

WE FOUND Bluffroll's army along the way as we followed Death through the heaving, disintegrating world that had once charmed me utterly with its vibrant intensity.

"Who are they?" Margaretta had whispered in a tiny voice.

The head she was holding replied sagely. I thought it was Vireo's voice. "The army of Lord Bluffroll. Called, it would seem, to savage the mortal lands on the behalf of the Bramble King and to take for him the many kingdoms and sew their bodies and lives into the earth that they might feed a new age. Would I were not dead, that I might march with them."

"You would go with them? To destroy the mortal world?" Margaretta always sounded like life had surprised her all over again. "He said he was going to make the royalty of Pensmoore his footstools!"

"All the more reason to go. Have you ever had a prince as a footstool?"

"I ... no, of course not!"

Vireo laughed. "You might like it. Even the blushing bride Izolda found she had a taste for our ways once she was inducted into them."

"By *your* treachery," Grosbeak reminded him.

"And I'm not even asking to be repaid," Vireo agreed. "I'm a generous soul."

I did not speak, merely followed our silent guide through the ranks of the army of Bluffroll. They looked like him — green of skin, with pronounced lower incisors that peeked up through their lips. Male or female, all were built large and broad, their hands so full of weapons and their backs strapped so generously with them, that they resembled porcupines. Their armor was fanciful, created with swirls of metal, turtle shells, some kind of scales the size of saucers, and webs of woven gold and something black that looked like lace made of spiderweb, but could have been broken dreams for all I knew.

Some rode on lizards like the men who had surrounded Coppertomb before the hunt for the Hounds of Heaven and all watched us pass through their midst in owlish silence.

"What was the point of the Hounds of Heaven?" I asked Grosbeak. "They showed up, raging and howling and shredding, and then were quickly dispatched. Why come at all?"

"They're a portent. Portents must portend. They can't very well remain sleeping comfortably beside the fires of hell when there are warnings of the end of the world to give, now can they?" he snapped.

"I thought they were Hounds of Heaven, not hell."

"Heaven, hell, what difference is it to me?"

"As a dead man who may eventually find himself in one or the other, I would have thought a great deal."

"And there you would be wrong, for I have bet all the coins of my soul on this one afterlife with you and I will not taste either of the other options. Don't die, or you'll make me regret that."

"I'm dying already," I said grimly. My racing heart stuttered as if to emphasize that. The tips of my fingers were numb.

"For now. Unless you can talk your way out of it."

"You can't talk your way out of death by poison or it wouldn't be used so reliably on unwanted government ministers."

"Ha. That's a good one. For someone with no sense of humor, you occasionally surprise me."

"For someone without a shred of human decency, you surprise me, too."

"Do not go soft on me. We don't have time for that."

We found Bluffroll in the center of his bustling army, gathered around a table of maps with what had to be his generals. Death stopped in front of him, staring down his long pale nose.

Bluffroll's eyes narrowed and then darted quickly down to me and procession of wives carrying heads and then back up to Death.

"You've no business here. Either of you," he said calmly.

"Can I bargain with you not to go where Coppertomb leads you?" I asked, hopeful. I would spare my people if I could. And Wittentree's. I'd promised protection for them as well.

"You cannot. Be glad to keep your head after such an insolent offer."

But there was an edge to his tone that I caught. I lifted my chin.

"Ah, so you know then that you are the last living competitor who worked against Coppertomb for the throne of the Bramble King," I said calmly. "I saw his assassins eat Wittentree alive."

His jaw clenched but he merely spat. "I'm no Wittentree, mortal, and you will not sway me with pretty warnings. I care not whether you live or die. Be off with you."

I stared at him a long time and then I said, "I march to Death's lands with only these mortal brides and our severed heads as my army. And together we will draw back the heart of the Bramble King and restore the Wittenhame, while you and your shining army go down to unleash your frustrations on innocent mortals. I have learned just now that even those of powerful build and stern jaw may have craven bones and runny coward hearts."

Bluffroll reached into his collar and pulled out a long double-looped string on which hundreds of thick ragged pieces of dried meat had been strung.

"Tongues," he said with a lift of his brow. "I collect them. Yours is of poor size, but the sizzle of it might make it worth a place with the others."

There was a general murmur of laughter and a few glances at me, but the generals looked away quickly every time they caught a glimpse of Bluebeard's face resting against my shoulder. While I'd been distracted a hummingbird had built a thimble nest just over his ear and its prospective mate was trying to lure it with a side-to-side dance.

Interesting. So much life seemed to center around this man they all named dead.

But perhaps they understood in their bones that he was their true sovereign. For they dared not cross him even when they thought him dead.

I swallowed.

"I can smell the Neverseed on you." Bluffroll leaned back in his small camp chair. "You'll be dead before we see another moon. And what are you doing here? Are you trying to walk the Path of Princes by following Death as you do? A dying wife with a dead husband clutched to her like her last remaining coin? Good luck with that."

"I am, in fact, doing just that," I said coolly, "and you would do well to help me with it, for when I succeed, you will be as much under his rule as any other Wittenbrand."

Bluffroll's eyes flicked from Death's pale face to mine and back and he leaned back, drawing a dagger and pretending to trim his nails, but I saw by his quick glances up at me that something about my actions worried him.

"There's no way a mortal can walk the Path of Princes."

"What if I don't walk it for myself? What if I walk it to fill full the Arrow's purpose?"

Bluffroll swallowed. "I have no quarrel with the Arrow."

"And yet you plan to sack his mortal lands."

Bluffroll jammed the dagger into the table before him. "They were only his for one play of the Game. He won't be attached to them."

"And yet, he seems to be attached," I said. "What do you think will happen if I bring him back from the barrow?"

Bluffroll looked up at the crumbling sky and then casually caught a goblet that moved across the table as the earth shook again. He glared balefully at me.

"Tell me this, little buzzing bee. Can death be turned back? Can a broken glass be mended? Can time restore my beauty?"

"You had beauty?" I asked, doubtful.

His laugh was a harsh bark. "Some things cannot be reversed."

"And if they can be?"

He considered and then pointed at Bluebeard. "Then my head will decorate his wall."

"It doesn't have to end so," I warned.

"Doesn't it? It feels to me as if the great tides of fate have been tugging on us all, surging us where they will, and if we are shattered on the rocks then that is as the song has been written and who can deny it?"

"As keeper of the singing flowers," Grosbeak whispered to me so loudly that everyone could hear. "Bluffroll is a master of song and music. His flowers can bring the rain or turn back the tides."

Bluffroll inclined his head in acknowledgment of Grosbeak and said, "But they cannot turn back this tide. It will roll in and bear away the last of the Wittenhame."He looked around him sadly. "And I shall do all that I can so that my kin will not suffer unduly in the depravations of the pale, miserable, mortal world."

"This does not have to be," I warned. "Bargain with me. Do not harm my lands and I will carve a place for you."

He smiled sadly. "While your audacity enchants me, and your misplaced confidence tastes of citrus and cinnamon, I will not make a bad bargain with you. I have tongues to collect, souls to harvest, and slaves to take from the ranks of the mortals. No hand will turn back what I unleash."

"Then we are enemies," I said grimly.

"I cherish the knowledge of it."

To my surprise, his answer felt more like a prospective lover accepting a memento from his beloved than a dark Wittenbrand Lord making an enemy, but that was the Wittenhame.

"The game is over, Izolda Savataz, wife of the Arrow. The chips have been wagered and lost. I've already lost my favorite two stallions, Coppertomb came to collect three of my consorts — and they were not the three I wanted to wager — and my foot aches from where my toe was taken from me. That's a loss, mortal woman."

For the first time, I could see the bitterness. But I shook my head as I followed Death from the war camp of Bluffroll, and I wondered if the mortal world would wash out the violence and delights inherent in the Wittenbrand, or if the Wittenbrand would set the mortal world ablaze. I rather thought both would be true and in the mingling, they would bring out the very worst of each other and dull the best parts.

"I can see you thinking," Grosbeak murmured. "And if your thoughts are that you and your Bluebeard have been each other's undoing, then you are correct. Star-crossed lovers doomed to die tragically. The woman who trips up the great man and brings him down. The pair that marry for love only for their children to savage the world and squander their inheritance. These occur again and again in stories for a reason, and you are playing out the piece before us like a pantomime."

I gave him a long look.

He laughed. "Don't stop. The entertainment is worth the price of admission."

"Your life?" I asked incredulously.

"I think you'll have to stop teasing me about that," he said smugly. "Now that you are dying, too."

Chapter Sixteen

IT WAS ONLY ONCE we finally left the army behind that we found the place beyond them — Bluffroll's Estate — and it was to there that Death led us.

"Whistleroll," Grosbeak said. "It's what he calls this place."

"I need to stop finding myself astonished by what I find in this land," I breathed.

"It would certainly save time."

Bluffroll — thick, heavy, gauche Bluffroll — lived in an estate made of spun glass and crystal. Its towers rose fancifully high, twisting in sugar-spun shapes that seemed impossible and utterly impractical and yet stole my heart away the moment I saw them. His home was spun of the palest lavender and rose glass as if formed by the clouds at sunrise. It was whimsy and fairy dust and the exuberant joy of spring meeting the delicate wings of a butterfly.

"Whistleroll," I gasped. "It seems nothing like him."

"Well, how would you know? You've barely spoken to the man. We are not how we look on the outside. I would have thought a plain thing like you would realize that by now."

"Consider me chastened," I said coolly, but I felt the other brides behind me relaxing as we drew closer to this estate. It had none of the terror of the other Wittenbrand homes. No hideous dead things gathered or displayed, merely very impressive gardens, all flowering at once though there was no possible way that all these flowers could be in season at one time. Lilacs bloomed alongside roses, which in turn bloomed alongside peonies and orchids. Perhaps these enchanted flowers were permanently in bloom. Their scent was heavy in the air, making each breath thick with perfume, though the ground continued to heave and roll and the flowers with it, timed to my husband's lurching breath.

When we were close to the tower, Bluebeard doubled over, sliding down my back, and coughed a terrible, wracking cough, and as he coughed the ground shook so intensely that one of the glass-spun towers of Whistleroll came crashing down in shattering pieces, tinkling and sparkling as it collapsed.

I drew in a shuddering breath. I was losing him.

I do not know why you must walk, my husband, but I fear you need help now, I told him in his mind and he certainly did. He could not seem to rise from his bent state and his breath was so shallow I could barely hear it, his eyes shut tight. With a sigh, I crouched down, set Grosbeak on the ground, and then maneuvered Bluebeard onto my back, slinging one hand under him to hold him in place even as I lifted Grosbeak's lantern pole again. I was bowed under Bluebeard, even though he was not heavy. Somehow, he seemed to make me bend beneath the figurative weight of all he was. But it was no matter. I would never let him go. Not now, not ever.

Another tower fell as he coughed, clinging to me as if to salvation. I felt his bare chest heaving and clenching against the bare skin of my back.

He was getting worse. Time was running out. We had to make haste.

I blinked back hot tears that insisted on welling up even when I willed them away.

I turned to look back over my shoulder but the other brides were silent, though their lips formed words and their eyes were wide. Margaretta pawed at her face, panic rising in her eyes and then Corinnian turned to run, only stopped by Tigraine who seized her arm and forced her forward again with a grim expression.

"What manner of madness is this?" I gasped, glad I could hear myself, but none of the heads responded, not even Grosbeak who clearly wanted to, as he opened his mouth only to shut it with a furious grimace. We'd been silenced to each other, caught in our own bubbles of stillness.

Had all sound been removed from the Wittenhame then? But no, glass crunched under my feet, and as we moved around the broken castle to a new part of the garden, the perfect flowers became still, frozen, in time though they whistled and sang as the wind moved through them.

There were small signs hanging over the paths of the garden as it split off into five different paths between the whistling flowers, and to my surprise, Death stopped there and would not go on, crossing his arms over his chest and raising an eyebrow at me.

"This is for me to decide?" I asked, a little huffily.

But there would be no help — not from Death and not from any of my advisors. Annoyed, I read the signs.

Paradise

Hades

Pennstein

Angstbite

Desire

What a truly eclectic list of names. And now I must choose a path with nothing more than the names to go by. I hummed, trying to think, and to my surprise, the glass flowers all shifted with a tinkle and turned toward me. How odd.

Death shifted, and then suddenly faded away.

No! No. No. No. My breath was caught in my throat.

I turned in a circle in a panic, but he was truly gone. There was no one here with me except the silent parade behind me, and my beloved on my back.

Bluebeard? I asked in my mind, reaching for him mind to mind, heart to heart. *Arrow?*

He was not there. I carried nothing but a fading corpse. I was on my own.

I needed to choose a path and walk down it and I needed to hurry before I lost Bluebeard entirely.

Should I follow the path marked Desire? Perhaps I would find what I wished at the end of it. Or perhaps I should journey to paradise to find my lost love. Or hades. Pennstein sounded like my home and tempted me, but it was the name of the fifth path that arrested me.

Angstbite. The name of the marriage sword Bluebeard had given to me.

He'd known all along that we would come to this path, hadn't he?

He had warned me to be silent, he had chosen me as his sixteenth bride and married me in the Wittenbrand way. One of the first things he'd given me was the golden key that opened the door to his other wives — to the blood of nations I would need to rescue him once he had given himself to the grave. Did it not make sense that his very first gift to me — my marriage sword — might contain another clue?

With my heart in my throat, I set down that path, only to have the glass flowers shuffle, tinkling as they moved, and barring my way. I turned, but they had sealed the way behind our parade, too. The big eyes of the wives and advisors met mine, glaring at me, demanding that I do better. And Grosbeak stared at me with slitted eyes like I should know the solution.

Sing for your Sovereign.

Perhaps, I should try that.

I began to sing, a song about a horse and rider but as I sang, the glass flowers pressed in, the nearest one slicing my arm and leaving a red weal. Grosbeak's cheekbone was slashed, too, and when I glanced behind me my fellow brides were also marked.

Wrong song, perhaps?

But what song should I sing?

So I tried singing the song I had grown to loathe, and as the first words fell from my lips,

"Fly with the arrow," the flowers backed up, and by the second line they cleared a path for us. I was already walking by the third line as — to my shock — the flowers joined in. Tinkling, whistling, shivering, they sang with us in pristine voices as if glass itself had been given a voice. The singing flowers were joined by my followers, and by the fourth line, I heard the entire chorus joining in the song.

Grosbeak's clearly reluctant baritone was quickly joined by Vireo's unwilling tenor and Margaretta's soprano and then we were singing in a powerful chorus and the flowers relented, allowing us through. I could tell by the expressions of those around me that the song was pulled unwillingly from them, as unwanted as the forced silence had been, but there was nothing I could do to ease their frustration. We had to walk this path. All of it.

It felt as though we traveled for hours. My legs grew so tired that I often tripped. My throat was dry and parched and my tongue stumbled over the repeated words, etched so deeply now into my brain that nothing would ever remove them.

And as we walked, the ground beneath us began to melt, to drip like wax from a spent candle, but our feet trod on air as the ground dripped away, leaving nothing but the black broken heavens above with their dissipated sun, and the black void of the missing ground below.

My stomach dropped with them and my hope melted. Surely, I had finally gone insane, lost to this world. Lost to all sanity. I tried to look over my shoulder at my beloved, tried to find solace in his presence but his head lolled lifelessly on my shoulder and his mouth had fallen open, his eyes no longer closed but open in a slit and what I saw of them was insensate. Within me, my heart sunk.

I'd taken too long. I had not made enough haste. My husband's breath no longer shook the earth. He no longer breathed at all.

And then all light winked out and I was left in utter darkness.

Chapter Seventeen

WHEN I BLINKED AGAIN, there was Death. And there was light once more from a huge white moon.

We were no longer in the Wittenhame. Or at least, I did not think we were. The smells around me were faint and tepid, the wind did not bite as strongly nor the moon shine as brightly as it did in the Wittenhame, and when I shifted, a coney shot out from the underbrush, running in a wild back-and-forth pattern, and then disappearing into rustling bushes. Since none of them came alive and ate him, or turned to glass and sang, this could only be the mortal world.

I swallowed, nervous now because time passed differently here. That single rabbit escape might have used up the last of my time. And as if to agree with that, my body lurched, the numbness I'd felt in my fingers now running up my arms and legs so that using them felt strange and foreign, as if they were not my limbs at all. My mouth tasted of acid and my belly flared with pain.

I was — most certainly — dying.

It was hard not to panic at the thought. For some reason, memories of my mother and father swam to the surface of my mind as I fought down blind fear. My mother murmuring over me when I was ill as a child. My father's strong hands steadying me on a horse. Had they been fearful when they had died? Had they wondered about me then? Their missing child, snatched away forever by a stranger from another world?

"I hate the stench of mortals," Grosbeak said in a voice that seemed to creak from overuse. "Lead on, Master Death. I have no desire to linger here."

But Death was in no hurry, his eyes flicked from face to face as if counting us, and then he raised a hand.

"Ask your friends to form a circle with us," the head wearing the coronet said gruffly. Her voice also sounded worn and rough.

"Form a circle," I said, and yes, my own voice cut out on some words and burred on others. How long had we sung, that we struggled now to speak?

My fellow brides stumbled into the circle, eyes dull, feet heavy, hands barely holding onto their burdens as they hung at their sides. We were a ghastly group worthy of nightmares. Likely, Death would reap a great harvest if we stumbled into a mortal community. Folk would die of shock and horror at the mere sight of my band of tattered brides and me— at their head — the worst horror of all.

I looked down at my living hand, only to see it was black from the poison and that blackness trailed right up my arm to my elbow. I sucked in a wavering breath and glanced backward at my husband. He hadn't so much as flinched in hours. He was cold as night to the touch. Was I already too late?

"Thirty makes a quorum," Vireo said sourly. "He planned this well. Are you calling on us for our vote, Death?"

At the nod of our spectral guide, Vireo laughed long and bitter.

"He picked *us*?" the mermaid asked, her gaze flicking toward my dead husband.

His ruined hands were blackened, too, I realized. Again, I clung to thoughts of my parents to keep panic at bay. My mother sewing in her chair and laughing over a story she was telling my father as he ate his breakfast.

"What manner of madman picks his enemies to judge in the end?" Vireo asked acidly.

Grosbeak's laugh was familiar. I knew this one. It was the one he used when someone was in deep trouble and he was entertained by their possible grim death.

It was the coronet head that spoke, her voice firm and even. "One who must have been very certain that he would win so thoroughly that even his enemies must judge it so."

They were silent then for a long beat and I was so tired, so very tired. I wanted to sit down and sleep on the ground right here. I did not dare. I was running out of time.

"What's going on?" I murmured to Grosbeak.

He turned his horrific grin toward me, his missing ear seeming to stand out in the mortal moonlight.

"Death has called on a quorum of dead Wittenbrand to vote. And you are lucky enough to have thirty dead Wittenbrand with you — the exact number needed for a vote — minus me, of course."

"Why not you?"

"You can't have friends vote. Conflict of interest."

"Does that make you my friend?" I asked tiredly, but when he wouldn't answer I asked instead, "A vote for what?"

"Can we please get on with it? I grow weary," Vireo interrupted.

Death lifted his other hand as if in response.

"A Vote of Esteem," Grosbeak whispered to me. "If a Quorum passes a Vote of Esteem a mortal may be elevated to the ranks of the Wittenbrand. But this never happens. The requirements are too high. You must have succeeded at an impossible task and be respected for it — oh, and you will die very painfully if you fail to achieve the esteem of the quorum."

"Me?"

"Well, who else would they be voting on."

I looked around at the heads. They were all winking — one eye closed. I did not know what that meant.

"I am already dying," I said grimly. "Indeed, I am nearly dead."

I could no longer feel anything beneath my waist and my heart was slowing, each ka-thump a little more erratic than the last.

Death lowered his arms, his hair and beard dancing in a wind I did not feel.

"Well, I suppose you'll die as an honorary Wittenbrand," Grosbeak said, and was that *pride* in his voice? "The Quorum has spoken. You have risen in Esteem."

"Wait ..." I said as Death began to walk again and I hurried to keep up. "Esteem. Have I walked the Path of Princes?"

"It would seem so," Grosbeak said, his voice breathless in awe. "To have achieved this, Izolda — even if you die in the next few moments — is an honor that will trail behind you beyond death."

"How lovely," I said dryly. "I can parade about with it when it no longer matters a single whit."

"Don't be crass," the head with the coronet said in a clipped voice. "You've been granted an honor you do not deserve by those unhappy to give it. Take your honor and show some respect."

I swallowed, for she was right. Was this why he collected these heads? Had he foreseen the need for this, too?

Death strode ahead, his hair flowing behind him as if it were weightless, the tiny skulls on his robe clinking. Shadowless, he floated over the mortal grass, but he did not walk up the great hillside ... he walked into it. And with my heart in my throat, I followed, stepping with my eyes closed and my breath held.

"Open your eyes, Izolda," Grosbeak whispered and when I opened them, there was only blackness for a moment and a creeping sensation like I was feeling the earth and worms and roots pressing against my skin, even though I had no feeling anymore in most of my limbs, and then I stepped through, and I was within the hill.

Or maybe I was not.

What I saw on the other side chilled me. There was no moon or sun, though I could see just fine. There was no color. And when I looked to Death, he was white and pale and the brightest thing to be seen. He flicked a hand and then my own living hand in his possession snapped its fingers, and he was gone.

I gasped, startled.

"Where did he go?" I breathed as the brides filled up the space behind me and I looked at what lay before.

"Your bargain is complete," Grosbeak reminded me. "He brought you into the barrow — into his land where the dead are stored until the end of the age."

I stepped lightly down the path, barely willing to take any step at all.

I had to pick my way with great care to stay on the path, for it was overrun and tangled, as were the rolling hills in every direction. What it was tangled with horrified me to such a degree that I dare not step off the path at all.

The ground, in every direction, was littered with the dead, displayed as though they had been brought directly here from their resting place. They were not laid out respectfully, but rather one still figure was curled over herself as if she had retched to death, and another, half tangled over her, had been disemboweled. His foot was thrown haphazardly over a man missing a head and a hand, and he, in turn, was draped over a woman still clutching the snake wrapped 'round her bulging throat.

They were all white as Death as if their passing had leeched all color from them. White and cold and frozen in agony.

I retched, gagged, and retched again, trying with great difficulty to follow the path without stepping on limbs or hands or — sweet mother of mine — someone's eye.

"No one said the path into the barrow would be an easy one," Grosbeak growled.

My lips were numb — whether from horror or the poison killing me — and my voice came out high-pitched with despair, "But how will I find him here?"

Jumbled as the dead were, their state was made worse by infestation. Colorless beetles scuttled between them, cobwebs draped wildly from one to another, as if some mad spider were intent on working a last masterpiece. Pale squirrels chittered and scrambled round and round one leg, and then a face, and then darted into a nest somewhere below. I did not wish to notice the flies, but it could not be helped for the milky infestation of them crawled on everything as if an army seeking to devour the world.

"Death set us on this path," I said and my words were clouded by the thickness of my numb lips. "It must take us there."

Behind me, the other brides murmured or sobbed or hiccuped their distress and in their hands, their heads advised them likewise.

"Stay on the path."

"Do not tarry."

I swallowed and forced myself onward through the hills, which I now realized were uneven heaps of the dead.

"No wonder you prefer an afterlife with me, Grosbeak." My voice was faint even to my own ears. "I half wonder that all of the Wittenbrand do not beg for such a half-life if it would avoid this place."

Grosbeak laughed boorishly. "This is not the afterlife, Izolda. This is merely a waiting place. When the age turns, all these will pass on to what is to come."

"I thought the age turned with the change of the Bramble King and the end of the Game," I said and it was getting hard to speak. My lips and tongue were too numb. I stumbled, not even feeling when my ankle rolled under me until I looked down and saw myself standing on ankle rather than foot.

"It lends credence to your blind hope that you carry the Bramble King with you even now, does it not?" Grosbeak said lightly. "But I fear you will never make it. Already you stumble and trip. And you have all this vast land to search." He made a happy sound in the back of his throat. "Ahh, but I love a fated hero. Doomed to die. Destined to perish. Yet forging forward, writing her own damnation with every decision she makes."

His eyelids fluttered with pleasure.

"Curse you, Grosbeak," I murmured. "Curse you for not helping. Were you not son and husband once to those who will be found somewhere in these heaps?"

He spat, and think if there were colors remaining, he might have been flushed. "How do you know about my wife?"

"It was spoken at your funeral."

"What else was said at that funeral?"

"It was mentioned that you were tall."

"Ha!"

"And that you had a herd of Clay Horses."

He grew silent at that, and we were nearly to the next hill when he finally said, "I had forgotten that. Lend me your fingers, Izolda."

"I do not care what you're planning," I said coldly. "I absolutely won't agree to *that.* Is it not enough that I have bargained away my hand again and again?"

He scoffed. "No, it's not. Here at the very end, the least you can do is lend me what I ask for. I said *lend* not *give.*"

"In exchange for what?"

"You're too Wittenbrand for your own good, fool of an Arrow's wife! In exchange for my help, is that not good enough? Lend me your fingers and I will lend you my help."

Behind me, I heard murmurs of interest from the heads. But I cared not. I had but hours left, if that. Why not take any gift offered me?

"Fine. What do I do with my fingers?"

"Set the pole down. No, not there! Gross! Fine. Yes, that's fine. Right there. Lovely belly you have here, lady corpse, don't mind me while I rest on it a moment. And now, Izolda, if you'll put your first two fingers in my mouth."

"You accused me once of not having the imagination to dream of what you might do with only a head. If this is a part of it, then I beg you not to go on."

He rolled his eyes. "Before you had too little imagination, now you have too much? Just shove them in there and spread them wide."

Grimacing, I acquiesced.

To my surprise, Grosbeak pursed his lips around them and made a piercing whistle that seemed to echo far over the heaps of the dead, reverberating back and back until it returned to us. He repeated his whistle twice and then around my fingers he spoke.

"Et em oww ow."

I took my fingers out.

"I fear that has turned my stomach," he said, looking miserable.

"*Your* stomach?" I repeated as I wiped my sticky fingers on my dress. "You must be joking. I am the one with dead-person spit on me, and I should note it smells of rotted fish."

"You're one to talk. If I had an hourglass I could only watch a fraction of the sand run before I'd have to give a speech at *your* funeral." He paused to pull a long face. "She was wishy-washy as dishwater, never grabbing hold entirely of her opportunities, but never having the good grace to be properly stamped into the ground either, and those who most hoped she would be a practical heroine were most devastated to discover she was human after all."

"If I die in the next few minutes," I said as I heaved myself back up and then his pole with me. "Then I shall die cursing your name for all the gods and angels to hear."

"I would have it no other way."

But before he was finished speaking there was a tremble in the ground like the sound of many horses and as my eyes were still widening, they came thundering over the dead toward us, kicking up cobwebs and insects as they went.

"You had these at your disposal all along?" I asked him in wonder.

"I forgot until you mentioned it, but I think I wouldn't mind a last ride before I die."

"I'm sure you wouldn't," I said absently, watching as the great mass of bodies thundered toward us.

There were maybe fifty of them — great stamping, hearty warhorses. Had I been buying for the king, I would have bought every single one, even knowing they were made of clay and not able to breed more. They held their necks in perfectly formed curves, ears back properly, hooves and limbs still bearing marks as if they'd been cut from premium clay by a fettling knife.

They moved like real horses, not cracking or jointed like a man-made thing, but their expressions changed not one whit, and their eyes were lifeless. With all the furor of a cavalry exhibition, they ran up and wheeled in front of us, stomping and neighing and throwing back heads as they approached.

"These will take us to your husband," Grosbeak said.

"A kingly gift," I said a little breathlessly.

"Not a gift," he objected. "Not at all. You've done tasks for everyone else. You'll do one now for me."

"Don't you see I am running out of time?" I asked, almost wailing in my despair.

"Which is why you must do this first," he insisted, his horrible face screwing up in hostility. "Or else you'll be dead and it will be too late."

"Fine then," I practically spat through my numb lips. "What will it be? Shall I give my other hand? A foot? My still beating heart?"

"Take my pole and strike the nearest horse in the neck."

"You're mad!" I said, furious now, but I did exactly as he said, hitting the horse across the neck as hard as I could. I did not want to look at its feet for fear of what those clay hooves might have done to the bodies sleeping in eternal rest, so I did not see what size of shards the head and neck broke into, but they shattered like struck clay pots, leaving only a jagged stump where once had been a head and neck.

The other horses did not care.

"I think it's best you mount," I told the other brides. "If I survive his task, there will be little time to ride."

"Follow me!" Tigraine said jubilantly as if her whole life had been leading up to the moment she could ride a clay horse over a heap of corpses.

I turned to Grosbeak. "You have what you wished."

"That is only the first part. Now. Jam my pole into the hole in the neck."

Easy enough. In fact, if I were to be rid of him, I may even glory in it.

"Now," he said, his voice still commanding as he swung from the empty neck of the horse. "Use one of the shards to dig the ground. Dig up earth and clay and form for me around this pole, a body."

"Out of dirt?" I asked, incredulous. "It will be terribly inferior."

"Do it, or see no help from me."

And this was the Grosbeak I remembered from life. The furious, demanding Wittenbrand who wanted me dead. And it was he who I was now bargaining with, so with the last of my energy, I dug until my nails were torn and my palms bloody from the edges of the sharp shards. And I built him a patchy thick body, slumping dirt shoulders, and long, lumpy arms.

"There," I spat. "You have your ugly dirt body and I hope it falls to dust in your face."

"Place my head upon it," he demanded and with relish, I jammed his dead, fly-infested head into the earth. "And now, lady of dust, bound to Pensmoore, Ayyadmoore, and Rouranmoore, give me one last thing. A drop of your blood, if you please."

Easy enough. My hand was already cut and bleeding, though it was a moment before I realized it was red in this black and white world.

"On my cheek, Izolda. Draw your husband's sign. Give me one last taste of his power."

"He's too worn to work magic," I said.

"And yet there's enough power still in his sign alone to grant me this one last wish."

"Just be done with it," I muttered, and I traced the bloody tear trail down Grosbeak's cheek and when I was done I looked down, and then up again, as he rose above me. I gasped, for there was no longer a clay horse and a rotting head before me.

There was, instead, a living, breathing centaur.

"Stop staring and mount up — or if you're too dainty and lily-livered, then just die already. I have no need of you to carry me anymore, and no desire to wait around here," Grosbeak said with a very horsey toss of his head, and to my surprise, I found myself scrambling numbly up his back.

Chapter Eighteen

WHEN YOU ARE the master of a herd of Clay Horses you can direct them anywhere you wish and Grosbeak did without so much as consulting me.

"Fan out, you fools," he said to the other wives and advisors, grinning like a mad man. "And stop gaping like fresh-caught fish. Your jealousy at my elevation could not be more apparent."

For my part, I did not care that he was going to lead the search. Relieved of his lantern pole, I slid Bluebeard around my body so I could cup him to my chest. He was limp and did not move easily, his head lolling, the wound in his side bleeding so sluggishly, that it seemed not to bleed at all.

I let my tears fall freely over him, washing his face as I moved it to my shoulder and held the back of his head as though he were an infant.

I couldn't feel the hands touching him or even my own cheek when I pressed it against the top of his head.

Here in the depths of the grave, I did not know if it were day or night, and I did not dare trigger the curse still lingering, as if I still hoped there could be salvation even now, so I did not speak aloud to him as I would have liked.

I spoke, instead, inside my mind.

My husband, Lord Arrow of the Riverbarrow, I do not know to what destination you fly now. I fear that — king though you are of all lands both

Wittenbrand and mortal — you are a dying king, a passing sovereign. I wish only to say one last word to you. It has been an honor to travel these past seven years as your wife. I would not bargain them away. Not even to spare myself such pain as I have eaten and such bitterness as I have drunk. You chose well when you chose me. For I have married you both in heart and soul and I cling to you yet, here in the lands beyond death.

And as we rode, I spoke back to him our vows, one final time.

As long as rivers run and moon shines, as long as the earth has bones and death has claws, as long as the ages pass and fail – that long shall I be wife to you.

Little had I known the bones of the earth would be his and that Death would sink long claws into both of us.

Flesh of my flesh and bone of my bone you will be.

I would give my own healthy flesh to make him whole — had I any left to give.

Spirit of my spirit, heart of my own heart, fall what may, we shall be one. Your days shall be mine and your happiness my own.

We would spend the last of my days together, shared. Halved. And yet somehow multiplied.

My body I dedicate to none other. The bounty of my wealth is yours. If ever it be otherwise, may I waste away with sickness and may famine eat my strength, and may my enemies overtake me, and siphon from me the blood of my life.

Well. They could get in line.

We were riding up a hill — an actual hill still strewn with the dead in their age-long sleep, not a heap of the dead.

"You will owe me a thousand thanks, Izolda Savataz," Grosbeak said happily. "For look what I have found? Is that not your husband, the Bramble King, seated on his broken throne and dead as dead can be?"

I leaned forward, twisting to see around his clay torso, and gasped for he was right.

At the top of the great tor — so massive in size that it dwarfed all else — was a throne made of a Wittenbrand rib cage half submerged in the earth. The broken-ended ribs grasped upward toward the sky —fifteen of them and one broken off to a bare stump. Fat chains wrapped in brambles ran from each rib to snake around a pale throne and trussed there on the throne —

bound so thoroughly that limbs and torso were lost in the jumble of chain on chain — was the form of my husband, his dead eyes open but unseeing, one dead hand reaching out, grasping, the broken rib crown displayed on his head.

I looked back and forth for a moment from the dead man on the throne to the dead man in my arms and back. Two halves of a whole? Two representations of the same man? Or something more? I did not know. This land of Death bent the mind to uncertainty.

I was leaping from Grosbeak's back before he'd stopped moving.

"Sixrteen locks with sixteen keys," I murmured, following each chain back to the rib and seeing on each rib a complicated lock-like shape where a depression had been carved into the ivory rib — a depression just like a seat. "I wonder if it matters how they are arranged."

"I rather think so," Grosbeak said, seeming as absorbed in the puzzle as I was. "He always did seem very precise in how he placed them on those pedestals."

At the base of each rib were two impressions like shelves. For the heads, I realized.

But who could be such a seer as to have seen this coming in every detail? Who could have planned it all and yet trusted that one mortal woman would have gathered up these all ...

"The blood of nations," I murmured. "All the prophecies come true here."

"All what prophecies come true?" Tigraine asked from just behind my shoulder. "Margaretta would you stop petting him? He was a bodiless head just a moment ago!"

"I bid you pay mind to your own business," Grosbeak snarled.

I did not turn. Whatever nonsense he was getting up to was no longer of concern to me. Before me, lay the last puzzle.

Here lay Wittentree's riddle and I said it aloud as my eyes ran over the ribs. They couldn't be *the* ribs, and yet here they were. Perhaps they were a representation of them, just as I carried one husband while watching the other chained there, just as the world could not fit entirely in the chest of my dead husband, Bramble King though he may be.

"What once stood in a line, now missing a brother. What was taken for wealth and refined by another. What holds life or death in the gap left behind. What holds endless damnation in similar kind."

There was still something missing. I chewed my lip for I could not tell what it was.

"I suppose we find our places in the seats?" Tigraine asked, looking at me.

"Wait." The word ripped from my tense lips. "Wait only a moment."

"Ah, she's remembered then," Grosbeak said, amused. "It won't be endless damnation, then?"

The blood. The blood of nations.

"Each of you come to me here," I said, a little breathlessly. And with a kiss of apology, I slid my husband's dagger from his belt and as each stepped forward I made his mark down her cheek. Bold Tigraine — first of course, right through to trembling Corinnian and Margaretta who was stealing little flirtatious glances at centaur Grosbeak — I wanted to roll my eyes at that, but this was no time for distractions. Last of all, Ki'e'iren received her mark.

"I hope you do not damn us still, last bride," she breathed. "You have little time to get this right."

"Thanks to you," I returned coldly.

"Give me neither your disdain nor your condemnation. They are not my just dessert. Suffering belongs to us in a way that it belongs to none other, for it was given to us as a gift from our husband. I merely deepened yours."

"I do not think he will see it that way."

"Will he see anything again? That, last wife, is the question."

I cleared my throat. I was having trouble bringing breath into my lungs, my eyes watering constantly now that blinking was an effort.

"Find your places, but do not yet sit," I said thickly and my sister brides arranged themselves as they had been in the Room of Wives, setting the heads they carried in the nooks made for them.

I carried my dead husband across the last steps, heart in my throat, as I brought body to spirit and I had not the time to so much as kiss him goodbye because the moment my fumbling foot connected with the pale frozen man on the throne, the one in my arms vanished and the one wrapped in deep chains flushed with color — color, in this world of white on white on white.

With a dry throat and a thick tongue I spoke the last riddle.

"Sixteen locks with sixteen keys. From grip of death, the vict'ry seize,

Silent brides for silent lord, unravel back time's cord. Bought by blood and claimed in oath, only one holds bitter troth. One hand living, one hand dead, she finds the place where hope has fled. Now let her choose what comes last. Freedom now or holding fast."

I swallowed and spoke again.

"I think you sit. And when you do, I think it is goodbye." I looked up and met their eyes one by one. "Either we have succeeded or we are doomed."

"You most certainly are. Your lips are black," Ki'e'iren pointed out."

"Yes, thank you," I said repressively, but then my expression softened as I looked around at them. "Thank you all for achieving this with me."

My throat was thick. I didn't know what else to say. But it did not matter. Ki'e'iren sat before anyone could say anything and the moment her seat touched the carved slot in the rib, she vanished in a flash along with the heads at her feet, and the chain that led from her to Bluebeard's throne uncurled from around him, and snaked back into the rib on which she had sat.

"I was glad to fight with you," Tigraine said boldly.

And then, as if by mutual accord, the others sat, almost as one, and they vanished in sudden flashes of light and gasps of surprise and little scream from Margaretta and as they sat all the chains retracted with them leaving me alone holding the hand of a dead man — unchained now, but still lifeless.

"Oh," I said aloud. "I thought that would work."

"I think it did work," Grosbeak said, stomping a horsey foot. His tone was hushed. "It's just not complete."

All the chains were gone. My beautiful Arrow lay there still, motionless, color in a world of monochrome, but he spoke neither in my mind nor with his newly freed lips, merely lay there, still sleeping in the barrow, still waiting to be brought back somehow.

I looked to the last rib where it was broken and cracked. And when I looked back at my Bluebeard, Death was there, standing beside him.

"Nrrgh, that one gives me the creeps," Grosbeak said, taking a step forward and flicking his clay tail with a pottery clatter. He sounded delighted as he spoke in hushed wonder. "But of course he's back. Because it's decision time, isn't it Izolda? And how excellent is this? We stand now, on the brink of a new age, the old age and old world are melting away, but who will reign in this new era and how? A mortal will decide. A mortal who we have mocked and made merry with. A mortal stolen from her home. I could never have predicted this."

"What do you mean that it's for me to decide?" I asked, barely managing the words through my thick lips. "I see no choice here. There is simply a broken rib and a king who will not wake."

"The riddle was clear," Grosbeak objected. "Freedom now or holding fast. It speaks to a decision."

"But what is the decision?" I wailed. "Why can these things never be clear? How am I supposed to decide blindly?"

"Where did the brides go?" He pushed.

"Bluebeard said they were meant to go back to their own times and places."

He smiled beatifically, "Then I think that is the freedom you could choose, is it not, Lord Death?"

We both looked to the pasty specter and he inclined his head in assent.

"Or?" I asked.

"Or you die, I think," Grosbeak said. "You hold fast to his damn fool dream and you die here with him just like the song we sing and I think that might be enough magic to repair the rib. If greed broke it, then perhaps generosity will repair it."

"Perhaps? You think?" I asked, aghast.

"Well, I'm hardly the expert here," Grosbeak huffed. "And I don't think Death is going to give us any answers."

The world was spinning. I had to reach out and catch myself on Bluebeard's dead shoulder to keep from collapsing.

"I mean it makes sense with what we know, right?" Grosbeak said. "We know it's a choice of freedom or stubborness. We know the rib needs repairing with something that counters greed. We know that to finish fulfilling the song you'll have to die. So it doesn't seem too big a leap to say that you have about four or five more breaths to pick one or the other and get on with it."

"But I'll be dead!" I objected. "I won't know how the story ends!"

"Well," Grosbeak considered, sounding cold when he finally spoke, "I will, and that's who counts."

I couldn't make out his face anymore. My vision had darkened too much. But I could easily guess he was grinning. He'd wanted to see me die, after all.

"Hop to it, mortal girl. You're just about dead already. Go sit on the seat in the base of that rib and unlock your chance to go back in time and marry that fat horse lord and have his babies and never know a moment of any of this ... or lie down on your dead husband's chest and die with him. But choose quickly, because I see your spirit becoming unmoored, your body quaking. You have not a day left to spare, I fear."

His voice felt like it was coming from far away. But it had never been a choice, had it? Not really. Not from the moment I realized that I loved Bluebeard and that I'd do anything for him.

"Not an hour," Grosbeak's voice came from a long way off.

Well. I was a sensible girl. I could accept death just like everything else. I reached blindly to his side, wounded here just as it was everywhere else, dipped my finger in his blood, and smeared it over my cheek in his sign. The line I drew was nothing more than a smear, my hands no longer worked.

I could only hope it had just enough magic left in it.

"Not a minute."

I tried to lean forward to kiss him one last time, dead though he was, but I had not the control to manage it. I fell, sprawling over his chest, my heartbeat erratic, my breath caught somewhere in my throat.

My lungs would not expand. My poor eyes would not close. I was staring at the blue of my husband's beard.

Blue.

Not white anymore but blue.

"Not a heartbeat."

I felt the last thump and tried to reach for it, but it shivered away.

"Well, I suppose that's her choice then, don't you think? I would have bet on her choosing the other way but I've never been a good judge of what fool mortals might do with their mayfly lives. At least I got to see the end. I do hate it when a story is unfinished."

A white hand pressed over my mouth, my nose, my eyes as Death stole what was left of me, unwilling though I was to leave those I loved. Just as once, long ago, my husband had plucked me from a mortal life, so I was plucked now from a Wittenbrand one. Just one more head of grain harvested by the Great Reaper.

Chapter Nineteen

THE WITTENTALES my mother told were always full of strange magic and stranger magicians and those poor mortals found within those stories were never more than leaves swept by on a current or coins tossed into a fountain. Happy fortunes and living forever after were never theirs to claim. Only the Wittenbrand ever found justice for ills done to them or reward for their great deeds. For mortals, the best that could be hoped for was to be entirely forgotten.

I woke, forgotten.

My eyes blinked awake slowly. A small bird sang in the tree, a simple trill followed by the response — and I did not know why that made my heart ache cruelly, or why I clutched at my chest and shook with silent sobs. I felt as though I had lost something I never knew.

I rose from my bed in my father's house in Northpeak and I readied myself for a day in my third best dress — noting that the stitching needed repair around one of the cuffs. I dressed my hair and then I sat on the edge of my bed and I listened to the bird again.

My room with its simple wood furniture and carved lintel felt odd. Unreal. As if I had not been living within it for the past nineteen years.

I couldn't quite remember ...

I shook my head. I did not know what I had forgotten, only that it was terribly important. The broken memory ripped at me and tore at the seeming tranquility of the morning, as if my heart could hear a trumpet blast of warning that bypassed my ears entirely.

I made my way down to the Common Room, nodding idly to Raisa, one of the maids who I'd known all my life. Seeing her face made me feel surprise, but why would I be surprised when surely I had seen her only yesterday?

In the Common Room, my father spoke quietly but firmly with my brother Rolgrin over something regarding the rotation of grazing land on northern fields. My mother sat with them but her gaze was dreamy as she looked out the window. I paused in the doorway of the room, uncertain why I was blinking back tears or why the mere sight of them caught at my chest.

Svetgin ran in, bumping into me on the way past. It broke the moment. I stepped forward and moved to kiss my mother's brow.

"Izolda, my sweet girl," she said with a smile.

And the pain in my chest moved me around the table to kiss my father's brow, too. He paused long enough to look up at me with a warm smile before returning to his instruction. My brothers, I did not kiss, though Svetgin winked at me from across the table and Rolgrin caught my eye and offered a tight smile of greeting. And then I was breakfasting with my family, smiling as the wash of their conversation calmed me, and the busy mundane seized both time and energy.

I spent my morning moving from task to task, feeling as though I were in a dream, not understanding why the sight of Svetgin red-cheeked and laughing brought to mind a sudden image of a broken, drunken man looking toward me with desperate eyes, or why, in that moment, I felt the urge to glance down at my hand and be sure it had flesh on it.

When I helped Rolgrin bring up supplies of parchment and ink to our father's business chambers, I did not know why, when I saw him, I also saw a grave young man only a little older than me asking me about a battle.

When my father gave me one of his rare embraces, I did not know why it felt as though the dead had come back to life.

And when — every time she passed me in a hall, or brought me a little bit of something to eat or drink — my mother kissed the top of my head or cheek or drew me into a cuddle, it made me shiver and cling back twice as tightly.

"My affectionate girl," she whispered into my hair. "My sweet outdoor girl."

And in the afternoon, when I rode my horse out to the pasture, and down to where the North River was swollen with spring melt, I did not know why I was drawn to the banks of the turbulent water and found myself leaving my mare to graze while I stood and watched the vigor and froth of the mighty river sweeping down from the mountains and swelling powerfully.

I studied the furor of the water and felt the spray upon my face and I felt a loss I could not name and a hollowness in my belly to which I could put no place. I only knew that it gutted me, hollowing me inside so that I could hardly breathe, my thoughts flying frantically within the confines of my mind like trapped birds.

I stared a long time at the raging waters before I returned home for the work and routine of the evening.

I returned to the river the following day to see it had swelled further.

And the following day.

And the next.

Until my father joked that at least we would have warning if there was to be a flood, and my brother joked that perhaps I had grown bored of my maidenhood and wished to be swept down the river to whichever hold had an empty spot for a mistress and was willing to take a half-drowned noblewoman to heart.

And still, I went, as the rains came, pounding the earth and filling the river, until great trees were swept down with blocks of ice and the last of the melt broke out the dams of both ice and beavers, and brought the flotsam of winter down our hills, intent on sweeping out upon the plains.

It was there, as I rode along the deafening banks of the swollen North River, that I saw the water foam up and rise — but rather than crashing back immediately it continued to build and shift until it was a great pawing stallion garlanded in river weeds. Branches that had been washing down the way formed the tail and nose and great legs and water, moving, foaming, rippling water filling out its form and spirit.

The great beast's neigh was loud enough to be heard even over the crash of the river and to my surprise, it looked directly at me and I felt something release deep in my heart — something that somehow had been waiting for this, though I knew not how.

Something that was one with this great river kelpie, that soared with excitement even when the creature snarled and showed not horse teeth at all but massive gleaming spike teeth that were as apt to rip a creature apart as any predator's.

This — this impossible legend, this fanciful nightmare — was what I wanted more than my own life.

I leapt from my horse's back. He tore the turf up in clumps as he fled to safety, but I — I stood before the creature head flung back and arms spread wide, letting the freezing droplets of the river wash over me.

I did not understand myself at all. Never in my memory had I done such a wild, untamed thing. I had not reason to seek death, no motivation to fling myself upon the cold, uncaring draught.

Practicality demanded that I return home to my loving family. Good sense bid me now at least turn and walk away.

And I threw it all away as I offered myself to the rearing, pawing water horse, my heart pounding to nearly bursting in my chest and my lungs heaving with what seemed to be sobs though I couldn't remember why I was crying and I couldn't understand why — when I saw this impossible equine creature formed of magic and likely a good dose of insanity — I felt a surge of loss so great it nearly overwhelmed me.

And then a fractured memory I could not place split into my head as if someone had stabbed a knife into my mind.

A man with a white face and a tongue like a slug leaning over me.

My vision growing narrow and dim.

And behind that man, another rising like a king from his throne, his bare chest crisscrossed with silver scars, his pale skin growing suddenly flushed with life, his short beard blue — blue like a horse or a dog. A crown was on his head, and as he stood he plucked a rib from the crown, and thrust it into the neck of the pale white man with the beard that flowed like milk over rocks. And the creature choked, spitting blood white and thick as cream, and my vision spun and faded as the man called my name, stepping forward with a look very like panic in his rolling eyes.

"Izolda! Izolda!"

And now, this strange horse made of river and shadow rose up over me and rolled his eyes in just the same way and something in me called back to him.

I gasped, and though I did not know how I knew the name or why it made my whole body tremble, the urge to utter it was overwhelming.

"Riverbarrow."

With water flinging in every direction, the kelpie spun in a sudden circle and as it spun, it grew smaller and smaller, and then, drenched from head to toe, the water washing right down him in sheets, a man stood where the kelpie had been.

I gasped at his beauty for surely no mortal man could look so lovely and so yet terrible. His short hair and beard shed water, darkening his already black hair and the strange blue-grey of his shadowed beard. Despite its color, his face was not old. Nor was it young, though I felt like I once knew it younger than this.

It had an agelessness that could have been thirty or fifty or perhaps five hundred and fifty and his eyes were the eyes of cats. The pupils dilated as they came to rest on me and a thrill of fear shot through me for he was naked to the waist and had the build and crisscrossed scars of a feared warrior.

On his head, the twisted crown looked more like thorns than anything else. In one hand — marked with a ragged hole in the center — he held a rib stained with white and in his side where that rib might have originated was a thick knot of scar and a hole that seemed to be punched straight through his body though it was neither bloody nor gory.

He did not remain still. He was striding from the river to me and to my shock he threw himself to the ground on one bent knee and lowered his glorious head.

"Oh," I gasped, stepping backward in my surprise, "Sir, your obeisance is not warranted."

"Speak to my riddle," he said and the face he turned up to me was twisted as if he mocked me, and yet his eyes shone with a joy so bright and full, that it hurt to watch it. I had to look down and bite my lip for a moment lest I be swept into any machinations he might please, for I was powerless beneath both its intensity and the desire to share in so great a joy. "Speak to my riddle, you stern visage, you startling aspect. Who has walked the Path of Princes? Who has broken the curse of the rib and set free the blood of nations? Who has flown with the Arrow? Who has danced with the Sword? Whose heart lay bleeding in the barrow? Who now — tell me who, if you can — has died side by side with her Lord in the realms of death, beneath his feet and his dominion."

I swallowed, my mouth and throat suddenly dry. "I know not, my lord."

The twist in his mouth turned to a smile of devastating triumph and he stood, suddenly, catching my hands in his and leaning down in a predatory way that made my mind scream at me to run, and yet, I held fast and met his eyes with my own.

"One last choice remains to you, Izolda, and I must ask this with you blind to the consequences. You have behind you all you once held dear. Mother, father, brothers. Hale and happy they are. Soon enough, your father will ride to the capital and find for you a good husband who breeds lovely horses fit for a king. And soon enough you will give to him fat babies and live out your life in simple satisfaction."

"If you say so, my Lord," I said, blushing at his implications. His hands on mine felt so familiar. As if they were a matching set, a team of horses trained in draft together.

"Or," he let the word hang in the air and I waited, swallowing. "Or, you can leave all that behind and come with me ... one more time." He leaned his forehead against mine in a way far too familiar for a stranger and there was a vulnerability in his eyes and a softness to his voice as he lowered it to speak this last part. "And this time, fire of my eyes, I will not bid you descend with me into the grasp of hell but instead help me birth, into the fresh age, a paradise beyond anything you've ever tasted."

I swallowed. I did not know this man. Or at least, I did not think so.

And then he lifted my hands, bringing the knuckles up to where his lips grazed them lightly as he spoke, his warm breath sending little tingles down my hands and wrists and arms where gooseflesh broke out. My heart began to race again, not out of fear or danger but out of a sudden, overwhelming attraction. I swallowed and without meaning to, I stepped forward, causing his lips to curl slightly as he kissed my knuckles and whispered.

"Heart of my own heart, fall what may. I have bought you by oath and blood, and made you my wife, and though you have been snatched from me by the currents of time and washed up upon this shore, my vows to you remain. Stay here if you wish. Enjoy the life you might have had apart from me. Or come with me now, and take your rightful place at my side, be queen to me and cherished wife, until the sands of time have all run out, and the earth has rotted away like spoiled fruit, and Death himself is so long past that the stars have burned to dust."

"I don't know what any of that means," I said, and yet ... I could feel some tug to him. It was something that went beyond my attraction to this man I'd never met, beyond how he spoke to me with such intimacy. It was something deeper and longer though I could not have guessed what it might be.

He bit his lip looking up at the sky, releasing my hands with a frustrated huff, and then turned to me with his fists on his hips. I worked very hard to keep my eyes up on his face. He cut a very fine figure. Enough to make a girl of nineteen blush.

"Speak to my riddle, wife," he said.

"Wife?"

He made a brushing gesture as if his title for me did not matter. "What is better? To lose without knowing, or find you have gained too much?"

"To lose without knowing," I said firmly. "If I must lose, then I shall bear it, but woe to the man who takes from me without expecting me to notice."

"Ha!" He laughed as if I'd solved a problem and the fretful worry on his face evaporated as he snapped his fingers.

I blinked.

And my memory was restored.

With a gasp, I turned to him and for the first time since the joust, he watched me with uncertainty in his eyes as if he did not know whether I might attack or smile.

"Do you remember, my wife?" he asked hesitantly.

"Everything," I whispered and I did not wait a moment more to claim what was mine. I strode forward with certainty, took his bearded face between my hands, and fed myself on his kisses, taking them with softness at first, and then with greater hunger and deeper intensity. Did he truly think I would choose a life without him given the chance? Did he truly think it was a mercy to leave me bereft of him?

I pulled back from him long enough to gasp, "And I choose you every time, Lord Riverbarrow."

His laugh of triumph made my heart sing.

Chapter Twenty

"I HOPE you do not set much store in titles, wife," Bluebeard said, pausing to lean once more and take for himself a swift, almost violent, kiss. "For that one is passing away now that I have claimed by blood and life the title of the Bramble King."

As if on cue, his crown rustled and the thorns rearranged themselves even though the material it was made from appeared to be black metal.

"And the curse must be broken, for I can hear your voice speaking to me, though it is day," I said, but though I felt shy to be speaking directly to him, I refused to pull back and break out of our embrace. The long days of him pressed to my back as a corpse had returned to my memory, and I was in awe now of how whole he felt — how warm and alive. I skimmed my palm down his bare chest, reveled in his shudder, and slid a finger — feather-light — around the edge of the wound in his side. His wet clothing soaked right through mine and I cradled my head to his chest and listened for his voice in my mind.

"No hold may bar me now," he said aloud and it echoed in my mind, too. "And though you can hear my voice alight upon your ear, still my heart speaks to you as the moon calls to the sea. I will not give up this rare intimacy, even though we have leave to share in others."

"Share in others?" I asked breathlessly.

I pulled back just enough to see his eyes and his quirking half-smile, and before I could demand that he confirm my suspicions, he had caught my jaw between finger and thumb, angled my face as he pleased, and pressed his lips to mine, sliding his tongue between them to open them, as if it were key to my lock.

"Do you choose to come away with me then, my one true wife?" He asked a little breathlessly when he seemed to be sated for a time. His hand was tangled up in my hair as he spoke and he seemed fascinated with it even though I was rolling my eyes. How did he always manage to untangle my braid any time I wasn't watching?

"I do," I agreed. "And will you tell me, then, how this curse was broken?"

He scooped me up before I could finish speaking and held me to his dripping chest, pausing only long enough to bite his lip as if concentrating, and then lean in to nip my cheek so that it bled his sign.

"The first Bramble King, when his rib was stolen —"

"I thought it was the creator's rib who was stolen," I objected, still a little breathless from the sting of his bite. My husband always made my head swirl with his unpredictability. Who would have expected a bite rather than a kiss? Not me.

"One and the same," he assured me with a boyish grin. "He placed a curse on men and Wittenbrand alike to fall upon them in the last age — this age — unless one soul dared step up to take on the challenge of the curse. If he did, then the curse would fall on only him, but that man must risk all for the rest."

"And you risked it," I said, certain I was right.

"And I won," he says, his grin turning cat-like.

"So you did. And will you answer all my questions now?"

"If I have a mind to do so."

"Will you answer at least a few, my husband?"

"Say that name again, Izolda Savataz, Mad Princess of Pensmoore, wife of the Arrow, Lady Riverbarrow, darling Queen of our current Bramble King."

And I did not need to guess what he wanted, not when I could turn my lips to the curve of his neck and whisper it so my lips brushed his skin and let me taste his shiver.

"Husband," I whispered.

"My true wife," he agreed burying his face into my hair, and then he spun quickly away.

Before I could catch my breath, he was once again the stomping water horse of the river, and he surged forward under me, catching me up upon his back. My fists sank into seaweed and froth when I tried to hold on, but he did not drop me as he reared, came down hard, and ducked into the river, dragging me behind him like an anchor.

It seemed I did not need to breathe as I usually did, or at least I did not need to breathe when I was with him, for I sank beneath the water and into the cold, clammy depths and I smelled the fecundity of creeks in spring, and the sharp tang of a river in autumn, the scalding ice of winter flows and the warm caress of summer streams, all at once without having to take a breath of air.

And when we emerged, it was not the mortal world we emerged into, but the sparkling, flashing, dance of the river that flowed through Riverbarrow.

I gasped.

"Am I not to be made mad then?" I asked him, as I plunged my fingers deeper into his watery mane and his fluid muscles bunched beneath me and sprang us across the width of the river to where the white pavilion formed of growing stone roots spread wide in welcome.

"Not when you are with me," he spoke into my mind.

"And what of when we are apart?" I asked, probing, for though he was here with me now, I felt very uncertain.

"Forfend that it ever be so," he spoke into my mind, and then he whirled again, scattering water in every direction and leaving me too dizzy to properly see the transformation from watery horse to half-naked, dripping man, though the one carried me on his back and the other in his arms. He ducked his wet head in close to me and when the tips of our noses touched, he drew in a long breath as if he were drinking me in and he whispered, "I journeyed through the folds of time and climbed across the tides of space to find you and pluck you out of your life and home and gather you up into my arms. What manner of thing could exist that would ever tempt me to leave you, love of my love, heart of my heart? Speak a new riddle and tell me of what villain could separate we two now, or what terror could part us. Tell me of what wonder or charm might steal your heart from mine, or what

cataclysm rob from my grasp what has been bought by blood and bone, by sweat and cold death?"

"None," I gasped and his lower lip trembled for a moment before his lips parted lightly, his eyes closed, and he tilted his face just enough to catch my lips in his and drink deeply of me.

I could never tell what had bought me such fortune as to be chosen by one like this, to be swept away into madness and sanity by so precious and powerful a ... man? A king? A champion.

I did not know what to call him, but I had been given this tiny chance to leap from mortality and into his arms, and I dared not lose it, so I leapt with him not knowing where I might fall, only that it would be with the husband I had married thrice: once by law, once by vow, and once more by choice made in death.

To my startled surprise, he leaned me against the pillar of the pavilion and took his time unraveling my hair from the rest of its braid as if *that* were the main concern rather than that it was cool and he was soaking wet and mostly unclothed. But he did not look cold as he combed his fingers through my hair and then asked me, "Would you wear my token in your hair, wife of mine?"

"I'll wear whatever you like, my Bluebeard," I said, scraping his rough beard with my fingernails boldly.

"I crave your touch, wife. Do you require further invitation?"

"I rather think I do," I said shyly, watching his eyes as they warmed to me and the lines of his face as they tightened in a half-smile.

"Did I not vow to you the dedication of my body?" His eyes darkened as he watched me and his throat bobbed with a swallow. Was he — somehow — nervous, too? Though he was Bramble King now and resurrected from death?

"But was that you as a man, or you as a king, or you as a river, or you as a kelpie?" I asked. "And how many husbands am I to have, precisely?"

"Sixteen wives were required of me, and only one of my own desire," he said, his expression turning sober, though I shivered when he said the word desire and licked his lower lip in emphasis. "Who are you to demand that you will be gifted fewer husbands?" He paused and made a sound like a growl before finishing his thought. "But know this, Izolda my wife, all of them will be me."

"And what will these husbands do with me?" I asked boldly.

His grin was like lightning. It lit his face fast and violent. "Whatever I wish."

And this time when he kissed my neck, he nipped me with his sharp teeth, and when I gasped he shifted so suddenly that his movement was more like a striking snake than a mortal man, and he caught the gasp of my lips in his, and laughed as he kissed me long and deep, trapping me against the pillar so that I must submit to his kisses and the strength of his steaming body against mine.

I was happy enough to allow him this, and to add to it my own embrace and another boldness as I ran my fingers lightly over his cheeks and up to the tips of his ears and then threaded them through his hair and when he gasped and shuddered and his eyes lit with delight, I caught his gasp and stole it back and looked him in the eye, as I demanded more kisses with urgent lips and drew him closer still into my embrace.

"I have waited long centuries for this, bound to one path and one passion," he gasped when I finally allowed him to pull free, "and like my victory in all else, I have made plans to savor this, every moment, and every touch. So we must wait a little while longer, for many things require my sovereignty to set them right once more."

"I thought you were master of time herself," I gasped, lifting a leg to catch his hip and pull him back to me.

He laughed low and deep and bit his lip, "And so I am, wife of mine, but have you ever feasted a week long and learned to pace yourself a bite at a time? One small morsel of each delicacy?"

"I fear I have not," I said wryly. "My life in the mortal world was far more frugal and your world has fed me only on pain and fear."

"Then I shall teach you," he said with a decadent smile that told of pleasures to come. "And you shall attend well and learn from me how to savor each taste to its full extent."

I swallowed as he stepped back and the sight of him from head to toe made my cheeks hot. "I'm savoring now, I think."

"But only for a moment, for I fear we both present poor rulers as we stand and must clothe ourselves more ably for what is next," he said but he did not look ashamed of his current mode of dress as he strolled out across the pavilion and up the steps to the great rooted tower that presided over the waterfall. I followed him, admiring him as he walked and climbed, and worrying that perhaps I did not have his ability to savor a meal over many days for my own thoughts were hot and sharp and fast and very unbefitting of a virgin bride — if I could be such a thing now that I was seven years and one death married.

The tower was sparsely appointed, but he led me to the uppermost room and there we found three things. A pool, his mirror — which I had thought was gone forever — and a long empty bed with a ring set on it.

Bluebeard gestured to the pool and when I balked he said, "Surely, it will be more embarrassing to walk around smelling mortal than to bathe before your husband."

I had no idea what it meant to smell mortal.

"Orderly thing of designations and logic, this must appeal to you," he said lightly but he turned his back and bowed to his mirror. "We'll be needing fitting accouterments, mirror."

I stripped out of my homespun woolen dress and underthings as quickly as I could, taking advantage of his turned back. I was already briskly bathing myself in the warm pool when he began to dress, and I could not help it, my eyes roamed over him, admiring him as he outfitted himself in strange clothing — no underthings at all, because I supposed a king required no modesty, breeches made of something that seemed to be dragonfly wings woven into cloth. They fitted like fine silk and had he been less of a man or lower than a king he would reasonably feel shame in such strange attire.

The jerkin to follow was spiderweb and both it and the more scandalous portions of his breeches were masked by a crisscross of hand-thick belts that both accentuated his lithe figure and were used to sling various swords and knives and even a pair of curved sickles, about his person. His doublet — when it was produced — was lined with rabbit and sewn all over with what appeared to me to be the moment he was placed in the land of death, his wives surrounding him in the embrace of the jutting ribs. There was even a small Grosbeak picked out as a centaur and the brooding figure of Death.

I gasped at it and could not tear my eyes from it even as he cloaked it with a short cape made entirely of living moss, and then took out a sickle no larger than my finger and set to work trimming his beard until it was nearly clean shaven, revealing only enough of itself to remind us it had been there until moments ago. I was still staring when he turned his boyish grin to me and let his eyes light at the sight of me.

So enamored was I by the light in his eyes, that I forgot what he was seeing for a full breath before sense came over me and I felt the heat of my blush fill my face and climb up my ears.

"Shall I be dressed so gorgeously?" I asked, trying desperately to stay cool under his careful scrutiny.

"I care not," he said, flicking an idle hand as if to dismiss what I might wear. "But I'll not deny that it will delight me to know you wear this flesh beneath your garment, for I missed it when you wore the flesh of another."

"The hand, especially," I said dryly, flexing my flesh hand that once was a skeleton and stepping out from the pool to see what the mirror had spat out for me.

"On the contrary, the hand is the only part that pains me to lose."

"Not the perfect hourglass figure or the heart-shaped face?"

"Indeed no, for you wear this sober visage much more fittingly. "The hand, however, set you off most magnificently, and I shall think long on whether to restore it to you."

"I rather think that should be my decision."

He made a moue that was almost a pout, but inclined his head in agreement. "If you say so. Though you did dedicate your flesh to me in our wedding vows."

"I imagined you using it differently."

That pleased him. He smiled broadly. "And you shall tell me of all these imaginings. Later."

And then he leaned against a post of the bed, clearly intent on watching me as I dressed.

I did not think it was possible for my face to grow hotter. I was wrong. But I swept up the offerings of the mirror and dressed with my chin held high, bold as you please. I had nothing to be ashamed of and I refused to hide girlishly from the only gaze I sought.

Fortunately, the ban on underthings did not seem to extend to me. I dressed in a filmy silk shift first — real silk, not spiderweb, though I supposed there was little difference — and then carefully fitted on the dress offered by the mirror.

It was backless, of course.

"I left the scars. I hope you don't mind," Bluebeard said quietly, referring to my back with a gesture. I paused.

"*You* left the scars?" I felt a little breathless at that admission.

"When I brought you back from the lands of death and restored you to your place in time. I gave you back the hand, and healed your wounds, but I left the scars. They are dear to me. You took them for my sake."

"Very sensible," I said, though it was not at all sensible. It was sentimental and something about it made my heart burn so hard that I wanted to ignite his, too.

The dress was fitted around the bodice and boned for shape and support, with soft draping white fabric emphasizing the faint curve of my breast. No one would notice the top of the dress, for the skirt was in a style where the ivory outer skirt swept up to show a layer of filmy petticoats underneath, but from the arch of the brocade outskirt hung a great plentitude of swords and knives and daggers of sizes as long as my femur, to as small as my littlest finger hanging down from silver and gold chains decorated with thick brambles. They ought to have been ridiculously heavy and yet by dint of magic — most likely — were no heavier than brocade. And rather than the clatter they ought to produce when I moved, they made a sound like faint wind chimes and swirled gracefully with my every movement. They were woven in and out with more silver and gold chains all fitted to drape from a woven belt of brambles as wide as my hand that clasped around my waist.

"This is rather much," I said calmly as I beheld myself in the glass but I did not think my husband agreed for his face was lit with pride. He bit his bottom lip as if he were holding back a laugh or perhaps a snarl, and he moved to stand behind me and look in the mirror at the pair of us.

I shivered under his scrutiny and then barely kept myself from melting when his head tilted, and he put his hands in my hair. With a look of concentration, he teased and tangled it until it looked as wild as he was, and only when I appeared as if I were a warrior queen out of a Wittentale, did he finally stop.

"Perfect," he declared with a smile. "My fearsome bride, ready to work her will across the face of the earth."

I did not think it suited me any more than all these impractical Wittenhame creations did, but I did look more fit for a Wittenhame court than I did in my threadbare wool dress, so I smiled my agreement.

"And now," Bluebeard said, turning to the bed. "We deal with something long overdue."

Chapter Twenty-One

I SWALLOWED NERVOUSLY but found myself blinking when he said, "Sparrow. She who was faithful until the end is owed what she was promised."

And before I could say one word or another, he picked up the ring from the bed and I realized it was a small silver one in the shape of a Sparrow.

"She bid me hide her token here and it is well I did," he told me, smiling as if sharing a secret with me, but I did not know what he meant by that until he led me out of the room and down the steps and back out to the pavilion. I was nearly out of breath when we reached the spot overlooking the river and misted by the waterfall but his boyish grin told me he was about to do something amazing. "Ready?"

I nodded, though I did not know what I was agreeing to.

And then he lifted a hand, easily, as if he was waving to a friend, and there was a ripple in the water. Then out of the river, good as new, Sparrow walked out, dripping wet. She was perfectly whole, no longer a severed head and missing body, and the smile she gave my husband made me feel both nervous and jealous. After all, had she not died with me unable to prevent it — twice? Would she bring a complaint to my husband?

"My captain," Bluebeard said smiling with a powerful pride as he looked at her. Unlike her master, she had the decency to exit the river fully clothed. "Come to your due."

And she was smiling, too, as she walked up to the pavilion, mounted the steps, and then knelt gracefully to him as he offered her the ring.

"I give back to you both your ring and your life, dedicated in my service and lost for a time. My gratitude you had already, my respect you have now earned."

As he spoke there was a flutter of wings as songbirds came drifting in from the open sky, landing on his head and shoulders. He looked over his shoulder at me and his eyes softened.

"And I believe you have a gift for her, fire of my eyes?"

I felt my brow furrow and I tried to think, but no answer came to me. What gift would I have to offer? I looked down at myself, thinking perhaps one of the daggers might suffice.

"It is gift enough that she is no longer dogged by that grim pet of hers," Sparrow said lightly, but she was watching me, too, not yet standing as she awaited my gift.

"A name, I think, that you no longer require now that you find yourself to be wife of the Bramble King," Bluebeard prompted me and I gasped.

"Lady Riverbarrow," I realized as I said it. He was giving her his landhold, wasn't he? Bequeathing it to her as if he had died, which of course he had, but he was alive again now. Alive and king. And that meant he must relinquish direct reign over his former landhold.

I met Bluebeard's eyes and saw the sadness there, lingering, like watching your former home from decades past. And then he reached into his shirt and drew out a pendant — the very one I had worn with the pearl of Riverbarrow strung on it — and he passed it to me and I offered it to Sparrow.

She took the pendant, smiling. "I knew that in the end, you would conquer all your foes, Lord Arrow."

"Of course you did," Bluebeard said lightly. "How could I not?"

And I barely managed to hold back a laugh at how light his tone was over such a very narrow miss.

"And as you took on the risk of my defeat and with it lost your immortality, so I give now to you, your portion of the reward. Your Wittenbrand life is returned to you, and with it my lands, the lordship over Riverbarrow from the boundary of the northern snows to the southern heat, from the western mountains to the eastern sea. I offer to you the care of my people and disposition of the wealth and power inherent in this place. Along with all of it, I bequeath to you the name Arrow. Fly from my bow, Lady Arrow, and accomplish for me all the things that must be made so from beginning to end."

He took her hand and drew her up on her feet, and I couldn't help my pang of jealousy as he put his hand on her shoulder and escorted her out of the pavilion and then stepped to the edge of it, drew from the waves a great horn, and blew it soundly.

As if they had been waiting for this exact moment, his people appeared. Small and strange, great and shambling, they came. Toads in top hats and mice in waistcoats, strange branch-and-root creatures that shuffled across the ground, a massive creature large as a tower made entirely of rock and her two sons also made of rock, a pair of dragonflies, and an elderly beaver carrying a spear, and more besides, each odder and wilder and further from the mortal world than the last.

And when all had assembled, Bluebeard stood before them and simply breathed, in and out. They waited for him, seeming to hold their breaths, but with every breath he took, I realized things were changing. The creatures grew larger and stronger and brighter, backs straightening, bodies healing from wounds I had not noticed, eyes brightening. And with each breath, the world around them greened and flourished, and they began to dance and sing as more and more of them came, being healed and made whole.

This, then, was what they had been pleading for when they had come to him in his home. One who looked like a tree winked at me as he passed by and all placed a kiss — or something like a kiss — on Sparrow's hand and she looked both eager and shy all at once as they processed past her, making their obeisances. This was the healing they'd asked for. This was the restoration.

Each time I glanced around me, Riverbarrow was brighter and more flourishing, the river swelling, the trees growing before my eyes, flowers bursting from the ground and fruiting, pink returning to the cheeks of children, and a bounce coming back to their elders' steps.

It was like watching Spring come to the world in a single hour instead of months, and my heart swelled to it. I felt the warmth of pride when I looked to my husband who was fulfilling all his promises to his land and people. They would be well now. And they would be happy.

"My folk," Bluebeard said gravely when they seemed to be all assembled and they crowded around him with a familiarity I envied, some going so far as to sit on his shoulders and head, as he spoke and others crowding right up against his legs, one large furry horse with her head bumping against his shoulder so often that he had to fight to keep his balance. "You pled with me for mercy and it is yours. You asked for prosperity, I have given it to you four times over. My heart would have been very glad to go on being your lord, to lead you through this dawning age of delight and prosperity, but my place is with all of the Wittenhame now, and thus it is not to be. And so I offer to you Sparrow, once my captain of war, now my captain of peace, first a member of my Court of Fools, then a counselor of the wise when my wife sought aid, now pledged to me and to you as the Arrow, the shot of the Bramble King out into the world. May she strike true and strike down your fears and worries."

There was a cheer — a strange one as it came from the lips of both men and beasts — and it rippled out from among them and Bluebeard lifted his voice and said, "The Lady Riverbarrow has taken my place as Lord and as your river. May her reign over you be blessed and may I offer both her and you this one last gift."

And then he closed his eyes and opened his hands and flowers burst up from every plant and tree and ripened and exploded into fruit — all kinds, all at once — raspberries and strawberries, peaches and apples, watermelon, and honeydew, and grapes and I was still in awe when he whispered loudly to Sparrow.

"They all have wine at the core. Your festivities tonight will be the envy of every landhold in the Wittenhame."

And to my surprise, I realized she was crying. At first, I thought it was from gratitude, but after a heartbeat, I realized he was crying too, and he leaned over suddenly and wrapped an arm around me, gently displacing the creatures who had been resting on him, and it was only when he spoke that I understood.

"I will not see you again, my people. This place is hidden from all but those of Riverbarrow, and though my life and strength will sustain you, this is no longer solely my realm. I will visit you here only as Bramble King. But I wish for you untold blessings, for by your faithfulness and steadfastness you have remained mine through ash and dust, and so now you must reap fruit, wine, and happiness with the guardian I have set up for you."

And he nodded once to Sparrow — the new Arrow and Lady Riverbarrow — a brisk nod of finality.

And then a cloud of songbirds poured in from every direction and swept us up and away, and I was not at all surprised when my husband's arms wrapped tight around me and turned me so he could bury his face in my belly, ignoring the sharp blades of my skirt or how the chains tried to catch on his crown of brambles as he shook with what I thought might be the tearing pain of walking away from a place that had anchored him from a time before Pensmoore was even an inkling in the mind of King Pen.

I knew this feeling. I'd felt it myself, not just once, but twice when I was ripped from the family I loved into the arms of the unknown. I felt my own eyes smarting as I felt the echo of his pain through his mental voice and I leaned into it, caressing his silken hair and whispered into his ear.

"All things pass, but some things remain."

"Remain with me then, wife," he whispered into my ribs and I let my hands drift to his sides and hitch him a little closer to show that I agreed. And though I was comforting him, I had never felt so comforted myself as his lightly furred arms — stronger than tree roots and just as hard where they wrapped around me — gave me the feeling of being encircled and guarded all around. His tears, though they soaked my white dress, felt like spring rains. They brought with them the certainty that something old was passing and something new was yet to be discovered.

"I will remain with you all the days of our lives, my Bluebeard."

"Do not forget that name, fire of my eyes," he whispered and I felt the move and pull of his lips through the cloth of my dress against my sensitive ribs. "For I am quickly losing every name and title ever bequeathed to me except this last one, and though I must become the Bramble King, it pains me to lose what I once was."

"I will not forget," I whispered, leaning my head down so that I might let my own lips brush the shell of his ear, and let one of my hands fist in his hair as I held him even closer. "Though places and ages pass, never will I forget you."

Chapter Twenty-Two

I DID NOT KNOW how far we flew like that or where we went, not even whether it was in this time or the next but when the birds let us down it was in a forest on the edge of a river. The water of the river was pewter and the forest shades of grey and white of mist. The mortal world, then, for nowhere in the Wittenhame could be so plain.

"Will you bring restoration to every place then, husband?" I whispered as his arms unraveled from me and we found our feet. "To all who served you? Will they dance for ten years like in the story of the Wittenbrand?"

In answer, he drew out a key from around his neck — my golden key. My hand flew to my chest where it had been before.

"Shall we look at this room one last time before I close it forever?" he asked as if that would answer my question.

I did not want to go back into that room and watch my days disappear, but I nodded gravely to him.

"How was it, husband, that you triumphed over Death in the end?" I whispered as he set the key in my hand and he leaned in to where he could speak over my shoulder as he replied.

"He could not forbid me rise. Not when I had brought all things to a close. Not when my blood had graced the Wittenbrand and bought a new age. He did indeed try to hold me down, and I fought him for what felt like an age and half an age but in the end, the Bramble King wins, and all those who set themselves up as his enemies must fall — even Death himself."

I made a sound of agreement in the back of my throat. Had I not once been his enemy? I found that I much preferred a world where Bluebeard was Bramble King, for while I could not predict all that would mean, I knew it would be a world much better than the alternative.

"Do not hesitate too long, wife," he whispered in my ear. "For our enemies still roam across this earth tearing apart its sinews and nesting in its bones. I feel them as if they were an itch within my own body. I own a violent urge to drive them out and drink their despair as a tonic."

"Don't let me slow you, then," I said dryly and I turned the key in the air and strode into the room before I'd taken in what I was seeing.

The moment I did, I froze.

The hourglass at the end of the room was shattered, not a garnet was in sight, and there was broken glass and bent, molten metal on the floor where once it had been.

"My days," I gasped.

"Gone now," my husband whispered to me and when I looked at him he licked his lips nervously, pitched his voice low, and met my gaze with a burning look in his. "I fear, true wife, that you are burdened with me for many centuries to come for while I shared in your days and spent them like water while you still lived and I had perished, now you spend my days for yours have all run out. We drank too deeply of them and found their end just as the poison sapped your strength."

I swallowed, feeling slightly ill. "And how great is the store of your days, Bramble King, can you spare even one for me?"

But his laugh was the type that restored strength to the bones like a hearty broth. It rang out full and deep and echoed through the chamber and he smiled so widely at me that I found myself beginning to smile too, when at last he was able to answer me.

"Speak to my riddle, Mad Princess. How deep is the ocean, how many are the stars, what number will you give to the insects that crawl upon the mortal earth? Know you that my days number more than all these."

"Oh," I said, feeling too stunned to say more.

"And now, bid your sisters goodbye for you'll not see them again," he said firmly, and I looked around at the crumbling walls, the ceiling that had fallen in revealing a blank sky, and the pillars crumbled to dust. Nothing at all remained of the room except for the books the others had kept.

I walked to the nearest one and opened it. I was Margaretta's. And when I opened it, I saw a pretty girl of about nineteen dancing at a ball in the court of Pensmoore and there was the king I had known, only he was a child, and she danced and danced with a mortal man. I flipped the page and she held a baby as soft and golden as she, flipped another, and she ran with him as a toddler, and with every page I flipped I saw her life as if it were a story spooling out into children and grandchildren and the bounty of life and when the story was over the book faded from my hand.

"She lived the life she was meant for, her days returned to her with interest," Bluebeard said, leaning casually against a crumbling wall and kicking at a piece of mortar. "Will you read the others?"

"I think I ought to," I said, swallowing. "Someone should remember them."

"I remember," he said firmly.

"And do you miss them?" I asked, raising a single eyebrow. He cocked his head in confusion.

"I honor their sacrifice, though in the end, it was no loss to them, as I did try to tell each of them when I stole her as a bride."

"But it might not have gone that way," I reminded him, sensibly. "And you were never very clear on what you meant."

He waved a hand. "Success was never in question."

"I rather think it was," I said acidly, because it was all very well and good to be glad of a victory but rather silly to pretend it had been a sure thing when it had been anything but that.

I read through the books and he watched me read, and I was pleased to see his foxy first wife find a brutish-looking husband who treated her kindly and gave her fifteen sons. Happier still to watch Tigraine become a mighty warrior queen. She did not marry at all, but ruled until she died in battle when her hair was white and her strength faded. Each wife lived a life full and long — even Ki'e'iren whose life I did not wish to honor seemed settled in a palace and if she looked somewhat distracted and seemed to peer into shadows that were not there, that might only be her suspicious temperament at work. When the last book was shut and winked out, I looked at my smug husband.

"And so you kept these promises, too. For all sixteen of your wives."

He held up a single finger.

"Speak to this riddle wife. If a man has sixteen coins but has never had fifteen of them, how many does he have."

I rolled my eyes. "You can hardly pretend you were not married to all these other women."

He shook his single finger at me, a look of repressed mirth in his eyes. "Have you no answer to the riddle, then?"

"One," I said dryly. "He has one coin."

"And I have one wife," Bluebeard said, grinning in triumph, and then to my shock he sprang forward and flung me over his shoulder, laughing as he bounded from the room in one leap and tossed the key over his shoulder.

The room closed behind us, and it took its secrets with it. Though I lived a very long time — forever by the reckoning of mortals — I never again saw the room nor the wives who had helped me fight for the life of our husband, but that did not stop me from teasing the man relentlessly about them for what else was there to do?

Chapter Twenty-Three

HE BROUGHT me out to the misty clearing between the dark trees and I revised my opinion of this place. It might not be the mortal world at all. I stood in one place and turned, frowning, as he lounged against a tree. He was letting a small bird dress his hair for him as he studied his fingernails.

Around us, pollen thick as snow drifted through the faint breeze. As the mists lifted, the pollen grew thicker and I felt some grand shift in the land — the passing of one into the other. Night was falling, soft, orchid-toned, and billowy.

I yawned and Bluebeard made a rumbling sound much like a growl.

"Where are we now, Bramble King?" I asked him, feeling a little wistful. I was a queen without a castle or so much as a loft to call my own, and I was very tired.

"The Wittenhame burned and melted and collapsed into the mortal world," Bluebeard said, lifting his chin and preening a little as the small nuthatch put finishing touches on his grooming. "This spot is one of those where they melted together."

"So it is both mortal and Wittenhame," I said, studying it. The tiny clearing was hardly bigger than a space where a pair of deer might bed down, but it was soft with moss and drifts of pollen. I could not see the Wittenhame here at all.

"A fitting place to spend our first night after we have walked death's land, don't you think?" he asked me with a slight smile and his own wistful look in his eye.

"A bed and a warm fire would not go amiss," I suggested a little daunted by the idea of camping in this glen with no tinderbox or blanket, wearing a cold hard dress of knives. And how would he stay warm clothed in spiderweb and insect wings?

He swallowed in a way that suggested to me that pollen and nuthatches were all he had to offer me tonight.

"I shall keep you warm and pillow your head on my chest — if you will consent to spend this night here with me."

His eyes were shadowed as he spoke and they seemed to darken with his words, catching my breath a little as if it were fabric sliding along a rough fence post. I had to swallow to find my voice.

"If this is your home, then it is mine, lord of the Wittenhame," I said, a little breathless.

He made no move toward me, regarding me from his place against the tree. The little nuthatch leapt from his shoulder and away and he pulled the crown of brambles from his head like a girl might drag down a drooping daisy chain. He toyed with it in his hands as it rustled and shifted and then he looked up at me with blazing eyes, and behind them, I saw not a great king of power who had defeated death but a nervous bridegroom approaching his new bride. He bit his lip, catching it between his teeth, and drew in a long breath.

I waited. His thoughts were opaque to me.

"Something troubles you, husband?" I said carefully. "You, who have flown on the backs of birds and broken the neck of Death?"

His chuckle was grim. "Here I stand before you and I find I must clutch at courage to take another step." He paused and swallowed, hanging his crown on a broken stub of a branch sticking out from one of the trees encircling our hollow. "Can you accept me as bridegroom, Izolda? Can you embrace me knowing I am this man but also this hollow in which we stand? That I am the river you hear bubbling, and the moon that rises to limn your lovely skin, and the nuthatch who flew away just now?"

"You are all that?" I asked, teasingly. "How shall it all fit in this hollow, then?"

But he was not wrong to ask, for how could a mortal mind accept all that and also bring him into her bed?

"Tell me true, wife," he said, still keeping himself across the hollow from me.

I spread my hands wide and spoke my heart. "If I cannot accept that, my Bluebeard, then where shall I go? For you are not only everywhere by right of Bramble King, you are also everywhere to me by right of heart and vow. When I look at the moon I will see you, whether you are moon or mortal. When I hear the bird sing, it will be your voice echoing in my mind whether you are bird or memory. Such is the way of a heart anchored deep in love."

A faint smile appeared on his lips, but still, he hung back. I was not much of one with words — not like him. Perhaps mine were not enough to assure him.

"All these must be our children," he said, gesturing to the singing frogs along the river and the birds in the trees nearby, bedding down for the night. "For as Bramble King, I cannot give you natural-born little ones."

I swallowed. "Are you saying you cannot make love to me as a man to a woman?"

For some reason, this question left me feeling raw inside in a way I had not expected.

His eyes darkened further and this time he took a sudden step to shorten the gap between us. He looked surprised at that, as if he had not meant to move.

"That is not what I am saying at all. I shall feed you on love until you are overflowing. I shall drink of you long and deep as a thirsty man who finds water. I shall pour into you all the wild passions of my untamed soul and find in you the rest I have long sought and never acquired. You are order to my chaos, stillness to my energy, feather to my flint, and I shall love you as no mortal had ever loved, as no Wittenbrand has ever dreamed of, and you shall never lack but I fill it, never want but I sate you, never tire of my endless offerings at the altar of your heart."

I swallowed, somewhat overwhelmed, and this time it was I who took a slow step forward and I gestured to the land around us, "Then I shall take all these to my heart, my husband. And I shall take you deeper into it, too. Together we will tend your land and people as though they were children to us."

He made a humming sound in the back of his throat. I thought that perhaps he was pleased. But I had worries of my own as we stood here, finding our places as man and wife.

"But what of my life, Bramble King? For I am dust and ashes. I will fade and die in what will feel to you but a moment."

"Ah," he said and now he was smiling as he took the last step between us and cupped my cheek with his hand. The look in his eye was triumph as if he had won yet another battle. "But I am now and I am later, I am this moment and I am what is to come. And as you are one with me as my wife, so are you the same."

I turned my face and kissed his palm and he let me, his lips parting slightly as if he were enjoying the gesture. I certainly was.

"Tell me then," I whispered into his palm, still confused. "How are you one with time and the land?"

"Each life and moment is sustained by me."

"And me?"

He leaned forward and put his forehead to mine.

"I sustain you, too. More than any of these, since our days — both in number and substance — are shared." He leaned down and kissed me softly. "I could never stop breathing this life into you. How could I? I have made you my very heart. Given to the barrow. Taken back by my own hand. I refuse to surrender you to another. All challengers must hear and tremble, or find themselves lost without land or time to succor them."

"Well," I said between his kisses, a little breathless as they turned fervent and wordless. "I suppose that settles it then."

And my own kisses joined his and for a time our language was the language of affection and reverence and there was no room for words or rational thoughts. I did not miss them. This new speech filled my mouth and heart and hands and left room for little else.

He was right, it turned out. The hollow was warm enough and his chest made an excellent pillow and the sword dress was not an issue at all. It hung in the tree next to the crown and sang pretty wind chime songs as the moon rose high and watched us. But it was not spying for it was not only the moon but also the lover I held in my arms, just as the hollow held me while the man kissed and adored. Had I never tasted the Wittenhame, I might find such contradictions impossible, but I had walked the Path of Princes and found now that I did not care if my world was comprehensible so long as it was full of my Bluebeard.

Chapter Twenty-Four

I WOKE with my head on my husband's warm chest and his breath in my hair. His arms came around me, warm and secure, a gentle weight on my skin.

"I dreamed all the world blossomed for you and you sang to me of the stars," he whispered into my hair and I pressed my cheek to his chest and pushed up so I could meet his cat's eyes gaze with my own and our shared smile shot through me with warmth and security.

"I slept like the dead," I said. "And I would know exactly how they sleep for I have seen their grim repose." I paused there for a breath. "But I woke in your arms this morning, just as I woke to life from death by your word."

"So you have," he agreed, and his smile was so full of burgeoning joy that it was almost painful to watch. It washed over me with the rise of the bright sun, its beams just as warm and golden.

The kiss, when our lips met, sent thrills of joy straight through me and I thought that perhaps he felt the same, for he lingered there a while with me, inhaling deeply as if to memorize my scent, and offering gifts of small kisses to grace my skin. I offered the same, for while my affections might be lesser than what he could give, they held within them all the yearnings of my soul.

"Would that we might linger here, wife, in the heart of the forest, but you and I have work to do this day."

"I am no shirker," I teased, offering one last kiss before I found my feet.

His smile and the twinkle in his eye made my heart flip over and my breath catch.

"Will you let me dress you?" His voice was low and tinged with what I knew now to be desire.

I nodded, mutely, and with a wink, he snapped his fingers, and we were both fully dressed — not what I had imagined, but with him things never were.

My garments were rough and painful and when I looked toward him with a question in my eye. I saw his were the same.

"We go to do grim work today, fire of my eyes. I thought it fitting that we dress for the occasion."

I nodded, taking in his clothing — breeches of woven nettle and bramble belts that wound 'round his hips. Boots of the same. A garland of thistles hanging loose like a baldric across his naked, scarred chest, showing very plainly where his rib had been ripped from his side. A small half-jacket of living brambles that came down to the middle of his rib cage but rose up in a tall collar around his neck and ears. In the brambles, small creatures climbed — beetles, luna moths, and even — I thought — a small saw-whet owl. He reached for the Bramble Crown and set it upon his head, and when it met his brow, the sun itself seemed to grow warmer and more golden as if it, too, were pleased to see its king crowned.

He arranged my hair himself, to my blushes, combing his fingers through the tangles and weaving it across one side and then down to the other. My boots, belt, and short jacket matched his — though, thankfully, the living brambles were not inhabited — and my dress was of woven thistle.

When he had finished my hair, he wove for me a crown of thistles and with red, painful-looking hands, he set it upon my brow and his smile lit my heart and flooded me with warmth and contentment enough that I did not care that my skin was aflame from our garments.

"Grant me a request, my wife," he whispered.

"Ask it," I whispered back, and he lowered his head until his lips were a breath away from mine and then ran his reddened knuckles down my jaw with gentle appreciation.

"Let me take your flesh hand for the breadth of a day."

I gasped, surprised by his request, but what could he ever ask for that I would not give?

"Take it, then," I said and he snapped his fingers and my left hand was bone once more.

"And now we go to the land of mortals and dispense the pain and discomfort we share," he said, smiling as he took my skeletal hand in his and led me through the swirling pollen and out of our hollow.

I expected us to step into a forest, but I was not surprised when we did not. I had lived too long with my husband to be surprised anymore by sudden changes of place and time. I was, however, startled and somewhat horrified by what I saw.

We stood before the palace in Pensmoore, the city fanning out behind us. If I had not been with him, the swirling clouds of pollen and the way every plant in sight was in bloom — from the vines that crawled up shop walls to the grasses growing between cobblestones — might have stunned me. But I was not stunned right now.

"Pensmoore seems very fecund," I murmured.

"My presence has that effect now," he murmured back, shooting me a wicked look that made my cheeks blush hot, and before I could say anything else he led me straight through the gates and directly to the guards standing before us.

They wore blue. They were not mortal.

"Where is the Pensmoore green?" I asked, my voice hard with my worry.

"An apt question, wife," Bluebeard drawled but I knew by the sharp look in his eye that his casual tone was a ruse. "Care to explain, guard?"

"We do not answer to outsiders," the Wittenbrand said. He was a great hulking creature with a massive polearm held in one hand. I said "was" because he quickly became so when Bluebeard snapped his fingers and with a shivery tinkle as if gemstones were being shaken out of a bag, little sparks of green leapt from his heart to Bluebeard's hand and then he collapsed, so dead that he already stank before he hit the floor.

"Who else would call his king an outsider?" Bluebeard asked, eyeing the other Wittenbrand who had stood with the first.

When none spoke, he strode past the stunned guards, mounting the steps to the palace. They trailed behind him like lost puppies.

After so long away, the palace seemed small and dull to me.

A Wittenbrand who was dressed like he thought he was something hurried toward us. His short cape swept behind him, sewn all over with what I thought might be human ears and his doublet was stitched with finger-bone beads as decoration. His face had the faint greenish cast that Bluffroll shared, and I smirked at the concern on his face.

"Lord Bluffroll is not seeing guests in the court at the moment," he said, his voice coming out choked. He must have already heard about the guard Bluebeard had killed.

Bluebeard made a brushing away motion and kept walking and I strode at his side, just as cold-faced and dead-eyed as he was.

It was not a show for me. While Bluebeard had all the attention of the yipping Wittenbrand, my eyes had been searching for mortals, and what I saw deeply troubled me. The staff was not right. There were servants, most certainly. But they scuttled around with heads down and walked with limps or faces hidden. Some bore terrible scars across their faces. Others were missing fingers or even hands. I felt ill at the sight. My family ruled this land and it was bound to me. Why had my people been so mistreated and who would set it right?

"Save it up, my grim monstrosity," Bluebeard murmured to me. "Save it for the ones responsible."

The Wittenbrand following us was still trying to protest when Bluebeard reached the throne room and flicked a finger. There had been two rows of Wittenbrand guards in full regalia there. There were none standing now. They lay on the ground stone dead and already rotting. I swallowed down bile as I stole a glimpse at my husband's face.

"Think you their punishment too great? I do not think you will judge so for long."

He was right. When — at a flick of his wrist — the doors to the throne room opened wide, I certainly did not think his judgment was too harsh. If anything, he had been too merciful.

This was not the throne room as it had been in my brother's day nor even as it had been in the old king's day when first I had broken the Law of Greeting and won for myself a husband. This was entirely different.

Just inside the door, a statue had been erected in bronze and I grimaced at what I depicted. Someone had cast a very recognizable depiction of me — my one hand skeletal and the scars on my back through my open dress were dead giveaways — but they had cast me on all fours, crawling on a slab of rough-hewn rock that I thought was meant to be mud. A leash in a ribbon of silver ran to my captor's hand and one of his feet was positioned between my shoulder blades. The Wittenbrand depicted in this role looked a lot like Bluffroll — but larger, broader, and more handsome. The sculptor had spent time lovingly adding detail upon detail to his bare muscled torso and there were even small details brought to life like the exact angle of his lower incisors sticking out of his lips and the precise curl of his long hair.

I shuddered at my first sight of it, and my husband stiffened enough that I felt it through our clasped hands. I was so shaken by the casting that it took me a moment before my eyes moved onto the rest and when they did I was horrified.

The only mortals in the room were mounted on the walls — not dead as one might expect, but fully alive, just hung up and nailed to the walls through the spot where the chest met the shoulders. They were dressed in blue — forbidden in Pensmoore — and I wished that was the worst shock of what had been done to them. They stared at me through a glaze of pain and hopelessness. And to my horror, each of them was missing their left hand, severed at the wrist.

Well then. This must be why my husband had bid me show my skeletal hand.

On either side of the throne were a man and woman I assumed were king and queen. Her, I did not recognize, though she had the look of Rouranmoore about her. He, however, was my nephew Rolgrin, and on his head was his crown, melted in such a way that it looked as if it had been jammed onto his skull while still hot.

I swallowed down bile and managed to voice my question aloud.

"Why are they dressed in blue?"

The Wittenbrand assembled in the court took this to mean they could laugh, which I rather thought was a foolish response, for if my husband had stiffened at the sight of the degrading statue of me, then he flinched at the sound of their laughter and it was not a flinch of pain or fear or even embarrassment.

Fury radiated off of him like heat and he tilted his head slightly to the side as he looked past the rows of opulently dressed Wittenbrand dressed in the garb of mortals — perhaps dresses made of living squirrels or flowing waterfalls were too hard to maintain in the mortal world — to the throne where Bluffroll lounged with a shining golden crown on his head and a wide smile on his lips.

"Is this how the Bramble King is to be greeted?" Bluebeard asked quietly. "With laughter? His wife degraded, his people maimed, his court reduced to rubbish?"

"Wear all the brambles you want, it doesn't make you Bramble King," Bluffroll's voice boomed out from across the room, but he straightened on the throne as if he were suddenly less comfortable in the seat. "This place was gifted to me by the true Bramble King who was once Lord Coppertomb, he whose Coronation Ball looms close. It is mine to do as I please. And did I not please well?" He gestured now, coyly, at the statue. "There was a bronze casting of the Mad Princess, Savior of Pensmoore, when I arrived here. She held a sword aloft and was missing a hand. Apparently, she guided their king to victory and prosperity and united this land with Rouranmoore, and on and on. I showed these people who they ought to worship. There will be no savior for them from Bluffroll. And I have put an everlasting reminder in their flesh and in their throne room to keep that ever in their minds."

The green banners in the throne room that once depicted the white horse of Pensmoore had all been replaced by blue, as well. I was too horrified to ask all the other questions I wanted to ask. Instead, I tried a variation of my first question.

"Why blue?"

"Bluffroll takes liberties with my wife's people," Bluebeard said quietly.

And that was when Bluffroll laughed, his booming roar filling the throne room and echoing in the voices of his enthralled court.

"The mortals believe blue is bad luck. They wouldn't wear it. And I agree. It's terrible luck to wear blue. Look what happened to them when I dressed them in it and made them cook their own hands for my dinner."

I swayed, so filled with horror that I could not focus. I had brought this upon my people by coming here and guiding them for the battle. I had brought it on them by being Bluebeard's true wife and defying Coppertomb and all of his folk.

My eyes sought Bluebeard's but his were riveted on the casting.

"Marvelous, don't you think, Arrow?" Bluffroll taunted him. "Surely a man who has clawed his way back from the grave can appreciate a good reversal."

The court laughed with appreciation.

"Your filthy fantasies about my wife ..." Bluebeard said, letting his words hang in the air until the court quieted. "...annoy me."

And perhaps they did not know him as I did, because they laughed at that, even as I tried to draw in a shuddering breath, for fear had gripped me hard and held my heart. Not fear of these monsters, but fear of what devastation my husband might unleash now that I would witness.

"And what will you do, Arrow? You cannot kill a competitor," Bluffroll said smugly. He reached for a chalice of wine and drank it down, leaning forward as if he were anticipating some pleasure. "You can only run away with your tail between your legs while I take new delight in stripping your pride away with every torment I inflict upon the people who saw you as their patron saint."

"I compete for nothing now," Bluebeard said, and his voice was so quiet that I saw the court straining to hear it. "But you will, Bluffroll. You will compete and so will your court. Let us see who will be first to be eaten by worms and forgotten by history."

And then, without any warning at all, he released my hand and spread his hands wide and there was a clinking rush as sparks of every color flew from the Wittenbrand assembled there into his hands, and then they fell like scarecrows when the stick is removed. He marched across their limp bodies as they stared at him, powerless to move as his boots crushed hands and legs and faces. I could hear the crunch of their bones from where I stood. I watched him move with a mix of horror, awe, and a sense that perhaps — finally — there might be someone to right wrongs and turn tables and bring all the violence inflicted upon my people to a sharp end.

Even now, as Bluebeard walked through the throne room, puffs of pollen swirled out from him, settling on his foes and coating the ground.

I picked my way more carefully through the mass, remembering all too well what the land within the barrow had been like.

"There's no need for such dramatics, Arrow," Bluffroll said, looking nervous at the approach of my husband. "The game was won by Coppertomb."

"Speak to my riddle, Bluffroll," Bluebeard said, taking his time as he strolled over the breaking bodies of his enemies.

He paused to examine one and scoff before moving closer. Bluffroll, for his part, stood, seeming to realize that on the throne he was at a disadvantage now that he had no guards to defend him.

"Who spits in the eye of the hurricane and survives? Who pokes the unicorn and is not gored? Who dances with Death and does not descend to the barrow?"

"Is it you? Is that what you're telling me?" Bluffroll said, trying to keep his tone light, but it shook with the fear he had not managed to leash. He leaned down and plucked a massive two-handed sword from the grip of one of his fallen guards.

As Bluebeard grew closer, their disparity in height was highlighted. My husband was not a short man, but Bluffroll was nearly a head taller.

"Well," Bluebeard said, smiling slightly and then flicking his wrists and like magic — or maybe by magic? — a pair of curving swords appeared in his hands. "It certainly is not you."

I saw Bluffroll swallow from where I stood. And out of the corner of my eye, I saw Rolgrin twitch from on the wall. His eyes were following the pair. When I looked around to check, I saw that every set of eyes in the whole room was following them.

Bluebeard spun his swords and then tossed one and caught it with a laugh.

"I could snap my fingers and take your days, Bluffroll."

"You can't," Bluffroll growled, but he didn't sound entirely convinced.

Bluebeard's laugh this time was rich and full as if he were deeply enjoying himself. He danced in a swirling pattern, tossing and catching swords as if this were a show and he the principle showman, not a confrontation between what had been equals.

"I don't wear nettle and bramble and thistle for the joy of their sting," my husband said conspiratorially. "I am your true king."

"Coppertomb," Bluffroll tried to say.

"Is a weak imposter. Or did you not consider that no true Bramble King would watch the Wittenhame melt and do nothing to stop it?"

"It was the old Bramble King. It melted with him," Bluffroll said, clinging to the lie as he circled the throne, trying to keep my dancing husband in front of him. "And who cares? This mortal world is fun. I have inflicted cruelties upon this place ... this Pensmoore ... that would make the bravest Wittenbrand tremble."

"I don't doubt it," Bluebeard said and I thought that perhaps Bluffroll took his smile as approval, but I knew that smile. Every time I saw it before was right before he took a head. As if thinking the same thing, he said, "It's a shame I don't collect heads anymore. I have no proper use for them now."

Bluffroll laughed. This is all a big game, is what his posture said. We're joking, we two, is what his laugh said. It was all a bluff, just like his name, and I knew it.

"I had planned to let you live, you know," Bluebeard said. "Better the devil you know than the devil you don't, and of the remaining Lords and Ladies the only other one I know well is Sparrow."

"Your lieutenant?" Bluffroll scoffed. "Tanglecott ate her for breakfast, I heard. Better than roasted boar."

"I'd suggest you try to tell that to the new Lady Riverbarrow, but I'm afraid that I don't plan to let you live long enough to try it," Bluebeard said, feinting lightly now and forcing Blufroll to extend an arm to parry. It felt like someone trying something out to see what might happen. My breath caught a little in my chest.

Bluffroll's eyes flicked to me. "Is that not the Lady Riverbarrow?"

"Keep up," Bluebeard barked as his blade slapped Bluffroll's, forcing him to change his footing and lunge at Bluebeard. My husband was somewhere else when the heavy blade landed, the flat of his curved sword slapped Bluffroll's rear. "That's the Bramble Queen, second only to me in the rule of the Wittenhame and your sovereign."

"That's not how it works," Bluffroll said, his breath growing heavy as he tried to match Bluebeard's frenetic pace. I could barely see their blades in the air, but I could see the sweat forming on Bluffroll's brow.

"Speak to this riddle, then, Bluffroll, last of your name."

"Last of my name? You can't declare that!" He sounded panicky now.

"Who speaks and it is so? Who holds the world in his breast and the fates of men and beasts between his fingertips."

Bluffroll was much quicker this time. "You do."

Bluebeard paused in his swordplay and leaned in to wink at him. "Yes."

And then he was rolling away again, spinning, blades dancing in the air as if to unheard music. "And Izolda Savataz of House Northpeak, of Pensmoore, of the Mortal Lands, known heretofore as the Mad Princess, is my true bride and the Queen of Brambles and she will have your honor."

Bluffroll shot a wild glance at me and then at the statue he had cast in bronze and his mouth opened and then shut and then his face turned hard.

"I regret nothing," he growled. "And were I to do all this again, I would do it in exactly the same fashion."

Bluebeard shrugged. "It seems you wish to hurry your meeting with Death. Do be my most honored guest."

He flung his swords outward and to my surprise, they flew right past Bluffroll and stuck in his gilded throne, and before I could even gasp, Bluebeard had lunged forward, picked up Bluffroll in his powerful grip, and thrown him against the wall behind the throne.

He landed with a smack right between my nephew and his queen, and Bluffroll did not slide down the wall, because brambles erupted through the stone, winding quickly around him. Another branch of them grew — as if by decades, but all done in a heartbeat — right out his open screaming mouth, and two more curled and tangled out his eyes.

I sucked in a gasp as Death erupted from the ground, white and swirling. He bowed once to Bluebeard, and then his slug tongue shot out and sucked something pale from Bluffroll's body. Before I could blink, Death burst apart like smoke in a high wind and was gone and nothing remained of Bluffroll but his grasping rictus of a skeleton caught within the brambles.

"I do hope you'll leave that up on your wall," Bluebeard said, seeming to address my nephew from where he hung beside Bluffroll's desiccated remains. "It's a far better tribute to my beloved wife than that monstrosity. I'd stand on the throne if I were you, wife."

I knew a command when I heard one, gentle or not, so I scrambled up on the throne as Bluebeard raised a single eyebrow and the bronze statue melted, collapsing like water falling from a bucket and eating through the mass of Wittenbrand on the floor, burning them to nothing and bronzing the entire throne room floor in the time it took for me to accidentally let out a little cry.

I recovered myself enough to straighten and draw in a breath. "I prefer your choice of decor, my husband."

"Indeed," he said, smiling cruelly and then stepping up to join me on the floor. "And now, shall we go find Coppertomb and ruin the fun of his Coronation Ball?"

I smiled, but just like his smile, mine did not touch my eyes. "As much as I would love to hurry to his destruction, I think you're forgetting something."

"I forget nothing," he said, waving a hand.

The spikes popped out of the shoulders of the mortals hanging on the walls. And with their removal, some spell was broken and I heard their cries of pain and sorrow and relief as they scrambled to one another, heard my nephew cry, "beloved" and fling himself into his wife's arms. I thought, from what I saw, that he had healed their wounds, though their left hands were still missing.

"All restoration costs something," Bluebeard breathed into my hair. "Days or pain or something else. Their freedom cost the lives of those I melted away under the shame of that terrible rendering."

"Of course," I agreed in a whisper. But though we spoke quietly, I could see the terrified mortals around us watching the strange pair standing together on their king's throne.

"Will you pay a price now? One to restore them?"

I swallowed. "Name the price, husband of mine."

He made a happy murmur in the back of his throat and lifted my skeletal hand, touching the end of each finger with his flesh fingers. "Give up your flesh hand forever and I will restore all of theirs."

"Could you not restore them without such a sacrifice?" I asked, my voice trembling a little. I had liked having my flesh hand back. I did not want to give it up again.

He lifted an eyebrow. "Who values what is not bought at great price? Who treasures what is given for nothing?"

"I do," I said firmly.

"I leave the choice in your excellent hands," he said and I looked from his mercurial expression to the huddled people — maybe a hundred of them — who had just been set free of the curse that pinned them to the walls and I swallowed. He was not going to restore them on his own. That much was clear.

He loved me. I knew it.

And yet he could only be who he was. Incomprehensible as it sometimes was to me.

"I agree to your bargain," I said calmly, though my voice shook a little. "My hand for theirs."

He huffed out a breath as if in relief and leaned in close to breathe me in.

"Well chosen, wife of mine," he said and then he kissed me so thoroughly that the sweetness of his lips dulled the sadness that welled up in me at my loss and when I opened my eyes it was to the sound of mortal awe.

"Remove the blue from this place," Bluebeard said curtly. "And when next I attend these courts, I expect a more fitting tribute will be erected for my queen."

Rolgrin bowed to him, spreading arms wide in agreement and his court and queen were quick to follow.

"And now we ride," Bluebeard said.

"Wait," I interrupted. "I should be sure my folk are safe."

"Is that not what I just accomplished?" He seemed confused by the request.

"I should ascertain that my kinsman is in good enough health to reign."

"He stands, does he not?" Bluebeard gestured at Rolgrin.

"Aunt," Rolgrin said from where he stood, and his throat was dry. "I thank you for your concern. And I assure you all will be well. Only ... please ... we are but mortal. Please withdraw your glory from us."

My mouth fell open and I had to shut it with a click at the look of fear and admiration directed at me from my nephew. None of the others even looked at me. Their heads were bowed in what I now realized was fear.

"If you wish it," I said faintly.

"Please," my kin begged and Bluebeard took my upper arm in his grip and turned me to meet his lifted eyebrow.

"Now we ride," I agreed and he smiled, blinked, and we were no longer in Pensmoore.

Chapter Twenty-Five

IN THE WITTENTALES that my mother told, the prince would come — or the woodsman, or the firebird, or the deadly Wittenbrand prince — and the fair maiden would be swept away with him after many trials and difficulties and they would kiss and then my mother would say, "And they lived happily ever after."

And I, fool that I was, never asked, "What was that like? Did they have a nice bed and regular meals? Did they have comfortable clothing and make fat babies?"

If I had asked, I suspect she would have given me a mysterious wink, for what other option would she have had? Mortals have no ken of what the Wittenbrand do, or of how their ever afters might be, and the firebird is as like to consume a maiden as live with her, the woodsman is sure to have many days of poverty and grinding exhaustion, and the human prince might have his entire court forced to cook their own hands.

And so, if I had turned my sensible mind to the matter, I might have realized that there would be no such life of luxury for us. My choice of the Bramble King — the mystery prince who had, through boldness and cunning, defeated death and ushered in a new age — was the choice of a man who did not toil nor spin, nor did he worry about human concerns. There was no feast of delicacies or comfortable fire that he brought me to when we finished restoring Pensmoore. Rather, we emerged in the heat of a summer day on the banks of a river that was certainly in the Wittenhame, for no mortal water sparkled so, nor was any human place so heavy with the sweltering doldrums of the ripest summer. Pollen swirled so heavily, clouding all else so that at first I saw nothing but thick puffs of white pollen and the water my feet stood in up to the ankle.

The river ran with bubbling charm up and over my ankles but beneath my feet was firm black stone.

"Let us shed these robes of justice, fire of my eyes," Bluebeard said and I nodded, fighting back a sudden burst of fear.

The judgment we had just rendered was fitting and right. I was not sorry for it. But it had highlighted what I already knew — that I could not return to the mortal world. That there was no place there for me.

"Something troubles you beyond the prickles of the nettles and thorns you wear," my husband said, gently beginning to undress me from my painful garb.

"I fear I have no place now, Bramble King," I said quietly. "I am no princess of Pensmoore any longer, nor am I a daughter of Savataz. I have not a home nor a place."

He was quiet for a long while as he rent my garments and removed them one after another. As he worked, the pollen swirled back, revealing that we stood on a rock shelf and the water ran behind and before us, washing over short waterfalls only as high as my waist or my knees. Cool water flowed from one level to the next, only as deep as ankle or knee.

"Sit and wash yourself of the pain of what we have just done," my husband said but his face was considering as he removed his own ruined clothing and sat with me in the river.

The cold water did, indeed, ease the pain, but I lifted my hand and looked at my skeletal fingers and I sighed.

"Do you regret giving yourself for others?"

"I merely find the consequence grim," I said, blushing a little as I said, "I had hoped for a happy ending."

"And is your ending not happy with me?" he asked, and I realized he was close enough to murmur in my ear. I turned to see him beside me, his face very serious and eyes grave.

And I did not know what seized me for it was not the reasonable, sensible thing to do, but instead of airing my woes to him or asking clearly for a place to call my own, instead, I turned to him and embraced him, body to body, and brought my skeletal hand up to cradle his cheek. I could not feel it, but I could gasp with the pleasure of watching him close his eyes and turn his cheek into my broken embrace.

"I consider your sacrifice a treasure," he whispered as he let his eyes open enough to meet mine and then leaned in very slowly to steal a kiss from my lips. "For it mirrors my own and in all this world, who else will know what it is to be me except you, or what it is to be you except for me? Please, wife of mine, do not give your heart to another."

"I will not," I gasped as his warm flesh arms wrapped themselves around me, reminding me that he remained broken, too, with holes in his palms and his side that would never be whole again. My mind was dazed at his touch and his warmth, and any discomfort the nettles and thorns had left behind was thoroughly gone at the brush of his fingers.

"Do not give it then to comfort, for he is not me," Bluebeard whispered. "Nor to prestige for he is no Bramble King, nor to riches for they are not my affectionate touch."

"I will not." I sounded breathless now, my heart stolen away by his plea. He asked me for so little — only my heart.

"Let me feed you, and clothe you, and show to you what our life together might be."

"Will it be bathing in these falls with all our clothing drifting away?" I asked as my thistle crown fell to cover one of my eyes.

He laughed, catching it between his teeth and then tossing his head to send it into the falls and then he kissed me again.

"If it is those things, are you sorry?" he asked me gently.

"I am not," I gasped, leaning my forehead shyly against his strong shoulder.

"And if I tell you I am slowly making this world new again and that I require your input on some of the most intimate parts of it?"

"Then I will bid you take me to those parts and show to me all your secrets," I said shyly, peering up at him through my lashes.

"And if it will mean deprivation and the loss of many things?" A ghost of his smile has returned.

"Then I will give them," I said, kissing his bare shoulder.

"And if it will mean that I gift you with one good thing after another?"

"Then I will consider all those gifts small beside the gift of your heart," I breathed and to my surprise, he did not answer but instead he ducked down and caught my mouth in a kiss and he was laughing through the kiss and he did not stop kissing me even as he slowly drew me to my feet.

He pulled back only long enough to pounce again. Drew back a second time, his fingers threading through my hair, only to nip at my bottom lip. But the third time he held my gaze with his intent one, and leaned in to press the softest of kisses along my jaw, and when I was drunk with them, eyes half-lidded with the drug of pleasure, he finally stepped back.

When I looked down, I found myself dressed in a gown of soft white with sprays of lace decorating the edge of the deep v-neck in little patches as if it were frost. The full skirts opened to become three great grey owls who fluttered and snapped and hooted with deathly glares at both me and my king.

I was still staring at them in wonder when a movement made me look up and I found my Bluebeard clad similarly. He wore breeches woven of witches' hair today, his feet bare beneath them and his doublet was formed entirely of living hummingbirds which sometimes hovered close to his body and sometimes took flight, flew laps around him, and then returned to their posts and while he wore his bramble crown, the thorns had grown longer and sharper and bore white roses. He smiled and produced for me a crown that was the same and set it upon my hair, before lifting my hands to kiss the backs of my knuckles.

"I'm making all things new," he said sweetly, kissing each knuckle individually. "And your time of waiting and torment is over, wife. Never again will you go hungry. Never again will you be cold. Your place is at my side and here you are Queen of the Wittenhame. Need you a home beyond this?"

I looked around where he was pointing and I realized that as we had talked together the pollen had retreated further and further leaving our shallow waterfall at the top of a great vista that was spread before us, filled with sweeping hills and roaring rivers, green lakes and moss-encrusted bogs, white beaches, dusky forests, and purple mountains. The pollen continued to spread far past what I could see, stretching out across the land.

"When you say you are making all things new ..."

My words trailed away.

"I meant I was rebuilding the Wittenhame for my people. They must not live with mortals on their plane. They must enter this age fresh and new."

"You made all this?" I said, stunned, pushing my flower crown up.

And when I looked back he was grinning with mischief in his eyes. "And I have more yet to make. Will you weave it with me and bring to this some of the order of your practical soul? Be the straight line to all my twists and curves, the sharp edge to my soft billows?"

I smiled. "So long as rivers run and moon shines, so long will I be wife to you."

"Then I shall see that they continue in their courses age upon age," he said and then he turned from me, took on a look of concentration, and then snatched at the water brimming over the closest step-fall and when his hand came out he had a sleek rainbow trout in his grip. "But first, I will cook you breakfast."

And perhaps happily ever after meant eating fresh-cooked fish beside a fire burning with white and purple flames while your husband created pink and gold clouds in the sky.

Or perhaps it didn't, but it did for me that day.

Maybe the next day it would mean something else. Maybe with Bluebeard, I would never know what it would mean.

"And what will I do in this world you're making?" I asked him between bites. "I feel like a rake in a world without gardens. Like a sword in a world with no enemies."

"Do not fool yourself, once-mortal wife," he said and there was a dangerous glint in his eye. "For I am tied to you as you are tied to me. There will be no blossoms if you fade, no sunshine if your smile ceases, no warmth if your love for me runs cold. All this I have created, but it was made for you, and each day you will bring newness to it."

"And will I have an occupation beyond this marvelous existence I seem to have inspired?" I teased, but I was truly worried. I was not one to sit idle.

"I fear you may have the hardest occupation of all," he said gravely, taking a bite of the fish.

"Loving you?"

"That is easy enough. But someone must keep me from growing bored or I may forget to bother with setting the seasons in turn, one after another."

"But you have to or everyone will die of starvation," I said, aghast.

His eyes twinkled. "See? You are at it already. If I do not feel challenged enough, I may forget to order the sun to rise."

"You wouldn't," I said with huge eyes.

"I might," he teased, making his eyes grow big and biting his lip as he drew in close to me. "I might forget."

"You can't," I choked.

"Help me," he said, hands spread wide and eyes also wide with feigned innocence.

"For how long?" I asked, giving him a wry smile.

"As long as rivers need to run and the moon needs to shine," he said, putting on a sorrowful expression. "I fear that you will be stuck with me for exactly that long, for who else would remind me of the necessity."

"That will be forever," I warned.

"So it will." And his smile was beatific again. "And will you take the occupation?"

"I fear that if I do not, the world will fall to chaos," I said grimly.

"Your fears are well-founded."

"Then, I will take this occupation," I agreed and his laugh was deep and rich and told me he had tricked me into being his compatriot in the very best of ways because he dropped his teasing and the rest of his fish and swept me up in his arms and we were busy for a long while like that until our fire went out and he had to remake our crushed flower crowns.

"Can we stay like this forever?" I gasped.

"Soon," he whispered. "But first, we have one last snake in our garden and I fear we must root him out ourselves. Let us hie us to Coppertomb's Coronation Ball for a Battle of the Kings."

Chapter Twenty-Six

I EXPECTED him to snap his fingers and take us there like he had so many times before, but to my surprise, my husband took my hand instead and knocked on the rock we'd been standing on. It began to shake, rumbling and rising. I had to grip his hands in mine as tree roots shook loose and soil and river all tumbled off the rock. And then a seam opened up, and out of the seam, a fire flared up hot and rich.

"My fire," Bluebeard said happily. His smile was the kind of smile that could melt the rock itself, holding the light of a lantern in the darkness, the warmth of a welcoming hearth, a kind of glowing, pulsing satisfaction.

"My King," the fire rumbled, hissing and popping.

"I require your service."

"I am honored to serve," said the fire.

"Is there a fire at my adversary's Coronation Ball?" my husband asked.

"Of course," said the fire.

"Then you shall deposit your King and Queen there, my fire, and await my orders." Bluebeard turned and looked at me and there was a teasing smile in his eyes that turned fierce as he said, "Are you ready to turn tables and upend designs, Queen of my Heart?"

"I am," I said firmly.

"Are you ready to untangle tangles and unravel ravelings?" He leaned in, his half-smile teasing in a way that made me melt a little.

"I'm also ready to tear down what has been built and unmake what was made," I said dryly.

"Ah, excellent. Then we are of an accord." He bent in to steal a sizzling kiss, his fingers trailing lightly over my waist. And then, before I had time to so much as take a breath he whirled me as if we were dancing, right through the air and into the fire.

The fire grew, burning bright and hot, though I was not scalded by it, and when it cleared enough to see out through the flames, there was a great statue that looked as if it were a depiction of Death himself, for it accurately showed his beard and fluttering cloak and it held in its hand a severed hand — my hand, I thought. But the statue was old and beaten by winds and weather to the point where the glazed-over eyes and slug tongue were worn to nubs and the face was unrecognizable.

"Where are we?" I gasped from within the fire.

"The Plains of Myygddo," my husband whispered in my ear, leaning around me so we could both peer up at the statue. "Recall how I required you lead the armies of mortals to fight here on these very Plains? Recall also how Coppertomb thought he had won the day before the fight occurred. He called me 'ancient' even among my own kind. What he never guessed was that ancient people hatch ancient plans. This statue, I had placed here over a thousand years before."

"This statue?" I asked with a cocked brow. "This one that holds my severed hand? How could that be?"

"Some things must be, one way or another," he murmured.

"So you ... what? Crafted it out of magic?"

"Not at all," he said and his eyes were far away as if in memory. "There was a mortal with clever hands, Halifast, I think his name was. And to him, I granted riches and power and showed him the face of Death that he might set the depiction in stone."

"I don't remember seeing this when I was on the edge of the Plains with Rolgrin," I said frowning. "I would certainly have remembered."

"Indeed," my husband breathed, "but the Plains are vast and this image is often obscured by the rising mists and the sun baking the nearby ground and disturbing the vision of mortals."

I nodded. "Well enough, but why place it here at all?"

"When it was complete, I set it under a geas, that if one who shared my days and wore my token led an army to this Plain, then the magic stored within would pour out and lend aid to her armies. None who fought under my standard could be so much as touched while fighting in the shadow of this statue, nor afflicted by deadly thirst, nor poisoned by draught. You may recall that my adversary was very sure of himself. He'd had the local water sources laced with poison."

"But did anyone know there was protection here?" I asked, my brow wrinkling as I turned to him. It was so Wittenbrand to offer a way to win and be safe without ever telling anyone what it was.

"I was not there when King Rolgrin fought," Bluebeard said, scratching his beard as if thinking. "But I know much more as Bramble King than I knew as a mortal, and I can see that battle in my mind's eye. The fight was grim and tight. A near thing, indeed. But when your people rallied at the base of the statue, sheltered in the cool shade, they fought like lions, and were untouched by blade or arrow until their enemies lay scattered at their feet."

"But what if I'd failed?" I asked, aghast. "Or what if I left before I brought them to the edge of the Plain? None of that was a certain thing!"

"Did I not instruct you to bring them to the Plains? Did I not bid you succeed?"

"You did," I said. I could so easily have failed, for he had not told me of the importance. How many other things like this had been very close with me utterly blind to their importance?

"I had every confidence in your fidelity," he said with a kiss pressed to my cheek.

"I hardly dare imagine what would have happened had I not followed your commands precisely." I was still having trouble drawing in a full breath with this new knowledge hovering over me.

"I did not need imagine it. I know you too well, my sober monstrosity. You would not have drawn up short. Not then or ever."

"Your confidence in me is too great," I said grimly.

"It was not then, and is not now," he said with a last soft kiss to my cheek. "But come now. Explanations grow dull. Let us go and act instead."

He spun me, still in the flames of the fire, and we emerged from a new fire. This fire was set in the very middle of what was most certainly the Wittenbrand Court in Exile.

Around the fire was the grandest display I'd ever seen. Dancers by the hundred rushed around the fire and then closed in toward it, only to back slowly away with dragging steps, huge fans like the tails of birds were in each hand and they used the fans to mask their forms or accentuate their beauty, to tantalize with revealing, and then disguising, their loveliness.

Mortals had been set to play the music, their eyes dreamy and far away, as if they were drunk on wine or the seeds of the poppy. I rather thought this was a Wittenbrand trick done to them. A stealing of their wills, and perhaps even their memories.

They were not alone, other mortals served food from silver platters with glazed expressions and slow movements. I frowned at those chosen to serve. They were of every race and mode of dress known to me, but without exception, each stolen to serve was of great beauty and lithe in form. Curse the Wittenbrand and their obsession with taking everything beautiful for themselves.

"I took you, my beautiful one," Bluebeard whispered in my ear as if he could hear my thoughts.

"Then you failed in your task, for I am not beautiful," I whispered back.

He lifted my skeletal hand in his so that they hovered at shoulder height and he escorted me forward as if we were partners in a dance of our own.

"I see none other with so singular a hand."

"A hand you demanded of me," I challenged.

"But did I?" His eyes met mine, blazing with intensity. "I think rather that you chose this. For you are my match, rib for rib, hand for hand, ambition for ambition, and who better to remake the whole world than the two who wish to drink it all up whole?"

And what could I say to that? For I knew myself entirely from our time apart, and I knew I was not content with the mortal world or with mortal power. I had been willing to shipwreck my very self on the rocks of the Wittenhame if only I could seize hold of his soul once more, and I knew to my very bones that I would do it all again exactly as I had before if I were given the chance.

He knew me too well. I withdrew from the thought, lest I be distracted from our task, and focused instead on our surroundings.

I did not know where we were as we emerged from the fire, only that it seemed to be a series of isles with a low river trickling between them. The water was no higher than my ankle and limned by the light of the huge, golden hunter's moon.

On each island the trees were in full blossom, the moonlight making pale the soft pinks of the petals that fluttered down in little rains and showers. Between the trees, white stones stood out like sharp teeth and claws, and they had been commandeered into tables and chairs. Adding to them, human chairs and tables were set and heaped with delicacies. And these were not plain chairs or tables, but those from royal courts, carved and inlaid, upholstered, tufted, and brocaded. As if all the wealth of the mortal world had been scattered here, and indeed, did I not see a brightly colored woven rug spread out under one tree, a wine barrel overflowing with gold jewelry under another, and an open chest spilling out pearls under a third?

The island where we emerged was treeless, the fire being the central feature. It had been the focal point of the dancers, but rising before it was a greater island still, set back across the gleaming water a little. Upon that isle, someone had carved a great statue to rival the statue of Death — and the sharpness of the features and rough edges of the work suggested it had been erected in great haste. It was a true likeness of Coppertomb with the rib crown on his head and the Wittenbrand arrow in his hand as a scepter and his lifeless stone eyes faced outward with unflinching calm.

And at the foot of that statue, a throne had been set on a narrow dais, and on that throne sat Coppertomb himself, looking down on us.

Before the dais, a smooth granite dance floor had been carved out of the stone and polished to perfection, ringed in tiny lights and garlanded at intervals with more pink flowers. Drifting petals washed across the slick surface and piled on the edges and I could not help but notice that there were smears of blood hastily wiped from the very edges of that dance floor.

It was the blood smears that made me look more closely at the scene and oh, when I did, I wished I had not.

The dancers were not Wittenbrand. That was my first observation, and whatever magic made them dance had made their feet bloody and broken, and indeed, some had bone sticking through the flesh or were so ragged that every footstep was awash in blood. I was still gagging at the sight when I turned my eyes to the musicians to see their hands were similarly worn from ill-use by those who thought them playthings and not playmates.

And hanging in the blossom-laden trees were broken mortals, ruined by the Wittenbrand and tossed aside like used handkerchiefs. How they had been used was graven on their broken bodies and rent flesh and I fought hard to remain upright as I took in the hidden horrors done to my people under this veneer of ethereal beauty.

I turned to look away from one woman whose huge staring eyes would never see life again, only to set my eyes on an enchanted server offering a platter of fruit to a horned Wittenbrand. He took an apple from her platter, bit it, and then, quick as you please, bit into her flesh and tore a bite from it, too, and all the while she stood motionless, eyes glassy as she was so used.

My heart sped. This could not be allowed to continue. This must end. Immediately.

"A weak display for a weak king," Bluebeard said in an undertone. "Already their magic fades and their pomp is but the crowning riches of mortals. Dust and ashes and fixed forever within the bounds of time."

I hummed agreement. "But I am far more concerned by the abuses to my people."

"Patience wife, for we have come to end exactly that."

I swallowed down the demand that he end it immediately. Had I not seen him make things right with Bluffroll in Pensmoore? Surely, I could trust him with this, too.

Instead, I cleared my throat. "All of this must have taken time to organize. And Coppertomb told me his Coronation Ball was to be in two days' time. Surely, that was more than two days ago."

"But only two in the Wittenhame." I glanced at him and saw his tight jaw and calculating eyes as his gaze swept around us and the certainty there brought me relief.

"I know you know all things as Bramble King, but how would he know that?" I asked, meeting Bluebeard's eyes. They twinkled at my admission that he was more than a mere man now.

"All the Wittenbrand will feel it in their bones. They are not of this world, but of another, and just as your mortal body tells you without fail when it is time to sleep and rise in your world, so their bodies do the same. It is the second night at home. And all present here know that."

"How nice for them," I said coolly.

He laughed but not in delight. This laugh was more an acknowledgment of all that was and it held a bitter mirth. We stepped together with that laugh, breaking the dancers apart with his inexorable strides. At first, no one seemed to notice except for the dancer he nearly trod on, but three steps in, the music stopped and a gasp tore from every throat at once.

And if there hadn't been enough proof before that I was married to the King of the Wittenbrand, all it would take was the looks on their faces to confirm it. I'd been there once when General Thistwaite returned from conquering the barbarians in the north and Svetgin had greeted him in estate. The General had marched his great white horse right into the throne room, its hooves still bloody with the deaths of our enemies, and the gasps in the court that day had been nothing compared to the gasps of the Wittenbrand now. They were like lazy children found out by their tutor, thieving servants discovered by their lord.

They knew a conqueror when they saw one. And I knew him, too. For he was my Bluebeard, the Bramble King.

Chapter Twenty-Seven

"AH, COPPERTOMB, MY DULCET DARLING," my husband said, startling me even as his measured pace led us through the flowing water and toward the dance floor. "You've put yourself out on my behalf. To have crafted so generous a Coronation Ball on such short notice must have cost you great expense in both wealth and worry. Your endeavor is noted." He looked to me with mock admiration. "See how he has even kept my seat warm for me, wife. Has ever a manservant been so attentive or a vassal so abundant in generosity?"

Coppertomb came to his feet so suddenly that his throne fell backward, crashing into the feet of his statue with a clatter. His fist wrapped around his arrow-scepter and his mouth twisted into hatred. His face — so much younger than my husband's — was pale beneath the rib crown he wore, but his fine mortal clothing — fit for any king — looked plain and ephemeral opposite his true king.

Bluebeard's shadow, long and dark from where he stood before the central fire, was cast across the expanse and it shrouded our adversary so much that I could barely make out those with him.

"This is not *your* coronation ball, Arrow," Coppertomb said in a poisonous tone.

"Is it not?" Bluebeard said, looking around in mock surprise. "And do not call me Arrow, for the title belongs to another."

"Who inherited it?" Coppertomb spat the word "inherited" as if to remind us that Bluebeard had died at his hand.

"She who was once called Sparrow, now Lady and Ruler of the lands of Riverbarrow and honored by the title of Arrow."

"She will have to pay her tribute to me," Coppertomb said, hand drifting to the sword hanging from his waist.

"There will be no need for that," Bluebeard said, waving a hand. "She has already repaid her king tenfold."

"And yet I see no largess in my coffers," Coppertomb said, snapping a finger as a pair of winged Wittenbrand scurried to stand his throne back on its feet.

Though he was diminished in his mortal garb — and so were the rest of the Wittenbrand, I was conscious, suddenly, that we were surrounded. His court closed in slowly. They were armed — with any mortal weapons that weren't iron, but armed all the same. And there were thousands of them.

With the music abruptly ended, and the swirling bubbles and petals falling to the ground, with the eating and laughing paused, they seemed quite threatening. I looked around as subtly as I could as my husband led me closer still to his shadowed rival.

The Wittenbrand had been eating and drinking. And as was common for them at these events, there were some bearing bloody wounds and others with red-tinged blades. Some ran naked through the crowd laughing or growling. Some rode mortal beasts — tigers and boars who tore at any in their path, horses, of course, but also the grand fable elephantas of the jungle lands and the dusky camels of the deserts. And they bore on their persons trophies from the many lands the animals represented. Crown Jewels. Scepters. Prized pieces of armor and coronets.

I was looking, I realized, at a raiding party. But not a raiding party as I was used to in the mortal world, a raiding party that had *ravaged* the mortal world and rallied here with their slaves and plunder to spend a night in evil and debauchery.

And while I was not surprised at all to see that they were doing exactly as I expected Wittenbrand to do I was very surprised to find one notable person missing.

"Where is Grosbeak?" I asked aloud.

Coppertomb shot me an irritated look as he shifted, trying to move out of Bluebeard's shadow without being caught at it. My husband shifted with him, keeping the shadow in place, but the movement shed light on the figure standing to the left of Coppertomb's throne.

A centaur with a rotting yellow face and lank hair regarded me balefully.

"You ask, 'Where is Grosbeak?' but where were you when I was forced to wander the lands of Death bereft and alone?" he said, and for a moment I thought he hissed at me, but it turned out it was only a giant black mamba creeping down Coppertomb's statue and spooling around the base of it who was hissing, and when it thrust its head forward, Coppertomb placed a hand possessively on its head.

"I have many pets, mortal woman. Grosbeak is only one of them," Coppertomb said "And I fear you are too late. You were to come to my Coronation Ball."

"As I have," I interrupted. "And my dead is raised."

"Not by your power," Coppertomb said, smiling now as if he had won.

"He is not buried beneath the ground."

"But he was, wasn't he?" Coppertomb said smoothly. "And what was my ruling? That you, bride of the dead, would give yourself to me at the Coronation Ball."

"I cannot give you what I no longer possess."

"You were to be my bride."

"I am already married to another."

He laughed then. "At one time, such an objection might have stymied me, but I have now a worthy advisor. Your own friend and confidante. Is it not so, Grosbeak?"

And his gaze flicked to my old friend and mine turned to horror as I realized that Grosbeak was sweating so much that his face seemed to be malforming like hot wax.

"Feeling the effects of a geas, horrible revenant?" Bluebeard asked quietly, his fingers steepled under his chin as if he were considering something.

"I feel them," Grosbeak said and I swallowed because I remembered the geas Bluebeard had put on him — that if he betrayed me, he would feel the effects of his betrayal in his own flesh. Was that what was happening now? But how, then, had he betrayed me?

And then I saw her step from the shadow. Ki'e'iren. Her eyes were narrowed and she smiled cruelly when they met mine. I felt my blood run cold as ice.

"I have found one who has a prior claim," Copeprtomb said, and his smile slowly grew as around us the silent Wittenbrand began to murmur in delight, and then — like an avalanche, a murmur grew to a chuckle and it turned to the kind of wicked laughter that takes its delight from cruel turnabout.

"But she was returned to her time," I said, feeling suddenly lightheaded. This woman had tried to kill me once — had, in fact, succeeded — and that was when she could benefit from my survival. How much more likely was she to try to kill me now?

"And offered a chance a second time to wed a bright Wittenbrand and live the life of grandeur promised her," Coppertomb said smoothly, and his smile was growing by the moment. He reached up and adjusted his crown with a look of triumph in his eyes. "Will you deny, Arrow, that she is your wife?"

"That's no longer my name," Bluebeard said slowly, but his expression was considering and he tapped his steepled fingers to his chin as if in thought.

"But will you deny that you married her first?"

"I will not."

The Wittenbrand calmed again, hanging on his words. They could sense drama in the air as a pike senses blood in the water.

"Or that she has a prior claim to you? To your wealth and your body?"

"I will not," my husband said, but he shot a look at Grosbeak that promised punishment later.

There was a murmur of excitement from the crowd.

I risked a glance at my old friend. Despite the warmth of the firelight, he looked green and grim and cracks were forming in his clay horse's body.

"Why would you betray me?" I asked him in a low voice.

"Why would I not?" he replied with an up-thrust chin. "What did I owe you? You, who paraded my corpse and humiliation through this world and the next."

But he would not meet my eye and I knew not what to do, anxiety rising in my throat until it seemed it would choke me.

"And if she is your living wife, you may not have another," Coppertomb said grimly. He spread his arms wide, addressing the crowd like a showman. "Look upon this would-be usurper, Court of Wittenhame! See how his weakness is exposed. Who can rule us who is ruled by a mortal? The dead fly in his perfume is this mortal wife of his — the error in his judgment, the flaw in his weave, the hole in his barque. It is this wife who claims him — this wayward mortal. She is usurper and fraud, a wife only in name, for she knew from the first of the existence of others, that they were not properly dead or buried and had prior claim to him. How could she lie to our court as she did and not face consequence? How could she lay claim to one of ours and not face punishment when we reveal she has grasped too high and risen too fast? This one's mortal wife, last of her kind, is incriminated in every way, and therefore is not his at all, but by right of the Wittenhame, ours to do as we please with. And we shall revel in her punishments. We shall feast on her terrors. We shall find joy in her screams. And he shall be made to watch all of them to remind him that he is but a vassal to us, but a supplicant before the throne of the Bramble King."

Coppertomb stepped forward, offering his hand to me as if he expected me to take it, but his eyes were on Bluebeard. And if he expected my husband to flinch or back up, then he was disappointed for Bluebeard merely tapped his steepled fingers against his chin and regarded us.

Coppertomb took another step forward as if trying to show his threat was serious.

I stared at Bluebeard, willing him to look at me. Had he not planned for this? Were we taken unawares after everything?

Behind us, someone began to beat a low rhythm on a hide drum and my heart beat in time with it as I looked between my accuser and my husband.

And I shouldn't have panicked. Not after all that had taken place. For had he not saved me again and again? Had he not planned all things for my benefit? But I could not help it. The threat was too near. The accuser too ... accurate. I had never deserved any of this, and by my husband's refusal to gift me with his gaze, how could I be sure he would ever look upon me again at all?

I swallowed hard and then I forced the words out — the only ones I could think of to save myself.

"I challenge Ki'e'iren. I will not have my place taken. If she wishes to displace me, then she will fight me."

There was a murmur of appreciation from the crowd. The Wittenhame adored a good challenge. I was counting on it.

"It is not your role to defend," Coppertomb chided. "You have been found out. You have been exposed. And you will suffer your due."

"But the role of wife is mine if I take it by right of challenge," I pushed. "That is the Wittenbrand way. To take what you can by force or violence, is it not? And I will take it. I have walked the Path of Princes. I have wandered the lands of Death. I will not be cheated of my right now."

"You cannot deny her this," Bluebeard said to Coppertomb and when I looked at him his eyes were twinkling. "None of you can deny her this. She has issued her challenge. Let us see her make her play."

And the roar of approval that swept the Court of the Wittenbrand left me trembling, for I did not know how I was to defeat anyone, much less my savage enemy, but all our fates depended now on me.

Chapter Twenty-Eight

"MEET ON THE DANCE FLOOR. We shall observe the challenge there," Coppertomb announced, spreading his arms wide as if in a joyous announcement. I noticed his cheeks were brushed with gold dust. He looked young beside my Bluebeard as a willow whip looks beside a mighty oak.

Bluebeard cleared his throat, and I barely held back a smile when I realized that all who were gathered hesitated, waiting for his command.

"I rather think this dais a better place for a contest," he said mildly, still tapping his chin, but now with a look of devilry in his eye. "After all, if my wives are to battle, I think all deserve to see the result. Do you not, Wittenbrand?"

Behind him, another cheer rose up and Coppertomb flushed hot.

"The dance floor is just as adequate," he said firmly.

"But if we adjourn there, how will we admire … this?" Bluebeard asked, his voice dripping with disdain at the word "this."

He motioned toward the towering statue of Coppertomb and then he twisted his hand and as he did so the arms of the statue moved. They dropped the arrow scepter. It fell amongst the crowd, igniting screams of terror as it hit with a crunch that I was certain was not just rock on rock but rock with bodies smashed in between.

"He still has Wittenbrand magic," I heard a voice quaver and I shot a glance at the crowd where a horned woman leaned to whisper in the ear of a magnificent courtier whose face was pierced all over with golden rings. "Is it possible that he really is the Bramble King?"

"Tricks," the courtier sighed, but the sigh was a happy one.

And then Bluebeard twisted his hand to lay flat horizontally, and the statue moved to cup its hands at the waist.

"A better place to display a battle of the Queens, don't you think, Coppertomb?" he asked easily, swiping a drink from one of the trays passing by and toying with it.

The murmurs of appreciation around us were growing.

"You think to impress us by wasting what little Wittenbrand magic lies still at our disposal?" Coppertomb asked tightly. "We are not impressed. But I ask you this — man who is no longer the Arrow, Nameless One, Ghost of the Past — have you a stomach to gamble?"

"Always," Bluebeard said, downing his goblet with one quaff. He coughed. "Mortal wine? Were there no glow spirits? It's hardly a proper Coronation Ball without Wittenbrand draught, Coppertomb. We might as well be mortals. And here I had such confidence in you, I nearly had a mind to make you my steward."

Coppertomb's lip twitched manically and my eyes widened. My husband was goading him to the breaking point, and while I should not have found that funny, I must confess that I did.

"We don't need dramatics," Coppertomb said firmly. "I have won my crown by right and trickery."

Bluebeard snapped his fingers and then Coppertomb's crown was in his hand. The Wittenbrand lord shook with fury but, impressively, he kept his face impassive.

"Cheap tricks. Go ahead," he said with a nod to me. "Use the last of her days on them."

Bluebeard smirked and then looked around at the crowd. "What say you? Shall I use all my magic on cheap tricks?"

The crowd laughed. Their eyes were bright and they'd abandoned their torment of the mortal servants to become spectators to the drama here.

"It's settled then, Coppertomb. I'll be displaying every cheap trick I know for the delight of my fellow Wittenbrand."

That garnered him another laugh.

"And I must confess, my young friend," my husband said, gliding around to where he could drape an arm over Coppertomb's shoulders. "You've presented me with an interesting riddle. Perhaps those assembled here can help us solve this. Who owns a thing? The originator, or the current possessor?"

"If you mean to ask if you are worthy of the crown because it's in your hand, then I shall tell you succinctly, no. The current possessor is not the owner."

"Ah," Bluebeard said, spinning the crown on his finger. "But I am the originator, for that is my pale bone thrust through the grip of the crown. How ... crass. Don't you think?"

"Then it does not belong to the originator, either."

Bluebeard smiled. "The first originator, then? He who made my rib? The Bramble King?"

"It belongs to me." Coppertomb clipped every word as he snatched the crown back and replaced it on his brow.

"But it bears no Brambles," Bluebeard said, looking confused.

I crossed my arms over my chest and looked at him wryly. He was delaying the inevitable. I would have to fight Ki'e'iren no matter how long he drew this out. One of my owls hooted as if to remind him of this and another made a powerful effort to fly away. He could no more leave my skirts, though, than I could leave this clever trap.

"The wager," Coppertomb said through gritted teeth.

My husband tugged him closer as if in a half-embrace. "Of course I'll gamble with you, dear Coppertomb. Nothing would please me more. After all, I could stand to win some of my own back after all your triumphs."

There was a murmur of appreciation from the crowd. They were loving every moment of this.

"Then offer me this," Coppertomb said, disentangling himself from my husband's brotherly affection. "Your most recent wife will stand as your champion, and your earlier one will stand as mine, and whoever loses, will leave the Bramble Court forever, never again to make a nuisance of himself."

"I would never call you a nuisance, Coppertomb," Bluebeard said sincerely. "All kingdoms need their flies or who else would dispose of the rotting flesh?"

"Take my wager, craven fool." Coppertomb's eyes sparkled and his mouth drew into a severe line. "I have plans for the Wittenbrand now that we own the world of mortals. We shall start the Games anew. But we shall start them without you and your onerous presence. You had not the good grace to die. At least have the dignity to leave when you are not wanted."

"Not wanted?" Bluebeard pressed his hand to his chest as if surprised. "I? Who brings with him such violent delights?"

There was laughter again and my husband winked at the crowd.

"Take. The. Wager." Coppertomb's eyes were bright.

"A bargain is struck," Bluebeard said and his eyes were dancing as he took Coppertomb's hand in his and grinned.

He had, of course, received exactly what he wanted but I wished he hadn't bet so high ... again. For now it was all resting on my performance and I was no warrior. I was not even as tall as my rival or as strong as she. I was certainly not so bloodthirsty. I had lost even my guide to the Wittenhame.

My guide.

Who had been suspiciously quiet.

I shot Grosbeak a mistrustful look and saw he had a mild, peaceable expression of slight boredom on his face. That was not right. Grosbeak, for all his terrible traits, was never peaceable. Never mild. Certainly, never bored.

I frowned, but before I could question him, Coppertomb waved a hand. "How are they to climb to the hands?"

Bluebeard flicked a finger lazily and steps formed leading up the sides of the statue to the hands.

"To every problem, a solution," he said, plopping down lazily on the throne and flinging his legs up, one over the arm and the other over the back as if he were a child and not a man.

I could practically hear Coppertomb's teeth grinding from here, but he did not bother to challenge my husband's right to sit on his throne. Or drape over it, as was the case now.

"Then no more delays. They shall fight, and as Bramble King, I have the right to determine their weapons. I shall choose —"

There was a loud clearing of a throat, followed by a hacking cough and all eyes turned to my green-faced former friend, lover of mermaids, traitor to all, Grosbeak.

"Need I remind you, my King, of the terms of our agreement?" he asked with a silky sweet voice. When was Grosbeak ever sweet?

"You need not," Coppertomb said tightly. "But, I pray you, remember who your sovereign is and who will remain your lord when this is past and you are nothing but a cracking clay horse with a Wittenbrand's head."

"Would that I could forget, my lord, and yet it is seared into every thought," Grosbeak said acidly.

"Care to explain, Coppertomb?" Bluebeard asked and his fingers were steepled under his chin again. I was starting to be skeptical of that gesture. It seemed to indicate that he knew what would happen next and when he caught my gaze, he winked at me, confirming that fear. He knew how I must fight, and like the rest of the Wittenbrand, he was longing to watch me acquit myself against my rival.

"It was the revenant who offered me the suggestion that I turn to one of your former brides, and he who suggested that I drain the last of our residual magic to walk through the sands of time and draw her back to us," Coppertomb said and his smile was superior now. "And was I not correct to ask him — as I did — how to gut you? Was I not correct to assume you would crawl back here and try to take what is not yours? Was I not prescient to gather all I needed to defeat you one last time?"

"So prescient," Bluebeard said. "Perhaps when we are done here you may practice your visionary talents as an oracle to those similarly afflicted with poor planning and cowardly hearts. When I journeyed through the lands of Death I noted a pretty spot along a river of corpses that might serve you well."

"I'm glad you noted it, for it will be home to you hereafter."

"And what did our friend Grosbeak garner in exchange for this intelligence?" Bluebeard asked, smirking.

"He won the right to choose the challenge," Coppertomb said. "For he rightly guessed that your current mortal bride would wish to defend her position, and would gladly give of her last breath in your defense."

"Then perhaps Grosbeak should serve as oracle," Bluebeard said wryly.

Grosbeak sounded ill when he spoke. "I'll predict — accurately, I might add — that you'll father no children and live with no palace or lands."

"A grim fate indeed," Bluebeard said lightly, but his eyes were on mine when he said it for we both knew that whether Grosbeak mean to insult him or was truly psychic, his words were true. "Come then, my old enemy. What battle awaits my two wives in their quest to have me once and for all."

And there was silence as the Wittenbrand waited with held breath to hear what my former friend might say and his wicked smile told me that whatever it was, I would not like it in the slightest.

Chapter Twenty-Nine

GROSBEAK HAD ALWAYS HAD a head for drama and he was not to be deterred by the mere fact that his body was now clay or that he had four feet instead of two. He clambered up the steps to the hands above us and looked out and over the assembled mass, his voice raised as he spoke.

"Lords and Ladies of the Wittenhame now in exile! Dukes and Duchesses, Counts and Countesses, fairy friends, centaurs, mermaids, and brownies, demonkind and angelic watchers, mortal dust and dreary human whelps — all who love tales of trickery and vice lend me your ears!"

"I see he's prepared a speech," Bluebeard said confidentially to me. "Your next pet should be voiceless, wife of mine."

"I'm certain you'll make it so," I murmured and he seemed to like that. His eyes lingered on me before he stole another glass from a passing tray and sipped it as Grosbeak carried on.

"We stand here together to determine a contest of wives — or Queens, as one of the competitors has suggested."

There was a general cheer at that.

"We all know the legend about the one who draws out the Wittenbrand arrow from the stone," here he gestured at Coppertomb. "He will bring milk and honey with him and we will all dance for ten years. He will shepherd in an age of glory. He will marry the finest woman who has been revealed through her actions to be pure in spirit, and all the land will see peace."

There was a silence after that. Perhaps his Wittenbrand kin were not so certain that they wanted peace.

"Who better to help find this worthy partner than I? I have plumbed the great depths where Death keeps his horde. I have been carried down the Path of Princes — for I am not one to walk, and my feet grow sore with any effort."

That garnered him a hearty laugh from the crowd. I noticed that drinks were flowing again and the people were merry as if this was going according to some internal script I did not know. The only individuals who did not look well pleased were Ki'e'iren, me, and Coppertomb.

"It was my pleasure to betray the Arrow to the Sword and make an attempt on his wife's life. And why should I not have? It was spoiling the game to see him take a new bride every time and drain her days, only to take another. The vampirian have always been a legend we despise in the Wittenhame."

"Hear, hear!" the crowd called back.

"But, I was caught in the act, my head taken, my will snatched. And I was bounced from place to place, passed from hand to hand — even dragged once by magic from Bluebeard's vaults to watch him as the Sword pried that very rib from his chest while he stood naked and bleeding. That was a grisly sight. And I don't mean the theft of a bone."

More laughter. He was nearly as good at this as my husband was.

"I won't explain or justify myself. I was a true son of the Wittenhame. I did exactly what suited me and bettered me at each juncture. And now here I am, gifted with twice the number of my original legs and with the great honor of declaring to you what challenge my former mistress will face ... oh and also Ki'e'iren who once I kissed while she was living and her husband was not looking."

Here he winked at Ki'e'iren and to my surprise her face colored and her eyes grew even harder. My gaze shot to Bluebeard, but he was drinking from his goblet, unconcerned at this revelation. I knew he cared not at all for his wives, but I did think he would care that Grosbeak close to cuckolded him. I was wrong.

"And with that revelation, and my assurance that I have thought long and hard on this matter and considered every possible battle a hopeful

Queen of the Wittenhame might have need to endure, let me reveal the one I have settled on."

"This century, if you don't mind," Coppertomb said, drinking from his own goblet. His neck was almost puce, but he was still rigidly straight.

Grosbeak chuckled one of his evil chuckles. "Do not think I did not have you in mind, my darling audience, when I made my choice. For I know you. You are me. You have seen every possible physical and mental feat in your time. Arrows shot from horseback do not impress you. Nor does swordplay, nor do drinking games. Nor do knife fights, nor do bids of endurance where each member of the challenge slowly slices their own body parts off one by one."

Had that been an option? I was suddenly more worried than I had been. I glanced at Bluebeard and saw he was watching me with a hard, considering face. This was just like the hand. He needed me to go through with it, just as he did. And he would respect me if I tried, and suffer the consequences of my cowardice if I did not. Well. I was not giving up my place by his side. I was not backing down. No matter what challenge Grosbeak had settled upon.

"What we want, brothers, sisters, flesh of my own flesh," Grosbeak said, his voice rising in a crescendo. "We want novelty. We want drama."

I swallowed down a lump in my dry throat and shot my beloved a last look. There would be no help from him. I had made the challenge. He would watch me see it through.

"We want our competitors equally matched, equally likely to fall into the pit and never return. Equally likely to be humiliated and ruined. And we want them to do it to themselves!"

The crowd roared and my belly lurched. What would Grosbeak force me to inflict upon myself? What revenge would he take now for all the wrongs done to him while in my care?

"Ki'e'iren!" he called, "take your place here as the former of Riverbarrow's wives."

"You can't call me that," Bluebeard said calmly. "It is not my name."

"Fine," Grosbeak said, grinning hugely so that his terrible, leering mouth looked like a gash in dead flesh. "We shall call you by Izolda's name for you. *Bluebeard's* wives will join me here in the gracious hands of the Bramble King."

I felt my cheeks grow hot as Bluebeard laughed at the name I gave him but it was not a happy laugh, it was a sardonic one and he watched me as I ascended behind my rival. Would that my husband's moods were easier to read. Would that he were like mortal men in that, at least. But as ever, he was as mysterious to me as a fish of the sea is to a bird of the air.

I mounted the steps and I could see now why Grosbeak was grandstanding. From here, you could see all the land around. Fathoms and fathoms of moonlit islands, laced with the silver river and set off with blossoming trees. Between them, the Wittenbrand were gathered by the thousand, and all were watching me.

My palms grew sweaty and my breath hitched as I looked out over them. But why should I fear? Had they seen Death's lands and returned? Had they been made to watch everyone they love pass and their most beloved die before them? Had they survived all that and more? I did not think so. I would rip Ki'e'iren apart limb by limb with my own hands if I must. I would spread every drop of her blood over them like christening water. I would rend every one of them apart. I would do anything I must to stay by the side of my husband and confirm his choice in me. And I would not be afraid.

When I met my old friend's eye, here on the platform, it was with steel and determination and when he saw that look in my eye his own expression shifted to delighted excitement.

"We are ready," he said a little breathlessly. "Let the Game Commence. I name it for you now. The lives of these women and the fates of those they represent shall be determined by ... the Blind Man's Jape!"

The crowd gasped, and I did not know why or what I was to do, but their gasp turned to cheers and Grosbeak's grin grew broad and wicked as he lifted his hands in victory and reared in the air.

"You must be joking," I heard Coppertomb snarl from below.

But though I did not know what a Blind Man's Jape was, I knew one thing for certain. Grosbeak was not joking. And he was claiming his right and that meant whatever this terrible fate he'd chosen for us was, we must endure it or fail utterly.

Chapter Thirty

"WHAT IS A BLIND MAN'S JAPE?" Ki'e'iren snarled as Grosbeak turned to us. "None of this is what was promised to me. I was promised little contest, if any. I was promised the right of supremacy!"

"You're trusting in promises now, faithless ally?" Grosbeak asked her wryly with a wink to me. He smiled like he was savoring this. "You were not content to stay in your old life. You had to crawl back to us little mousie mousie and you've landed in a trapsie. What else did you expect?"

She turned red. "You jest. When I was stolen by the Wittenbrand, that was a promise of power and riches to come. Or it should have been. Why should she inherit what was meant for me, merely because she's the last?"

"Precisely," Grosbeak said, his grin widening as he turned to me. "Why should she, indeed?"

"I'm the one he chose," I said coolly. "Does a man not have the right to choose his own wife?"

"And that is why Izolda is here," Grosbeak whispered confidentially to Ki'e'iren. "Because she lets other people do the choosing. You and I are better at seizing the reins, though if you win, it's not like you'll receive the power and riches you hope for. But that doesn't matter, does it mousie? It only matters that you are here right now to play with us."

"The Bramble King will wed me," Ki'e'iren said with a dangerous smile.

Grosbeak's laugh was delighted. "Did he promise you that? How delightful. I must admit that I'd enjoy the sight of him constantly humiliated by the presence of a mortal wife. So gauche. So terribly mortifying."

"Bluebeard took *her*," Ki'e'iren reminded him.

"Yes, well, he's mad even for a Wittenbrand," Grosbeak said, waving a hand. "Coppertomb is far too sane to enjoy that."

"We had an agreement," she insisted through gritted teeth.

"But did he promise you exactly that?" Grosbeak asked, leaning in as if imparting a great secret. "Because I'm willing to bet that he did not. Despite all my posturing just now, he is not looking for a bride, mortal or immortal. He is only looking to win."

Ki'e'iren's eyes widened and her jaw stiffened and she shot me a look of death. "Don't you have anything to say, usurper?"

I shrugged, trying to appear more detached than I was. In truth, my heart hammered and raced within me. I needed to stay sharp for whatever this contest would be.

"What is there to say, poisoner? You killed me once. You would kill me again. You would take from me all I hold dear for the entertainment of others. But I am not the mousie Grosbeak calls us. I will not scurry away in fear."

"Ladies," Grosbeak interrupted with a vicious smile, but he said the word slowly as if he wanted us to talk right over him. I shut my mouth with a snap. "We'll blindfold you now, and tie your hands behind your backs. There's to be no touching."

Below us, the crowd had begun to grow noisy again. I wished I could see those directly under the platform. It would have been helpful to pick up any cues from my husband, but he was entirely out of sight.

"No touching what?" Ki'e'iren made her objection sound like an Imperial decree. "How can we fight with no eyes and no hands?"

"It's a contest of skill," Grosbeak said leering at her, and there was something about how he did it that reminded me of something. My eyes narrowed. What was it? Oh yes! The time he'd told me about his harem of mermaids under the sea, he'd had that exact same expression on his face. "The Blind Man's Jape is as old and time-honored as a Three Day Bind. Did not Foinen the Terrible use the Blind Man's Jape to humiliate his wife Issarra? Did not Horace of Hagglesphere declare a Blind Man's Jape in his challenge to Surricus and win his entire wine store as the prize?"

"Can we get on with it?" Ki'e'iren asked testily.

She was remarkably irritating for one so lovely, though her white-haired beauty was so great that she nearly looked Wittenbrand. Perhaps she did fit this place better than I. Perhaps. But she would not win. I had fought for every inch of Wittenhame I'd tasted and I would fight for the rest of it, too.

"Let him tell his stories," I said dryly. "They are all he has."

Grosbeak offered a tiny bow in my direction and a nasty grin.

"The rules of the game are simple enough. Neither of you will leave the platform until a winner is chosen or that is a loss. You will not stop to eat or drink, or that is a loss. You will not remove the blindfold or free your hands or that is a loss."

"And then when she dies it's over?" Ki'e'iren pressed. "I do not object to killing my rival."

"Clearly not, since you did it once already," I agreed pointedly.

Grosbeak's eyes met mine and he laughed as if we two were having a marvelous time.

"This will be a delight," he said in a low, menacing tone. "Your funeral was not nearly long enough, Izolda. It makes the heart happy to see you back for a final showdown and a proper drawn-out death and burial. These pleasures should never be rushed."

"I couldn't agree more," I said dryly. Let him stew on that.

Grosbeak waggled his eyebrows but his tone returned to lecturing as he laid out the next part. "Your skill will be tested. She who finds her prize may claim it. She who does not, will receive her doom. I confess, I would dearly love to compete. I have the exact skillset required for such a challenge."

"Is it ugliness?" I asked. "Because I fear to inform you that I have the edge over my rival on that one."

Grosbeak scowled. "I will have you know that despite your husband's constant jests, I am glorious to behold, a delight of the eyes, a jewel among the Wittenbrand. I have been reliably informed on more than one occasion that my smooth wit and golden tongue bring delight to the ladies and I take every opportunity to practice and improve upon them. A skill you may soon wish you possessed as well."

"What are we testing?" Ki'e'iren asked as beneath us a song broke out among the Wittenbrand. It was the old "Fly with the Arrow" tune again, sung badly but with great enthusiasm from thousands of throats and Grosbeak half-closed his eyes at the sound as if reveling in it. "Is it the skill of means of death? I can kill a thousand ways."

"I'm sure you can," Grosbeak said, amused.

A Wittenbrand hurried onto the platform bearing four silk scarves. Two were white and two were black. Grosbeak held them up and looked back and forth between us before settling on white for Ki'e'iren with a wink for me. Yes, yes, very ironic to choose her as the innocent. I rolled my eyes at him. I was used to his antics by now and though I could barely suppress the storm in my insides, I thought I could at least manage to do this with dignity and a sense of humor.

The assistant, a Wittenbrand with long ears that ended in tufts of fur, and eyes so black they looked like night, deftly tied our hands behind our backs, making the knots so tight that they hurt.

I wondered if Bluebeard had stayed to watch. It would have been a comfort to see him in the crowd. That he held me so dear and yet with such light fingers hurt the heart just a little.

Can you hear me, husband of mine? I asked with my mind, but there was no response. Perhaps I'd lost the skill. Or perhaps he merely was not listening. Well. I'd chosen this. I'd have to see it through.

"... and she cannot manage a single one," Ki'e'iren was saying as they lifted the blindfolds to our eyes.

I stole one last glance at Grosbeak who cocked an eyebrow at me, and I could not tell if that was cruelty or kindness in his eye as mine were bound shut. With him, it could very well be both.

"And now the terms," he said when we could no longer see him. His growling voice sent shivers up my spine — and not good ones at all. The world seemed a madder place with my eyes and hands made useless. "You both claim to be the wife of one man. Who should know him better than you? You must choose him now from among all the Wittenbrand present. The rules state that none here may speak to you with their lips, nor touch you with their hands, so do not press them to do either."

"But how shall we find him then?" Ki'e'iren said and it was almost a wail. "This seems impossible!"

Grosbeak laughed, a cruel, delighted laugh. "Doesn't it? And that is the charm of it. Why did you think it was called a Jape? This is not meant to entertain you, but to entertain us. Whichever of the Wittenbrand who so will, shall parade themselves up to this platform and by their salutation, you must identify your husband."

"What does that mean?" Ki'e'iren asked, sounding irritated. A chill crept over me. This could not be as simple as it sounded.

"By their blandishment, they shall make themselves known."

Uh oh. I was starting to suspect ...

"I do not follow." She bit off every word.

"By presentation of endearment, so shall your fate be recognized."

When neither of us spoke, Grosbeak huffed out a frustrated breath. "Everyone gets a chance to kiss you and you have to pick which one is your husband or you lose. Is that so hard?"

"But which am I to choose?" Ki'e'iren asked. "The original or the Bramble King? He who was named Coppertomb before?"

"You tell me," Grosbeak said. "I'm no expert in matters of your heart."

And at our surprised gasps he laughed so hard that I heard him yelp as his hooves skittered sharply on the slick surface of the stone hands and his cry grew fainter as he — I was quite sure — fell from the platform to the crowd below.

I was not worried about him. It would take worse than that to kill my old friend and adversary. But my mouth was dry at the prospect of kissing half the Bramble Court in exile and my heart hammered in my head. What if I chose wrong? What if I did not know my Bluebeard by his kiss? So much depended on this.

I should have known that Grosbeak would choose something so ...icky ... as the means of our battle. I had seen Wittenbrand with the lips of serpents. I'd seen them with double layers of teeth. I'd seen Grosbeak's rotting mouth and tongue. My stomach heaved at the thought of kissing him. I was no mermaid to brave that. This was not the easy option. I could very well die of this. Slowly, from disease, rather than quickly from the edge of a blade.

Worse still, it would not be so easy to identify my husband for there were just as many angelic Wittenbrand as there were horrific. Just as many with thousands of years to learn to bestow perfect kisses. With no guide to who was who, I would be lost.

"I suppose you're feeling superior right now," Ki'e'iren said in an undertone. "But you should know that I have an advantage here. I have vision that exceeds that of most mortals and guess what? I can see through this blindfold. It's blurry, I'll admit. But I bet it's better than what you are bringing to this contest."

And she wasn't wrong, because I could see nothing at all. I was truly blind, and if I were to win this, it would take all the memories of all the kisses that I'd ever had to help me find my beloved.

Chapter Thirty-One

I UNDERSTOOD the drinking and singing now. And the sudden bursts of giggles. And Coppertomb's annoyance at Grosbeak's choice. And Bluebeard's amused steepled fingers. They had all known from the very start what this would entail.

More annoying than having to participate in this farce for their entertainment, was the blindness. I would have liked to see who reacted to what when it took place. As things stood, I was required to focus only on the task at hand.

The first footsteps on the stairs leading to our platform — or perhaps I should say the first hoof-steps because they clattered — set a spike of dread down my spine.

Someone laughed nearby and someone else said, "Look at the face the ugly mortal is pulling. She's practically green. Where's Bluffroll? He likes them green. He should be here."

"He'll not trouble this world again," I said precisely. "And if you kiss me, you may find the same fate for yourself."

"She's cold as ice," the first one said, disapprovingly. "What was the Arrow thinking?"

"He's not the Arrow anymore. We can play with his toys all we like."

And then I was surprised by a very sudden, very wet kiss. I felt like I could hardly breathe, but I was certainly not going to open my mouth to draw in more air. Not after that. I swallowed, feeling ill at the smell of cheese that now wafted into my nose, and then I was kissed again, by someone new, I supposed, who at least smelled like wine and seemed to be less drippy.

I wiped my mouth on my sleeve and frowned. This was already horrible.

Beside me, I heard Ki'e'iren complain, "Don't waste my time. It's clearly none of you."

I opened my mouth to ask her how she knew and then my lips were caught by a pair that were petal-soft and caressed mine with loving gentleness. Like I said, it was going to be confusing, but I knew this was not my Bluebeard. This person smelled of honey and freesia, not mint.

Ki'e'iren seemed to like that kiss more, though. I heard her sigh.

But her sigh was cut off by a sound from below. Someone spoke in a low, menacing tone I could not quite catch, and then there was a scream that cut off suddenly followed by a second one that went on and on and then stopped.

I drew in a long breath — from my nose, I wasn't stupid — and steadied myself. There would always be violence where the Wittenbrand congregated. They were mortals with no veils, not bothering to disguise their peculiarities or passions. Where a mortal might kill your reputation, the Wittenbrand went for the literal throat. Where a mortal might silently plot revenge, the Wittenbrand plotted it openly, gathering support and offering riddles and challenges.

The next kiss thrust upon me was sharp and bold, as if the kisser were screwing up his courage to kiss me at all and then the one after that was hard and furious and followed by a laugh. I could almost have sworn that was Coppertomb.

There was a lull for me and I had the feeling that Ki'e'iren was receiving no lull at all. I heard wet smacks and moans from where she stood — in between screams and begging below us.

There was a metallic clash and the sound of sword on sword. Perhaps betting on the results had gotten out of hand. I'd seen that among them before.

And then a set of lips met mine that were tender in their touch but tasted of dead fish and rot and the teeth of the kisser nipped me as he finished his kiss. I spat to the side.

"I know that was you, Grosbeak. Are you happy to get it out of your system?"

He didn't break the rules by addressing me, but his laugh was as familiar as my own, and I frowned.

Honestly, how dare Bluebeard smirk and steeple his fingers knowing this was coming for me? Why did he not warn me if he knew, or stand to prevent it? How many times had he taken a blow for me and how long had I carried him pressed against my bare flesh, and now he stepped aside and allowed anyone who pleased to kiss me? It wasn't right, and I found I felt betrayal at his disregard. I had expected more from my husband. I had expected possessiveness and fidelity.

No one was kissing me now, and though I was grateful, it was not enough to assuage my fury. When I won this challenge — and I would — I would make him pay for not championing me.

Oddly, Ki'e'iren was still receiving kisses at a steady rate. They went on for some time and I was almost beginning to grow concerned — had I failed somehow already and been disqualified? — when a dry pair of lips met mine, but before the kiss could end, there was a strangled sound and a thump and the lips vanished suddenly from mine as another set claimed them, fitting my lips precisely, drawing mine into the embrace of his. I gasped and the kiss deepened, a forceful tongue sweeping between my lips in claim, and the roughness of an unshaven face brushing against my skin, and through the kiss I gasped his name.

"Bluebeard."

And his murmured laugh of victory was followed by a second kiss as a hand met my jaw and caressed it and then swiped the blindfold from my eyes.

My husband's cat's eyes met mine and I drank in the sight of him.

Behind him, Grosbeak was cursing. "You've ruined the whole thing. It's just like you not to be able to take a joke! You couldn't let it go on for a few hours, could you? No. Not Bluebeard. You couldn't just let a few Wittenbrand have a little fun, could you?"

"None other is to touch my wife," Bluebeard said easily.

"And yet several have kissed me," I said dryly, meeting his gaze with my steely annoyance.

"So they have, wife, but I suffered none to live."

"You …" I looked down at the corpse at my feet. The one he had killed while the man was still kissing me. "Oh."

"He was courageous, that one. To kiss you when he's seen me kill a dozen others already for the same offense. Courageous, but foolhardy."

He reached behind me and my bonds fell away.

"Is this perhaps an overreaction?" I asked, chilled as I saw the bloody blade in his hand. How many had kissed me? How many were dead now?

I peered around him to where Grosbeak was nursing a black eye. His clay body was cracked and he was missing one hoof — likely from the fall. A sword stuck straight through his clay body, wedged in the hard torso.

"He stabbed me, too, in case you were wondering, and I'm already dead," Grosbeak complained. "I set the rules for this game. There was no mention of stabbing."

"I am Bramble King," Bluebeard said and as he said it he turned and drew me with him to the edge of the platform, looking out over the gathered mass below him. There was evidence of … a battle among them? I was hard-pressed not to gasp at the sight. Bodies were strewn across the ground, red-flecked weapons in most hands and some were still locked in the conflict, breath heaving, arms grappling, their attention barely even on the platform.

This time his voice snapped like a whip. "I am your Bramble King."

He made a flicking motion and thorny vines began to grow from his hand. They tumbled to the ground and crawled across the surface, multiplying and blooming with white flowers which turned to dark berries, still growing and branching and tangling around the feet and legs of the crowd, forcing fighting Wittenbrand apart enough to still them. Their wide-eyed silence was all I needed to know that this act was his true win, not this game we'd just played.

"Challenge me with any wall to vault, any sea to cross, any army to fight, and I will show you again and again that I am your sovereign," he said but he didn't sound victorious, he sounded like he was threatening them. "But do not think to take or sully what is mine. I will have your respect — whether it is given freely, or whether I must take it with the edge of my blade. Choose today who you will serve. Is it to be me, or Coppertomb?"

And as he spoke, his winding vines rose up in the air, lifting Coppertomb, as if he stood upon the rising back of a sea monster. His teeth were gritted and his cheeks flushed and I realized that for the first time since I'd met him, there was uncertainty in his eyes.

"You thought to win by theft, Coppertomb," my husband said in a menacing tone. "You thought to steal my sacrifice and pretend it was your own. You thought to pull strings from behind the scenes rather than fight with your own hands. You thought to rip out my very heart and feed it to the grave. And you thought this would make you king."

He snapped his fingers and the silver arrow slipped from Coppertomb's hand, slicing his palm as it went and showering red upon the white blooms below his feet. It shot, as if launched from a bow, toward my husband and Bluebeard lifted a hand, and the arrow pierced into the gap in his palm created by the knife that had held him fast to the pillar of the sea. It stuck there, lodged in the ragged gap.

"This," my husband said, "Is mine. Bought with my deeds. Bought with my blood. Sign of my power." He turned back to his people. "And you are mine by the same merit. Now, choose. For those who choose to serve me will return with me to the Wittenhame."

Coppertomb scoffed. "There is no Wittenhame to which we may return."

"I have rebuilt it from the bones out," Bluebeard said, and as if on cue a swirl of pollen emitted from him like a cloud. "It will serve as home once more to my people and to their magic."

I heard a whisper then of, "magic" in the crowd. It sounded almost disbelieving.

"And those who will not serve, will go with Coppertomb to his fate."

"Fate?" Was the new whisper I heard echoing through the crowd.

"Fate?" Coppertomb said, crossing his arms over his chest and lifting one brow. "It is not for you to determine my fate. You have no authority over me."

"I am the Bramble King, he who was once the Arrow, Lord Riverbarrow, now your sovereign. All authority is mine for I have conquered Death," Bluebeard said in a low tone.

"Then what fate have you determined for me?" Coppertomb asked, annoyance in his tone.

"Patience," Bluebeard said, holding up a single finger to him. He turned back to his people. "Decide, now, or go with this old serpent to his destiny. Any who would go with Coppertomb, raise now your token."

But though we waited in silence with nothing but the trickle of water and shush of the wind to answer, there was no response.

"Swear, then, before me," he said and the crowd looked at one another. One of them rose as if to come and kiss his ring but he said, "There will be no pomp and ceremony. Swear now, all together, or await your consequence."

As one, they fell to their knees, despite the thorny vines, and from the throats of thousands came the rush of their vow, like the sound of a waterfall.

"By height of night and light of moon, we give our fealty. Be ye our sovereign and dispense justice, sanity, and fated destiny to your people to the end of the Age."

And then Bluebeard spoke,

"By height of night and light of moon, I so swear to you. You will be my people and shelter within my bones until the end of the Age."

And Coppertomb's sigh was what told me it was finished. For I had never heard such a sigh of defeat before.

"And so it is done," he said bitterly as he plucked off his glove and revealed his missing finger for all to see.

Chapter Thirty-Two

"BUT NOT ALL DONE," Bluebeard said. And to my utter surprise, he slit his cheek with the tip of his sword to make his mark, and then, taking a drop of his blood on his fingertips, he flicked it out over the crowd and the ground shook, and the mortal world fell away and there was a feeling of being ripped from the earth and transplanted.

I reached for his hand and gripped it tightly as the almost-familiar madness of traveling between worlds gripped me, shook me, caved me in, puffed me out, and sent me spinning into the madness.

And when I recovered, we were once more within the Wittenhame, in that familiar place where the trees rose miles above the ground and the mushrooms were as large as houses, where the roots of trees were roads and the flowers could shade a whole family.

Everyone — the entire assembled crowd — had come with us, and they were arranged among the bramble vines exactly as they had been in the mortal world, but without their mortal servants or their weapons. Instead, between them, were banquet tables loaded with piping hot food and drink, covered in white cloths and piled with white flowers and dazzling with leaping sparks as if from a crackling fire.

It was day here — high noon, if I was any judge — and bunting was strung around the clearing, a strange kind of bunting made of clouds and shifting rainbows. Frogs the size of horses leapt from table to table with more good things borne on their sleek backs.

When my mind finished reeling and sanity began to trickle back in to join the memories that mixed with nightmares that mixed with hopes, I realized we stood at what must be a head table, placed on roots high above all the others. And to one side, was the glittering sea. It shone soft azure under the light of the brilliant sun and mermaids flipped up out of the water with porpoises beside them like huntsmen with their Hounds.

"Welcome," Bluebeard said, pollen swelling around him and tiny songbirds darting down to cover his shoulders and arms. The birds sang riotously. "Welcome, my folk, to my marriage supper."

There was a general cheer, though that was just as likely for the food as for anything else.

"Be at ease. Eat. Drink. Delight. For my bride is worthy of celebration, and she who bore me through death is worthy of your honor. But before I feast with you, it is customary for a new-crowned king to receive gifts, and the gift I demand is from my queen."

He turned his body to me, and I turned to him also, but with a raised eyebrow. What was this gift to be? Was I now to kiss all the mermaids in the sea and watch them be slaughtered for their trouble?

"Willst thou, bride of mine, pass judgment in my name, as your gift to me," he asked, offering me his hand. I placed mine in his.

"I will give whatever you ask of me," I said steadily. But I hoped this would be the last of the tasks, for I was tired and even the smells of roast chicken and peaches and honey rolling out from the supper table were not enough to tempt me. I needed sleep.

"Then stand now, in judgment of my enemies," he said, sweeping a hand to where I found Coppertomb, Ki'e'iren, and Grosbeak still embedded in vines.

"I have never been your enemy," Grosbeak said, pouting. "And have you not already run me through with your sword?"

But I could see that his outburst had directed the eyes of my husband's people toward him as if to question whether this would be tolerated, and an acid rose in my throat. I needed to get this right or my Bluebeard would lose the respect of his newly sworn people.

The Bramble King flung himself into one of two large oaken chairs at the head of the assembly — Wittenbrand thrones, I realized. His moved with a constant shifting that made the knots in the wood look like faces. No, not look *like* faces. They *were* faces. I caught sight of the former Bramble King within and my heart caught in my throat, even as my husband lounged with one leg flung over the arm of his throne and a bunch of grapes in his fingers.

He smirked at me, lifting a brow.

I was up for his challenge. So, with a pale face, I stepped up onto the seat of the other throne-like chair. Fortunately, this one seemed to shift from flower to flower rather than face to face, though that still was unsettling in a piece of furniture.

"You cannot mean for her to judge us," Coppertomb said in a low, throaty voice. He sounded like he might growl at any moment. "She is mortal."

"No more," Bluebeard said, pausing to suck a grape from the vine before seeming to remember that he was speaking. "I have granted her equal share in my days."

There was a gasp from the crowd. And I will never understand the Wittenbrand because, as if this declaration were a signal, they all seated themselves and began to dig into the spread, watching me from time to time as if I were their entertainment.

"Do go on, wife. I am burning with curiosity to see what fates you will find fitting for my enemies."

"You have already defeated your enemies, my Lord," I said clearly. "You have stood on the neck of Death." His pleased laugh made me bold. "But under your authority, I will speak so that each here receives what is fitting."

"I have every confidence in you, as do we all," Bluebeard said and then winked dramatically at the crowd. They laughed, but it was a nervous laugh as if they were afraid they might be caught up in "receiving what is fitting." They had good reason to be worried. They had been complicit in all of this.

"To Ki'e'iren who tried to usurp my place," I said forcefully so that all would hear, "I assign this fate: go back to your time and place and dream no more of the Wittenhame. Be mortal in every way, and remember forever how you betrayed us."

"Ooohhh," the crowd whispered together. To them, the fate for forgetting this place was a fate far worse than death.

Ki'e'iren gasped, clearly unhappy, but then the vines drew her in and she disappeared, sent to her fate.

Bluebeard quirked an eyebrow at me and I felt the blood rush to my cheeks. Had he thought that too harsh, or too light? I could not tell. Or perhaps he found it too predictable. The Wittenbrand did not like things to be predictable. He flourished a hand as if bidding me to continue.

"To Coppertomb who conspired against my husband and tried in every way to make him stumble and fall, who, at the end, stole his beating heart and gave it as a feast to the barrow. Execution is too good for him. One death can only be enjoyed once." There was a murmur of approval from my husband and a mirror murmur from the crowd. Better, then. They turned their sparkling eyes on me, ready to see what torture I would gift to the one they had followed into tormenting the mortal world. "Coppertomb, I condemn to banishment." There was a disappointed sound from the crowd and I saw the man in question begin to smile. Until he heard my next words. "I banish you to the lands of Death to wander until you succeed in walking the Path of Princes." My heart was racing as I uttered his judgment in full and my voice rose as it gained confidence. "Languish there among so many whose fate you wove. Drink deep of despair with them. Make friends with Death — your only companion. And learn the lesson hubris teaches all of us: that in the end, we are all equals. Rich or poor, mortal or immortal, in the dark of despair, there is no great and small. We all are lowered even into the dark embrace of death. And how shall we bear up under his crushing weight?"

"I hardly think," Coppertomb began with an easy smile, but his words choked off and he gasped and the crowd gasped with him, freezing, as a white figure in long robes strode forward.

Death's beard and hair flowed delicately in a wind that was not there, and he walked over the waves of the sea without his feet so much as getting damp. In one hand, he held my severed hand, and he twisted it so that it beckoned to Coppertomb, and with a look of horror, Coppertomb looked down at his feet and when he saw that they were moving of their own accord to follow Death, ignoring any will of his own, they danced a complicated step as they went. And in this moment, he was no higher or greater than those poor mortals who were made to dance until their feet were in tatters. He let out a choked cry that cut off as if he'd bit his own tongue.

And when he had danced half down the aisle, following the white specter, his breath hitched into panicked short breaths, he threw a look over his shoulder and spat. "I will see you again, mortal Izolda. If not in this life, then in the next."

"I'm counting on it," I said. "For my husband bid me dispense justice and so I have. But if ever I lay eyes on you again, I shall dispense injustice and that to fulsome measure."

And my husband's barked laugh was the last thing Coppertomb heard for Death leaned in, kissed him, and he was no more.

I swallowed and we all took one long minute to breathe before Bluebeard slurped his wine noisily and startled us back to reality.

"More judgments, wife?" he asked with a lifted brow.

"Yes," I said in a shaky voice, for Bluebeard was looking at Grosbeak, but this next judgment I planned to go elsewhere. I turned in place again and looked out over the feasting crowd. "Folk of Wittenhame," I said clearly. "I judge that you, too, have wronged my husband, uniting under his rival." I risked a look at Bluebeard and saw him frozen, regarding me warily. "And so I sentence you with this. For the duration of my husband's reign, you shall not cross the barrier into the mortal world. You shall not harry those made without magic, nor reward them, nor use them in your schemes. You shall not know them at all. They shall be insulated from you, and you from them, for an age and half an age."

And the silence that met me was far deeper and far more sober than even the silence that met my judgment of Coppertomb.

"Wisely said, Bramble Queen," my husband said in a low voice.

The murmur that followed his was part resigned despair and part awe, and I felt I needed to swallow to go on.

"But there is more," Bluebeard said, nodding toward Grosbeak. My old friend had his rotting chin thrust up into the air, his clay arms crossed over the jutting hilt of the sword sticking from his chest. "Loathe though you may be to judge he who was once your ally, he is enemy to me, and he shall be punished. Doom him now, with your own tongue."

I reached down to the table and drew up a goblet and drank, and then I turned and I strode to Grosbeak and offered him the cup and to my surprise, he met my eyes silently, his twinkling with humor, and he took the cup and drank it to the dregs.

"Think not that you can best me, Izolda. For I know all your secrets and all your lies." His voice had an edge.

"This much is true."

"Strike then, your harshest blow. I shall drink your cup of wrath."

It took great courage for me to meet his eyes then. For though he may have been enemy to my husband, I owed him as many thanks as I did punishments. And so I took a long breath, tossed the cup aside, and turned to the crowd.

"To Grosbeak, treacherous ally, betrayer of plans, criminal of heart and mind, I give this punishment. Lose now your clay body and be delivered to the sea in the flesh you wore before you were dead and buried. And the sea shall have you until she tires of you. And you shall be our ambassador to both her and her kind. A punishment and a gift knit together for both the good you did and the evil, that you may know the emptiness of great power and find, perhaps, at last, what love might exist still for those who seem beyond all redemption."

And when I looked back at my old friend he was laughing and as he laughed, his clay body fell away, and his face crumpled to nothing and out of the wreckage of what had once been Grosbeak a man rose to full height and stepped out, his skin perfect and unmarred, naked as the day he born and — to my shock, for I had forgotten his face from before death — surprisingly good-looking.

He bowed to me once, folding at the waist, and then a great wave rose from the sea and splashed over him, sweeping him away, and for a heartbeat, I thought I saw four mermaids, two holding each arm, one cradling his head and a third tangled around his waist and they carried him off to the heart of their mistress.

And the last I saw of him was a wink.

I could not claim I would not miss him sorely, or that I was not sad to see him leave, and I do not know how long I stood, looking out to sea, only that after a time, my cheek was tickled by whiskers and warm breath and arms wrapped around me from behind, and my beloved's voice purred in my ear.

"And now, fire of my eyes, I think it is time that you, also, receive your just reward."

Chapter Thirty-Three

MY BLUEBEARD SWEPT me up in his arms and carried me, hooting owls and all, out across the azure waves as if it were no more difficult for him to walk on the rolling surf as to walk on the sand, and I should have been caught up by the silver gleams of the wave-tips or the soft deep blue of the cloudless sky, or the pollen that still followed my beloved in a golden swirl, stirring up new life in his wake. But it was not these things that I dwelled on. Nor was it the white sandy beach of the island he took me to, nor the great leafy fronds of the trees there that cast the cool relief of shadows over the sand.

No, it was the depth of the world held in his shining cat's eyes and the hungry longing that hovered just beneath the surface of them. It was the warm arms that held me safe in their embrace and the gust of his breath as he carried me, the quirk of the edge of his smile as we drank each other in wordlessly. Those were what caught my heart.

"Is this to be my reward then, or yours?" I whispered, my breath caught slightly in my throat for in all the wild, tangled fairytale we'd woven together, I'd had little time to dwell on what "after" might look like and I found myself to be almost overwhelmed now that it was upon me.

"Can it not be both, bride of my heart?" He murmured to me, his voice pitched only for my ears.

"I suppose it could," I said, considering, but I would not be myself if I were not practical and as he set my feet down on the white sand, I could not help but press him with what still troubled me. "But I must confess, I find I am still quite grieved by your actions before your folk. You allowed me to be kissed again and again against my desires. Am I to expect that treatment in the future."

He paled slightly as he looked at me as if the thought of what had happened wrung some emotion from him.

"I killed each one who set his lips to thine."

"So you did," I said, lifting my owls — who had gone to sleep with their heads tucked under their wings — so that I could wade into the foaming surf. I was trying to appear confident, but I was deeply troubled. "And yet, you allowed the violation. I agreed to the challenge, but I had thought it would be some contest of merit. It did not occur to me that you would leave me to such an exercise in humiliation without preventing it."

And when I turned, he was standing before me, and he had stripped off coat and weapons and jerkin as if he planned to bathe in the sea. The great gaping hole in his side distracted me for a moment. He wore that for me. For always.

It was hard to be angry at a man marked so.

He froze, biting his lip and looking at me intently.

"And is this your last doubt of me, my wife? I have given you my flesh, my bone, my death, and my fidelity. I have honored you as my queen and made you secure in that position forever. I have invited you into partnership with me, into a share of both sufferings and reward." He paused, eyes blazing and I felt a small quake of fear. "But you harbor one last doubt, hmm? Will I uphold your honor in the future? Will I never again suffer a violation to your person? Is this the last question that must be answered before you can find happiness in my arms?"

"Yes," I said, lifting my chin steadily. "It must be answered. For how can I trust the rest of my future in your hands without an answer to that?"

He nodded, looking down and his expression was thoughtful as he waded into the sea with me. When he reached me, he took my hands in his and my owls hooted and tried to fly away when I dropped my skirts. They made such a protest that I was forced to hold my skirt in one skeletal hand to keep them from the sea and his hands in my flesh one.

And when his gaze met mine I felt myself swallow at the purity of the emotions I saw there. His eyes radiated finality.

"You know the old hymn. You've heard it sung. You followed it onto the Path of Princes."

"Yes," I whispered.

"Sing it for me." He stepped nearer, leaning in so that all I could see was his dear face and his parted, wanting lips. He drew in a breath like a backward sigh.

"I sing very poorly," I said, cheeks heating.

"Sing, all the same." One of his hands left mine to caress my cheeks with the back of his hand, drawing my attention to the holes in his palms which he bore even as Bramble King, and would bear now forever. He gave me that. Could I not give him this?

My lips trembled, but I sang for him.

"Fly with the Arrow,
Dance with the Sword,
Give Your Heart to the Barrow,
Die with your Lord

And if ever you be broken,
And gasp on the ground,
Hold up your fine token,
And join with the sound.

Sing for your Sovereign,
Bow to your Dream,
Make Haste for the Fallen,
Rise in Esteem.

And if ever you be broken
And gasp on the ground,
The word may be spoken,
And salvation found."

He tilted his head so that his lips brushed my cheek as he whispered, "There's more to the song."

"But that's the Path of Princes," I said, leaning back so I could narrow my gaze and meet his. "The whole of it."

He smirked. "So it is. But the rest is the Way of Kings."

And my lips fell open and I felt as if I could not catch my breath as he sang to me, sweet as any songbird,

"*From the Kiss of your Enemy,*
Your Home Restore,
Bring each one to Justice,
Fairness Adore.
And if ever you be broken,
And troubles abound,
Know vow is Unbroken,
For your King is Crowned."

"But how," I gasped. "How did you know."

"I've always known," he whispered, leaning in to rest his forehead on mine. "While others walked the Path of Princes, I was walking the Way of Kings and you were walking it with me."

"It might have been nice to know," I said wryly, finding it harder and harder to resist his charms as he kissed down my neck and buried his lips in the flesh where my chest met my shoulder.

"Mmm," he murmured.

"But now there will be no more surprises?" I asked

His head whipped up in that odd lightning-fast way he sometimes had.

"Well," he said, smirking mischievously, "maybe some surprises."

And then he spun me gracefully around to show me what was fluttering down from the sky and onto the island — our old Grouse House. A black raven was nestled in the thatch and it croaked at me balefully.

I gasped. "I thought that was lost forever."

I turned enough to see his glowing smile directed at me.

"And I thought you said you could have no home. I thought a life with you would be sleeping in tangled tree roots and eating wild berries."

"The Bramble King has no home," he agreed. "But who is to say that the Bramble Queen may not have one? Perhaps, my dearly beloved Queen of my heart, you may see fit to invite me within, to share your sup and fire ... and perhaps even your bed."

He paused and I loved how he held his breath to hear my answer.

"Oh, so now is reward time," I said dryly. But it was hard to be cool and dry on the outside when on the inside my pulse thundered and my blood ran hot.

He smiled so sweetly that his eyes went crinkly around the edges and his dimples showed. I could barely breathe with the beauty of it.

"I hope so. I hope it will be reward time for a very long time. An age and half an age, perhaps."

"And what is to be *your* reward?" I asked, quirking my lips to tease him.

His smile washed away and he fell to his knees in the surf but I would not let him bow before me, so I threw myself to my knees with him while my owls coughed and sputtered, half-drowned and furious.

He took my face between his palms and his eyes were deep and dark, his voice full of longing. "Be my reward, Izolda, fire of my eyes and flame of my heart. Be everything I gave myself for."

"I will," I gasped. "But only if you will be my consolation in return, for I love you, my Bluebeard."

He leaned in then, gathered me in his powerful arms, and drew me to him, until I was clasped tight against his chest. He leaned in tenderly to kiss me long and deep. And then, he leaned back to lie in the shallow water, bringing me down over his chest in a tangle of wet cloth, foaming water, and glittering pollen. And there, as I lingered over his warmth and strength, he kissed me and ran his fingers through my tangled hair, until my poor owls begged for mercy and had to be set free. And when they were released, he made up for the moments spent freeing them with kisses upon kisses as if he would gift me all those he stored up over the ages of his great quest.

The Law of Greeting stole me away. The Law of Love brought us together. And kept us together.

And if Happily Ever After is how a fairytale ends, then ours ended here. But truly, it had only just begun, for love is like that. One peak is crested only to reveal another. One depth plumbed, only to uncover greater depths still, and a thousand years from now, when we are nothing more than terrifying legends to the mortals who were once my kin, we two will still be learning our love as one learns the heights of music, the breadth of art, and the deep deep depths of the written word.

And if my old friend Grosbeak saw me from his place within the sea, then he may very well have noticed that I had a very bold imagination after all — one that might have put even him and his mermaids to shame.

It certainly made my Bluebeard laugh and sigh, and it is for his happy sigh that I live — for an age, and half an age, and forever.

THE END

THE MORTAL WIFE
THE BRAMBLE KING

Author's Note

Bluebeard's Secret is my heart and everything I love about fairytales laid out on a platter. It's a story dear to my heart with characters who are alive in my mind and will continue to remain alive whispering to me. I think the best stories have the same heart — one of love, sacrifice, and seeking restoration. And if they can have some humor and a nod to how dark things can be before that restoration takes place, then all the better.

If you enjoyed the series, you will likely enjoy the series of stand-alone paladin fantasy romances that I'm planning for 2023. That world is already shaping up in my mind. (You should follow me somewhere so you don't miss news on this.) You'll also likely enjoy my Fae Hunter series and my Mayfly World stories which are featured as short stories in various anthologies and also published as short novels (*Stolen Mayfly Bride* and *Married by War).* You'll find links to all of that at www.sarahklwilson.com.

Thank you for reading and being part of this journey with me. We are friends now in heart, even if we never meet.

Special thanks to Grosbeak. Without him, I'd never have found my way through.

And to Melissa who loves all this as much as I do.

Behind the Scenes

USA Today bestselling author, Sarah K. L. Wilson loves happy endings, stories that push things just a little further than you expect, heroes who actually act heroic, selfless acts of bravery, and second chances. She writes young adult fantasy and adult fantasy.

Sarah would like to thank **Melissa Wright & Eugenia Kollia** for their incredible work in beta reading and proofreading this book. Without their big hearts and passion for stories, this book would not be the same.

Sarah has the deepest regard for the talent of her phenomenal artist Erion Makuo who created the gorgeous cover art that accompanies this book. Without her work, it would be so much harder to show off this story the way it deserves!

Thanks also to the Noble Order of Female Fantasy Authors who keep Sarah sane – sort of. And for her beloved husband, Cale and sons Neville and Leif who are endlessly patient as she talks to them about bookish passions.

And a HUGE THANK YOU to Sarah's patrons during the writing of this book, **Mike Burgess, Jennifer Wood, Victoria Churchill, Ken Baker,** and **Carly Salsbury** for their support. She couldn't do this without readers like you!

Want to keep track of Sarah's future projects? Follow her on social media @sarahklwilson or sign up for her newsletter on her website www.sarahklwilson.com.

Visit Sarah's website for more information:
www.sarahklwilson.com

www.ingramcontent.com/pod-product-compliance
Lightning Source LLC
Chambersburg PA
CBHW020345310726
48979CB00015B/2508/J

* 9 7 8 1 9 9 0 5 1 6 5 2 8 *